THE KI

She lay on her back
side. He was breat
the odour reached her, the strong acrid odour of
horses. It enveloped her, sweeping over the bed so
strongly that for a moment her confused, sleepy
mind suggested that there were horses in the room.

The stench filled her nostrils so that she gagged.
There were sounds outside the chamber. Downstairs? She opened the bedroom door a crack. The
sounds magnified . . . she heard heavy breathing
just below her. The stench was too much and the
bile rose in her and then — as her eyes probed the
black infinity — she found movement there. Something gleamed and shuffled and pawed . . .

Cold terror flooded through her, bringing the
hairs erect on her arms, and she backed away from
the gallery rail, into the bedroom, slamming the
door between her and whatever was down there,
waiting.

THE
KILLING GLANCE

D. G. Finlay

ARROW BOOKS

Arrow Books Limited
62—65 Chandos Place, London WC2N 4NW

An imprint of Century Hutchinson Limited

London Melbourne Sydney Auckland
Johannesburg and agencies throughout
the world

First published by Century as *Watchman* 1984,
Grey Regard 1985, *Deadly Relations* 1986, *Graven Image* 1987

First published in this edition by Arrow 1989

© D.G. Finlay 1984
© D.G. Finlay 1985
© D.G. Finlay 1986
© D.G. Finlay 1987

Printed and bound in Great Britain by
Anchor Press Ltd, Tiptree, Essex

ISBN 0 09 955860 2

For Y. G.
In eternal gratitude
for four years of firm
but gentle guidance and
encouragement

Glossary

BENDER	tent
BENG	devil
BOK	luck
BOR	friend
BOSHOMENGRO	fiddler
CHAV	child
CHIRIKLO (endearment)	little bird
CHOVIAR	magician
DADRUS	father
DIK AI	look out!
DIKKER	look
DINELO	fool
DJILLIA	song
GORGIO	non-Romany person
GRAI	horse
GRAUNI	gem or jewel
GURNII	cow
HOBBEN	food
HOTCHIWICHI	hedgehog
JALLING THE DROM	travelling the roads
KANNI	birds
KAULO	black
KENNER	house
KUSHTI	fine
MOKADA	unclean
MORT	woman
MULLO	ghost/spirit
MUSHGAYING	spying out the land
NARKRI	dark, dank or unpleasant
PEN	sister
PIKIES	Romanies expelled from the tribe
PRAL	brother
PURI DAIA	grandmother

RAWNI	lady
ROM	Romany husband
SAP	snake
SAR SHAN	good day/hello
SCRAN	food
SHURA	headman/master
SIMENSA	cousin
VARDO	waggon
WOODRUS	bed

Contents

BAYLESS FAMILY
TREE
1660-1952

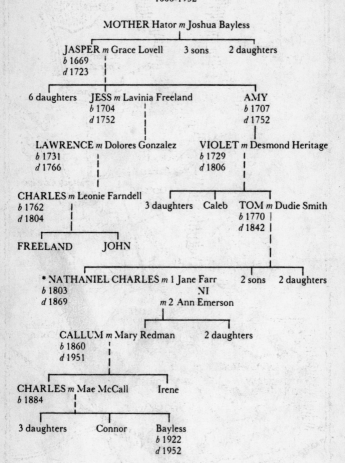

MOTHER Hator *m* Joshua Bayless

JASPER *m* Grace Lovell   3 sons   2 daughters
b 1669
d 1723

6 daughters   JESS *m* Lavinia Freeland   AMY
                b 1704   *b* 1707
                d 1752   *d* 1752

LAWRENCE *m* Dolores Gonzalez   VIOLET *m* Desmond Heritage
b 1731   *b* 1729
d 1766   *d* 1806

CHARLES *m* Leonie Farndell   3 daughters Caleb TOM *m* Dudie Smith
b 1762   *b* 1770
d 1804   *d* 1842

FREELAND   JOHN

* NATHANIEL CHARLES *m* 1 Jane Farr   2 sons   2 daughters
b 1803   NI
d 1869   *m* 2 Ann Emerson

CALLUM *m* Mary Redman   2 daughters
b 1860
d 1951

CHARLES *m* Mae McCall   Irene
b 1884

3 daughters   Connor   Bayless
                                b 1922
                                d 1952

* Illegitimate son of Dudie and Charles Bayless

Part One

1704-1737

JESS AND AMY

Prologue

Jess Bayless was just past his fifth year when he was deemed fit to join his cousin Fedor in the daily scouring of the woodland for hedgehog or rabbit or even the chance of a fine fat bird. It was the first time he had been given the grub sack and he was dragging it happily after him as he worked through that part of the wood which surrounded the old Roman brick kiln.

Something stirred nervously in the paper-dry leaves ahead of him and he stood quite still, hardly daring to breathe. It was a baby hedgehog, too young still to have been separated from its mother. The little creature seemed suddenly aware of danger and scuttled away through a patch of warm sunlight and shifting grass.

Jess, crouching low, followed as quietly as his inexperience permitted. His whole attention was focused on his prey as he thrust his head through a curtain of whippy hazel wands into a small dell — and it was as though he had stepped over a cliff into space. He spun, falling like a stone, his heart huge and thunderous in his chest. Then he realized that he was sitting in a pool of warm light which seemed to come from around him rather than from the thick interlace of tree branches above his head. Everything was bathed in strange golden blandness.

The little hedgehog had vanished.

Jess leaned back on his elbows, giving way to a warm languor. The blood singing in his ears still sounded like thunder, but he no longer felt afraid. He waited, feeling something seep into him, filling him from the top of his dark curly head to the soles of his bare feet . . . coursing through him in a warm, smooth tidal wave of elation and strength — and power.

He was too young to know what power meant, but he was well able to recognize the bursting sensation of pure strength and — unaccountably — he seemed to have the muscle and knowledge of ten men. There was sound after that — and a kind of fear and anger grew in him as voices spoke in a tongue that he could not understand, for there was a veil over the surface of this new awareness and behind it was movement and great heat and a young voice calling . . .

He opened his eyes. The bright light had left the glade. Now it was just a pretty little dell with a moss-covered floor and for company some old grey stone boulders, mottled with dried lichen, half submerged in the under-growth. He stood up uncertainly and pushed his way out through the leafy curtain. The hazel and nettles sprang back into place behind him.

He notched a couple of tree trunks with his gutting knife to mark the entrance.

1

Amy Bayless was aware of her deformed foot by the time
she had learned to walk, for she quickly discovered that
she was not able to skip and run like Jess and her elder
sisters. Her frustration was soothed by the presence of
Jess, who appeared to have decided from babyhood that he
would be her protector against the rest of the world. They
were rarely out of each other's company, and the rest of
the Romany clan quickly came to think of them as a single
unit . . . Jess 'n' Amy. Amy and Jess. They closed ranks
and were content.

It took Jess a long time to decide to share the Place with
Amy. Even then it was not really sharing, except the secret
of its locality, for he forbade her ever to go there on her
own. It was the only thing in all his life that he felt he
owned completely, and it was just not possible to share its
mysteries, even with one as deeply loved as Amy.

Had it not been for Jess and his protective instincts,
Amy's life would have been almost unbearable in those
early years of life, camping beside the saltpans with the
other members of the Bayless clan. It was difficult enough
to be a daughter of Jasper Bayless without also being his
seventh girl. Her misshapen left foot was turned inward
and the leg that supported it was wasted. As an infant she
had lived in a box under the waggon, and from the first it
was Jess who took her to their mother when she was
hungry and Jess who slapped his sisters to get them to
remember to change her and clean her small sore behind.

Grace Bayless died during the winter wandering of
1714-15. Amy was not quite nine years old at the time. She
studied Jess's grief at the passing of his mother with

17

interest for she had never felt any emotion at all towards the calm gaunt woman who quietly governed the lives of Jasper and all his brood. The elder girls were married off or sent into service in Chichester and all of a sudden the overcrowded vardo held only Jasper, Jess and little Amy.

It was during the summer of 1716 that Jess met John Freeland. Jess often took Amy with him on hunting expeditions, for it involved little walking once a suitable location had been selected. On this occasion they had come up on to Apuldram Common through the fields, skirting Manor Farm and following the river inland to a marshy patch where the wildlife was plentiful. They settled down to wait for fowl. The day was muggy and overcast, with a hint of rain in the air.

Amy curled herself up small, content to watch Jess using his special gift. Flaming his quarry required complete concentration and she had learned very early to meld with the bushes and remain perfectly still until he came back to her.

A family of ringed plover splashed and hunted among the reeds over to their right. Jess squatted in the muddy water, watching, selecting. His face assumed a waxy pallor, his body a rigidity in which only his eyes moved, following a fat young male bird through the water. There was a period of total suspension. Amy held her breath as she sensed the enormous gathering together that was being manifested in Jess's head. Then there was a distinct flash — as though the sunlight winked sharply for a moment on a ripple of water. The young plover dropped like a stone and the others flew upward with a thunder of frightened wings and swooped away, rising and dipping over the common to sink back to the springy turf round a bend in the stream. Jess stood up among the reeds and sloshed through the water to where the bird lay. It was warm, unblemished — and very dead. He stuffed it into his satchel with the rabbit they had downed on the edge of Hempstettle field and waded back towards Amy, grinning at the size of the fat plover.

He noticed John Freeland immediately. He was sitting further upstream among the bulrushes, fishing with a cane rod and a length of cord.

'You'll never catch nothen' with that.'

They surveyed each other, taking in the contrasts between them in speech and dress.

To the young fisherman, the boy on the bank seemed like an apparition: tall, even graceful, in spite of the raggedness of his clothing, with a face of such dark beauty that he could do little but stare up at him. The little girl beside him hung back shyly, the tangle of wiry black hair almost hiding her face.

'I'm John Freeland,' he said to them politely. He was square-shouldered and almost as tall as Jess. His hair fell in light brown ringlets over a round, friendly face. He looked with regret at the undisturbed water and slack line curving idly against a lazy current.

'I known who you are,' Jess said shortly. 'Seen you often enough.' They settled down to the serious business of fishing, the ragged teacher and his eager gorgio pupil. Amy sat close by, watching and silent, content to be with them and sensing the start of a pattern of companionship which would remain between the three of them always.

Childhood proved to be an uneasy battleground for Amy's loyalties. There were so many contenders for Jess's affection, and top of the list was Yoshi. Yoshi had been their waggon nag ever since Jasper had picked her up as a yearling at Tavistock Goosey Fair nine years before. She was a stocky, rough-coated little cob, placid and affectionate, with an apparently limitless supply of energy. Jess loved her absolutely and gave more attention to her daily welfare than the rest of the Bayless clan gave to the whole string of their horses put together. When chance offered a mating between Yoshi and a fine Arab stallion during the clan's wandering, Jess began to plan for a great new line.

Jess's attentions to Yoshi constituted no great threat to Amy. Even his friendship with John Freeland was not too

difficult to accept, for he was a cheerful and uncomplicated companion and always treated her with a courtesy
that she had never received from her own people. But the
way Jess's eyes lit up whenever little Lavinia Freeland
came into the conversation somehow turned her stomach.
It mattered not at all that the child was still in her baby
frocks. Instinct put Amy's hackles up at the mention of her
name and she would inch closer to Jess and slide her hand
into his for reassurance.

The birth of Yoshi's foal was a magical event for the
children, in spite of the fact that they had seen many of the
waggon horses foaling over the years. Yoshi was a calm
little cob. Motherhood came easily to her. The long-legged
and graceful foal was of unusal size and colour, and she
inspected him with pride, cleaning the membrane and
secretions from his nose and eyes and coat. She was on her
feet within half an hour and in no time she had nuzzled
and nudged the little cob on to his wobbly feet.

'Oh, look at him, Dada.' Jess had said to his father. 'He
has just one white sock. May we call him Olivas?'

And Olivas he became, as surely as he was also Jess's
own horse from the very first moment.

The stolen mating of Yoshi with a wealthy gorgio's fine
Arab stallion had been a most fortunate union, for Olivas
developed the strength and health of his sturdy little
mother, combined with the grace and fine proportions of
his sire and the promise of speed and endurance in his fine
shoulders and quarters. Within months of his birth, it was
clear that, in Olivas, the Baylesses now possessed an
animal whose value was quite beyond their wildest
dreams.

1721 was a difficult year for Amy. Just after her fourteenth
birthday, Jasper Bayless collapsed in the lickering shed
and was dead before his brother Piramis could get him
back to his tent. Piramis and Sarey Bayless discussed the
futures of Jess and Amy at length and eventually found
work for Amy up the road from the saltpans in the Manor
Farm kitchens.

It was a wrenching separation for Amy. It was strange and frightening to find herself in a house of bricks and mortar for the first time, separated from the sounds of the countryside and the comforting wind in the trees. But there were compensations because, for the first time in her young life, she found that she was being depended upon — and the responsibility pleased her. She was able to visit Jess each week on her free day.

She was growing tall and straight so that the game leg was scarcely noticeable until she moved. The cowman began to take an interest in the Manor Farm kitchen maid and it was remarked that John Blunden from Rymans was over delivering messages a great deal more often than he had before. Amy ignored both her suitors and concentrated on her cooking and cleaning. Her eyes were on her work and her mind was away in the woods with Jess.

After Jasper's death it seemed a natural move for Jess to build a bender in the woods, for he had always preferred his own company. The glade he chose was, of course, the Place — full of unseen spirits who seemed to disturb his uncles and cousins, for instinct told them it was filled with unaccountable menace. Jess was unconcerned at their distrust. It would ensure that he was seldom disturbed by the clan unless there was a good reason. The excitement that stirred in him strengthened his resolve to build with bricks and mortar a proper home on the very spot so that he could protect his invisible Spring from . . . .It was odd but he could never decide just what it was that might endanger the Force in him. Its strange pattern of soundless voices in his head had been the same for so many years that he knew each inflection by heart. The only worry he did have — and it grew with every passing day now — was that the strength of his instincts was gradually lessening. He began thinking of life without the Power. The realization that time was no longer his ally finally decided him to form his own smuggling gang.

He chose John Freeland, Thomas Blunden, Richard Farrington, Anthony Fowler, James Hunt, Andrew Lawr-

21

ence and finally Nicholas Smith. It was not easy for Jess to convince Mr Tovey that he was as competent to organize a night run as his father had been. Jess was only just eighteen and although he was already a commanding figure over six feet in height, broad in the shoulder and undoubtedly strong as an ox, the cautious merchant was loath to trust an investment of several hundred pounds to an untried boy. Against his better judgement, he gave Jess permission to do a trial pick-up the following week.

After they parted he sat in the dark cubbyhole of his counting house behind the shop in East Street, and wondered what had made him give in so easily. It was something to do with the way the lad had looked at him, he would swear. Those amazing grey eyes had looked deep into his very soul and he had been caught and his mind bent to an invisible will — and he had heard his voice agreeing with young Bayless, even as he had tried to protest and shake off the strange, compelling languor that had gripped him. Those gypsies were odd folk, he knew. Some of them seemed to have the reputation for some pretty ungodly practices but he'd never imagined that Jess Bayless was one of those.

The drop had gone without a hitch.

The group, grinning at each other from soot-blackened faces, christened themselves the Apuldram Blacks and were delighted to accept the guinea and half-anker of spirits that was their night's fee. It was the beginning of a brotherhood that would continue for a decade. The financial rewards were great for them all. It was, however, the excitement and trust in each other which held them together. For Jess the growing size of his fortune was the cornerstone of his now single-minded campaign to possess the affections of John Freeland's sister Lavinia.

Jess felt unusually diffident as he rode over to Rymans. He had taken a great deal of trouble to wash himself from head to foot and was clothed in new breeches, shirt and cutaway coat. He had combed his hair until the tears started from his eyes and now it was fastened into the nape of his neck in a neat cue. His face was freshly shaved and he smelt of wood smoke. Olivas had been given the same treatment and gleamed like burnished copper as he picked his way over the pot-holed road, lifting his elegant hooves with proud grace.

Horse and rider made a fine pair, Thomas Freeland decided, watching their arrival in the yard through an open casement. Young Bayless might be a gypsy and something of an opportunist but there was considerable panache in the way he sat his horse — and the energetic and precise manner he went about any work that he took on called forth a grudging respect, even from his superiors.

He thought that his own son, John, had been influenced for the better by Jess over the years, for he now emulated Jess's strict code of ethics and was far steadier than he had been as a child. True, there was that owling business which was a dangerous as well as unsavoury occupation, but young men must be allowed to work the wildness out of their systems before settling down to the serious business of living.

He strode through the house to his office and was still considering the subject when Blunden ushered Jess into the room.

'Come in, come in,' he said, waving Jess forward as he settled himself behind his huge mahogany desk. 'Sit you down then and make yourself comfortable.'

He surveyed Jess through pince-nez that were perched on the end of a long and angular nose. A twinkle softened his stare.

'By George, Jess — you're looking prosperous. Not thinking of getting wed yet, are you?'

Jess's long face puckered into an expression of acute alarm. 'God forbid, sir. There can't be a maiden in the parish that could be doing with my habits.'

Freeland bowed his head with a half-smile.

'So — how may I help you?'

23

Jess grinned across at his host. 'Well, sir . . . you know all about my family. We come from mixed Romany stock but we've worked the saltpans for two generations now and hope we might go on doing it for two more. Although we're travellen' folks by nature, there's enough gorgio blood in our veins for some of us to want to settle in Apuldram in proper homes. I'm one of those, Master Freeland — and Amy's another. I've always had a powerful urge to better myself, sir . . . to own a house of bricks and mortar and go into business. I can read and write pretty fair now and so can Amy, for Mrs Chatfield gives her lessons each afternoon and she's as quick as a clerk with her numbers. Well, sir, the long and the short of it is this. There's more ways to make money than workn' the fields and the saltpans, as you know . . . . '

Freeland flashed him a quick look from under bushy eyebrows. They were both well aware of the activities upon which Jess's interests were founded. He did not condemn the practice and even occasionally passed on to his son some small snippet of information that might be useful to the Blacks. His well-stocked cellar and his wife's elegant French window-hangings were evidence of their appreciation.

He nodded and dug into his yellow waistcoat pocket for his snuff box.

'Well, I've ben thinken' along these lines, sir. I've more than enough money to invest now in the builden' of a house. Not a cottage . . . a real decent house about the size of your own. Apuldram 'as been the only home I've ever 'ad and I'd not be happy to put my roots down in any other place. Would you be good enough to ask Mrs Smyth's trustees whether they'd consider leasen' Salterns Wood to me, sir? I'd want to clear a few acres north of Copperas Point and west of New Barn field and build me a fine house there, with access along the west boundary and into Salterns Lane. I plan to put Olivas to stud, and breed a strain off him and some of the New Forest and Devon cobs that my people use. Then I'd put the rest of the woodland to grazen' swine. That would soon clear the

24

undergrowth there and give the oaks a better chance of growen' . . .'

He stopped. It had been a very long speech for him and he found that he was perspiring freely under his shirt. He sat forward on the edge of the ladder-back chair, his stomach muscles suddenly knotting with tension.

Freeland took a clay pipe from his desk rack in silence. He lifted the lid of the tobacco humidor and carefully selected one leaf after another with apparent concentration. He pressed them into the bowl and tamped them down. Jess watched the long tapering fingers preparing the pipe with unhurried skill.

'Tell me, what sort of acreage are we discussing?'

Jess rubbed his smooth jaw, frowning. 'Forty . . . maybe forty-five acres, I'd guess.'

Freeland struck tinder to steel and applied the flaming taper to his pipe. He sucked and puffed and sucked again, knot-veined hands cupping the bowl. The tobacco caught and he leaned back, pulling the aromatic fumes into his lungs with deep contentment.

'Bought with your ill-gotten gains, no doubt,' he said quietly, watching Jess's face.

Jess agreed with a shrug. 'That may be where the first of the cash comes from but the whole business of free trading is too chancy to rely on for long. It is my intention to invest my savings wisely and stop the night runnen' entirely, before I settle down in a good solid business partnership.'

Freeland took the pipe from his mouth and banged his fist on the desk top. His enthusiasm for this young man grew with every word.

'Wisely said, my boy — very wisely said, although men with far more experience than you have been caught out with those same sentiments. The investment market is still in the doldrums after the disaster of the South Sea Bubble, y' know.' He spoke ruefully, from the blow to his own pocket after the collapse of the great South Sea Company in 1720.

Jess looked at the old man with understanding, well

aware of these events. It was because of their financial pressures that John had allowed himself to be drawn into the Apuldram Blacks.

'How much money have you got?'

Jess was ready for the question. 'Seven thousand pounds and three hundred silver crowns, sir. I would like to spend five thousand pounds on the house and land and invest the rest in a marine partnership.'

Freeland blew fine blue smoke out through his nostrils. 'I can't argue with that, Jess. Countless numbers of our peers enjoy the comfort of large estates and fortunes today, simply because of the irregular practices of their forebears.'

He sank back into another of his pondering silences and Jess watched as the old man mused, tapping steepled fingers together.

'Now, I'll tell you what I am proposing to do. I shall recommend that the trustees of the estate lease you thirty-five acres of untended woodland north of the salt-pans; the condition being that you agree to clear a percentage of oak wood, the felled trees remaining the property of the estate. Further, that you build a dwelling house of a design and size to be agreed with the estate — the whole messuage to be on a renewable lease of twenty-five years. I can't agree to your having the entire tract of the south woodlands because other uses are already planned for the land that runs westward from the highway. There will be one other stipulation, Jess . . . I'd like an unwritten promise from you that there will be no further night-running from Copperas Point during your tenancy.'

Jess stared at him in consternation.

'For God's sake, man — if you're going to live there, you won't want to sully your own nest. That fine mansion of yours is going to house your wife and family one day, yes? If your ideals are as fine and honourable as you imply, you would not wish to risk involving innocent women and children in the violence and danger of that work, would you?'

26

The craggy hardness of his face relaxed. He stood up slowly, rubbing the ache from the small of his back, and then stretched out his hand across the desk top.

'Give me your word and your hand on it, Jess — and I'll be glad to speak to the trustees for you at the earliest opportunity.'

Jess rode home, listening to the clop-clop of Olivas's hooves on the road. Bricks and mortar . . . bricks and mortar . . .

It was impossible not to dwell on Lavinia Freeland, and after a while he gave in and feasted his mind upon her — John's sister . . . still only a child of ten but golden and delicate and surely the most perfect specimen of young girlhood that nature had ever created. She was only just aware of him but already she would pick up her skirts and fling herself at him whenever he appeared with John at Rymans. He accepted her admiration with secret pleasure but was careful not to encourage it openly in case it caused offence to Mr Freeland. Thinking of her, he groomed Olivas, working on the gleaming coat as though his very life depended upon it.

Jess's mood was subdued after the next two runs — even though one of them was a consignment of unprecedented proportions which involved fifteen men and the whole night to distribute the shipment amongst waggons and light carts. The night's work was undisturbed and earned each man the sum of ten guineas. For Jess it meant nearly four thousand pounds to add to his assets.

A lease was arranged for Salterns Woods, and one December morning Jess signed his name to the parchment document in Thomas Freeland's Chichester office and exchanged it for a pouch of two hundred guineas. It was an oddly moving moment for him and afterwards he paced his new boundaries, from Copperas Point through uncultivated scrubland to the marshy banks of the Chichester Channel.

Thirty-five acres of oak and beech wood . . . just asking

to be set in order. He strode into a biting wind, noticing nothing of the frost-laden day. A flight of geese scythed the crisp blue air over his head and wheeled in tight formation across the Bosham farmlands before circling in to land against the Chidham shore beyond. Jess saw only his trees and the little glade which housed his bender. The house would be built with the Place at its heart.

The clearing operation progressed through the winter months and well into spring. It would not have taken so long had it not been for the rate at which the casual labour abandoned the work. The brooding watchfulness in the atmosphere was certainly so strong that it even had Jess's uncle Piramis looking over his shoulder. He breathed a sigh of relief when the last tree had been uprooted and the site was ready for the footings to be started.

It was no real surprise when the masons, digging foundation trenches, came upon evidence of another, infinitely older building on the site of the Place. Jess insisted that the old stones must remain as they were. The masons crossed themselves and murmured together that the gypsy was building on unhallowed ground and no good would come of it. Their mood deteriorated even further after an incident which occurred soon after the trenchwork began.

There were eight labourers, and the youngest of them was Will Tregus. He was always the first on the site each morning, well before dawn, and was hard at work by the light of one of Jess's lanterns by the time the others arrived.

Jess rose one morning and prepared himself a parcel of food for his midday meal. He could hear the boy moving about in the half-dug trench across the glade. As he hung his night blanket over the wood pile to air, an odd scuffling made him pause. It sounded as though Will was in conflict with one of the woodland pigs who were at their most aggressive at this time of the year.

'What's amiss with ye, Will?' he called, ducking out of the tent to see for himself.

Dawn was still an hour away but the density of the night

had thinned into milky greyness. By the lantern's light he could just make out Will's head bobbing up and down in the foundation trench. He went across to investigate, alarmed by the muffled grunts the boy was making. By the time he stood over Will Tregus, the boy was on his knees with his arms clasped tightly round his head as if to defend himself from a vicious attack. There was nothing in the trench with him — and no sign of the muddy earth being trampled by anything other than Will's own large feet.

'What's up with ye, bor?' Jess called down into the trench.

The boy curled himself up into a tight ball and his only movement was the trembling of his whole frame. Jess jumped down beside him, realizing that something had frightened him so deeply that he was almost paralysed. He was still trying to get some sense out of Will when the other men arrived for work.

Will had been struck dumb, unable to do anything other than slobber and mouth unintelligably.

It was much later that same day, after the sullen men had finished work and left the site, that Jess noticed the marks on one of the precious boulders. They had been cut deep into the stone so that they stood out clearly like a branding mark. There was a crude heart flanked by two sets of initials. W.T. on the left side and P.L. to the right. The blade of the knife had slipped on the L, leaving a deep, pinkish scar running away from it down the boulder.

Jess stood looking at the stone for a long time.

The Watcher, seeing the shattered remains of the old totem, was suddenly exhilarated. So that was what was at the root of the whole thing — the evil of the house, the rottenness in its owners. The stones . . . the stones must be lying there, beneath the paved floor, waiting to be found. Waiting for him to tear them out of the heart of the Place. He must tell Frances right away . . . and Robert too. The old monolith was the core in the whole dreadful situation.

The moment the foundations had been dug and laid, the

men collected their money and withdrew in haste. Young Will Tregus was unable to relate what had befallen him for he never recovered his speech or his senses.

When the walls were up to the eaves, Jess stood in the gap which would one day be his main entrance and stared across the shallow slope of the cleared ground to where the water of the narrow channel winked and sparkled on its way to the open sea.

LAVENHAM. The name sprang up from the spongy earth and filled his head. LAVENHAM . . . The bricks and mortar of this house should be named for the woman who was already becoming the cornerstone of his whole ambition. Woman? He smiled at the thought, the whole of his face softening at the bold assumption that such a precious and eternal child would ever become woman.

Lavenham . . . for Lavinia.

The new house squatted in its ancient foundations, opaque moonlight flowing over its unfinished walls and jutting roof timbers like warm milk. The woodland and cruelly scoured clearing stood out sharply in the white, uncompromising glare in harsh slashes of black against the silver water. The sour smell of the saltpans hung about its skeletal rooms and paneless windows.

As soon as the ground floor was completed and the roof sufficiently advanced to give protection from the weather, Jess struck his bender and moved into the kitchen quarters.

The following February, Amy stopped working for the Chatfields and joined Jess at Lavenham. By that time, the roof was complete, the fluted chimneys in place, and Amy was quite content to sleep on a pile of straw near the kitchen hearth until the upstairs chambers were ready for occupation. She and Jess were back together once more by their own fireside, and the look in his eye promised that she need never leave him again.

The house sat serenely amid a jumble of brickwork which would one day be its outhouses and stabling. The soft pink brick was offset by dove-grey window mullions of Bembridge stone, and the windows themselves were of leaded glass, reflecting the opaque blue of the sky.

'Sar shan, bor.'

The quiet voice at his elbow jerked Jess from his contemplation and he turned with a smile as he recognized his cousin Manfri Bayless.

'Builden's comen' on a fair treat,' Manfri observed after a pause.

Jess grinned at him. 'Bricks and mortar, bor,' he said, eyes twinkling. 'They're no bad way to build, after all, are they?'

'Good for some of us, maybe . . . .'

Manfri was small and wiry, the top of his unruly head little higher than Jess's shoulder. He was older than Jess by four years and looked more, for the flesh of his gaunt face seemed already folding into lines and creases. The fine blue Bayless eyes topped high cheekbones over which the olive skin was tightly stretched. He would have had a foxy look but for the humour in him and the relaxed upturning corners of his strong mouth.

Knowing that his visit would not be a social one, Jess waited quietly for enlightenment.

'How's that boil healen' on Olivas's hind quarter?'

Jess clapped his cousin on the shoulder. 'You're a real choviar . . . come and see for yourself. The swelling is down and the wound as clean as lambs in clover. He's as right as rain now, bor.'

They made for the north meadow, where Olivas cropped contentedly, close to the wattle hut that was his stable. He lifted his head as they approached and whinnied his welcome.

'Thinken' of putten' him to a good mare yet?' Manfri asked casually after examining the fast-healing wound.

It had been in Jess's mind since they began the barn foundations. Olivas was eight years of age. He was ready for special mares.

'I can get you a real little beauty for three goldies.'

31

He laughed at the surprise on Jess's face. 'Et's no great mystery, bor. Young Edmund Gibbons — over to Runcton — he won this pretty little mare at the gamen' tables off of that bleeder, me Lord Sherwood. Next night he lost all his ready cash the same way he won it . . . . Now he's offeren' it to me for three guineas. She's a beauty, Jess, just three years old and in good health. Thought you might be interested in haven' her . . . and maybe I should pitch me bender here and make sure the two of 'em thrive and give you a fine stable?'

Within a month of Manfri's arrival the roof timbers were being set and Manfri's little bender was established against the side of Olivas's wattle shelter. Olivas and Glimmer grazed side by side, obviously much taken with each other. There had been no trouble from the young mare and Jess was delighted with her. By the time she came into season, Manfri was ready for her. The covering went perfectly, and afterwards Jess hitched a piece of sacking from Olivas's groom box and rubbed the sweat from the horse's steaming coat with strong strokes.

'There y'are, my fine fellow,' he said softly to Olivas. 'A good performance, bor . . . . A few more like today's and I reckon you'll have made a fine little 'un for us. What say you, hmm?' Olivas was still breathing as though he had run a race but he turned his head into Jess's chest and snorted against his coat. He knew all about the threads of his master's dreams.

2

Jess stood on his wide stone terrace, rocking back and forth on the balls of his feet, surveying his building work with critical complacency.

The geese were doing a fine job of keeping the grass short between the gravel forecourt and the slope down to the creek. Light airs sang through the summer-clad oaks and stirred the rushes at the water's edge. Away to the right, beyond the new dutch barn, Olivas cropped stiffly in white-spatted dignity, and Jess could just see Glimmer and her foal sauntering across the second paddock beyond. Her movements were slow for she was again heavy with foal.

Behind Jess lay the house, its rosy brickwork and grey stone blending with the first tints of early autumn. Contentment was his companion; achievement his balm.

Warren Chaldecott, the Chichester silversmith, had been the first to suggest that Jess should make loans. It was a great deal more profitable than simply storing coinage in his chest in Tovey's strong room.

'Plant your sovereigns 'n watch them grow,' he'd said — and judging by the growth of his own fortune, Jess could see the wisdom of such advice.

Now, just one year later, there was enough money, and more, for him to think of the next step. He heard the sound of hooves and watched as a horseman rode round the Dutch barn and into the forecourt.

John Freeland raised his crop in greeting and slid down from his horse.

'Sar shan, bor.' He clasped Jess's hands and hid his surprise at the change in the man since his last visit, eight months before. Jess looked older — far more than his twenty-five years. He had filled out and was simply but expensively dressed in strong cord breeches and a well-tailored brown leather jacket over fine lawn shirting. His unruly curls had been cued neatly into the nape of his neck and the grey eyes danced with pleasure as he pumped John's hand. It was Jess's face that had startled him, for he had always known it as the bright, open arena for all his friend's moods. It was still as handsome — possibly even more so, but new lines made a stranger of him, deep creases round his mouth and below his eyes. John wondered, as they turned towards the house, what strictures the place was laying upon one who was so essentially elemental.

'Amy . . . come and see who's here,' Jess bellowed as they crossed the hall towards the parlour. There was a light dragging patter of feet behind them and Amy came through the kitchen door, wiping her hands on her apron. She had a dusting of flour on her nose.

'Master John — how good to see you. You've not been home for such a long time. You will stay and eat with us, won't you?'

He was swift to accept, glancing from sister to brother and thinking how fine they both looked. Tall and straight-backed, they had a dignity about them that he found most endearing.

Amy was willow slim, her hair bushed out from under her cap and spreading down the back of her dress like charred gorse. Her sleeves were rolled up to the elbows, showing a creamy expanse of olive skin. Something stirred in him and contemplated her. She was startlingly handsome, with the piercing blue eyes of all the Baylesses except Jess. No coquetry about her, though. She simply didn't try to project her womanliness, so that there was a lack of animation about her that cooled any ardour her looks inspired.

The parlour had changed dramatically since he last saw it as a bare place. Panelled and shuttered by an army of

34

carpenters, now it had become a delightful room. The pale wood gleamed with polish, and there were heavy yellow damask curtain hangings to draw across the shuttered windows on cold nights. Jess's desk dominated one end of the room. It was a magnificent piece of carved and polished mahogany, its leather top cluttered with a mess of papers and scrolled documents.

The fine seascape hanging over the fireplace had been John's personal thanks for Jess's many small services, not the least of which had been his timely rescue of Lavinia and her maid when a bullock had run amok through the Autumn Sloe Fair in Chichester. His parents had also been warmly grateful and had made Jess more welcome at Ryman's since the incident. Now, as they settled themselves in comfortable leather wing-chairs, John slid to the dream which he knew most occupied his friend's mind these days. 'Are you any closer to achieving that particular desire yet?'

Jess nodded. 'Next time you visit these parts I should have my own vessel in commission. She's being built in the Birdham yard now and Ferris reckons that if the work on her continues to progress at the present rate, she should be down the slip and into the water by the spring.'

'Ha then,' John said, seating himself in one of the chairs and hunting in his pockets for his snuff, 'I shall be here in that case, to wish her Godspeed — for I take my articles in September and come back to Chichester in time for Christmas to take up an appointment with Joshua Daley, the West Street lawyer.'

Jess sat forward, legs splayed out in front of him. 'Will you represent me then — or am I too great a risk for your expensively acquired new reputation?'

'I'd be honoured to act for you. I shall be starting with no reputation at all, Jess — until I can show my paces — and your business is liable to be as complicated and laced with litigation as any freshman could wish for.'

Jess's eyes twinkled. 'There's the gravest danger of my becoming a respectable citizen in the very near future, you know. I have met with a man of extraordinary vision, not to mention an impeccable background. His name is Thomas Benson. He seems to have more contacts in France and Spain and even as far as the Orient and India, than any other man of my acquaintance. He hails from Barnstable way . . . a far cry from here, I grant you, but that may be no bad thing when I tell you that the law seems only to have been created for the express purpose of trying his wits against it. I think he gets more enjoyment from cheating the very government he represents in Parliament than anyone I've ever met. I'm thinking of using him as my contractor until I have made my own reputation with the foreign agents.'

They talked with the ease of brothers, knowing what was in each other's heart.

'May I bring Lavinia to call tomorrow?' John eventually said. He watched the quick flare in the grave grey eyes, as swiftly quenched.

'That would be a welcome pleasure for Amy — and for me.' Jess said lightly, his tone almost impersonal. 'She embroidered the cushion behind you — and gave it to me for Christmas. I treasure it greatly.'

He jumped up, pulling his watch from his waistcoat pocket. He flicked open the cover and took his time counting his numbers before tucking it back out of sight.

'Come on, bor,' he said. 'I nearly forgot my special news since you were last here. Olivas's dam, Glimmer, has produced the finest little foal we've bred so far. He's four months old now. Come and take a look at him before Amy starts complaining that we're spoiling her hot food.'

They leaned on the barred fence, watching the horses grazing in companionable silence. Olivas lifted his head, saw his visitors and moved towards them, swishing his pale silken tail and shaking the flies from about his head. He was unquestionably monarch of the field, magnificent in carriage and quality, even though he was now no longer young. He approached, whickering a welcome in the back of his throat.

36

Jess fondled the stately head. The three mares hung back, giving Olivas precedence with the visitors and then curiosity drew them slowly towards the little group by the fence, trailing their young as they approached. They were russet shades of autumn — except one.

'Look at him,' Jess said quietly, pointing.

The foal had been too small to catch John's eye at first, but now he came timidly towards the jostling horses at the fence, peeping at them from behind his mother. He was a completely golden creature, his coat the colour of wet sand and the still stubby mane and tail like liquid cream.

'Isn't that the most perfect sight you ever saw?' Jess's voice was husky, as though the air was knocked out of him afresh each time he looked at the little foal. They watched it quietly as it stood against its dam, staring at them with huge black eyes. Then, tired of the lack of action, it backed away and gambolled off across the paddock, bucking its tiny hooves as it went.

'Phew.' John realized that he had been holding his breath as he watched the foal's perfect movements. 'Beautiful, Jess. He's surely the most handsome little creature on four legs that I ever recall.'

Something distracted his attention and made him turn away from the horses. He swung round and leaned his back against the rails and looked at Jess, to find himself staring into grey pools filled with an intensity that quickened his pulse. Unable to tear his attention away, he was hardly aware of Jess's quiet voice.

'Midas is his name, bor . . . after the king who turned everything to gold. And John, I'd like to give him to Miss Lavinia, for he is the most perfect possession I have. Do you think I might safely ask your father's permission to do this? I . . . don't want to offend them so that they feel bound to refuse me. Will you mention it to them and see how they feel about it?'

The eyes held him. He felt weighted down so that neither his limbs nor his brain would respond. The deep grey pools swam round him like eddies of smoke in a fathomless black cavern.

Jess blinked — and the moment passed and might never have been. 'What do you think, bor?' Jess's voice sounded eager, no more, nor less, than any other young suitor on the verge of committing himself to a declaration.

He must be mad, John thought — he knew that the answer would be in the negative. Jess was a good and valued friend but Thomas Freeland would never permit his only daughter to marry a gypsy. He heard himself say, 'Struth, Jess — that animal will be worth a king's ransom in a year or two. Is it Lavinia you're after?'

'You know I am, bor.' The deep voice was gentle, patient, with even a hint of humour in it. 'You know me . . . I hate to be refused anything that I've worked hard to win. There's never been anyone else for me — and I've plenty to lay at her feet. I've watched her grow from a little child into the perfect young woman she is today. If worship is not too strong a word, you could say that that is how I regard her and always will.'

John put his arm round Jess's shoulder and they strolled back towards the house.

'You know that I'll do all I can on your behalf,' John said before he left. 'I'll speak to Father as soon as the right moment presents itself.'

Amy watched him go. There was an element of worry in Jess's cheery farewell. She hoped devoutly that his concern was justified.

Jess waited for word from Rymans.

Each day saw him in a different place, feverishly negotiating the sale of timber here, collecting interests on his loans there. He kept up a furious pace as though the need to add to his already considerable capital would ensure that his reception at Rymans was cordial.

Amy missed nothing — but then the surveillance of her brother had always been her main occupation. Something was worrying him, she could see. He was like a coiled spring of nervous energy, dividing himself at a furious

38

pace between the new Chichester office, the Birdham boatyard and Lavenham.

She allowed him to bring Polly Ayles into the house to help with the growing responsibilities of keeping the place the way the well-to-do gorgios liked their homes kept. Polly would never be a temptation to Jess. There was only Lavinia to contend with.

After a week, Blunden arrived from Rymans with a note from John. Jess read it in anguish.

> Dear Jess, I'm sorry about the lack of communication but the problems are legion and Mother and Father are in constant strife so that, so far, nothing is resolved. You will have to be patient because your appearance at this time would only exacerbate the situation. Lavinia is quite unaware of the cause of our parents' discord and is naturally most concerned about it. I fear that my father's increasing ill-health makes him unreasonable, but I think you have a right to know that Lavinia acquired a suitor during her recent stay in London. I understand that my father considers him an appropriate match.

The letter tore away the last of Jess's peace of mind. He went about his business in a state of thunderous gloom, snarling at his cousins and even shouting at Amy. She bowed her head before his misery, but only to hide the satisfaction she felt at the way things were turning out. He had broached the subject too soon, he saw that now and cursed himself for the foolishness of his timing. Thomas Freeland was a mortally sick man with fast failing strength — and after this next Nutbourne run, he would be having no further direct involvement with the Blacks, apart from making the arrangements and financing the operations. In a month or two he could have presented himself, not only as Jess Bayless of Lavenham, but also as owner of the *Grace* — a combination that should have impressed the most reticent of fathers.

'Leave me alone, Amy. I'm in no mood for company.'

She stared at him in surprise, in the act of settling herself in the chair opposite him as she did each evening.

'I won't distrub you,' she said stiffly, 'we don't have to talk, do we?'

He glowered up at her from his place on the sheepskin rug. 'Are you deaf, girl? I said I want to be alone.'

The colour flared up in her cheeks and she turned sharply so that her precarious balance slipped and she stumbled heavily against her chair.

Contrite, he put up a hand and took hold of her russet skirt. 'I'm sorry, pen. I'm a rude, evil-tempered bastard and I can't think why you put up with me so patiently. Come back and sit down here on the rug. Maybe you can cheer me up.'

She put her sewing on the chair seat and settled down beside him, the two spots of high colour still bright on her cheeks. She could feel the torment in him and, knowing the source of it, gloried in his pain. Let him suffer . . . his hurt will turn to indifference one day, she thought.

The look was in his eyes and, recognizing it, she said nothing, but sat quietly gazing into the embers of the fire in the basket grate. He took her hand and smoothed it across his knee and she let it lie there, comforted by the gentle stroking motion.

He stared into the red coals, concentrating once more upon searching within himself for the Power, calling to it and feeling only the emptiness of total loss. Its influence was there in another, more subtle way but it was quite different now, filling him with compulsions of such sensuality that he groaned aloud, stirred by erotic fantasies of Lavinia which would never be fulfilled.

He saw her delicate face in the glowing embers, staring back at him with parted lips and a reflection of his own longing in the huge blue eyes. He saw her mouth upturned in laughter, the pink movement of her tongue moistening her lower lip, gleaming, full. He felt Amy's soft hand under his and began tracing the contours of each finger with the tips of his own. Thin hands; long and strong and the nails as smooth as glass. Warm glass.

Warm hand laying across his thigh like a small waiting bird . . . caught in the shadow of the hovering hawk; knowing . . . submissive, almost entranced by the knowledge of its own danger.

Lavinia. . . . Hear me . . . need me — want me. . . .

The pent-up feelings of years seemed suddenly to flow outward from him, flooding through him without warning and he groaned aloud again, knowing that it controlled him. He stared at Amy as her arms went round him in comprehension, drawing him against her.

Soft warm skin with the clean woman smell, the scent of excitement — of wanting him. He wept with the vastness of his need, of her fast, shallow breath beneath his hands, of her urgency, the overwhelming response of her. He drowned in the smooth length of her body — olive skin against the olive of his own, blue Bayless eyes submerging in the hard cold steel of grey rage. He hurt her and the very infliction of the pain was sweet pleasure and her pleasure roused him further until images blurred and the fury drained from him.

The Watcher groaned. Here it was again: life being made within these tainted walls. He steadied himself and homed in on that tiny new seed in its moment of creation. There was resistance. Strange, he thought. New life had always been easy to obliterate but this one was deflecting him. He would wait — and take it at the moment of its birth.

Thomas Freeland died just before dawn on 24 March, 1729. He was sixty-nine years old. The funeral attracted mourners from every walk of life for Freeland had administered several estates and had been a wise and respected steward. When the service was over and the coffin lowered into the earth, the family and closer friends returned to Rymans, where refreshments were served in the great hall.

Jess had been surprised and touched to receive a note from Mrs Freeland inviting him to attend the funeral. It

41

had done much to lift the heavy mood which had afflicted him since the day of his last meeting with Freeland.

He did not stay long at Rymans after the service. He attended to pay his respects to Mrs Freeland and John and Lavinia, not to drink at their table. He took Abigail Freeland's hand and bent over it.

'I'm truly so very sorry for having been such a burden to him at the end,' he murmured against her black bonnet. She drew back from him, keeping his hand in both of hers and her face was gentle in private grief.

'I was afraid that you might not come, Jess,' she said, 'but I prayed that you would, for at the end he asked that you be invited here today. He was sorry too, you know, for he had quite an affection for you in his own way.'

He paid his respects to John and Lavinia, spoke most courteously with the Controller of Customs, John Carr — and left the house without dining. He could not bear to be under the same roof as Lavinia without telling her how he felt. He had tried to keep his eyes averted from her but it was impossible not to feast his gaze upon the small graceful girl in her mourning black, which only enhanced the milky beauty of her skin and the silver gilt lustre of carefully coiled hair.

He rode slowly back to Lavenham afterwards, with Lavinia fresh in his mind. He threw Olivas's reins to Manfri and strode into the house, slamming the door behind him and shouting for Amy as he shrugged himself out of the uncomfortably formal black coat. There was no sign of Amy.

'Hey, chika . . . where are you? Come and help me off with these confounded boots. They're stopping the blood in my legs.'

She came to the door, wiping her hands on her apron. She looked drawn and ill.

'What's the matter?' he asked sharply, suddenly aware of her mood.

She shook her head and her face was the colour of parchment. 'Just a little off-colour. Nothing to worry about.' Her voice was like the murmur of distant waves on shingle and she came forward to kneel and take the foot of his uplifted boot.

Jess watched her as she pulled and tugged, keeping her eyes on what she was doing. The boot came off and she put it behind her and turned to tackle the other.

'What's wrong, Amy?' he said quietly.

She looked up, squatting before him. Her blue fustian gown was the same colour as her eyes.

'I'm with child.' Her voice, sharp and ugly, was the faintest whisper.

They stared at each other, shocked by her vehemence. She had never spoken to Jess like that before — never spoken in any way other than with love.

He put his hands on her shoulders and drew her against his chest. They stood very close together.

'I'm truly sorry,' he said, and all the grief of the day and his own self-condemnation was in his voice. 'I'm so sorry, chiriklo. It should never have happened and I'll never forgive myself . . . .'

'Why shouldn't it have happened?' she said fiercely into his shirt front. 'I'm glad it happened. I love you more than I can ever show you — so how else do I express myself? You know you have always been God to me, Jess. You know that you always will be. I feel like a woman with you, so it's only right that I have your child to express it. You could never have given me more.'

He held her away from him and stared down into the white, mutinous face with great tenderness and then gently put her from him. He went into the kitchen and picked up his working boots from the yard door.

'I have to think and then we'll talk about it later,' he said.

The arrival at Lavenham of Rueb Bayless was fortuitous, for nine horses were more than even the tireless Manfri could cope with. When the house mares foaled there would be four more to care for. Rueb — Piramis's youngest son — was the obvious choice. He was, at fifteen,

43

a big silent stripling with an admiration for Jess which knew no bounds. He had no special skills except for a limitless capacity to keep going in whatever he was about. He took over all the occasional jobs in the stables and the main house, an occupation which kept him going from dawn until dusk. His industry ensured that Lavenham was run on oiled wheels and prospered daily.

Apart from Lavenham, there were only two houses of any importance in the parish of Apuldram — Manor Farm and Rymans. The farm was a pleasant brick and quarry-stone building, with a spread of barns and cattle shed on one side and a large orchard on the other. Rymans, on the other hand, was a unique structure of such unusual design that there had always been conjecture about its past.

Lavinia loved Rymans with all her heart. It had been the Freeland home since their father brought his bride, Abigail Pay, there in 1700, and it was where she and John were born. It was surrounded by fields, and the path to the little church ran along one of its boundaries. Saint Mary's was only a hundred yards away, standing alone in Church Meadow, with the grass growing high round its Saxon stonework. Lavinia could look out of any of the Rymans windows as far as the eye could see and the only other buildings were their own out-houses, the church and Manor Farm. The rest of the village was long gone, ravaged by plague and then fire nearly two centuries before and abandoned now, save for the nocturnal passings of furtive men about their unofficial business.

Loving hands had levelled the ground on the west and northern sides of Rymans, creating lawns and flower beds and a well-stocked orchard and vegetable garden. The children had a swing here among the trees, and John Blunden's father had even made them a see-saw with little chairs at each end of the long plank. At the bottom of the orchard huddled a mess of bee skeps, tended with devotion by a very old man whose name no one seemed to remember — he was always referred to as Beezer.

Lavinia might have been a solitary child, since John was eleven years her senior, had it not been for the mysteries and fascinations with which Beezer occupied most of her early life. She felt undoubted affection for John, of course — and also for his close friend, the gypsy boy Jess Bayless, who never ceased to fascinate her — but best of all, in her young days, was her special friendship with old Beezer and the strange and wonderful bees with their industry and almost human life-style.

Very early in her life, Beezer had been content to talk to Lavinia about his charges. From as far back as she could remember she had listened to his often unintelligible ramblings, wide-eyed and attentive to everything he told her. It was that very trust which had started their rapport, for he said very little to anyone else. She had always been able to understand the garbled speech — and mostly it was about the bees.

'Be good to the little furry folk,' he would say, 'an' they will be good to you. Move carefully near their hives with kindness in your heart and they will never sting you — even though you walk naked among them. But put a hand upon their house when there is hatred or skulduggery in your mind, and you'd best beware for they know . . . they know what is in you — and if it is bad they will surely go for you.'

Lavinia became aware of her father's failing health after a particularly uncharacteristic exchange over his wish to send her to London for the winter season. 'Why is Papa so crabby these days?' she asked.

'Don't cross swords with him,' Abigail Freeland said gently. 'He has a wretched pain in his stomach which is very worrying and Doctor Sanden doesn't seem to know how to ease it for him. Be a good daughter and do as he asks. Spend this season with Aunt Julia, as he is urging. Please.'

And, of course, she did as they wished.

After the London season was over, she returned with relief to Apuldram, walking with a new decorum, perfect

45

manners, an ability to converse with assurance — and a firm determination not to repeat the previous three months.

Unfortunately, she also left behind, with no regret, a suitor who had refused to take her dismissal of him seriously. Her flat rejection of Toby Rathfarnon angered her aunt, so that heated letters to Rymans followed her departure from Kensington. Because she was so shocked by the deterioration in her father's health during her absence, she dared not be too forceful in her opinion of Lord Rathfarnon. She began to feel that she was being thrust into an impossible position and, seeking to wipe the odious young man from her mind, her thoughts turned instead to Jess. The unavoidable comparison between him and the wretched foppish Toby only made her more unhappy.

Two weeks after her return to Rymans Jess had still not made an appearance, his name had not once been mentioned and Abigail returned again and again to the subject of Rathfarnon and his suit.

'Dearest girl, we only want you to be secure in the future and happy in the company of your equals. By this time next year, I'm afraid that our finances will be sadly diminished and the possibility of doing another season may well be out of the question.'

Lavinia did her best to keep the impatience out of her voice. 'Mama — dearest Mama . . . when will you accept that I absolutely will not do another season? I only did this last one for Papa's sake. I don't like most of the people I've met at Aunt Julia's. They are empty-headed and prattling. I enjoy the soireés because of the quality of the music, which was always delightful — and I love the theatres and rides in the park. But truly, dear Mama, I don't at all care for the rest of it — and Lord Rathfarnon in particular. He is foolish and drooling and he smells quite dreadful.'

Seeing the displeasure her words were causing, she gave her mother a contrite hug. Abigail Freeland smoothed the fine golden hair from her daughter's forehead. Dropping her guard for a moment she looked at Lavinia with all the love of a woman for the last child in her life.

'One day it will come to you, I know. One day you will be in such a hurry to get to the altar — just as I was when I was your age and your father came into my life. One day . . . .' She stopped, seeing the sudden flush steal across Lavinia's face. She stared at the tell-tale colour and her daughter's downcast eyes — and turned away quickly, biting her lip. 'So . . . you reciprocate the gypsy's feelings, do you?' she thought, suddenly knowing it all. Had he already spoken to her, then? Had they perhaps been meeting all this time? She closed her mind to the possibilities, torn by feelings of betraying Thomas's wishes and a grudging spark of private approval. He was so handsome — so full of life and vigour and bounding ambition.

Thomas Freeland died in his sleep at her side soon afterwards.

Since she was the most forgiving of women, it was Mrs Freeland's own curiosity which, after a suitable period of mourning had elapsed, finally brought Lavinia and Jess face to face for the first time since the funeral. The intriguing daily spectacle of his barley sugar chimneys being built on her horizon became more than she could bear. She let it be known through John that an invitation to inspect the house's progress might be graciously accepted.

Jess was struck dumb by the unexpected message. Then he became a whirlwind of activity, urging Polly and Amy to polish every stick of furniture again and again until Amy locked herself in her room to rage at him unheard.

He chose a fine day when the mud churned up by the passage of countless builders' carts — which still surrounded the house — was fairly firm, and the entrance was made more negotiable by the laying of fresh gravel. The sun shone warmly on their heads and the surrounding woods were filled with birdsong. John drove his mother and sister the flat mile between Rymans and Lavenham. It gave him a special pleasure that his close friendship with

47

Jess was finally being recognized and accepted by the two women.

'You'll be pleasantly surprised,' he promised them. 'There is nothing left of the barefoot boy about Jess these days. He is a very delightful companion, Mother. Just you wait and see.'

Jess was waiting for them on the front terrace, a tall, broad-shouldered figure, well dressed in fine-quality breeches and a creamy silk shirt beneath his dark green jacket. His voice was deep and musical as he greeted them and handed them down from the trap. He watched as Mrs Freeland looked about her, surveying the outside of the house with open curiosity which quickly became smiling approval.

Lavenham sat serenely amid a jumble of unfinished brickwork that would one day be its stabling and out-houses. The sun shone blandly on the bright backdrop of neatly husbanded fields and well-culled woodland with a sparkle of diamond water among the reeds where the Chichester Channel flowed by to the harbour and open sea beyond.

Lavinia stood close to her mother and said nothing. Her eyes remained firmly fixed on the back of Jess's head.

He ushered them into the hall, where carpenters from Hershall Kimber's yard were fitting pale limed oak panelling to the walls. The noise of saw and hammer was deafening and he hurried them through to the kitchen quarters with apologies and closed the hall door on the dust and industry.

Jess, as John had promised, proved to be amusing and delightful company without once abusing his position. Watching him surreptitiously, Lavinia could only admire his composure, for he did his best to give her mother his complete attention, when he must surely have been re-membering the times that they had assembled and played tag in the Rymans kitchens. Who would have imagined in his wildest dreams that that ragged and cheeky youth with the warm grey eyes and infectious laugh would now be

master of his own small estate, entertaining the gentry
with such easy courtesy? As though he read her thoughts,
Jess caught Lavinia's eyes on him and winked. She
coloured and lowered her eyes, but the corners of her
mouth fought a losing battle with the smile which trembled there.

All in all, it had been a most successful visit and
Mistress Freeland returned home with Lavinia, filled with
praise for Jess's aims and achievements.

There were regular visits to the Bayless house after that,
and at last Jess was made welcome at Rymans, for he
played a fine hand at cards and was more than happy to
partner Mrs Freeland when John and Geoffrey Tovey
were visiting.

Small parishes have few hiding places from prying eyes,
and news of the birth of a daughter to Amy Bayless spread
through Apuldram like wildfire. She had not called in the
Birdham midwife but had had the baby, as the rest of her
clan did, in the bender of Aunt Sarey Bayless, attended by
her own sister Saiforella and other Bayless women. Heads
were shaken, the disapproval compounded when Amy
refused to name the father — or to have the child churched
and baptised.

'Violet is her name,' she said with uncharacteristic firmness, 'Violet Bayless. What blessings can church and
Parson Kelway give her that she does not already possess?'

The gossips had a field-day and rumours concerning the
identity of the baby's father spread through the cottages.
Amy was quite unmoved by the commotion. She stayed
quietly at home and waited for the novelty to wear off and
for another topic of scandal to draw the attention from her.
It did, of course, but not in the way she had hoped.
Romance and the Baylesses were to provide even more
excitement in the parish before the year was over.

3

Jess stood in the middle of his driveway, sniffing the autumn air. It smelt pungently of sun-warmed earth, tinged with the sharpness of charred stubble. Over his head — high in the blue sky — trailing feathers of swiftly moving clouds streamed, riding the currents of the upper air like galloping horses' tails.

'Sloe Fair tomorrow,' he thought, vainly trying to keep his mind off his approaching guests. He smiled to himself, remembering the old camel that always appeared in Chichester on that day, giving a heady excitement to the throng and a ride to remember for the fortunate few who were able to stay on his back. Sloe Fair, with its colourful stalls and tumblers and travelling players and minstrels. He would offer to accompany Lavinia this year — and her mother too, of course.

They were coming. The phaeton clattered into view with Lavinia driving a smart little piebald. She waved her whip at him as they swept past, round to the front door. He hurried after them as young Rueb Bayless ran from the saddle room to take the pony's bridle, and was beside them with hand outstretched to steady them, before Mrs Freeland was even ready to descend from her seat.

'At last, at last,' she said gaily, giving Jess her neat black-gloved hand and leaning on him quite heavily as she stepped from the carriage.

'You always seem to bring the sunshine with you, ma'am,' he said with grave affection. He turned to Lavinia but she was already beside him. 'Good day to you too, Miss Lavinia.'

She grinned at him, acknowledging the adult address he

had awarded her. She was sixteen now and had entered the realms of maturity. The sharp breeze whipped spots of bright colour into her cheeks. She hooked her arm through her mother's and all three strolled into the house, pausing on the threshold to admire the finished effect of the limed oak panelling in the hall.

'Why have you not taken advantage of the elegant new-style sash windows? They are quite the vogue now in town,' Mrs Freeland asked, surveying the beautiful hall with approval.

Jess led the way into the parlour. No entertaining in the kitchen this time. 'I don't like the idea of them here. That is to say — I like them well enough in a town house where the streets give protection from the elements and the maximum glazed area is needed to bring light into dark rooms . . . but here, ma'am, we have plenty of light, as you see, and we have to contend with savage gales in winter, so transom windows are, I think, better suited.'

They settled in deep comfortably upholstered armchairs with bulging arms and high backs. The room was indeed light without being cold. A cheerful fire blazed in the basket grate and the room glowed with colour and polish and freshly cut flowers.

'Will you take tea now or after I have shown you round the garden and paddocks?' Jess was saying. Abigail Freeland noticed with an inner smile that he was looking at Lavinia with an expression that could only be described as heavily controlled joyous anticipation.

'Well, my dear, you may have noticed that my feet are not very steady these days on uneven ground. I suggest you show Lavinia the paddock and let me rest here and take in all this elegant newness.'

She watched them through the window as they sauntered across the close-cut grass below the terrace, making for the river bank beyond. Then they moved out of view, hidden by the Dutch barn. The sun went behind a cloud and for some unaccountable reason she felt an icy chill course through her.

'Good day to you, ma'am,' Amy said behind her.

Jess and Lavinia stood atop the river bank, watching the marine traffic slide by on its way to and from Dell Quay and Fishbourne Mill. Lavinia's mint green bonnet was level with Jess's cheek. She was small and neat as a doll, tempting as a cream cake with her matching outdoor habit and cape edged with white rabbit fur. He resisted an urge to draw her close to him and, instead, put a hand under her elbow and guided her along the bank towards the paddocks. They leaned on the wooden fence and watched as Olivas raised his beautiful head among his mares and foals at the far end of the field. He tossed his mane and moved slowly towards them, nodding a sage welcome as he approached.

'This is perfect,' Lavinia said under her breath. 'I love every corner of Apuldrum — but I've never found a more tranquil corner of it than this.'

Jess glanced away from the advancing horses and looked down at her upturned face with a smile.

'Mama feels that we should remove into Chichester or even New Fishbourne, now that father is gone. John takes his articles any minute now, as you know, and will then be returning to practise in Chichester. She feels that we should be more conveniently placed for him — and that Rymans is too large for us these days.'

'I'd hate to think of Rymans without Freelands in residence,' Jess said, 'and there's another thing too. Chichester would not be very convenient for all sorts of reasons. I have waited so long for permission to call on you — I hope very much that your mama takes her time before deciding on a move of any kind. Besides, I have a gift for you which might be difficult to accept if you were living in the town.'

Her eyes sparkled like blue stars.

'How exciting . . . what is it? Do tell me quickly, Jess. Oh, I do love surprises. I can't even guess what it could be.'

She was suddenly another Lavinia. All the carefully learned good manners of the schoolroom vanished — and she was sixteen years old, bouncing on the balls of her feet, the half of her who was all grave young womanhood instantly submerged in the excited girl. She grasped both his hands and tugged impatiently at him. He felt old and infinitely protective — and shook his head in mock severity.

'Patience, patience. How would it be if I gave it to you on your birthday?'

'Jess, how can you be so tantalizing? I would have to wait for another four whole months. How could I possibly contain my curiosity for a third of a year?'

'True, chiriklo . . . and I doubt whether my gift could wait that long either. Maybe I should give it to you today, after all.' He was teasing her, and she made a face at him and pretended to turn away with a mock pout.

Olivas came up to them on the other side of the fence. Behind him trailed the herd in a long straggle. 'How beautiful they are,' she murmured, stretching out her hands to them through the railings. They were golden and chestnut, the colours of autumn — fine-legged, high-flanked with proud arched necks and coats like well-polished wood.

'Why do you call your horse Olivas?' she asked, fondling the warm pink nose and letting him blow inquisitively into her hands.

'It's a Romany word . . . means socks or stockings. He has just the one white sock as you see.' Beside them Olivas lowered his head and cropped patiently, content to wait upon his master's pleasure before going through his pockets for the customary reward.

'How special you are,' she murmured to him, and he raised his head and sniffed the faint steam of her breath on the chill air, and whickered softly in his throat to her.

'He obviously thinks that you are very special too, Linnie.' She began to turn her head towards him when something caught her eye among the converging horses.

53

'Oh, Jess . . . just look over there. Have you ever seen anything more beautiful? Here, little thing — come here, here . . . . ' She strained her arms through the fence rails, wiggling her fingers at a colt who stood pressed against Olivas's flank, and peered at her with wide, tawny eyes.

He was a yearling, slim and immature and filled with apprehension at the sight of them. He jerked his graceful head from side to side, watching her . . . tempted. He was shades of golden sunlight like ripe corn, with mane and tail the colour of bleached flax.

'That's Midas,' Jess said quietly, moved by the sight of their meeting. 'He is my gift to you.'

The words took time to sink in, for all her attention was on the shyly approaching colt, but then she turned, wide-eyed and shaking her head firmly.

'Oh no, sir, I couldn't possibly accept such a gift.' And suddenly there was no trace of the child about her. His heart sank.

'Linnie, just look at him. From the day he was born I have wanted you to have him. He is the most perfect foal that Olivas has sired so far and it is important for me to give you something as precious as that. Something as perfect as you are yourself.'

He had taken her hand without realizing and now he looked down at it, resting with such trust in his own large brown one. The sight was too much.

'Linnie, I've carried about with me the image of that perfect little girl ever since we first met — when I was just a barefoot boy. Baylesses were all simple gypsy folk in those days but the sight of you — and my friendship with John — changed my whole life. Because of you, I began to dream of better things than living round a camp fire. You know what happened. John took it upon himself to begin my education and I have not wasted one chance of improving myself from that day to this. And I've done it, haven't I? I'm twenty-seven years old this month and you could say that I'm a well-respected fellow in these parts today, couldn't you? I've a fine house and a newly built

54

brigantine in Birdham yard on which I owe not a penny to any man, and I've a healthy mortgage business which, without even considering the marine side of things, brings me in enough income to support my own family in comfort.'

He stared down at her in an agony of expectation. 'Please accept Midas, Lavinia. I want you to have him so that he will be with you always as a reminder of me, nothing more, I promise. Only let me say that he represents all the devotion that this unworthy creature before you has to give.'

Her eyes were enormous, the blue irises flecked with tiny golden speckles round the pupils. She nodded slowly and the freshening breeze snatched a golden curl from under her bonnet and sent it bobbing across her cheek. He smoothed it away with a tender finger and tucked it out of sight, then took her hand and raised it to his lips.

'Miss Lavinia,' he said with a formality that stopped at his eyes, 'may I have the honour of calling on you tomorrow?'

Suddenly a puckish look of pure sparkling happiness filled her luminous face and she nodded with such eager pleasure that they burst into laughter. The tension broken, he took her arm and they turned away from the paddock and, bathed in a new intimacy, strolled slowly back towards the house.

Parson Kelway read the banns between Jess Bayless and Lavinia Freeland for three Sundays in May 1730. The parish watched the courtship in astonishment, for although he was now regarded as being the wealthiest and most evocative member of the community, Jess Bayless was still a gypsy in their eyes. Wealthy and influential he might now well be, but heads were shaken in deep disapproval that he should aspire to pay his respects to a lady of Miss Lavinia Freeland's gentle breeding — and that her mother should permit him to do so.

Having once made her decision on the subject, Abigail

Freeland countered the back-wash of disapproving comment by briskly pointing out that three generations before, the Freelands of Aldingbourne had also been simple peasant farmers — and that her own grandfather had been a peruke-maker in Chichester. Jess, she insisted, was not only a most presentable young man but his ambition and reliability were only exceeded by his extraordinarily kindly nature. He was, she said firmly, an excellent match for Lavinia — and she looked forward exceedingly to having him for her son-in-law.

Both Rymans and Lavenham became hives of industry from the moment that Lavinia accepted a ruby and diamond betrothal ring from Jess. Three months were scarcely long enough for all the weaving and sewing, furniture-making, brewing and cooking which preceded the wedding. Lavenham began to glow with new colour as Lavinia's chosen materials were sewn into heavily lined curtains and hung in the living rooms and chambers. The days sped by.

Each Sunday Jess now accompanied the Freelands to morning service and appeared to listen to Parson Kelway's simple sermons with undivided attention. Afterwards, the offertory bag always yielded a larger harvest. Jess again, the old man decided, because it had never contained more than a few pence before Jess began to worship at Saint Mary's.

June is always a favourite time for parish weddings and the day before the Bayless-Freeland wedding found most of Apuldrum involved in one way or another over its preparation. Mistress Chatfield from Manor Farm had organized Sarey Beer — who had only recently married a Bayless herself — and five other parish women into decorating the little church. The saltpans Baylesses had demurred at joining in this pleasant chore but had come to the church door, bearing armfuls of pink and white apple blossom, yellow field gladioli and ragged robin, march orchids, moon daisies and bluebells. They were all gladly accepted and heaped into deep window recesses and arranged in copper milk churns along the communion step. By nightfall, the little Saxon church had been transformed into a place of bright and simple beauty.

The seamstress arrived at Rymans the afternoon before the wedding. She and her three needlewomen had the wedding gown with them. Lavinia was borne up the wide staircase to the solar for her final fitting, jostled and teased by two young Freeland cousins and her aunt Pay. They laughed and joked among themselves as they unbuttoned her from her working gown and petticoats and then stood back as the seamstress moved in with her small army of cutters and tuckers. The wedding gown was reverently lowered over her shoulders and there was a murmur of delight from the onlookers. The heavy Indian satin shimmered like polished ivory, a perfect complement to the golden lustre of Lavinia's hair and the creamy purity of her skin.

She stood very still, a quiet pool of contemplation amongst the chatter of her attendants, letting them turn her this way and that as every smallest detail was checked. She was thinking about the Baylesses. Jess had laughed when she tried to question him about Romany customs. 'Just wait and see,' he had said, putting a long arm round her and planting a kiss on the end of her nose. 'Don't worry, little one. They won't dance round you brandishing their knives. You'll enjoy it all just as much as you'll enjoy our churching, I promise,' and she had had to be content with that. It wasn't that she was frightened of the Baylesses, in spite of the wildness of them all. The presence of Jess would be enough to ensure that she was well treated by his relatives.

A pin pricked her and she started out of her thoughts. They were just in the act of raising the veil to drop it over her head.

'No . . . don't do that now.' she backed away from the upstretched arms of the sewing women. 'I mustn't put it on until tomorrow . . . . Jess's sister Saiforella told me that it's bad luck to try on the veil and the wreath before

57

the wedding day itself.'

'What nonsense, child,' Mrs Freeland said with spirit. 'We have to try it on, just to check that it sits snugly beneath the wreath.'

But Lavinia pressed her lips tightly together in an obstinate line and shook her head with finality. She felt close to tears and her audience, quick to sense her mood, tutted and soothed her, understanding the natural tensions that she must be feeling on the eve of the most important day of her life.

In no time the gown was off, the petticoats unbuttoned and she was helped into her night robe and seated in a comfortable chair with a hot posset so liberally laced with good French brandy that it soon brought the colour flooding back to her cheeks. Then up came Lizzie Beer with a platter of sweet cakes and Bohea tea, and Annie Heberden after her, panting under the weight of the cider jug. Mrs Chatfield joined them and soon the solar was filling up with last-minute well-wishers.

Rymans was astir well before dawn, and by the time Lavinia woke the fires had been lit, and the halls and kitchens scrubbed. Preparations for the feasting were well under way in both halls and the big barn. She wrapped her dressing gown round her and knocked on her mother's door. They breakfasted together, keeping out of the way of Mrs Blunden and her army of helpers.

Lavinia allowed herself to be fussed over by the women. Her hair was brushed for a hundred strokes and long shining ringlets made with the hot tongs until they fell sleek and golden down her back and her head was ready at last for the veil. They lowered the heavy satin gown over her shoulders and she stood up for it to be buttoned and patted into place. Standing submissively, she realized that she would not sit down again until she was Mistress Bayless.

She was ready at last and they stood back and surveyed her critically and clapped their hands and exclaimed at the

beauty of this cream and golden young bride. Mrs Freeland gave her daughter a kiss through the cobweb folds of
the tulle veil.

'You look so very lovely, my darling,' she said softly,
eyes bright with unshed tears. 'I'm very proud of you.'

For a moment they held each other tightly and then
Lavinia noticed that, for some time now, she had been
hearing the church bells peeling at the back of her mind.
The sound lifted her spirits and she straightened her back,
kissed her mother again and gave her attendants a dazzling
smile.

'Shall we go, then, my ladies? The hourglass is empty
and the sooner we get to the church, the sooner these
craven worms in my inside will cease their churning . . . .'

She was late.

Jess felt as though he had been standing at the chancel
steps for half a lifetime. He stole a glance at his sponsor,
who was swaying beside him like a tree in a gale.

'He looks sick enough to be the groom,' he thought with
great satisfaction.

'Suffer, you son of a shit shoveller,' he said unkindly to
Richard out of the corner of his mouth. 'You'll be feeling
even worse when this day comes for you, I give you my
word.'

The stalls were filling with whispering, rustling people;
heads straining round this way and that to see who was
present and who was not; eyes swivelling to watch the
door for the moment when the bride would appear on her
brother's arm.

There was movement outside the porch and a ragged
cheer went up from the crowd standing along the path and
straddling the grave-stones. In the warm sunshine the
sound of a flute mingled with the double clarion of the
bells. Then Lavinia was there, at the end of the church —
walking slowly up the aisle towards him.

Amy sat in the stubbly grass with Violet in her lap,

watching a family of shelduck foraging among the reeds below the bank. Behind her, her sister Saiforella and all the Baylesses still living in the area worked over the huge fire and spread of food and ceremonial drinks. The sound of their laughter and ribald banter echoed across the water. It was some time since they had celebrated a wedding and this one was particularly special. Jess had become a monument to them and his time for 'jumping the broomstick' must have all the very best trappings that they could muster.

Violet crawled off her mother's lap and reached for a dragon-fly which hovered, trembling translucent wings as it drew nectar from a head of pink clover. Amy watched idly as the little girl sat back on chubby buttocks, staring in wonder at the dainty quivering creature. She was suddenly reminded of something in the child's intense concentration. The round grey eyes stared as the dragon-fly drank until, replete, it suddenly swooped out and upwards, away from the empty flower — and straight into Violet's face. There was a blinding flash like sunlight on glass. Amy scooped the child into her arms as the dragon-fly fell. It lay on the grass like a curl of burnt bark, charred and robbed of its rich colours — and very dead. The little girl in her arms shivered, her baby's face a mask of shock out of which the huge grey eyes glared blankly — just as she remembered Jess's eyes in the moment of a Flaming.

Amy hugged the little body tightly to her, rocking and murmuring small meaningless words of comfort until the rigidity drained away and the little girl relaxed slowly against her mother's neck. Then Amy stood up and climbed the shallow incline towards the well-stacked fire. She passed by the family, the child still held tightly against her chest, and disappeared into the house.

Across the corn and the Dell Quay road, over the coppice of Roman oaks and Olivas's paddock, the bells rang out. The Baylesses had been waiting for that moment and lost no time in filling their tankards with Polly's best ale and toasting the absent couple in the way they knew best. Soon the real fun would begin — but until the newly-weds were with them they were content to swap long and flowery tales of past rummers and drink the health of their host.

The wedding luncheon at Rymans was a drawn-out affair, for the food was excellent and the wines without equal. Speeches were made and toasts by the dozen slowed up the tempo of the occasion. While the tables were being cleared in the great hall so that dancing could commence, Jess and Lavinia went through to the barn where the village and local tradesmen and their families were making merry and waiting to toast the young couple. After that, it was all dancing and drinking, and by the time it was the right moment for them to leave, decorum had long been cast to the winds.

It took time to make their way to the waiting open carriage, for everyone wished to give them his own blessing. Lavinia threw her wedding posy into the sea of expectant faces and then they were moving off down the drive, with John Blunden up on the driver's bench, and the crowd cheered and waved behind them. Lavinia settled back into the cushions and leant against Jess with a deep sigh of relief. Rice rattled and cracked beneath their feet.

They sat close together, speechless now, watching the orchards stream by. Then they were turning into Salterns Lane and, almost at once, into the Lavenham drive. They passed Lost Labour, filled with young corn, rounded a corner thick with hazel and holly — and Lavenham lay ahead, mellow pink and golden grey in the clear evening sunlight, its barley-sugar chimneys poised above a long roof with its two attic windows like surprised eyebrows on the face of a wind-browned sailor. Climbing roses already softened the contours of its newness and a fine young magnolia from the Goodwood gardens was out in full waxy flower beside the front door.

They drove round the house to the terraced front,

which faced the water, and pulled up at the entrance. Across the pebble drive the Bayless clan rose from their fireside and streamed towards them, bronzed dark faces bright with welcome.

The Romany ceremony took them through the late afternoon into twilight. By the time the dusk had deepened into evening, they had observed all the formalities of casting up the bread and receiving the gorgio girl into their midst. Dusk brought out the bats to swoop silently overhead against a vivid evening sky. Then it was time to dance. They danced for a long time, until the moment came when Jess rose from his seat beside Piramis and Sarey, and held out his hand to Lavinia. At once the music stopped and the clan raised itself, none too steadily, to its feet.

'It is time,' Jess said to them, and added something in Romany that brought smiles to the men's faces and a softness to the women. He held Lavinia's hand and the children raced past them, eager to be the ones who laid the brooms across the threshold of the house. When it was done, the children stood back in a huddle, suddenly shy and watchful.

There were no farewells this time. The clan stood quietly in the dim glow of their dying fire, mute witnesses to the final ritual.

'Come on — we just jump over them.' Jess was pulling her across the grass now, breaking into a run. 'Pick up your skirts, chika, so that they don't touch the besoms. It's bad luck for anything to touch them . . . .'

She scooped up the full skirts and petticoats and trotted beside him across the gravel and up the terrace steps.

'Jump with me.'

She was up and over, and then they were standing in the dim hall, laughing and breathless, arms round each other.

'Welcome to Lavenham, Mrs Bayless,' Jess said, and suddenly the laughter was gone and she lifted her face to him. It took a long time for them to exchange their welcome. He had not kissed her with anything other than light affection before, and now there was all the time in the world to savour his mouth and to feel the first shafts of an excitement coursing through her which became almost a sweet pain.

There was a sound above their heads.

Lavinia jerked guiltily away from Jess. She had thought that they would be completely alone in the house and the sound of a creaking board jolted her. There was a flicker of movement in the gallery above their heads as though something withdrew into shadow.

'Don't worry, my darling,' Jess said in her ear. 'It's only Amy.'

4

'Everyone should marry in June,' Lavinia said, walking with Jess in the gardens. He glanced down at her and quickened at the sight of her vivid upturned face brimming over with happiness in this new ownership of her surroundings. She was having difficulty in keeping pace with him, it seemed, for each rustle of her blue striped skirts suggested that she would rather be dancing ahead in a twirling jig of sheer high spirits. They approached the north paddock and leaned on the gate, waiting for the horses to acknowledge their presence.

'Come up, Midas — come up,' Lavinia called. Jess put his arm round her waist and kissed the top of her shining hair as they watched the colt lift his head and break from the herd to trot, high stepping, down the field towards her outflung hands. There was always something touchingly beautiful in the coming together of these two golden creatures, he thought. He drew her away at last and they wandered back towards the house, skirting the newly completed barn and following the path along the river bank.

'I think we should consider discussing the household duties, don't you, my love?' he said, tucking her hand into his arm and covering it with his own.

She nodded eagerly. 'I know that I've a great deal to learn, but Amy will help me, won't she?'

'Of course she will,' he said abruptly. 'She's not an easy person to understand, I do realize, but I hope that you will make allowances for her various misfortunes. She is subject to occasional fits which Doctor Sanden puts down to epilepsy . . . but Polly and I are quite used to them and there is a routine treatment which you will quickly learn. Amy can be very surly at times, but once the strangeness of your presence here has worn off, I'm sure that you two will become good friends.'

Lavinia bowed her head. Amy was proving to be hard work already, quite impervious to the open friendliness of her new sister-in-law. 'I do understand, Jess. This was Amy's home right from the beginning and I would hate her to feel that I am wresting her rightful place from her. Maybe I could start by just being responsible for the duties that I have always done at Rymans — I'm quite deft with my needle, if you recall — and then there are the bees, of course. I love my bees, and old Beezer has trained me well in the making of honey.'

She stared up at the brooding, watchful windows as they crossed the lawn towards the house. It was looking as beautiful as ever, but there was something oddly chilling about it this morning. She looked away quickly. They strolled round the side of the house just as a cart trundled into the barnyard and pulled up with a slither.

'Why, Beezer,' Lavinia exclaimed, starting forward in surprise.

The old man gave her a wide and toothless grin. 'Thought you might be lonely without you'm little friends, ma'am,' he said through a jumble of mouthings. 'Brought over four skeps. Too late for swarmen' this month but I'll see ye away with 'em come September.'

All at once she felt much more at home. What a wise old fellow he was to have guessed at the spark of loneliness already there inside her, she thought.

Rueb helped old Beezer to set up the skeps in the orchard of young apple and plum trees.

'Well, if that's where they're to be, you can pick the fruit in autumn by yourself,' Amy muttered when Lavinia told her of their arrival. 'I can't be doing with the creatures,' she said, seeing the look of surprise on Lavinia's face. 'Nasty-tempered, they can be. A bee-sting's a powerful pain . . . to me, at any rate.'

'But I've been tending bees since I was quite small,' Lavinia protested indignantly, 'and I've only had a couple of stings in all that time — and that was my fault because the poor things became tangled in my clothing. Really, Amy, you must see if you can try to commune with them. They are very intelligent creatures and quickly sense whether or not you are a friend.'

Amy turned away with a shrug. 'You can make friends with whoever you want,' she said shortly, 'but don't expect me to, for they're no friends of mine, nor ever will be.'

Jess asked Amy for the house keys and presented them to Lavinia with a flourish. The two women stood either side of the kitchen table, watching him stride away from them. Upstairs the sounds of Polly sweeping in the chamber over their heads were movements from another world. The baby Violet slept in her day cradle beside the settle. Now and then she made small moos in her sleep. Lavinia bent down and watched her.

'How pretty she is, dear little thing,' she said, smiling up at Amy, eyes pleading for a spark of response.

'They'm never pretty at that age.' Amy began taking jars down from the dresser, pushing past Lavinia and gradually easing her away from the cradle.

'May I not help you? Or I could gather in the eggs, at least.'

Amy flung her a look of open scorn and her mouth curled. 'I cleared the nests before you were out of my brother's bed this mornen'.'

The insolent implication brought a deep flush to Lavinia's cheeks. 'I am married to Jess, you know,' she said quietly. She took a step forward and opened her mouth to say more, but Amy turned away from her. With a sigh, Lavinia left the unfriendly kitchen and closed the door firmly behind her.

'Has Amy done the inventory with you yet?' Jess asked that evening. He watched a cloud shadow her face and the animation fade from it.

She shook her head. 'She was busy.' She spread her

hands out across her lap and stroked the rose silk lightly. 'I — I didn't want to get in her way by asking her again.'

A nerve jumped in Jess's cheek and he stood up. 'Look, chika,' he said grimly, 'I'm sorry this is turning into a bit of a nonsense. It'll have to be stopped here and now.'

He left her and she heard him crossing the hall and going into the kitchen. She sat very still. There was a pause and then he returned with Amy trailing behind him. He waved her into a chair and closed the door firmly.

'Now, look here, Amy — and you too, Linnie. I'm a very busy man, and when I say that the two women closest to my heart are to run my house in harmony and make every effort towards the happiness of us all, I expect this to be carried out — with a good grace. Amy, I asked you to take Lavinia round the house today and to go over the inventory of furnishings, silver and other chattels together. You have made no attempt to do this. Why?'

Amy looked back at him darkly, jutting her chin. 'I baint her nursemaid,' she snapped at him, ignoring Lavinia. 'I've got more than enough to do about the house without having to wet-nurse your wife.' She stood up then, tall and close to him, her eyes only a little below his own. He saw the tremor in her body and the tell-tale flicker in her pupils and put out his arms as she swayed and began to crumble.

'Oh, Jess,' Lavinia started forward.

'Out of the way — don't crowd her.' His voice was sharp and she jerked backwards as he lowered Amy to the ground and crouched over her, gently turning her head to one side, soothing the jerking body with tender hands.

'There, there, pen. It's all right — just relax. Just try and relax.' The sing-song voice spelt out a long familiarity with such situations and he murmured over the fallen girl without once looking up at Lavinia, until the spasm passed and Amy lay damp and pale beneath his hands. He wiped the saliva from her mouth and pushed back the hair from her face. Only then did he remember Lavinia and he raised his head with an apologetic grimace.

'This is the only way to help her at these times, he said. 'It's because of these fits that I must have her here with us — where we can keep a close eye on her and make sure that her life is not more difficult than is necessary.'

So that was it: Amy in permanent residence was the price to be paid for Jess and Lavenham. She nodded, unable to find the right words to express her dismay — and her acceptance of his terms. He carried Amy up to her chamber and called to Polly to make her comfortable in her bed.

Lavinia woke from a deep sleep. She lay on her back, feeling Jess's arm against her side. He was breathing deeply, peacefully. Then the odour reached her, the strong acrid odour of horses. It enveloped her, sweeping over the bed so strongly that for a moment her confused, sleepy mind suggested that there were horses in the room.

She sat up in bed. There were sounds now . . . and the smell was sharpening into a stench. She slid out of bed without being sure why she did so, seeking without knowing what she sought — aware of a dream-like detachment.

The stench filled her nostrils so that she gagged. There were sounds outside the chamber. Downstairs? She opened the bedroom door a crack. The darkness of the hall was total. Even the night-light in Amy's room thrust no faint glimmer beneath her chamber door. Lavinia moved like a sleep-walker towards the bannisters and strained her eyes to see down into the black well of the hall below. The sounds magnified . . . she heard heavy breathing just below her. The stench was too much and the bile rose in her and then — as her eyes probed the black infinity — she found movement there. Something gleamed and shuffled and pawed . . . .

Cold terror flooded through her, bringing the hairs erect on her arms, and she backed away from the gallery rail, into the bedroom, slamming the door between her and whatever was down there, waiting.

'Who's that?' Jess's sleepy voice cut across the panic waves that rooted her, disoriented, in the middle of the room. 'Linnie . . . why are you out of bed?'

The blessed familiarity of his voice calmed her. She crept towards the comfort of the sound with outstretched hands, slid thankfully into bed and pressed herself against him.

'Can't you smell it?' she said against his shoulder. He put his arms round her and cradled her against his chest.

'Can't smell anything except you, darling. Nice, herby, lavender girl-smell.'

It had gone. The terrible bitter stench of that creature's passion. The sounds in the hall below them. She must have been dreaming, after all. Just a nightmare — but what a terrible fantasy. She shivered and pulled Jess even closer to her.

'I was just thinking how like Jess's eyes Violet's are,' Lavinia said to Amy one day, shortly after the little girl's first birthday.

Amy ruffled Violet's mop of dark curls. 'Fine eyes, they are,' she agreed, with a smile that stopped short of her own blue eyes. 'Fine grey ones, as you say — just like Jess's. We never did know, in the family, how 'e came by those, for there baint no other grey ones among the Baylesses, only his'n. And now Violet, too. Makes 'er look more like 'im than ever, don't it?'

Lavinia clenched her fists, suddenly shocked by the bald implication in the woman's words. 'Children often resemble their uncles and aunts more than the parents,' she said stiffly. 'Mother always says that John takes more after her father Pay than after the Freelands.'

Insolent amusement turned Amy's melancholy face into that of a cruel angel. 'The blood in Violet's veins be closer than that,' she said with the contempt in her voice that Lavinia was coming to hate. 'There be only Bayless blood in Violet so 'tis to be expected that she be like him.' She watched as her words sank in and found the tender spot at

69

which they had been aimed.

Tears pricked the backs of Lavinia's eyes. She stared back at Amy for a moment, the terrible hurt giving her unexpected strength. 'You are despicable,' she said quietly. She put aside the basket of pea-husks she had been shredding and left the kitchen, stumbling out of the house, over the yard cobbles and down towards the bank of the river.

Violet was Jess's child.

The impact of the statement smote her again and again, twisting her insides. It was almost too much to contemplate . . . that Jess — the beautiful, tender man who was her husband and who clearly loved her more than life itself — had found it in him to lie with his own sister; had lain with that gawky woman and taken the same pleasure in her body that he found so constantly in Lavinia's.

By the time the harvest was in, Lavinia had been at Lavenham for four months. She spent more and more time in her mother's new little house in Fishbourne as autumn drew the chill days towards Christmas. She appeared to need wise council at every turn these days, Jess thought wryly. Watching Lavinia working at her lace pillow, he realized that she was looking brighter and happier than she had been for some weeks.

'Rest your eyes and talk to me,' he said, patting his knee. She smiled across the hearth at him, the dimple in her left cheek deepening. Obediently she laid aside the pillow with its gaily coloured bobbins and came across to him. He could see that she was bursting with news, hugging it to herself with a little girl's secret glee, waiting to be persuaded.

'All right then, chiriklo, let's be having it. You've been holding something back from me ever since I came home this evening. What secret wickedness have you been up to?'

'Aren't you perceptive, my Jess. Well, I didn't wish to speak of it in front of Amy, so I couldn't talk before, but . . . I'm with child, Jess. I had been hoping that I might be, but now Mama tells me that I certainly am.'

He gathered her up, hugging her close to his chest, and the evening chill was forgotton in the plans and dreams that a first child always generates.

In the kitchen, Amy sat beside the fire with Violet on her lap, knitting a red shawl for the little girl to wear through the cold weather. She could hear the murmur of Lavinia's voice and Jess's replying rumble.

'Can you hear him talking, russli? Can you hear his voice?'

The dark little head nodded vigorously, curls bouncing.

'Who is it? Tell me who that voice belongs to?'

Violet considered, her attention sliding to the closed kitchen door before returning to her mother.

She beamed and clapped her hands then as enlightenment dawned. 'Dada,' she said happily. 'Dada . . . Dada . . . .'

Occasionally the south of England finds itself in the grip of a winter so cold that the seasonal pattern is thrown badly off balance, putting farmers and merchants into confusion and making the cycle of natural life a struggle for existence. The winter of 1730-31 was the coldest for thirty-two years. Frost came early, riming woods and hedgerows in icy sculpture, destroying the tender shoots which had already begun to sprout in fields and vegetable gardens.

On the downs behind Chichester the sheep suffered, and in the oak forests even the wild pigs froze to death. Freezing mists penetrated the densest thickets, embroidering everything they touched with a lethally beautiful silver lace and chilling the hardy swine through their thick protective fat. In two nights the whole herd of Lavenham pigs was lost, and every cottage in the parish was set to smoking joints of pork in their chimneys.

Jess moved his offices to more spacious premises in Little London, off East Street, just before the frosts began. In the town street directory he described himself as

'Jess Bayless — Banker and Importer'.

John Freeland was also establishing a fine reputation as a lawyer in Chichester. At twenty-nine, he was already an authority on maritime law as well as being a kindly and astute representative of all who sought his help. His chambers were conveniently near to those of his brother-in-law, so that time would not be lost in document bearing. He handled all the complicated legal side of Bayless's Bank and the Bayless Shipping Company.

By the time Lavinia was brought to her confinement in the summer of 1731, the graceful schooners, sailing under the Bayless pennant and carrying all manner of precious contraband goods in their 'special compartments', were making huge profits for the company.

Lavinia went into labour on a humid June evening and Jess lost no time in dispatching Rueb with the light-cart to collect Mrs Whittle, the Birdham midwife.

Lavinia was content to rest in a chair near the window of her bed chamber, loth to retire to bed as her mother pleaded, for there was little likelihood of rest for any of them in the hours ahead. Everything ached: her muscles, her legs, her back. Jess massaged her, as he often did when she was weary, but the gentle rubbing no longer eased this kind of tiredness.

The cradle stood ready beside the hearth, the first little gown aired and folded over its carved oak side. Now that the time had come, Lavinia was undecided whether she welcomed or dreaded the unknown burden ahead . . . for the preceding months had been ordeal enough and she could only hope and pray that the birth of her child would put an end to her morbid fears.

She had begun to 'see' and 'feel' strange things soon after the baby quickened. Reason told her that what she felt — and sometimes thought she saw — could only be caused by the heightened state of her body and mind. Yet there was something grossly unnatural about the atmosphere at Lavenham. Amy revelled in referring to its soul — and the disturbance of its peace by Lavinia and her gorgio ways. Even Jess, that most down-to-earth of men, had gently admitted that he believed that the place was in a state of possession, for he had built over ancient stones which were clearly of a special significance.

Lately, her fantasies were even beginning to focus on such complete innocents as Violet and her lovely Midas. Without being able to understand why, she had begun to feel the oddest sensation of fear whenever she visited the paddock — and, latterly, when Midas was brought to the terrace below her chamber window. His greeting and obvious pleasure at the sight of her was overshadowed by an uncharacteristic show of aggressive arousement, as though Lavinia actually titillated him.

And then there was the problem of Violet. Whenever Lavinia entered a room or sat in her chair, Violet would materialize at her side. Always, Lavinia was treated to the same unblinking scrutiny — until she felt she would scream.

'What are you looking at all the time?' she would ask, doing her best to keep the edginess out of her voice. 'Here is my brush, Violet. Would you like to dress my hair?' She had discovered what a popular pastime this was with the little girl. It kept Violet happy for hours — and also ensured that she stood behind Lavinia, so that she was not obliged to wilt beneath the unblinking glare of those intense grey eyes.

'Polly, close the casement, if you please. The smell of the stables is really quite overpowering today. Can you not smell it?'

The terrible stench which, it seemed, only she could smell began to make her jumpy. It took Lavinia a long time to realize that these odours were more severe when Violet was with her. So was the occasional intensifying of shadows which would suddenly bunch up on the periphery of her vision, to assume fluid but almost finite shapes. They vanished as soon as she looked directly at them, but she could not help noticing that they were there most often when the little girl was with her.

73

At first she tried to share her fears with Jess, hoping that it would halve their threat, but it was as though he considered them simply an extension of her pregnancy. Women were meant to become more fanciful at such times . . . .

In fact, Jess was deeply concerned about the whole thing, though he did his best to soothe her. He watched in growing fear as the happy golden girl of his heart slowly battled alone and paled into an anxious, delicate-looking young woman who jumped at the slightest sound and was afraid to sleep at night.

Now, sitting beside Lavinia as she checked through the pile of infant clothing in her lap, he decided that she had a right to know at least some of the circumstances which had led him into building Lavenham where he did. It might even help her during her travail to know there really were Forces about the place that were not of her imagining.

He began the story of his discovery of the Place as a small boy and slipped, without realizing it, into the sing-song lilt of the Romany story-teller. As she listened to him, astounded by his words but increasingly comforted by them, the child within her began the first soft thrusting of its journey into life.

Jess talked Lavinia through the night. At one point, after Mrs Whittle arrived and examined her and found that all was as it should be, he had put Lavinia to bed and lain at her side, holding her as he continued his story. Now and then she would interrupt with a question and he was obliged to break his train of thought. But it was really an impossible task, in any case, for how could any man explain how it was that he had until quite recently possessed a power that was, in Christian circles, attributed only to the Devil?

Some time before dawn they both fell asleep, and when daylight woke Lavinia again, it was to realize that the child had been making its own progress without her. The dragging pain that had been gnawing at her back slewed round and gripped the base of her stomach – and twisted hard.

She gasped, doubling up at the unexpectedness of it —
and Jess woke with a jerk.

Doctor Sanden called during the day. Mrs Freeland
arrived from Fishbourne and would not be persuaded to
make herself more comfortable down in the parlour.
'Certainly not,' she said firmly when Jess begged her to
leave the room and take some refreshment. 'A mother
should always be close to her daughter during her confinement.'

Sarey Bayless appeared at the door, not to offer dubious
assistance as Mistress Freeland feared, but with the good
wishes of the clan — and with the Dannerin' Stone.
Kneeling beside Lavinia, she patted her hand and folded
her fingers round a pale smooth pebble.

'When it gets so that you want to cry out, bite on the
stone and it will help,' she said.

The surge began: the violent thrusting which
threatened to tear flesh from bone — and with it came
another agony that had nothing at all to do with the child
and its battle into life. This was the culmination of all the
nightmares, her body imprisoned in fire. She cried out
with the torture of the vast weight which held her down,
crushing the life from her, mashing flesh and bone into
burning pulp . . . .

By late afternoon the leaden skies suddenly gave way to
a storm that drove in across the harbour from the south-
west, obliterating the land in a blinding deluge. Huge
waves were whipped up and clashed against the shore,
uprooting trees and sweeping away a flotsam of wood,
livestock and boats. The house shook to its foundations as
thunder rolled in across the Manhood, thick yellow sulphur clouds scudding so low that they were almost at tree
level. The Birdham windmill was struck by lightning and
burned to the ground; an abnormal tide smashed into
Itchenor boatyard and bore off the hulls of two nearly
completed vessels.

The tempo of Lavinia's pain changed and tore her apart,

and in the midst of disorder she heard a voice screaming. The words had no meaning for her and she was carried along within the great agonizing wave. Her body worked of its own volition and there was singing in her ears. The voice was there in her head with its high, shrill warble — calling to the Great One, begging to be released from the torment and admitted to the High Place.

Then she was empty. It was done . . . and yet not done, for she knew that she still struggled weakly to be free of her broken body.

She opened her eyes and watched the candles guttering in golden haloes round the bed — and there was Mrs Whittle bending over the crib, and Doctor Sanden's rubicund face floating near her. A hand came down on hers and she smiled, knowing that this was Jess, for there was his familiar tender touch. She sighed, refreshed by the strength which seemed to stream from him into her. She closed her eyes then and slept, cradled in the comfort of his presence.

Summer sunshine proved to be the best cure for Lavinia's weakness. Jess and Amy joined forces to oppose Doctor Sanden and threw open the windows to let in the mild fresh air so that it could do its cleaning best upon the ill humours in her fragile body. She did not fall prey to chills and lung infections as he insisted she would. She breathed in the sweet salt air with relief, feeling its purity heal her tiredness and bring back the colour into her cheeks. After three weeks she was well enough to sit by the window in her comfortable armchair so that she might watch the boats streaming by and throw sweetmeats to Midas, who was calm and disciplined once more.

Little Lawrence was never far from her, tucked up in his crib by her side so that she could study his soft fuzz of blond hair and one perfect pink shell of an ear. There had been no trouble with her milk and he had taken to her from the first so that, already, there were encouraging signs of robustness about both his appetite and his lungs.

Lavinia, blessedly free at last from all daemons and torments, knew only that some kind of battle had been waged with the elemental evil in the house — and that this time she had won.

Violet spent as much time as possible up in the big bed chamber, sitting on a scarlet footstool against Lavinia's legs and giving her undivided attention to the baby. He was very much a Freeland, except for the suggestion of his father's high-bridged nose — and the huge eyes which would certainly be grey and which already dominated his miniature face.

The eyes gave Violet a shock the first time she saw him awake. He was lying quietly on his back, staring up at the vague moving things that floated round the perimeter of his vision. As Violet peeped at him, his eyes suddenly focused on her and there was in them a burning light which had hurt her in her head so that she recoiled from him, crying, and hid herself in the folds of Lavinia's peignoir.

She kept her distance from the cradle for some time after that but, by the time he was able to focus properly, curiosity had overcome her fear. It was not long before the two children seemed to share a special bond of understanding. Lavinia did not notice this until Violet turned to her one day from beside the cradle — and two pairs of identical eyes regarded her with solemn appraisal. Something caught at her throat and she drew in her breath, aware of a stirring at the backs of their luminous greyness. Then Lawrence closed his eyes and slept and Violet climbed into her lap and asked for the piggy story on her little fat fingers.

On a damp September evening, Jess strolled through the woods where, as a small child, he had hunted the hotchiwichi, chasing it into a little dell out of which he had never again escaped — till age released him.

Violet had the Power! He recognized it now in the grey intensity of those beautiful black-lashed eyes of hers, and he had seen it happen when she had flamed one of Lavinia's bees. The shock of her own reaction had driven her, shaking, into a corner of the parlour where she had been playing beside the open window. He had looked away, numb with the discovery — to find Amy smiling at him with all the triumph of a striking snake in her eyes.

He suddenly felt the desperate vulnerability of both Lavinia and the baby Lawrence — and even himself, for Amy was surely telling him never to move them away from Lavenham, as he had been considering lately. With such a weapon to ensure her wishes, he would have to bow to that demand.

He had done his best to establish himself positively in Violet's affections without admitting to being her father. All too often, though, she had long been asleep in her cradle and was not aware of the nightly vigil he kept at her side, stroking the curve of her little cheek with a forefinger and marvelling at every clear Bayless feature — and the promise of beauty — in every baby line. He did his best to have her close to him wherever possible so that Lavinia, too, might enjoy her company, for he was quickly made aware of Amy's jealous guard of her daughter during the hours that he was out of the house.

Violet permitted herself to be indulged by Jess, but he was wryly amused to observe that Lavinia — with her youth and golden looks and gentle affection — held more fascination for his daughter than did her father.

'Dearest, we just cannot risk exposing you again to the kind of stress you suffered before Lawrence was born,' Jess said firmly to Lavinia one night after they had retired and the subject of another child was raised. Lavinia nestled into his shoulder and shivered — but then shrugged off the dread of that still-fresh memory and smiled up at him, the dimples coming and going in her cheeks.

'It was only my condition,' she said lightly. 'I don't really mind whatever it is that dwells here, now that I'm getting used to the feel of the place and now that Lawrence is with us, safe and sound . . . and besides, I've had no trouble at all since his birth, have I?'

'I'd like to feel that we shall have other children,' he murmured, cuddling her close to him. 'I have been thinking about it a lot, you know. Maybe the best answer would be for you to go to your mother in Fishbourne when you find yourself with child once more. Have your confinement under her roof, where you know you will not be disturbed.'

She tucked her hand into the crook of his arm among the pillows of the high, curtained bed. 'We have not reached that problem yet, my love,' she said softly, snuggling against his long body. 'I shall certainly do whatever you think best, though, when the time comes.'

The winter passed by, mild and dank, setting the farmers' heads shaking even more dolefully than they had throughout the winter the previous year. There was no frost to break up the soil and set the sap running in the dormant seedlings. There was no snow at all, and very little to differentiate between the seasons since the previous spring.

Lawrence thrived and, growing fat and strong on his mother's milk, was much admired by the visiting matrons of the neighbourhood. Time suddenly hung heavily on Lavinia, in spite of her duties with Lawrence and those that Amy grudgingly permitted her about the house. She enjoyed her flower-arranging and apiary well enough. She loved every moment spent with the tiny blond-haired boy who would one day look so like his mother. She counted the minutes each day when she could visit the paddock to ensure that her beloved Midas was still in perfect health and as eager to see her. She could think of no time in her life when she had been happier than she was in the company of Jess, the most desirous of husbands, and Lawrence, the most perfect of sons — but even with this roll of delights, there still remained that other, darker side of the picture, which was reducing her happy nature into one of constant anxiety. Lavenham and its intrusive brooding; Amy and her implacable hatred. She ignored it and tried to pretend that it did not exist.

Jess rode Olivas home, sharing the road with market waggons and huge drays which rumbled and swayed over the muddy, uneven highway. He went slowly, thinking with wry amusement of the offer which had been made to him that day. What strange quirk of fate had made the Sussex collector, Pusey Brookes, offer the Chichester collectorship to him? What magnificent irony that it should have been offered at all to Jess Bayless of all people, gypsy turncoat, one-time leader of the Apuldram Blacks and still importer of some of the most costly treasures being illegally landed in Britain. There was a fine humour to be found in the innocence of such an unlikely offer but, somehow, a heavy weariness robbed him of laughter.

His chest ached, as it had done once or twice before, and he frowned, suddenly aware of a certain shortness of breath. Twenty-nine and becoming short-winded! What kind of life was it when all the money in the world was not enough if your own body decried the sour air of ill-ventilated and odour-ridden buildings? There had never been bad air in the benders of his people. There was, he decided, a high price to be paid for ambition.

He was in pensive mood that evening, miles away from Lavenham and the problems it wove about itself. Lavinia, seeing his abstraction, wisely muted her chatter. He looked pale, which was unusual for him, and seemed constantly to be rubbing his chest and hunting for breath.

'Just a touch of indigestion,' he said shortly, in answer to her question. 'Maybe a draught of Amy's peppermint water will ease it.' She went with all speed to make him some.

'Ugh . . . '

Lavinia, returning with a mug of hot mint tea, saw Jess double up in his chair, cradling his body with crossed arms. She flew to him, putting the tea on a table at his side, and massaged his back in great fear as he continued to gasp for breath, his head on his knees.

'Jess, try and drink some of the mint tea . . . it will ease the chest pain.' Hands on his shoulders lifted him deeper into his chair. The sweet pungence of the liquid was hot against his lips, scouring his throat, going down into his stomach . . . soothing. The pain — the pain was excruciating. It seeped downwards through his chest, his right arm, into the muscles of his thighs. Hands rubbed his back and he felt the blood pounding in his head, through the channels of his body like a river in spate: furious . . . out of control . . . .

Then it was easing. He felt more of the soothing liquid against his lips. He swallowed gratefully and with difficulty, then slowly the room ceased its gyrations and slid back into focus. Lavinia knelt beside him, holding his head and guiding the cup of hot peppermint to his lips. As his pulse slowed to a less furious pace he opened his eyes.

'You look as though you have seen a ghost,' he said weakly, in a vain effort to make light of his pain.

She did not return his wobbly smile. 'I thought for a moment back there that I had.'

Her gentle eyes filled with tears then, which spilled over and coursed down her ashen cheeks.

He lifted a hand to wipe away her tears and found it immeasurably difficult. 'I'm all right now, dearest. It was just severe indigestion.'

5

Lawrence sat in the arms of his favourite tree, watching the house. From where he crouched, knees up under his chin between two bulbous branches, he had an uninterrupted view of the south and west fronts. From this vantage point he could watch the changing moods of the place and sense when it was about to gather itself up into one of its sly manifestations. The windows seemed empty, save for the reflections of light from the river, which glinted and slid across the glass, creating an impression of movement within the casements. There was no Watcher behind the house's blind eyes but the pulse was present, the latent heart-beat of its restless soul.

A spider crept along the branch towards his hand. It had a tiny round body and long, double-jointed legs which spread out round the wood bark with neat, fastidious movements. He smiled at the spider, gathered his energy into a ball of pure strength within his chest — and flamed it as it approached his fingers. There was a flash of light — orange, tinged with something metallic . . . lethal. The spider simply disappeared. A small scorch mark scarred the branch. He stroked it smugly with a forefinger. It was still very hot.

'Never,' Dada had told them, 'ever Flame anything unless you have to. You have a gift which is given to very few. If you are like me, it will fade as you grow up — but maybe things will be different for you, and you will always carry the burden of Flaming.' He had looked at the two of them with grave sadness — Violet leaning against his knee, tall for her age at eight; and Lawrence, five years old and not yet breeched, lying on his stomach at his father's feet.

He had their total attention for once, for it was the first time that the Bayless Power had been openly discussed and both children were fascinated by their father's admission that he, too, had been able to Flame things in his youth.

The Power, however, was just about the only fun in the boredom of Lawrence's life. He enjoyed Flaming things and he was sure that Violet did too. Why shouldn't they? No one else would ever know, for no one else seemed to have the same gift. Aunt Amy certainly did not, and it was as well that this was so. Polly had no idea of its existence in the children and once, when he had tried to explain it to her, she had pinched his cheek and told him what a clever boy he was to have such a vivid imagination.

Amy appeared in the terrace doorway. Lawrence shrank back into the foliage of his oak tree and watched her. Tall and straight-backed, she stood with her face uplifted as though she was smelling the air. Maybe she was, he decided, because when the house filled its rooms with the stink of horse sweat, it made Aunt Amy rant and rave and sometimes brought on one of her turns. Perhaps his parents had told her that she and Violet were to be sent to live somewhere else, he thought.

As he watched her, the light seemed to shift on the rosy walls of the house. A dark shadow passed across the sun and extinguished all the diamond points of light in the upper windows. The climbing creepers seemed to close their leaves, wilting against the brickwork. A hot wind swept through the oakwoods behind him, rattling the branches, and he clung to his trunk and steeled his mind to deflect the coming onslaught.

Nothing happened. He saw Amy open her eyes and look about her, disillusion turning her face from its momentary beauty into the ugliness of sudden defeat. She limped across the terrace, dragging her game leg painfully.

Twenty yards from the oak tree she saw him. Their eyes met, mutual hatred glaring between them. His pulse stopped in the depths of such venom. Something small and young shrivelled inside him. I wish I dared . . . I just wish and wish that I dared, he said to himself.

'Lawrence, get down from that tree this instant — and go inside.'

He swung his leg over the damp branch, taking his time, clung to the bowl of the tree and slid carefully to the ground.

'Why is it that you seem bent on giving yourself more coughs and colds than the rest of us put together?' She grabbed him by his fustian jacket and hustled him into the house, scolding and shaking him roughly as she shooed him upstairs to change his stained shirt and breeches. Her eyes were red rimmed and their colour like flat stones at the edge of a winter sea.

There are too many women in this house, he thought gloomily as he stomped up to his chamber. Dada was in Chichester all day, so that inevitably he was left to the mercies of Aunt Amy and Violet. Thank goodness for dear old Polly. She was a secret supporter when the others weren't looking. He'd been whipped more than once for creeping off to the saltpans to see his Bayless cousins. He'd been whipped even harder for leaving the paddock gate open and letting the horses out. That was last year, when four of the foals had died. Violet said that he had Flamed them — but he had not. He was not allowed to go fishing because they said he came home wetter than the fish. What *was* he allowed to do which would not break one rule or another? Now he must also be punished, it seemed, just for sitting in his favourite tree and doing no harm to anyone.

He sat in his window, watching the birds swooping over the south paddock until his nose told him that Polly had the broth on the hob and it was time to eat. Quickfare at midday was always a swift and silent business. Manfri and Rueb bolted their broth, dipping Polly's crusty bread into the thick liquid to cool it faster. They would always demolish half a loaf each, wiping the bowl clean with the last twist, and then were up and away with little more than a touch of a forelock. Sitting with the women for quickfare was boring because Amy and Polly took their time and the children must chew every mouthful thirty-six times before swallowing, to aid their digestions. He wished that he were Manfri or Rueb, who could gobble and suck at their food and make all sorts of splendidly rude noises without earning a scolding.

Violet lowered her head over her food but Lawrence could feel her watching him out of the corner of her eye. Well, she wouldn't catch him out this time. He ate quietly, cursing his lack of years and the indisputable fact that his nose was still so close to the top of the table. Violet's taunting pulsed between them and he felt her challenge, daring him to look at her.

'Oh, no . . . I shan't fall into that trap again,' he thought. He had looked back at her one day, making a rude face and staring right into her eyes for just a second — to show her that he was nearly as strong with the Power as she was — and his platter of meat and potatoes had shot out from under his spoon, skittering across the table and knocking Rueb's dish on to the floor. There had been a terrible fuss with all the mess of food and gravy spattered over the table and floor. He had gone to bed hungry that day, his small rump throbbing from the beating he had received. He would never permit himself to be so careless of Violet again.

It would not be as bad as this when they were gone and Mama was in complete charge at last, he comforted himself. Mama and Dada loved him, even if Aunt Amy and Violet did not. But Mama had to spend all her time up in her bedchamber now, of course, for the new baby would come soon and she was not allowed to tire herself. All the same, she was always there for him to run to when things became too bad with Aunt Amy.

But Aunt Amy hated Mama even more than she did Lawrence. Mama did her best not to show it, but he could see that it upset her. Still, things would soon be better, he thought with secret gladness. Did they know what was in store for them yet? Had Dada told them that they were moving from Lavenham? He guessed not, for there would be terrible scenes once it was made public — and his own knowledge was only through having overheard his parents talking about it in the privacy of their bedchamber. He finished his food with unusual meekness, sitting straight-backed and eating without a single sound or dribble.

'Away with you,' Amy said at last. She stood up and Polly began to collect the bowls. Violet would wipe them and put them away in the dresser and then settle down with her mother to mend sheets. The kitchen was very much their domain.

Lawrence tugged on his outdoor boots and went out into the misty yard, leaving the door swinging open behind him.

Jess was always at his desk by eight o'clock in the morning and his staff would have preceded him by at least an hour. Ships' business occupied the early hours of each day, and twice a week Jess visited the little wooden office on the muddy shore at Dell Quay, where a clerk dealt with the Bayless vessels.

There was a move afoot, through the present landlord, William Hamilton, to build up a new quay so that ships might dock alongside the jetty, rather than in mid-stream. Colonel Hamilton proposed granting building concessions to a few of the merchants who regularly used the quay and Jess, naturally, had been the first to submit his application.

Afternoons at Bayless's were filled with loans business, and he finally rode home to Apuldram with the last of the day's waggon traffic. The sun was declining into Old Park Woods by the time he clattered into the yard and slipped stiffly off Olivas's back.

'Manfri . . . ' he shouted as Rueb came forward to lead the animal away.

Manfri poked his head out of the saddleroom door. 'In 'ere, bor,' he called, 'see'en what blacksmith've made us. Come an' take a look.'

It was pleasant to linger for a while among the horses and chat with Manfri and unwind from the pressures of the day. Later, as he made his way into the house, his mind was filled with thoughts of the collector's appointment and all its connotations. He was being pressed for a decision. He could put it off no longer.

The three lurchers bounded across the hall from their vigil before the hearth and Lavinia's hand-bell tinkled upstairs in the bedchamber. He went up to her, taking the shallow stairs two at a time. She was sitting in her comfortable chair beside a coal fire, a red rug across her knees.

How frail she looks, he thought with a jolt. Her burnished hair was neatly rolled into bunched ringlets on either side of her face. She wore a loose manteau of pale blue camlet, embroidered with pink roses. The colour accentuated the violet shadows under her eyes. Her forehead was hot beneath his lips.

'You do look jaunty,' she said to him happily enough, seeing the vigour in his face. 'Have you had a fruitful day, dearest? You look as though nice things have been happening . . . .'

It was always such a pleasure to come home to Lavinia, for she was instantly aware of whatever mood he was in and matched her own to it. Today he was not only having to consider Pusey Brookes and his suggestion but was also full of the wager he had accepted with the Duke of Richmond that forenoon — to race Midas against the Duke's prized runner, Bolton Red. It was an unexpected chance for him to advertise the qualities of the Lavenham stud, he told her. At worst they would lose the race, but as long as Midas gave Bolton Red a good run for their money, the name of Bayless would still be well promoted in equestrian circles . . . and if Midas actually beat Bolton Red — well, the Frenchman, de la Guerinière, who was Master of the Horse at Versailles and presently staying at Goodwood, would certainly consider breeding from Midas, which would open up the French studs to him.

So many dreams, my Jess, she thought, listening to the

excitement in his voice, and you have the facility for making dreams into reality. The colts in the north paddock were proof of that dream. At this moment there were three lovely yearlings out there with qualities akin to Midas, although he was still the undisputed king of them all. She looked at Jess's animated face, seeing life surging in the sparkling eyes and wishing joy to all those bounding hopes which lit his normally calm, saturnine features.

Feeling the depth of her regard, he paused in mid-sentence and stooped down to kiss the top of her head.

'What a selfish monster I am to be so full of my own pursuits as to forget the most important person in the world. Tell me how you are feeling, chika . . . and where is that scamp of a son of mine?'

She leant her head against him. 'All is well with me, Jess — though the baby weighs too heavily for comfort now. My valise is packed and everything is ready for the trip to Fishbourne next week.'

Jess tugged at the bell rope. 'Let's have tea,' he said, 'and afterwards Polly can open the floodgates and send up the children. Maybe they will stop bickering for long enough to tell us what they have been doing with their day. Since you are so determined to take Lawrence to Fishbourne with you, I think it might be the right time to broach the subject of Amy's and Violet's move to the new cottage.'

Lavinia paced her chamber, made restless by the fresh abrasive currents scouring the house. In the past few hours, Amy's hatred had begun building up to a violent climax. The tension was unbearable. It was, of course, all to do with the decision to move Amy and Violet to the new Salterns Cottage. She had known that there would be scenes and had half hoped that Jess might spare her by telling Amy once she was out of the house. Now she must just steel herself against the worst that Amy could do to her and pray for the week to pass quickly.

It had taken six long years of small daily humiliations,

pleadings and tears before Jess finally agreed to such a move. Violet was not the trouble, for she was an intelligent and affectionate child by nature, though sadly torn between loyalty to her mother and a genuine love for Lavinia. The trouble was — and always would be — Amy.

The sheer animosity in the woman had deepened sharply since Lavinia quickened with her second child. It simply made life even more difficult to cope with, since she had begun to feel unwell almost as soon as she announced her condition. Periods of double vision, constant sickness and malaise had marked every stage of the pregnancy since then. She sensed Jess's unease, though he never spoke of it. All the same, she knew that he was worried about Amy, and when he unexpectedly appeared in the kitchen one day in time to hear the invective being flung at Lavinia, it must have been the last straw for him. A short time later he said to her, 'I have leased a small parcel of land on the corner of Salterns Lane and the Manhood road. I shall build a cot there for Amy and Violet. We won't mention it until the place is built and there is something to show them — but it won't be long, chika, before we are just the four of us here. I know what a relief that will be for you . . . . '

Now, months later, the time had come and Jess had chosen this day to break the news to Amy.

The kitchen was a haven of quiet at dawn, after breakfast had been cleared away. 'Don't rush away,' Jess said to Amy with something of the old gentleness in his voice. She sat down obediently. She didn't look at him but stared down at her hands as she had done for a long time now whenever engaged in direct conversation.

'Pen, look at me,' he said.

Violet was still sitting at the far end of the long refectory table. She studied their faces, the brother and sister — her parents. She noted how the different aspects of their lives had eroded the similarity between them. The height was there and the colouring and the jutting cheek-bones — even the olive skin. But where Jess was like applewood hewn into perfect sculpture, the sap had run dry in Amy and it was as though she had fossilized into a living cadaver. Her skin was sallow and dry on the bones of her face, stretched into a bitter mask which turned the echo of early beauty into a sallow death's head. Her only animation was in the rictus of epilepsy and the increasingly frightening rages when all reason left her.

'Pen, look at me,' Jess said again and Amy, recognizing that special tone in his voice which had, all their lives, been reserved especially for her and her alone, looked obediently into Jess's warm grey eyes and allowed herself the luxury of drowning in the affection she found there.

And then he told her.

'I have bought some land from Walter Bartelott at the corner of our lane, at the end of the drive,' he said carefully. 'I have been building a well-appointed cot there for some time, as you will have seen, and it is almost ready for occupation now. I have been building it for you and Violet, Amy. It is to be your very own home and you shall choose your own furniture and have a maid to live with you and care for you — and a garden boy too.' His voice went on and on, with a tinge of anxiety coming and going and his eyes mourning over the blank shock in Amy's face. 'With Lavinia so close to her time now, it won't be long before we run out of rooms here, pen, as you will appreciate . . . we only have the three upper chambers and I do not plan to extend Lavenham at this time.'

'Dada. . . .'

Jess dragged his eyes away from Amy and turned to Violet in surprise. He had forgotten that she was with them. She had not moved since he began to speak.

'Dada, please don't do that to Mama. You know how she feels about this house — and about being here with you. Please don't hurt her, Dada.'

The tears came then and contrite, he leant along the table and drew her to him, cradling her against his shoulder.

'I have to find you somewhere else to live . . . you know

that, my chavi. The situation has been getting more and more difficult between us and is fast getting out of hand. With the new child to think of, I *must* plan ahead for us all, must I not? In the meantime, Aunt Lavinia is going to Fishbourne with Lawrence, and you and Amy will keep me company until they return and it is time for you to go to Salterns Cottage. It will be quite like old times, won't it?' He looked over Violet's head at Amy, asking for understanding — pleading for it.

She stared back at him and gradually the life came back into her. She laid her long hands flat on the scrubbed surface of the table and watched as they curled themselves into white-knuckled fists.

'Old times,' she said, and her voice was as dry and grating as metal against stone. 'Old times, you say. Yes, pral . . . you wanted much of me in those old times.'

She dragged herself up on to her feet and came round the table to stand over him.

'Will you be wanting me again, pral? With your little simpering rawni gone from your bed . . . ? Will you want to lie with me again out there in the hall beside the fire — just like old times? Will you want to take me and pump your seed into me with all the rotten lust of your greedy soul — just like old times?' She spat at him and the gobbet caught him on the forehead and slid slowly down his temple.

It was a bitter joke that, before this pregnancy, Lavinia had almost forgotten the ordeal she suffered prior to the birth of Lawrence. Time blunts the edge of memory, so they say, and certainly she had given little thought to the formless things that had dwelt in her very soul in those months of nightmare. The years between had been blessed with so many fulfilments, despite the anger and underlying viciousness always present in Lavenham's heart. There had been three unaccountable mis-carriages but they had all been very early ones and her natural good health ensured her recovery.

There had, miraculously, been no miscarriage this time. She was young and healthy, and the relief of knowing that she would be under her mother's roof for the actual lying-in did much to ease her mind. There was, meanwhile, a long period of waiting to be got through, for Doctor Sanden had been adamant that she should do as little walking about as possible in the last months. As a result, the large, airy bedchamber became the four walls of her existence, and there was time — plenty of it — to brood over her situation and the house with all its repellent shadows and odours and strange influences.

She wondered whether it was Amy or the house which threatened her most. Mama thought that Lavenham was a delightful place and so, she knew, did her brother John. The Bayless clan seemed to shy away from it, though, and Manfri had been heard to mutter about mullo's being its guardians but that was just gypsy talk. Taking stock of the alien influences in the house, she began to realize that Violet worried her, once again, almost as much as Amy did.

Violet was, by any standards, a strikingly beautiful child with an excess of restless energy that made life in her company quite tiring at times. She was, like her mother, going to be unusually tall for a woman. Already her fine-boned young body had a leggy grace which brought to mind the foals gambolling in the paddocks. She was wilful and moody, full of affection one moment and sulks the next. Recently, she had taken to watching Lavinia again — with the same unblinking constancy that had so embarrassed her before Lawrence's arrival.

A hardness in her stomach made her feel breathless and she shifted constantly in her chair. There was a tiresome ache in the small of her back and she pulled herself to her feet and began to pace to relieve the discomfort. Really, she wondered, maybe it would be better if I were to go to Fishbourne before Jess's race. Then, if the child were to start coming sooner than expected, at least Mama and her staff would see that all was well for me. She suddenly distrusted the waiting feeling at Lavenham. Even Polly and Rueb might be elsewhere if she needed them in a hurry — and Amy was much too fey and strange to rely on at all these days.

The small ache became a worry until something distracted her attention. The children were sitting huddled over their school work on either side of the card table in the chamber's west window, the chalk slipping and squeaking in their hands. From the far side of the room she stared at them, for it seemed that shadows crowded about each child — and yet they were in bright sunlight. She blinked, as there was a dull red reflection in the room. It faded and she moved towards the children, suddenly filled with a shivering foreboding. I must get out of this house, she thought in panic. I will tell Jess as soon as he comes home and we will dispatch Rueb to warn Mama.

Leaving the children to their studies, she opened the chamber door and went out on to the gallery to stretch her legs. She leaned against the bannisters and stared down into the hall, remembering that night soon after her wedding when the dreadful sensation of horses down there in the dark well had turned the centre of the house into a place she ever after preferred to avoid.

Amy was standing close to the dining table, quite still, as though she was listening and Lavinia, seeing that her eyes were closed, wondered whether she was about to have one of her turns. She paused in the act of calling to Polly, suddenly aware of the expression on Amy's face. It was so weird that it sent new shivers along Lavinia's spine. Amy was standing with bent knees, her shuttered face filled with an ecstasy so intimate that Lavinia backed away, flushing to the roots of her golden hair. She returned to her chamber and closed the door very quietly and leaned against it, disturbed and strangely revolted.

It had looked as though Amy was communing in a most erotic fashion with some unseen entity.

Jess hastened up to the bedchamber and bent to kiss

Lavinia, the tiredness of a tedious day made better by the sight of her.

'Jess, I want to go to Fishbourne in the morning,' she said urgently, taking his hands and pulling at them as she had done as a young girl. He was startled — his mind filled with the coming race the next morning.

'What is it, my love? Do you feel close to your time? The child is not due for another two or three weeks yet.'

'I know, I know . . . I don't care when it's due, Jess. I just feel that I must get out of here — as soon as possible. There is something wrong here in the house, threatening me . . . I'm really afraid. Please let me go tomorrow.'

He soothed her, seeing her agitation. 'Of course you must go, chika, if it is your wish. It is important for you to be happy and confident at this time. I do understand. I'll dispatch Rueb first thing in the morning to warn Mistress Freeland of your arrival, and it won't take long to pack you and Lawrence off as soon as you've had breakfast. You will be comfortably settled in by the time I return from Charlton with the Duke's wager in my pocket. How does that sound to you?'

Her relief was touching. He sat with her late into the evening, until she had drifted off to sleep, aided by one of Amy's sleeping draughts. Then he went down to the stables to inspect Midas and to talk long and deeply to Manfri and Rueb.

Amy stood in the centre of the hall, pressing herself against the refectory table. It was going to work this time — she could feel a vast gathering of forces in the shimmering air around her. She breathed deeply, raising her face as though to the warmth of the spring twilight outside.

'Go to it,' she said to the house. 'I have surely weakened her enough for you this time. Now it's up to you.'

It had been fascinating watching the very slight but accumulative daily effect of the tiny doses of monks hood crowns she had put into Lavinia's sleeping draughts. She had been most careful about the quantities so that there was absolutely no evidence of sudden poisoning. It was most encouraging to note the extreme slowness of her gradual decline. The pleasure it gave was all the greater, knowing that if Lavinia succumbed — as she must — she and Violet would not be leaving Lavenham as had been planned. It made her laugh aloud now and then, when she thought of all Lavinia's efforts to part her from Jess.

'Oh no, my fine rawni,' she said aloud, 'it won't be long now.' She heard Jess's feet clattering into the kitchen and sighed, turning away from the hall into the parlour. She stood behind the door and listened to him going up the stairs and into the chamber above, doing his best to tread softly.

'Not long now, bor — not long now. . . . .'

6

'Hold 'em still there, bor. Acha 'doi, Midas. . . .'

Manfri gentled Midas's nervous prancing till he stopped backing and bowing among the grooms and onlookers and allowed Manfri to tighten his girths for the third time. Jess sat easily in the saddle, stroking the horse's gleaming neck. He could feel Midas's excitement heightening his own.

The race was to be run over a circular course, starting and finishing at the Richmond hunting lodge at Charlton and taking in such great houses as Selhurst, Halnaker and Goodwood. Jess and Manfri had ridden the course, setting the mare, Gilda, and Midas an easy pace with no pressure. It had been a wise move. Now, sitting comfortably astride his dancing mount, Jess sniffed the cold morning air. A light breeze was coming from the west, dry and fragrant. The Duke's horse appeared amid a thin scatter of onlookers, led out by a groom and surrounded by a gaggle of jostling stable lads. The jockey was already mounted, dressed in a bright emerald green shirt with a yellow fox emblazoned on his back and white kersey breeches. It would not, Jess decided dryly, be difficult to keep him in sight.

Someone had strung a cord across the road and the two horses moved up until their breast-bones were against it. The onlookers crowded back on to the verges of the dirt track and the Duke, coming forward from the hunting lodge gate, pulled a brightly coloured silk kerchief from his pocket and held it above his head. He made a short speech of appreciation to the crowd, published the terms of the wager and was clearly impatient for the race to commence.

There was a moment's silence while Jess murmured to the dancing Midas, who had backed away from his opponent. Gradually he eased him back to the start. The moment his nose touched the hemp, the silk kerchief flashed downward and the rope was dropped. The two competitors rocketed away and were quickly lost from view in a cloud of dusty earth. The onlookers sighed in appreciation of the excellence of such a clean start and settled themselves on the grass with their backs against the stable walls, to share a hunk of bread and flagon of ale as they waited and speculated and laid bets among themselves as to the outcome.

Jess was content to let Bolton Red set the pace and they settled into a steady loping canter, traversing the curving hill which fell away beneath their hooves, down to a winding stream below. East Dean was quickly behind them and they headed south-east over the hump of the Downs into the unkempt swathe of Selhurst forest. Jess eased Midas into an effortless rhythm which he felt they might be able to keep up indefinitely. The forest behind them, a hedge stretched out ahead and Midas gathered himself joyously and took it with Jess tucked against his neck. They were down and streaking across scrub land towards the next incline before Bolton Red's hoofs struck the ground behind them. He let Midas make his own pace then, and they slithered down steep slopes into thick carpets of dead leaves and clambered up banks of loose earth thick with daffodils just past their blooming. Overhead, the first haze of new leaf growth softened the cave-like silence of the hollow woods, magnifying the song of nesting birds. They burst out suddenly into early sunshine and Midas laid back his ears with a long snore in his nostrils, gathered himself under Jess — and streaked towards the distant shape of Halnaker House.

'Why can't I go and watch Neeley unloading?'

Lawrence's full lips pouted like two raw sausages and he scowled darkly at Amy, hoping that she would be too busy

97

shortly to check that he intended creeping off to Dell Quay, whatever she had to say on the subject.

She cut short his hopes. 'As far as I'm concerned, you can go where you please — that's if you are not going to your gran's with your mother,' she said curtly, peering into the great iron pot which hung over the cooking fire, filled now with water for upstairs. Small silver bubbles were just beginning to rise up in a necklace round the rim. 'Take your chalks and slate and do some copying from that book your mama uses with you — and you'd best stay in your chamber until the carriage is ready.'

He turned away from her and picked up the slate and the little tin of chalks from their place on the kitchen dresser.

'I'll be up shortly to see that you're doing as you're told.' Amy's parting shot floated up the stairs behind him.

I'd like to Flame her, he thought, and sucked in his breath at the idea of such wickedness. He hesitated outside his parents' door but, hearing no sound from within, turned away and made for his own room.

The boxes were all ready at last. Lavinia rested, feeling the definite tell-tale contractions of the onset of her labour. She decided there was no need to mention them — she must let nothing impede her departure.

The carriage crunched across the gravel to the front door and Rueb leapt down from the buckboard seat and looped the reins into a wall ring. He opened the door in readiness for his two passengers and leaned inside to give the leather padded seats a final wipe with his sleeve.

'Hey, Rueben — will you come and take the boxes down now,' Polly called from the gallery.

He went up awkwardly, wiping his hands on either side of his breeches. He had never been in Jess's bedchamber before — never been in any kenner bedchamber for that matter — and his embarrassment was intense.

Lavinia was sitting in her deep chair, dressed in her best blue travelling cloak. He noticed her pallor making the skin of her oval face shine damply.

'Mornen' Miss Linnie.' He touched a finger to his forehead and bobbed his head shyly as she smiled back at him, a small troubled grimace. The cradle and boxes look as though she will be gone for some time, he thought uneasily. Cain't blame the poor rawni either, for this is a terrible kenner. He hefted the largest box up onto a broad shoulder and staggered down to the carriage with it.

'I'll just see that young Lawrence is ready, m'am,' Polly said to Lavinia. She hesitated and then put a hand shyly on Lavinia's shoulder. 'We'll miss you, Manfri and me, m'am,' she said with affection. 'The house is always kind of gloomy when you are out of it. I know that sounds silly — but I shall be a lot happier when you are back with us again.'

They regarded each other with the mutual respect that had grown easily between them in the six years that they had been mistress and maid under the same roof. Lavinia patted Polly's hand. 'I won't be gone for long, Poll,' she said as the girl turned away. She stood up then and began her habitual pacing. Quickly, quickly . . . why was Rueb being so long with the boxes?

'Is Lawrence ready?' she asked as Polly came back into the room. 'Don't 'e fret, Miss Linnie. Master Lawrence is so keen to get to his gran's that he's already downstairs and sitten' in the carriage since Rueb brought it round to the door.'

Lavinia resumed her pacing as Polly went down with the last of the bags. It was a cold day but starkly bright. A good day for Jess and his race. She wished him well, her lips mouthing the little message as the ache deepened in her back. There was something very wrong with the light in this chamber, she suddenly saw. Even as the thought occurred to her, she felt the familiar dread of pounding vibration closing in on her. The features of the elegant room slowly drained of colour and shape — and she was standing among strangers in a coldly pulsing wilderness. She put her hand out, groping in panic for the safety of her chair. The room seemed to waver beneath her feet, and then it was there, curling round her in noxious waves that brought the bile to her throat — the stench of the horse. . . .

She could hear her heart thudding wildly — or was it the thunder of hooves down a thousand years . . . ? The light was changing, a faint glow seeping into the heavy shadows — and with the orange glow came the first waves of the heat.

She forced herself to move; forced her leaden limbs to carry her out of that place, away from the thing that stretched out to take her, to trample her beneath its flailing hoofs and grind the child within her to pulp. She lumbered headlong out of the bedchamber, unaware of anything but the hideous odour, the reaching of that murderous following presence. She ran — and then there was nothing beneath her feet and only the impact of blows upon her body. The pain was almost welcome when it invaded her for it was at least something finite, a reality to which she could cling. She ground her teeth into the agony and let herself drift away.

By the time the entrance to Goodwood was in sight, Midas was blowing hard. There was an ache across Jess's shoulders which seemed to tear into him with every jarring movement. They skirted the front of the sprawling old house, scarcely noticing the flutter of red kerchief which heralded his approach, for Bolton Red was right behind him, the horse's breath blowing against Midas's straining flanks. They rode close together now, the squeak of leather and snorting breaths intermingling with the jingle of harness and the winded encouragement of the two riders. Then the ground was rising steadily ahead of them once more, and the smooth breast of St Rook's Hill reared up sharply, cresting over to their left and crowned with the ruined chapel of Saint Roc. Bolton Red levelled and began to draw ahead.

Lawrence sat disconsolately in his favourite place, in the

window-seat of his little room, where he could survey a broad view across the fields. The turret of Rymans and the little wooden bell tower of Saint Mary's rose distantly out of a misty line of trees. The land was quite flat and open and it was possible to see any visitor to Lavenham from the moment he turned off Salterns Lane and into the Lavenham drive. If he was not allowed to be with poor Mama, at least he would be the first to know when Dada and Manfri returned, so that he could race down and tell them that Mama had fallen head-over-heels all the way down the stairs — from the very top to the very bottom. She had banged her head and her baby and now Doctor Sanden was in there with all the others.

Blood pounded in Jess's head. Progress was frustratingly slow as the horses struggled up the almost vertical incline. Bolton Red was half a length ahead. The going had slackened to a snail's pace. As the ever distant rim of the hill cut across Jess's vision, Midas saw it too — and seemed to generate an extra burst of energy, straining up close to Bolton Red. Then they were cresting the hilltop and feeling the sudden scour of March wind cutting across them and the sun on their faces. They raced downwards towards a distant stream at the base of the hill, parallel now with Bolton Red.

Without warning, the Duke's chestnut faltered and in a moment was down, body twisting and kicking as momentum continued to carry him past his rider, who had nimbly leapt clear. Jess glanced over his shoulder as he drew away from the flailing horse and, seeing Steele picking himself up, gave the rest of his attention to getting himself and Midas safely down the slope into the narrow valley below them. He felt as though they had been riding all day but the sun was just clearing the trees across to the right. Tension in both of them eased without the sight of the other horse forever ahead of them — and Midas slowed to a walking pace, picking his way daintily over grassy hummocks and hidden rabbit burrows.

It took another ten minutes to reach the floor of the little valley. The brook was shallow here but steep sided and altogether too wide to jump. Jess rode along the edge of the bank until they found a place where it had crumbled away into the water. As they went down its loose side and splashed across to the flatter northern bank, they heard the chestnut coming down the hill behind them. Jess dared not risk a look over his shoulder until they were across the stream and tackling the shallow incline beyond. Steele was hard on their heels again — miraculously little time had been lost from his fall — and urging the mud-spattered Red downwards in a clever zig-zagging movement.

Jess drove his heels into Midas's heaving sides. By that time they had made a gradual ascent and there only remained a light gradient before the crest of the last ridge came into view. Bolton Red was climbing out of the stream as Midas reached the top of the rise. Below, a line of small foothills broke to left and right, fringed by straggling woodland. The ground dropped sharply into winter corn, which lapped the scatter of buildings that he knew was the finish. He straightened his stiff shoulders. Midas sensed the closeness of the stables and strained forward eagerly. They plummeted down off the bare hillside, traversing sharply. They loped and slithered, Midas blowing flatly, sweat creaming round the edges of the saddle leathers and dropping in frothy bubbles from his bit. Pebbles waterfalled across their track and Jess glanced up to see Bolton Red on the hill above, plunging down with Steele lashing his flanks grimly. 'Not long now, my kushti grai,' he muttered to Midas, patting the heaving sides. 'There they are, the Charlton stables . . . just keep our lead the way it is, bor. Keep going, then . . . just keep going.'

Sunshine warmed the earth, stirring the juices in the growing things. Midas seemed to get the scent of his promised hay-bag and his ears sent signals, pricking and pivoting as they followed the cleft between two cornfields. Bolton Red snorted down the slope behind them. The ground opened out ahead and a path led them between a long tithe barn and the main stable block.

Sensing the chestnut drawing in behind him, Jess dug his heels in sharply, the edges of his riding boots grazing the tightly stretched skin across Midas's ribs. The horse snorted with shock. Jess had never lifted a finger against him before and the sudden pain in his ribs sent the adrenalin pumping through him. Head down, he dragged himself together and lumbered onward, spurred further by the sound of Bolton Red's whistling breath directly behind him.

They passed a blur of colour and thundered onwards before Jess's mind registered the fact that they had passed the finishing flag. He released the iron vice of his knee grip and brought the reins sharply up against his chest. Midas checked and slowed lumpily, breathing hard through his nose. They took several deep breaths between them to get their thumping hearts back to a more comfortable pace, and then turned and walked quietly back towards the cheering crowd.

The light was brighter in the room, as though they had pulled back all the window curtains. Voices murmured softly and hands moved her legs.

'The poor dear lady, she really has taken a terrible fall,' Doctor Sanden's kind voice said to someone beside her. She tried to smile her thanks at his red, comic face with its bushy clown's eyebrows drawn together now with worry — but her body seemed to belong to someone else and nothing responded to her efforts.

'She always said this house didn't like her having children.' Polly sounded tearful, as though she too was on the verge of breaking down. 'Every time she's with child there's some sort of calamity. Oh, I'll never forget that sight, doctor — never get the picture out of my mind. She came screamen' out of this room as though all the devils in hell were after her and then she just seemed to jump into the air instead of coming down the stairs. She rolled over and over, poor young soul.'

Dear loving Polly, don't let this hurt you as it has hurt me, Lavinia thought. Thunder in her head. Thunder without lightning, but no — it was some part of her body bursting apart . . . in the head? The explosion in her raked every nerve and she cried out, for the child was tearing itself from her, ramming itself out into the world. The shadows closed round her and she saw the face of the Watcher emerging from the red mist. He had always been there, it seemed — always watching, waiting. It was strange, she thought, as the abyss yawned upwards to claim her, that there was an expression of tragic regret, even grief in the infinite depths of his great grey eyes.

The child, a girl, was born too small and bruised for any chance of survival. She died within minutes of her birth. Mistress Whittle wrapped a cloth hastily round the little body and handed it to Amy. She put the bundle into the waiting crib and returned to where Mistress Whittle was peering over the doctor's shoulder.

'Bleedin's stoppin'.' the woman said with relief.

He straightened his back and drew the covers over Lavinia's legs, felt her pulse and put his head down on to the quiet mound of her chest. The two women stared at him as they watched him gently raise an eyelid and press his cheek to her mouth.

'I'm sorry,' he said, getting up off his knees and dusting his breeches. 'I'm afraid that fall was too much for her, poor lady. There must be internal damage, both in her head and in her body. I'm afraid that she is dead.'

Amy closed the door of her chamber and stood against it, feeling the smooth silken surface of the polished wood under the palms of her hands.

'*My* door . . . *my* chamber,' she said to herself with fierce joy, for now there would be no move to the cottage on the muddy highway. Now Jess would need her again, just as he had needed her when first this house was built. She gripped her arms tightly across her chest and hugged herself until her ribs hurt.

'Amy will care for you, my kushti chal . . . Amy is all

you need. Take your women in the taverns and the fields, bor — just as you did before — but Amy is here to see to everythen' for you now . . . . ' A laugh bubbled up in her throat and she sank on to the floor as her body began its puppet jerking. She rolled over on her back and the laughter tore up from the pleasure in her heart, melding with the onset of the spasms. She stared at the ceiling, seeing Lavinia's face there, and she spat at it with all the venom of the victor — and allowed the seizure to take her into oblivion.

The Watcher turned from Lavinia's bed, engulfed in an anguish of grief. How beautiful she had been in life. There was no guilt in her, no sin as there was in him — and yet he had had to erase her, for the child had carried the Evil. He observed Amy, thrashing and twisting alone in her chamber — and withdrew, locked in the revulsion of recognition. His roots were embedded right there in the centre of that furious madness.

Violet stood outside the door of Lawrence's chamber.

She opened it soundlessly and peeped inside. He was sitting curled up in the window-seat, staring out at the sprawl of bare trees which barely hid the entrance to the drive.

'They're dead . . . both of them.'

She spoke sharply, getting an empty kind of comfort from the cruelly flat statement. He looked such a good little boy, sitting there with his golden curls shining in the fading light. How could such innocence compound the taking of life — of his own mother's life — even for the reasons of jealousy which must have been at the back of it all this time?

He turned his face to her. The rounded cheeks were streaked with tears. 'I know . . . I felt it all, did you? It was like the dream I have, but Mama was all right in that. I felt something horrible reach out — and then she went, and the baby too . . . '

Violet inched in through the door and closed it behind her. She stood with her back to it, looking at him.

'We didn't want that baby, Mama and I . . . but at least I would never have Flamed it. You disobeyed Dada, you know that?'

He clenched his fists and stood up, and the light made snail trails of the tears on his cheeks.

'I know well enough that you didn't want the new baby here — nor Mama. You don't want any of us — except for Dada . . . So I know that it was you who Flamed them, not me. You don't want me either, do you . . . but you won't find me so easy to get rid of.'

The Power blossomed from him without warning, the force waves so strong that they were visible, like the petals of a great red poppy.

Violet recoiled and was slammed hard against the door as the shock struck her. The shield went up round her but she could feel him draining her, dragging at every nerve in her body. Sudden pleasure erupted, pouring through her and turning the whole world golden.

She found herself smiling at Lawrence, suddenly loving the weapon he carried. 'Oh yes, Lawrence, I do love you really. We are all we have left for each other, you and me . . . I really do love you.'

Part Two

1746-1768

VIOLET AND LAWRENCE

1

The poacher paused, leaning against the damp green bark of an oak tree where Mr Bayless had lately cleared another tract of woodland for pasture.

The soft blanket of sea fog was thinning as daylight grew, bringing with it a flotsam of noisy gulls which circled and dipped in and out of the mist, feeding from the first sprouting of freshly seeded grass. The poacher watched their spiralling activity, bemused at their deftness, that so dense a cloud of screeching life could move in such freedom without collision. Left to their own devices, the gulls would leave little growing in the ground. Nature teaching Mr Bloody Bayless that not everything he touched turned to gold. Grim satisfaction cracked his gaunt tinker's face into a black-toothed grin.

Across the field, a figure stood against the hedge, also watching the swooping activity of the gulls. Seeing him materializing so suddenly and unexpectedly, the poacher eased back into shadow until the tree hid him completely. The unwelcome sight of another human presence was alarming and there was something about the concentration of the youth across the field which was puzzling.

He stood on the edge of the tilled earth, tall and straight-backed, his pale gold hair unqueued and loose about his face. Even at a distance the expression of rigid absorption in the gulls made the poacher hold his breath. The daylight brightened, bringing into focus with over-sharp clarity the tension in that slender body. His head and hands were bare and the poacher watched the youth's fists clenching and stretching at his sides as though to keep the blood working in them. Between the two humans, the gulls swooped and rose, screeching over the succulent new seedlings, the arch of their grey-white wings like scythes in the cold air.

Something dropped among them, plummeting downwards like a stone. The flock rose up in screeching thundrous alarm.

The poacher stood rooted to the spot, mouth open. Another and another body fell from the wheeling, panic-striken cloud of birds. He pressed his quaking chest hard against the trunk of the tree, grateful for its tangible stoutness, and watched with growing terror and disbelief as a rain of gulls dropped out of the air — until the field was carpeted with inert bodies, a soft warm harvest of grey and white with a frosting of black-tipped feathers.

A single gull scudded wildly away over the bare tree tops and out across the harbour.

The boy stirred, arching his back and flinging his arms outwards and up over his head. The sound of his laughter bounced off the hedgerows, filling the heart of the poacher with a primeval fear that galvanized him into movement. Dropping the half-filled grub sack, he crashed away into the tangled heart of the wood. The sudden movement caught the boy's attention and he turned his head and focused on the fleeing figure. The Power still pulsed and thundered within him and the temptation to Flame the rascal was almost overwhelming, but he mastered it.

It would be amusing to listen to the wild tales that would be woven out of the fellow's experience; he smiled to himself, giving the gentle contours of his handsome face a charming innocence as he moved out into the field and began to gather the bodies of the seagulls into a heap against the hedge.

Giles Croucher stood on a bulging bank above a small stream swollen after three days of torrential rain, surveying the wreckage of the little footbridge which he had only recently completed. He had laboured on the bridge footings since before Christmas and had been well pleased with the seemingly sturdy structure, which now lay in ruins in the muddy waters below him. He cursed himself at length and the urgent, swirling stream in particular.

'Strong words don't make strong structures, Mr Croucher.'

He whipped round, feet sliding on the muddy bank. At the top of the slope a horse and rider stood against the murky morning sky. The girl smiled down at him, her face wet with rain.

He pulled the stocking cap from his head and bowed. 'Mornen' Miss Violet. Looks like the rains cut out my bridge work fair and square. I should keep your mount well away from the bank all the way along, for the ground is none too secure.'

She nodded, leaning forward slightly in the saddle as though to hear him more clearly. She looked, he thought with a great lurch of the heart, irresistible on the golden horse, her own dark colouring contrasting to perfection with its creamy mane and burnished tail.

'Take the footpath up through Denmans Piece and cut northwards across the open land and back on to the highway south of Rumboldswyke,' he advised, trying to keep his eyes discreetly averted from the gentle curve where the well-fitting jacket of her riding habit swooped down from small breasts to a tiny waist.

She watched the expressions washing through his up-turned face. Such an exciting procession to see there. Such an honest, open visage. Strong and clean, with the bright sparkle in his eyes and a certain mature composure about him that belied his twenty years. The words they uttered mattered little, for the important part was the sound of his voice with its musical warmth — and the time the words afforded them in each other's company.

Their eyes met and locked. It was as though they had joined their bodies and Violet blinked, feeling the colour flooding into her face.

'Well, good day to you, Giles,' she said, tightening her grip on the reins and making her horse dance beneath her.

They hesitated a moment, loath to bring their interchange to an end but lost suddenly for further words.

Giles bowed again as Violet turned the gelding, thrusting the heels of her boots against its shining sides. He stood where she had left him, his earlier irritation with the ruined bridge replaced by a feeling of buoyant good humour, and watched the graceful figure in its soft blue riding habit until she and the golden gelding had merged with the misty rain amongst distant trees.

Violet rode through the Lavenham archway into the cobbled yard and Rueb, emerging at that moment from the harness room, came over and held Songster as she swung her skirts across his rump and slid to the ground.

'Yer Dadrus be looken' for you, chavi,' he said, catching the reins she threw to him and rubbing the horse's nose with a calloused hand. His brown face was creased as a walnut shell beneath untidy black curls, an ugly caricature of her father's handsome features. But cousin Rueb was as loyal and devoted as Manfri and she loved them both dearly.

'I'll wager that means I'm in for a ribbing for putting Golden Harvest over the jumps yesterday. Wish me luck, cousin . . . your poor Violet has been in the wars with Dada nearly every day lately.'

'Manfri reckons your Dadrus bain't too well,' Rueb said. He spoke slowly, pondering each word before parting grudgingly with it. Speech came hard to him and he always used it sparingly. Observing folks was more profitable — and seeing young Violet grow from a fat little tickni into this breath-stopping beauty had long been one of his most absorbing occupations. He watched his words cast a shadow over the classical lines of her oval face, clouding the great grey eyes with instant concern.

'You may be right. I hadn't thought of his health,' she said, the imp of a moment before changing to a thoughtful angel. 'I'll go to him right away.' She hurried through the grey stone archway which led to the main house, tapping the side of her riding habit with her crop, a small frown of concern still creasing her forehead. In the hall she collided with a small running figure. She put out her hands and steadied the girl.

'Do forgive me, Lettie. I was in such a hurry — and you were too, it seems . . . . '

'Yes, mistress, oh dear . . . I was going to fetch Polly, mistress. Your mama is taking one of her turns and I can't for the life of me get her up on to her bed.' Alarm painted bright spots of colour on the girl's cheeks and she fidgeted nervously, glancing up the stairs over her shoulder.

Violet steadied her. 'Quite right of you, Lettie. Polly knows the routine. Away with you quickly then.'

Jess Bayless looked up from the untidy, document-strewn desk in front of him. He didn't smile at the sight of his daughter. Instead, a little frown of irritation came and went. 'Yes? What is it?'

Violet closed the door behind her and came across the broad expanse of bright turkey carpet. 'Rueb said you wanted to see me, Dada.'

'That's right, I did . . . but not when I am engrossed in mortgage ledgers, if you please, miss. I'll see you immediately after luncheon. I have to go to Portsmouth early in the afternoon and will not be home before dark, so I must not be delayed now. It seems I am never able to find you when you are most needed, Violet.'

Violet smiled at him, not at all put out by his sharpness. He was not a difficult man by nature, rather a benevolent and humorous mentor who gently curbed her headstrong nature and countered her wilder actions with common-sense alternatives. This brusque mood of his was not in character and must be soothed away.

'I'm sorry, Dada. I'll try to be around when you want me.' She hesitated and then leaned across the desk and put her hand over his large one. 'Can you not ease up just a little from your work? You are looking so tired these days and it seems a very long time since we walked in the woods and hunted the hotchiwichi. . . . '

He sighed, putting down his quill and passing a hand

across his eyes for a moment. He took her hand and put it to his cheek. Weariness suddenly softened the granite jawline.

'Maybe I am overdoing things a little at the moment. Getting a mite tetchy in my old age too, I'll warrant. There's a mountain of work to oversee, and since Lawrence shows no interest in the business, I have recently come to realize that I may well be obliged to take a partner before long — and that's enough to make a man like me more than a little irritable.'

He looked at her with the affection and pleasure which usually tempered their association.

'I shall not be here forever,' he went on. 'Recently it has been worrying me that Lawrence seems so disinterested in the family's affairs. Our vessels have a certain pull for him as you know — but the hard-nosed day-to-day running of the shipping company makes him yawn whenever I try to involve him in it. He's only interested in the more dubious aspects of the *Grace* and *Golden Dawn* and has no eyes for *Lavinia* or *Heron* at all.'

Words were unnecessary between them for they well knew the reason for Lawrence's interest in the two larger vessels. Both had been constructed with skilfully hidden compartments in their hulls to facilitate the importation of certain precious cargoes from the Indies which were not on the ships' manifests. Jess's long connection with the illegal importation of precious goods had attracted notice in other quarters, however, and it appeared to have been the visit to Lavenham of Mr Thomas Benson of Knapp which had suddenly focused Lawrence's attention on the *Grace* and *Golden Dawn*.

Lawrence had been profoundly impressed by Mr Benson. Although it was Jess he had come to see, it had been Lawrence who engaged much of his attention. Lawrence, at sixteen, was well above average height and promised to fill out to match his father's broad-shouldered physique. Beyond that, apart from the same grey eyes which he shared with his father and sister, he was pure Freeland —

with his mother's rich golden hair and the fresh, whole-some features with which all the Freelands were blessed. That he was inclined to be wilful and cared little for learning was forgiven by the whole family and put down to his youthfulness. Another year or two would see reason beginning to cool his spirits, they thought.

It was not the looks but the daredevil in the boy which endeared him to Thomas Benson — and Benson's growing reputation as smuggler and privateer, as well as Member of Parliament for Bideford and Sheriff of Devonshire, fascinated Lawrence.

Benson had stayed at Lavenham for three nights, closeted with Jess in the Bayless shipping office at Dell Quay by day. Lawrence, imagining every kind of possible contract between two brilliant smugglers, was left in a state of buoyant excitement.

'What a leader,' he said to Violet. 'I've never met a man like him before.'

'What nonsense you talk,' she scoffed. 'How can you think so well of a man who accepts office in Parliament with one hand and then robs it wholesale with the other?'

He grinned from ear to ear and sliced the air with an imaginary sword feint.

'Master Benson is an opportunist of the finest quality, little sister,' he said loftily, unable to erase the ring of admiration from his voice.

She said sharply, 'How many people are going to entrust their Member with their problems when it is common knowledge that the honourable gentleman not only cheats His Majesty's treasury but turns to his own advantage the very problems with which his constituents seek his aid?'

He looked at her with pity. What did a girl understand about a man of fire like Mr Benson? One day . . .

There had been — and still was, in many ways — a close bond between Jess's two children. After Lavinia's death they had drawn together and presented the world with a united front behind which they quarrelled and fought only in the privacy of the nursery. In recent years, however, a certain jealousy had begun to mar their relationship.

That other talent shared between them became, in their emergent years, a secret weapon rather than a precious Romany gift entrusted to their care, as Jess proclaimed.

To have the Sight was one thing — but to have, in addition, the Killing Glance was a burden of a different weight to both of them. In Violet, her childish lack of wonderment for it gradually resolved into something close to fear. She loved and respected most living things, especially those creatures of the field and hedgerow who led their lives on a level closer to the pattern of her gypsy forebears. It became repugnant to her to Flame any of them and there was nothing in her nature which would permit her to take the life of another human being.

Lawrence matured very differently. Where he had been almost timid as a small boy, proud of his special powers but also terrified of using them where Violet might intrude and inflict retribution, as he grew towards manhood, he began to assert himself and to forge that inner strength into a weapon for his own devices.

The brotherly affection he felt for Violet began very gradually to assume a different importance, for he became more aware of her newly emerging shape and found an uncomfortable excitement in it. They clashed on two occasions only — and both times Lawrence had suffered. It was not in his nature to realize that the only superiority Violet possessed was in her more disciplined control and use of the Power.

She left her father to his ledger work now, knowing with sudden certainty that Lawrence was not the cause of his weariness. Something to which he was not admitting was draining his energy. Maybe he was not aware of the condition. She stood in the hall, as she had so often seen her mother stand, listening to the heart of the house, feeling that faint, familiar discord within the heavy silence which surrounded her.

'What is wrong with him?' Violet asked the house. She stood very still and probed the singing silence with every one of her senses as her mother had done in days gone by. But nothing responded. The house was still, except a momentary change in the air currents of the high-ceilinged hall.

The Watcher, standing in the doorway between the parlour and the hall, turned away from observing Jess Bayless and gave his attention to the girl.

He was proud of Violet. She had such strength. The beauty of her was certainly a gilding of what was already great excellence but it was the refining of all that was Bayless and all that was Hator in her which was so fascinating. Here was the coming together of Romany and gorgio at its very best. The Watcher recognized that in himself, there was more of Lawrence than there was of Violet. Even the boy's sexual attatchment to her, of which he was scarcely aware, found an echo in him. He shrank from the tell-tale quickening of the blood in his veins at the mere suggestion of the Power which was always there now, poised and ready to thunder through his body and burst from him in a hideous trail of destruction.

He groaned to himself and bowed his head, trying to shut out the image of Jess Bayless and the failing of that stout heart, already beating with a falter in his great chest.

Jess Bayless pored over his architect's drawings, biting the inside of his cheek in concentration. Discussions for the proposed additions to the house had been going on for months and now the results were spread out on the desk before him. The family's needs had altered over the years but he had resisted change until now, loath to tamper with anything which had been created with such dedication for Lavinia.

Lavinia. . . . Her name still brought a softness to his eyes. Eleven years had rolled away from that memory of Lavinia's young face, tranquil in death after the battle she had fought and lost. His anguish was still as great as it had been then, but now it lay deeper, rarely acknowledged except when he woke from sleep and felt the echo of her presence close to him.

His eyes slid back to the drawings. He was seeing the architect, Dalziell, in Chichester later in the day to give the final consent to the plans. He studied them, forcing himself to concentrate on the new wing. Dalziell could not understand Jess's reluctance for further foundations to be dug — but then why should he, for he had not been present during the building of Lavenham and knew nothing of the incident which had started all the tales among the villagers. There were only two local men still living who had been involved on that long ago day. John Kidd had been a jobbing labourer on the building site and was now verger at Saint Mary's. He still crossed himself at the mention of that dark day in the winter of 1725. Will Tregus himself was the other — and he was in the asylum where they had put him when he was still little more than a boy. Jess had seen him once, a poor mindless, gobbling creature who had said nothing to anyone since the day Jess had found him in one of the foundation trenches, kneeling against the earth with his arms wrapped round his head as though to protect himself from something.

Behind closed doors and over teacups, the country gossips slowly wove a web about the Baylesses of Lavenham. Fortunately there was little evidence of such superstition in Chichester, where Jess was both liked as a man and respected as an honourable and imaginative negotiator.

Jess raised his head from the house plans and leaned back against the leather padding of his chair. Poring over his work for many hours in the day often gave him a chest cramp and uncomfortable shortness of breath, and now it smote him afresh without warning. He closed his eyes as the pain tightened round his ribs, imprisoning him in an iron grip. He sat still, willing the moment to pass, feeling the ache creeping down his side and through his upper arm muscle. A light sweat broke out over his body. He felt the blood pounding in his veins as though he had been running. The moment passed.

Amy pushed through the undergrowth of Salterns Woods, the medicine pouch swinging at her waist. The woods gave her a great sense of peace for, beneath the bastion of protective branches, there were no disturbing influences whirling through her head as there were in the house. Living creatures watched her passing without fear. It was quiet in the woods, even though a chill wind whined and rattled the branches over her head and the undergrowth was drenched from the overnight rainfall. She wore only her dressing robe and thin house slippers but noticed nothing of their saturation as she stumbled painfully through the trees towards the saltpans. The saltings were empty.

'Jess,' she called, sure that he would be somewhere near the lickering shed at this time of day. Her voice was swept away in the blustering wind and she stood uncertainly, her misshapen leg throbbing. Where was he? There were the benders over in the corner, at the lane end of the pans. She could distinctly see smoke curling up lazily from the three hearths and figures moving there in shadow.

'Jess,' she called again, but he didn't come and she turned from the empty pans. She headed back towards Lavenham and plunged into the undergrowth, looking for the path.

The wood became alien. All at once the gently dappled light held menace and the leafy green canopy overhead was filled with faceless demons. She was lost in the heart of a vast forest which had no boundaries. Struggling against the barriers of brambles which barred her path, she stumbled and, falling, lay down on wet leaves, face pressed against the mossy ground, weeping with fear.

Hands lifted her and transported her, with a murmur of voices.

'Coom oop, bor . . . that's right, I'll take yer now. Let go me sleeve then.'

The voice was familiar but she could not conjure up the name or the face.

'There, Mama — Rueb has you safe. You'll soon be home . . . Oh, poor soul. She's so wet and bedraggled. . . . '

Violet — Violet with her big eyes and black curly hair and the dimples in her little elbows — and there were two more dimples where her fat little bottom joined her spine.

'Hush my kushti tickni,' she crooned to the baby. 'Amy knows what you want.' She tore at her bodice, rummaging for her breast but the clothing had no opening and her breast was thin and empty and she beat her fists against Rueb's grizzled head until he swore.

'Coom up, simensa,' he said gruffly to Amy. 'Stay quiet a while, an' we'll soon have yer back in yer woodrus. . . . '

'Really, I'm at my wits' end with Mother,' Violet said later to Jess. 'That's the third time this week that we've found her wandering in the woods in all weathers. She'll catch her death of cold one of these days if we can't keep a closer eye on her. I'm afraid the only certain solution is to lock her chamber door.'

A door slammed in the hall and a shrill yelp from one of the lurchers meant that one of them had earned a well-aimed kick from Lawrence's boot.

Jess's head jerked up. 'Lawrence, in here a moment, if you please, sir.' His voice had remarkable carrying power, without his making any apparent effort to raise it.

Lawrence poked his head round the parlour door.

'Your servant, sir. Oh hello, Violet. I thought you were always about the cottages, doing your mercy round at this time of day.'

'Charity begins at home,' she said mildly, refusing to rise to the banter in his voice.

'Spare us the details, if you please.' He went across to his father and, suspecting a rebuke of some sort from the sharp tone in which he had been summonsed, turned upon Jess the full charm of his sunniest smile. For a moment it worked — as he had hoped it would, for he knew just how closely he resembled his mother and how certain express-ions shot his father through to the marrow with the yearning he still felt for her.

Jess hesitated and his craggy, weary face softened at this uncanny replica of Lavinia's puckish, slightly hang-dog grin — the look she had always assumed when she knew that she had done something which she enjoyed but of which Jess would disapprove.

But this was not Lavinia. This was Lawrence.

'Did you Flame a great pile of gulls that Bob Wickens found in Boorscroft this morning?'

Lawrence looked blameless but surprised. 'I found them going for the seedlings again,' he said. 'That field never seems to grass decently and I knew you wanted it for grazing next year.' He caught sight of Jess's expression and his voice became defensive. 'Oh, come on, Dada. I was doing no harm . . . I only thought to help rid you of those confounded parasites.'

The softness in Jess's face had gone and he regarded his son bleakly.

'Bare-faced lying will do you no good, sir. You Flame things simply because you enjoy the experience — so don't try and dress up such mindless acts of barbarism in fawning excuses. Now just attend me, sir. I will not stand for these unnecessary slaughterings, Lawrence. You are becoming a menace both to yourself and to the family. I learned to respect the Power and only used it for the cooking pot or in my own defence. Violet has made very little use of it at all — but you, bor, you have to scour the countryside when the mood is in you, taking out a sheep here or a flock of birds there. It has just got to stop, sir, d'you hear?'

Lawrence nodded, head down and staring at a speck of mud on his shining boot. He would have liked to listen and obey, for he truly respected and loved this man who was his father. But lately it seemed that he *had* to keep Flaming things, that he was being manipulated by a will far stronger than his own. He had just taken his first woman and had made a most intriguing discovery — that in the act of ejaculation he experienced the same almost unbearable pleasure which came flooding through him when he Flamed things, and Flaming was so much swifter and easier than tumbling girls.

Jess's voice cut through the thought before he had time

to explore it further. 'I've not put a stick to you since you were a nipper, bor — but, strap me if I don't give you the leathering of your life if one more Flaming comes to my attention. D'ye understand me, Lawrence?'

Seeing that his lecture was over, Lawrence excused himself and closed the door with a slight slam behind him.

Lawrence sat in the window-seat of his bedchamber and surveyed the paddocks and fields beyond the sweep of the drive. He could oversee Boorscroft through the trees surrounding the house, and one small stretch of the drive just before its junction with Salterns Lane. The rich tilled earth of the field stretched out before him in cold sunshine. Above it a couple of crows swooped and lifted and veered away into the feathery green tops of the distant trees. There was no sign of the gulls which contantly fed there. He smiled to himself. Dada might rant and rage at him but he had had trouble seeding that field ever since it had been cleared and ploughed, for the birds picked it clean as soon as it was planted. It looked as though they would give it a miss though, from now on.

Voices floated up from below and Violet came into view, strolling beside Giles Croucher, who was leading his horse and gesticulating avidly with his free hand. They walked close to each other, absorbed in themselves. Lawrence watched them, feeling the intensity of their preoccupation. It came to him suddenly, from the vibrations flowing from her, that Violet was falling in love — and the thought drove through him like a sword. They had been antagonists all their lives, but a long time ago — after the death of Lavinia, his mother — they had arrived at a kind of unacknowledged truce. They both possessed the power to Flame things, and when they were very young, had frightened themselves considerably by trying to use it on each other. Their own defensive systems had been the saving of their lives then, and it had actually brought them together.

It was something of a shock, now for Lawrence to discover just how strong that attachment apparently still was. If Violet became betrothed she would soon depart from Lavenham to a home of her own, which was unthinkable. There would be no one to rise to his defence when he annoyed Dada, no one to take the burden of the household — which might even mean that Dada would consider marrying a new wife to run Lavenham. This last thought was so appalling that it quite overshadowed the other feeling, deep down inside him, that she was giving Giles Croucher the full benefit of her affection and that he, Lawrence, would not engage her attention at all while another dwelt more rosily in her thoughts.

He closed his eyes on the now distant figures, who had stopped in the drive and were looking back towards the house.

Violet suddenly stopped in her tracks and swung round to look back at the house.

'What is it?' Giles asked, seeing the odd look on her face.

She stood straight and still as though she was listening, eyes fixed on the house. 'I don't quite know.'

Her voice was puzzled, far away — as though she had heard a sound that she was not able to place. She turned back to him. 'I must go now,' she said, holding out her hand.

He took it and put it to his lips. It was small and warm and the fingers tightened briefly in his hand, giving him their own private message.

Lettie Heberden was not long past her fourteenth birthday when Miss Violet Bayless engaged her to help in the kitchens at Lavenham. She was shown into the servants' room off the kitchen, where she would sleep, and stood beside the narrow bed, looking round her in delight. It was a small room and bare in the extreme but she had never had a room of her own before, nor a bed that was not shared with her sister or another of the press workers.

Polly took her round the house, which she found spacious and awesome but in no way frightening. Later in the day she watched Jess Bayless riding into the stable yard from Chichester. There again were the distinctive high cheek-bones and dark foreign looks of their gypsy blood, but how much more refined and strikingly handsome was this man compared with Rueb's and Manfri's rough homeliness, she thought. With the exception of Polly and Master Lawrence, they were all a darkly foreign breed. Still, they were kindness itself to her, and who was she to question their antecedents when they made her welcome with such grace?

She had been at Lavenham for two days before she saw Lawrence. She was in the hall, rubbing beeswax and turpentine into the already shining surface of the dining table, when feet clattered down the stairs behind her and she straightened as a young man passed her, heading for the kitchen. There was no greeting, for he was clearly in a hurry. The door slammed and she could hear Polly chiding him with good-natured exasperation. He was only about a year older than herself, this young master — but tall. He was so tall that she would have to crane her neck to catch his eyes, she thought, attacking her work with new vigour and pink cheeks. He was very pleasing to look at, with a fresh complexion and fair, almost golden hair. He and Miss Violet both had their father's high-bridged nose and grey eyes, though. He looked very pleasant, Master Lawrence.

When, on Christmas morning, Lettie appeared in a new gown while the rest of the family prepared for church, Lawrence began to study the girl unobtrusively and found her quite pleasing. She was like a small robin, brown eyes and brown haired, with a small, thin, heart-shaped face that had no beauty but still held a certain appeal. Everything about Lettie seemed to turn upwards. Her eyes turned up at the corners; her mouth was well shaped and much inclined to smiling. She was slender to the point of skinniness, but there was still an interesting suggestion of small high breasts beneath her bodice and a remarkably neat little waist, which he noted with increasing attention. He did nothing to attract her attention that day, even when the heavily laden table and generously flowing wine brought a flush to the cheeks of all the guests, relaxing

124

much of the formality in their manners. All the same, she was very conscious of his eyes, which strayed in her direction constantly.

'Where do you come from?' he asked one morning as she knelt to dust the fat bowled legs of the dining table.

She peered at him through fine strands of hair escaping from her pinner. He had seated himself on the bottom step of the stairs with his back against the carved lintel. In the strong light from the casement behind him, his neatly queued hair gleamed like old gold. He looked across the hall at her with polite interest, the glint in his long-lashed eyes carefully veiled.

'Well, from the Witterings, really, sir,' she said with some hesitation. 'Leastwise, me gran lives there for me mam's dead these past three years an' we never knew where me father went.' She grinned at him and resumed her polishing. There wasn't much to tell when you were born of a long line of bastards.

'Have you had any schooling? Can you not read nor write?'

She shook her head and squatted back on her heels. 'Lawks a mercy, no, sir. Where would I have been teached me letters? Me mam never had no learnen' . . . nor me gran. I can see me name when 'tis writ down but that's the beginnen' and end of it. What would I do with learnen' in any case, sir?'

'If you had a bit of education you'd be able to get a better job and earn more money,' Lawrence said patiently. 'You would become a more valuable asset as a wife and might catch the eye of a tradesman. Would that not be better than your present lot?'

She shook her head, smiling at his earnest face and flattered at his attention to her.

'I be real happy right here, sir. I've the roof over me head and victuals aplenty and a room of me own to sleep in. That's a wonder in itself, I can tell you — why would I want to change any of that for a bit of learnen' and a husband who, like as not, gives me a kid each year an' nothing to feed an' clothe 'em with?'

He uncoiled himself and stood up, stretching. 'I tell you what I shall do, if it pleases you. I shall teach you your numbers and letters myself. I tell you, Polly will be delighted if you can master your numbers as you'll be able to give her a hand with the dairy accounts. You know how she hates doing them.'

Learning her numbers and her letters became a very mixed blessing.

'We will keep it to ourselves,' Lawrence said firmly before the first lesson. She agreed happily enough but soon discovered that concentration on her sums and alphabet was none too easy. It was not that the content of the lessons was beyond her but rather because of the close proximity of Master Lawrence himself.

Lawrence produced slate and chalks and discovered a patience within himself which surprised him. He was well aware of Lettie's nervousness and embarrassment, but her shy admiration of him was flattering and provoked a state of heightened consciousness whenever he sat close to her. Watching her bent over her slate with the chalk scratching its way laboriously through CAT . . . RAT . . . MAT . . . , he studied the lines of her little face as she frowned with the effort of her concentration. She had a small nose, dusted with freckles and turning upward at the end, the nostrils flared. Her full-lipped mouth was slightly open, and now and then the tip of her tongue slid like a pink lozenge over her bottom lip, leaving it glistening. The smell of her was not displeasing, he found. She worked hard in the house and perspired freely and the warm odour, far from being repugnant, quickened his pulse.

'Put a longer loop on that G,' he said, reaching over her shoulder to point at the mistake. He stared down at the pale nape of her neck where her hair, spilling from its cambric pinner, parted on either side to fall over her shoulders. The soft brown hairs were fine and curling there, like a baby's, and there was something infinitely vulnerable about a nape so trustingly exposed. He put his lips to the enticing place.

Lettie shivered and froze.

He slid his hand under her writing arm and cupped her left breast, teasing the nipple into hardness with his fingers. She turned her head, eyes frightened and excited and the protest forming on her lips. He silenced the words before they were uttered and they sat very still on the bench, twisted towards each other, savouring the sweet surging that the joining of their mouths provoked.

'Oh, no please, Master Lawrence . . . please don't.'

Her distress clamoured at him through the blood pounding in his chest and he dragged himself back from the slippery slope of nerve-edged excitement with reluctance.

'Sorry,' he muttered into her hair.

She completed her exercise and held up her slate for his approval. A new nervousness in her made him take it brusquely.

'What did I tell you about those loops?' His voice was harsh, and at the sound she was filled with dismay. That small familiarity had broken their easy companionship, putting them planes apart from each other.

She bowed her head. 'I shall practise on them this evening, sir — when I've finished me work,' she said humbly.

There was no sign of Lawrence the following day, nor the one after that. By the fourth lessonless day it dawned upon Lettie that maybe the young master was so angry with her that her reading and writing might never be acquired. Her abstraction turned to silent mourning and even Polly's good-natured teasing did nothing to ease it.

She did her best to continue the learning that Lawrence had begun. When the household retired and she had finished scrubbing the kitchen floor and damped down the cooking fire, she settled at the table and spread out her lesson books around her. Five days after the incident in the dairy, Lawrence walked past her without even a nod as she was clearing away the remains of the family's breakfast. The cool rebuff brought tears to her eyes, for it proved — more surely than any words could — that his brief interest in her was gone.

Lawrence avoided direct contact with Lettie for two reasons. It made him feel quite guilty to see the habitually cheerful little maid now flitting silently about her work, head down, as though to efface herself completely. He also knew that the incident had set him alight where Lettie was concerned, and the memory of what had been intended as a quick fondle had become a constant yearning in him.

When the fifth day without speech with her had drawn to a close, Lawrence retired to his chamber but found that sleep eluded him. The memory of the neat firmness of her warm breast and the earthiness of her body odour brought him up from his bed.

There was an uneasy restlessness in the atmosphere of the house. A heavy pulse-beat in his ears like a drum sounding its warning on a distant hilltop. For some reason there seemed to be a peculiarly strong odour of the stables in his nostrils, which he sniffed with distaste. Those bloody horses make themselves felt everywhere, he thought. He cocked his head and listened, for it seemed that he could even hear them. That was mighty odd at this time of night. Behind him, yellow candlelight streamed from the open doorway to drown in the gaping stair well. The heavy pulse-beat was all about him, vibrating in the air he breathed, filling him with a growing excitement. It was the way he felt before Flaming a quarry — deeply disturbed and filling up with overwhelming . . . intention. He moved slowly down the stairs, carried like a sleepwalker in the grip of an outside will.

There was a chink of light under the kitchen door and he stood in the stone-flagged passage between the hall and yard doors, listening for sounds of movement in there. He took a step forward and turned the handle very softly, opened the kitchen door an inch and put his eye to the crack of light.

128

Lettie sat hunched over her slate and a pile of books and testers, completely absorbed in her work.

He watched her in her pool of candlelight and saw her look up, searching the shadows around her as though she sensed his presence. Concentration broken, she fidgeted between her slate and books for a little longer and then rose with a sigh, gathered them up and padded across to her room.

Lawrence waited, watching shadows on the kitchen wall weaving languid reflections from the dull glow of the cooking fire. Lettie came back into view and picked up the candle in its pewter holder. She glanced around her and the soft light lapped her face, highlighting the unease in it. Then she was gone and he heard the snap of her door closing.

He pushed the kitchen door open, slipped through and closed it silently behind him. The coals were banked up in the grate and he moved across towards their faint glow and sat himself down in Polly's rocking chair.

He rocked the fireside chair quietly.

The odour of horse . . . sounds of squealing creatures in pain and terror . . . the pounding heartbeat thundering in his ears — all were centred in the heart of the house.

Finally he rose from the rocking chair and padded towards the door of Lettie's chamber.

Violet stirred and woke suddenly, pitchforked out of sleep by waves of liquid sensation flooding through her body and down her legs. The air throbbed about her, shot through with distant sound. Whinneying — terrified, squealing whinnies and the crashing of stamping kicking hooves.

The horses. Something was going on out in the stables. She tumbled out of bed, fumbling for the tinder box on her chamber closet, before something made her pause and, standing very still, reach out her mind to test the strange vibrations pressing in upon her. A thickly acrid stench of excrement filled her nostrils, making her gag for an instant. Horse dung . . . but overpoweringly strong, sickeningly putrid. She put her hands up to cover her nose, feeling the protection shield curl up round her.

Across the room, Amy slept on her back. Violet padded over to the shadowed bed and stared down at her mother, searching the serene face for an echo of her own deep disturbance. There was no sign of reaction in Amy. She lay, free of the twitching and gasping which usually accompanied her sleep, legs bent into blanket-covered steeples. She was so still that had she not been breathing deeply and regularly, she might have been mistaken for dead.

A great coldness pervaded the room. Trying to control the trembling in her body, Violet crept back into bed and sat, hugging her knees and remembering the nightmares of childhood and the terrible dying of Aunt Lavinia.

Amy floated, wallowing in the pleasure of pure sensation. Streams of nerve responses coursed through her body in well-remembered joyousness.

Jess . . . Jess's hands upon her, tingling every inch of her bare flesh; Jess's mouth wandering, teasing . . . so lightly that the very nerves beneath her skin jumped; Jess within her moving so sweetly while the exaltation grew and flowered and the pounding of their bodies echoed the thundrous drumming in the air around them.

The house lived.

It was pulse of her pulse, surge of her surge. It fed upon the responses of her body and, knowing it, she was further uplifted — a willing vessel with sudden purpose. She gave herself up to the wishes of the Place, washed by the house's excitement — purified by its hunger.

Lettie kicked off her slippers, rolled the woollen stockings off her legs and removed her apron and working gown. The little room was cold, for there were draughts round her window, which came whistling through the cracks of the shutters when the winds were easterly. She scrambled

130

into bed and lay curled up, with the covers round her chin.

Something creaked.

Her blood froze and she held her breath, eyes staring sightlessly into the darkness.

'Lettie. . . . '

There was movement by the door — then the click as it snapped shut. The sound of breathing came towards the bed, hands groped along the side of the mattress.

'Lettie, don't quake so . . . the whole bed is shaking. It's only me — Lawrence.'

Lawrence. . . . By the time the name sank in, he had found her feet and the curve of her legs. He sat down on the edge of the bed and searched the darkness for her hand.

'Lettie, don't be frightened. You know it's me. I won't hurt you.' His voice soothed her and the fright eased. She struggled up from the covers and felt him move closer. His arm went round her shoulders and she snuggled against him, her fear fading into a new excitement.

'Oh, sir . . . I bin tryen' so hard to get me sums and letters right. I bin studyen' each night and I thought you wouldn't. . . . '

'I know what you thought.' Lawrence's disembodied voice had an uneven quality to it. His breath rasped against her ear, his lips touched her temple.

She put her arms round him in the darkness and turned her face up to him. There was a terrible longing suddenly in her, a huge striving for him which made her feel light-headed. She clung to him, allowing his hands to roam over her, his fingers to unbutton her shift and tug at the tapes of her petticoat. He had forgiven her, the dear young master. He actually liked her still.

'Oh sir, thank you . . . thank you.'

Dawn found them locked together in exhausted sleep. Beyond the closed chamber door, Polly came banging into the kitchen with the milk buckets and Lettie started up in fright at the noise, scrambling from the bed in panic as Polly called her.

'I'm coming . . . I'll be with you directly.'

She threw the covers over a still-sleeping Lawrence and pulled her clothing on, frightened that the door might open at any second and that Polly would come in to scold her for not having the fire already burning in the grate.

Pulling her cap down over the mass of her tangled hair she hastened out into the kitchen, slamming the door sharply behind her. Master Lawrence would be able to slip away while they were in the dairy, she thought — if he woke at the slam of the door, as she had intended.

2

Lettie was having difficulty in sleeping. She twisted on her side and felt for lantern and tinder box, then sat up in the soft yellow candlelight with her arms hugging her knees, trying to control the trembling in her body. If honesty permitted reflection, the cause of such long sleepless nights must surely be the simple knowledge that she was with child.

For weeks she had been shying away from the growing suspicion of her condition. Until recently Lawrence had often visited her after the family was abed and, worshipping him, she wanted nothing to change the way things were between them. His flattering attention had swiftly created a doglike devotion which she was now having difficulty in keeping to herself.

During the daylight hours she did her best to continue mastering her letters and numbers. She made gradual progress, although her tired mind was slow to absorb each new lesson, and Lawrence's impatience confused and alarmed her.

'Damn it. Lettie,' he stormed at her over and over again. 'Can't you even remember a simple nursery rhyme?'

She bowed her head in wretchedness over each rebuke. There was no point in telling him that she was so tired that she could scarcely keep awake now to hear what he was saying.

Eventually Lawrence noticed the black hollows under her eyes. 'What's happening to you?' he asked. 'You used to be so full of energy — a real little wanton. Now you droop like a limp weed all day and are even more miserable when I visit you than when I don't. Would you prefer me to take my attentions elsewhere?'

She clung to him then — begging his forgiveness, pleading with him not to leave her. She was sorely tempted to admit that she was carrying his child but something stayed her.

She kept her worries to herself and blocked the thought of eventual confrontation from her mind.

There came a time when she realized wretchedly that Lawrence had not been near her for more than a week and that he had not bothered about a lesson for twice that time. He scarcely acknowledged her presence in the house and turned away if she tried, as she often did, to catch his eye and rekindle his devotion.

Polly observed Lettie with growing concern. Lately she had begun to look quite ill. There was no doubt that she was sickening for something, for her usually pink-cheeked countenance had become pallid and her eyes sunken shadows in hollow sockets.

'Are you ailing, Lettie?' she asked eventually, after the girl had been unable to eat her evening meal.

Feeling the tears pricking the backs of her eyes, Lettie looked down at the mess of food on her plate and shook her head.

'No, mam — thank you kindly. I ben sleepen' badly these last weeks and I'm mighty tired . . . that's all.'

Polly said no more but her eyes missed nothing. She was beginning to reach a fairly accurate conclusion as to the reason for Lettie's sleeplessness.

So too was Violet.

'Lawrence, there's something going on between you and Lettie, isn't there?' she said bluntly to him one day as they drove the open carriage into Chichester.

He stopped staring out across the common at the tall spire of the cathedral rising slender and beautiful behind a misty line of elms, and looked at her blankly, his square-jawed face empty of any guilt or deceit. His grey eyes were large, untroubled.

'Well,' He stretched his legs out and smiled lazily at her, and she watched the small glint come and go at the very back of his eyes. 'I have been engaged in teaching her to read and write these last weeks, if that's what you mean.'

She looked at him steadily, at the smug contentment on his face as he listened with obvious enjoyment to her words.

'Come on, admit it for once. You have been dallying with her, Lawrence, haven't you?' Violet leaned across the carriage and slapped him sharply on the leg. 'That girl has been like a ghost lately. Polly says she looks quite ill at times and all the sparkle has gone out of her.'

'I really haven't noticed, sister dear.'

Lawrence stoutly denied any intimacy with Lettie and began to fume and bluster, red spots highlighting his round cheek-bones.

It did not matter; she would speak to Lettie and get the truth out of her.

Relaxing back against the padded cushions of the carriage, she looked at Lawrence's angry countenance and was well pleased.

'Lettie, you are so sad these days. What troubles you? May I help in any way?'

Lettie looked up from the pile of straw at her feet. The late afternoon sun stole behind a cloud and she shivered as a sharp gust of sea breeze drove across the garden and ruffled the fichou of her gown. For a moment she regarded Violet, and her face reflected a stream of conflicting emotions. The straw in her hands shook slightly. She lowered her head.

'T'is nothen', mistress . . . I'm not quite meself at the moment. I'm not getten' any rest for I'm haven' such bad dreams at night. Must be somethen' I ate, maybe.'

She glanced at Violet through lowered lashes, her instincts warning that she had said enough. The lovely face of her mistress was grave and she was touched by the gentleness and concern she found in those liquid grey eyes.

'Such nightmares are usually caused by disturbance of the spirit.' Violet's voice was soft and low and there was compassion in it which reached out to Lettie's starved and lonely soul. 'A problem shared is a problem halved.'

Violet watched the girl's unhappiness wrestling with her conscience. Two large fat tears slid down Lettie's cheeks and dropped on to the golden straw in her lap.

'How can I tell you, mistress? I never had a home before I come here, see, an' if you know what trouble I'm in, you'll only show me the door for tis no more than I deserve, you can be sure. . . .'

Lettie put her hands up to her face and the tears streamed through her fingers. 'Oh, mistress, I'm sore afraid. . . .'

The words came tumbling out and, doing her best to piece together the facts from what the girl was saying in her discordant way, Violet felt her indignation turn to anger as Lettie's situation unfolded.

It was infuriating that Dada still insisted upon a formal classical education, whatever his eventual occupation might be, Lawrence fumed. It was a confounded waste of time having to spend his mornings under the attentive eye of Master Crabtree. There were so many more interesting things to occupy him at the moment. The letter from Thomas Benson burned in his lorgnette pocket and he itched to take it out and read it for the umpteenth time.

'Attend, if you please, Master Bayless.' Crabtree's thin rasping voice cut through his thoughts, and he dragged himself back to the classroom and the other students crouched at their desks around him, their quills scratching the page in their exercise books.

Mr Benson had agreed to discuss with Dada the possibility of employing him on Lundy. His heart leapt afresh as the implications of that one small fact blotted out the scrawl of writing on the page before him. It was as though their personalities, recognizing something unique in each other, had come together like metal and magnet. Lawrence turned it over in his mind for three months after Mr Benson had returned to the West Country. He had finally penned him a letter, asking for employment in any form in

Thomas Benson's service.

The memory of his conversation in the carriage with Violet made him sit up with a jerk. He must see Lettie this very night. She must not be allowed to disclose their liaison in case Dada, thinking him irresponsible, chose to decline any offer that Mr Benson might make. He would have to control Lettie and — if necessary — Dada also. It looked as though he was strong enough now to succeed without much trouble. Smiling to himself, he bent his head over the exercise book and finished the sentence with a flourish in a fine clear hand.

Lawrence slipped downstairs after the rest of the household had retired. He had not visited Lettie for more than a month. All the same, she had been an exciting lay for a few weeks, for she had learned certain tricks which were almost unbearably titillating. Thinking of them provoked him sharply so that, by the time he had padded through the dark kitchen with his candle and turned the handle of her door, he was in a state of heightened anticipation.

'Hello,' he said, wreathed in smiles.

She was sitting up in her bed with a green shawl round her shoulders, brown head bent over a book that was propped against her knees. She looked up, startled, as he slipped through the door, closing it after him with his foot. Colour flooded into her pallid cheeks, giving her face sudden animation, and she smiled back at him timidly, reminding him even more teasingly of those things which had first attracted him to her.

She laid her book on the table beside her bed and drew him down against her.

He wallowed in sensation. Really, he had been most foolish to withdraw from Lettie. . . . He was surprised anew by the depths of his gratification, for she was so young and, in spite of being very sure of herself in the ways of the heart, had still been a virgin when first he had taken her.

It took some time to remember the main reason for his visit.

'Lettie, Violet spoke to me of you this morning,' he said casually, keeping his voice light and stroking the soft inside of her arm closest to the curve of her breast.

She turned her head quickly and he saw with a jolt that it was too late. Her face was as easy to read as a child's sampler, and alarm and guilt and fear were chasing each other across it in quick succession.

'My God, she's wormed it out of you, hasn't she?'

She nodded dismally, staring up at him with frightened brown eyes and thrusting her small body further into the tangle of bed covers.

'I couldn't help it, really I couldn't, Master Lawrence. She seemed to make me confide in her, it was weird really — but I didn't tell her the other — I swear I didn't.'

It took a second for her words to sink in. He stared down at her, anger making an ugly gargoyle of his cherub's face.

'What other? What do you mean?'

She stared back at him and there were no tears any more. She took a deep breath and a kind of dignity wiped away the timidity and fear. 'I am with child, Master Lawrence.'

Her words were like a body blow. Somehow he had assumed that she would know how to prevent such things happening, since she was so skilled in other ways.

He looked down at the timid, curled up figure among the covers and felt the other pulse quickening through the whole of his body. He said nothing but gazed at her with limpid grey eyes. Lettie stared back at him, her whole body suddenly tense, as a rabbit stares at a stoat.

Something gathered behind his eyes; something hot and vast and immeasurably deadly. For some reason she found she was quite unable to move, unable to struggle out of bed, away from those terrible hot eyes in which the grey orbs were even now growing, gathering like whirlpools to sear right into the depths of her soul.

In the instant before it happened she realized that this was part of the nightmares — this moment was the essence of all her fears. There was a white flash, fringed with scarlet. She smelt the dreadful odour of her dreams, heard the crackling of immeasurable flames, felt the heat of their greedy burning tongues curl round her, devouring her flesh in screaming pain. Something exploded in her chest and she spiralled downwards, away from all sensation, away from the flash of sudden understanding which had come to her as he struck.

Lawrence sat on a dead tree branch and watched four labourers removing brine from the saltpans and taking it into the long lickering shed. From within came the clash of the dippers as the liquid was poured into great cauldrons to be boiled and rendered down to the various degrees which would result in the medicinal salts and crystals for which the Apuldram pans were known.

Dadrus, he thought. Dada knew what was in his heart. He must have recognized what had once been in his own, for at the same age Jess Bayless had been busy all along the Sussex coast, running contraband goods from one end of the county to the other. There had been nothing boring and lack-lustre about Jess Bayless's life in those days. He had used his special Power to protect those night forays from the militia and the riding officers and had killed dispassionately without any hesitation when the need arose.

Lawrence jutted his chin grimly. Dada had used it to further his own ends — and so would he. It was his right, after all, and no one could dictate to him as to its uses — except maybe Violet. He glowered at the thought of her. She was being damnably difficult, blocking him with her fury over Lettie's Flaming.

The household mourned, for she was so young and death had not visited the house since Lavinia Bayless had been taken from them, eleven years before.

Violet knew at once that Lawrence was responsible. She watched him like a hawk over the breakfast table and saw the defiance in him. For days he did his best to avoid her, but she finally cornered him as he was about to climb into the carriage with Polly to go to his tutor in Chichester.

'A moment alone with you, if you please, Lawrence,' she said, and there was something about her which made him obey her command without protest. He jumped down from his seat and walked with her down the drive.

'You Flamed her, didn't you?'

There was no question in her voice. It was a flat statement and he became flustered, for this was not the warm and protective Violet who had defended her young brother through all the years of his childhood. This was not the Violet with whom he had struck up a truce after his mother's death. This was the Violet of their earliest years — a dangerous opponent, with whom it was most unwise to tangle.

He recognized the pure strength of her will and was, for a moment, cowed by it. He nodded sulkily. 'I couldn't help it, bor — she was putting me in a hell of a difficult position.'

'She was but fourteen . . . a servant in this house. How could she refuse you when you forced yourself upon her?'

He kicked viciously at the gravelled drive with a shining boot. 'I had to do it. She was deliberately seeking to compromise me and to feather her own nest. I've plans for my life, pen — and they don't include supporting a host of bastard children fathered on casual tumbles.'

She stood back and took in the tall, almost stooping figure with its golden head and long sulky face. He would be even broader in maturity than was their father — a lion of a man — and twice as dangerous with the deadly Power that Jess Bayless had passed on to the two of them.

He turned away and began to walk back towards the waiting carriage.

'Lawrence.'

Violet's voice made him pause between one step and the next.

'Dada has forbidden you the use of the Power upon people — except as a weapon of defence. If you use it again, I will punish you.' There was a softness in her tone

140

which was almost a caress but he felt the iron in her words.

Giles Croucher put out his hand and took Violet's in his.
He held it in his large palm, looking at the fine blue veins
and the texture of the olive skin, tracing the shape of her
nails with a forefinger. He brought it to his lips and kissed
it with tenderness. It remained passively in his. He had
half expected her to snatch it back in indignation, but she
stood close to him and the tips of her fingers curled into a
light pressure in his palm. He put both arms round her,
found no resistance to his impudence and embarked upon
a long, pulse-leaping exploration of the contours of her
sweet-smelling face.

The progress of their courtship had been very gradual.
Violet Bayless was a young woman of considerable beauty,
much sought after in Sussex society despite the dubious
nature of her parentage. She was, after all, the only
daughter of a wealthy and respected merchant, and her
arresting looks and cultured intelligence overrode the
undesirable aspects of Jess Bayless and his past. Of course,
there were many who wanted nothing to do with the base
child of a brother and sister. Such accidents were not
uncommon, but few people of quality aired the situation
with such indifference as did the Baylesses, accommodat-
ing the offending sister under the same roof. It mattered
little to the gossips that the poor woman was demented
and, as rumour had it, kept behind locked doors.

Seeing Violet growing up three fields away across the
Manhood highway, Giles Croucher had decided early in
his life that no other woman of his acquaintance came
anywhere near her in comparison. When Violet was
eighteen and already the centre of much speculation in the
parish, he watched her during a reception at the assembly
rooms. She was surrounded by admirers, and he realized
with a jolt that if he failed to make a move soon, in no time
at all someone else would claim her.

Violet drew back from Giles and sighed contentedly. He
was such a completely honest person. He didn't prevari-

cate once he had made a decision — and she had known as soon as she saw him that afternoon that he was, at last, about to declare himself to her. He was not above average height, so their noses were almost on a level — but his hazel eyes exuded a sparkling good nature which never failed to lift her spirits.

Nothing in the moment of their coming together disappointed her. His mouth was strong and firm and his attentions were so long hoped for that she returned them with a fervour which delighted him.

'If you had taken much longer to do that,' she said against his coat, 'I think I would have come over to Crouchers and declared myself to you before summer.'

He stroked her cheek. 'Oh no you would not, miss. There is too much pride in you for that. You would have found another suitor a thousand times more worthy of you.'

'Well, maybe I would have contented myself by weaving all kinds of Romany spells about you and drawing you to me in that way.' She was testing him, in spite of the lightness of her tone, and, perceiving the watchful edge to her appraisal of him, he grinned and tightened his arms round her.

'You must have done that when you were a very small raggle-taggle gypsy then, because I was still in the schoolroom when I decided to let no other rascal have you.'

Lawrence was in ferment.

He had held himself in check for nearly eight weeks, assuaging his appetite by Flaming insects and concentrating on reaching out to the distant West Country. Thomas Benson was, even now, buying the lease of an island off the North Devon coast in order to put into practice a daring project he had touched upon during his last visit to Lavenham. It was so impertinent a plan it might well succeed, for the wealthy Member for Barnstable would be above suspicion where piracy on the high seas was concerned.

142

There were only two important things in Lawrence's life now: finding a way to join Mr Benson — and preventing Violet from wedding Giles Croucher.

He had to admit that there was no real reason why he should feel the jealousy which raged through him every time he thought of them together, and it was only gradually, after Giles had been to ask Jess for Violet's hand, that other aspects of a Lavenham without Violet began to come to him.

Once Violet was gone, Jess would turn his full attention on his son. The question of his inheritance would come into focus more clearly and he would be obliged to take on all kinds of unwanted responsibilities with which Violet had been coping up to now. What would happen to Aunt Amy? Who would run the house? Would the new situation of a household without a woman to run it pitchfork Dadrus into another marriage?

He withdrew from Giles's easy friendliness the more he thought about the whole business. He became sulky and short tempered, and saved the pleasanter side of his nature for his Freeland relations, who always tended to make a fuss of him in any case.

Lawrence's surliness was not lost on Giles.

'What's amiss with him?' he asked Violet after Lawrence had bowed sulkily and left the room as they entered it.

Violet shrugged. 'I suppose he must be a little jealous of you,' she said. 'He has had my company and full attention all his life, and it is possible that he has not thought about the fact that sisters fall in love with other men and marry them in time.' She tucked her arm into Giles's and squeezed it tight. 'He'll soon get used to having an older brother. In time he will come to depend on you, rather than me, when he needs advice and company — just you wait and see.'

Violet frowned, looking up from the bedsheet she was repairing. There was an air of unrest in the house which was laying its finger on everyone. Tempers seemed short

143

this day. Even Polly had snapped at the kitchen-maid after one of her frequent disasters with a china meat-dish. Jess had come home briefly from the Chichester office, wolfed down a plate of meat with scarcely a word to anyone and ridden off to the shipping office at Dell Quay. He had been curt and preoccupied and poor company.

Amy was more than usually restless upstairs. She had had a bad epileptic fit the evening before and it had taken both Jess and Violet most of the night to quieten her down. Violet had had to give her a strong potion to make her sleep, but even that had been so rent with bad dreams that she had had little rest.

The house was like that sometimes. It had distinct moods, which were immediately reflected in those who lived within its walls. Weeks would go by when its atmosphere was benign and tranquil — a delightful place with pools of warm sunlight shining on fine panelling and furniture and gleaming in copper pots of wild flowers, a small perfect jewel of a house in the serene setting of oakwood, paddock and sea shore. Then, for no reason that she could ever perceive, a moodiness would descend upon the place, taking the glow so that a grey pall seemed to hang over everything, wiping smiles from faces, deadening even the lively colours in the parlour carpet and curtains, as though a thunder cloud had stolen across the sun.

Amy was always at her worst at these times. She wept and yelled and tore wildly at her clothing so that even Jess had difficulty in calming her.

It was like that now. Violet could feel the brooding anger all about her. She bent her head and concentrated on the torn sheet in her lap, but the vibration in her ears pounded relentlessly, a living heartbeat which sent a familiar excitement racing through her body. She bit her lip, resisting it, and filled her mind with Giles.

He was to dine with them that evening. They would discuss the date for the announcement of their betrothal. It was regrettable that Mama was so disturbed at the moment. Violet had been hoping that she would be in a quieter mood so that she could come down to the parlour and sit by the fire, as she sometimes did. Then Giles would have a chance of talking to her and judging for himself the problem she was giving them — for she would suffer no one but Violet to tend her, other than Jess, and it was unthinkable to move her to Crouchers.

Up in the second bedchamber, Amy sat hunched against her pillows, listening, claw fingers plucking at the covers.

The house was gathering itself together for something.

'What ails you?' she asked, raking the charged air with eyes sunk deep into their sockets. The drumming was in her ears, louder than the other sounds, the turmoil and the fear of things long gone. 'My friend . . . you are my friend. You know that, don't you?' A deep anxiety consumed her and she raised her arms and looked searchingly at them, for it seemed that the house was already holding her down.

'No . . . no . . . leave me. I promise not to hurt you.' But the snakes were wrapping themselves about her body and arms and she screamed at them, tearing at the thick warm coils that began their slow tightening about her — which she knew would end in squeezing the last breath from her body.

'Jess . . . stop them, Jess. *JESSSSS* . . . '

Down in the kitchen Polly cocked her head.

'Oh, dear heaven, she's at it again.'

She turned on the kichen-maid sharply at the girl's careless words. 'That's enough of your lip, Etty. The poor soul cannot help it. Just be grateful that you are not living in her kind of torment. Time was, Miss Amy was a fine woman, working her fingers to the bone in this house and everything shining and tidy . . . better than it is these days, I tell you. Crippled or not, she never allowed a speck of dust to settle. It's a real tragedy to see her now, after knowing her in them days. So just you spare a little human charity for her.'

She turned away from the girl. She was feeling edgy and

regretted the sharp tone in her voice, but Etty was so slapdash, so clumsy. Now and then the sheer irritation of the girl's lack of sense penetrated through even Polly's abiding good humour, and Etty would get her ears boxed.

'Go and tell Rueb and Manfri that I can't wait all day for them to come and eat,' she said to the girl. 'Pottage has been on the hob this past hour. Master and mistress are both fed. Master Lawrence must be away to Chichester.'

The Watcher closed his eyes.

Projection was definitely weaker. It seemed that he was no longer completely competent to invoke the right period, for he felt himself sliding further back towards that which he knew was the ultimate darkness. He gathered his will about him and sought out the boy, for there was a huge force field building up there and it just might be possible for him to divert it.

Lawrence sat in his window-seat, staring out at the drive and new paddock with unseeing eyes. His head ached and he could not control the intermittent trembling of his body as though an ague was in him. On the other side of the house, the sun was going down on another mild spring day, drawing with it the scents of new growth and mourned by a choir of settling birds. A faint pink glow suffused the rolling meadow grass and tipped the woods with spun gold. He saw nothing, for the conflict within him blotted out all other awareness.

Something black and ungovernable in him was slowly materializing. There was a frightening excitement in the pit of his stomach, a sweet loathing which was as attractive as it was repellent.

Keep away from Giles till the mood is past, he thought . . . but I cannot.

The meadow was suddenly shrouded in dusk, distant trees merging softly into a flat blur. Shadows in the room became one, gathering behind his rigid body.

Something moved at the furthest corner of the drive — a

horse and rider trotting briskly towards Lavenham's inner gate. Stay very still. . . . Concentrate on doing nothing, he told himself, digging his fingers into his palms until the nails pierced the skin. Stay where you are. Don't move. Look away . . . look away.

Uplifted for one instant, he gloried in the perfection of annihilation. Nothing could resist him. Nothing could hide from him . . . Giles Croucher was dead.

Dead.

Dead as Lettie was dead.

Then it was gone. Even as it left him and his body was filled with trembling exhaustion, something else came through to him.

Violet.

Violet had registered the Flaming.

In one movement he leapt to his feet and ran. He tore down the stairs, across the hall and out of the yard door, leaving it hanging open behind him. Feet thundering and sliding against the yard cobbles, he burst into the barn.

'Rueb, Rueb − saddle Hator *quickly* . . . '

Rueb's startled face peered round one of the open stall partitions. Seeing Lawrence making for the saddle room without waiting for him, he put down his pitchfork and hurried after him.

Lawrence returned, brushing past him, arms already full of saddle and harness. 'Come *on*, then . . . I've got to go now.'

The near panic in Lawrence's white face alarmed the slow-moving Rueb. He took the saddle from Lawrence and slung it over the dozing Hator's back without daring to ask the reason for such desperate urgency.

'Tighten those girths more . . . Quickly, can't you, damn it.' Lawrence was already up in the saddle, reins in hand. Then, with a jerk of the reins and Hator's hooves slithering on the stones, he was gone before Rueb had even tightened the last girth. Puzzled and alarmed, he stared after the flying figure as it tore out of the yard into the gathering dusk.

Violet stood in the driveway and looked down at her feet. The tips of her pale green slippers rested against Giles's cheek. He lay on the gravel, arms spread as though he were trying to embrace a world too large for him to encompass. His face was calm, its expression serene. The fine dusting of freckles on his nose and cheeks stood out sharply against the new pallor of his skin.

He had not been aware of attack at the moment of death. At least that was something, she thought.

From the moment she was smitten by the sheer force of Lawrence's Power and went charging out of the Long Paddock, knowing . . . knowing . . . to see the fallen figure out in the drive, his black mare standing disconsolately over him, her mind had folded inwards to probe and search for him. But he was already gone.

3

It took nine days for Lawrence, riding his horse Hator, to cover the two hundred and thirty miles from Apuldram to Bideford. By the time they rode into the Devon town, the softness had gone from Lawrence's body. He was lean and fit and filled with a new contentment. Lavenham and his sins were behind him, and for the first time in his life he felt as though an immense weight had been lifted from his shoulders. He rode slowly through the busy, stall-filled streets, down steeply cobbled alleys flanked with leaning timbered houses, to the quay and the first sight of green water since he had turned his back on the Sussex shore.

Finding Thomas Benson was easier than he had expected. He rode into the yard of the first inn he came to, threw his reins to a stable lad and went stiffly in search of a pot of ale. The smoky taproom, rafters ringing with noise, teemed with sailors and merchants, and he pushed his way across the room to where the landlord was filling battered pewter mugs with frothing ale from the banks of wet barrels. He straightened up at Lawrence's question and surveyed the dishevelled figure whose clothing was greyed with the dust of many roads.

'Well, zor, t'is Thursday noon about now. Mr Benson's vessel, the *Catherine Vellacott*, be unloaden' so he won't be far away from the quay. Call in at the Anchor, zor. Anyone in there will direct you to 'is worship.'

Lawrence spied Benson as he thrust through the crowd on the quay and approached the berth of the *Catherine Vellacott*. His broad-shouldered figure stood out from the group of haggling merchants and labourers humping sacks from the ship's hold. Benson stood with one foot raised on a bollard on the edge of the quay, black haired, black jacketed — with an emerald green cravat knotted at his throat — directing the men's progress down the three gangplanks and into a warehouse at his back.

If Benson was surprised at the unexpected sight of young Lawrence Bayless, he showed no sign of it. 'Welcome to Bideford, Master Bayless. What good fortune brings you to these parts?'

Lawrence started forward eagerly. 'Good day to you, sir. I hope you forgive my intrusion, for I see that you are busy. May I beg a word with you in private when you can spare a few minutes?'

Benson regarded him from under bushy black brows. He was slightly shorter than Lawrence, but his breadth gave him a formidable presence, of which he was well aware. He noted the youth's diffidence and the eagerness overlying it.

'Get yourself a platter of meat at the Royal Inn,' he said briefly. 'Order me a tankard of ale and a Genefa and I shall join you within the hour.'

Lawrence retraced his steps to the Royal and, true to his word, Benson joined him before half an hour had passed. He pushed through the crowd and clapped him on the back with a hand that was heavy as a meat dish.

'Pick up your platter,' he said, wheezing cheerfully at Lawrence's side. 'I've a private room here where I do my serious drinking. Come and join me and give me the news from Sussex.'

They sat by a well-banked fire and picked at strips of roasted pork and hunks of fresh bread, washed down with Genefa and a chaser of ale. The conversation dwelt on Sussex and the activities of the Bayless vessels. Benson seemed relaxed and in no hurry to discover the reason for Lawrence's unexpected arrival. Seeing the tension in the boy, he guessed that the tale would not be long in coming.

'Sir,' Lawrence said eventually, 'I have come to Bideford to offer you my services.' He hesitated and then went on with a rush, 'You have known of my wish to join you, sir, ever since your first visit to my father — and you have been good enough not to discourage me in that hope, from the tone of your letters. Would it be possible for me to work with you — right away? I have had a disagreement with the family and was obliged to leave home in a hurry.'

Benson pulled deeply at his pipe. He regarded the boy, liking what he saw. It was a point in his favour that he had recognized the harm of an over-protective family, as the Baylesses obviously were, and had shaken himself free of it.

'How old are you, Lawrence?' he asked.

'Sixteen, sir — but ahead of my fellows at the tutor's and more than passing keen to prove myself to you.'

Benson's eyes twinkled. He pressed his double chin into the green cravat. 'Keen you may well be, young sir, but what do you propose I do with an untried lad of tender years who has never left the family apron-strings before? I'm a busy man, with a constituency as well as a fleet of vessels to administer. If I put you aboard one of my ships you'd have no protection from me against the rude treatment you'd be bound to attract from the crew. We have picked this subject over in letters for nearly twelve months already.' He chewed the end of his pipe. 'I would most assuredly want your father's blessing before committing myself to an agreement to — '

'But, sir, I have left home without my father's consent. He has no idea that I have come to Bideford, and I would be most grateful if he remained in ignorance until I have proved myself.'

Benson looked at the boy's earnest face. There was something in those grey eyes that was mighty compelling.

'Very well, Bayless,' he heard himself say with surprise. 'I'll take you on trial for a year. If yer jib don't fit in that time, it never will. I'll send you over to Lundy first, where you'll meet the other crews and get some of that polish rubbed off — and then we'll take it from there.'

The big bos'n was muscular and lantern-jawed, with

151

greasy black hair held off his face by a stained kerchief tied round the head. One eye was purely an empty socket slashed through with a livid scar. The other eye regarded the new crew member with horrible distaste. He had a drooping moustache which trailed despondently from his upper lip, on either side of a mouth full of blackened tooth stumps.

Instant dislike of each other was openly mutual.

Lawrence followed him down three ladders to the crew quarters, where bos'n Creasey pointed towards a corner locker. 'If ye think ye can lift one, that's where hammocks be stowed, yer honour. Ye'll have to find a safe 'aven fer yer jewels and fine linen, which no doubt ye'll be wanten' if yer workin' alongside us dirty buggers.'

Lawrence, ignoring the sneer in the man's voice, thanked him coolly and looked about him. Three men were bent over a locker playing cards and a fourth lay in his hammock, snoring lustily. There was a strong odour of linseed oil mixed with tobacco and unwashed bodies. No one raised their heads or acknowledged Lawrence standing uncertainly among them. Creasey had vanished without another word, so he went across to a corner between two bulkheads and sat himself on a roll of sailcloth.

There was an air of dinginess and grime about the place, which told its own tale of neglect. The decking was filthy and had clearly not been scrubbed down for many a trip. It was depressingly different from the pristine conditions Jess Bayless insisted upon in his vessels.

'Oho, lads . . . who have we here? What good fortune has brought so fine a peacock into our humble lives?'

Lawrence looked up into a wizened face whose black pebble eyes stared with exaggerated astonishment at the new arrival. 'I'm Lawrence Bayless,' he said, liking the look of this muscled gnome. 'I've just joined the ship.'

The old man shook his grizzled head in wonderment. He was small and hairy, with arms so roped with sinews that they appeared to foreshorten the rest of his body.

'What was you thinkin' of doing here, young gent?

Teachin' us our manners maybe? Or how to eat our dinner off a fork instead of our dirty fingers?' There was a twinkle in the deep-sunk eyes in spite of the banter in his words, and Lawrence — seeing the mildness in that granite face — grinned back at him.

'Play your cards right, bor, and I might even do that. But not until I've learned to do everything that you can do — twice as well.'

His new friend was called Delaney. He was the oldest member of the twenty-man crew and had, he said with pride, been in Master Benson's employ for more than eighteen years. By the time they had toured the ship and returned to the lower deck, Delaney's skill as a raconteur was warming up and reaching new heights of embellishment — 'and when we boarded her, by Dickery, what did we find but a bunch of women an' childer makin' fer the Colony of Virginny. We took the best of 'em, o' course. . . . '

They clattered down the ladder, bare heels slithering on wood made smooth by the passage of countless pounding feet. Creasey was leaning against the bottom of the steps.

'Right, Bayless — I've bin lookin' fer you,' he said. 'Found a few little duties as befits a gent of your station.'

Seeing the gleam in the man's single eye, Lawrence's heart sank. He was going to have trouble with this one.

'I've a nice little list to keep you occupied for a while. Bucket, scrubber and pumice-stone over there in that bulkhead locker. Let's see yer get to it, down on yer hands and knees and scrub out the whole of this deck. *Now*. . . . '

Lawrence looked about him, at the shambles of personal clothing and refuse littering the deck between the hammocks.

'Would it not be better for me to do it when all this is cleared away?' he asked.

Creasey's lip drew back from the black stumps of his teeth. 'See this?' he said softly, pointing to the ugly socket with its jagged red scar. 'I lost that eye in the service of Master Benson and I 'ent goin' ter insult the other by havin' ter look at the likes o' you in our midst, mincin' round the deck as if you'd a right to it. Get that fancy shirt off, double quick . . . go on, off with it — and then down on yer kness and give every inch of these planks the best scrub out they've ever had . . . *see*?'

He put his face close to Lawrence's and exhaled deeply, his one eye daring Lawrence to recoil from the horrendous tooth decay on his breath. Lawrence bowed his head in silence. Stripped to his breeches, he was still scrubbing doggedly when the ship put to sea that evening. The setting sun in its last dying surge of jewelled gold, cast burnished shafts of pink light upon his glistening back.

The same sun gilded the wide sweep of lawn which separated Lavenham from the river. Violet, reading on the terrace, lifted her head and stared up at the deepening extravagance of clashing colours. Something about the sheer vastness of the fiery canopy about her made her shiver, for Lawrence was out there somewhere in the world — and one day they would face each other again.

Lundy presented itself to Lawrence on a perfect June morning, emerging with the dawn from a blanket of low sea mist. Entranced, he paused from hauling up water buckets to watch the land materialize slowly as daylight thinned the pearly haze, the ache in his tired body momentarily forgotten. The island rose like a grey curtain, its hanging valleys choked with undergrowth and stunted trees, the soaring cliffs topped with bracken. Within minutes of their arrival, the air teemed with birds — shrieking gulls, black-winged ravens hanging over the headland, colonies of smaller birds fussing about the crumbling cliffs.

The *Catherine Vellacott* anchored in a small bay at the south-western end of the island. At this point the ancient cliffs crumbled from a hammer-shaped headland, topped by a half-ruined castle, down to two small islets which gave fair protection to the bay. Had the bright morning not been so warm and peaceful, Lundy would have presented an uncompromising face. As it was, the bland sunshine gave it an air of provocative mystery. 'This,' thought Lawrence, scanning the terrain with approval, 'is going to be just right.'

'Have you noticed,' he said to Delaney several evenings later, 'how Mr Benson seems to be provisioning this place as though he was expecting a siege?' They had been working from dawn until the last of the daylight and now sat with their backs against the wall of their sleeping quarters, a cattle byre outside the castle gates.

Delaney drew deeply on his pipe and tapped it against the tankard held between his bony knees. 'I heard tell this mornin' that we've a human cargo to pick up at Rotherhithe this trip.'

'Passengers? But she's not equipped for them.'

The old man grinned, stump-toothed. 'Plenty of room in the main hold for passengers — as long as they be travelling under a deportation order. Mr Benson, he signed a contract with the Transport Office more'n a year back. Did that soon after he was made Member for Barnstable. Never misses an opportunity, our master.'

Before Lawrence could question him further, Benson's servant arrived and bade him attend his master at once.

Benson was sitting at his desk, poring over a thick document as Lawrence was ushered into the room. His solid frame overflowed the chair, the rich black beard and thick curly hair giving him the look of a comfortable demon.

'Well, Bayless, you seem to be settling in without too much trouble. What I called you in for was to talk to you about your father. You have probably heard that the *Catherine* is sailing at first light — and that I shall be aboard, also, this trip.'

Lawrence nodded. News in any form was never confidential for long among the crews, and speculation as to the reason for his presence had produced some wild rumours.

'I have urgent business with Master Bayless,' Benson said, pressing one broad hand flat across the document in front of him. 'We shall pass through the Solent waters. I shall make a brief break to our voyage and anchor off Bracklesham Bay so that I may visit Lavenham and save the two of us a great deal of time. Now, what is in your mind, concerning your presence aboard? Do you wish me to tell your father that you are with me or . . . ?'

'*No.*'

The word cracked between them like a whip-lash and Benson bowed his head before more was said. 'I had a feeling that that was how you felt but had to make sure.'

How strange it was, Lawrence thought, as he left Benson's quarters, to hear the names of his father and Lavenham on other lips. It was some time since he had even thought of them, so that they were like strangers in another world.

They weighed anchor on the morning tide and headed out into the Bristol Channel, the *Catherine* dipping her bows into a choppy green sea. There was a jaunty cheerfulness throughout the ship; it was good to be heading away from the land after weeks plying between the Devon mainland and Lundy. They made good progress south, following the Cornish coast down past Trevose Head and the Carracks, and by the time they skirted Cape Cornwall, Lawrence was completely in his element. The weather was perfect and they creamed through deep, purple-troughed seas with the thunder of sail over their heads and the salt spray flailing their faces into hard brown leather.

It was after they left Plymouth that Lawrence began to feel uneasy. By the time they anchored off the South Bar and Benson had gone ashore, he was in a ferment of fear. Something was calling him, something deep inside keened for its very roots. He was unable to sit still and paced the deck, half of him tempted to go over the side and swim for the shore. Maybe it was Violet trying to draw him back to Lavenham, where he knew without a shadow of doubt that

156

she would destroy him. He ground his teeth and concentrated on making good the rope locker.

Benson returned soon after sunset and sent for Lawrence.

'You were mighty swift to answer my summons,' he said to the boy, noting the almost hawkish anxiety in the young face. 'I have been to Apuldram, as I intended — but came away with my business uncompleted,' he said. His face was serious and Lawrence's heart leapt as the rumbling voice continued. 'I regret to be the bearer of ill tidings, Lawrence, but I'm afraid that your father has suffered a serious stroke. I feel that you should go to him without delay.'

Lawrence stared at him, grey eyes huge in a suddenly bloodless face. His head shook slowly from side to side. 'I cannot, sir.'

The words were little more than a croak but the eyes were like tortured steel.

Benson shrugged, compressing his lips into a thin line of disapproval. 'Very well. I cannot make you — but consider the grief of your sister, who is still in mourning, so I was told, after the death of her betrothed. Do you not think that she deserves your support?' The golden head shook briefly once more. 'I cannot explain, sir, but I may never return to that house, even for Father.'

The *Catherine* weighed anchor at dawn and continued her passage along the south coast, round the eastern bulge of Kent and into the mouth of the Thames. Lawrence appeared, to his companions, to have temporarily lost the bright good humour which usually stood him in good stead. He had little to say to anyone, even to Delaney, until they had been anchored — in mid-stream — at their Rotherhithe berth for several days.

London in summer stank like a vast midden. Its riverside streets and alleyways teemed with paid-off men returned from the wars with France, Spain and even a young pretender to the English throne. The sloop was

157

made ready for her human cargo by the beginning of August, and the first contingent of prisoners was boarded without delay. Lawrence, up in the rigging, watched the ragged trickle of filthy humanity struggling over the ship's side, to be herded below by their guards. He caught a whiff of that special rank odour which pervaded every prison establishment and to which he would soon have to accustom himself. When they sailed, it was with ninety-two convicts and guards aboard and not an inch of desk space to spare. The long voyage to Jamestown, Virginia, was not going to be a comfortable one.

Summer storms dogged their passage and kept them well out to sea. They had been battling against mountainous seas for five days before the weather cleared and gave them an horizon.

'That's mighty strange,' Delaney said as they descended from the rigging to the bucking deck. He scratched his grizzled head under the grey sock he always wore on it, and peered at the outline of a distant headland rising on their starboard bow. He screwed up his eyes and cupped his hands round them against the daylight.

'Can't think why, but I'll wager my life against a farthing that that's Trevose Head. . . . '

He was right. The Cornish coast slid by and it soon became clear that Benson was taking the ship, not towards the distant shores of the American colony but back to Lundy. Now what was the devious master up to?

Lawrence was on lookout duty as Lundy rose out of the evening to welcome them. By the time the deckhands had lit the ship's riding lanterns they were sweating over the anchor chain and the *Catherine Vellacott* was once more straining at her cables in the little cove below Marisco Castle. The longboats scuttled like water-beetles between the ship and the shore and by midnight all the convicts had been disembarked and taken up to the castle.

It took the crew three days of hard labour to scrub out the holds and remove the special bulkheads that had been fitted in Rotherhithe to accommodate the prisoners. They were all tired, all ill humoured, when Bosun Creasey began sending them ashore in small groups, to stretch their legs.

When Lawrence's turn came he found himself with Delaney and Tupper, the boot boy, who had taken to dogging his footsteps — eager to serve him. The day was fair, with a keen breeze which held the scent of gorse and the distant heath. Lawrence sniffed the air, reminded of Apuldram Common and fishing with his father in the Lavant.

'How about hunting some fowl or a bit of rabbit for our supper?' he suggested as they stood on the beach and watched the bumboat bobbing back to the ship.

Delaney looked up at the gulls shrieking and wheeling above them. 'Might as well,' he agreed, for there was little else to occupy them then.

They turned their backs on the water and plodded up the steep cliff path with Tupper trailing, puffing, behind them. Lundy was a wild and unkempt place, the sanctuary of generations of wild birds, apart from the colonized southern tip. They reached the heathy summit and struck out through tall grasses, laurel and fiery yellow broom, towards the distant northern tip. The sun shone on their heads, the heat cooled by the ever present wind.

Delaney stood still and took a small catapult from his belt. He grinned, pointing over to the left, where a copse of leaning trees broke the flat landscape fifty yards away. A pair of large, black, long-billed cormorants perched close together on a dead stump, preening each other in the sun. Delaney fumbled in a pouch hanging from his belt, brought out a small white pebble and sighted on the birds through slitted eyes. His brown face was a mass of fine lines, beaten into the skin by a lifetime of brine and wind.

The pebble left its sling with a sharp *thwack* and flashed away from them. The birds rose vertically, their great black wings beating in alarm as the pebble found its mark on the tree trunk beside them with an audible *clunk*.

The little Irishman cursed profoundly and Lawrence

grinned at him. 'Old age taking your sight, now, is it?' Tupper sniggered beside them and Delaney silenced him with an angry snarl. They pushed on through the high ferns and bramble towards a small coombe which hung high above the sea. Standing at its edge, they watched a family of seals sunning themselves on the granite rocks far below. Bees droned lazily in the yellow gorse nearby. There was a light, sweet fragrance of wild mint in the air. It seemed as good a place as any to take a rest, and they lay down and idly watched the antics of the hosts of gulls over their heads. The sun began to slide below the cliff top at their backs, leaving a new chill in its wake.

'Nothin' to take back fer the pot, after all, then,' Tupper complained as they started back towards the cove path. He looked at Lawrence for a while and then nudged him. 'Get us somethin'. You know . . . like you can do.'

Delaney said nothing. Lawrence had shown them some very strange tricks since he had joined the ship, telling them of his gypsy blood to explain it — though none of them could see how there was gypsy in such a fair-skinned and yellow-haired fellow. Those odd tricks had not failed to impress the men — even if they had not endeared Lawrence to most of them. Still, there was no doubt that they respected him, all the same. He watched Lawrence's youthful face out of the corner of his eye as they walked, seeing the conflict that scudded across it.

'All right,' Lawrence said at last, 'why not? We'll take a brace back, but I'll want your word that you don't mention how we came by them. Understand?'

They squatted down in the bracken and the inquisitive gulls swooped lower over their heads. Lawrence focused calm grey eyes on one of them. Delaney and Tupper watched intently. They felt the aura in him building, gathering strength, emanating outwards so that their own bodies began to tingle. The sensation excited then frightened them, and they drew back and sat, shoulders pressed against each other, seeking comfort in the physical contact.

There was a moment of singing silence. Then, from amongst the soaring gulls above them, a bird dropped earthwards, its grey wing feathers splayed grotesquely in the churning air. It hit the ground with a dull thud a few yards away and lay still, the breeze ruffling the soft underfeathers of the broken wings.

The old seaman looked at Lawrence's serene face as he stood up and went across to the fallen bird. It held nothing in it but a quiet pride in something well accomplished — but there had been an instant, just as the bird hit the ground, when something else had peered out of that fresh boy's countenance; something old and infinitely dangerous.

The sun was long gone and the island washed in dusk by the time they reached Marisco Castle, looking for the alehouse. They carried a brace of rabbit, three herring gull and an orange-billed oyster-catcher.

Hard work and the ship's routine made a fool of time and Lawrence's dogged industry did not go unnoticed. When the *Catherine* put into Bideford to take on a cargo of leather for the last trip of the year across the Atlantic, he was put in charge of the longboat. By the time they dropped anchor in Plymouth Bay, New England, he was industriously studying charts, rutters and books on navigation, and the ship's master, Truby, was pleased to encourage him.

They landed their cargo and turned for home before the winter closed in, returning via the Grand Banks fishing grounds off Newfoundland. They sailed up the Torridge towards Bideford with holds groaning with the best catch of prime cod that they had ever netted. All the same, morale was none to high for it had been an eventful voyage.

They had ridden out a patch of vile weather for three long weeks, hove to under bare poles in mountainous seas. The first mate was washed overboard — and the promotion ladder moved up a rung. To everyone's surprise,

Lawrence Bayless was elevated to second mate; it infuriated Creasey that this inexperienced stripling should have been promoted over his head. The rest of the crew accepted the move, knowing the hardness inside that young body and fearing the power they sensed in Lawrence. They were content to wait and watch and see who eventually won the contest between the two men.

'See that the watch get that jib in before it flogs itself to ribbons,' Lawrence said one day to Creasey. There was a biting wind blowing and the ship was still labouring under perilously heavy canvas as she strove to make up the time lost while hove-to.

'Jib's needed,' Creasey said shortly. 'Just wants trimmin' a bit.' He was already turning away, his craggy face contemptuous.

'Creasey.'

There was something in the quiet voice that made him hesitate and they stood close together with the canvas roaring above their heads.

'Haul in the jib, Creasey.' Lawrence looked at the man's pugnacity with something akin to gentleness, feeling the depth of his own hatred for this foe with bland pleasure. He fixed Creasey's answering glare with the heat of unfurling power and smiled as he watched the lines fade from the granite face into unfocused emptiness.

'Get that jib in right away, Creasey,' Lawrence said softly, 'and then you know what to do next . . .'

He turned away and went below. The deed was as good as done. He was reporting to Truby when the cry went up. 'Man overboard.'

They hurried out of the master's cabin in time to see the three figures over their heads scrambling down from the rigging like frightened monkeys.

'Don't know what happened at all, sir,' they said later, when all efforts to sight the missing man had been made. 'Bosun shinned out on to the beam with the three of us. He went to grab the trim-line and the next we knew . . . he'd gone, without so much as a cry, sir. He's worked those

162

beams longer'n any of us, so I can't for the life of me see how he could have missed his hold like that.'

The *Catherine Vellacott* creamed on towards her home port with a gravely subdued crew. Two deaths in as many weeks seemed a mighty bad omen. What, was in their minds, would happen next?

The tempo of life on Lundy quickened when, in the summer of 1753, a chance survivor of one of Benson's sea attacks identified him positively. It was not until the following spring that the government's slowly turning wheel of justice finally pronounced Thomas Benson MP guilty of piracy on the high seas. He was stripped of his parliamentary powers, fined £5,000 and banished from Bideford and Barnstable chambers of commerce. Benson's reply to such trumpetings of officialdom was to sail across to Lundy with all his vessels and set up a stout defence of the island which would have done justice to the Tower of London.

Besides the transport contract, Benson had warehouses in Virginia, Maryland and Newfoundland for the storage and disposal of the cargoes he pillaged from other merchantmen. It was, therefore, certainly not simple financial greed but, rather, a strange quirk in his nature, which demanded the constant excitement of those piratical forays. Maybe he would not have contemplated those attacks so readily had Lawrence not been at his side, but to Benson's sharp eyes, young Bayless's uncanny control of his men was so absolute and Truby's seamanship so good that the combination was too excellent a partnership to waste. Illegal privateering was proving infinitely more profitable when no portion or Bounty Tax went to the Crown.

After the isolation dictated by a long winter, Benson was once again entertaining guests, an occupation close to his heart for curiosity was great among his mainland friends.

Lawrence sat across the table from his host, giving scant attention to the banter between Benson and two of his three visitors. They were business acquaintances and had been to Lundy more than once, but the third man, Edmund Lamprey, was a stranger to Lawrence. He was not at all the usual type of visitor whose curiosity concerning Lundy and its community was often rooted in a wish to participate in Benson's rich hauls. He was elderly and bowed and there was much of the scholar about the way he would lean forward with eyes tightly shut, one hand cupped to his ear, the better to hear what passed between the other guests. But for the most part, he sat quietly at the table like a benevolent gnome, eating with neat little movements and chewing his food very slowly. Before the first course was over, Lawrence became aware that he was being closely observed by Lamprey — and that something was worrying him. He could feel the old man searching his memory. Lawrence reminded him of someone — and he would eventually realize that the high-nosed, clean-cut features and Saxon colouring were those of his old friend and Lawrence's grandfather, Thomas Freeland. Lawrence cursed his bad luck — for word would now get back to Lavenham and his whereabouts would be discovered at last.

Benson rose to stretch his legs and went to the window to stare out across the twilit water.

'Come, my friends, and look out here. Tell me what you see.' His guests crowded round him, peering out of the long uncurtained casement. Hartland Point was a purple smudge in the evening haze and the lights of small mainland villages twinkled across the channel like a bracelet of yellow jewels. Seven vessels rode at anchor out in the darkening sea roads beyond the little cove. In the morning they would leave and slide into port up the Torridge and the Taw.

Benson looked at them with satisfaction. Much of the conversation at dinner had been centred on his supremacy on Lundy.

'I should like to illustrate the completeness of my rule here, gentlemen — to show you just how well I have already trained the mariners who use these seaways. If you would join me at Marisco at sunrise, you may be amused to observe the daily ceremony and enjoy the little niceties accorded to Benson's sovereignty over the Kingdom of Lundy.'

The party broke up a long time later. Lawrence made his way back to his quarters in the old castle, his mind mistily dwelling on Edmund Lamprey and the uneasy feeling that Lavenham was reaching out to him once more. His unease was compounded when, at sunrise, he found Lamprey at his elbow as they stood in a cold, silent group on Marisco's outer bastion, longing for the warm beds they had just left.

'It came to me in the night,' Lamprey said, his chin shivering in the gusts of briny air, 'that you must be a Bayless of Lavenham. Am I right, sir?'

Lawrence nodded. 'I am the son of Jess Bayless, certainly,' he said and, excusing himself on the pretext of urgent duties, moved away towards the flag mast with alacrity. No questions . . . no mistakes.

The three guests, with Benson in their midst, leaned on the parapet and watched as the little fleet of merchantmen completed the laborious business of weighing anchor in the early light. The distant rasp of their chains being raised echoed across the choppy water. Over the visitors' heads, a pennant was being raised under Lawrence's orders and, secured at the pole pin, unfurled with a crisp *thwack* in the gusty morning breeze.

Benson regarded the vessels intently through his spyglass as first one and then another began to move away from their mooring. A courtesy pennant was hauled up into the rigging of the leader and was gradually followed by the others. Benson beamed with satisfaction and pointed to the little strips of red and yellow cloth winking their message across the widening slate sea.

'There you are,' he said to his guests. 'They are conforming to the required custom, acknowledging my supremacy on these shores and thanking me for my hospitality. I'd bloody soon teach them their manners if they didn't.'

One by one the vessels raised their colours and turned away — with the exception of a single brigantine flying the Harwich flag. Benson watched the vessel frowningly as she swung away into wind, dipping her bows into the swell. When, within moments, it became clear that here was one who would not doff its cap to him, he pushed away from the parapet and strode along the bastion to a cannon emplacement manned by three suddenly alert men.

'Fire a broadside at that impertinent bugger,' he snapped at the gunner, who, after one nervous look at his master, leapt to do his bidding. 'Quick as ye can, damn it . . . or she'll have slipped out of range before she can be chastised.'

There was immediate agitation among Benson's guests. He could not, surely, fire on his own countrymen?

'Hurry, gunner,' Benson roared over his shoulder at the gun crew, completely ignoring his visitors.

'It was but a small discourtesy, after all,' Lamprey was saying to him in disbelief. 'The master has probably not been in these waters before and knows no better.'

'Then he will soon learn,' Benson snapped. 'Ignorance is a dangerous cliff to climb, sir. Knowledge often comes with a sting in its tale. The sting I shall deliver will be a salutary lesson to all of them, would you not agree?' The thought pleased him and restored his good humour, and he returned to the cannon — where the barrel was being set and primed with commendable precision.

Within minutes the order to fire was given, the gunner jerked his lanyard and the air was suddenly filled with the detonation and acrid smell of sulphur. The visitors watched with smarting eyes as, through the billowing smoke, they saw a gout of spray rise up beside the brig's port bow. Even before the ball hit the water, the cannoneers were busy repriming and ramming another ball down the hot barrel. They fired a second salvo, and this time the ball holed one of the fleeing vessel's topsails. There was a cheer from below them and, looking down, they saw a ragged group of convicts thumping each other on the back and roaring their delight at this unexpected entertainment.

'Sir, I beg you to desist from this folly, before you sink her,' Lumprey said angrily.

Benson gave him a smile of guileless charm. 'No need, I assure you, sir,' he said airily, 'the lesson is already learned. See, they are hoisting colours now. You will be certain, my friends, that you see before you a vessel whose master will remember in the future that Lundy is in foreign waters.'

Lamprey turned away from the group in disgust. 'Where is your conscience, sir?' he said as a parting shot.

Benson watched the old man go and then turned to the others. 'I've long since withdrawn from my conscience,' he said with a wide grin, 'for to harbour such an indulgence with my chosen mode of life would create a battleground of emotions I feel unfit to be party to. Live for each separate moment in our short span, I say, good friends — and let the other moments take care of themselves.'

A matter of hours only had passed before Benson found himself staring at a scrap of paper brought in by carrier pigeon from the mainland. He glowered down at it and then screwed it up and flung it with all his strength into the fireplace.

'Raikes . . . ' he roared at his servant, 'Get Master Bayless here at the double. Quick now, not a moment to spare . . . . '

Lawrence was up in the charthouse of the *Catherine* with Truby, poring over their manifests, when Raikes panted into the cabin. They were sailing in thirty-six hours for Oporto in Portugal and he was irritated by the peremptory command for his immediate presence.

Benson was a good master, but sometimes the pressures he laid upon his officers and men made them wish that he was still involved with his parliamentary duties. That bounding mind of his was no longer fully extended, virtually exiled as he was on Lundy, so that the plans he hatched were of a reckless nature and, they feared, eventually would bring all of them into danger. Like the foolhardy plot he had dreamed up for the old *Nightingale*, which was already, this very day, being set in motion. Benson had insured the old brigantine and her cargo for an enormous sum, and was at this moment transferring that cargo to the huge cavern he had fashioned in the cliff-face. The ship would put to sea and then be scuttled by her crew, in sight of other vessels which would pick them up safely. Benson would then claim the insurance on both vessel and cargo. He had been studying all the implications for weeks and felt that he now had a fool-proof plan. *Nightingale's* master, John Lancey, would do as he was told, whatever his feelings in the matter, for he was financially in Benson's debt — and there was no more to be said. It was up to him to square it with the rest of the crew, buying their silence where necessary.

Lawrence felt the flaws in the plan. They smote him like a flay — but Benson had been adamant and now the project was under way. He jumped down into the bumboat impatiently, wondering whether Benson had had second thoughts, after all.

Benson was pacing his office floor with mounting impatience. 'My God, you took your time getting here,' he rumbled as Lawrence appeared. 'Look, Lawrence, I've had to make a few last-minute changes, damn it. I've just sent over a message to Master Truby advancing the *Catherine's* departure time by a day and I shall, after all, be travelling to Portugal with you.' He saw the surprise in the boy's usually impassive face and pressed on. 'The reason I had to see you is because several things have happened simultaneously which require me to do quite a feat of juggling with the vessels and their movements. News has just reached me that the authorities have confiscated my estate at Knapp and are on their way over to Lundy to arrest me and to seize my goods here, the buggers.'

Lawrence suddenly saw that the man was completely unpanicked and was, in fact, thoroughly enjoying the situation. 'Are you thinking to defend Lundy then?' he asked.

Benson went over to the fire and stood there, warming the backs of his legs. 'I haven't spent all this time and money on Lundy's defence just to lay down my arms at the first pop-gun,' he said, grinning sourly. 'I just regret the fact that it would not be expedient for me to be here when the attack takes place. Jerry Magra and his little regiment can certainly hold them off for quite some time and I will see to it that they do — but I must leave the defence to him and slip away before the fun begins, or they'll have me swinging several times over for all the charges they look to be gathering against me.' He became serious then. 'I need you with me in Oporto, Lawrence. I have the villa there and can give you a roof until you find one of your own, but we still have oceans to range, you and I.'

They looked at each other with complete understanding and Lawrence bowed his head.

'Right then, that's settled. Now we just have to get Lancey and the *Nightingale* out to sea, and her first mate replaced as he is making trouble and must be silenced. Will you replace him? When the survivors are picked up and landed, you can make your way down to Dawlish, where the *Catherine* will pick you up . . . .'

Darkness came early for the wind had veered, bringing a lumpy sea and driving rain squalls.

It was close to midnight by the time Lawrence and Lancey had completed the exchange. He felt heavy at heart as he was rowed away from her towards the dark slab of the *Nightingale*. She had been his home for over five years, during which time he had grown from a green boy into a man valued by Benson and respected and feared by those under him. Old Delaney was dead, snuffed out by a lung infection the previous year, but Tupper was now his servant, closer to him than any of the others. He sat in the boat with him now, arms round the two metal trunks containing all the possessions Lawrence had accumulated.

Two hours after midnight Benson boarded the *Catherine*, and the vessel drew up her anchors and stole away out to sea. At first light, *Nightingale* followed, wallowing heavily with all the ballast in her. It was gratifying, Lawrence noted, to see Lancey's relief at having Lawrence at his side, and the master's unease reduced as the last of the night drained away and dawn was suddenly a glimmer to the east.

Their new lieutenant's calm efficiency soothed the jumpiness of the crew. 'Brace the after-yards to port . . . . You there, bosun, get your men to clear away all that raffle forrard. This deck looks like North Street at Goosey Fair . . . .'

He kept close to the gangs, working them hard as the time slipped by. Dawn slashed the gloom with fiery light, the lanterns were doused one by one and order was firmly established on deck.

'Square away, Master Bayless,' Lancey called, and set a man to the helm. *Nightingale* slipped from the lee of the Rattles, out into deeply corrugated seas. When it came to the point, Lawrence was too busy to bid farewell to the *Catherine*, but as they butted into heavy seas he did have time to wonder whether he would actually make the rendezvous at Dawlish with her. The weather was less calm than they would have liked, but most of the crew comforted themselves with the promise of the bounty they would receive in return for their cooperation and rigid silence once they were picked up.

'Sail fine on the port bow.'

The look-out's cry was faint, snatched away in the thunder of squally gusts in the shrouds.

Up on the half-deck Lawrence met John Lancey's eye squarely. They had been examining the approaching vessel through their spy glasses and recognized her as the *Charming Nancy*, a Philadelphia-registered vessel whose master, Zeb Nicholson, was known to Lancey. Even as they watched her approach, the wind dropped suddenly as though a door had slammed shut.

The two vessels seemed to drift slowly towards each other. The time to abandon ship would never be better than it was now. A familiar warmth sprang into Lawrence's chest and the Power began to seep into his veins. He looked at Lancey, who nodded and turned from him as Lawrence made for the main deck.

'All hands on deck,' he roared, and heard the order echo down into the belly of the ship. They had been waiting for this moment since the anchors had rattled into their beds, but it still came with shock to some and excitement to others. The carpenters and two seamen were already down below, loosening planking in the bilges. Bedding and sacks of gun cotton had been heaped in strategic places on the lower decks and then saturated with melted grease. The cargo on the manifest was bale after bale of beautiful French lace and embossed damask. A lantern smashed in the steep seas would be blamed for the fire which was about to engulf the *Nightingale*.

'Light the bundles,' Lawrence ordered in an undertone. The *Nancy* was only half a mile away now and nothing must go wrong. Smoke began to eddy through the ports, and the men came streaming up on deck, sooty and expectant. The longboats were launched, the crew went over the side and down the trailing ropes like jack rabbits and finally Lancey and Lawrence followed — with Tupper pressing close behind, clutching a single valise of Lawrence's as though it were more precious than life itself.

They cast off as the sudden stench of burning waste turned to the billowing black of tarred and burning wood. Gripping the slippery side of the longboat, they sat and watched as the boat pulled away towards the approaching *Nancy*. *Nightingale* was suddenly etched in orange flame. All eyes were glued to her as she settled and began to tilt in the heaving sea. The oarsmen pulled them clear, cresting on great black rollers and sliding sickeningly down into troughs from which they feared they might never emerge. Saturated and baling furiously, the three longboats struggled towards the oncoming vessel.

4

The death of Giles Croucher caused deep sadness in Apuldram, for the community, though small, was closely integrated and Giles had been well respected. Violet mourned the loss of Giles privately — in her own fashion. In public there were no tears, but overnight the exuberance of youth seemed suddenly to drain out of her and she went about her daily duties with head down and little to say to anyone.

Jess watched his daughter with growing concern as the classic beauty, of which he was so proud, lost its animation and she moved with a new listlessness which was badly out of character. He was alarmed to notice the likeness to her mother at the same age. Amy was now locked away in a small room in the new wing and her occasional ravings were the only reminder to startled visitors that Jess Bayless even had a sister still living at Lavenham. The lease of Croucher's farm was taken up by William Challen, who was erecting a cider tavern on the highway nearby. As a gesture to Giles's passing and the fact that he had also purchased Giles's fine mare, he named the little inn The Black Horse.

Where it might have seemed natural for Violet to seek and find comfort for her grief from the Lavenham stud, whose horses had always been such a large part of her life, she went instead to her bees.

The five skeps had been kept in the orchard ever since old Beezer had brought them over from Rymans for Lavinia, seventeen years before. It was Lavinia who had taught Violet to care for the little creatures, and they seemed to understand her mood, caressing her softly,

172

coming to her in twos and threes, brushing her with their furry bodies and then veering away again. It was as though they were showing her collectively that they would not intrude upon her thoughts but she was, nevertheless, to know that they loved her. She was soothed by them, and a little of the bitterness went out of her. The hour spent daily in the orchard was not wasted in self-pity, in spite of her preoccupation with Giles and the nature of his passing. She sat on a wooden seat in leafy shade beneath the fruit trees in quiet meditation, oblivious to the bees' gentle circling for she was patiently casting the air waves for the slightest awareness of Lawrence.

Strangely, the only time she felt his presence was a few days after their father's stroke. Jess had been slowing up perceptively since Giles's death and Lawrence's disappearance. One day he came home unusually early from Chichester. Polly and Violet were still clearing away the debris of the midday meal with Manfri, Rueb and Polly's three children.

'What ails you, Dada?' Violet started across the kitchen as he appeared in the doorway and leaned heavily against the lintel, hunching his shoulders. His long gaunt face was grey beneath its olive tan.

'I have a terrible dyspepsia, I think.' His voice was hoarse and she saw that he certainly must be in considerable pain. She and Polly helped him through the hall and into his comfortable fireside chair in the parlour, where he sat, hugging himself, with his eyes tightly closed. The skin covering the bones of his face seemed tight and brittle, the colour of parchment. Polly, hearing sounds of strife in the kitchen, rushed away to silence them.

He said in a rasping whisper, 'Be a kushti rakli and fetch me one of your peppermint teas. That should shift it.'

Violet fled to do as he asked, for he only lapsed into Romany these days when he was under stress. Hurrying back with a steaming mug, she knelt beside him. It was a strong brew, not too hot, but he drank it all and it seemed for a short time to ease the pain. Then it was on him again and he curled up in the chair, the breath dragged from him in agony.

Without wasting more time she flew out into the yard, where Rueb was waxing saddles.

'Quickly, bor, get a horse and ride for Doctor Sanden. Dada has suddenly been taken ill.'

'Your father has suffered a severe stroke, my dear.' Sanden straightened up from the bed where he had made them carry Jess. 'We are just going to have to wait and see what the effects are and whether his poor heart and brain can weather the punishment they are taking now. He has always had a strong constitution, so it is quite likely that he will survive. We will know, during the next few hours. You must also be prepared for him to emerge from all this partially — or even wholly — paralysed.' He patted Violet's arm comfortingly, moved by the stricken look on her face. Really, the poor girl had had more than her fair share of tragedy, he thought. An imbecile mother, a runaway brother, the sudden loss of her betrothed — and now this.

The house seemed unnaturally still. It waited, holding its breath, the very pulse at the centre of life suspended into heavy silence. The three lurchers lay close together beneath the dining table in the hall and did not stir as Violet and Doctor Sanden passed them on their way to the parlour. She allowed the little doctor to settle her in Jess's chair and pour her a glass of his finest brandy. The fieriness of the rich tawny liquid gradually brought back her colour and reduced the tremble in her limbs which had started as soon as she released her hold on her father's hand. She had held him tightly, tightly to her until the ugly snoring breath eased and Polly lifted her away from the bed.

They were quietly discussing the situation when Polly called down the stairs to them and they hurried back to the bedchamber. Jess was swimming slowly back to consciousness and they watched closely as he opened one eye and gradually focused on them.

'What is the matter with his face?' Violet whispered,

aghast. The left side of Jess's face seemed to slide as he opened his mouth to speak. The eyelid remained closed and the left corner of his mouth dragged down towards his chin, giving him a strangely sardonic look.

'It is the effect of the stroke upon his nervous and muscular system,' Sanden said, cupping his fist and putting an ear to Jess's chest. She bent down and kissed her father's forehead and smiled at him with such sparkling love that he sighed, comforted by it, and rested his head against her cheek.

'You must not worry about anything at all, kushta da. We will take care of everything together, you and I.'

It was after that day that Violet became aware of Lawrence. She was in the orchard cleaning out one of the bee skeps after a particularly difficult morning. Amy had been restless and abusive for several days past, especially when she was being washed and dressed and her room scrubbed out, as it had to be all too often. Violet had ceased to think of Amy as her mother these days, but rather as a daily duty for which she had a deep repugnance. The last vestiges of affection had long gone, for Amy no longer represented that proud Romany woman whose blood she shared. She had become, instead, a drooling, incontinent creature whose grey apathy was punctuated by long fits and violent tantrums which were sometimes severe enough to require Rueb's assistance to control. How was it possible, the guilt in her asked again and again, for Violet to recognize the hawkish animal who ate her own faeces and screamed vile and incoherent curses upon her as her own dear crippled mother, whose tragic life had brought her down to this state?

Caring for Jess had, instead, become the central pivot of her life, for he was completely immobilized down his left side and she and Polly were obliged to move him from bed to chair, and chair back to bed each day. His speech was slurred and he struggled with terrible anguish against a situation which they all knew would not now ever improve further.

The orchard was the most peaceful of places. It was a

175

long grassy stretch, with fruit trees bordering the Chichester Channel on one side and the back of the main stable block on the other. It was tucked out of sight of the house, behind the stables, so that the water traffic was the only sign of humanity to be seen beneath the green roof of its foliage; a soft and leafy place, filled with the sweet smell of bruised grasses and a lingering silence, apart from the soft sigh of air in the trees and the comfortable drone of bees. In the orchard it was possible to expand the spirit, away from the brooding strictures of the house. Considering this, it dawned upon Violet that she was beginning to hate Lavenham. For all the bland charm of its exterior, the house's heart was in perpetual ferment, a deeply disturbing state of which she had been aware since babyhood.

Lawrence . . . .

Violet sat back on her heels with a jerk as the feeling smote her like a blow to the head. She examined the sensation warily. Yes, it was a tiny grain of absolute certainty — a registration of fact. Her sharpened instincts were screaming a warning that Lawrence was somewhere out on the edge of her field of consciousness. She stood up, brushing the dust and dead bees of the skep floor from her apron, overwhelmed by a distress she had not felt for weeks.

Lawrence on his way back to Lavenham? Every fibre of her being rejected the very thought. She had loved Lawrence in a strange, abrasive fashion, despite the fact that he had long been a daily reminder of her own unacceptable beginnings. She had done her best to curb his fascination for Flaming things, but he had always enjoyed the very power of such a gift, disobeying their father's stern injunction that the Power was only to be used for their own protection. It was probably this wilful streak, she realized, which had led him, through jealousy, to the Flaming of Giles. Now Lawrence was somewhere out there, almost within her reach. Casting about, she was only aware of a moving miasma between them.

'Miss Violet . . . are you there?'

Polly's voice made her turn from her dreaming perusal of her hands and she waved at the distant figure coming across the lawns towards the orchard.

'It's a visitor . . . a Mr Benson. To see your papa, of course, but I've told him of his indisposition and he would like to see you, if you can spare him five minutes.'

They hurried back to the house, and Violet went through to the parlour, rolling down the sleeves of her black gown and casting off her working apron as she went. An impressive figure rose to greet her.

'Your servant, Miss Bayless. I was most concerned to hear of your father's illness.'

She bowed her head, bade him return to his chair and allowed him to question her about Jess. He had been a friend to the Baylesses for some years now and she had always liked the strength of his colourful personality, the underlying warmth and sensuality she sensed there.

'He is making a little progress now but is still not well enough to receive visitors, I'm afraid. I am doing my best to carry out his orders concerning the business and we are most fortunate in having such a well-selected and competent staff at Bayless's, in both the Chichester and Dell Quay offices. They miss him sorely, of course, and it must not be easy for them, receiving their instructions from him through me — a mere woman.'

She smiled at him, a little impish sparkle lighting her flawless face. 'I have a suspicion that Mr Trew in the Chichester office thinks little of having a woman young enough to be his daughter telling him what is required of him. He complies with much less grace than does Mr Woolgar at Dell Quay.'

The smile suddenly vanished, snuffed out like a candle flame. 'When my brother Lawrence ran away from home, did he go to you?'

The question took Benson by surprise although he had been expecting some reference to Lawrence. He looked at Violet with studied innocence. 'Your servant did mention that your brother was no longer here to assist you at this sad time, ma'am, but I did not know that you are still ignorant of his whereabouts. He did not approach me at Knapp — nor at my headquarters on Lundy.'

The approach had been made on Bideford quay, so the denial — though not quite the truth — was still not wholly untrue either.

They looked at each other and Violet knew the lie of it.

'No matter,' she said lightly, 'he is young and headstrong and will do what he has to do, whether it be right or wrong.'

He was out in Bracklesham Bay aboard Benson's vessel. The clamour of him in her mind was sure proof of it. He was hiding there, an unwilling prodigal. He would not be making an appearance under their father's roof. The fierce urge to take him and extract just retribution for his crime was tempered with a deep relief, all the same.

It was cold in the small room, the air rank and chill in spite of the sunlight making harsh squares on the opposite wall. Amy wrapped her bed blanket round her shoulders but still her body shivered. Sometimes she stood at the casement when it was open, with her face pressed against the iron bars, smelling the clean fresh air with its beautiful bouquet of the woods and flowering things out there; savouring it with longing — even the noxious contrast of rotting salts from the lickering sheds beyond the trees . . . . What memories that sour brine brought with it. But the sun had a cold heart today. The voices were raucous in her head. They clamoured and screamed, begging for a release she had no power to grant. Every moment of her existence was a purgatory as her mind was pulled and buffeted by them. As each day slid by she sank further into a state of constant muddled confusion — a vessel within which a dual of strangers was being fought.

Footsteps . . . footsteps ascending the stairs towards her. She shrank into the furthest corner, feeling the angles of the walls pressing against her fleshless spine. Bolts were drawn, a key rattled in the lock and a young girl slipped into the room with a tin platter of food and a mug of goat's milk. She threw a nervous glance at Amy and put the food down on the window sill. There had been a table in the room once but Amy had destroyed it. Now there was nothing. A nice little creature, Amy thought. A fresh little thing with sprigs of yellow flowers on her gown and a green hair ribbon peeping out from under her pinner.

'Who are you?' she asked with interest and pleasure. There was something the matter with her voice for the words came out in a mewling growl, so she pushed herself up the wall on to her feet and took a step forward, the better to persuade this nice child of her good intentions. Alarm flooded the maid's young face and she backed away, feeling for the door latch.

'Don't be afraid, dear. I shan't hurt you,' Amy said kindly, moving across the bare boards with awkward, jerky steps. She seemed such a nice little thing with her pert, freckled face and mop of auburn curls beneath the crisp cotton cap. It would be such a comfort just to stroke that pretty little face and find a smile in those round blue eyes.

The girl gave a frightened gasp and fled. She slammed the door behind her and the light footsteps clattered down the staircase and faded beyond the hall. Amy sat down again on the edge of her bed and thought about the new servant for some time. It was difficult to count how many faces had come and gone over the years, but they never seemed to stay for long.

It was the house, of course. It was always the house. It did not like strangers, would never suffer change. It was sad the girl had fled from her like that. She would have liked to talk with her . . . to ask her how Jess was these days . . . how Violet looked in the new gown she had seen her sewing down there on the terrace in the sun.

But the girl had run away. They always did . . . .

There was something missing. Some part of the ritual of her imprisonment was incomplete. Sounds of activity floated up through the open window from below. She

179

went across and stood against the wall out of sight, watching Violet climbing into the carriage before the front door. The tumult in her head had changed its tempo and was suddenly soothing and pleasing. She felt quite well for the first time in . . . .

What is time, in any case? she thought dreamily. There is no such thing as time really, for there is no reality against which to judge it . . . .

The little thing that had been missing from the ritual suddenly occurred to her. *Click*: There had been no click and slide. There was always a click beforehand and another click afterwards, but today there had been no after click. No sliding of the three bolts. That was wrong — it had to be. She went to the door and watched her fingers straying like pale spiders along the wood, following the grain, careful not to make any jerky movements . . . and tried the latch.

It lifted right up. The wood bung had not been pushed through the lock from the outside. The iron key had not been turned. She opened the door without a sound and stood, hesitant before such unlimited freedom. The voices in her head were still quite gentle, so she was able to think calmly — and it occurred to her that she must be alone in the house, for Violet and Polly had gone off in the carriage, Jess was always out at this time of day and there was no sound downstairs to indicate that the servants were in the kitchen. They were probably making butter in the dairy. The whole house might even be hers to explore, to feast her eyes upon its colour and splendour after the empty greyness of her prison. It was, after all, her house . . . her furnishings and her industry that kept it so clean and bright. Why should she not look over her own property?

There was the wide gallery with its long casement in the stairwell which Jess had insisted on putting in . . . . It was so pleasing, he had always said, to be able to see the whole panorama of the garden, woods and harbour while ascending the staircase, and it made the upper gallery a light and gracious place, fit for the portraits of Baylesses in the years to come. There were several portraits on the gallery walls now. Jess and Lavinia hung in the centre of the long wall facing the stairwell. She averted her eyes, knowing that the sight of that delicate, golden creature would excite the voices again and make her do things.

Quite near to her right hand was a plain door similar to her own. There were two more at the other end of the gallery. Memory stirred and brought recognition. The left-hand one was her old bedchamber, which must now be Violet's . . . and Lawrence's was opposite. It was strange that she had not seen Lawrence for a long time. Maybe he was dead, as his mother was . . . .

She moved out along the gallery and, holding on to the balustrade, looked down into the hall, as she had so often done in the past. It was quiet down there, shrouded in shadow, empty of the usual pack of lurchers who dwelt under the long dining table. There was great comfort in the familiar tick of the long-case clock standing beside the parlour door. She leaned against the bannister rail for some time, listening to the slow, strong pulse of its metal heart. Memory conjured up two figures leaping across the threshold, hand in hand and pausing breathlessly to kiss, arms entwined about each other. Rich red velvet coat, gleaming black hair caught and cued as the gorgios did. Golden hair bedecked with summer flowers . . . billowing creamy wedding silk. A blur of pale faces and the flash of startled blue eyes . . . and Jess's voice, low with pent-up emotion. 'Don't worry, my darling. It's only Amy . . . .'

It's only Amy . . . only Amy . . . . She swung away from the stairs, bitterness like bile in her mouth, beating clenched fists against the air. It was always 'only Amy' in this household. Only Amy who created a splendid home out of the bricks and mortar that Jess had built. Only Amy who, all her life, gave him the whole of her love and her loyalty; only Amy who gladly bore him his child, his only full-blooded Bayless child. The other was a pale weed by comparison, a blight upon this place as his mother had been.

She lifted the latch on Lawrence's door and stood on the

threshold, taking in the emptiness of the room. No clutter of clothing, no sign at all of occupation. He must be gone from Lavenham.

She turned aside, the image of Lawrence already fading, and moved across the hall to the door of her old room. It squeaked as she pushed it open. It had always done so, and the sound was achingly familiar; tears sprang to her eyes and coursed down her cheeks. She began to feel dizzy as she smelt the sweet freshness of dried lavender in newly laundered linen.

The colour and femininity of the room smote her. It had always been beautiful — a young girl's room. White paint and limed-wood wall panelling. Curtains rich with embroidered peacocks and swathes of flowers . . . orange and scarlet and brilliant pinks in a sea of subtle greens. Her soul had been crying out for colour ever since she had been moved into the stark little room in the new wing. There was no colour there, just bare boards and window shutters. She moved across to the bed and stroked one of the curtains. Her very own handiwork such a long time ago now, when the new kenner and Jess were all she had wanted from life. Now they were Violet's — now they were the property of her own child.

Someone coughed.

She straightened up guiltily, letting the curtain fall and waiting for the scolding and the firm hands on her arms taking her back to the empty room. Her heart began to pound like a hammer. The cough came again, far away . . . at the other end of the gallery.

Jess's chamber.

Jess? Oh Jess, how I need you, she thought. How I long to see that dear face with the teasing twinkle in those smiling grey eyes. How badly I want to shelter against you as I used to do. Take my hand, bor . . . I cannot run over the stones like the others. Wait for me, lift me up.

She turned her back on the lavender-scented room, its sweet memories forgotten, and hastened with her awkward shambling gait along the gallery towards the open cavern of her prison doorway and the closed door to its left.

The cough came again, sharp and dry — the cough of an old man. She looked at the open doorway of her chamber, knowing it was where she should go now. Authority would wish it. The small sounds behind that other door were no business of hers. They were too much for her curiosity, all the same. She lifted the latch quietly, pushed the door open and stepped into the main bedchamber.

Jess drowsed and dreamed of the vardo and the peaceful sway of its passage along the highway towards the west. He could feel the familiar jolt and rocking movement of the vehicle as Yoshi hauled them over roads that were pitted with gaping holes that broke many a felley along the way. It was a better life in those days, he decided, better even than when he had become the mainstay of the tribe — and of the whole parish of Apuldram.

He gave a grunting laugh. You and I have come full circle after all, Amy, he thought. We began our lives close to the earth and we rose above it — but here we are now, close to it once more. For there's no place for us to go, pen — except back into it . . . .

His hearing ear picked up the sound of breathing in the room behind him. It was a fine day, with sunshine pouring through the room, and Violet had placed his chair close to the window so that he could watch the drive and the horses grazing in Salterns paddock.

'That you, chavi?' he said in his drawling slur.

'Avralie, bor. Sar shan?'

The blood froze in his veins.

Amy. How had she been able to leave her room? There were three bolts on the outside of her door and they were always secured, now that she had become so violent. A knot of fear twisted his stomach. He was quite defenceless if she chose to become difficult. He clenched his teeth and drew in a deep breath, trying to twist his head so that he could see her.

'Sar shan, pen . . . . Don't hover like that. Come over here and pull up a chair where I can see you.'

183

She heard his voice before she saw him, and started forward towards it, gabbling her welcome. A great tide of joy swept through her as she hurried round the great bed where life and death had struggled and Lavinia had lost — with her help. There was only Jess and Amy now, her beautiful Jess with his strength and heart-lifting handsomeness . . . .

She stopped in her tracks and swayed back on her heels as the hunched figure in the window chair turned slightly and raised a feeble hand in welcome. The face that greeted her with a lop-sided grin was the hideous mask of a stranger and she recoiled as though she had been hit.

'Jess . . . where are you, Jess?'

Her eyes hunted frantically, for the slurred voice had certainly been Jess's — but here was a stranger sitting in his chair. This was an old man, with grey streaks where there should have been shining black waves; a sickly visage with features dragged out of line where there should have been the strong, straight jaw and widely upturning mouth . . . a sunken, closed eyelid which wept at one corner instead of those great grey pools with their curling black lashes into which she needed so badly to sink and be cleansed of all the hatred which soured her restless soul.

One side of the twisted mouth curled up in a bitter smile but the voice was gentle. 'Yes, it is Jess you stare so sadly at, pen. Just the same brother Jess inside this travesty of a body. I have been ill, you see. Now I am useless down my left side and cannot get about any more. That's why I've not seen you for such a long time, my dear. Come and sit with me and take a glass of sherry and let us talk together as we used to do in the old days.'

His pulse pounded through his right side as he fought to keep his voice calm and soothing. Violet had gone to Chichester with Polly and he could not reach the bell-pull to summon Grace. Amy looked quite deranged, hovering over him like a skeletal wraith, the few wisps of remaining hair on her head falling across her suddenly enraged face.

'No . . . you are not Jess. My pral is fine and strong,

184

and you are not he for you are old and ugly. What have you done with my Jess, mullo? Give him back to me . . . I must have him here − give him back, give him back . . . . ' She lurched forward, and her fist shot out and hit him a glancing blow across the side of the head. He was not able to raise his arm to ward off the next one, and her knuckles punched his blinded eye, sending an agonizing pain through the mobile side of his face.

'Amy, stop it . . . it's me, chiriklo − your brother Jess. Come round to my other side, pen, and you'll see. I'm all right on the other side . . . . '

But the rage had taken her over and she no longer heard him. This abomination was pretending to be Jess. What had he done with him? Why was he sitting there in Jess's chair − in Jess's dressing gown? She reached out for a brass candlestick which stood on the table beside Jess's chair and brought it down on his head with all the strength of her pent-up fury. She saw nothing of the great gash which opened across his forehead under the blow; nothing of the bright gout of blood which burst from him. Her arm seemed to move up and down of its own volition − up and down, like a swing.

When she became tired, she stopped hitting the creature and wandered away to look for Jess. She went down the stairs and out through the open front door on to the terrace. She had forgotton what a nice place the terrace was on sunny days like this. When she had found Jess, she would bring him to sit here with her, as they had often done at this time of the year when the afternoons were warm and the birds sang sweetly from the woods. She strayed across the grass, luxuriating in the feel of its springy coolness beneath her bare feet.

The orchard caught her attention. 'Lawrence . . . I can see you up there hiding. Come down from that tree this minute,' d'you hear?' Disobedient little dacker, she thought. Sly as his mother with her simpering ways and her fool's love for those treacherous bees . . . .'The bees are restless today,' she would say. 'When the children are naughty it makes them restless . . . . '

Foolish Lavinia. Dead from the poison. Dead with the weak brat she made with Jess's seed. Not like her Violet.

The straw skeps were at the far end of the orchard, amongst young plum trees growing on the bank above the water. The sight of the five neat domes sitting snugly in the shade, like a group of old wives at their knitting, infuriated her and she broke into a shambling run. Bees — bees were like Lavinia Freeland. They fussed amongst the flowers and gave out their sweetness on the one hand and turned and stung you on the other. They were as treacherous as their simpering guardian . . . wicked thief that she was.

'Jess, where are you? You were here and you called to me. I heard you, Jess.' The epileptic darkness slammed down on her without warning and she stumbled — and, falling, knocked over the nearest of the five skeps. As she slumped across it the frenzy enveloped her and she tore at the plaited straw with claw hands, uttering strange animal ululations as the madness invaded her jerking mind.

From the moment that Amy's lurching figure appeared between the trees, the lazy murmur of a summer's afternoon was shattered. The orchard had been a quiet haven, with the chuckle of water in the reeds and the soft hum of drifting bees over their hives the only sounds to break the peace. The bees, sensing the approach of danger, began to agitate, to rise and fly nervously from tree to skep and back. The person came, emanating terrible vibrations which brought them up in a frenzy of defence — too late to protect the first skep as it crashed over on its side, crushed by the weight of the alien creature's body and gouging hands. They shrieked and trilled their warning, and the message of the queen drove them up and outward in one sweeping movement. Out of all the hives they poured, rising in a great black arc, to home down upon that thrashing body, striking as they swarmed over it.

The orchard was rent of its gentle mantle as the afternoon waned into early evening. Nothing stirred in the dusk-blurred cavern beneath the canopy of green leaves. A few dazed bees buzzed aimlessly around the standing hives, disorientated by the presence of so much death.

Lights went on in the house.

The sound of shock and tragic grieving scarcely equalled the despair of the bees in the loss of their queen.

5

Violet stood beside the gaping hole and stared down at the two coffins. They were made of polished wood and embellished with handsome brass handles and plaques. She had just thrown a handful of earth down into the pit and it lay scattered across the burnished lids in untidy dry lumps.

It seemed that she was always to be standing thus — saying her farewells to those she loved — since that first funeral when Lavinia had been laid to rest and she had pressed against her mother's skirts and wept for the gentle woman who had married her father.

She felt a hand grip her arm lightly and looked up at John Freeland, standing at the grave's edge by her side . . . .

'Come, my dear,' he said gently, the depth of his own emotion roughening his voice. Aunt Lavinia's only brother and, in all the years that she could remember, the only Freeland to offer her the same sort of uncritical affection that Lavinia had given her so unstintingly. She leant against him for a moment, grateful for the depth of his compassion. Then she took a deep breath. The parson had finished his prayers and there was no more to be said over the bodies of her mother and father. Materially they had ceased to exist.

She allowed him to turn her away from the open grave and, with Aunt Mary Freeland on her other side, walked slowly between the tomb-stones towards the church path. So many people laid to rest here beneath the trees who had helped to fashion her life in one way or another. Lettie Heberden over by the wall; Giles and his father, John

Croucher, in the same plot.

Lavinia Freeland and her newborn baby daughter.

Now two Baylesses had been added. Two Romanies whose belief in Christianity had been purely superficial. They had no real place in this leafy, daisy-strewn gorgio burial ground. They should have been laid to rest in the fashion of their forebears, but it would not have been Jess's wish.

'It's ironic,' she thought bitterly, that poor Aunt Lavinia must even now share her grave, as she had shared her life, with Amy as well as with Jess.

'Stay on with Mary and me, my dear,' John Freeland urged as they walked slowly down the church path towards Manor Farm's gate, with the rest of the congregation trailing after them. 'Don't think of returning to Lavenham after the guests have gone. The house will be lonely for you during the next few days and it will do you good to be in other surroundings.'

What a good man Uncle John Freeland was, Violet thought. He exuded an air of comfortable stability with his broad shoulders and pepper-and-salt whiskers. Violet tucked her arm into his. He must be suffering a special grief at Jess Bayless's passing.

'Thank you, Uncle — but no. Lavenham is my home and Dada would have wanted me to return there. Manfri and Polly will look after me well.'

She smiled at him and knew what was in his mind, for he had long been aware of the tensions and mysteries of Lavenham and of the unnatural capabilities of Jess Bayless and his children. He knew and had long ago chosen not to challenge such gifts. To be able to stop the heart of any living creature at a hundred yards was beyond explanation, but he had seen Jess do that very thing many times during their youth on their hunting expeditions. It had been part of the privilege of their friendship and the gift of Jess's confidence.

It had also been a prime part of Jess Bayless's fascination.

'Don't worry, Uncle. I am not afraid of Lavenham or its ghosts,' she said, seeing what was in his mind. They walked on in silence, for both were aware that she spoke of the house rather than of her parents.

'So much death here,' she thought later, looking at Lavenham's beautiful façade with loathing as the carriage halted before the front door. Manfri and Rueb, sitting awkwardly on either side of her, had been silent as they drove away from Manor Farm after the funeral reception.

She picked up her skirts and stepped down on to the gravel carriage sweep and strolled across the lawn with her back to the waiting house, feelings its will boring into the back of her head. It waited, crouched over the worn boulders that were its very heart.

She stood on the bank, looking down at the water. In the sparkling reflection of the clear blue sky, a mirrored feather of thin cloud evaporated into diamond stars as a piece of wood floated past. Three moorhens shot out of the reeds and sailed away on the fast-flowing current. Sunlight glinted on the undulant water in shafts of shattered silver.

A lighter passed, heading out towards the harbour, water creaming round its black tarred bows. The sweating seamen labouring at their oars gave a ragged cheer at the sight of her. She heard nothing of their yelps and whistles.

Something touched her cheek lightly.

She put her hand up and a bee crawled on to her fingers. It vibrated its delicate double wings at her and then sat still, exploring the surface of her knuckles with its proboscis. Violet looked at the tiny black and brown creature. It seemed to feel her scrutiny, for it ceased its probing and waved its antennae at her. She watched it with love, knowing that the feeling would be received and acknowledged. After a few moments the bee flew off her hand and droned away towards the fruit trees in the orchard.

She turned her back on the water and followed the little bee under the trees towards the five straw skeps. Three were now empty and abandoned. They had not been cleaned out since the tragedy of the two deaths, and the honey in the half-completed combs had begun to seep through the bases. She stood and watched the listless driftings of the little colony which remained. They seemed despondent and idle, with little of the bustling activity they normally showed at this time of the year.

She could still see that terrible swarm . . . still hear the heightened sound of their furious single purpose, still see the dreadful writhing mass moving like a black blanket on a boulder. When they brought her to the orchard, nothing had been touched. Amy lay across a crushed skep in a pool of liquid honey and dead bees. The defending swarm still covered every inch of her body, which was so bloated from their stings that she would scarcely have been recognizable, even if every particle of hair, skin and clothing had not been covered with the dense swarm of small furry bodies . . . .

Sounds of children's laughter shattered the stillness of the day: Manfri and Polly's twins playing in the stable yard. Even the solemnity of a double funeral in the family was not enough to douse their twelve-year-old exuberance.

She stood in the shadow of Manfri and Polly's cottage, close to its corner wall, watching the west front of the house. There was always an element of awareness to be found there somewhere . . . watching her and waiting like a thief in an alleyway.

Lavenham lay like a jewel against a backdrop of leafy oakwoods, its dove-grey stonework dusted with mellow gold in the late afternoon light. Already the Virginia creeper, which Lavinia had planted in the first months of her married life, and which had gradually spread over most of the west wall, was sending orange feelers across the stonework of the new wing.

The house stood mute before her scrutiny. Deep within the heart of its foundations a pulse beat softly. Something stirred behind the gleaming casements as though a silent multitude closed ranks within its walls.

The will had been read by John Freeland after the funeral

191

to all those who would benefit from it. There had been quite a large gathering of them — which was hardly surprising in view of Jess's generosity. Every employee was rewarded for his service to the Baylesses, and the parish was left a princely sum for the improvement of its roads and waterways and for the care of the needy. Even Parson Wilks, who had come to Apuldram on the death of old Thomas Kelway, was left an annuity which would ease his inadequate stipend.

To Violet was given the Chichester business, and the stud, in partnership with Manfri. Lawrence had been left the shipping company at Dell Quay and Lavenham itself.

At the end of the will a codicil had recently been added. If Lawrence did not claim his inheritance within five years of the date of Jess's death, the house and all other assets left to him were to revert to Violet and her descendents.

Listening to John Freeland's voice as he read the words, Violet bowed her head to hide the sudden trembling of her lips. The words were a committal to a life sentence in a prison whose bars were in the mind and whose retribution was in the soul.

Apuldram suffered a severe winter in the early part of 1753. The Chichester Channel froze above Dell Quay all the way up to Fishbourne Mill, and a fire at Rymans destroyed the roof of the whole building apart from the tower.

A pair of elderly sisters took the lease of Salterns Cottage. There were many times, after signing away the lease, when Violet looked at the mullion-windowed little house with longing. There were no ghosts there to follow her from room to room; no echo of Amy's tantrums and epileptic fits.

Her new responsibility to Bayless and Co. in Chichester kept her busy from dawn until dusk each day. She discovered that insurance and banking were much to her liking; she had a natural aptitude for figures which quickly impressed the chief clerk, John Trew. But it was her trustee interest in the Bayless Shipping Company which was her greatest surprise, for there was a strong element of romance in the beautiful vessels which sailed in and out of Chichester Harbour under the Bayless pennant, bearing cargoes as varied as the seasons to cities the length and breadth of the world.

John Trew, in the Chichester office, was a meticulous man with a passion for his ledgers. The East Street business was run with precision and orderliness and needed little of Violet's time, she quickly discovered. Her most necessary contribution was her signature. Knowing this, she still insisted on a daily attendance to become thoroughly familiar with each and every transaction that was negotiated. Sometimes she was able to offer suggestions that would save Baylesses time or money but, for the most part, the firm ran smoothly under the competent guidance of Trew and the legal assistance of John Freeland.

Within a year Violet had made them both partners in the business and changed the name to Bayless, Freeland and Trew.

The shipping office at Dell Quay was a very different affair for nothing was ever predictable about its transactions. Sailing schedules were fluid, cargoes haphazard, and it did not take her long to discover that both the *Grace* and *Golden Dawn* had concealed compartments in their hulls and did a thriving duty-free trade in brandies, liqueurs and small consignments of precious metals and jewels from the Indies. There was something about these illicit transactions which appealed to a part of her spirit which hungered for an excitement her life had always lacked. It must have been these cargoes which had drawn her father and Thomas Benson close.

She took nearly two years to realize that she was also having to struggle to control the increasing intrusion of Lavenham itself upon her.

One afternoon in 1754 she watched a rider enter the drive and went forward to meet him.

'Good day, Uncle. What a pleasure to see you here at this early hour.'

The eagerness in her voice made John Freeland study her closely as he returned her greeting and climbed down stiffly from his horse. He was beginning to feel his years, for his hip joints were stiff and often painful these days. He put his arm round Violet's shoulders as they went into the hall, and Polly hurried out of the kitchen to take his cape.

'I have news, after a fashion, of Lawrence,' he said, settling himself with relief in the parlour chair that had been Jess's. 'It's not very good news, I'm afraid, my dear.'

He saw the blaze in her grey eyes cloud over and patted her arm comfortingly. 'There has been an article printed in the *Gentleman's Magazine* referring to a rascal by the name of Thomas Benson who was known to your father — and I believe to you also?'

She nodded, recalling florid good looks and old-fashioned courtesy which almost hid the sheer bounding energy in him.

'He came here several times to visit Dada. I thought him rather a fine person,' she said, wondering what was coming next. 'He was certainly a gentleman — and of considerable wealth at that. I always understood that he was a Member of Parliament and very respectable.'

John grinned at her and his eyes twinkled under their bushy grey brows.

'That would not necessarily endow him with the gift of virtue. There have been many villains involved with the running of our country, and it would seem that he is one of them. The article reports a most perfidious deception regarding the Sun Insurance Company, for it would appear that Master Benson filled the holds of one of his vessels with pewter and linens and insured the cargo and his ship for a princely sum. Then his captain put to sea and scuttled it just out of sight of land, having first ensured that there were other vessels within call to pick up the crew. The deception would not have come to light at all had it not been for the conscience — or maybe the mischief-making — of one of the survivors. The plot was reported to the authorities but Benson, with Lawrence close behind him, fled to Portugal, where they are both now residing.'

He smiled at her and said gently, 'I have to write to Lawrence, now that we know where he is living, to tell him of his father's death and of his inheritance. There are still eight months left of the five years before the property reverts to you, my dear, and it is only fair for him to be given every assistance to realize his claim — although I very much doubt whether he will be prepared to risk his freedom to make it. It seems that he was aboard Benson's vessel, you see, when the deception was perpetrated. The article in the *Gentleman's Magazine* goes into quite fine details and reports that a man called Lancey, some relation of Benson's, was commanding the *Nightingale* and Lawrence was first mate. They are both liable to hang, my dear.'

On the twentieth of October 1754 Violet became sole owner of the Lavenham estate and principle shareholder in the Bayless Shipping Company.

'This calls for celebration,' John Freeland said, as he watched her put her signature to the last of the documents which sealed her fortune.

Violet put the quill back in its holder and reached for the sander. 'It has been a long time since we entertained at Lavenham,' she said hesitantly. 'People are not as friendly to me as they were when Dada was alive. I would hate to send out invitations and have them refused.'

'Then we shall have a reception at Manor Farm with you as our guest of honour,' he said gently. He reached across the desk and put his hand over hers. 'You are a beautiful and wealthy young woman with enough to offer any man to make you an excellent match in any circle, so do try not to be intimidated by the murmurings of the Chichester gossips.'

He raised his hand as she began to protest. 'Oh yes, my dear, I realize that a husband and family are not as high on your priority list as they are with most young women, but procreation is the ultimate reason for our existence, however independent we are. You have been getting more and more isolated from young people since your father's death, and too much work and no play makes for a dull companion, you know.'

It was true. There were few callers to Lavenham, and the associates with whom she brushed shoulders in business hours received short shrift from her when the inevitable references to her womanhood and good looks were made.

'I don't feel the need of close friends,' she said shortly.

'Nonsense, my dear. Everyone needs them. You were not put into this world looking the way you do and with an intellect as sharp as yours simply to waste yourself on horses and ships' manifests. Let me speak with Mary and arrange a suitable celebration . . . please. Indulge an old man's fancy this once. It will give us both great pleasure, for you know how Mary loves organizing banquets and I can think of no lovelier guest to honour than you.'

On the morning of the dinner party Violet was in the Dell Quay office early. *Golden Dawn* had arrived off Cockbush at the entrance to Chichester Harbour on the previous evening's tide, and the lighters and bum-boats had begun bringing her cargo and passengers in soon after dawn. She had sailed from Boston, Massachusetts, with a cargo of timber and hides.

There were five gentlemen on the passenger list. Two of them were merchants from Chichester whom she knew, one was a London silversmith and the other two names were unknown to her.

She settled herself at her desk beside the main window, from which she could see the full length of the wharf to where the channel curved away round Bosham Hoe and fanned out into the wide harbour basin. The water sparkled in early sunshine, a million tiny diamonds

196

drowned in the dip and spray of oars from the busy morning traffic, as she pored over the thick wedge of documents that was *Golden Dawn's* cargo manifest.

'Number nine comen' in, sor. Hides and two passengers.'

She raised her head as the cargo-handler on the wharf sang out his message to the tally clerk. There were three or four vessels being offloaded into the warehouses but she knew the voices of the Bayless men. She idly watched the longboat approaching and the rowers shipping their oars smartly as they slid alongside the slimy wooden piers to the jetty steps. The morning tide was in, and offloading the hides would be a simple operation.

The oarsmen leant upon their dripping oars and waited for their passenger to climb the steps on to the jetty, his servant close to his heels with a heavy valise. He stood on the top step and waved his thanks down into the longboat, looked about him with evident pleasure and then turned and headed towards the office.

Her eyes followed him, taking in his purposeful stride and the weather-tanned face under his travelling cut-wig as he passed the window and made for the Crown and Anchor tavern next door. He disappeared through the open doorway and she was left with a feeling of heightened interest, which surprised her. Her finger slid idly down the manifest to the passenger list.

Master Desmond Heritage, of Seel Place, Boston, Massachusetts was the only one in company with his servant.

She honed her mind as she had done from time to time all her life, sending its searching fingers to examine him — and was shocked when nothing happened. She frowned and concentrated harder, squeezing her eyes shut and willing herself through to him.

Her mind remained static.

She sat back in her chair, staring up at the ceiling, letting the impact of this new development sink in. A fly crawled along the window ledge and she fixed her attention on it and gathered herself into a knot to draw the

Power within her. There was no response, no familiar build-up of heightened pulse and body heat. She was empty.

The Power was gone.

She sat in her chair, with a sense of loss that was too profoundly deep for explanation — she had never welcomed her gift and had long refused to exercise it. Jess had lost his power in his late twenties. She was twenty-five. On reflection, it might even be a relief to be freed of its burden. With the ability to Flame and to probe the minds of others, she had been a creature apart — a fact which was sensed rather than known by all who came into contact with her. Maybe now they would lose the reserve that held them away from her.

It was like being cleansed of infinite sin.

In the evening, all problems laid determinedly to one side, she dressed herself with care in a deep crimson gown of crushed velvet. Polly tonged her hair, gathering it up with jewelled head-combs into a shining waterfall of blue-black curls which cascaded down from her crown to the nape of her neck.

'My soul, Miss Violet . . . you look so fetching. I 'ent seen you look so fair and happy in a long time.' She stared with wonder at Violet through the dressing table mirror.

'I'm really quite looking forward to this evening's entertainment,' she said lightly. 'It's been a long time since I had the chance to wear this gown. Dada brought the material for me in Paris, if you recall.'

She stood up and surveyed her reflection critically; tall and straight-backed, perfectly coiffeured hair framing a flawless face and white swanlike neck. The *décolletage* was low, displaying a creamy expanse of breast, a perfect contrast against the rich crimson. Her stomacher was plain but for a line of tiny bows which plunged from her cleavage to the centre of her slender waist. An ornate Swiss lace undercoat peeped from the trailing half-sleeves. A ruby and pearl necklace and earrings set in chased gold which her father had given to her mother long ago. Her gloved hands were unadorned, the long tapering fingers ringless.

'Will I do?' She pirouetted slowly round in the centre of the bedchamber, hands clasped demurely.

Polly watched her and nodded her head, overwhelmed. 'Oh deary me, miss. You'm better looken' than any of them ol' crotchity madams goen' strutten' round the Assembly Rooms at them balls. You'm just about perfect . . . perfect.'

She turned away and busied herself with the curling tongs, for the lump that came to her throat threatened to bring tears to her eyes. It was such a dreadful waste to see the young mistress looking so lovely and no husband in the offing to appreciate that breathtaking beauty, she thought, not to mention her great goodness of heart. Those withdrawing room tattle-tongues were all too hasty to label Violet Bayless because of her beginnings, which were, after all, no fault of hers. They had never seen the patient, long-suffering child growing up under the weight of such a yoke of disapproval — and still managing to be well balanced as well as beautiful.

'I'll take your cape downstairs,' she said, gathering up the scatter of petticoats and slippers that littered the floor. 'Just you go on down and have a nice glass of Madeira wine beside the fire until the carriage comes for you.'

Violet picked up her reticule and pecked Polly on the cheek. 'Dear Poll,' she said softly. 'I don't know what I should do without you. You and Manfri and the twins.'

Manor Farm was ablaze with lights when the Lavenham carriage bowled in through the gate. Violet, thinking that she was early and that there would be time to snatch a few quiet words with her host and hostess before the evening began, was surprised to see several other carriages already taking up much of the barn yard, and another clattered through the entrance as she alighted.

John Freeland stood in a shaft of yellow light in the open doorway and put his hands up to his eyes in mock confusion as she greeted him.

'My God, Violet. It's almost indecent being as comely as
you are. You'll have all the men eating from your hand,' he
said in delighted admiration, the bushy pepper-and-salt
eyebrows shooting up and down like signalling flags.

'And all the women scratching your eyes out,' Mary said
tartly from behind his shoulder.

'Nonsense, my dear.' He kissed Violet soundly on each
cheek, enjoying the fresh lavender smell of her smooth
skin. 'The ladies, bless their hearts, are always in a twit
over each other. Violet will render them speechless, for a
change.'

Mary snorted and turned to greet the next guest. She
had never had much time for any of the Baylesses, save for
Jess, whom she had found most charming. His bastard
might be handsome but she was as hard as stone and as
unyielding. She had never found anything to say to Violet,
apart from the basic civilities.

'Good evening to you, Mr Heritage,' she said with
ceremony to the latest arrival. 'How delightful to have you
back in our midst.'

Violet felt a deep flush seep through her and forbore to
turn her head. What an extraordinary coincidence, she
thought, as she gave her cape to a bobbing servant girl and
swept into the brilliantly lit drawing room on John's arm.
She knew that she was looking her best and for some
unaccountable feeling, the inclusion of Mr Heritage in the
guest list gave the evening especially interesting overtones.

There were several couples already in the room, sitting
and standing around a wide high-mantelled fireplace,
engrossed in the preliminaries of polite conversation.
They looked up and, recognizing her, became guarded.
The conversation thinned. She felt the women's veiled
antagonism and the men's covetous glances.

John squeezed her arm. 'Here she is, this lovely niece of
mine,' he said cheerfully to the gathering in general.
'Come, my dear. You know Mistress Calthorpe and
Master Calthorpe, don't you? Permit me to introduce

Master Lennox and his good lady . . . . '

They circled the room, going from group to group, and then he raised his hand and waved over the heads of his guests to the man who had just entered the room.

Violet was exchanging pleasantries with the elderly Doctor Sanden's wife, Tilly. Mrs Sanden had known Violet since her husband brought Lawrence into the world. Violet remained, in her eyes, the ragamuffin she had been born, her looks and brains being little more than an impertinence. She had to admit, though, that Violet Bayless looked well and behaved with decorum, even if the designing minx had the attention of every man in the room. Her voice was low and pleasantly pitched and she seemed genuinely interested in Mrs Sanden's work in the new poorhouse which the doctor had recently presented to the city. All the same, she was relieved when Mr Freeland brought another guest into the group.

'Oh, how nice to see you again, Mr Heritage,' she said warmly to the smiling stranger.

John Freeland looked at Violet with consummate pride. 'My dear, may I present Mr Desmond Heritage. I don't think you have met before, for Mr Heritage lives in New England these days and has only lately arrived . . . . Desmond, my niece by marriage, Miss Violet Bayless.'

It was there immediately — the mutual recognition of a magnetism she had felt that morning as he passed the office window, unaware of her presence and bent only on the happy anticipation of his first tankard of Sussex ale.

She looked into Desmond Heritage's smiling hazel eyes and bowed her head over a modest curtsy.

'How do you so, sir?' Fight it, she said fiercely to herself. Fight it now.

He bowed over her hand, and as she looked down at the top of his white peruke there was a painful sinking feeling in her chest.

'I am honoured, ma'am,' he said, and his voice was deep and clear and the fine hazel eyes seemed to glaze at the sight of her. He quickly recovered himself and smiled —

and something strangely tender passed between them.

'Why have we not met before, sir?' She asked at the beginning of dinner, finding him seated at her side. 'Uncle says that you are from these parts, and yet I do not recall having heard your name before.'

'I have been in the colonies for some years, ma'am,' he said. 'I went over to Massachusetts with my father and three brothers when my mother died. I was only a babe at the time, and I have returned to this country lamentably infrequently since then.'

He was, it seemed, an importer of goods from England and France. Wool and fabrics were his special interest, and Chichester was his primary source for good South Down fleece.

She listened as he sketched a picture of life across the vast Atlantic, highlighting all the benefits of space, and freedom from many of the social mores which so stunted Georgian English society. She liked the musical pitch of his voice and was infinitely soothed by it.

It seemed quite unimportant that he was not young. She studied his face whenever it was turned her way and could count the lines round his eyes and mouth. It was a mobile, intelligent springboard for a host of expressions, an endearing face rather than a handsome one, for his nose was over large and his jaw almost too square.

'Of course, the facilities are much improved now, compared with the way they were in 1716 when we first arrived there . . . . '

If he had been two years old in that year, he would have been born in 1714, she calculated. He must be all of forty years old now . . . just a decade younger than Dada, had he lived.

She did her best to climb out of the bittersweet pit into which she was gently but certainly sliding. She engaged in an animated and even slightly flirtatious conversation with Nicholas Reemer on her left, arguing the costings of English-made salt against the cheaper continental varieties which were now being imported into England.

202

'How can it benefit the country in anything more than the short term, to remove the salt tax? I agree that there are plenty of imports which are grossly overdue for tax clearance, but our English salt-refining is of superior quality to the continental product and it means that those with lower incomes have therefore to bear the brunt of buying this impure stuff whilst their fellows in France and Holland and Denmark live off our own good produce.'

Nicholas Reemer was entranced. It was quite an achievement to instil an element of suggestibility into such a dry subject, and this dark beauty was positively throbbing with intensity. He moved closer to her and pressed his thigh against the side of her leg.

It had, after all, been an excellent evening, she decided as the carriage took her home. At the back of her mind lurked Desmond Heritage, and she veered away from the memory until she was lying in her bed and searching for sleep — which suddenly seemed to elude her. As she had taken her leave, he had clasped the hand she offered him and lifted it to his lips, holding it there for an instant longer than was strictly necessary so that she had felt the warmth of his breath through the lace of her glove.

'I would very much like to look over the horses in your stable, ma'am,' he had said. His voice was casual, as it would be when mentioning a possible business transaction — but his eyes looked into hers and they were not concerned with horses. They regarded her with infinite tenderness; the desire in them had none of the open lust which she was accustomed to reading in other men's eyes, but rather the humble acknowledgement of her sensuality and an almost embarrassed awareness of his own.

I know nothing of this man, she thought in sudden panic. He may have a wife over there in Boston . . . he may be a woman-beater. I have no defence against treachery without the Power — so how is it possible to consider the affection of a stranger when I am at my most vulnerable . . ?

When sleep finally came, it brought with it strange, disturbing dreams from which she awoke in the small hours with the sweat of fear on her forehead.

She had been in a wooden building, sitting in the centre of an open space. There were stone columns encircling a fine mosaic floor. They made her feel imprisoned, though the oval place was spacious, even draughty. She sat cross-legged and her body was heavy with child. There was a low nagging pain within, as though the birth was imminent, but she knew that this should not be so.

She was very frightened. The feeling swept through her, making her shiver until her teeth chattered. The tiny clattering sound only heightened her growing terror.

They were coming for her.

She could sense their approach through the tangled oakwoods . . . the clank of their weapons, the heat of the torches they bore.

'Deivos . . . protect me,' she found herself praying with a fervent despair in a language that was quite different and which she understood even as she heard the strange sound of it. 'Help me, Deivos. Help me now.'

She scarcely heard the crash of falling masonry, scarcely registered the blue flash that burned through her closed eyelids. The sudden stench of horse dung filled her nostrils, making her retch.

Violet woke with a jerk and sat up in bed, her body still shaking from the agony and the sickening odour.

It was still there in her nostrils. She shrank from it and pulled the sheet up to her face, breathing shallowly and schooling her jumbled senses back to the reality of her bedchamber.

A bad dream, that was all, she told herself. Caused, no doubt, by Aunt Mary's rich hare with all its concentrated syrups and juices. She made herself take a deep breath and forced herself to quieten the mad pumping of her heart.

The stench persisted. She sniffed the air cautiously, puzzled by the strong stable smell in the room.

She could even hear them out there now. Manfri must

be having trouble with a sick horse, for faintly came the shrill whinny of a frightened animal, then hooves struck against stone, kicking and clattering.

She sat, listening, the fright of the dream still half real in her mind. They seemed nearer than when she had woken up. A horse neighed shrilly, and the sound made her jerk upright. It seemed close enough to be inside the house . . . somewhere below her.

The screaming horse was somehow not quite right, for there was agony and rage in it which tugged at her memory, bringing with it a dread for something which was just beyond her comprehension. She felt herself move, drawn out of her bed from under the protection of the covers.

She stood on the carpet in her nightgown, clenching her fists and trying to resist the pull towards the sounds.

'Help me, Deivos,' she said to herself, and shivered as she remembered the plea in her nightmare. It was becoming difficult to separate reality from fantasy. Gritting her teeth in an effort to clear her mind, she felt herself drawn towards the door. She opened it cautiously, afraid of what might be beyond.

Silence reigned in the blackness surrounding her. She stretched out her hands and moved step by step towards the invisible bannister rail, listening to her own breathing. The longcase clock in the hall ticked away the seconds.

As her hands touched the smooth wood of the bannister, the night exploded into a harsh blue light which burnt into her eyeballs and etched the long gallery window in harsh relief. She stood riveted to the balustrade, the blood frozen in her veins, heedless of the rolling crash of thunder which followed, for the shaft of lightning had revealed an impossibility —

A great black stallion was rearing up at her from the black well of the hall, screaming his hatred through great bared fangs and gaping nostrils. The leap from below was prodigious, but he was huge and wild and nothing at all to do with reality; and the blue light shone on the gloss of his coat, the shining, killing hooves flailing in their rage. She could see the red flare of blood in the creature's furious nostrils, the rolling lust in its molten eyes.

There was no time for fear . . . no time to cry out . . . .

She fell beneath the crushing weight of its pounding body. The creature's screams and the dreadful reek of its excretions engulfed her. Something pounded her head and she slid away from the whole maelstrom of terror into blessed unconsciousness.

'Oh, dear child, thank goodness you are awake.'

Polly's anxious voice filtered through waves of nothing and she opened her eyes. Sunlight poured through the partially drawn bed curtains.

Polly's kindly face swam before her and then came into focus. She lay still, trying to remember why Polly was there and looking so worried.

The black stallion.

She hid her head in the pillow at the memory and felt the tremors returning to her body.

'Miss Violet, please say something. We've ben that worried. Should I send Rueb for Doctor Sanden? Did you have a fainting turn?'

Polly's voice steadied her and lessened the horrors of the night. She turned over and put a hand up to take Polly's and squeezed it tightly, seeking and finding a comfort in its rough warmth. 'Poll, I had such a terrible dream. It frightened me so much, I must have lost my reason. I'm all right now. Just let me stay here for a little while. There will be no need to have Doctor Sanden in.'

The relief on Polly's lined, good-natured face was almost comical. She sat on the side of the bed, rubbing Violet's hands in hers. 'Hester came upon you when she started to sweep the stairs at dawn,' she said. 'There you were, all of a heap on the top step an' it gave me such a turn, it did. Them stairs claimed your aunt Lavinia. I can see her now, as clearly as I see you, lyen' on the ground at the bottom in just the very same position as you was a'lyen'

206

at the top. It made me feel right queer, it did. The storm must have frightened you, dear. Such an odd one . . . just the one great flash of lightning and one mighty clap of thunder right overhead. Frightened the horses half to death, that did. Took Manfri and Rueb most of the rest of the night to calm 'em down. Hester said she could hear them right through the house to her chamber at the back.'

'I heard them too,' Violet said. 'I expect you are right. It must have been the thunder.'

She fought the fear that Polly's words had brought back. 'I feel quite well now, truly — but my nightmare was so real, Polly. I thought I saw a horrible black stallion here in the house . . . down in the Hall it was. I know now that I must have been dreaming, but in the middle of the night it was so real — and then it seemed to jump right up at me from below and came down on me and it was all erected and terrible as though it was going to mate with me.'

She hugged herself, shaking again as the full memory of it flooded through her.

Polly stared at her. 'Oh, Miss Violet . . . don't say that.' She crossed herself and sat twisting the ends of her apron in her fingers. 'Your aunt Lavinia had dreams like that sometimes. She used to tell me that they worried her *dreadfully* but that your dada was always able to comfort her and send them packen'. I thought her a trifle fanciful, I admit it — but there've ben a few times when I felt something real unpleasant too, down there in the hall. Nothing really to see, you mind . . . but just feelen' that there was somethen' strong and bad and vengeful close to me — and that dreadful smell . . . . '

Violet was recovering her poise as she listened to Polly's words. There was nothing new about the Presence at Lavenham. It could be felt in the hall and the parlour and sometimes up in the main bedchamber. Something was in the house with them but no one had ever been inclined to give it a name. It was not a ghost that stalked the corridors at night, nor was it a devil that disturbed the furniture as was the case with the Old Rectory at Palingthorpe.

Lavenham was permeated by another kind of atmosphere.

The Watcher cursed at the sight of the two figures strolling along the paddock fence and pausing to examine one fine horse and then another. They walked close together without actually touching, but an aura of intense feeling emanated from them in a strong yellow glow.

More hate, more suffering — more death. The antithesis of the depth of the love they were fashioning together.

He clenched his fists and beat them against the sides of his legs.

Mea Culpa . . . mea culpa. Forgive me this genocide.

He stared down at the ugly burns on the palms of his hands, knowning they were all part of the punishment that something here at Lavenham must extract from the blood line. He must ensure that this eternal sentence of death was erased.

6

Desmond Heritage rode out from Chichester at a walk. Although he was drawn towards Apuldram by the thought of Violet Bayless, there was much on his mind to give him cause for considerable concern.

He was visiting England for six short weeks, during which time he would travel to London and Plymouth, purchasing merchandise for his warehouses in Boston. His berth was already secured for his return to the New World. It was against his cautious nature to permit anything to disarrange plans which had been laid with precision months before, but there was no getting away from the fact that Miss Bayless had completely captivated him and it was difficult, all of a sudden, to envisage life without her. The physical excellence of her was more than enough to get every head in Boston turning, he knew. Her sensuality charged him in a way that he had not felt since his youth.

It had never been like that between him and dear Betsy. Theirs had been a gentle coming together of souls for the betterment of two families. She had been taken from him when smallpox scourged the town, and for a long time he felt that part of him had died also. There had been other women, other attractions, but in the twelve years since Betsy's death he had never seriously considered re-marrying, for the few ladies suitable held no interest for him.

Violet had taken him unawares. She had exploded upon him with such force that he was still reeling from the vastness of this unheralded feeling.

He rode slowly down the Manhood road against a stiff

breeze and lifted his face into it, sniffing the burden of its light scents with pleasure. Such different smells here in the Old Country from those across the ocean. Here was the smell of the Solent, and the briny sharpness of the saltpans; the faint suggestion of ripening apples, the smell of warmth and cut corn and the Chichester tannery.

Violet smelled of lavender. Her skin was so smooth, free of the slightest blemish, like warm polished ivory . . . .

He turned off the highway into the leafy lane which twisted and curved its way down to the saltpans. The Lavenham driveway led off the lane, and he noted with satisfaction how well she kept the carriage track. No ruts or gaping holes here, but a well-tended surface, recently gravelled. It was the same with the paddocks on either side of the drive. Carefully laid hedgerows separated the fields, and iron railings lined the drive so that it was possible to admire the grazing horses without interruption all the way to the main entrance in front of the house.

He waved as Rueb, hearing the clatter of horse's hooves on the cobbles, came out of the main barn, wiping his hands on his breeches.

'Good day to you,' Desmond called.

Rueb hurried forward, recognizing Violet's American buyer. 'Is Miss Bayless at home?' He slid down and handed the reins to Rueb, whose wise brown eyes had not missed the jaunty air this gentleman sported. He looks to be sniffen' around like a dog to a bitch, Rueb thought. Interesting.

'She is, sor. She's not too fit though, so I don't rightly know if she be receiven' this mornen'. Polly in the house will find out for you.'

Polly greeted him with her customary comfortable warmth but looked dubious when asked whether Miss Bayless would receive him. 'I'll go up and have a word with her, sor,' she said. 'She had another very bad night and she was sleeping an hour back, but let me just peep round her door. I'll not disturb her though, if you don't mind, if she is still at rest. Unless you have urgent business which cannot wait, of course.'

They smiled at each other, knowing that of course his business was urgent. He could scarcely bear to be here and not see her at once.

'No, Polly. My business is purely social,' he said, aware that she was almost certainly a party to this delirium which had overtaken her mistress and himself.

He waited, half of his mind listening to her footsteps mounting the stairs and then the soft pad as they crossed the carpet in the chamber above. The other half examined his surroundings and registered uncomfortably its contrasting atmosphere of cold hostility beneath the charm of rich colours and well-polished furniture.

It was like a beautifully furnished crypt, he decided. How was it possible for such a warm and vibrantly alive woman to live in a place which emanated such an atmosphere? He stood in the middle of the room, trying to identify his feelings. He knew only that the chill in the beautiful room had nothing to do with the sun being obscured behind thick banks of blueish clouds.

It was a terrible house. She would be better off as far away from it as possible.

A wry smile turned the Watcher's mouth into a bitter curve. How naive and ignorant of this man to imagine that distance had anything to do with safety. He might scoop her up and take her from here, if the house permitted it — she was but one link in the chain of revenge. He was, himself, the living, tortured proof of that.

Polly returned. 'She is awake, sor, and will see you if you will be good enough to excuse her from rising. I have persuaded her to remain where she is, for she would have dressed and come down rather than deny herself the pleasure of your company. But you will find her very weary, sor.' She studied him and then seemed to make up her mind to speak further.

'She thinks very highly of you, sor, and I am sure that it

will cheer her up considerably to see you. Maybe you would be good enough to advise her too, sor, for this house is the root of the problem. Either persuade her to admit her fears to Doctor Sanden . . . or go and ask the help of Parson Wilks . . . .'

Violet was lying with her eyes closed as Polly ushered him into the bedchamber. As the maid bustled over and drew a chair forward for him to sit in, Violet opened her eyes without moving and regarded him drowsily.

'She is still full of the posset I made her drink a while back,' Polly said, plumping the bed pillows up around Violet's dark head. 'Wake up now, my dear. Your visitor is here and will have plenty to talk to you about, it being quarter sessions an' all.' She pushed dark tendrils of curling hair back from Violet's forehead with a proprietary hand.

'Poor lady, she's not at all well, sor. I'll bring up a tray of chocolate and sweetmeats for you. I won't be but a moment. Make yourself comfortable.'

She was gone and instantly forgotten.

Desmond leaned forward and took one of the hands that lay so limply on the coverlet. 'I'm most troubled to see you so unwell, Miss Bayless,' he said, bringing it up to his lips and kissing it. There was a faint answering squeeze from her fingers and he sat forward in his chair and retained the hand in his.

'I feel very tired. Silly really, for there is nothing else the matter with me. Just a dreadful lack of sleep — and peace of mind.' Her voice was far away but her eyes took him in from beneath half-closed curling lashes, and a faint colour washed through her ashen face.

'Do you often get turns like this?' She shook her head. 'I'm rarely bothered with ill health,' she said, and there was a faint spark of the old Violet in her voice. Encouraged, he kept talking.

'Have you had the doctor out to examine you? There is fever in the town, I'm told, ma'am, and it may be that you have contracted an infection.'

'No, sir — It is nothing like that, I assure you.' The musical voice had become sad again. They looked at each other.

She is in need of me, he thought.

He looks so concerned. Would it sound too hysterical if I tried to tell him? she wondered. He was suddenly too important for her to risk being thought nervous in any way. She sighed and pulled herself up among the pillows but left her hand in his.

'This is a very strange house, sir. It has a most alien atmosphere at times — which none of us has ever been able to explain, so I will not try now. All I can tell you is that I remember it being a terrible place as a child but the feeling seemed to go away. Now, suddenly, as soon as I go to sleep, I am beset by nightmares which are quite terrifying. My fear of them leaves me exhausted on waking and when I try not to sleep, I now find they manifest themselves about me in my conscious state. Truly, sir, I am becoming mentally and physically exhausted and I am wondering — pray, do not laugh at such a thought — whether there is something going on in this house which seeks to harm me.'

She stopped and lay, biting her lower lip and waiting for the soothing, cajoling words of one who disbelieves but seeks to comfort all the same.

He frowned, and the pressure on her hand tightened.

'I do not know you well yet, Miss Bayless, so I cannot say whether or not you are imagining these visitations — but at the same time, I feel that I know you well enough already to have the greatest respect for your integrity and intelligence. I don't think that you are imagining things for I, too, feel something very unsavoury about this place, although there is nothing but pleasantness outside in the stables and your charming garden.'

They sat close together and the comfort between them gave them strength.

'Must you stay here?'

She closed her eyes, for the question had been in her own mind for a very long time and was still unanswered.

'Sometimes I feel that I must get away but then I think how difficult it would be to move the stud. Its reputation, after all, is here at Lavenham, and I would not be happy if I had to be without it, for I have always involved myself with my horses . . . ever since I was old enough to ride.'

'Whatever it is, don't attempt to fight it alone,' he said seriously. 'You have already indicated that both Manfri and Rueb are related to you. If you must live in such a destructive situation, protect yourself by having them here in the house too, I beg you. And I would be willing to stay with you also, you know that. I realize that might well be an unwelcome intrusion upon your privacy — but if you find you need me, I shall be at your service.'

Polly had the children to protect, for she would never leave them to Jasper's tender mercies, Violet knew, any more than she would allow them to live under Lavenham's roof. Manfri and Rueb might help, though. They knew about the house and about her, without having to have anything explained. She yearned to pour the whole thing out to Desmond but it would sound too ridiculous, the highly coloured imaginings of a foolish mind.

'Thank you. I know that you would be true to your word, sir, and I thank you for it most devoutly. But I cannot accept your offer, not yet. I shall arm myself with Manfri and Rueb this evening, and if we are troubled as I have been these past two nights, then in the morning we shall bring in the clergy and see if they can rid Lavenham of whatever besets it.'

He remained with her for an hour, drinking the chocolate that Polly brought them and suffering her presence with needle and linens in a seat by the window, a firm but tactful chaperon.

When he rode away, his mood had changed from pleasurable thoughtfulness to one of deep concern. He headed for the deanery.

The Watcher did not see him go. He was back in the parlour and was in the process of removing an area of

214

pavings in the worn flagged floor with hammer and chisel and a pickaxe. If he could reach the temple stones and learn to control the impulses emanating from them before he was drawn back into their period, it was just possible that he could avert his own destruction as well as Violet's.

He worked for a long time on the first paving. It had lain snugly in place for a very long time and had been pressed more snugly into its foundations by the passage of countless feet. The day had long departed by the time it finally moved and he was able to lever it up gently with the point of the pickaxe.

Violet rose and dressed herself during the afternoon. Desmond Heritage's visit seemed to have cleared the air a little. She had slept peacefully after he went and woken much refreshed. There was something very comforting about his presence, as though he had known her a long time and would be a constant companion in the future. It was difficult to see how that could be, though, she told herself sharply, for he lived many thousands of miles across the ocean and would be returning there in less than five weeks. The thought turned her heart over.

Manfri came in to see her just before sundown. 'I couldn't come before, simensa . . . had Autumn Gold in trouble with a lump on 'is fetlock an' had to cut it out. Rueb 'n me, we'll come in an' stay with you tonight, see? Somethen's goen' on in this place, chavi . . . we c'n all feel it — even Polly an' Hester an' they 'ent of our blood even.'

She nodded, so thankful of their support that she could have hugged him. 'Mr Heritage felt it too. I'm so worried, Manfri. What do you think is causing the house to go bad in this way so suddenly?' He grunted. 'Et's always ben bad, Chavi. It was bad when yer Dadrus was abuilden' the place and et was bad afore that even. 'Et's ben bad all the years I've known it . . . but not as it is now, not since our Jess wed Miss Lavinia.'

He rubbed the stubble on his long chin. 'She put up with such troubles from this place, for the sake of yer

215

Dadrus. A real saint, she were. Mind you, she 'ad 'im there to give her support, which must have helped, but there were times — when she were with child especially — when she looked fit to drop.'

He stared at Violet in sudden alarm. 'You ent with child, are yer?'

Violet flushed. For some reason such an idea was most offensive.

'Of course I'm not,' she said brusquely.

'Keep yer hair on. I'm only wiggen' ye. Don't like ter see ye the way you are, chavi. It's not like you, is it?'

She shook her head and the sudden tenderness in his gravelly voice brought tears welling up to prick behind her eyes.

'Let's see it out together, chavi, an' if it's too much, then we'll have ter send word to Saiforella an' Naffie in the forest by Lyndhurst and get 'em over to try an' rid us of these mullos.'

The thought was an added comfort. Aunt Saiforella was Dada's eldest sister and it seemed that she had inherited something of the Romany gift of the six senses.

'Let us all eat together after sundown,' she said, feeling suddenly optimistic for the first time in two of the longest days of her life. 'Polly and Hester can then return with Jasper and the children to your cot, and you and Rueb and I will build up the fire and have a good night reminiscing. There will be no time for mullos if we can make it so.'

There was a kind of anxious jocularity about the evening meal which was out of place with the situation. Everyone seemed in lighthearted mood, as though all would change on the morrow but that this evening was to be enjoyed to the full. Even the children seemed infected and there was more laughter and enjoyment at the kitchen table than Violet remembered for a very long time.

The gathering broke up with regret long after darkness fell. The two women left Manfri and Rueb settled by the hall fire with Violet and a brace of house dogs, and shooed Jasper and the protesting children back to the stable cot.

Without the twins' excited trebles and gusts of laughter ringing in their ears, the house intruded once more upon them and they became aware, each in his own fashion, of the yawning blackness of the gallery above their heads and the coldness which accompanied the night, despite the size of the hearth fire and the pile of logs beside it.

'Tell me about the Hators and the Baylesses,' Violet said to Manfri. When she was a child she had made him relate the story over and over again, for her father was always too busy to be approached thus and it was mostly Manfri who had kept alight in her the pride and curiosity of her blood.

He stretched out his legs towards the leaping flames and took a swig at the ale pot on the table beside him. One of the lurchers moved across from under the dining table and lay down against his feet.

Rueb packed his pipe and lit up, sucking noisily as he drew. He enjoyed these story times as much as the young, for he knew each and every word that would be said — and there were one or two things that he could contribute of his own, if only he could find the words to express them.

'A long time ago in Northern India there was a tribe goen' by the name of Hator . . . . ' Manfri warmed to his story as the words flowed out. He never tired of story-telling. After all, narration was in his blood, for the Romanies are as good at fable and the spoken word as they are at mimicry and seeing the humour in every aspect of living. ' . . . and then they came to Greece and it was a good place to put down for a while. They stayed for a long time, picken' up the language and the customs of the people, and then they moved on again — no one knows why, except that there was always this urge to move in the heart of each of them, to keep moven' towards the West.'

The longcase clock in the hall struck the hour. Eleven long fluting notes.

Violet looked across at the faint glow of its flower-painted face in surprise. The time was passing swiftly and easily. It might be all right, after all.

Rueb reached across and flung another log on the fire.

217

'Gets cold this time o' night,' he said, giving the wood an encouraging shove with his boot and watching the sparks fly up into the chimney-well in a long plume of orange.

It had certainly become much colder since they settled down for the evening. Violet took the shawl from the back of her chair and wrapped it snugly round her shoulders. In the brief pause while Manfri lubricated his vocal chords with another pull at his tankard, she became aware of something in the hall with them.

The house was gathering itself together.

Her heart began to thud and she swallowed, pressing down the fear which lurched into her chest. Don't say anything to the others, she told herself. If it is all in the mind, they will not feel anything, and if it is clear that they are not being affected then it will surely cure my own terrors.

'And the word gypsy, Manfri. Tell us how that came about . . . . '

'Aye, I wonder who was the joker there.' Manfri put down his pot with a bang. He had been drinking steadily for three hours and the fumes were beginning to have an effect on his movements. Rueb had matched him pint for pint but remained stolidly unmoved.

''E must've ben someone like our Naffie, then,' Manfri said. 'Naffie'd tease the sun out 'f the sky if'n it suited him.' He stopped smoking as Rueb's expression caught his attention. He was sitting bolt upright in his chair, listening, head cocked to one side.

'What's up with ye?'

Rueb frowned. He dragged his eyes away from the darkness beyond the pool of candlelight in which they sat, and shrugged uncomfortably. 'Dunno. Nothen', I dare say, bor . . . but dordi, dordi — I suddenly felt as though a snake had passed over my grave. Thought I could see somethen' out there on the stairs but et b'ent there now's I'm talken' about it.'

'Yes, it is,' Violet said quietly. She sat forward in her chair, hands gripping the arms tightly. The coldness in the air had been increasing and now she felt no warmth at all from the fire. Indeed its bright flames had sunk to a sullen glow and, even as she watched, they faded altogether and vanished.

The air was tinged with acrid odours and Manfri sniffed. 'What's that stink, for lummocks' sake?'

'It is what has been trying to get at us all since Dada built this place,' Violet whispered.

She stood up and the two men stood with her, closing together so that the comfort of contact with each other was the one tangible reality.

There was nothing to see. The hall swam in darkness so complete that no light from the lamps penetrated even as far as the stair balustrades.

It occurred to them all in the same moment that the house had become charged with an alien essence drawn from some other place, a being with a will and the power to destroy. Something was watching them. They could feel it as clearly as if they could see it, but all there was beyond the wavering pool of light was the stench of ordure and the faraway sound of frightened horses.

'Pooker it, the horses've got wind of it too.'

'No, Manfri, it's not our horses,' Violet said under her breath. 'It's the ones that come with the creature . . . . '

They stared at each other, and he put out a hand and gripped her arm tightly, seeing his own fear reflected in her face. 'It's all right, Chavi. Rueb an' me're here now. We'll see you safely out of this. Come on, we'll go to the cottage and sleep there.'

She shook her head and a shiver ran through her. 'It's too late. It won't let us . . . . '

Thudding hooves in the turgid air; the shriek and snorting whinny of terrified horses. Hearts thundering in their chests, they pressed together, their bodies jerking with shock as it loomed out of the shadows suddenly and stood, tossing its head on the edge of the lamplight.

'O God in Heaven.' Rueb sucked in his breath.

It was not quite engulfed in shadow, and the guttering

candlelight picked up the wet gleam of its rolling eyes, the sheen on its jet body. There was a froth of slime about the red flare of its nostrils and something dreadfully familiar in its regard. They stared in ghastly recognition as the huge grey orbs fixed them with a glaring lust.

It uttered a shrieking whinny at the back of its throat and lunged forward, beating the stout oak of the dining table with its hooves. There was an explosion of flying splinters like tiny daggers . . . pricking, cutting wherever they buried themselves.

Between the two men, Violet gave a small whimper, slipped down and lay curled at their feet. Manfri and Rueb, rooted to the spot in their terror, scarcely registered the movement of her collapse . . . but in the same instant the creature was gone and they were huddling together in the middle of the empty hall.

They stood quite still, searching the blackness, trying to prepare themselves for the next onslaught, distrusting instincts which knew that it was no longer with them.

'It went when she swooned.' Rueb's voice was husky with shock and he bent down and gathered Violet up in his arms to hide the shaking of his limbs. He took his time settling her back in her fireside chair, patting her hands tenderly between his large rough ones.

'Don't do that,' Manfri said sharply. His cheek was pouring blood where a splinter of wood had cut a jagged graze. 'While she's like that it has nothing of her to fasten on to. It won't come back, see. Pick 'er up and let's get out of this stinking mullos' place.'

The Watcher stood in the gaping cavity in the middle of the room. Only rubble — and more rubble. He was tired from his exertions — so tired that he allowed himself to be borne away, out of that room with its empty hole now two feet deep and seven by four pavings in diameter. The answer was right there, though. Of that they were both agreed.

220

7

As soon as he had celebrated matins, Parson Wilks hurried over to Lavenham in response to Violet's urgent summons. Rueb was waiting and took him across the yard to the stable cot, where the company was gathered in the little kitchen. He was shocked at the sight of Violet's haggard face and the state of Polly Bayless — and even young Hester, the kitchen-maid. All three women seemed to be in a great agitation — Miss Violet, that epitome of coolness and level-headedness, in particular.

Always direct, she lost no time in coming to the point. 'Parson, there is something in my house which is preying on us all and which has reached the stage where we are convinced it means to do us a damage. We all shared a most frightening experience there last night and we have come to the conclusion that whatever inhabits Lavenham at the moment needs to be exorcised.'

He was shaken by the unexpectedness of her words. This was most unlike the Violet Bayless he had known for the past seventeen years. He was accustomed to her sharp mind rejecting the fancies of old wives' tales and idle rumour, but there was no getting away from the fact that, judging by her agitation, she had been greatly disturbed by something.

'I would not presume to argue with such a request from a patron as sensible as you, Miss Bayless,' he said gently. 'What has been happening here?'

He looked from Violet to Manfri and Polly, who hovered behind her. He could not recall having seen such fear in any three faces.

Violet took a deep breath. She was deathly pale and a

light perspiration stood in tiny diamonds on her brow. 'Without putting too fine a point upon the situation, we are being sorely tried by an ungodly presence here.' Her voice was husky and he watched the clenching and unclenching of her fists in her lap. 'At first it was only I who was troubled by nightmares of fire and death and the trampling of horse-like creatures upon me. That began just three nights ago, parson, and I've slept little, if at all, since then. I would have put these dreams down to some failing in my own mind or health in normal circumstances, but last night Rueb and Manfri stayed in the house with me and they, too, were witness to the visitation.'

She paused and clasped her hands together. The parson could see that she was trying to stop the tremble in them.

'It is like nothing that any of us has ever seen before . . . . It is as though we are in the presence of a vengeful spirit which is determined on my destruction, for we are agreed that it is I who am the target. Please, I beg of you, help us.'

The story that slowly emerged under his close questioning turned his disbelief into astonishment and then serious concern — for the apparition was not of human form, they insisted, nor yet was it all creature. It had the appearance of a gigantic horse but at the same time all its responses were human ones, and the feeling that all the Baylesses agreed upon — and little Hester also — was that the thing had not been there before its first manifestation on Wednesday, the twentieth of October, three days before — but was now gaining strength with every visitation.

'I shall go back to the parsonage now,' he decided. 'I will collect the utensils for a blessing of the house and return after Evensong to keep vigil with you through the night. If I am not satisfied by the morning that the disturbance is in your own minds, then we shall approach the bishop and seek permission for a full exorcism. In the meantime, let us go over to the house now and see whether it is clear of trouble during the day.'

It was not easy to return to Lavenham with the memory

of that vicious menace still fresh in their minds. Polly and Hester shook their heads and hung back, but Violet pursed her lips and grimly made for the yard in Parson Wilk's wake. Rueb hesitated and then growled at Manfri. 'C'mon bor . . . give 'er a hand.'

The front door stood open as they had left it. They hung back on the threshold behind the parson, feeling the air, ready to turn and run. The sun was just emerging from the trees which fringed Salterns Lane. It cast a clear pale light over the hall.

The oak refectory table in the centre of the room was as they had left it — its heavy six-inch panels splintered right through as though cleaved by a monstrous sledgehammer. One end had fallen on its side.

Halfway between the hearth and the shattered table, the body of one of the lurchers lay spreadeagled, rigor mortis stiffening its legs into wooden stumps.

Parson Wilks crossed himself and clutched the crucifix he wore in his belt. He stepped nervously into the hall and stood still, testing the atmosphere.

There was nothing . . . no sense of another presence, no sound of those distant horses, no stable smell. Lavenham sat quietly within its foundations, bland as summer sunshine, innocent of all guilt.

'It's all right,' the parson said to the Baylesses crowding the front door. 'Whatever was here last night is not here now.' Three days, Violet thought numbly, later that morning, after the parson had left them. The daily routine had to go on, whatever the interruptions, and she settled at her desk in the study and did her best to concentrate on a sheath of documents from the shipping office. It was only three days since Desmond Heritage had stepped on to the Dell Quay jetty from *Golden Dawn's* longboat and into her life, but already their growing involvement was being shattered by her utter exhaustion and bewilderment.

The Power was completely gone and she was defenseless against the malevolence growing like a canker within the four walls of the house. Desmond had felt the tension in

223

her from the start, and it was going to be impossible to keep him in the dark about the nature of the pressure they were under. But, with Manfri and Rueb as her witnesses, he would surely not dismiss this nightmare as a woman's foolishness.

Violet sent a message to Desmond Heritage's lodgings and he appeared at midday and took luncheon with her while she told him of the previous night's events.

He did not dismiss her explanation as a fanciful woman's dreams. How could he, when she related the whole story standing over the splintered wreckage of the long refectory table. He stared down at it, frowning and biting the side of his lip.

'I do believe all this, incredible as it is,' he admitted in the silence which followed her story. 'It is not the first time that I have heard of such violence. About sixty years ago a whole settlement not far from Boston was afflicted by devilish possession. Can you imagine the horror that that conjured up? It spread through two hundred and fifty families and brought death, disgrace and terror to adults and children alike. The settlement was called Salem and the name is still synonymous with witches and the devil.'

'Lavenham has been afflicted ever since it was built,' she told him. 'We know that it was erected round a group of very ancient boulders, which my father described in detail. He had always felt that they were the foundations of a pre-Christian place of worship. We accepted that whatever dwelt there, or was worshipped there, has an influence still within these walls. But it has never manifested itself in this way before. What have I done in the last three days to anger it?'

'You have met me,' he said quietly.

Eager to be free of the brooding atmosphere of the house, Violet took Desmond Heritage across to the stables, in search of Manfri, for advice on the final selection of the breeding pair of Lavenham horses for him to take back with him to Boston.

The atmosphere was utterly different in the yard, where

the beautiful golden creatures stood nodding and flicking their milky manes in the bright gloom of their stalls. Violet relaxed visibly in this safe and enduring atmosphere of life and activity.

Desmond stood close without actually touching her. He was appalled at the state of her distress, which she clearly imagined she was keeping to herself. There was something very wrong indeed here. He did his best to give his full attention to the lovely Lavenham mare being paraded before him, but the even lovelier owner was deeper in his mind. There were several suitable horses and Desmond was hard put to decide between a beautiful Lavenham-coloured mare and a roan with the Lavenham mane and tail. He eventually selected the former, and settled for a magnificent dun yearling with a white blaze on his nose and white socks. Manfri approved. The colt would be a fine cross with the mare, Golden Star, since his sire was in direct line to Olivas and the chances of breeding a perfect Lavenham were high. The animals would remain at Lavenham until Desmond had completed his business in London, then would be taken in easy stages to Plymouth, whence he was to embark on his return journey to Boston.

He tucked his arm through Violet's as they left the yard, feeling well pleased with his purchases — and acutely aware of her warmth against him. It was a most familiar move and would certainly have been frowned upon in public, but she seemed to welcome it, all the same.

The afternoon had sped by. 'Stay and take tea with me,' she said as they returned to the house. 'Unless, of course, you have more pressing things to do.' There was pleading in her tone and he tucked her arm more closely against him. 'Parson Wilks is coming to bless the house later and I would much prefer to have someone like you here with us to keep our feet firmly on the ground. This sort of situation could so easily degenerate into a sort of superstitious drama, don't you agree? And we'd end up thoroughly daunted and frightened by our own imaginations.'

He examined the face turned so pleadingly up to him.

There was fear again at the back of her eyes, despite the common sense of her words. She might appear to have complete assurance, this tall, cool girl, he decided, but at the moment she was only a bewildered soul, casting round for reality in the midst of nightmare. He put his arms round her without thinking further and held her close against his chest, cradling her head, stroking the gleaming cascade of black hair beneath her lace pinner.

'I shall not leave you in this place until every shadow has been eradicated,' he said, and knew, even as the words were uttered, that this was what he wanted — a woman of Violet's beauty and strength who needed him with the intensity he could feel in her now.

Violet rested her cheek against his ear. She had not meant to provoke a physical contact which was, after all, most unseemly; but now that it had happened she clung to him, safe for this moment and quite unable to tear herself away. Eventually it was Desmond who gently drew back.

'Come now, let me bid Polly give us tea and then I shall insist that you take a little nap until Parson Wilks arrives. Nothing will disturb you, I promise, and we'll have this whole thing cleared up before nightfall.'

He was so comforting. There was authority without dictation in his voice, and she obeyed him gratefully. They had two glasses of madeira wine before Polly bustled in with a tray of tea and sweet cakes and buttered fruit buns. Violet did little more than pick at the food, but afterwards she allowed Desmond to settle her into her chair with cushions behind her head and a shawl over her knees. The nearness of him was a balm, and she ceased to jump at every sound. She watched him on his knees beside the hearth building up a good blaze in the grate, for the house was cold, in spite of the bright autumn sunshine outside. She drifted into a deep, dreamless sleep.

Desmond wandered along the bookshelves which lined the west end of the long room. He found much of interest and finally took down a slim volume of sonnets by John Donne. He settled himself opposite the sleeping Violet and tried, unsuccessfully, to read the lavish poems. The dreaming figure resting so gracefully before him drew his eyes away from the pages, again and again. He sniffed the air, feeling something of its antagonism, watching and waiting. He raised his eyes and looked round the room, probing the shadows and registering the faintly acrid odour of the stables. Odd that, for he had been most impressed by the very sweetness and cleanliness of both the yard and the stalls themselves. He frowned over the little book. The odour sharpened until he stood up and went across to the window and opened the casement. Warm sunshine and sweet autumn air flowed across his face and he drank in the peaceful sweep of lawn and trees curving down to the river bank. There was no stable smell outside the house. It must be coming from somewhere in the room.

He stood, rooted to the spot, heart pumping in his chest. For just an instant, something was reflected in the glass behind the mirror image of his own head. It was gone before he had time to snatch his hand away but it was almost as though it had actually been between him and the glass itself. He spun round, raising his arm in defence — but there was nothing in the room. He examined every corner, feeling guilty at the fear still coursing in his veins. The room was serene and peaceful but for the soft sound of Violet's sleeping breath. She had not moved in her chair and lay as relaxed as before. He stared down at her, frowning, remembering the after-memory of that split second: the furious hatred and red-rimmed animal eyes — huge eyes with distended black pupils and great grey irises.

Parson Wilks appeared again after Matins, as he had promised. He was accompanied by two other clerics.

'On reflection, I decided that there appears to be something here that will give you no rest until we grant your request and not only bless this house, but also carry out an exorcism, Miss Bayless,' he said. 'May I introduce the Reverend David Fishwick, dean of the cathedral, and Augustine Talbot, his curate — with whom Mr Heritage has already spoken on the subject of this place.'

Violet shot a startled look at Desmond, who smiled back with his eyes, straight faced. The tall cleric bowed over Violet's hand. 'Forgive the unheralded visit, madam.' His voice was soft and high-pitched, light as a woman's. He was thin, pallid-faced, with limp strands of dull hair receding from a broad-domed forehead. His pale, lashless eyes inspected her narrowly as she introduced Desmond, noting her tiredness, the quick nervousness of her movements.

'It is some time since such a report has reached me and I confess that I am most interested in the subject of possession. How long have you suffered this affliction, madam?'

Violet regarded him with veiled distaste. 'I am not possessed, sir,' she said tartly, showing signs of her natural spirit. 'You are welcome to examine me if you feel that it will help the situation, but the possession is in the house itself — and it is the house I wish to have purified, not myself.'

Fishwick smiled thinly at her. The woman was obviously stubborn. He would have to control her completely before her devils would leave her.

'Madam, I have no doubt that you believe the culprit to be the house, but buildings are but inanimate things with no soul for the devil to inhabit. Many are the places that I have investigated after reports of violence and evil manifestation, much like your own — but alas, human affliction has always been the root of the trouble. Every time, I assure you.'

Violet sat back in her chair and closed her eyes against the veiled insolence in the man's smoulderingly unclerical expression. 'Then I suggest that, on this occasion, your diagnosis is not correct, sir.'

They stared at each other, suddenly open antagonists.

'This house does not need me to be present in order to

manifest its evil. It has been a place of threat and fear for as long as can be remembered — well before my own lifetime. Please do not come into the house with preconceived ideas, for you will not find ghosts nor poltergeists to grapple with.'

Parson Wilks seated himself beside her and patted her hand comfortingly. 'Calm yourself, madam,' he said quietly. 'We are here to rid this place of its afflictions and the dean has been very skilled in this field for some time past. Pray give us your help, my dear, and try not to be offended by the questions he really must ask you.'

The anger was still in her. 'Lavenham has a living evil in its very heart and always has, you know that to be so, don't you, parson?' she said to him, trying to keep her voice from reflecting the anxiety in her. 'We have done our best to keep the tempo of our lives smooth and untroubled in recent years and there has been no great disturbance for some time — but suddenly, just during the past few days even — something has stirred up a hornet's nest of unpleasantness here and I could think of no better way of getting rid of it than to ask the help of the Church.'

Parson Wilks nodded, a man troubled by his own knowledge of this unhallowed place and its history. 'We will do our best for you, madam. With the help of the good Lord, you will surely be freed of your troubles here before the night is over.'

Something passed between them, disturbing the air as though a gull had swooped across the room. Wilks jerked backwards into the depth of his chair. Fishwick frowned, aware of something; unwilling to acknowledge it. The fine hairs shivered along his arms beneath the sleeves of his cassock as he beckoned his curate forward with a valise of equipment.

'Where may we prepare a small altar?'

The Watcher observed the preparations with interest.

What an intriguing experiment. Would an exorcism in the house eradicate him? It certainly wouldn't dislodge the

229

*Presence, merely add fuel to its fires, for it would thrive on
the blind faith of these men with their incantations and
mouthings. Faith was but an extension of love and could
produce a similar state of seminal ecstasy. He awaited the
inevitability of the outcome with rapt attention, his mind
deflected for an instant from the smoothly mottled boulder
at the bottom of the pit, which he had been brushing free of
earth and gravel with a soft hand-brush.*

'Who has been involved with this apparition, besides your
good self?' Fishwick asked Violet.

Desmond, standing behind her chair, put a hand on her
shoulder. 'In the last three days it has been witnessed by
Polly and Manfri Bayless, Rueben Bayless and Hester the
kitchen maid,' he said.

'How about you, sir? have you seen anything of an
unnatural nature?'

Desmond hesitated, remembering that flash of reflection in the casement glass — and then shook his head.
'Nothing specific, but I am very aware of a most unpleasant atmosphere in the place — as you must also be,
sir. It is here with us at this moment, isn't it?'

Fishwick drew down the corners of his thin mouth and
shrugged. 'Suggestion is the culprit of that, sir. The place
is said to have ungodly spirits . . . and so the human
condition creates them in our minds. No, we must stick to
hard facts, and the first is that the witnesses to the
emanations are all from the one family, but for the servant
girl. This implies, would you not agree, that we may well
be looking at the suggestion of one person influencing the
minds of the others. The evidence from the servant girl
may be taken with a pinch of salt, I feel. I assume she is
the one who took my cape. She seems of the mentality that
would believe anything her mistress tells her.'

Desmond opened his mouth to argue, but the Reverend
Fishwick held up his hand to indicate that no response was
welcome. He turned away to the table that Polly had
brought forward so that the curate could set upon it a

cloth, a pair of small candlesticks, a Bible, a small hand-bell and a crucifix.

'This will not take long, madam. I shall want every member of your household in here in order to bless them and to cast out from you all the canker which is in you. Then we shall tour the house, from attic to cellar, blessing each room — and, afterwards, I have no doubt that you will feel the benefit of God's presence immediately. I do not envisage difficulties — unless they come from you.'

Violet regarded him stonily. This hateful man, so smooth and contemptuous — he was not the equal of whatever dwelt here, however confident he might feel, He was also the wrong person for what he was attempting, since there was no genuine goodness in him. He would only stir up more trouble than he was capable of controlling. Oh, Dada — how I wish you were here, she thought.

Polly went to fetch Manfri and Rueb and the children. They came reluctantly, with Hester, for it was a busy time of day after the horses had been bedded down. They were also in mortal fear, although reluctant to admit it, after the previous night's violence. To set foot over the threshold now seemed to invite disaster.

The twins, James and Grace, came shyly into the parlour, ducking their heads at the three churchmen, and sat on the carpet against Violet's skirt. Jasper, tall and gawky as Rueb and intensely uncomfortable at such goings-on, hovered close to the door with his father and uncle. Polly, with Hester at her shoulder, joined the little group beside Violet within arm's distance of the twins. Manfri and Rueb, never easy in the house, surveyed the scene with blank faces. They had known this kenner since Jess had been unwise enough to build it. They had seen what Violet had seen. They had their opinions on the subject of chasing out mullos — and the antics of these gorgio tompads was already laughable, for how could their beliefs have any strength when they were grounded on a holy war within their own ranks, so that the very essence of their faith was now thinned down to negligible

231

strengths? The old Romany invocations would have been a better weapon with which to attack this enemy.

Fishwick stood at the improvised altar with his back to them. The day was already fading into twilight and the candles had been lit. They flickered like long yellow dancers, casting an uncertain aura about him as he prayed, head bowed.

'O Lord which are in Heaven, have mercy upon these your sinners who are gathered here before you. Forgive them their wickedness and the lust in their unworthy bodies . . . .'

Disgusting creature, Violet thought in contempt, the only lust in this room is in your own body, you wretched crow . . . .

His incantation became heated, the light voice rising to a shrill clarion. 'Forgive the violence you see in this house, where death walks at the side of innocence, unholy alliances are tied and lives taken without retribution . . . .' So — he has been making enquiries, Violet realized. Are we to be subjected to the Inquisition here now?

Outside, the evening sky deepened into a sunset burnished with every shade of orange and red. It filtered in through the parlour windows, flushing their faces, washing like heatless fire over the room's white walls.

Fishwick turned. In his hand was the crucifix, which he raised above his head.

'Cast out the vile daemons from this place, O Lord. I charge you, all you unholy spirits, in the name of the Father and of the Son — be gone from here.' He stood in the rosy light like a hard granite rock, long spiky arms raised high above his head, the cross gripped in his right hand like an avenging weapon. In the last light of the dying sun he was flushed like a man on fire. On either side of him, Wilks and the young curate stood with bowed heads and folded hands, their lips moving in silent prayer.

A nerve twitched coldly at the back of Desmond's collar and he shivered and glanced at Violet. She appeared to be listening to something outside, for her head was cocked in the direction of the hall, her face once more drained of colour.

'Listen,' she said. 'Can you hear it? Listen . . . . '

'Silence, woman,' Fishwick said sternly. 'Say your prayers and await your deliverance.'

But his ears had caught what she was hearing and he turned his head slowly towards the doorway, searching the sudden silence. Manfri, Rueb and Jasper backed away and stood against the wall, the first edge of fear drawing them together so that they stood like rigid soldiers, guardians of the room.

The pulse was all about them in the air, drumming like the beat of a monstrous heart in the bowels of the house. It pervaded the room and became the very blood pounding in the ears. Grace began to weep softly.

'How can you bring innocent children into this,' Violet said furiously to the dean. 'They have no part in the sins you spoke of — and they've never been involved with the house at all. You are bringing down upon us all something more terrible than you can possibly imagine. Stop your incantations and let us go, sir, before this place is the death of us all.'

'There is evil here, woman — and evil must be cast out. It is manifested in *you* . . . the sinning seed of vile fornicators.' His eyes glowed at her and he held the cross in front of him with both hands and made a four-cornered sign with it before turning away. 'Lead me round the rooms,' he ordered Hester, who shrank back behind Polly, shaking her head.

'I am familiar with the geography of the house,' Parson Wilks said timidly. 'I will guide us.'

The three men left the room in slow procession, surplices swinging, and made their way across the dim hall and up the staircase. The Baylesses sat very still, listening to the tinkle of the altar bell and the soft sound of slippered feet on the floor above.

'I don't think the children need be witness to any of this,

you know,' Desmond said quietly to Polly. 'Why don't you take them back to your cot and give them their supper? As your mistress said, they are not involved.'

She shook her head, 'I couldn't let them out of me sight now. We've always been troubled by this place and now we've got to be rid of the badness in this house, for Lavenham's our liven', you see, sir. It's Manfri's and my home and our children's . . . there ent no other place for us to go.'

The sun had set but still the red glow persisted in the room, filtering through the window hangings and casting weird shadows across the walls, wine dark and menacing. The pulse beat remorselessly through their heads, and with it came the stench of the stable midden. The lurchers were nowhere to be seen.

The feet of the clerics creaked over their heads and then went out to the upper gallery, the muffled sounds of their prayerful passage floating down to the tensely listening group in the parlour. Far away in the stable block, the horses were restless, disturbed by something deep down in the forgotten memory of their past. A horse whinnied somewhere closer by, from within the house.

'I want to go home, dai.' Grace whispered to Polly. Her teeth were chattering with fright and she twisted a fat fold of Violet's rose brocade gown in her fingers. 'I don't like it here, dai . . . please let Jamie and me go back now.'

Polly bent and kissed the small upturned face gently. The fear she saw there smote her, reflecting her own.

'You can both go in a little while, I promise. Just wait until the parson has finished blessing the rooms and then we'll go together — and you shall have beef dripping on your bread for a treat.'

The three men drifted away from the open door and joined Violet and Polly. Instinct drove them together and they huddled protectively round her as they had the previous night. She stood up but retained Grace's hand in hers. The clerics were coming down the stairs. Something trembled in the very heart of the house. She suddenly knew with terrible certainty that she must move — now.

'Come quickly,' she said to them all, whisking her skirt round her and pushing the twins in front of her through the doorway. They all moved as one, Manfri and Rueb and Jasper, and Desmond shepherding Polly and a shivering Hester, all streaming out of the parlour on Violet's heels and into the lightless hall.

The little group of clerics stood on the lower staircase. Beyond the yellow candle-glow their shadows loomed monstrously up the stair-well behind them, like crouching animals. There was movement now in the very air, disturbance within the dusk itself: a terrible gathering of unseen forces. An echo of red sunset flickered around them.

The crash which suddenly stayed Violet's headlong flight for the open front door was two-fold. The little altar table in the parlour exploded without warning at their backs, showering Rueb and Jasper with splintered wood and the shattered remnants of the anointing bowls. And ahead of them, in the hall itself, a vast piece of masonry seemed to be tearing itself from the upper walls, for there was the rumbling thunder of falling masonry. Then, with a crash of sickening immensity, a huge, pinkly iridescent column of mottled marble collapsed in a cloud of dust and stone about them.

Pressed against the wall beside the front door, they stared at the shattered stone in horrified disbelief — for there was no marble in the house, no stately pillar as this had once been.

A dreaming kind of recognition drove the breath from Violet. 'Run . . . run for the water,' she screamed, feeling the rising presence seeping over them like mist in a winter marsh, the terrible upsurge of sheer power from beneath the house even now materializing about them.

They cowered, hugging themselves with terror as their heads were filled with the thunder of monstrous, scything hooves — and then it was there, between the hearth and the wrecked dining table, rearing up over the heads of the three clergymen . . . the great stallion with its shining black body and its stench of hatred.

The air shivered about the three men huddled in the centre of the hall, clutching their candles and crucifix, faces livid in the dull violet glow that filtered from the great hall window. The creature billowed like wet black curtains in a high wind, carrying with its image the shrieking of its own agony of destruction. The tall figure of the dean seemed to leap up into sudden height, a vast angular scarecrow as he lifted his gaunt face and screamed at the onrush of those deadly mutilating hooves.

Hands grabbed her and Desmond flung her backwards through the open front door, and they fled out of the house, across the terrace and away down the sloping lawns towards the bulrushes that fringed the river bank.

It was only later, as they crouched wetly among the reeds and watched the house burning, that the words of the dean's screaming incantation − and their appalling meaning − smote her.

I banish thee, vicious Glory, most hallowed Lord . . . I, the servant of Deivos . . . .

He was part of the nightmares which had troubled her childhood and now her nights. He was uttering the words which she remembered with a terror she could not understand. *I am your servant, Deivos . . . I offer myself to you . . . .*

But now it had destroyed itself, for the house was burning. Lavenham was finished.

She felt Desmond's arms tighten round her shoulders and, leaning against him in the chuckling water, allowed herself a sigh of pure relief.

1766

8

John Freeland was feeling his age more and more, he realized with a certain nostalgic regret. He peered at the woman seated across the desk from him. She was not quite handsome, no longer in her first youth, but carried herself with great dignity. She must have been a fine-looking maiden, full of the fire and passion of her Portuguese blood, but now there was just the tiredness of a bitter battle for survival in her sallow face. She sat, black-gowned, on the edge of her chair, one hand stroking the head of the small boy who stood shyly beside her.

Freeland turned back to the documents spread out before him. Their contents brought back a flood of memories and an echo of the strange mixture of fear and excitement which had washed through Apuldram for months — even years — following the exorcism of Lavenham. He had never expected those dark memories to be resurrected. He spread out the largest page, flattening its curling edges with hands as gnarled and soft in age as well-worn tree roots. He had not recognized the writing when he first began to read, and Lawrence Bayless's signature sprang out of the vellum at him like a blow. Looking at it now for the third time, he still felt the recoil of that first shock.

To whom it may concern

The bearer of this letter is my lawful wedded wife, Dolores Bayless, whom I married in Vigo, Portugal, on the tenth day of April in the year Seventeen Hundred and Fifty-Five. I, Lawrence Freeland Bayless, do write this so that, in the event of my death, she and any issue resulting from this marriage may claim my rightful inheritance from my father, Jess Bayless.

Lawrence Bayless

Lawrence dead? Time was a cruel master, cutting down so much life before its allotted time, without apparent rhyme or reason. Why should he himself still be soldiering on at sixty-seven when youth was being laid to rest all about him? Lawrence would still have been quite young — not more, surely, than his mid-thirties. It was so long since he had turned his back on Lavenham that there was no image to be conjured up of Lawrence the man, only of that wilful and attractive boy, so similar to the child who stood before him now, leaning against his mother's knee and looking at him with such shy attention. Lawrence was there in every feature — and his mother, Lavinia, also. Remembering the sweetness which had been the mainstay of his little sister's character, he winked at the child in the heavy silence and watched an answering smile animate his cherubic features.

He turned to the second sheet and found it to be an affidavit written by the priest who had performed the marriage ceremony and, later, baptized the child Charles Thomas Hernando Bayless. The document was counter-signed by a Narcissus Hatherley, Lawyer.

The third document was a letter — a hastily written scrawl, also from Lawrence but obviously penned with some difficulty. The page was stained and some of the ink had run, as though water had been poured across a corner of the sheet.

My Dearest Wife: I commend this note to my good companion, Bernard Lacey, for I am grievously ill of a knife-thrust in the chest and fear I shall not survive the voyage back to Lisbon. Documents which will ensure the futures of you and our little Charles are lodged with Advocate De Pero and, upon receiving this communication, I beg you to retrieve them with all haste and go to Chichester, to my uncle John

238

Freeland, so that Charles may claim the birthright denied him by his father's selfishness.

The security which my lawful Apuldram inheritance will give you both should, at the very least, provide you with the security which our mode of life in Estoril denied you and with the ease and gentility with which I should have provided you in the years of our marriage. I trust, from the bottom of my heart, that Lavenham will enhance the remainder of your lives and the lives of our descendants.

Dear Dolores, I ask also for your forgiveness.

Lawrence

John Freeland raised his eyes and shook his head at the woman, and the regret in his heart was tinged with a pain that etched itself across his lined face.

'Madam, please rest assured that I fully accept the validity of these letters.'

A small sigh escaped her and she sat back in her chair, relief lightening the tiredness in her face. It was all too clear that she had imagined they would not be made welcome in this cold English place.

He continued gently, 'I recognize my nephew's signature and see his likeness even more clearly in your son — but there is a grave misunderstanding concerning the inheritance, Senhora, for your husband's father left very precise instructions in his will, which have, over the years, been carried out to the letter. Lawrence was to inherit the family home of Lavenham and also the shipping business at Dell Quay, as he told you. I wrote to tell him of all the aspects of the will as soon as I discovered where he was living. It is most unfortunate that Lawrence was obliged to stay out of this country in latter years because of the court order for his arrest and the price that had been put on his head. As a result of that absence and inability to claim his inheritance, the house and the Dell Quay Shipping Company went to his half-sister, Violet — who married and went to live in the New England colonies. The shipping Company has been sold, together with her other assets in Chichester. Bayless and Company is no longer in existence.'

Bewilderment replaced the woman's relief. 'But what about the house, sir? Is there not even a roof for our heads, after all?'

Freeland began to perspire freely. He wiped his forehead with his kerchief. 'The house is unoccupied, Senhora, and I expect that it is perfectly tenable,' he said quietly, 'but it is not possible for you — or anyone else, for that matter — to live in it. Tragedy has always followed tragedy there from the moment that it was built and, about ten years ago, Mistress Violet sought to rid it of whatever evil dwelt there by bringing in three men of God to exorcise the whole building.'

The woman stared at him with dark, uncomprehending eyes.

'I was not present on the actual occasion and so I can only tell you what Violet and the other witnesses testified to afterwards. It is a terrible and very frightening tale but we much believe the sworn oaths of no less than nine people, even though it sounds inconceivable. It seems that some terrible presence invaded the house, bringing images of fire and destruction with it. Vile words were put into the mouths of the clergy who were trying to banish the devilish presence. Feeling themselves beset by unthinkable evil, the others ran out of the house and fled to hide in the rushes at the edge of the river. But the clergymen were held by the thing in the house — and, tragically, they died there.'

He paused, clearly much distressed.

'At the time, all the witnesses vowed that the house had become a furnace of flame — but when the parson and his colleagues did not appear the next day and I went with some of the villagers to investigate, we found them dead in the hall — and no sign of fire or destruction, apart from the dining table, which was utterly destroyed. So Lavenham stands today exactly as it stood ten years ago. The furnishings and family treasures are there, ripe for the taking by any ruffian who dares to enter. None will, though. Lavenham has its own guardian, it seems. Now it is avoided by every man, woman and child in the area.'

The woman crossed herself and drew the little boy close to her. Defeat was back in her face, in the dejected droop of her shoulders. The old man smoothed out the letters with hands that shook. 'There are some things in this life of ours which will never be explained, my dear, but that house was both the making and the breaking of the Baylesses. Keep this charming little fellow of yours well away from Lavenham, for it may still reach out to harm him if he once sets foot there.'

He smiled at the child with infinite sadness, for in him was the essence of Lawrence and all the golden innocence of Lavinia. 'It was quite correct of you to come here to see me, as Lawrence instructed, for we are not without means in the family and it would smite my conscience to think of my sister's grandchild growing up in impoverished circumstances through my ignorance. I shall certainly make you both an allowance suitable for your needs out of my own purse.'

Her head jerked up and gratitude lit her face.

'I have no doubt at all that Violet will wish to do the same, once she is advised of your existence. She has three daughters but no son of her own yet, and I am sure that she still retains the same affection for your husband's memory that she had for him during their childhood.'

He stopped her stumbling thanks, leaning across the desk to drive home the seriousness of what he must still insist upon.

'I am quite certain, though, that there will be one proviso from Violet — and that is that you will be supported by the family on condition that neither of you ever sets foot upon Lavenham soil.'

He watched indecision chase across the woman's olive face and then she nodded. The boy leaned an elbow on his mother's knees and scuffed his foot up and down along the carpet. He twisted away suddenly from her restraining hand and came to stand against the desk, pressing his

241

small chin upon its leather top. The yellowing film over John Freeland's eyes made distant objects blurred so, for the first time since they had entered the room, the boy came sharply and suddenly into focus.

They smiled at each other across the desk — and something in John's heart twisted suddenly, for he found himself drowning, as he had done long ago, under the scrutiny of another boy's wide-eyed grey regard.

Part Three

1800-1804

TOM AND CHARLES

1

In the event, it was easier than he had imagined to detach himself from the pain of having the dressings on his hands changed. The removal of pus-encrusted lint and bandages was an agony which he discovered could be forced to the back of his mind — as long as he kept the centre of his attention upon the other, even greater, issues of the moment. He struggled with them now, eyes tightly shut against the sight of Frances's solemn young face bent over him, with a tiny frown creasing the smooth area between her eyebrows. She was good at her job, deft and swift, and the tenderness with which she worked on the burns across his palms was no more than she gave to all her patients, he knew.

'Try not to twitch. I'm being as quick as I can.'

He veered his thoughts away from the pain and concentrated on the stone upon which he had spread his hands. It had been red hot; it was impossible to take that in, for it was just a very ancient boulder embedded in the hardpacked earth beneath the house's foundations. But it had been hot enough to strip the flesh from his palms. The shock was almost greater than the physical blow; and now, even after half a day, he could see no glimmer of explanation. He had given himself little rest during the last five days and nights. God . . . was that all it was since he had opened the oak door, carrying a rucksack and a box of stores, and walked straight into a terrifying kaleidoscope of personalities who bore his own genes imprinted upon their faces.

'There we are. All done. How do they feel?'

The Watcher opened his eyes and looked up into the girl's face.

'Better. Much better, thank you, ma'am.'

They regarded each other for a long moment, which seemed to stretch . . . stretch . . .

After the first terrible months of Tom Heritage's captivity, when every new moment was a nightmare of utter degradation and hunger, the daily act of waking followed a familiar pattern. An inexplicable timing mechanism in his head seemed to set up a warning, moments before the hatches were flung back and the night guards' hoarse bellows dragged him back into the unwanted presence of another day. Sleep was rarely a haven of rest – of forgetfulness. For most of them it was another kind of nightmare, often as violent and uncontainable as the realities of each day. It was, as always, a gradual procedure, the seconds stretching as he hung back, pushing his fear against a force which propelled him, like a leaf on the surface of a stream, inexorably towards that chink of light which was consciousness.

He was, as usual, aware of his own body before the senses acknowledged the enormity of his surroundings. His bladder was full. His stomach was empty. The lice were once again breeding in his crotch.

The sudden screech and grind of the hatchbolts being drawn back brought movements into the reeking air below decks. Dawn was still two hours away, but the guards' raucous urgings spelt the beginning of another featureless day for six hundred and thirty men, prisoners of war aboard the mastless frigate *Fortunée*.

'Two bells of the mornen' watch. Turn out yer hammocks . . . . '

Any icy shaft of frost-laden air drove down from the open hatches through the slats of the deckladders. Men stirred and rolled, groaning, from their hammocks. Moving blindly in the pitch darkness like maggots in the rotten heart of the old hulk, they groped for whatever extra covering they might be fortunate enough to possess, too tired and demoralized to care for the elbows that jutted into each other's ribs, the stench of their night breath and body odours.

'Off yer butts, ye stinken' buggers . . . . On deck at the double or ye'll feel the warmth of me boot up yer funnels.'

The rasping voices, the foul language, the debasement, slid off Tom now so that he scarcely heard the message of contempt in them. Twenty-six months of it had created a defensive shell about his mind and body so that only deeply within himself would he admit to the private but continuing survival of Thomas Bayless Heritage, individual.

He wrapped his thin wisp of blanket round his shoulders, crossing the corners over his chest and securing the ends in his string belt. The trailing corner would cover the flapping rent in his breeches until he could persuade one of the Rafalés to mend it for him in exchange for the week's soap ration.

The reeking air was cold and his teeth chattered like castanets. February was even colder than January this year, and it seemed that English winters went on and on until it was almost halfway through the year before the sun came to warm the slimy timbers of the old frigate.

There was general movement now towards the ladders, and Tom let himself be thrust along among the press of bodies until his bare feet snagged against the bottom rung and he put out his hands and pulled himself upward and out into the pure and freezing air.

A hand gripped his shoulder and thrust him forward impatiently among the gathering swell of men on the windblown main deck. Teeth chattering uncontrollably in the seering cold, they stood hunched close together for warmth, blowing into grey, cupped hands as the dirty tide of ill-clad men continued to erupt from the open hatches. The dawn muster of prisoners on deck: a shifting, pathetic

247

sorting-out of spiritless souls who had once been men fighting proudly under their country's new flag. Tom no longer felt the old repugnance which had threatened his sanity when he and the nine others from his ship had arrived in Langstone Harbour following their capture. They had been thrown amongst ravening creatures who had also once been men; some of them had been confined in this and other prison hulks for ten years and more. There were few amongst them who still resembled self-respecting human beings, for there was little of the human left to respect in many of them. He had shrunk from the ragged, menacing scarecrows with their comical, moth-eaten beards, afraid that he too must soon wear the hollow-eyed uniformity of their despair. There was such desperate depravity in the rotting and shredded humanity, whose only remaining aim was to sustain life at its lowest moral level.

Death became a close companion as dropsy and scurvy and other mortal ills that went hand in hand with over-crowding and disease took their toll — and many sought it as the only escape. Others, like Tom himself, devoted themselves to the very science of survivial. More than two years later, he stood shoulder to shoulder amongst them with almost complete indifference to filth, insanity and constant humiliation, still able to recognize, beneath the matted growth of lice-filled beards, the tiny differences between each bag of bones. Some were Americans and others French or Dutch, and there was even a peppering of mercenaries from Sweden and Africa.

Peering down the shuffling line, he caught the gleam of white eyeballs set in ebony and winked under the bulkhead lamps at Li'l Moses across the deck. A dim toothy flash signalled the answering grin and both men straightened their backs and knuckled their fists at their sides.

"Tenshun!'

The hoarse cry echoed thinly through the ranks. Then the rattle of leg irons being shifted and dragged was stilled.

The master of the *Fortunée* was beginning his inspection. Herbert Furze paddled slowly between the lines of slouching, shivering men, with the first mate at his side and a pair of red-coated marine artillerymen bringing up the rear with upraised lantern poles. This was always the worst part of the master's job, the dawn muster, for he had but lately rolled from a warm bed and breakfast was yet to come. His baleful glance bounced over the ranks, left . . . right . . . left again, like a mouse caught in the bread locker. His gross stomach rumbled anxiously. Suddenly angry, he stopped before a Frenchman slumping half-naked against his companion in a futile attempt to protect himself from the bitter dawn wind.

'Where is your jacket? Were you not issued with one just last week?' The little captain's nasal voice echoed down the lines but few bothered to crane their heads and watch. The Rafalés were always in trouble — and small wonder, for they gambled away their possessions with such fanatical zeal that naked Frenchmen were becoming a serious problem to the authorities, or so it was said. When clothing was put upon their backs, they promptly gambled it away once more until the winter weather finally laid them out. There were few old hands amongst the Rafalés, but those few were the toughest and most vicious men aboard. The skeletal creature grinned back at the *Fortunée*'s captain, his sunken pebble eyes roaming insolently over the overstuffed figure of his gaoler.

'*Allez-vous f'foutre, Cul,*' he said softly through a wisp of drooling moustache, making the insult sound like a caress.

Furze stared back at him suspiciously. He knew few words of the French language and certainly none of the sort that these animals used. 'Get yourself covered or I'll have you put in the black hole while you contemplate my orders . . . and get your hands off that man. I will not have your disgusting wickedness on show before my officers.'

He moved on before the Frenchman's hot eyes could scourge him further. They were little better than a pestilence, these morally corrupt Rafelés, and he thanked

249

his good fortune that there were only a handful aboard now. The colonial rebels, of which there were many, were a much more orderly and controlled group, in spite of the high mortality among them.

He paused once more, beside Tom this time, and turned to the first mate.

'This is the man I was speaking to you about. You, fellow, They tell me that you are an educated rebel and have been giving lessons to some of your less fortunate collegues.'

Tom bowed his head. The intense cold brought tears to his eyes, which irked him. The fool would probably think that he was moved by being spoken to by his master.

'A little mathematics and astronomy, sir.' he said, looking at Furze from a height. The ship's captain was a clear head and shoulders shorter than he, and almost as wide as he was high. He nodded ponderously now, shifting the weight of his grotesque body from one stout leg to the other, and broke wind ponderously.

'Report to the orderly office after muster and get yourself shaved,' he said to Tom over his shoulder, leading his party onwards down the line.

'The man I have in mind is as presentable as he can be in the circumstances,' he said later to his wife across the breakfast table. 'I suspect he fancies himself as being somewhat superior to the rest of us, in spite of his present situation. His papers show that he served for some years in rebel vessels, including two owned by his father, and he was captured west-sou'west of Cape Cod while carrying dispatches. It was in my mind to offer his services to you after he is fumigated, should you feel inclined to make use of his education. What think you, m'dear?'

Mrs Furze's plump, good-natured face lit up and she smiled her pleasure across the white damask cloth. She would never refuse such a rare offer, even though she was unsure what actual use might be made of the poor man. She was in great sympathy with those pathetic wretches so cruelly herded in the hulks — and had been the mediator many times between her husband and the prisoners' committee, as they liked to call themselves. Living in comparative luxury in the master's suite and being a constant reader of her Bible, she felt the deepest anguish at conditions below decks. She had no official voice to raise, and certainly Herbert Furze, with his bullying nature fuelled by the small man's demand for assertion, had little inclination to heed any advice she might offer him — but there were ways and means of making herself heard now and then, and none of those moments had been wasted since she had brought the five children to live aboard the *Fortunée*.

'What they talk to you 'bout durin' muster?' Moses asked as they swabbed down the orlop deck.

'Nothing much. Something about reporting to the orderly office after this and getting a shave. Reckon they might be going to fire our little cannonball at the Frenchies as their latest secret weapon and offer me the command of the *Fortunée*.'

Moses sniggered through clenched teeth. 'Ooh Jericho Jeeeezuz, he don' need no cannon! The way he bin manufacturin' natural gases lately, they jus' gon' point that li'l old man at the French fleet, fill him up with kidney beans . . . and man alive, just listen to him *go* . . . .'

They laughed, heads down, their shoulders shaking, till chest cramps stilled them. They finished sluicing their deck area and Tom threw his bucket and cloth into the slop locker. Somewhere further along the lightless deck a man groaned as his bowels vented themselves. There were too many dropsical men, too many suffering the first symptoms of scurvy, for the benefit of attention in the already overcrowded little sickbay. Mostly they just lay in their hammocks until the last of life flickered out. Five more had died during the night.

He gave Moses a thump in the stomach. 'Save your clowning for our porcine friends. See you later.'

Tom did his best to make himself presentable. He put

251

the comb he had fashioned from a ham bone through his hair and fastened it tidily off his face with a piece of string from his belt. The orderly would see that his stringy beard was shaved before his audience with Mr Furze. A pity — for, scrofulous as it was, it kept a little of the frost off his face. Tightening his breeches and straightening his hop-sack shirt, he tucked the tail neatly into the breeches belt. No stockings to straighten. No shoes to polish. No jacket to check for food stains. He arranged his shawl more closely about his shoulders and made for the orderly office up on the half-deck.

'Ha, it's you.' Furze was sitting behind his desk, a self-important gargoyle, with one square foot resting on a pile of ledgers, busily engaged in exploring the holes in his tobacco-stained teeth with an ivory pick. 'Took yer time, didn't cher?'

Tom looked at the captain's brown and mottled face with inner disgust. The man was such a hideous individual — handpicked for this thankless job, no doubt — with thin gingery hair, receding from a broad forehead, red-rimmed eyes of an indeterminate blue, an angular hooked nose and a gash of a mouth which seemed to rip his head in half, the narrow lips constantly agitated by a nervous twitch.

'I came as soon as I had finished deck duty, sir. Gotten a shave, like you said, too.'

He stood across the desk from Furze and submitted to a long, silent stare from the baleful, deeply pouched eyes. His lower face felt indecently naked. There was a broad area of white chin and jaw that had not felt the chill air for a very long time.

'All right . . . now tell me about yourself. I'm consider-ing you for certain duties which will be more to your liking and education than your present situation. Hence the need of a shave. Name first, then age and background with qualifications. Speak.'

'Heritage, sir. Thomas Bayless Heritage. Thirty-two years old and unwed. Seaman by profession. Born and brought up in New Midhurst by Boston, in the State of

Massachusetts, Continent of North Anerica. Three older sisters and one brother, sir.'

'What nationality are your parents?'

Tom gazed at Furze's hawk nose. There was a dewdrop forming on the tip. Others had formed and fallen before it, for there was a damp patch on the left lapel of his blue jacket.

'Why, they are Americans, of course, sir.'

Furze banged the desk with a pudgy fist. 'We are not here to have a political discussion, Heritage. Give me a straight answer. Where were your parents born?'

Tom smiled at the man's antagonism. He was a person of limited intelligence and they were both well aware who was really in charge of the interview.

'Well, sir, it depends on how closely you wish to refine their ancestry. They were both born in Sussex, not far from here, in fact, but my father has lived in New England for near on fifty years now. My mother — well, she was born close to Langstone but she was a gypsy and they have a mixture of foreign bloods in them too varied to learn much of. I always reckoned my mother was more continental than English.'

He watched a series of expressions chase across the captain's stolid face. The drop of moisture trembled in one ginger-haired nostril. It dropped on to the damp stain on his lapel.

'Thomas Bayless Heritage, you say. Is the Bayless your mother's name, by chance?'

Tom nodded, suddenly wary.

'Well, well, well . . . . ' Furze speared a thin string of chewed meat from a newly discovered cavity in a back tooth. He gazed at it for a moment before flicking it off the point of his toothpick on to the floorboards. He changed the subject abruptly.

'I wish you to attend Mrs Furze and my sons each morning after your deck duties are completed. You will ensure that you are clean and free of lice, and then make yourself useful to her in any way she sees fit to employ you. You will clean-shave yourself daily and be neat and respectful at all times. She will receive you in my stateroom immediately. Go.'

Tom, bowing, withdrew and stood outside the office door for a moment to collect his thoughts. He had long hoped for this position. Service in the officers' quarters was the job most sought-after amongst the prisoners, for it meant working in warm rooms, in a greater state of cleanliness, and there were already two prisoners acting as mess stewards to the officers. But to be with Mrs Furze meant kindliness as well as the possibility of little gifts of meat and fruit. He took a deep breath, straightened his shoulders and made his way down the passage to the stateroom, putting from his mind the captain's odd reaction to the name of Bayless.

Mrs Furze was no more comely than her husband, but there was about her such an aura of good nature that it stood her well in stead of beauty. Beneath her pinner, her round pudding face was accentuated by the bunches of fat, mousy-coloured sausage ringlets bunched on either side of her red cheeks. Her eyes were small and struggled to do their job from between twin bulges of cheek and brow. There was a large brown mole sprouting a couple of strong black hairs beside one nostril. She was taller than her husband but had spread nearly as widely, and the wrap of her fichu and the whale-boning of her corsetry were hard put to keep her body in a recognizable shape. At the same time there was a comfortable easiness in her manner to which Tom warmed as he stood inside the stateroom door, respectfully attentive.

She had been quite excited at the thought of having a servant of her own, and she was impressed by the look of the gaunt, dark-haired man standing quietly, one shoulder leaning against the lintel. In some prisoners this casual stance might have implied a certain insolence, but she saw none in this man's pinched but serene face.

'Come over and let me see you better.' She said, motioning him forward.

He smiled and came across the room and stood with his hands holding the top of a high-backed chair, as relaxed as though he were in the presence of someone known to him.

He was older than she had imagined, but maybe it was simply the privations of his existence that had lain those extra years upon once young shoulders, she thought. He was tall and, despite the wasting in him, she could see that his was a lightweight frame with broad shoulders and long legs. His blue-black hair was neatly tied back into the nape of his neck and the pale-chinned face that returned her perusal with quiet courtesy was filled with a private strength within its gentleness. The eyes that regarded her from beneath straight brows were the colour of the sea in winter, but there was no chill in their expression, only a calm dreaminess that was content to await her command.

Her questions were about himself and his capabilities, and he gave her the answers willingly, knowing that they held no traps.

'I can teach your sons mathematics, ma'am,' he said, seeing that she wished to use his mind while appearing to utilize his body. 'I can teach them to navigate by the stars and, were we living on the shore, I could show them the ways of the small wild creatures that live in the undergrowth. As it is, from here I can only tell them of the birds that fly overhead and of the fish that live in the sea beneath us.'

'That would do very well for a start,' she said quickly. 'My children are not making progress in their studies with Mr Dalby in Emsworth, and it would be so much easier for them to have their lessons here with you for four hours each morning than for them to be taken ashore in all weathers, as they are presently doing. I shall be going to Portsmouth tomorrow to visit my mother and will take the opportunity of equipping the boys with slates and chalks. They will be ready for you to commence your duties on the third day from today.'

She stood up from her chair and moved round the table towards him. Her gown was covered in a pattern of fat pink roses unsuited to her girth.

'I hope that you will find some relief from your troubles in these mornings with us,' she said with a little hesitation. 'Before you begin, I shall give you some of my own concoction to rid your hair of unwanted passengers.' Her eyes twinkled at him.

He looked down at her shiny red cheeks with the bunches of ringlets framing the kindly face and the very tenderness of those light words smote him.

'I thank you most kindly, ma'am.' he said gruffly, and turned from her, bowing his head.

A bitter wind lashed his face as he emerged from the master's quarters. He felt nothing, his mind already sifting through the events of the morning. He tucked his freezing chin against his chest and, butting through the icy gusts which scoured the main deck, scrambled down the main hatchladder in search of his companions.

'Apple pie for luncheon from now on, my brave fellows,' he said, coming upon the little group, heads bent over rough-hewn dice. He squatted down and they made room for him.

'I'm to teach our Toad's little tadpoles in the mornings. Mrs Furze is a good, warm-hearted woman, and I foresee some tasty little titbits coming the way of the *Free States'* crew in the very near future.'

A wizened face peered round the bulk of the capstan. There was something in the sunken eyes that was not quite envy, not quite hunger.

'Judgen' by the size of that one's titbits, reckon you'll soon find you've bitten off more than you can chew, brother.'

Tom turned his back on the man.

It was only much later that the thought occurred again to him: Why had mention of Mama so interested the Toad? The question kept nibbling at him, burrowing deep. It still hurt to think of home, for it conjured up a haven of peace and plenty, where Mama ruled supreme in the house and Papa governed all beyond. They were a united family — Jane and Philippa married, and dear Catherine long promised to Caleb's best friend. Caleb too would be wed by now, for arrangements had been underway before Tom's capture.

If only there had been some way of making the tenuous postal arrangments more secure, the men would have felt less abandoned even by their own Revolutionary Council. Letters kept them alive in their dungheap of a prison, kept their imagination filled with hope and their tongues wagging. But letters were such infrequent treasures and there had been no news from home for several weeks now. There was a great closeness between those of the crew of the *Free States* who had remained in one group. The rest of their crew, including the captain, were scattered between Forton Prison at Gosport and Pendennis Castle in Cornwall, where all American prisoners were taken immediately after capture, for redistribution.

The men on the *Fortunée* acknowledged Tom Heritage as their first mate and leader, and had a healthy respect for one whose father was a member of the Revolutionary Council. It had, after all, been Desmond Heritage's persuasive arguments which had inspired many of them to volunteer their lives to free their country from arrogant and distant Georgian misrule.

Prison had not, they discovered, made equals of them all, even if their sufferings and humiliations were shared equally; there were a few who resisted the fall into insanity and sickness, and they were the rocks to which the others clung. Tom Heritage was one. The giant African Moses another. The two men, instead of competing with each other for the men's support, closed ranks together in friendship and mutual respect. One day soon the parole board would register their existence and give a little more freedom to some of them. One day soon a more fitting captain with kindlier feelings for American rebels would replace the Toad. One day soon . . . .

'Ooh man, I heard the sweetest li'l tale today you ever did hear,' Moses said to Tom after they had been battened down for the night and most of the lanterns extinguished. 'Me and Osgood were abowlin' our bales into Hayling warehouse and came to rest to hear talk between two overseers. It seems that our very own li'l Toady is being prosecuted by a local farmer. Remember those sheep he had us round up in the marsh a fortnight back? Well, we thought he'd bought them, didn't we? But oh, no'dy no . . . he just up an' took 'em all without so much as a "please, sir" . . . and when he came to present them at market for to gain the full price, rumour led the rightful owner straight to Furze and there was a fine scene — and now he is to pay dear for his greed.'

The men who had heard the whispered tale knew in their hearts that they slept, for once, a deal easier than did the captain of the *Fortunée*. They hugged themselves with glee at his discomfort and plotted in the reeking darkness to contribute to it further.

Muster the next morning was a livelier affair than usual. Furze sensed an unusual anticipation in the silent men as he came out on to the main deck in the biting dawn. Another heavy frost had rimed the ugly clutter of wooden shebangs growing like warts from the upper decks; they housed the galley and sickbay and gave the old hulk the grotesque, top-heavy appearance of a hunchback. Furze had completed the length of only one row and was halfway down the next when an odd commotion made him pause and cock an ear. Far away at the very back of the ranks a muffled bleating filtered through the packed rows of men. The corners of his mouth turned chinwards as he passed slowly down the lines. There was, he saw, a growing insolence in the wolfish faces on all sides of him. He quickened his pace. The sound grew until it seemed as though a flock of monstrous sheep had invaded the *Fortunée*. Furze's nervous tic fibrillated his lower lip furiously.

Now the scarecrow men were openly *baa-baa-ing* around him and he turned on his escort in fury.

'Stop them immediately!' He roared, bouncing up and

down on the balls of his feet with rage, in which ill-disguised fear now played a keen part. The marines shouted round him at those men within their reach, threatening them with raised muskets.

The prisoners took no notice except to increase the volume of sound. Weary and dispirited throats suddenly caught fire and were uplifted, and the message of their contempt broke from them in exalted howls, catching the heartbeat of the next man and then the next. *Baa! Baa!*

'Silence!' roared Furze, a dark flush turning his pumpkin face into beetroot.

BAA BAA . . . BAA BAA . . .

With horrible, dawning embarrassment he realized that they had learned of his summons. Almost beside himself with rage and mortification, he puffed his chest out until he seemed in danger of exploding.

'Get back below decks, all you maggots! Go on, get down there – *now!*'

The guards were frightened by the sheer uniformity of the revolt and were all too aware of their inadequate numbers. They laid about them freely with the flat ends of their muskets, the toes and heels of their boots, with elbows and balled fists. Frail bodies fell beneath the blows and trampling feet, and were swept back down the hatches into the unaired miasma of their night's expulsions. The pen, roped off from the deck-ladders to other levels, was suddenly empty. When the last man was down, the hatch covers were slammed shut and bolted – and the *baa . . . baa* continued, a chorus muffled and contemptuous below the damp deck planking. The din continued for the rest of the day and by four o'clock in the afternoon a boatload of port officials, alarmed by the distant sound of rebellion, arrived with complaints from the authorities.

Six hundred and thirty men were put on half-rations for the following two days. It emphasized the ache of hunger in their stomachs and increased the mortality rate, but there were no complaints. It had been worth it just to see the rage and fright on the Toad's face and the worried consultations of panicky port officials.

Five days after the 'Sheep Revolt' a new supplies contractor for Langstone came aboard to inspect the *Fortunée*. It was a day of watery sunshine, the first of that year of 1802, for January and February had been filled with icy snowstorms. Now, as the end of the month slid into March, a lull brought sudden clear skies washed clean and pearly to silver the harbour waters lapping the four decaying hulks.

'The new contractor's on his way,' Mrs Furze said to Tom as he prepared the day's texts for his five pupils. They were dull children, but clearly found him more personable than their previous tutor and did their best in order to ensure that he stayed with them. Their mother always looked into the schoolroom at the beginning of each teaching session, and sometimes during the morning, to reassure herself that they were not misbehaving.

'Let us hope that he is of a more generous inclination than was his predecessor,' Tom said to her with a rueful little smile that took the sting from his words.

Captain Furze brought the new contractor into the schoolroom an hour later. He opened the door and ushered in the visitor as Tom stood behind the chairs of the two eldest boys, looking over their shoulders at the sums being wrought so painstakingly upon their slates.

'Here are my sons, sir, hard at work as befits their years. Their tutor is an American prisoner being put to good use, as you see.' His mahogany face was like a polished turkey cock's and the tic in his lower lip trembled furiously.

What's eating him, all of a sudden? Tom thought.

Furze seemed to swell, as he often did from both anger and extreme personal gratification. 'This man's name is somewhat similar to your own, Bayless. Did you not tell me that your mother was born in these parts, Heritage? That her name was Bayless also?'

Tom's head lifted from the perusal of a slateful of bad sums. He looked across the room at the tall figure standing behind the little captain, doing his best to appear unconcerned.

'That is correct, sir.'

The new contractor was elegantly clothed in plum brocade, bringing a welcome splash of colour into the little school cabin. His head was proud and wigless, and crowned with a fine thick growth of clean crimped hair the colour of a new guinea. There was something a little foreign about the palely aquiline features, but as the two pairs of eyes met, silent recognition passed between them.

'How interesting. I'm afraid I must hasten on now, Mr Furze. Be kind enough to continue our perambulation.' He inclined his head to Tom and turned away. Furze followed, disappointment turning his face into that of an unhappy gargoyle.

Bayless — Furze had called the new contractor Bayless. Something suddenly lifted in Tom's chest and fluttered there like a bird caught in cupped hands. They had looked at each other with Violet Bayless's great grey eyes and the instant shock of recognition had been mutual.

2

The acute discomfort of the *Fortunée*'s captain over the
heavy damages awarded against him brought unexpected
benefits to the prisoners. They lost no opportunity in
poking fun at their gaoler by literally bleating him off the
vessel if he issued orders which their prisoners' committee
thought to be unjust. The result, during the following
weeks, was a definite easing of the pressures laid upon
them by the guards. A further improvement in the misery
— which had nothing to do with the Toad — went
unnoticed by most, and that was that the new contractor,
whilst cutting down the spending of the officers' mess, was
definitely delivering bread, soap and victuals with greater
regularity than had any of his predecessors.

Charles Bayless's dourly elegant appearance quickly
earned him the nickname of 'the Snake' among guards and
prisoners alike. There was something slightly repellent
about his gaunt countenance, with its bloodless coldness
and the washed-out grey-blue eyes, deep-set in shadowed
sockets. His long, stooping figure was always impeccably
clothed, with no hair on his head out of place, however
windswept his passage out to the hulk might have been.

He made no effort to engage Tom in conversation;
indeed he ignored him completely on the few occasions
that they met. Although Tom was certain by June of that
year — after receiving confirmation from his family — that
the contractor was his first cousin, there seemed little
chance of claiming this relationship.

Mrs Furze was not slow to notice Tom's interest in Mr
Bayless when he was aboard to dole out the weekly rations
or check on his officiating clerks. After his duties were

262

completed he could usually be induced to take a glass of claret in the stateroom and the pleasantries of their conversation would naturally include enquiries after the health of the contractor's family. By such casual means, she was able to give Tom a fairly detailed précis of Charles's family life.

'I have just been taking tea with Mr Bayless,' she said to him one afternoon, as spring at last warmed gently into summer. He was in the stateroom, squatting on the floor beside an open casement, mending a chair whose leg had buckled under the unreasonable weight of its owner. He looked up quickly, and for just a moment his eyes were filled with such eager anxiety that her heart bled for him. He dropped his head again and addressed his attention to the evil-smelling fish glue beside him. The contents were beginning to congeal and would have to be reheated.

'He tells me that he has two sons. His home is in Chichester, you know, so he is not greatly inconvenienced by travelling to Langstone.'

Another time, she said, 'Mr Bayless spoke of his elder son's birthday this week and that he shared a tea party with the lovely young daughter of Lord Lennox at Goodwood House.' She sighed and smoothed her little fat hands across the flowered taffeta of her gown. 'How pleasing it would be to move in such refined circles. Of course, it is clear that Mr Bayless is accustomed to such company, for he is so cultured, don't you think? How my boys would enjoy the freedom of a property such as Goodwood — but to be sure, I'm talking to the air, am I not, for you have not been there and cannot know of the sumptuous new mansion the Duke of Richmond has just built from the old place.'

Slowly Tom formed the beginnings of a picture of Charles Bayless. He was about ten years older than Tom, which surprised him for he looked more, his parchment skin already etched with a tracery of fine lines. The two Bayless boys, Mrs Furze told him, were close together in age and their mother was always in delicate health, with lungs which gave cause for concern during the months of winter. It sounded a rather remote family. Not at all like ours, Tom thought with longing, for theirs had been a noisy, happy, loving upbringing by parents who cared for each other as much as they cared for their sons and daughters.

Lessons with the five Furze children ended each day at two o'clock in the afternoon. Tom was then given meat and pickled cabbage with his bread, and sometimes there was even an apple — a rare delicacy. He ate in the schoolroom after the children had gone, and it was an hour that he enjoyed for he had the peace and privacy of the little cabin to himself while he ate and slowly corrected his pupils' work.

He was sitting at one of the children's desks after school one day, busily swabbing up the meat juice on his dish with a crust of fresh bread. He looked at the long gash on the back of his hand with grim satisfaction, for another of those creeping French varmints was laid out in the sick bay with scant hope of survival.

Life had become so cheap. His whole attitude to the sanctity of life and death had altered during his confinement. He wondered, without greatly caring, chewing the gravy-soaked bread, whether he would ever again feel guilt and regret for terminating the life of another human being.

He had not intended to maul the little rat quite so badly. It had all been too quick for rational behaviour. One moment he and Moses and Dick Sturdee were leaning against the deck-rail, watching the shadows lengthen over the distant shore, and then he sensed something behind them. He whirled round just in time to see the man put skeletal fingers deftly into the pouch swinging at Moses' hip. Something welled up in him and he clutched the man by the throat and turned him round. The Frenchman gasped and twisted like an eel in his grip. There was a flash of metal, and the little knife which was suddenly in his hand flicked upwards and across Tom's knuckles. Blood flooded out of the gaping cut and streamed across his wrist and down on to the man's thin neck. The sight of it had an odd effect. Something exploded in his head and he took the skinny body with a strength he had not guessed at, slamming it again and again against the deck-rail.

Others sought to part them but he had a two-fisted grip on the Frenchman's throat, and he gritted his teeth and squeezed, ignoring the rattle in the man's throat, the terrified eyes bulging in their sockets. Kill him . . . tear him apart . . . blot him out, something raged inside him. Hands grasped his rigid fingers and prized them apart. The man fell away from him and was pushed aside.

'C'mon, brother.' Moses' voice in his ear was soft, persuasive. The fury faded and the red glare in his eyes drained away, leaving him trembling and filled with confusion.

'Don't know what got into me there,' he muttered, as the three of them left the little crowd grouped round the crumpled body of the Frenchman. 'I saw the little runt go for your pouch. I was just going to give him a good hiding and then something seemed to make me want to squeeze the life out of the thieving little sod.'

'Should've let 'im get on with it too,' Dick Sturdee grunted. In his opinion, those filthy Rafalés were a constant danger to any God-fearing man aboard.

The incident was only one of many, but Tom had not been involved before. Now he was shaken by the memory of the event, not because of what had taken place but because of the ferocity of his own reflexes — and the extraordinary pleasure that had, for just an instant, lapped through him as he had squeezed the man's throat and felt the life jerking out of him.

The door opened behind him. He turned, thinking that it was Mrs Furze coming in to discuss her children's work with him — but it was not. It was Charles Bayless.

'I hope I'm not disturbing your meditation,' he said with unaccustomed diffidence.

Tom shook his head. 'I was just finishing the food

265

which Mistress Furze kindly provides.' He waited for Charles to explain his presence.

'Well, cousin . . . I thought it was time for us to have a quiet conversation, for it seems that we *are* related. I had doubts until I discovered that you are the son of my aunt Violet. It is regrettable that we have to meet as our countries' enemies rather than as blood brothers. May I join you?'

He unbuttoned his coat and sat himself down across the schoolroom table. They inspected each other, taking in the facial lines, the contrasts in colouring which divided them — the grey eyes which betrayed their bond. Tom still said nothing. In truth, he suddenly felt an unexpected mixture of fear and attraction for Charles. The washed-out colouring was the antithesis of what he might have expected from any relative of his, knowing that the Baylesses were all dark with an almost Latin look to them. Since Charles had also had a Portuguese mother, it seemed inconceivable that this very blond, almost foppish English gentleman was so closely related.

'You don't much resemble any of us,' he said at last, embarrassed by the drawn-out silence.

Charles laughed, and with the laughter came a softening to the coldness in him and his face warmed into an almost shy pleasantness. Tom felt himself relax a fraction.

'I'm told so,' Charles said comfortably. 'It seems that I am a throwback to my grandmother, Lavinia Freeland, who was very blonde and fair-skinned, much more so than my father. All my Freeland relations are on the fair side. I have bridged the gap in my sons, it seems, for one is as dark as my mother and the Baylesses, and the other is Freeland again and very fair. Are you wed? Do you have a family of your own?'

'No,' he said. 'I have been at sea for too long. There was a girl but . . . . ' He shrugged and grinned ruefully. War had been his only love since he was old enough to offer himself to it. 'I have three sisters, apart from my brother Caleb. They have been women enough in my life to make sure I kept well clear of matrimony for as long as possible. All that squabbling and tale-telling. I miss it now, though. I reckon I shall surely settle down and be the quietest of husbands once this strife is resolved, and make me some sons — all the better to defend our country in the next generation.'

Charles leaned back in his chair. Bright daylight, slanting through the cabin ports, etched small pockmarks along his cheekbones.

'You and I may not admit to our relationship before others,' Tom said, 'for it would lead to suspicion and trouble for both of us, but here and now we are alone, sir. Pray, tell me more of yourself. Do you not live at all in the old family home now? Mistress Furze has told me that your home is in Chichester.'

He watched a guarded look leap into Charles's face. 'Look,' he said hurriedly as Charles opened his mouth to speak, 'What in heaven's name is the matter with Lavenham — for I see the same expression on your face now as my sisters and Caleb and I have seen on our parents' faces if ever we tried to question them.'

Charles rubbed one side of his long jaw as though he was trying to erase something from it.

'Lavenham is a cursed house,' he said finally. 'I was brought up within sight of it but I have not been there. My mother promised my great-uncle John Freeland that neither she nor I nor our descendants would ever venture there, for its history is such a record of death and disaster and things unexplained that he was convinced whatever lurks there seeks to harm the Bayless family — and any other who disturbs it, also.'

'I cannot believe that,' Tom interrupted. 'Your father was born there and so was my mother. They spent the whole of their childhood there without apparent trouble, and our grandfather lived there from a young man until he died.'

'Yes — and do you know how he died?'

Tom stared at his cousin. The pale eyes blazed and

there was something in them that he could not quite fathom. It was difficult to drag his gaze away. He shook his head. 'I understood that he had a stroke.'

'He did . . . oh yes, that is quite correct — but his death came about when the crippled sister, whom he had cared for all her life, bludgeoned him to death with a brass candlestick . . . .'

Tom stared at him, frozen. 'Who was that sister?'

'Amy Bayless.'

'But . . . .'

Charles dropped his eyes. He seemed suddenly uncomfortable. 'Look, cousin, there are many things from the past that are better left unsaid. It is more than fifty years since those tragic things occurred and, except for your mother, the participants are no longer with us. Things happened then which we cannot explain. Lavenham is a most evil house. May we speak of other things, if you please? I hate even to say the name of that place.' His pale face looked pinched and gaunt and more sepulchral than ever.

Tom sat silently chewing his lip for a moment. He had to know about Lavenham. The name, with such a delightful lilt to it, had always conjured up pictures of a charming sprawling mansion, dignified and huge with turrets . . . even battlements, for that was how, as children, they had imagined great English houses to be. From his earliest years it had called to him. Somewhere at the very back of his mind there had always been a need to be there — almost a yearning for something loved and lost.

Charles watched his face. Then he stood up, and there was kindness and regret and something else in the washed-out eyes as he held out his hand to Tom.

'I think I had better take my departure now, cousin. Think of what I have said of that place and let us not talk of it again.' He took Tom's hand and shook it warmly. The grip was firm and cool.

Tom watched Charles as he buttoned his coat and made for the door.

'If you are in need at any time, Mrs Furze will always be able to get a message to me.'

'I need only one thing, cousin, and that is my freedom.'

Charles bowed. 'The one thing that I can do nothing about. It is my great regret, I assure you, sir.'

Then he was gone as quietly as he had come, closing the cabin door behind him with scarcely a click. Tom slowly picked up his dish and empty tankard and returned them to the little pantry that housed the officers' tableware.

Lavenham! the name attracted him but repelled him also now. Why had mother not told them more about it? With an ocean as vast as the Atlantic between them, how could it harm them from that distance? Amy Bayless — he had known that she was Mama's mother, but that she was also Grandfather Jess's sister and not his wife had not once been even hinted at. She had died, they were all told, as a cripple, and in her last years had been confined to her bed. It seemed unlikely that she would be able to commit such a crime upon one to whom she was so devoted if she was unable to walk. So many questions — and out of each one, another and another now sprang.

He buried himself in thought, curled up in a corner of the main deck behind the galley, oblivious to the warmth of the sun on his head, to the flies which hung about the ship, settling on eyes and mouth. Food for serious thought was rare in such confinement, and today he had been given a veritable feast.

The letter which arrived from Tom in England had taken four months to reach the house at New Midhurst, four miles south of Boston. It lay in Violet Heritage's lap and she sat in her chair with eyes closed, pale-veined hands folded across the single, tightly written page. The questions that he asked had been asked by the children since they had stood at her knee, and yet they still created this hard knot of fear and loathing which churned her stomach. He had met Charles Bayless, described him, related the conversations they had shared. Charles — he was nothing to her, this child of Lawrence. It was enough that she had helped to finance his upbringing and education, that she had acknowledged his gratitude graciously enough, that he had not wasted her generosity but was well thought of in Chichester and now was obviously doing his best to see that the sufferings of the prisoners in the hulks were eased in any way he could. But he was Lawrence's son, and within him surely dwelt an echo of that weakness and cruel greed which had turned her from the father.

Time, in many ways had indeed been the great healer. She no longer thought of Lawrence with all the pent-up hatred of her youth. He had caused the death of Giles Croucher soon after their betrothal had been announced, but he was long gone from Lavenham by the time she had met Desmond Heritage. Her life with him had been filled with a happiness and contentment that she had never known in youth.

All gone now — all gone.

The late summer had taken him gently from her and now the fall was blanketing his grave with a carpet of yellow leaves.

How was she going to write this next letter to Tom with such news . . . that Papa was gone and now Catherine also, in childbirth? Dear child, dear sweet Catherine, with her father's bone structure and her mother's headstrong will. She had thought that Catherine would always be their youngest one — but then, five years after her birth, Caleb was born, and a year later, Tom. Sons at last to a man who had hungered for them while loving his three daughters with such gentle passion.

The years in Boston and then Midhurst had taken up all her attention so that she thought only very occasionally of Lavenham, and even then only when she woke in fear from some unremembered dream — and knew that her memory was reliving those last terrifying days and nights there. Now here was Tom, within a few miles of Apuldram and filled with curiosity that Charles's very fear of the place had only fanned into what seemed like becoming a dangerous obsession.

Uncle John Freeland had mentioned in one of his letters that Charles appeared to recall nothing of the occasion when, as a small boy, he had strayed into the Lavenham grounds and then into the house itself. Whatever had happened to him there was now lost deep in the furthest recesses of his mind, for he could recall nothing of that visit, save to cry out against the terrible bees in his nightmares.

The Lavenham bees.

How well she remembered the bees — and the sight of her mother lying in the leafy orchard rich with summer splendour — there had not been one glimpse of her beneath that dreadful droning cocoon of vengeful bees. Her body had seemed to undulate with the movement of their wings in a terrible brown wave of death.

She shivered and opened her eyes in an effort to wipe the picture from her mind.

Tom and Charles. Her heart cried out against the meeting. Tom was the only one of her children to bear his mother's great grey eyes, but he seemed to have no sign of the terrible Gift that accompanied their strange colour in the case of her father, and Lawrence and herself.

She had watched Tom closely as a child, in fear and dread of the possible consequences to them all if he showed signs of possessing that Gift of Death — but he had grown normally, an attractive and mischievous small boy, becoming a tough young patriot with all his father's devotion to his country's struggle. He developed a strong personality with a fine disregard for either the business, which Caleb managed, or for the daughters of their neighbours.

My dear son . . . . How am I to tell him that in the space of but half a year he has lost his father and the sister who was closest in his affections? Violet wondered. How am I to tell him that the answers to his questions are still too painful to put on to paper or even into words? You come from a kind of hell, son. That is how your mother was begotten and whence she came. Think only of your father, who was all that was good and had nothing in his

271

background of which he was ashamed. *Bayless*. To see the name written down in your hand brings sudden terror to me, my son. I thought that in this great world of ours, I had put a large enough ocean and sufficient miles between us all and that dreadful place and those who remained close to it, that the two might never meet until all trace of those memories had died . . . .

News of his father's and his sister's deaths reached Tom shortly before Christmas. The letter came with the first great bag of correspondence for the prisoners to be brought by the American agent, Joe Trotter, for close on four months. Trotter lived in London and appeared to trouble himself infrequently about the welfare of the Portsmouth and Langstone American prisoners.

Tom stared, dry-eyed, across the shining deck where wind and recent rain had scoured it of the litter of its overcrowded cargo. The landscape had lost its colour and was etched in shades of black and white, the marsh robed in thin mist. He saw nothing, felt only the shock of initial loss, that he would never again see his father – never again share his woes and joys with the ever sympathetic Catherine, loving companion of his childhood.

Charles's sympathy and concern at the news of Desmond Heritage's death was as surprising as it was genuine. 'It may sound fanciful to you, who had brother and sisters aplenty,' he said to Tom on hearing the tidings, 'but I was a solitary boy and my absent family was almost more real to me than were the ones with whom I grew up. I created my own images of my uncle Desmond and aunt Violet, and he always seemed such a colourful and romantic charcter, arriving at Dell Quay off a Bayless vessel, sweeping Aunt Violet off her feet and carrying her away from all the troubles she had here.'

He hesitated and then went on, 'In many ways, I can well appreciate what you are suffering, quite apart from the physical deprivations. I was such a lonely boy for most of my childhood, never close to the Freelands even though they had children of my own age. Mother and I were foreigners to them, I suppose. I'd have liked to have known old Manfri and Polly Bayless and their family a lot more intimately than I did. They lived for some time at Newbarn, quite close to our cottage — but they didn't heed me much, either. I wasn't a Romany — and I was my father's son. So I grew up with you American cousins as my private family and absorbed every small crumb of knowledge about you all that I could glean from Great Uncle John Freeland before he died. When he went, I almost wrote to your mother, Tom. Then I found that Great-aunt Mary had already done it. I wish now that I had had the courage to establish a correspondence with Aunt Violet, for she did so much to give my mother and me a stable and comfortable life.'

Tom, still filled with the grief of his loss, was scarcely aware of the significance of this sudden confidence. He thought only that he was being offered words of comfort.

He said nothing immediately of his loss to Moses, who, seeing that Tom's mail had brought him sober tidings, forbore to question him.

'I heard something today,' he said mysteriously.

Tom looked round at him, miles away. 'Oh?'

Moses tried again. 'I heard me a little gem this morning, while we was loadin' at Cut Mill. There was three, four men from the mill sittin' on the jetty while we was loadin' the flour. Talking about three prisoners on parole at Havant. They said there were many such men, French . . . American . . . the like, though mostly officers. They were saying that the South Coast towns are full of paroled prisoners these days, for there just isn't room for them all in the prisons and the hulks. What say we investigate this one? You at least might have a chance of being paroled, bein' an officer.'

Tom shook his head. 'We could look into it, sure. But I'm not leaving anyone from the *Free States* aboard while I swan it in lodgings. No, sir. The only way I shall leave here before a peace treaty is signed is by making a run for it — with as many of the lads as will join me.'

Moses grunted. 'We all say that, master — but no one from this hulk has yet found the chance. Ole Toady looks after us too well.'

There had been few break-outs from the *Fortunée*, and only two prisoners had succeeded in getting away for good. The others had been recaptured, and two had died in the gaseous slime of the marshes.

'Reckon there might be one way we could get out,' Moses said, staring across the distant smudge of bulrushes to the tree-line marking the shore. 'Remember last week we was down in the cargo hold, swabbing decks afore fresh supplies was loaded on? I sat me down in the hold for a quick crap and made an interestin' discovery. I leaned against the bulkhead, an' oh man . . . there's a piece of wood maybe three feet in length and eighteen inches in height which is soft as a sponge and I poked my finger right into it, right through it, by the Lord, for I felt the outer timberwork an' I swear that that's just as soft. Didn't think much of it at the time, except to wonder how soon we'll sink.'

Tom was now all attention. He folded his mother's letter carefully and tucked it into his shirt. 'Let's go see,' he said shortly.

Tom followed Moses down one ladder after another, through decks tightly packed with men in every stage of health and occupation, into the very bowels of the old vessel. The place reeked of excrement, mould, the rotting of her timbers and human death. They bowed their heads beneath cross-beams only four foot nine inches high and crouched their way through storage compartments to a space directly above the ship's black hole.

There was no light, and their eyes, even though accustomed to the gloom of scarcely lit lower decks, were no match for the solid blackness that surrounded them. They felt their way along the stacked barrels of grain and dried fish, the scratch and scamper of rats magnifying in their ears.

'Sounds like a herd of buffalo down here,' Moses muttered, invisible ahead of Tom. He stopped and Tom cannoned into him. 'Wait. I'm countin' the bulkhead stays from the hold section.'

'Well, keep talking and I'll follow your voice.'

Moses hummed under his breath, now and then muttering a curse as his foot slipped on the sticky decking.

Tom, fingers spread out along the dank timber wall, inched his way forward until Moses' mutterings stopped in a quick hiss. 'Here . . . and here . . . . Yes, I'm sure as sure I'm not wrong, Mas' Tom. Feel that — yes, and here too. It's as crumbly as soaked bread.'

Tom was beside him, and he reached out and guided his hand along the edge of a slightly recessed length of timber. 'Press.' His voice floated away in the black limbo all about them.

Tom pressed the tips of his fingers into the section under his hand. It gave under the pressure; it was like pushing into a piece of uncooked liver. Moisture seeped under his fingernails. 'My God, how much more is there like this?' he said, aghast.

Moses chuckled. 'Ya, I know what you're thinkin'. The bottom's goin' to fall out of this ole wreck one day — an' we don't want to be aboard when it happens. I went all the way along this side as far as the next bulkhead an' the other timbers are sound. Can't speak for what's in the storage hold, behind all them crates and barrels. All I know is, if there are more timbers like this on the starboard side, then Lordy me, I's gettin' off . . . . '

It was as Moses said: just the one area of rotten planking, which they worked at patiently for the next four days whenever any of the nine *Free States* crew used it as a latrine. The saturated wood fibres looked very much like the faeces they were required to bring up and dispose of. The possibility of escape was discussed at length, but after much whispered argument and head-shaking only two of them were prepared to brave the icy harbour waters in winter. The others were, however, more than willing to double up for them each muster until the gap in the outer timbers was discovered and a closer scrutiny was taken of the roll calls.

The four men were all emaciated, with little but their own despair to combat the freezing sea, but they gradually became fired with enthusiasm and the others, ripe for adventure of any kind to break the boredom, built up their anticipation with their own excitement.

'For God's sake, stop looking so pleased with yourselves,' Tom said to his crew, concerned that their absorbed, almost happy faces might be noticed by the guards. 'The plank is now cleared and we won't — daren't — start on the outer timber until we are ready to go.'

'When's that to be then, master?'

Tom smiled at the face of his carpenter, Stace Harbottle. Stace was as fit as the best of them and more so than some, for he was only just past his twentieth year and, uncomplicated and trustful by nature, tended to take each day as it came with commendable patience. It was unusual to see frustration on his face.

'Wind's been blowing hard all day,' Tom said softly. The men crowded closer, the better to hear his quiet voice. There were others nearby, for they had been battened down for the night and the sleeping hammocks were hung so close together that there was only an eighteen-inch allowance for the width of each man. Tom crouched on the deck beneath two hammocks in which his men lay on their stomachs, the better to catch his words. The others crowded in on either side, their backs to a group of Rafalés, who were so furiously and noisily engrossed in a game of plafend that nothing existed outside their circle. The only illumination at their end of the deck came from the Rafalés' tiny fat lamp.

'That means that it will either blow up again tomorrow and set into an all-out gale or else, by nightfall, it could have blown itself out. I suggest we try it tomorrow night. There's no point in waiting . . . the sooner we're out, the better our chances. All right with you, Moses . . .

276

Stace . . . Lunt?'

There was so much to go over. It would take the four of them an hour or so to hole the outer timber work — and even then, the hole must be too small for Moses to get through or its chances of detection before nightfall would be almost certain. There was a twice-nightly boat patrol which circled the vessel, so the hole must not be started until the dusk patrol had completed its round, and they must be gone before the midnight patrol was due. Work-time was narrowed even further, for the prisoners were battened down at sunset. They would have to miss the head count and hide in the storage hold, being careful to keep out of the way of the sentries and the fellow who inspected the black hole.

'What happens to us if we survive the swim?' Abel Lunt asked. He was the oldest of the four escapees. A hard man, he hated all Britishers, for General William Howe's soldiers had killed his parents and ransacked his home during the war. He wanted nothing but to carve his way out of England, cutting down in the name of his dead family all who crossed his path.

Tom turned his head towards the disembodied voice. 'Each man for himself,' he said shortly. 'We know nothing of the countryside, nor the people here. We know that there is some sympathy for the American cause here in England — but without names, one man's face is much like another's. There is just one aim for us all now: to take passage across the Channel with all speed. None of us has any hope of staying free for long while we are on English soil.'

Their location was discussed. Langstone Harbour was to the east of the southern shore, facing the Isle of Wight. They were in the vulnerable underbelly of England, where her coasts were most closely guarded against the threat of Napoleon's invading forces. Portsmouth, with its busy marine traffic, was a possibility but dangerous. Emsworth or Bosham were more likely places to pick up a boat, but exactly how far they were along the marshy shore was not

277

at all clear. They would just have to trust to luck — and the possible goodwill of some isolated farmsteader.

'I know where I'm going,' Tom said to Moses when the little meeting had broken up.

'Yeah, master, so do I. You'll be off looking for that place where you mammy come from. Not far, you've been saying all this time — but how far is "not far" when you're a stranger and cain't ask the way an' have no clothes to keep that pokey ol' wind off your jennies?'

'Not far is nearer than across the Channel,' Tom said, suddenly filled with longing by the thought of what lay ahead. To see Lavenham . . . to be there under the very roof that his grandfather had built. To roam the place to his heart's content, until he was familiar enough with every inch of it — and satisfied about the truth of its legends. Then to be able to leave and make his way back across the Atlantic.

'What do you plan to do?' he asked, suddenly aware that Moses had said nothing about his own ideas.

'How's about makin' room in that empty mansion of yours for a free black American? Cain't say as I'm overly hopeful of gettin' across that li'l old Channel being the colour I am. Jus' as likely to end up back in the slave pens unless I come with you.'

'You can travel at night. As long as you keep your eyes and your mouth shut, there's no one can spy a black man at night.'

'Reckon it'd be harder to stop my tongue from awaggin' and my eyes from arollin' than 'twill be to bust out of this ole wreck,' Moses said, the laughter in his voice making even deeper the rich oily tones. His good humour was in no way rattled by the possibility of recapture or, worse, that other option of losing his precious freedom at a slave auction.

'I'd be glad of your company, Moses,' Tom said to him. Indeed, he discovered that this was the truth. Moses had strength and dignity as well as that infectious humour. He was also an excellent discourser, with a hunger for learning

278

that Tom found exhilarating. It would be good to share Lavenham with this best of men — and later they would return to Boston and Moses, now writing and reading under Tom's guidance, would be the perfect partner in setting up a chandlery business with the money that Papa had left in trust for him. To hell with the disapproval that such a partnership would create among the doyens of Boston. He and Moses understood each other.

Moses clasped his hand and shook it hard. 'Thank you, suh.'

There was no more to say after that, for each knew the strength of the other and was glad of it. They settled into their hammocks and tried to rest their bodies for the coming travail.

3

Charles Bayless and his two clerks arrived during the next morning with the weekly soap allocation. The prisoners gathered on the main deck, heads bent against the salt-rimed gusts, standing shoulder to shoulder, waiting to join the queue, stamping their feet and blowing on their hands to keep the circulation going in the bone-chilling air. The contractor's desk was set up, as usual, in a corner of the deck with its back to the galley. His two assistants busied themselves, one with his ledgers and the other with sacks of block soap. Each greyish block had to be cut and weighed into two-ounce tablets, the weekly allowance agreed for prisoners of war. Slowly, the men began to form a queue and the laborious business began.

'Abbeville . . . Ansell . . . Amhurst . . . .'

They filed slowly past the desk, silent but for the shuffle of their bare feet, the wind barging through the untidy clutter of improvised sheds which housed the galley and sickbay, and the hoarse commands of the Snake's general clerk.

Charles sat, quill in hand, ticking off each man's name as he received his ration. There were not many contractors doing this irksome task themselves, but it was the only way to ensure that the prisoners were not short-shrifted by a light-fingered clerk. He saw little gratitude in the men's eyes, but then he expected none. Their well-being was of little consequence to him. His good reputation was, on the other hand, of prime importance.

'Haines . . . Herbert . . . Heritage . . . .'

Their eyes met for a moment as Tom took the dirty grey soap tablet from the weighing scales. They would not be speaking together this day, for Mrs Furze had taken the boys over to Portsmouth for the week to stay with one of her sisters.

Tom bowed over his soap. 'Thank you, sir.'

Charles raised his head, straightened his back and smiled broadly.

Surprised, Tom turned away thinking that he must be getting used to Charles's sepulchral looks — for he seemed almost handsome this day. The wind was having little effect upon his impeccable turnout, as usual, but there was a jauntiness about him that spoke of some private inner joy. Whatever it was, some hidden flame was burning strongly in Charles Bayless, giving animation to the sculptured features.

Tom was not the only one to notice the phenomenon.

'Snake was looken' pretty pleased with himself this morning,' Stace Harbottle said later.

The crewmen from the *Free States* were gathered together round the four who were to leave that night. It was difficult to keep the excitement out of their faces and inevitably some of their companions guessed that something was being plotted.

The whole group had clubbed together and bought jackets from the latest batch of prisoners to arrive aboard. Solly Abrams was this minute putting patches on the largest jacket so that it would accommodate Moses' broad shoulders. Each of the four had sewn his personal papers into his clothing in the hope that the salt water would not completely destroy those few letters and documents that were precious to them.

Tom insisted that they rest in the daylight hours. He lay with his eyes closed. Sleep eluded him. He tried to curb the racing thoughts which slid through his mind, but someone was singing the same little song over and over again nearby, and the irritation of the off-key, nasal sounds cut through any attempt to drift off. In the main hold, somewhere below him, two of the men were loosening the spongy fibres of the rotten outer planking while the

others were either keeping guard or hovering near to the
resting foursome, making sure that they were neither
disturbed nor robbed. He must have slept after all, for
someone was shaking his arm and a voice said in his ear,
'It's time.'

He was awake instantly. Darkness enveloped the orlop
deck, darkness shot through with the sounds of men
struggling with the nightmares that dogged their overbur-
dened dreams. Nearby, someone was weeping in muffled
gasps. Someone told him to be quiet with a snarl. Snores
and the small cries of uneasy sleep were all that broke the
reeking night.

'Wrap up well. The wind has died but now it's raining
and the sea is choppy and running fast.'

He rolled out of his hammock, grabbing jacket and
blanket 'That you, bosun?'

'That's me, Master Tom, sir . . . Moses be down in the
hold already. Stace an' Abel and yourself got plenty of
time, for it's two hours to midnight by the sandglass. We
reckon you should be away within the hour.'

Tom's eyes slowly became accustomed to the darkness.
At the other end of the orlop deck a light glimmered feebly
through the tightly packed hammocks. Somewhere nearby
was a suggestion of movement. The Rafalés were insati-
able and thought nothing of paying their debts in all
manner of Godless ways.

They crawled beneath the hammocks, avoiding floor
sleepers where they remembered them. Now and then,
draughts from the barred but open ports slid icy fingers
across their faces. Tom shivered. In a corner directly
beneath one of the unshuttered ports a rough trapdoor had
been cut in the deck planking. Each deck had at least one
of these 'private' hatches to the deck below so that it was
possible for the men to move freely and undetected
between decks. Inspections were almost unheard of, for
the pent-up feelings of seven hundred men might well
have found expression against their captors had they
ventured below. It was enough to give the prisoners light

and fresh air each day by opening the hatches and ordering them out on to the main deck and into the pen. What went on below was best ignored. The two men prized up the boards gingerly. Below was the main hold, which was patrolled by sentries several times during the night hours. It was vital that the loose boards remained undetected, for others would need the freedom of the vessel to assist their own escapes.

Below them, a whispered greeting floated upwards. 'C'mon there! Thought you'd decided not to try for it, after all, you bin so long a 'comin'. Patrol went by ten minutes ago by my counting.'

Tom lowered himself through the gap and swung for a moment, then let himself fall. Hands steadied him, and the bosun's whisper came after him: 'Good luck to ye, Mr Heritage. God go with ye.'

He heard the planks being replaced. They would be opened again for the other two.

'Take a grip on my jacket,' the man with him ordered. The sound of his low voice seemed magnified in the silent darkness. For a moment the little scurrying creatures stopped as though they too were waiting for danger, breaths held.

Tom felt for the man's coat and took a firm hold of the back flap of the jacket. They set off, moving cautiously along the gangway towards the little forward compartment. They had not gone more than twenty paces when it happened.

'Gotcha . . .' a voice snarled beside him and hands closed on Tom's arm with a vicelike grip. He spun round, heart thumping at the unexpectedness of the attack. One of the guards must have been lurking without his lantern and heard the descent from the orlop deck. He felt his companion tear away, and then his hands were on the sentry's throat and he was squeezing, feeling the Adam's apple gulping against his thumbs while the man struggled and tore at him with frenzied fingers.

He dug his nails into hard flesh and felt the man's eye

283

sockets under his fingers. He probed and gouged with all his strength and felt the squirming body jerk. A vast excitement welled up in his chest. The sentry began to scream and Tom pressed down on him so that the gasping shouts were muffled against his shirt front. Red rage filled him and he thrust at the man's eyeballs, feeling the oval softness of them bursting like fat plums beneath his jagged nails. The man went limp suddenly. They sprawled together against a bale of cloth and slid to the deck. Tom lay panting across the still body. The man was still alive, for his breath came in shallow tremors.

'Are you still there, Pinder?' he panted into the darkness.

'Whatchew done, for God's sake? You killed him?' His guide's frightened voice sliced through the silence from a few yards away.

'No. Just put him out, I hope. I can feel him breathing but he won't be seeing us go. Come on, we must hurry before he is discovered.'

Feeling their way, they dragged the unconscious sentry behind some barrels of pig fat, out of the way of the next patrol's lanterns. Then they made for the forward compartment. Tom could hear the man counting under his breath. With hands stretched out in front of them, they slowly paced the hold until they collided with a bulkhead — they must be close to the hull breech now.

'You there, Moses?'

'If you c'n see ma teeth, man, then I must be here . . . .' There was a small chuckle in the blackness and a shifting of bodies. The air was very cold here and spots of water sprayed Tom's face. He could see a faint grey glimmer. They had successfully breeched the ship's side.

'Best hurry up and go,' Bosun Pinder said. 'They'll be missing that sentry any time.' The anxiety in his voice made the words snap like a whiplash.

'We were jumped by a sentry back there,' he explained to Moses. 'I had to attend to him. Don't worry, I didn't kill him. Just made sure that he'll not see what we're up to.'

'You sure he's not dead, for Chrissake?' the Bosun grated. If a sentry had been killed, the whole ship would be in trouble. There would undoubtedly be heavy reprisals and twice the reward on the escapees' heads.

'No,' Tom said quickly. 'I probably blinded him, that's all, Give me your word you'll lay the blame for the sentry on me, tell 'em what a filthy temper I have, eh?'

They huddled round the open wound in the ship's side, sniffing the cold sharp saltiness of freedom. Water sprayed their faces as unseen waves troughed and peaked against the slimy timbers. There was a strong odour of briny tar in their nostrils.

'Right.' Tom gripped Moses' arm. 'There's no point in waiting for the others. Moses and I'll go now. Is Fred standing by for the signal?'

Above their heads a crewman waited for the knock on the wood beneath his feet. It would signal the moment for a diversion, and he was to raise his lantern so that the other watchman on the far side of the deck could see the sign and begin banging the bars of the open port on the starboard side of the vessel. With luck, the unexpected sound would bring the sentries running to investigate the rumpus.

Hands fumbled at his waist, looping a rope round him and testing the slip-knot which held the two of them together. Hands gripped him in darkness. There were no words for such a farewell.

He straddled the open gash of rotten planking, feeling the old hulk dip into a trough and then lift laboriously. When she had begun to sink into the next one he thrust his body outwards through the opening and into the teeming night. He fell, hurtling through the air for what seemed an eternity before the waves received him with freezing suddenness, sucking him down. He felt himself dropping like a stone, and held his breath until his head began to sing and the heart swelled in his chest. The sensation had been a sinking one but his head suddenly broke surface and he was flung roughly upwards. He caught his right leg in the rope and felt it seer across his kneecap. Then the blood thundered in his ears and he no longer felt his body at all. Time seemed to freeze with his limbs. Something struck him a blow on the trailing leg. He choked, drawing salt water into his lungs and spun, retching — the plaything of the relentless water.

His cheek was pressed into something soft. His chest hurt. He was so cold that it was moments before he recognized the ferocious sound in his ears as his own chattering teeth. He drew in a deep, agonizing breath of dry air into his lungs and groaned at the sharp pain which burned his chest.

'Shh, man. Stay silent.'

He opened his eyes. Daylight; the soft pearling of cold misty air. He was lying on marsh mud, penned down by tall rushes.

'Don't move a muscle.' Moses' voice was a breath against his ear. Sounds filtered through the sentinal reeds. Close to them the clunk and dip of oars.

'Patrol's searchin' the shore, in sight now. There's geese feedin' behin' us. Make one move an' they'll be up into the air in a moment. Sure giveaway.'

Tom closed his eyes. He had not drowned after all. This was terra firma at least, and Moses was still with him. He let his body relax and slept.

The cold brought him round. That and the stark white winter daylight. Moses was there, grinning his relief as Tom turned his head to look about him.

'Any sign of the others?'

Moses shook his head. Far away a ship's bell rang out the noon toll. They crouched in their cover, limbs stiffening while the search boats passed and re-passed. Dusk came swiftly and the restless geese settled close to them along the mud flats. A wind sprang up for half an hour as the day drained away, slicing through their bodies. Moses hauled himself on to his feet and almost lifted Tom as the pain in his leg made him gasp. The kneecap and ankle were swollen, and even his light weight was going to be a problem. He gritted his teeth, shook his head at Moses' outstretched hand and followed the big man away up into the woods. Hunger gnawed. Once within the thick protection of the trees, they found a hollow, burrowed into fern and dead leaves and settled down to sleep.

They woke to find a red morning sky turning the branches over their heads into fine black lace. It was not a good sign, but they left their warm lair and turned eastwards. The land was empty, stark with winter hostility — open common broken by straggles of oakwood and unploughed fields. They kept close to trees and hedges and crouched against the thicket when movement betrayed the passage of man. The swelling in Tom's leg had begun to creep up towards his thigh, the pain diffused by fever.

Hunger sent them rooting for bulbs and nuts. Moses managed to steal bread from a cottage and the intermittent rain squalls gave them water to ease their thirst.

When they spied the roofs of a sizable village it was Tom, with his bloated leg, who insisted on investigating it more closely. It was, as they had guessed, Bosham.

Tom limped painfully into the little town, leaning on a stick which Moses had made for him. It was a busy place, he discovered, even though mid-winter was approaching, and the muddy roads were choked with carts and pedestrians and noisy teasing children. He made his way down to the waterfront, settled himself in a corner of the sea wall and held his hands out to passers-by, with a beggar's touching supplication.

Moses had the best of the bargain. He was hiding in the luxury of a hay barn, for his dark skin and great height would attract too much attention. He fidgeted, frustration at inactivity and concern for Tom's state making a caged creature of him.

Tom, out of the wind in the lea of the wall, and seeing free humanity all about him for the first time in years, began to feel more relaxed. His outstretched hands were rewarded with several coins before the day was over. He sat with his suppurating leg outstretched before him and floated in his fevered state until someone tripped against his foot and staggered into him with a gasp. He had been dreaming, and the shock of sudden agony thrust a bellow of pain from him.

'Oh, sorry . . . I didn't see you! Sorry, bor.'

His head sang with the pain and he rocked his body, seeking release in movement. A hand touched his leg lightly, fingers feeling the pus-filled pouches around the dislodged kneecap.

'There is poison there, bor. Best get it seen to or you might lose the whole leg.'

Tom shook his head, eyes screwed up, not looking. 'I would if I had the means, but I have nothing.'

'I'll get you a poultice, since I have caused you even more pain than you had before. Sit quietly and I'll be back soon.'

It was only afterwards that he realized the voice had been light and melodious — a young girl's voice. Must remember to tease Moses about that, he thought. To talk with a woman after so long . . . . He sank back into a drowsing state until her voice woke him and hands moved over the leg, soothing, probing.

'Here, bor — I've some onions and bread for a poultice. Hold still while I wrap them round.'

He closed his eyes against the confusion of light and shade which danced about her. She was small and nearly as ragged as he. A long time after she had gone, he recalled the beauty of shining black hair, thick as a horse's mane. It would have been nice to stroke it . . . .

The next time he opened his eyes he felt better. The sun was beginning to go down and there were five coins on his lap. The right leg of his breeches had been neatly slit all the way up to his thigh and the swollen knee had been poulticed and wrapped in a green kerchief. On his lap lay a loaf of fresh bread, the warm, bland smell of it making his mouth water. Two small boys hovered near him, staring. He eyed them covertly, for the little ruffians might well be planning to rob him of his fortune. They watched as he tore a piece of the bread and ate it ravenously. The slipway was almost deserted now, shadows lengthening into evening. He tried to get to his feet, hauling himself up between his stick and the wall, but weakness made him dizzy.

'Hey, give a sick man a hand, will you?' he said to the boys. They stared at him with pinched, stony faces. Then the smaller of the two came forward and helped him up. The pain poured through him so that he stood, hissing through bared teeth. Then he hobbled away from them, up the uneven road, trying to remember the way he had come that morning.

'Don't know his face,' the elder boy muttered. 'Never seen him round here before. Not from these parts, by the sound of 'im.'

The day had stretched out without incident for Moses. Once he had seen Tom out of the barn, he made a warm nest for himself in the hay and was content to lie and savour the joys of freedom, albeit without the benefit of food in the stomach. Towards evening, Tom returned, his face grey with pain but bearing the greater part of a large fresh loaf. He was too weak by then even to do justice to such an unexpected feast, and Moses ate most of it.

'Apuldram,' Tom said. 'Must make for Apuldram.' He was clearly fevered and Moses watched him in alarm. His face was flushed, the grey eyes light bright stones. Wherever this Apuldram was, Moses knew he'd have to get him there pretty quickly or he'd have a goner on his hands.

'Heard them talking on the slipway,' Tom muttered, lying back in the hay and closing his eyes. 'Take the Dell Quay ferry across the water. That's what we've to do.'

'You don't look fit to move one pace, master,' Moses said, 'so how're you thinkin' of travellin' to this ferry, wherever it is?'

'East along the Hoe . . . that's what they said. We can travel after dark.'

There was a moon that night, skipping like a dancer from cloud to cloud. It was enough to light their way, but

Moses had to carry Tom now, for he was quite delirious and unable to stand, let alone walk. He moved quietly, keeping close to the high hedgerow. When they came to crossroads, he studied the angles and checked them with his mariner's eye against the clouded moon. A narrow cart-track looked the best bet, for it wound away from the road towards the twinkling of distant lights. Maybe they could hide there overnight and he could search for the Dell Quay channel in the dawn. He patted Tom's thin back. 'Just hang in there, master. Soon have you tucked up for the night.' His voice was more cheerful than he felt. What if those lights hid trouble?' There was only one way to find out.

The track was deeply rutted and although Tom was no great weight, he was enough to make their passage a perilous one. The track seemed to go on forever. Here and there, rocks from the fields had been used to patch the deeper holes, but the going was slow and mud coated his legs up to the knees. The track suddenly tilted into a slope and he paused, shifting Tom more securely against his neck. He moved forward again and was startled to find himself in an enclosed yard. There was movement round him: cattle in their stalls, tails swishing, a soft moo, a rump being rubbed slowly against the byre. Comforting farm sounds.

A hand gripped his arm and he jerked round, heart leaping.

'Hey, don't hurt me,' a voice gasped as Moses grabbed at clothing and pulled the man forward, peering down at him. 'Let go. I ent a danger. I bin waiten' here since sundown in case 'e come.'

'What d'you mean, waiting'? You don't know me.'

The man — he was quite old, Moses could see now — whispered, 'Keep yer voice down. There are six of them across there by the ferry. Waiten' for you. Come on into the kitchen, quick as you can. Safer in there.'

Tom sighed, a moan in his breath. Moses gripped him firmly and followed the blurred shadow of the old man round a wall, along a cobbled pathway and in through a small gate. They stopped once when a growl in the darkness warned of another watcher.

'Stay, Scamp, it's only me. Come in quickly, now. The patrol might be on the prowl.'

A door was opened and then closed without a creak. Warmth and the scent of woodsmoke and kitchen baking enfolded them.

'Fran, ye there? I got 'em.'

The heavy atmosphere was torn by the scrape of the tinderbox, then light scoured his eyes, a soft pink translucence held between cupped hands. Moses cradled Tom against his chest and stared at the two elderly figures suddenly etched in light against the yawning darkness. The woman held up the lamp as the old man smiled at them, relief and pleasure unbelievably shining in his face.

'We was told of one black an' one white, but not that you was such a giant.' The soft Sussex burr soothed the fear in Moses and he relaxed a fraction.

The woman came forward then and looked at Tom's white and fevered face. 'Poor soul. Best get 'im upstairs and into a comfortable bed with some good hot broth in 'im. Follow me but keep quiet.' She led the way up to a large, low-ceilinged chamber and, when Moses had settled Tom in the capacious double bed, brought him back to the kitchen, where her husband was stirring a beef broth over the range.

'News of yer escape has been published in all the towns and villages,' he explained at last, when Moses had been made comfortable with a steaming bowl of broth and half a loaf of fresh bread. 'It is yer good fortune that my brother and two of my sons emigrated to Virginia. Our sympathies are with the Colonies, so we've bin watchen' out fer the two of you. Yer friend upstairs was reported to the military by a couple of children today, so we knew 'e weren't far off.'

Moses wolfed down the food and tried, without success, to take in all that was being said. 'Our boy, Georgie, 'e went to war with England, just like you did. We don't know what happened to him.' The old man's eyes glittered across the table.

Ben and Frances Chase: Two old people risking their lives as an unspoken memorial to the life of a loved son. 'I thank you, sir, from the two of us,' he said to Ben Chase, and held out his hand to shake the old man's.

4

The rain turned to snow during the night.

Tom opened his eyes to a white and silent world beyond a strange window. He lay in long-forgotten comfort in a bed, with a bright chequered blanket covering him; he was warm and clean — there was even a hot brick at his feet.

'Moses' head bobbed up from beyond the end of the bed. 'Mornin', brother.' His eyes had lost their bloodshot look and he too seemed refreshed and ready to face the world. 'Slept here on the floor so that I'd not risk bumpin' your leg in my sleep.'

He grinned happily at Tom's astounded examination of their surroundings. 'Now, don' you ever say I'm not the brightest li'l ole Moses on two feet, findin' us the best billet in a strang land . . . .'

'Where are we, for God's sake? I remember nothing of last night apart from lying in a wet hedge.'

'Parklands Farm, that's where. Right in full view of the li'l ol' ferry and Dell Quay on the opposite bank of the river. Real kindly folk, these two old people. They was even on the look-out for us, can you beat that? The militia told 'em you was probably makin' for Apuldram. Old Farmer Chase, he was in his barnyard and stopped me from going down to the slip where there were soldiers hidin' in waitin'. They've gone now. Went just after daylight — and a right sorry-looking bunch they were too, after a night out there in the rain and snow. How're ya feeling?'

The fever was still in him and his leg was on fire, but he settled down among his pillows, relaxed and secure in the warm chamber. His hunger had gone, and so had the usual stink of his own stale sweat.

'I'm fine,' he said with a contented sigh, closing his eyes. 'I'm just fine.'

Ben Chase came upstairs to see his visitors at noon. 'Ye must stay up here until that leg is healed,' he said firmly to them both. 'The track past the farm is a busy thoroughfare during the day and any sight of strangers would have the authorities swarmen' all over us again. There is quite a stir in Bosham since you did your begging act there yesterday. Everyone's keepen' their eyes peeled for strangers now.'

'What happened to the other two who escaped after us?' Moses asked.

The old man scratched his head. 'I seem to recall the sergeant mentioning that they caught one and the other drowned and they hung his body up on the hulk as a lesson to your companions.'

'Won't be no lesson, sir,' Moses said. 'It's every man for himself in them hulks, and death be not a bad alternative to life there. Despair breeds scant respect for obedience.'

On the second day at Parklands Farm, Tom felt a little stronger. He allowed Mrs Chase to prop him up in a nest of pillows and put a comb through his hair. He watched her face with its network of lines and pouches under kind eyes, and knew that she was playing a private game of having her sons about her once more.

Neither Tom nor Moses had come across anyone answering to the name of George Chase. Looking at the sad affection in her face, he knew that he would try hard to discover the fate of this loved younger son.

'You must stay here with us until you are quite fit,' she said, when his head looked tidy enough.

'Ma'am, Moses and I are forever in your debt, you know that. There is little enough we can ever do to repay what you are doing for us — but we'll get some kind of news to you concerning George, that I promise. First, though, I must get back on to my feet and over to Apuldram.'

'Is that where your folks hail from? They said you'd be maken' for Dell Quay or Apuldram.'

He nodded. 'I know so little about them,' he admitted. 'That's why I must go there. Mama has always been very reticent on the subject of her family and I'd dearly love to know more. Her name was Bayless. I am Thomas Bayless Heritage.'

She was in the act of taking away his washing bowl and hesitated, the soapy water sloshing. 'Bayless — that seems to ring a bell. I'll ask Ben, for he was born and raised right here in this house and his father and granfer before him. There baint a family from these parts that'd not be known to him.'

Ben Chase came up to see them later. Moses was prowling the upper floor of the farmhouse like a caged animal. The regular food and rest had already renewed his energy, so that he longed now for nothing more than to be able to exercise and expend some of it.

'Pity I can't use some of your fine muscle out in the yard,' Ben said, seeing Moses' ill-concealed frustration.

'Maybe I could do a few jobs after dark,' Moses said eagerly. 'I'm strong as an ox, sir, an' gettin' fitter every hour with the 'tention Mrs Chase be givin' us.'

Ben smiled. 'It's a great joy for her to have a couple of chicks to fuss over again,' he said. 'She's a born mother, my Fran, and it was a grief to us both that we were only blessed with the two boys, for there were no more after Georgie. She'd have bin in her element with the house filled with little 'uns.'

He sat on the bed and studied Tom's thin face. 'Looken' better all the time, ent ye?' he said. There was something at the back of his eyes that Tom had not seen before. Uncertainty — fear?

'Is something wrong?' he asked, suddenly anxious.

The old man shook his head. 'No, no . . . the hunt for you has moved away towards Portsmouth now. Soon ye'll be forgotten, as long as ye don't show your faces to the wrong folks.' He hesitated. 'Fran tells me that ye're aimen' on taken' a look at yer mam's old home.'

Tom nodded.

'There ent a soul liven' there, sir. Hasn't bin for near on fifty year.' He narrowed his eyes and Tom watched indecision chase across the old man's weathered features.

'You say your mother was a Bayless?'

'Yes, sir. She was Violet Bayless, born and brought up across that river — and so was my grandfather, Jess Bayless.'

Ben stared hard at Tom now, taking in the thick black hair, the high-bridged nose. 'Yes — I see her in you,' he said slowly. 'I was no more than a sprig of fifteen or so when she went away with the American gentleman, but I remember her well enough, for she was a mighty striken' lady to look at an' most of us young 'uns would have given our week's wages just to speak to her.'

Tom grinned at him, delighted with this unsuspected aspect of his mother — and yet there was still this odd tension in his host.

'Tell me about her,' he said. 'Do try and remember. My parents were always so reticent about Mama's younger days. Father died last year and I have had no word from home for months now, so it may even be that she has followed him. She would be all of seventy-four or so, you see.'

Ben regarded Tom's intense white face. 'Reckon it's hardly my place to talk of things as intimate as that,' he said gruffly. 'There be other Baylesses about here as 'ud be more suited to tell you all you want to know.'

'I know it, for I have already met my cousin, Charles Bayless of Chichester. Since he is the contractor to the Langstone hulks, it was not difficult to discover our connection, once I knew his name.'

Moses had been standing, legs spread, before the fire. 'And he sure knows by now that his cousin was one of the escapers,' he said, his voice a deep rumble in the quiet room.

'I suppose he must . . . I hadn't really given him much thought since we left the ship.'

'Would you like me to make contact with the gentleman?' Ben suggested.

'No . . . no. That might prove a very bad thing for us all, for I was never very sure of where his sympathies lie,' Tom said quickly.

'Then may I suggest that another member of the Bayless clan comes to see you? I think I know just the person. It would be a most discreet visit.'

The two men looked at him without understanding and Ben, seeing the question forming on their lips, hurried on, 'look, sir, I'm not one for fancies − never have ben − but there are things I see'd with me own eyes that defy explanation in that Lavenham place. I see'd as clear as I'm seeing you now, that house burnen' to the skies one night − flames comen' through the roof an' rafters open to the skies. An' yet when mornen' come, there it was across the water with the lawns so trim an' the rose creepers growen' so sweet across the west face, and inside was three dead men − yes, I promise − dead without blemish. I tell ye, Master Tom, leave well alone. It's ben good and quiet over there for nigh on half a century now. Best leave it that way, do you please.'

He opened the door and paused as he went out. 'I'll bring you someone better fitted to tell you of those Baylesses, but don't ask me no more.'

He closed the door firmly behind him. Moses blew out his cheeks with a loud wheeze. His eyes had begun to pop as he listened to Ben's words. Now there was a greyness about his dark face which Tom had never seen before.

'Phew, brother − those questions of yours fair put the wind up him. What you goin' ter do now? Caint go crawlin' round a place filled with ghosties − leastways, not with me you caint. I feel those bad spirits a mile away, makin' ma skin creep and pluckin' the very soul from ma body. No, siree . . . I'm not goin' near a place like that.'

Watching Moses revelling in his superstitious fears steadied Tom's own shock at Ben Chase's words, and he lay back against his pillows, watching the big man's shoulders shaking like a young girl's and said placatingly,

'For God's sake, calm down, Moses. I shan't be going anywhere until this leg is better — so just take yourself off the boil. All I want to do is to see the damned house just once, so that I can leave this country and not have it nagging at me as it has done ever since I was a small child. When I'm fit enough I shall go over on my own for an hour — you won't have to come. I'll be back here before you even notice that I've gone. Will that suit you?'

Moses nodded, but the fear was still at the back of his eyes.

The swelling in the knee persisted painfully. Although Tom's fear had gone and he was feeling stronger every day, the heavy throb through his leg still restricted his movements. Though he tried to rise and move round the bedchamber, the pain was so great that he was always defeated after a few hobbling steps. Frustration began to chip at his temper and, to still it, he dragged from his memory the confused image of the little wild-haired girl with the long black lashes who had bound up his leg in the village.

Moses, on the other hand, was now quite content with his lot, for he would sleep during the daylight hours and work through the night, down in the barnyard, and had already chopped more logs for the wood pile than the Chases had had for many a long year. After someone commented on the sudden growth of Ben's log pile, he had to be content with rebuilding the inside of one of the cattle sheds. His richly burnished skin shone with his return to health, the tight black curls on his head gleamed with the animal fat he daily rubbed into it. His natural good humour made him excellent company and he was most warmly regarded by both his hosts.

Two days after the conversation concerning Lavenham, Mrs Chase brought them a visitor. Moses was sleeping on his back, stretched out on a feather mattress on the floor at the end of Tom's bed. His mouth was open and comfortable snores punctuated the peace of the room. Tom, drowsing as he half-listened to Moses's breathing, started at the light tap on the door. Mrs Chase put her head round it.

'Are you respectable?'

'As respectable as I shall ever be, ma'am.' he smiled.

'Well, I've brought someone to look at your leg.' She stood aside and ushered in her guest, saying over her shoulder, 'Don't worry about Moses there, he'll sleep for hours yet. Master Tom, this is Dudie Smith. She has a wondrous way with bones and infections and if she can't get you on your feet, I can't think who can.'

The girl, coming across the room towards the bed, smiled broadly at him. Tom gaped at her in astonishment, and she nodded her head, putting her basket on the covers near his elbow.

'Yes, bor — it was me as bound your leg that day in Bosham. I felt real badly about trippen' over such a swollen limb. How be you now? You look a lot better.'

He was struck dumb and just lay among his pillows, staring at her like a tongue-tied youth. His angel of mercy was wearing a clean blue gown this day, there were boots on her feet and the wild mop of springy black curls was tied demurely away from her face with a bright green ribbon.

She was even more perfect than his memory had painted her: tiny, slim as a willow and with an elfin sparkle of real amusement growing by the second in her heart-shaped face. She waited patiently for his reply, the light in her bright blue eyes threatening any moment to spill over into open laughter.

'Ma'am,' he finally mumbled, all too aware of his lack of manners, 'I'm mighty glad to see you again. I didn't thank you that day for your help — and I have your kerchief still.'

She examined the leg, clucking under her breath over the angry swelling; and the swift and tender way in which she removed the dressings said all that was needed about her skill. He watched as she took his knee in both her small, cool hands. She closed her eyes and her fingers explored the puffy skin, finger tips and thumbs probing every bulge and indentation.

'The knee-cap be out of place,' she said, eventually. 'It's best for me to manipulate it right away, if you can bear it, for the longer it is out of its cradle, the harder twill be to get back, especially as there be infection.' He was content to nod at the wisdom of her words and to continue his study of her, since she and Mrs Chase seemed quite content to do without his involvement. She had a most provocative cleft in her chin and one dimple on the left side of her full mouth.

The two women bent over the knee. Tom lay back and watched Dudie Smith. She looked quite foreign, with all those jet black curls and straight, full eyebrows. Her skin was unusually unblemished for a labouring woman, olive-tinted — translucent. She might well have a strong splash of Spanish in her blood, he decided. In spite of her gown and the well-brushed hair this day, she was still the lovely wild girl in a hurry who had haunted his thoughts since the first time she tended him.

'I think I'll try to shift the cap back into place now,' she said to him.

He smiled at her — anything you want, ma'am, as long as you stay this close to me, said his look. How could such a small girl have such an air of authority, and such enormous eyes? Delphinium blue, framed thickly by such long black lashes. He sank into the warmth of their regard. She could do whatever she pleased with him and he would thank her for it.

He didn't thank her a moment later, as she placed her hands firmly on either side of the swollen knee, adjusted her weight, then with a sudden sharp jerk twisted the whole joint. He reared up in the bed with a yell that shot Moses out of his slumbers.

'I told you twould be painful,' she said with an unrepentant grin.

'You didn't say how much, though,' he gasped, rocking

300

back and forth on the bed, the blood singing in his ears.

'Hey, what's goin' on here?' Moses complained sleepily. His eyes alighted on Dudie's broad grin then and they smiled at each other. 'Hey, brother — why should you get all the best nursin'? Have ya mentioned to this li'l lady about the ache in ma shoulder?'

Dudie, sensing that there was little more she could do for Tom, stood up and allowed herself to be ushered towards the door. Tom's head was still hunched over his leg.

'I'll be back in a day or two,' she said lightly, giving a little bow in Moses' direction.

'What a little doll,' he sighed after the women had gone.

Tom grunted. 'Some doll. The vixen half-murdered me,' he groaned, sliding back under the covers. It was quite some time before he would admit that she had done him any good at all. By then, he was, to his own surprise, on his feet and hobbling round the chamber in considerably less pain.

Dudie returned three days later, whirling into the room like a breath of fresh air. She was clearly in a hurry, wearing the same ragged skirt and shawl that Tom remembered from that first day. She greeted them both with airy friendliness but there were two bright spots on her cheeks and her eyes were asparkle, despite her casual attitude to them. Tom became visibly more cheerful at the sight of her. She was pleased with his progress though severe about the patient's new mobility, but he took his scolding stoically this time.

'The tissue holding the knee-cap in place is all torn and enflamed,' she tried to explain, tutting over the joint. 'If you try to use it before it is strong enough to support you, it will never heal. Stay in your chair by the window — and if move you must, then hop.'

'Yes, ma'am whatever you say, ma'am.'

Small and fierce, she stood over him, jaw set in a determined jut and the blue eyes pinning him into his chair as though daring him at his peril to defy her. He resisted a sudden desire to stroke the unruly tumble of hair, untethered this day and falling about her shoulders in a cascade of bouncy waves.

She and her brother, she told them, would be off to Portsmouth by the noon tide, taking pig iron across the harbour and returning with coal. There was time, she admitted, when Moses pressed her to stay, for just one cup of mint tea.

She sat between them and allowed herself to be bombarded with questions. She looked so small and child-like sitting on her little footstool, pink cheeked and smiling at their eager homage. Her name, she explained, was short for Boudicca, who had been a great warrior queen in eastern Britain a very long time ago.

Tom was intrigued. 'What was the great attraction for her?'

She laughed at him. How transparent these gorgios were sometimes. Gypsies were not meant to have any learning and he had almost said that.

'How can I say, sir? The choice of name was my puri daia's, Saiforella Bayless. She was the one who had the book learnen' among us.'

Bayless. Tom sat forward with a jerk that made him wince. 'Bayless . . . are you another Bayless, then?'

The smile was there again, shimmering out of her in the pure enjoyment of this secret that she had been holding from him. 'My name is Boudicca Smith, as I've said,' she told him primly, 'but my puri daia was the sister of your own granfer, Jess Bayless. So — yes, sir, we are connected. We share great-grandparents, Jasper and Grace Bayless.' She watched the emotions chase through his still pale face but was not prepared for the next question.

'Do you know Charles Bayless?'

Her eyes became watchful and the smile died in her face. She looked down at the cup of tea in her hands and gently swilled the contents round.

'Yes . . . I know him.'

For a moment she sat very still, as though the name had

turned her to stone, but then her head came up and she looked from Moses to Tom, defiant and vulnerable – and suddenly very young. The urge to gather her to him was almost unbearable. But then she suddenly went to the attack, as though the only way to turn him from unwelcome questions was to chastise this stranger.

'Mr Chase says you've ben quizzen' him somethen' terrible about Lavenham. You were born with money, bor – and all the comforts, and never had to struggle for your bread until you went to war. Why do you come pryen' into the past now? What is it you are looken' for from us? You and your kind wouldn't be proud of admitten' to haven' gypsies for kin – lest it be to mock them.'

'Now, that's where you are wrong, miss,' Tom said sharply. 'That may well be Mr Bayless's reaction to you but it is not mine. I simply need to be informed of the gaps in my knowledge of my family, that's all. Surely you cannot blame me for such a natural interest?'

She raised her head at last and gazed at him over the rim of her cup.

'What is it that had to be withheld from my brother and sisters all this time?' Tom pressed her. 'I am aware that my grandparents were brother and sister. Charles told me that. It was quite a shock at the time but I've heard of such things before. It has just made me all the more determined to know the rest of it.'

'It is the Gift, I suppose, that your mother felt she had to hide from you.'

He frowned then, mystified. She hesitated and then seemed to make up her mind for she gave a deep sigh and began to speak fast, as though the thing she had to say would be more acceptable if told at break-neck speed.

'All right, bor – here is what I know. Have you ever felt the presence of something special in you? No, I see that it means nothing to you. Well, this is goen' to sound like a foolish tissue of untruths but it is – I swear to you – no less than the absolute truth. Your granfer Jess was the seventh child of Jasper and Grace Bayless, and the only

303

son. My puri daia was Saiforella, the eldest of those children and your puri daia was the youngest, Amy Bayless.' She paused and sipped at her tea for a moment, fashioning the right phrases for him in her mind. 'Like others before him and after him too, Jess Bayless had the Sight. He also had another gift — and that was the Killen' Glance. Jess was able to kill by fixing his eyes on anything — animal or man — it made no difference. To have a gift of that kind is to bear a terrible burden in life.'

'Go on,' Tom said gently to Dudie.

'I know what be in your hearts, both of you. Fear is in you, Moses, for what I have just said ent strange among your people — but you, Master Tom, I see how difficult it is for you to take such words seriously. I can only tell you that it be the truth. Those grey eyes of Jess's seem to have had somethen' to do with the Gift because he had two children by blue-eyed women, and those children had grey eyes . . . also filled with that terrible Power.'

'Is there more?' he asked.

She shook her head. 'No — ent it enough? The evil of Lavenham is why Charles was never allowed to go anywhere near it as a child — and it is why we all beg and implore you not to go there either. You were not conceived or born in the place, which is probably why you are not infected by the wickedness there, but if you become involved with the house, who can tell what will happen?'

'And Charles, has he really never been there?'

She shook her head. 'He is always very unwillen' to touch on the subject but he did once say — after he had discovered as you were his cousin — that, as a very small boy he did once stray there but that he can recall nothen' at all of that time, save clingen' to iron gates and cryen'.

'Dudie, do you know Charles well?'

The still look came down across her face again. 'Well enough,' she said shortly. 'Ned and I be worken' one of his coalen' barges, so why should we not know him?'

She would be drawn no further. It seemed to him that she had no great love for their cousin.

304

'Oh, brother, what are you getting yourself into?' Moses said when she had gone. 'That family mansion of yours sounds as though we should give it a wider berth than the *Fortunée* herself. You won't never catch this one goin' there, I promise.'

Tom and Moses had been hiding at Parklands Farm for seven weeks before Tom was able to walk without a stick. His knee still ached if he put his weight on it for long but, by the time February came, he was taking short evening walks in the deserted woods which lined the river banks. It was nearly time for them to move on, they felt, and knew that the Chases were reluctantly coming to the same conclusion.

It was on a fine evening of almost springlike mildness that he found himself, through a tangle of brambles, almost level with a building on the opposite side of the river. He stopped and stared across the fast-flowing water, then moved along the bank, pushing through dead leaves, until he was close to the bank's muddy edge. Overhead, the birds murmured sleepily. The building was one of several barns. In summer they would be invisible from where he stood but now their outlines were quite easy to distinguish. A gaggle of old fruit trees, gnarled and unkempt like ancient gossiping women round a fairground booth, bunched together in a wilderness of dead creepers. He moved onward, treading carefully through clinging bramble — and suddenly Lavenham was there. The unkempt orchard seemed to draw back as the dying sun broke through cloud and shone low behind his head, filling his whole body with warm radiance.

Even emerging through acres of wilderness, the house was achingly beautiful. It lay at the top of an overgrown incline, an L-shaped building of soft pink brick and grey stone, with old-style casements and one huge gallery window reaching almost to the roof eves. The sun's orange light reflected fire upon its leaded panes through great swathes of creeper.

305

Lavenham — a huge excitement rose in him and spread. He stood and drank in the quiet scene, stripping the overgrowth away from the walls and terraced front, clothing it once more in all the graciousness which had once been its right. The sun slid away below the trees and blue shadows mantled the wood, bringing a sharp chill with it. His leg began to throb. He tore his eyes away from the house and retraced his steps, head bowed in thought.

'You've seen it, aint you?' Moses said to him later that evening as they ate their evening meal in the kitchen with old Ben and Fran.

Tom nodded. 'I'm going over there,' he said.

Ben Chase growled, exasperated, and then tapped the table between them. 'Tell ye what, then. Baint no good tryen' to stop ye when yer mind's clear made up . . . but go ye round the property only. Don't go inside that place.'

'I'm not going to stay for long,' Tom said, feeling the old couple's fear. 'I just want to satisfy myself about one or two things and then I shall be happy to go like a lamb and take that passage for France which you have so kindly fixed for us with Mr Timms. Would you not row me across?'

'Now look'e here,' the old man began to bluster, anger cutting through his apprehension. 'If'n I row ye over, in broad daylight it'll have to be — to Dell Quay. No one goes within half a mile of that land. Even the old hempen field where Mr Hamilton's built the dryen' barn 'ud be too conspicuous to land you. An' don't 'e go suggesten' us goen' over at dusk because I wouldn't even look at that place from this side of the creek, once the sun's down.'

'Moses could row me in,' Tom said mildly.

Moses rolled his eyes and his chin quivered fiercely. 'Told you, brother, I aint a-going near that devil's place, not now nor any time — even for you. I know when things are best left alone and this is one of those times.'

Dudie appeared later in the day. She came nowadays, they concluded, just to give them some company, for the leg was healing well on its own now and needed no more dressings. She sat herself in the window-seat and stared out over the cold grey afternoon. She was unusually quiet. Tom noticed shadows under her eyes, as though she had not slept.

'I have seen Lavenham,' he said, and waited for her reaction.

She turned towards him and there was nothing but a deep sadness in her, as though she already knew, and was grieved by it.

'It is callen' to you, bor,' she said in a low voice. 'Do not be enticed into Lavenham's web by its dangerous beauty.'

He was suddenly exasperated with them all. They were one more doleful than the other where Lavenham was concerned. 'For pity's sake, why can't any of you understand,' he snapped at her. 'I have absolutely no idea of living there — ever. My home is in New England and that is where I'll stay. My only wish is simply to go and look round the old place before Moses and I leave here. What possible harm can there be in that?'

She straightened up then and smiled round at him, taking both his hands in hers and turning them over so that she could examine his palms.

'You have so much luck in this life of yours,' she said, looking from one palm to the other. 'Your life line is a good strong one, only thin in the one place. It tells me that during the third decade of your life you will be in poor health. It is not my romancen' — look, you can see the thinnen' for yourself, simensa.' He was impressed, catching her meaning. He was in the third decade of his life right now. She went on, head bent over the upturned palms, 'See, the health line is this one, the heart line that. It says that you will not have many affairs of the heart — but whoever you give yourself to, there will be truth and sincerity in the relationship. How different your hand is to . . . . ' She stopped, and turned away.

'Dudie . . . dearest cousin,' he said very gently, 'something really bad is troubling you, isn't it? Please unburden yourself, if it will help you. You have been the very best of friends to Moses and me and we wish only to return your regard.'

Her eyes were suddenly bright blue stars of unshed tears. She sat very straight, holding herself away from him.

'It is just that thing that all women who are subject to harsh masters dread the most,' she said simply. 'I am with child.'

The first green shoots were springing from the cold earth. Night was a shining darkness, with no moon or stars but a strange clarity in the great black vault of the velvet sky. Moses rowed strongly, eyes down with deep concentration. A red woollen scarf was wrapped tightly round his head and nothing of his face showed but the whites of his eyes. The stern hunch of his shoulders bellowed his unwillingness to be there at all.

They traversed slowly across the current, butting through choppy water until they were in the lee of the east bank. It was easier to row into the oncoming current then, keeping close to the overhanging foliage which trailed right down into the water at high tide. At the point where the reeds and bushes thinned, Moses raised his head and worked his right oar so that the boat nosed through the rushes until its keel ground into the mud.

'Farmer says this's Hempsteddle field . . . I'm sure as sure not going further than this, brother,' he said grimly. He watched as Tom clambered stiffly over the bow, splashed through two paces of shallows and stumped up the muddy bank.

'Moses,' his whispered voice sounded rough in the silence around them, 'thanks, friend . . . I won't be long.'

Moses strained his eyes as Tom's crouching figure limped away along the bank. Then he was gone, enveloped by the twilight. It was very quiet. Somewhere in the heart of the woods something squealed once. Moses shivered and hugged himself, trying to control the trembling in his limbs which had little to do with the cold.

Tom moved slowly down the long field, keeping close to the hedge as he noticed the lights of a cottage beyond the far boundary. The dark mass ahead would be the Lavenham woods, for there was nothing south of Hempsteddle, so Dudie had told them, save for the Lavenham grounds and buildings beyond — and beyond them again, the Salterns oakwoods which screened the property from Ayles's saltpans and the marsh. He moved carefully, for his leg was still weak. Lavenham this night, said something inside, and then away to France — and home.

The ground was suddenly more springy underfoot. He was on ground which had been husbanded. A foot snagged on something hidden in deep undergrowth and he stood still, feeling the hardness of cobbles through the choked weeds. The sighing of the night air in the trees had faded away into total silence. The blood sang thunderously in his ears and he felt, rather than saw, the buildings on three sides of him. There was no menace in the night around him, no skin-prickling warnings. He lit the little lantern that Ben Chase had given him and raised it over his head.

He was in a barnyard, the weeds waist-high around him. Ahead was a massive Dutch barn, its great doors barred with rusty staves. To the right jutted a two-storeyed wing, to the left an archway joining it to another building and forming three sides of a square. He swung his lantern back to the arch and moved across the yard towards it. A slight gust of wind played round his cloak as he emerged into what must have been the main drive. The dense silhouette of the house loomed before him. He swished through tall grass and dead thistle, until his boot tripped painfully on an unseen step. There were three more, wide and shallow, and he climbed them carefully and found himself on a paved terrace. He stood still then and raised his lantern again. The house towered over him, its L shape enclosing him. The mellow Bembridge stone was cloaked in dead creeper which stretched the length and breadth of the building, covering the windows, drooping to ground level, even over the massive oak door.

The house waited. Tom limped across the terrace, shouldered through the creeper curtain and tried the iron door handle. It moved. Time had rusted the catch and hinges but, unbelievably, it was not locked. He put his shoulder to the wood panelling and thrust his weight against it. It resisted him and then gave way grudgingly, as though it was being held from within. The grating of the rusted hinges protested hollowly inside as he staggered forward, clutching his lantern, the weak leg wobbling uncertainly with his weight.

The Watcher groaned, feeling the familiar sliding beginning all over again. The pain in his hands faded — and he was standing at the top of the unlit stairs. So, this one had come, after all. Another piece of the jigsaw from which he was fashioned. There was nothing in this man that would spell out the recipe for disaster, no extremes of emotion on which the house could feed. Yet there was something gathering about him, even now. He probed the deepest recesses of the house and his heart sank, for recognition came to him then. His blood turned cold, but there was nothing that he could ever do to help this one, for he presented no case for death.

Tom stood in the hall, swinging his lantern from side to side. It was a large galleried cavern of a place, with a broad staircase. On the far side was a capacious hearth, and three doors opened away from him to the left and right. Dust and dried leaves lay in drifts about the paved floor. Countless tiny creatures had passed and re-passed in the dust, leaving the faint imprint of their passage in a pattern of aimless trails.

Someone had destroyed a long dining table in the centre of the room, smashing it into two splintered halves which lay on their sides. He sniffed the dry air, aware of vaultless silence which contained no menace, no fear. There was only a very faint odour of mould, overlaid by another, stronger scent — of sweet basil or maybe lavender, but soft

310

and essentially womanly.

The house waited quietly, presenting each of its secret beauties as the pale lantern-light picked out finely carved dining chairs, and a serving table, on which rested a clutter of blackened platters and cutlery and a large bowl. Tom picked up a dish and, breathing on the metal, rubbed it with his sleeve. A dull gleam of silver was his reward. He stared at it and then gently replaced it exactly as he had found it. Do not be tempted — take nothing from here but the memory of it, he reminded himself.

In one corner of the hall stood a graceful long case clock, its delicate filigreed hands stopped at ten minutes past nine. He held the lantern close to its ornate face, marvelling at the quality of the inlaid marquetry of its walnut case and the beautifully painted swags of flowers interwoven round each of the numerals. Ten past nine — in the morning or the evening? Had it stopped when the mechanism ran down or was it at that moment when the fury of Lavenham's soul had destroyed its unwelcome visitors?

He explored every room. Nothing had been disturbed and it looked as though it was all exactly as it had been left by his mother, half a century before. It made him feel very close to her. Up the wide stairs the gallery opened out, with portraits adorning the dim walls. His excitement led him past them with scarcely a glance. He could examine them later.

The rooms were like some forgotten fairy tale, for the beds were made up, their linen and blankets grey with dust. One room warmed him especially from the moment he opened its door and found the wood on the inside carved with wondrously delicate fruit and flowers. The bed hangings were heavily worked, their once brilliant colours long faded into cobwebbed age. A cushion in the winged fireside chair had a beautifully worked 'V' in its centre. He guessed that this had been his mother's bed-chamber. He sat down gingerly in the chair, for his leg was throbbing painfully. He placed the lantern on the ground beside him, rested his arms on its comfortable padded sides and closed his eyes. The room enfolded him. Even up here was that faint scent of lavender in the musty air and something touched him lightly on the forehead. He opened his eyes but the room was empty, save for the furniture dear to a young girl's heart and the almost audible beating of his own. That light caress must have come from a cobweb. He settled back to rest for a little longer, loath to leave this peaceful haven. He dozed and dreamed of loving hands stroking his face.

5

Charles woke with the sound of his own cry echoing in his ears. He lay on his back and felt the sweat clinging to the warm flannel of his night-shirt. His heart was still pounding hard against his ribs, and he made himself breathe slowly and deeply through his nose to try and bring it back to a normal pace.

The odour of his terror was sour in his nostrils.

It was the third time he had had the nightmare in the last month. He wiped the moisture from his face with a corner of the padded coverlet. It was not just the perspiration of his fear, but tears also . . . the tears of a small, terrified boy and, as always, his mind was even now closing upon the reasons for that fear, blocking all memory of the experience within moments of waking.

He had lived with this same doggedly repetitious nightmare for as long as he could remember. When he was a small boy, his mother had always taken him into her bed for the remainder of the night.

They were always the same, these fantasies. A yawning cave of a place, cold and dark and filled with stealthy movement beyond his vision. Without warning, every one of his senses was suddenly assaulted with appalling horror, for in the air about him, emanating from harsh slashes of light, was the deep-throated drone of bees . . . small vicious flying things which gradually formed themselves into a single deadly weapon of death.

Stench of an indescribable filth assailed his nostrils, making him retch, and above his head, descending a shadowy staircase, a figure floated like woodsmoke.

There was no firm shape to this central entity, save for

313

the impression of hatred in the angular blur of its face. Such loathing emanated from it in an uncontrolled babbling . . . a jumble of shrieking words which drilled themselves into him and shrivelled his very soul.

'GET OUT OF THIS HOUSE, LAWRENCE- . . . WHITE SPAWN OF A GOAT'S EXCREMENT . . . FILTH OF A DEAD COW'S WOMB . . . DRABANEYSAPA, SHAV . . . SHAVA NA KENNER . . . .'

There was no meaning to some of the words but they were always the same, always spat at him with such utter detestation that, by the time he came to manhood, they were engraved, without comprehension, upon his soul. In their wake, the droning burst upon him — and the bees were all about him, crawling on his body, his arms and legs, face and eyelids, and the terrible, agonizing stings were a million burning daggers in his flesh.

He screamed — and screaming, could not stop; his hands stretched out to ward them off and he took hold of iron bars and shook them with all his might. . . .

Then woke, shivering and terrified, for the instant before consciousness drove out the memory of what it was that brought him to such a state. It was all the stranger that the whole thing was gone from him soon after he woke, and it was never possible for him to remember the details of the dream in the morning — only that he was a child alone in that place and utterly, stupefyingly terrified.

He smiled bitterly, remembering the blessed relief and comfort of snuggling close to his mother's warm body and feeling her strength slowly wearing away the terror.

It was the memory of that warmth which had moved him to wed Leonie Farndell. The choice was not a good one. Oh, she had done her best, he had no doubt of that. She had given him two sons and regarded him with lofty respect — but she was too weak, both spiritually and physically, to retain his interest. A delicate chest in youth had quickly turned her into an invalid.

She also appeared to be increasingly nervous in his presence.

There was no offer of comfort from her now, no refuge from the terrors which still assailed him. She had always been frightened by the ferocity of his anguish, and removed herself from his bed quite early in the marriage — after the birth of John, their second son.

It was the private shame of a lifetime that Charles Freeland Bayless was still, in middle life, so afraid of the dark that it was a nightly act of bravery to climb into his single bed.

Weeks would pass and his sleep would be so deep and dreamless that the tension eased and he was able to go about his business with vigour and enthusiasm. Then it would be upon him again, and with the shock of his waking, the fear would gnaw at him for days and nights afterwards.

He had never before had a recurrence so close upon the last. He began to wonder whether they were actually generated in some way by the recent shock in his life.

Charles had recently taken on six new bargees and was surprised this day to see that one of them appeared to be a woman. He stood on the edge of the wooden jetty at Dell Quay, watching the baskets of coal being filled from the tar black barge moored alongside, hauled up to the quay on heavy sisal ropes the width of a man's arm, and stowed into the line of waiting carts. As each cart received its load it moved away, pulled by four huge punches, and another took its place.

He noticed that the slight figure at the tiller of the barge below him had a definite female shape.

'Hey, you . . . what are you doing there?' he called down into the boat. Six faces looked up at him; faces blackened by coal dust so that the features were blurred and only the eyes retained their sparkle.

The woman pointed to herself and he nodded.

'Your clerk took me on with me brother Nat, yer honour. I'm a good navigator an' he said that he could get another sack of coal from the weight saved in the boat.'

She grinned up at him, a smutty, ragged creature, entirely lacking in the deference expected of her, an air of cheeky independence in every line of her small body. She put her head on one side and regarded him intently, as though she was perfectly confident of winning any battle of words they might have.

He shrugged and turned away. If the clerk had hired her, she must be of some use to him.

He saw the gypsy girl again the following day as he rode out from Chichester to Dell Quay. She was walking ahead of him along the road from Chichester with a man at her side, a large basket of groceries on her head. The coal dust had been wiped from their faces, and he was struck by the similarity in their straight backs and features; her companion must be the brother she had spoken of. He had a brief impression of black hair and two pairs of piercing blue eyes raised to his, before he was past the two well-laden figures. He lifted his crop in greeting and was rewarded by that flashing smile again.

It stayed with him for the rest of the day.

He had the nightmare that night and, waking, found himself yearning for the comfort of a warm and loving refuge. Sparkling blue eyes and those long, strong arms about him. . . . He took her image and held it, burying his face in the memory of that riot of blue-black hair.

Gypsies had always intrigued him, for there was gypsy blood in him which was never referred to by the Freelands — nor by his mother, who knew of the story but, being from Portugal, had no clear conception of what a gypsy was.

Grandpapa Bayless had been a gypsy — albeit a wealthy one, or else he would not have been permitted to wed Lavinia Freeland. His blood still rankled in the family, though, so that Charles had been reared to conceal that relationship, to feel ashamed of it. He had, nevertheless, always nursed a deep curiosity concerning his Bayless relations, and because they were considered *persona non grata* they assumed an exciting importance in his mind.

Who were they? Where did they live these days? What was their situation? The questions had never been answered. Now, as casually as he was able, he rode up on to Apuldram Common in search of the encampment.

Summer softened the barren lines of the common. The few trees, huddling close to the river banks, had been fashioned into strange shapes by winters of fierce gales off the sea and grew at a slant, their tops scythed and leafless. Closer to the ground, new grass was a thick verdant green and the hawthorn bright with pink and white blossom. He came upon the little camp in the shelter of a stand of young birches, the lace of their upper branches heavy with witches' knots. A covered waggon was tucked into a flat strip of chalky ground where the curving bank of the stream sloped down to the water's edge. Two shaggy ponies looked up at him briefly as he slid off his well-groomed chestnut and knotted the reins round the silvery bole of a tree. Beneath the waggon a long-nosed lurcher dog growled at him, crouched behind one of the wheels. The fellies and spokes were painted in bright slashes of yellow and red.

The girl was there. She was squatting over a fire, behind the waggon, stirring something in a large iron pot. She looked up as he appeared and rose to her feet at the sight of him.

He raised his hat. 'Good morrow. I was crossing to Fishbourne and saw your waggon there,' he said, suddenly feeling less certain of his excuses than he would have liked.

She smiled then, and her face was suddenly alight with impishness. There was no indication of archness or servility.

'Sar shan,' she said. Her voice was deep for one so small. There was a softness, a huskiness there that he found delightfully pleasing.

'My clerk tells me that you and your brother are

317

gypsies,' he said, standing across the fire from her. A trail of thin blue smoke curled up between them. Something in the cooking pot smelt of bruised herbs.

She inclined her head and then pointed at the grass slope. 'Sit you down, sir. Will you take some refreshment at our hearth?' She glanced toward the waggon and back at him, making assessments. 'Nat, he be over to the quay. Should be back soon if it were him you was seeken'.'

He unclipped his cloak, shrugged it off his shoulders and settled himself down in the springy grass. 'I'd welcome some,' he said sniffing the aroma appreciatively. 'No, it's not Nat especially that I came to see. Maybe you could solve the puzzle as well as he.'

Her hair fell over her face in a heavy drape of unchecked waves and springy curls. She brushed it back over her shoulders and hurried across to the waggon. In a moment she was back, two large mugs in her hands. She dipped a ladle into the steaming liquid, poured it neatly into a mug and held it out to Charles.

He sat, cupping it in both hands. 'What is your name?'
She smiled at him. 'Boudicca Smith, sir.'

'I've not seen you or your brother in these parts until recently. Have you come far?'

She was squatting beside the hearth again, poking at the glowing embers with a short iron prong. Her hands were small and brown but very narrow, long-fingered — strong.

'Well, bor, we always travels in a circle, see. We keep on the move, except when we've work to do in any place, and then we stays until we have enough saved up and can move on to the next place.' She grinned at him, quirking finely drawn black eyebrows at him. 'Never outstay our welcome, simensa, if you see what I mean.'

It was very pleasant sitting in the shade of silver-dappled birch trees, sipping a strange and delicious concoction and listening to the soft husky tones of this small ragged, fascinating girl.

'You have a strange language,' he said. 'What does "Simensa" mean.'

318

She grinned at him again and her eyes danced. She had a deep cleft in her chin and she rubbed it.

'Cousin,' she said. Her face became serious, the clown's grin hidden away for the moment. "Simensa" means cousin of our people.'

'Do you call all visitors to your hearth "cousin" then? A very friendly term. I like it well.'

She shook her head, bouncing the sunlight off the shining waves of her hair. Laughter returned to her eyes. 'Not anyone, bor. Just you.'

They sat on either side of the fire, searching each others' faces through the thin ribbon of woodsmoke.

'I'm sorry,' he said at last. 'I don't understand you.'

'Think then, cousin. Did no one ever tell you that you get your name from Romany folk?' She smoothed the front of her brown woollen skirt with careful fingers. 'Put it this way, if you will. Your granfer Jess Bayless an' my great-granmer were brother and sister. He was seventh child in a family of nine, the only boy. My great-granmer was Saiforella Bayless, the oldest daughter of Jasper and Grace Bayless.'

She sat back on her heels, calmly watching the impact her words were having upon this coolly elegant gorgio. 'Under all your nice clothes an' learnen' — you're still a Bayless, bor. Just like Nat 'n' me.'

He sat like a figure of stone; shock, outrage and fascination chasing each other through his face.

'I know,' she said calmly. ''Tis a great shame to claim you for cousin when you see me with the coal dirt of your barges under my nails. Nat an' me, we're no prize, are we?' She watched the shock slowly fade from his face. 'We've not come here to shame you, sir. We only stayed by chance when Nat heard that there was work offered. No one will know from either of us of the blood we share.'

She put out her hand and placed it squarely over his. For a second he would have snatched it away from her, but she regarded him steadily with neither insolence nor familiarity. The warmth from her small palm steadied him and he took the hand and held it in both of his — and from it there seemed to flow a strength which softened his rejection, permitting him to relax.

Her eyes lifted and looked beyond him. She took her hand away to push the hair from her eyes again.

'Here's Nat, come back at last,' she said, and there was a faint regret in the way she said it that remained as a tantalizing echo in his mind after he had left them.

He threw his mount's reins to the stable lad and strode into the house from the yard door, his steps echoing down the passage as he went.

'Ah, there you are, Charles. We wondered what was keeping you.' There was a suggestion of petulance in his wife's voice as she looked up from her chair when he put his head round the withdrawing room door. She was entertaining four other ladies and a portly elderly gentleman wearing a most unfashionable periwig and frock coat. Charles, hovering in the doorway, bowed to the ladies.

'Good afternoon to you Mrs Wood, Miss Audrey, Miss Cecily, Mrs Pescod . . . How are you, parson?'

'Will you not join us then, my dear?'

He shook his head at his wife, his eyes cold. 'Forgive me if you will, but I must change and take the carriage over to Goodwood. I have business with his lordship at six o'clock. I shall have a word with Freeland and John before I leave. Excuse me, if you please.'

He bowed again and closed the door on the chorus of disappointment. Damned old maids' tea parties were not for him. He took the stairs two at a time. Really, he was feeling remarkably happy. What an extraordinary meeting that had been, out there on the common. What a fetching little thing his gypsy cousin was . . . and how pleasant her brother Nat also. A silent, watchful man — but there had been no animosity in him. If anything, the animosity had come from Charles himself at first. Rough and untutored peasants, that is what the Smiths were, and yet it was astounding to discover such simple pride. They truly

320

thought it was he who should feel honoured to claim relationship with the Hator tribe.

There were portraits in ornate gilded frames on the stair wall, mostly of Leonie's Farndell relatives, and a couple of Freelands. A huge and ornate chandelier hung from the roof in the curve of the stair. Its crystal droplets and flower petals glittered in a million reflected diamonds from its candle sconces. He had been proud of that purchase, for it was similar to a fine pair in the ballroom at Sibford. Now, suddenly, it looked a little ostentatious. He thought of the brother and sister at rest beside their camp fire, with the gentle pink light of the embers tinting their olive skins.

What a contrast. What a yawning chasm existed between his kind of life and that of the Smiths. Looking round the door of his sons' schoolroom at the two boys lounging in leather chairs with a table of cards between them, he wondered whether they might not have been much happier if they had been toasting chestnuts with Nat and Dudie.

It was not difficult to check on the Smiths and their movements, after that. A quick glance at the manifest books in the office at Dell Quay gave him all the information he needed to know. Dudie only went over to Portsmouth with the barge when the cargo was on the maximum load line. There were many days when Nat worked on his own with the other men. Charles soon discovered that on these days he would often be gone all night, for he caroused with his companions in the taverns — and if there was a woman to be had, would stay with her.

He returned to the camp often after that first day, drawn by the warmth of his welcome from both Dudie and Nat, telling himself that it was just to hear the talk of his forebears — and because this life of theirs was so fascinatingly different, so unfettered, compared with his own. At the back of his mind the other reason hid behind his fear of it. It grew a little every time he was with her.

He learned something new with every visit. He was always given the same cup and plate when he ate with them. 'A man and a woman must never use the same dishes,' Nat explained. 'If I ate from Dudie's plate or you drank from her mug it would be mokada. It is mokada if a woman steps across the plate of food you may leave on the ground. Then both the food and the plate must be destroyed. It is mokada to eat the flesh of a fox, a cat, a rat. These creatures are unclean, for they are meat-eaters.'

The Romanies, he discovered, lived off the land and ate mostly fruit, nuts and fish — with the occasional bird or hedgehog when the season was fruitful. Anything with bristles was clean and therefore acceptable to eat: the wild boar, pig and hedgehog — but even then the meat had to be cured with salt and saltpetre for several hours. The rules were absolute. They were never disobeyed.

It was one of the main strengths of the tribe.

The Smiths considered gorgios like himself — and all his cultured contemporaries — to be unclean in their habits and their hearts. To live in a house was to live in your own filth. Romanies moved all the time, rested on fresh grass and harboured no germs about them. They bathed in spring and summer and kept their bodies clean, as the Romans used to do. They suffered from fewer illnesses and lived longer than the gorgios. Their teeth were less inclined to decay and fall out. Their breath was sweeter. They considered themselves to be leading better lives than the gorgios and harboured no envy in their hearts.

Charles, astounded by this new angle upon his life, was inclined, upon reflection, to agree with them.

One evening he was late finishing the books at Dell Quay, so that it was past sunset by the time he swung up into the saddle and turned his horse towards Chichester. He took the new lane past Rymans and Saint Mary's church and cut out across the common towards the twist in the river where the Smiths were camped.

He saw the glow from their hearth through the trees and drove his heels into his horse's flanks. He was utterly weary. The night before had been shredded with yet another of the terrors that were slowly draining his health away. He just must see Dudie. Maybe she could help him. Her name drove his heart up into his throat. He thought of little else these days than the warmth and fierce tenderness of her, soothing the canker of fear and tiredness from him.

She was alone in the camp. Nat was off to Portsmouth and would be back on the morning tide.

Oh, Dudie, he groaned with longing.

She seemed almost to have been expecting him, for she came down from the covered waggon as he leapt from his horse. She was dressed in a bright red skirt that glowed like a great poppy, and a scarlet bodice that showed the froth of a white blouse beneath it. It was as though the sun in setting had left its reflection upon her. Round her shoulders was a shawl, knitted in a clash of brilliant colours. She had been combing her hair and now it fell about her shoulders in a shining cape.

'Sar shan, simensa,' she said calmly.

He picked her up from the bottom rung of the waggon ladder and swung her round in an arc. She was so light, like a doll, and she smelt of woodsmoke and mint. She steadied herself, gripping his upper arms.

He bent his head and kissed her for a long time. She did nothing to escape his embrace but put her arms round his neck and settled to the exploration of his mouth, the contours of his face, the vast longing which she found in him.

He thought that she had dressed herself for him, but this was Poorano Rarti, when the joy of their survival through centuries of hardship was celebrated with song and dance and every Romany man, woman and child dressed in their finest togs and gave their spirits joyfully to the occasion. It was sad that Nat was away on this festival night and that she could not go and spend it with other Romany families. But she had decided to prepare herself as though there would be others beside her hearth — and dance and sing and break panum on her own. At the back of her mind she had known that her evening would not be solitary.

He was such a deeply unhappy man, this Charles Bayless, she thought. Just how troubled he was, he obviously did not realize himself. He was badly scarred with the bruises of a past which were not of his making, but the wounds went deep and from them he would simply wither and decay if no joy were ever to enter his life. She sorrowed for his situation, and the sorrow brought with it a kind of love.

'Come,' she said to Charles, sliding out of his embrace and taking him by the hand. 'Today is a special day for all Romanies. It is the time for thanking God for our survival and asking for the continuance of the Romany tribes.'

He did not want to think of gypsies and their quaint customs. He had just discovered that he had, after all, a capacity to burn . . . to want . . . to love a woman. There had been such a feeling in him only once, some years before − for a young Arab youth of great beauty and tenderness. Their affair had lasted for seven passionate months. The boy had then turned his lovely, melancholy eyes upon an elderly but extremely wealthy duke, and had died the following year of a mysterious and agonizing illness. Now, suddenly, here it was again: that glorious liquid burning of the body and soul when his heart thundered in his chest and threatened to leap from his throat. He wanted just to take this small and vibrant creature and lose himself in her. He put an arm round her waist, but she turned to him, gently extricating herself, and a warning was in her eyes.

'Help me to celebrate, bor. Nat is away with the boat or we would be making very merry this evening. Drink and eat and dance with me . . . please?'

He did as she wished. Indeed, having settled among sheepskins beside the fire, he found that he was more than comfortable − and it was exquisite titillation to watch her as she brought him food which she must have been preparing all day.

For the first time in his life he ate hedgehog cooked in

the Romany way. The little bodies were wrapped in wild mint, packed round with clay and then baked slowly in the embers of the fire. When the clay finally began to crack and flake away they were scooped out of the ashes. As the clay was removed, the prickles and skin came away with it and the tender pink meat of the little creature was moist and succulent — and quite as fine a delicacy as veal or baby sucking pig.

She brought him cakes made from hazel nut and dried plum and plied him with a strong sweet liquid made, she told him, from elderflower three years before. It was a fine rich liqueur and he could feel it blurring the edges of his vision.

In a low, sweet voice she crooned strangely haunting songs in a language he did not recognize. She clapped her hands in time to the rhythm and then leapt to her feet and began to dance. Night came down and drowned the world, and there was emptiness everywhere save for the one globe of leaping firelight in which they dwelt in breathless isolation.

She came to him in the end, dropping down beside him, her breasts heaving with the exertions of her dance. Her hair had lost its sleek orderliness and was once more a mop of rioting black curls stuck about her damp forehead. He drew her close to him and wiped the dark tendrils from her shining face.

She let his hands discover the neat small breasts within the white blouse. Later she sat on the waggon step and let him unlace her bodice front.

When she was naked to the waist she took him into the waggon.

Dudie. . . . Her name kept flooding his mind like a great warm wave. Attending to the weekly soap allocation aboard the *Fortunée*, he shifted on his hard stool and closed his eyes so that the sheer glorious sense of well-being in him should not attract attention. She had taken him into her with touching tenderness and then with such mounting passion. There was so much, he discovered, that she had to give. He tried to veer away from the memory of her, but his body tingled afresh and he felt the hardening of his genitals like a guileless boy's.

He had remained with Dudie until dawn sent him sleepily home, to change his clothing and appear at the breakfast table in some sort of order. He had not wanted to go — but she had climbed over his weary body in the waggon bunk and fetched water from the river and washed herself from head to toe. Leonie had never stirred herself to do such a thing after the brief couplings which had brought them sons but no satisfaction. Dudie was different; another experience which put his nervous searchings to shame, for she had taken her time — and made him take his with her. She had used her body, her fingers, her mouth — and created in him a sustained excitement which had lasted through all the long hours of night, turning them into minutes. His continuing arousal at the mere thought of her only heightened his satisfaction. He had surely given her immense pleasure — but she had done something so much more astounding for him. She had, he decided, ennobled a manhood long made suspect. The secret dreams of his mother's warm body, which had brought him to his first climax, were washed away now — in his forty-third year — by a girl young enough to be his daughter, who had given him a taste of gratification as he had never before known it.

'No, you must not come back this evening,' she had said to him firmly as she parted. 'Nat will be back then.' Her eyes had softened at his disappointment and she had put her arms round his neck and nibbled the lobe of his ear. 'There will be other times . . . if that is how you wish it, simensa.'

Other times. . . . The thought buoyed his spirits through the ride back to Chichester and after, when he went about his business.

6

'What has come over you lately, Charles? You seem almost drunk all the time.'

Leonie was most concerned. She stared anxiously down the length of the breakfast table at her husband's flushed face as he tucked into an immoderately large helping of devilled kidneys.

'Are you quite well, my dear? You are surely running some sort of fever, for I have never seen the colour so high in your face before.'

Charles laughed. He wiped his platter clean with a crust and then leaned forward and helped himself to more bread and damson preserve. 'I am in the pink of condition, my love, have no fear,' he said with complete satisfaction.

Indeed, he was. He had never felt so vigorous, so truly alive, in his entire life. Everything seemed to be happening at once, and the last few days had made him certain that Fate was suddenly smiling with extraordinary benevolence upon him.

He had found the moment, kindly created for him by Mrs Furze, to talk, at last, with Tom Heritage. It had been a delightful exchange, lacking in any of the patriotic animosity that might have been expected, and would lead to more such meetings, he was certain. Added to that, a sudden and unexpected step had been taken in the direction of the private dream he was sharing with his young son, John.

Lord Egremont of Alfold had set the wheels in motion to float a company intent on building a canal system whose aim would be to join the River Wey with the River Arun, thus creating a commercial waterway between London and the south coast. Feeling as he did about the need for such a system between Portsmouth, Chichester and Arundel, Charles was now in a fever to see Egremont and, if possible to join the Wey and Arun Navigation Trust, once it came into being.

As if that was not excitement enough, he had been with Dudie again the previous night, when Nat had stayed in Chichester. It will fade after a few weeks, he kept telling himself. This feeling of light-headedness would settle down into its correct perspective and the visits to Dudie would become the natural expression of occasional release that a man should get from such warm womanly attentions.

The feeling of intoxication remained. Reason told him that it was certainly the result of his general optimism at the moment but he knew in his heart that all of it was Dudie.

She was a witch, that small, beautiful girl. She was like no other woman he had ever come across. Her skin was young and warm and smelt and tasted of fresh flowers.

She had washed her hair in the river at least three times since he had been visiting her, and afterwards rubbed into it some fragrant herbal juice which not only enhanced its luxuriant shine but gave it a curious scent of something which made his mouth water. Leonie's maid only washed her mistress's head two or three times in a whole year. There was some theory that the natural oils would otherwise be lost.

Dudie's black hair shone with health. There was no question of dryness or head lice.

She was so young and yet she had the most surprising attitude towards him, for she was not in awe of his age or his position. Rather the reverse, for she attended his mind — and, later, his body — with the same intense concentration upon every smallest sensation which might bring him even greater pleasure. And aside from such devotion, she regarded him with a strange mixture of motherliness and compassion.

It was not love with her. Maybe it was something more permanent. There seemed no words to describe what was now, for him, a madness of the heart. He was more than content to wallow in it and let the whole experience follow its own course.

He drained his coffee cup and reached for the pot to replenish it. Leonie seemed to shrivel before the bounding good humour of him. She coughed into her kerchief. He stared down the damask-covered table at her, seeing the livid red patches on either cheek.

'Really, Leonie, why must you insist on taking breakfast with me at this hour when you would be wiser not to leave your bed before mid-morning.'

She cleared her throat, biting back the pain in her chest.

'I am your wife,' she said simply. 'Other women may lie abed all morning, but this is the best part of the day and I like to try to have it with you during the summer months at the least.'

For the past three winters she had travelled abroad on the recommendation of Doctor Priestley in search of warmth for her thin body. The change of air and pleasant sunshine had helped in the beginning, but now the upheaval was becoming too much for her failing health.

Suddenly he longed to tell her about Tom. She knew his family history — though it was seldom mentioned, for the Farndells were wealthy millers and there were members of the family in many of the villages south of Chichester, including Henry Farndell in Apuldram, uncle to Leonie. Baylesses had made too deep an imprint upon the life of that village for the details of its dramas to be lost upon its neighbours.

She knew of his father — and the string of crimes attributed to him. She knew also of Aunt Violet Heritage and the strong memories that had been left of her in Apuldram, along with the oval portrait in Great-aunt Mary's hall at Crouchers.

No, he could not mention Tom, for the one thing that already overlaid their acquaintance was Tom's fascination

329

for Lavenham. Funny, he had not thought of the place for years. Yet now it was with him again, returning to chip away at his peace of mind — and all because he knew that in some way, by fair means or foul, Tom Heritage would find a way to set foot there at some time in the future.

The nightmare enveloped him once more that night.

In the morning, still sweating from the experience, it came to him that Dudie might be the saviour of his sanity — as she had been his saviour in so many other ways.

She was away with the barge, and the manifest book recorded that she would not be back before noon of the following day. He felt unreasonably bereft, as though he was denied the thing most precious to him.

He visited the Bayless camp on his way home that evening and sat on the steps of the waggon, out of reach of the long-haired lurcher, who still skulked on the end of her chain between the brightly painted waggon wheels.

It came to him, as though Dudie had suggested it, that he should go to Lavenham before Tom. He could hear her voice, hear the calm reasoning in it.

Go now? He simply could not endure the terror which instantly gripped him.

But ask Dudie to go with him? She almost certainly would, for the gypsy Baylesses still thought of the property as being their private province and there had been several sightings over the years of Romany caravans encamped on the overgrown west lawn.

The idea soothed the panic in his chest and he stood up, decision made.

As he swung up on to the horse once more and left the camp, a fine rain began to fall across the common.

Dudie inclined her head, as always the sage, his uncomplaining mentor.

He had a very pleasant voice, even when he was relating something as frightening to himself as his recurrent nightmares obviously were, she thought. She watched the frustration in his face as he struggled to recall any detail, but it was all buried too deeply. There was nothing to relate, saving that trapped feeling and the grasping of iron railings.

He buried his face against her hair and she held him tightly, feeling the tremor in him.

'There is one thing you can do, you know,' she said. 'Keep a pen and paper beside your bed — and when you have the dream, write it down while it is still clear in your mind.'

Such simple advice and so practical. Why he had not thought of doing this years before, he could not imagine. Within days of her words it happened again — and this time he was ready and wrote every terrible detail on two sheets of paper whilst the reality of it was still in him. Afterwards he lay back and fell into a deep and dreamless sleep, as though the conveyance of his experience to paper had halved its capacity to afflict him.

The essay, for that is how it read back to him, brought with it a great flood of memory — and with it, a strange peace. For the words were those of a small boy, long gone. With a deep sense of gratitude he took it to Dudie and she sat on the top step of the waggon, with the lurcher curled quietly round her feet, and read the whole piece slowly, silently mouthing the words to herself.

. . . They said I was not to look at the big house but the garden is so pretty. There are plums in the orchard and I can just reach a low branch. The sun is warm and the air hums. It feels so pleasant and safe here. . . . Who will ever know if I just look in these windows? There is a perfect rose growing on the creeper here. It is almost white on the outside but the middle petals are a lovely deep pink. It smells like Mama's perfume in the blue bottle on her dressing table. I will pick it and give it to her. . . .

There is so much dust on the windows, I cannot see very much of the inside. There is a big hearth across the other side of the room, and the carved staircase window beside me shows long sunbeams across one end of the room. . . . If I try the door, I shall only push it open, so that I can stand in the opening and look in without moving off the step. It is not even locked . . . the sound of the rusty hinges makes me jump.

It is a very large hall. Everywhere is dust and dried leaves which move with the wind from outside. If I go inside — just a little — I can see the whole staircase.

There is a funny humming sound all round me in this place. Suddenly the room is not so warm and pleasant any more and I am frightened when the door slams shut behind me with a sudden *crash*. . . . It is dark. The sun has gone from the long window. I wish I had not come here. There is something I cannot understand. Mama . . . Mama . . . I want to go home. The great humming sound is in my ears, all round me. The air is getting thicker now that the door is shut, and there is a terrible smell everywhere . . . terrible . . . I feel sick. Mama, help me.

Oh . . . the staircase — something is up there: a misty cloud, coming down into the darkness and yet I can see it . . . there is a face and a voice and yet there is nothing. I am so frightened. Oh Mama, I want you. . . .

The droning in the air picks up a dreadful gobbling voice. It hates me. It is coming to destroy me. I cannot understand what it is saying.

'OUT WITH YOU, LAWRENCE. OUT OF THIS PLACE.'

Please, I'm sorry. I did not mean to come in. I am Charles. I am not Lawrence. Something on my face . . . and then more and more. Things are crawling all over me, and suddenly they are stabbing me, burning my face and arms and digging for my eyes.

I am running . . . and the terrible screaming hate is mixed up with the drone of the burning bees all over my body.

'DRABANEY SAPA, SHAV. SHAVA NE KEN-NER . . . '

The words mean nothing but I know they are vile and cursing and full of a dreadful violence. I run crying, but cannot hear my own sobs, only the voice and the roaring drone of those furious, deadly bees. . . . I run into something but my eyes are too swollen to be able to see. My hands grip iron bars and I shake them in my terror, for I can hear my mama calling and I cannot get to her. Oh, Mama. . . .

Dudie looked up from the page in her hand. 'Do you remember writing this?' she asked.

Charles shook his head. 'It's extraordinary. I remember nothing but going to sleep, having the dream and waking, feeling oddly refreshed in the morning. Then I saw that I must have written it down, for there were the sheets, covered in my own handwriting, on the night table beside the bed. There was no fear or shaking. Just a sense of relief.'

She scanned the page and turned it over, then took up the second sheet. 'Here,' she said, pointing. 'Do you know what these words are?'

'No. They mean nothing at all to me. Maybe my imagination made them up the way that children do invent things sometimes.'

'No, Charles, you did not invent them. They are Romany words.'

He stared at her, his sandy eyebrows bunched low over his eyes. 'I will tell you their meaning. They are a curse, you see. They are words only uttered under the greatest possible provocation: "a curse upon you, snake spawn of a snake's rut. Begone before death in all generations. Death to you in my house. . . . " '

They sat close together, gripping hands, silent.

It was there, then, the reality of all the old tales. Strangely, he felt as though a great weight had been lifted from him as his eyes wandered over the pages of scrawled writing.

'I think,' he said, 'that it is Grandfer Jess's sister Amy. She was a cripple and insane in latter life. The Freelands have always maintained that she really hated Grandmama, and Papa too. My mother used to say that Papa had had a very unhappy childhool. Maybe *she* made it so for him. . . . '

They went to the gates of Lavenham together. They walked from the common down the new lane, past Saint Mary's church, and Rymans, with its single solid-looking watch-tower and the tall solar windows; past the empty shell of two workers' cottages and south to where the lane met the toll road to Dell Quay. They turned right and then left on to the track which led to New Barn Cottages.

Charles paused and stared at the untidy muddle of buildings. 'I remember these so well when I was small,' he said. 'There were Baylesses living there at that time. I used to play with the children but Mama thought little of them . . . Granfer's cousins, who used to run the breeding stables with Aunt Violet. In those days it was quite an honour to own a Lavenham horse. They were some of the finest horse-flesh in England, so Uncle John used to say.'

'He was right,' Dudie agreed. 'They are still around, you know. Less pure and not as swift and powerful as they were in Jess's day — but still the distinctive honey colour with white mane and tail.'

He was surprised. He had thought that the Lavenham Stud had ceased to exist when the Baylesses left Apuldram.

'Manfri Bayless and his cousin Rueb lived here for some years,' Dudie told him. 'It was Manfri's grandchildren that you probably remember. They are back on the road now. Manfri and Rueb are dead, and Polly, who was married to Manfri, she only died two or three years ago. She was a gorgio, of course. Polly Ayles. . . . '

Charles put his arm round her shoulders. 'You are a walking fount of knowledge,' he said, giving her a little squeeze.

She smiled up at him. 'It is the way we are reared. We all have our lineage firmly fixed in our heads from a very early age.'

They moved on down the rutted track once more.

'It's just as well, for it seems that I must spell out your own family tree for you as well as my own.'

The track curved suddenly to the left, and on the right side a pair of tall gates stood, choked in a straggle of twisted undergrowth.

Charles stared at them.

'This is the entrance,' he said, feeling his throat tighten.

The gates were of iron, wrought into a design of oak leaves in a central medallion with straight bars on either side. Creepers had long taken charge and imprisoned them in a blanket of convolvulus, so that little of their elegance was now visible. He tore at the clinging greenery and pulled it away roughly. Beneath the stringy tendrils the delicate metal leaves with their tiny acorns had rusted through the peeling black paint. The stone gate pillars stood firm, each topped by a single orb of Ventnor stone.

Dudie said nothing but stood on the grassy track and watched Charles tearing at the wild creepers on the gate. He worked silently as though time were running away with him. Then he stood back, rubbing the palms of his sap-stained hands down the sides of his breeches.

'Iron bars . . . ' he said. He gripped them with both hands and shook the gates with all his strength. Rust flaked and fell, showering his coat with red dust. 'These were the iron bars of my dream . . . I recognize them.'

'Except that it was no dream, bor, but a child's clear memory,' Dudie said softly behind him.

He turned and stared at her. She tucked her arm into his and held him close.

'Don't you see? What you've dreamed about all these years is the memory of what actually happened to you. You were very small, only five or six, and had no explanation for what befell you in that empty hall. So you pushed it right down into the back of your mind, denying its existence — even though you *knew* that it had happened.'

The right-hand gate suddenly swung away out of his grip and fell with a crash into the waist-high brambles of the overgrown drive. Charles, startled, leapt backwards with an oath, his face blazing white. Dudie held on to his arm and felt his whole frame trembling with shock.

'Come away now, simensa,' she said gently. 'I will come back with you another day and we will take it a step further. There is plenty of time.'

335

The dream deserted him. His nights were untroubled, save for the depth of his desire to spend them with Dudie. Sometimes he took the pages of his writing out of his night table drawer and re-read them; somehow, to see the events written down in clear pen strokes, to be able to go over each word again and again, seemed to remove the horror and his fear receded. With summer in full flood, he knew that he could bear to venture closer to the house hidden so securely behind the marching oakwoods.

Nat Smith was most concerned when she told him of the plan to visit the old house.

'Don' 'e go, Dudie. Let 'im go alone if 'e has to . . . but don' go too. That place is mokada. We all know it. Why defy what *is*?'

'I must go with him,' she said simply. 'He relies on my strength. You know that.'

'E wants too much from you. I'm not blind, bor. I c'n use my eyes when I have to. You'll be too clever by half, one day — just you see. You'll end up with that gorgio's chav and then you'll never see 'im again. Let 'im work out 'is own salvation.'

She turned away from him. There was no point in trying to explain her feelings, for he knew well that she felt no love for Charles Bayless — only a kind of compassion which had its reward in the obvious joy he felt in her. In the meantime, she would continue to sluice her genitals with the ointment made from ground ivy and to drink the concoction brewed from blue cohosh root which prevented conception. It had served her well up to now, but recently she had begun to worry for she had not been mokada for six weeks.

'Walk with me down to Lavenham and let us go mushgaying, bor. Let us get the whole thing over — now, this very minute,' Dudie said to Charles one afternoon.

He lifted his head from the pillow and leant over her on one elbow, searching her face, feeling a strange urgency in her. She lay on her back looking up at him, the question in the lift of her eyebrows. Her mouth was moist, upturned at the corners. She felt the peace and compliance in him after the purging of his passion.

It was high summer. Birds sang above the waggon in the highest branches of the leaning trees. Out in the harbour the gulls screeched and swooped over the dark hulls of the prison ships.

'Very well,' he said. 'If I think about it for long, I can always find an excuse for putting it off.'

They dressed after splashing in the curve of the little stream as Dudie had taught him. Cleansing himself after being with her was now part of the ritual of loving Dudie and he knew that he would follow this pattern always. Dressed, they wandered slowly over the common and down the network of high-hedged lanes, impervious to the sharp glances of passers-by. He was whole in her presence only — and she, feeling the depth of his well-being, feigned animation to cover the unhappiness slowly growing in her.

It was almost time for Nat to make the decision to go, almost time to withdraw from this complex and passionate man whose suppressed violence had begun to worry her of late. How would he react if she admitted that she was almost certain that she was carrying his child? She knew it was quite within his capability to kill her. There was more of his father in him than he realized. Still, if he was able to exorcise the fears of that house, he would gain the strength to manage after she had gone.

They paused at the entrance and then picked their way through the brambles, over the fallen gate. Charles leaned down, hauled it up and propped it against its stone pillar, before following Dudie through the high sweep of grass and fern which choked what had been the drive. They walked slowly, thrashing the overgrowth and staring about them. Trees had marched, unchecked, across an old paddock, and the wall of the kitchen garden to their right was almost invisible now. The house emerged slowly; first the roof, with a nest of small chimneys and what had once been two stacks of tall Jacobean chimney twists, broken now and long since tumbled invisible into the long grass. Charles gripped Dudie's hand and went forward, his face almost grey in the sharp sunlight. They skirted a fallen tree and came out into clear ground. The house was displayed before them. He sucked in his breath and Dudie watched him closely. She had no need to look at the house, for she and Nat had been here several times — as had most of the Bayless clan. None of them had felt the slightest sensation of horror. The beings that were here were within the balance of Charles's own mind.

They walked very slowly round the side of the house and on to a terrace whose flagstones were lifting under the growth of weeds beneath. To their right, a wild expanse of high grass was all that showed of the fine lawns which had once rolled in emerald perfection down to the banks of the Chichester Channel below Dell Quay. Here and there a sudden splash of bright colour drowned in undergrowth suggested the flower gardens of former years. As they picked their way along the terrace, a flock of noisy crows rose up in a frightened black swathe from the roof of the house and swung screaming out over the water.

Charles stood still. His hand gripping Dudie's was damp and the strength of his fingers almost made her cry out.

'It is here.' His voice was hoarse, almost a whisper. 'I can feel it. Hatred . . . withdrawal . . . warning . . . Can you not feel it too? Right here in the sunshine. Even on the outside of the place?'

She did feel something, it was true. There seemed to be a brooding watchfulness about its dust-blinded windows, as though it was drawing a cloak about itself and denying them the right to explore further.

'I only feel what you are telling me — because you are telling me,' she said gently. 'I have been here in the past with Nat and there was no atmosphere then — just a fine old kenner with a lot of valuable stuff inside that no one has ever felt inclined to take.' She laughed. 'That's the part that I have always found so strange. Not the tales of ghosts and evil happenings but the fact that it is furnished with paintings and fine furniture and even silver in there . . . and no one has taken a single spoon.'

They sat on the wall, looking up at the house. Let it get used to them, she thought. Let them absorb some of the atmosphere and get the pulse back to a normal rate.

'If you and Nat have been here,' Charles said, trying to keep the surprise out of his voice for she had never mentioned this before. 'Why did you not take a souvenir or two? I'm told that most gypsies have few qualms about seconding property that is left unprotected.'

'You do not take from your own clan.' She made no attempt to keep the disapproval out of her voice. 'In any case, we did look round, and Nat picked up a metal bowl in the hall to see if it was made of silver. He breathed on it and made to rub it with his sleeve . . . and an adder ran between the feet is a very bad sign, bor. You don't argue with the signs if you know them.'

She stood up. There was a slight singing in her ears and she realized that the suggestion of nausea which she had begun to feel as they walked through the lanes was now quite liable to erupt suddenly. If she were to be sick in front of Charles it was possible that he might guess the reason — and that was something that she had no intention of admitting to him.

'Come on,' she said shortly, holding out her hand to him. 'Let us go inside and see how it feels in the hall. There is plenty of light and we need not stay long. Just the hall today — and the rest of the house later.'

Rising, he took her hand and she felt the ice in him. He stood at the edge of the terrace, looking up at the soft pink brickwork. He was still very white and there was an almost blue tinge to his lips. A pulse beat strongly in his right cheek. She drew him towards the oak front door.

It was not locked but it needed all her strength, as she pressed her shoulder to the wood, to get it to open. Then it was as though something which had been holding it closed suddenly let go, and the door swung back on creaking hinges, almost unbalancing her.

The smell rushed out at them and Charles recoiled.

'No,' he said thickly. 'I can't go in there. The stench is still there . . . that same awful reek.' He flung her hand away and ran over to the side of the terrace and bent, retching, over the balustrade. The odour of decayed stomach acids and excreta was an almost tangible cloud pouring through the open doorway. For a moment Dudie could have sworn that she could see a creamy mass billow out past her and envelop Charles, but her own threatened sickness rose up then and she bent and let her stomach void itself into the brambles. When she was more in control again she raised her head.

Charles was lying on the terrace, rolled up in a foetal curl. The stench had gone and the afternoon was bright and blue and a little hazy. She bent over Charles and found that he had lost consciousness.

'Come on, simensa,' she said, crouching beside him and stroking his forehead. 'It's all gone now. There's nothing here. We'll go home . . . wake up, Charles.'

He stirred, and small animal sounds of fear came from him. She kissed his cheeks and patted his hands, repeating her comforting words of reassurance until he opened his eyes and looked wildly beyond her head. Then he seemed to grasp his position and where they were, and struggled to his feet.

'I can't go in there — not now,' he said, pushing her in front of him as he made for the end of the terrace.

They retraced their steps in silence. No word was exchanged until they had passed through the gates and were on their way back up the old carriage track to the Dell Quay road.

'You felt it too, I know you did,' he said, head down and eyes averted. He seemed to have no control over the depth of his fear, so that even a firm determination to override his feelings was no match for his instincts.

'I smelt a nasty old musty smell, yes,' she agreed, trying to play down that indescribable blanket of evil gases.

340

'It must have been just as appalling to you as it was to me, for I saw you vomit, just as I did, so do not try to dismiss it.'

She looked up at his pinched face. It was a death mask, cheek-bones protruding through the colourless flesh. His mouth was a cruel lipless slit drawn back from the teeth in a half-snarl. She could not tell him that her own sickness came from quite another source. Observing this new and strange Charles, she wondered whether his father, Lawrence, had looked this way when he Flamed things with that terrible Power of death in his eyes.

She put her head down. 'Nat will be back at the vardo by sunset. I must hurry to get his hobben into the pot.'

There were no words between them when they parted, almost like strangers. His thoughts were far away from her and he scarcely noted her withdrawal,

The following morning Charles heard that Tom, with Li'l Moses and two others, had made their escape from the *Fortunée*.

The whole ship was seething as he came aboard. Expressions of a varying nature were imprinted on the face of every soul aboard: anger, trepidation, exhilaration and just plain fear concerning the consequences. Furze was pacing his office when Charles looked in. His rage was so intense that he appeared to be puffed up in danger of an apoplectic fit. His resemblance to a great purple toad was quite startling.

'Can you imagine the wickedness?' Furze had to keep his voice low for it was striving to burst from his lungs in roar after mighty roar, and he thought that would only bring on his gout again. 'That double-crossing son of a sea cow, after all the privileges we have given him here in these quarters. . . .'

Charles flipped his coat tails deftly over the back of a stool and sat himself down calmly.

'Tell me what has happened,' he said in his most soothing voice. 'I gather from Sergeant Milburn that you've had an escape.'

The little captain winced and lifted his weight off the painful foot. He sucked in his breath and hobbled round the desk to slump back in his chair, the breath wheezing like a pair of ancient fire bellows in his chest.

'You could say that, sir, and you would be right. Four of the dirty lummocks, there were . . . literally dug their way out of the side of the ship, too. That's bad enough, but when I tell you that one of them is the fellow who has been teaching my own boys — Thomas Heritage, no less — you will see why I scarce know where to put myself. Heritage, that great mountain of Nigger flesh, Moses Abelson, and two others.' He banged his pudgy fists on the desk in front of him.

The mention of Tom was a profound shock to Charles. He had been well aware of Tom's determination to see his mother's birthplace before returning to New England, but they had both thought he would be one of the first paroled when the lists came through for Langstone. That Tom would take the law into his own hands and desert his shipmates had not once crossed Charles's mind. He scarcely heard the words that Furze was uttering, hardly took heed of the trembling in the man's body.

Tom would go straight to Lavenham. With an effort he closed his mind to all the hideous possibilities which might now be forming to destroy Aunt Violet's younger son.

'We caught one of 'em skulking in the mud on North Binness Island,' Furze was saying. 'Put him in the black hole forever, as far as I'm concerned. Till he's cracked, at any rate. That'll make the varmints think. Fished another of them out of the water. Dead as mutton. Had half the harbour in his guts. Strung him up in the bows as a pretty figurehead . . . just to remind the other sullen buggers what'll happen if any of 'em try that one again.'

'Have the other two been sighted?'

Furze snorted. 'You'd have thought a black monster might be difficult to conceal but, stap me, Mr Bayless, there's not been a breath of wind about him — or Heritage either — since they went two nights back. They've probably gone to ground with some Yankee sympathizer — or even taken ship across the Channel by now.'

Charles drank his claret in thoughtful mood and excused himself at the earliest moment. He felt the restless mood of the men as they filed past him for their ration. Anger and dejection overshadowed those who celebrated the continued freedom of Tom and L'il Moses. It was not surprising that a break had been made. The men had been imprisoned, for the most part, for nearly two years — some even more. Their bodies were crying out for fresh fruit and vegetables, for good red meat, for water in which to bathe the sores upon their desiccated skins. He averted his eyes from the boy who crouched almost double before him at that moment. He could not have been more than twenty, but the hands that were held out to take his ration were dried-up claws and his face was a nightmare of rotton tooth stumps, bleeding gums that protruded, spongy and swollen, so far out of his mouth as to give the poor creature an oozing, bulbous sneer, only contradicted by the utter grief in his eyes.

Scurvy . . . what horrors it made of men, he thought.

'Have you been to the sick bay?' he asked the boy, sickened by the terrible stench of putrefaction that emanated from him. There was no understanding the gobbled reply that came from that dreadful mouth.

Charles turned to one of his clerks. 'Get his name and see that he is treated before he drops dead,' he said.

''Twould be better if he did,' someone said under his breath.

Charles put his head down and ignored the aside. He could do little else but agree with it.

7

It was a day for making trap nets. Dudie sat cross-legged on a flat piece of ground, with three pieces of newly made hempen netting piled up beside her. The day was fine after the night rain, and the moisture in the mild air was just right for tightening the fibres.

She spread one piece out on the ground, smoothing it flat with her hands. It was about five feet square, made of a fine half-inch mesh which she had completed the night before and left upon the ground to absorb the dew. Over this net she laid a coarser one of the same size, then rolled the two up together and folded them over so that the wide meshing was underneath and the fine net on top. Finally she laid the third net, the same four-inch gauge as the first, on top of the other two, producing a netting sandwich which she sewed together with large stitches of hempen thread round the outer edges.

It was the perfect time of year for netting songbirds, mostly bullfinches, which were then mated with canaries, a very popular domestic pet, before being returned to the hedgerows. Dudie had three caged canaries, the largest a gift from Charles, who had also presented her with a Java sparrow, a lovely little creature with soft grey plumage and a pinkish red breast. Sadly, before there was time to mate it with an English finch, it had died. The canaries were thriving, however, and had already hatched one family each, which she had sold in the Chichester Tuesday market at a handsome profit.

The Romany method of trapping fascinated Charles, for there was no damage to the bird and the little creatures seemed almost unconcerned by the experience.

344

Dudie lifted her net and folded it over her arm and shoulder. She set out across the common to where a wild patch of scrubland divided the parishes of Fishbourne and Apuldram. Here there were birds aplenty and it was only a matter of minutes before she had marked a fine young finch. She spread her net in a gap in the hedgerow, over a ditch close to where the birds were feeding. After a few minutes the little creatures began to flutter back to the spot and Dudie, having stood well back from the hedge, now began moving very slowly towards it, driving the bird of her choice, step by step, towards her net snare. The colour of the hemp blended perfectly with the hedge twigs, so that it was not visible until it was too late. The bird gave a hop and a quick flutter. The movement drove it right into the net, through the first wide mesh into the fine second mesh. The impact of its small, frenzied body created a little pocket between the meshes and so it was held, secure yet with no restriction upon its body and wing feathers. Dudie gathered it up, removed it deftly from its open prison and thrust it into the safety of her stocking box. She caught three more birds in this way and then returned to the camp.

Nat was back from Dell Quay, by the time she had finished.

'Emsworth's all abuzz today,' he said, as she brought him food and tore a hunk of bread from the loaf he had bought. 'Ben a breakout from one o' them convict ships off Langstone . . . four prisoners cut right through the ship's side, cheeky saps. One of them drowned, they say, one got caught by the tide in the marsh and was hauled out like a mud worm . . . but the other two are still free. Good luck to 'em, I say. I'd not want to be battened down in them floaten' coffins. Prefer to chance me luck with the authorities, any time.' He sipped noisily at a large ladle of soup and swilled it round his mouth. 'Good luck to 'em, I says.'

She thought about the escaped men a lot that day. The following dawn would see her off to Portsmouth with Nat and the other bargees, and the camp would be unguarded until their return. She locked everything as securely as usual but left the bolt loose on the waggon door. Inside she put food which would normally have been buried in the cool box.

If the poor creatures came looking for refuge, they would certainly find a bit of a welcome here, she thought.

The night was misty again. Summer storms had swept through, leaving a period of still air and oppressive heat. They narrowly missed ramming a gentleman's yacht as they rowed out of the Channel round Bosham Hoe and made for the Thorney Cut. The barge was low in the water, weighed down by tons of large, rough-hewn coal from the Kent colliery. By the time Dudie had steered them skilfully through the Thorney and Hayling Cuts and they were approaching the Hilsea Stream, the day was brightening, a yellow lozenge of sun burning away the steamy dawn mist. They nosed their way along the narrow waterway which made an Island of Portsea and into the mud-silted reaches of Portsmouth Harbour, and then they were rowing strongly again, making good headway past Whale Island and on towards the busy dockland of the greatest seaport in the south of England. Away on the starboard bow, a sinister line of prison ships rode at anchor off Portchester Castle, like a rope of murky beads strung together by great rusting hawsers and attended, as always, by clouds of screeching gulls.

Dudie listened to the oarsmen's laboured breath and the occasional curse or joke tossed like small gifts between the striving of each mighty thrust. In . . . out . . . in . . . out. She leaned on the rudder and the boat veered a little to skirt a naval bum-boat crossing their bows.

She hated Portsmouth with its narrow streets and rank air, foul with smoke from the forest of chimneys inside the city wall. Her lungs seemed to clog up with the coke fumes when there was no wind to blow them out across the ocean. It was said that the dirty yellow haze over Portsmouth could be seen for miles out to sea.

She sighted the entrance to the coaling jetties and

turned the barge in towards the shore. Nat and the others would have to forgo much of their carousing this night, for they were due back in Dell Quay before midday — which meant leaving at dawn.

It rained in the night, scouring away the last of the sea-mists. The men were in cheerful mood and Nat's fine singing voice echoed through the Thorney Cut, as they made good progress with their light return load. Coal to Portsmouth, baskets of fish back to Chichester. There would be a fine meal for them all that evening. She remembered the escaped prisoners as they skirted the four hulks off the Langstone marshes.

Suppose they had been to the vardo and eaten all their victuals; Nat would not be happy, she thought.

'Drop me into Bosham,' she called down the boat to him over the heads of the three rowers in front of him. 'I need supplies from Mrs Priday.'

'No time,' Nat said shortly. He hated any deviation from routine, for delay could spell reprimand and they needed the work for a few more weeks yet. 'We 'm due in before midday and we'll need to keep goen'.'

'Hey, bor,' Dudie laughed. 'Look at the sky. Sun's up, riden' Birdham church tower. We've three hours in hand. 'Twon't take me but half an hour to fill my pannier and leave a message for Mr Chase that his baskets are ready for him to collect with the cart.'

He nodded, defeated as he usually was before her reasoning, and she leaned on the long arm of the rudder and watched the water cream in their wake as they joined the traffic entering Bosham Creek.

The tide was running away and a tiny boat like half a chestnut shell came out to bring her in. She clamboured over the side and sat high in its miniature prow as the fat ferryman poled her in towards the shore.

'I won't be long . . . wait for me, if you please, Dan.'

She hitched up her skirts, hopped over the side on to a mud bank and waded through the ankle-deep water and up on to the gravelled slipway. Passing the straggle of village houses, she swung her empty basket and hummed under her breath, her mind on those days, far ahead, when she and Nat would once more be jalling the drom. It was then that she fell over Tom's outstretched and reeking leg.

'Oi, dik ai, chav. . . . '

The dirty bundle of ragged humanity raised its head — and that fine, unbeggarly face found an instant niche in her mind.

That was her first meeting with Tom Heritage.

'Oh, sorry, bor . . . I didn't see you there.'

It was nearly a week after the incident at Bosham that a note was left at the Dell Quay office for Dudie. She picked it up as she collected her pay and stood against the wall outside the Crown and Anchor, next door to the office, to read it.

She was not a very fluent reader but the scrawl was large and clear and she recognized Mrs Chase's hand.

> Thank you for the baskets. They are just right — so strong and tight woven. Ben and I do have a favour to ask of you. We have a visitor real sick and I don't seem to be having much success with curing the malady. We'd be much obliged if you could bring your balms and pots of salve over to Parklands Farm at the earliest moment.

She was due to go to Portsmouth the following noon. It would be no trouble to pop across to the farm first, for it lay directly opposite the quay, a hundred yards or so across the channel on the Bosham shore. Besides, she had somehow sensed who her patient might be.

'There is something that you should know, Dudie.' Fran Chase told her when she had treated the Bosham beggar. 'That young man, Tom Heritage, is here with a purpose. His mother is Violet Bayless, born over there at Lavenham. He says he has come to look at his birthright.'

She had sensed the bond of their blood, even as he lay on the ground at Bosham. The Bayless eyes, not the piercing blue version that she and Nat possessed, bright stars generated by the first gorgio crossed with a Hator six generations before. No, these were the other eyes: the grey ones, which came and went without apparent connection, in one part of the family and then, for no apparent reason, in another part. It was said that Violet Bayless had possessed them.

So, too, did Charles Bayless. It had been the only inheritance from his father, Lawrence. Would the child within her have those eyes? But there was no sign in either Charles or Tom of the terrible gift that sometimes accompanied those grey eyes.

Word would have to be sent to Janatha and Prentice Bayless, the current heads of the family, over in the dense oakwoods outside Wickham. It was possible that danger was beginning to gather here, for both cousins, it seemed, were obsessed with the house that had brought such evil upon both the families.

'Sarah will have to go over to Wickham and tell them,' Nat said, when she broke the news to him. 'You cannot leave here in case you are needed across the water.'

He was sitting beside the fire, whittling a hazel twig with his paring knife. He raised the long twig and tapped her lightly on the arm with it.

'Best tell of your own involvement too, pen. I don' like it. He's too keen, Master Charles. That kind of feelen' c'n end badly if'n you handle it wrong. . . . '

She cupped her chin in her hands and stared into the hot embers of the dying fire. 'It has no roots, bor. From the first I offered him my support, not my love — for his soul was ailen', poor man. Bruised and witheren', it was.'

'So you say, but he's had enough now and just be usen' ye . . . he won't let it go easily for it's mighty convenient to have yer fine rawni on the one hand and yer poor girl to tumble when ye will on the other. He'll give ye trouble, see if he don', an when that happens I'd not stand by and watch. You know my temper. An' now, darn it to hell, there's this other one.'

She smiled and a little dimple came and went beside her mouth. He frowned, for there was suddenly a softening in Dudie's face. The vigorous strength in her became muted with uncharacteristic gentleness.

'Don' you go getten' involved there, for scran's sake,' he said sharply, even more alarmed by this sudden change.

'I'm not, prala.' Her voice was mild. 'I'm just nursen' him. He's got a knee there that could lose him his leg if I don't make him respect its critical state. He'll sail away to France as soon as he is fit — Ben Chase will see to that — and anyway, we shall be gone from here by then.'

He was not convinced. Dudie was a fine-looking girl who had turned down the attentions of Matthew Boswell and one or two others around their own tribe fire. When their mother died and Sarah married, Dudie had persuaded him to take her with him in search of work, away from the tribe for most of the year. She was a good companion and not given to flightiness. He had never had cause to worry about her until now.

Now, he did not at all like the look that was back in her face as she watched the fire pictures glowing between the half-burned logs.

'Why are you so silent?' Charles asked her.

He picked her up and brought her into his lap and sat with his arms round her, feeling the warmth of her body against his chest.

'I do not mean to be.'

'Are you sick?' he asked. She looked well enough and had suffered his eager coupling without complaint. He had even been able to bring her to climax, which still, after all these months, gave him the most powerful gratification. He turned her round and pressed his mouth against her breast. The nipple rose enticingly against his tongue and he buried his nose between the tight, full little mounds.

She drew back from him with a gasp. 'You're hurting me,' she said sharply, and there was a stiffness about her that he had never felt before. Her very withdrawal was a new sweetness. He lifted her so that she straddled his lap, and held her tightly against him, entering her hard.

She fought him. She beat at him with her fists.

'God, you're fierce,' he said hoarsely against her hair, holding her down into his lap. Suddenly she was like a wild thing, tearing at his hair, sinking her teeth into his shoulders, clawing at his face. It was exquisitely primaeval.

Afterwards he said to her, 'Why did you fight me like that? It was an exhilarating experience — but look, you are still angry with me. What have I done?'

But she only shook her head, avoiding his eyes.

Later, to change the subject, he said, 'Those two escaped prisoners from the Langstone hulk . . . have you heard anything about them?'

She stared blankly at him. 'Why should I? They never came here.'

She was still angry. He said gently, 'I need to know. One of them is related to me — to you too, for that matter, for his mother is Violet Bayless.'

He had her attention now. She was combing her hair, wet from the river. She stopped for a second and then continued with slow combing sweeps, her eyes fixed on his face with an empty waiting look.

'We know the history of Violet Bayless,' she said. 'If you knew he was in that stinking hole, why did you not arrange for him to be paroled?'

Here it was — the very thing that he had tried to avoid. 'I would probably have lost my contractor's licence if it came to light that one of the prisoners was my own cousin,' he said shortly.

'Is your business so much more important than your family, then? Certainly the Romany strain has been bred right out of you, which must be a relief.'

'Look, Dudie.' He changed his tone, doing his best to smooth away her uncharacteristic criticism. 'Of course I care about my flesh and blood. Maybe not as passionately as you people do —'

351

'We gypsies. We riff-raff. Why do you not come right out and say it, for that's what you mean, isn't it?'

'No, that's not what I mean. I think that the closeness of the Romany tribes is a most commendable and astonishing phenomenon, and there are times when I try to feel that way too, but I just cannot see the sense in jeopardizing a line of business that I have taken great pains to build into a very special concern, simply to give unlawful protection to one man who was a complete stranger to me until recently.'

She threw down the comb. It fell to the floor with a clatter and slid beneath the narrow bunk. He had bought it for her in London; a pretty thing made of bone with a silver inlaid handle.

'How quickly you forget when it suits you.' Her words were hard little lashes. 'Did his mother never do the same for you — a child she had never seen? Did she weigh *that* against your needs?'

He stared at her in astonishment. She was clenching and unclenching her fists, eyes blazing.

'For God's sake, Dudie, what *is* wrong with you? We are speaking of help for one stranger from another, not making accusations. The man is at large. It may be that I can now help him. I couldn't before.' He took her chin and turned her face towards him. 'Well I could not, could I?' His voice was soft, persuasive. The grey eyes pleaded. His thumbnail pressed the flesh of her cheek, insisting.

Dudie turned away from him in disgust. 'Look, master,' she said coldly. 'I have things to do before the morning. Be good enough to leave me now to get on with them.'

This was a new Dudie, an imperious and beautiful woman with complete assurance. God, what he would not do to gain submission from such a prize. He started to speak, to cajole her, but saw the look in her eyes and stopped, suddenly mortified. Damn and curse her. The vixen had dismissed him like any pot-boy.

He stood up and went down the waggon steps without a word. Before he had time to turn and bid her farewell she had closed the painted doors behind him with a sharp slam. He heard the bolt being drawn across.

She had sent him packing in a more summary fashion than many a titled lady might have done. Dudie Smith, a grubby little gypsy — in his own employ. He raised his riding crop to hammer on the door and saw Nat Smith silently watching, his dark face glowering.

'That sister of yours needs to curb her temper and keep a civil tongue in her head,' he said. Nat said nothing but stood like a stone. The stick in his hand had a heavy knob on the end. It usually lived in his belt.

Charles withdrew and rode back to Chichester with the anger in him slowly rising to fury. Bloody little vixen! What right had she to question his actions?

It was only later that night, when sleep eluded him and he thought back to the furious excitement of her beautiful angry, struggling, hurting body and the extra eroticism of mounting it, that it occurred to him Dudie might be tiring of him.

He didn't see Dudie for some time after that. His pride had been badly bruised and days slid into weeks and drove him into a private torment. His black mood swung into despair, through contrition and back again to anger, with the inevitability of a metronome, and was felt by his family and employees alike. He was, he realized, in the grip of a despair so great that the very magnitude of it shook him. His feeling for Dudie had become so intense that, should he ever return to her good graces, he decided to declare himself to her more positively. Maybe if he offered to set her up in her own home where he could visit her discreetly, she might be tempted. Then, when Leonie's declining health had finally broken and he had gone through the correct period of mourning . . . was it so unthinkable to consider wedding Dudie? Others in his family had married gypsies and not regretted it. He clung to such fantasies — and finally, buoyed up by the hope they gave him, returned to Apuldram Common to make his apologies.

The move was a grave mistake. When he saw the look on Dudie's face at sight of him, a stranger seemed to take possession of him.

'I came to apologize for my rudeness to you,' he started to say, and then the words stuck in his throat for she was standing by the waggon ladder, her slim body already turning to shut herself away from him. There was no warmth in her face, no forgiveness in her lovely features. With that proud lift of the head, she was a small empress dismissing a lesser mortal. She said nothing at all to him and he felt like a tongue-tied boy, mortified to realize that her rejection of him would have been more than justified in a young woman of his own breeding.

'Dudie, please don't shut me out. I was entirely in the wrong to have forced myself on you the way I did — and I apologize. I simply cannot live without your affection. I feel very deeply for you, you must have realized that — you probably knew it before I did. Forgive me, please.' He took a step towards her and held out his hand.

'Don't 'e come a pace closer.' Her voice was low and harsh. She moved then and he saw the gleam of a fletching knife in her hand. 'Oh, Dudie, dearest girl — I'm not going to hurt you. How could you imagine that I would?' The pain in his voice was so sharp that she hesitated and then laid the knife on the top step. He went forward and in one movement had his arms round her, burying his face in the thick black curls.

'Don't be afraid of me, dearest Dudie.' The ragged breath was almost a sob against her neck. 'See, I shan't even kiss you if that is what you want. I just need to know that you are not angry with me any more.'

She stood woodenly, saying nothing and he held her away from him, searching for a spark of warmth.

'Come and live with me. Let me find us a little cot somewhere which will be your very own — please?'

She said — and her voice was flat, featureless, 'We have no connection any more, sir, other than the accident of our births. This is all the home I want, now and ever.

354

It's what we was born to and Nat would not allow it to be any other way.'

'You and Nat. Is that the only man you ever think of, then?'

He was horrified at the sudden fury in his voice and the words that came out were being uttered by a stranger. 'You and Nat — is it common practice, after all, for gypsies to lie with their brothers rather than with other men?'

Oh God — why had he said that? It had never even been in his thoughts.

She jerked out of his grasp and dealt him a blow across the mouth with her clenched fist, splitting his lip. The salt taste of blood came off his tongue. His hands went out, gripping her shoulders, digging his fingers into the coarse oiled wool of her shawl, feeling the rounded flesh beneath. He shook her — and his anger mounted, shot through with the awful need of her. She saw the look on his face and brought her knee up into his crotch. He cried out and released her, curling up and rolling away in agony. She ran up the steps and flung herself through the door. He was in too much pain to hear the bolts being shot on the inside.

She told Nat of the coming child that evening.

Charles tried to see Dudie twice after that, but somehow she seemed always to be absent from the camp when he called.

When he made a wrong decision with one of his investments, he suddenly discovered that his abstraction was costing him dear.

Sitting in the farmhouse bedchamber, Dudie watched the blood drain from Tom's face, leaving it pinched and grey. Then the hard lines relaxed.

'Oh, you foolish girl. Why have you not told me this before? Moses and I could have given you our support, if nothing else. Are you happy to be having a child? Do you intend to marry?' He was talking without thought; she saw the anguish which was threatening to engulf him. His face was an open book of misery, struggling with compassion which told its own tale. He stroked the curve of her cheek, for she said nothing.

'If this is an accident,' he said then, 'surely there is a solution? Romanies have the answer to most things, so you always tell us. Have you not the answer in that medicine box of yours?'

She shook her head. 'We do not believe in killen' unborn babies,' she said. 'My worry is not in the child, for there is always room for one more beside our hearth. My concern — my curse — is in the father, and of what the child will therefore turn out to be.'

She sensed the struggle in him, the dawning of his feeling for her — and was warmed by it, knowing that this was the right kind of regard. The rest had to be open between them.

'The child is Charles Bayless's.'

In the morning, Ben Chase came across the common with the first streaks of a red dawn.

'Tom Heritage went over to Lavenham in the night,' he told Nat and Dudie in agitation. 'Moses rowed him across the water and waited two hours and more for him but he hasn't come back. Moses be mighty feared for him. Says that Tom had no intention of staying in that place alone an' now is sure that somethen' bad has happened. Go to Lavenham, I beg you both. Find him and bring him back to the farm, for there's a passage across the Channel arranged for the two of them in three days' time.'

Two bright spots flowered in Dudie's cheeks. Without speaking they began to gather up their cooking pots. Nat stamped the last of the fire's embers into the ground and they watched the old man, muttering to himself in his agitation, hobbling away across the common in the eerie red dawn. Before the light had softened into a bright early morning, they had saddled the waggon pony and were on the move.

'I see that Nat Smith has taken the coaler to Portsmouth this morning,' Charles said casually to his clerk later in the afternoon.

'No, sir.' The man looked up from his ledger and a twitch of annoyance brought his white eyebrows together. 'He should have taken the coaler but he's not turned up today. I had to put another man in his place.'

Charles hurried over the common to the camp as soon as time permitted, praying that he might find Dudie on her own for once — and found the place deserted. He stood where the waggon wheels had dug deep runnels into the clay soil and scourged himself, for she would not have turned her back on him in this way had he kept a tighter control of his temper. Now they were gone — and he would, he guessed, never see them in this place again.

The realization that he alone had driven them away stabbed at him. Dudie was gone — and Tom Heritage was gone. . . . It occurred to him that they might each have made for Lavenham for their own good reasons.

The Watcher stood back in shadow, watching the man limping painfully up the stairs, brushing aside long swathes of cobwebs as he went. There was a strange peace in the house. Lavenham seemed to be holding its breath, watching this seedling of its creator and beginning — even now — to probe his mind and the reason for his presence. There was no feeling of menace about this man; but then, he was not yet aware of the rules. The house would beguile him, smooth his way so that it would seem only natural for him to linger there a little longer . . . a little longer.

She *would be there watching over him. The Watcher could feel her presence already, almost see her luxuriating in this young man's innocence, the limping gait a parody of her own. She would smother him with the protective passion that she had felt for Jess, but even with all the strength of that suffocating love there was little real power in her to protect him from the Place.*

It was so eternally mystifying, the Watcher thought, that

he had the power of death at the first moment of life only.
There was nothing at all that he could do to warn this one.

8

A persistent jingle woke Tom and he sat up with a jerk that
made him wince. There was a brief moment of sharp fear
before he recognized his surroundings, expecting the
comfortable security of the farmhouse bedchamber, and
finding instead that he was curled up in a capacious
armchair in a chill and dusty room steeped in swathes of
enormous cobwebs, its heavy furnishings faded almost to a
uniform mouldering grey and the heavy silence accentuated by the scratchings of small scurrying things behind
the woodwork. He stared about him in confusion until
memory flooded back, and in the same instant he heard
again the distant silvery horse-bells which had woken him.

He levered himself out of the chair and went stiffly over
to the broad leaded casement, rubbing his aching leg.
Husks of long dead cockroaches hung in cobweb cradles at
the corners of the window frames. Dust coated the panes,
obscuring his view, and he rubbed one with the sleeve of
his jacket and peered out.

Dawn was just breaking in purple bands of light across
the night sky, shot through with growing slashes of a livid
red. The fiery bars cast a sullen bronze light over the
oakwoods and waters of the Channel, turning the outbuildings on one side of the house into monstrous black
sentinels.

Just disappearing through the archway leading into the
main stable yard was the back of a covered waggon.

He stood leaning against the folded shutters, momentarily shaken by the unexpected sight of movement, of life.
He had become cocooned in the silent contemplation of
himself and the house, closing his mind to everything

beyond the boundaries of this legendary dream which was suddenly reality. Now, feeling a rude jolt at the intrusion, it was almost as though he felt the disquiet of the house itself.

No one ever came to Lavenham, so it was said. Ben had been adamant about this, and Charles and Dudie too, though Dudie had added that the Bayless clan considered it family property and camped in the south paddock occasionally.

Dudie? Could it be that she had convinced Nat, after all, that they should come over to Lavenham? His spirit lifted at the thought.

He had only meant to wander through the house and return quickly to Moses, but there was something here which beckoned to him and made him feel unaccountably at home — and then there was something else which held him. Everything around him seemed strangely familiar, and his feeling of well-being spread into a warm euphoria. He had felt this way before, especially after drinking too many pots of French wine. Light-headed . . . happy. He had a ridiculous urge to sing aloud through the quiet, abandoned rooms.

He peered out through the single pane of clear glass, but no further movement caught his eye and he turned away, the waggon and its occupants put aside for the moment.

The house called to him *now*. Taking a deep breath of the musty air, he gave himself up to it and wandered across the room, making scuffs in the dust as he went.

He opened the chamber door and stepped into the gallery, pausing to study the portraits at length. There was no doubt who the subjects were, for they were an integral part of the Lavenham story, as easy to identify, each one, as if he had known them all his life. They stared down from their gilded frames with bright, youthful faces, his own features stamped on two of them and those of Charles Bayless smiling down at him from the others.

Charles. Something erupted in him without warning, a rage which had boiled deep inside him since Dudie told him of her condition. He had always been careful to control his behaviour, having inherited his father's strong sense of right and wrong. In this house, though, the thought of Charles Bayless brought blinding hate suddenly into focus and he snarled aloud as it welled up through every nerve in his body.

Whoa there. . . . Nothing is worthy of that kind of feeling, he told himself, startled by this uncharacteristic venom. Charles had always quietly done his best for the prisoners. He had offered Dudie a home — even though he was not yet aware that she was pregnant. Nor was it, in all honesty, Charles's fault that they were both smitten by the same woman.

There was something very odd about this place, for it was affecting him in a way that was most disturbing. He limped along the gallery, concentrating on raising as little dust as possible on the staircase, and made his way down to where he could get a better view of the waggon in the yard.

There was a stone passage leading off the hall and past the kitchens to an outside door. The hinges on the yard door had completely rusted and the noise he made trying to drag it open must have been heard all the way to Newbarn Cottages. He was hardly surprised when there was a sudden sharp hammering on the oak panels.

'Tom . . . is that you?' Dudie's voice sounded far away, disembodied, but the anxiety in it was unmistakable.

'Yes,' he said. 'It's me, right enough, as you'll see if only I can get this thing open. Push, if you will. The hinges are rusted solid.'

He heard a murmur of voices. 'Who's there with you?' he called anxiously.

'It's only Nat, bor . . . don't worry. I'd not bring anyone else.'

The door suddenly gave and crashed back against the passage wall, catapulting two figures across the threshold.

'Phew,' she said, grinning up at him in her imp's way from where she sprawled at his feet.

'Sar shan, simensa. Welcome to Lavenham.' She clambered to her feet and pulled her brother forward.

'This is Nat,' she said. 'We've left our camp on the common, for he and Charles had a few unfriendly words yesterday and, in his present way of thinken' it's likely he'd give us some trouble there. He won't come here though. Mr Chase came over not an hour gone, and warned us that you'd come here, so we thought we'd keep you company until it's time for you and Moses to go.'

The bulky shape of Nat Smith appeared at Dudie's back — foreign-looking, with his long, pale face, black curls, brooding, distrustful eyes, Tom thought. The high cheekbones and sallow skin were there in Dudie also, but they looked very different on her — giving her dark beauty a sharp sensuality.

'I'm pleased to see you. Thought you might have Moses with you when I heard voices.'

The disappointment in his voice was overlaid by something else and she narrowed her eyes at him in the dim passage, trying to read his face. He looked tired, but there was an excitement in him, a breathlessness as though he had made a great discovery and was hugging it to himself, loath to share it.

'Come on in.' He turned and limped away from them down the passage, back towards the hall. They followed, looking about them cautiously.

The red dawn had paled into a pinkly overcast morning. There would be no sun this day to burn through the heavy rainclouds which stood off the land on the horizon like great purple cliffs.

The hall in daylight was impressive. Its ceiling was lofty, like the nave of a church, with the stairs and gallery giving it unexpected elegance. The destruction at its centre added a sense of ancient drama, and the three of them stood uncertainly bunched together, eyes roving slowly over the smashed refectory table lying in two halves, its legs mouldering like broken bones amongst the dust eddies.

'I can scarcely believe the story of what was meant to have happened here,' Tom said, resisting the urge to whisper.

Nat moved away from the table. 'There be bengs here, all right,' he growled, the deep voice echoing back at them. 'Best to leave 'em alone, I say. They've done no harm these many years an' I'm all for leaven' it that way. You come back here and stir 'em all up again — an' who can guess at what might happen.'

He crossed to the parlour door, which was hanging back on one hinge. He stepped out of their sight and they listened to him moving about in the room.

Dudie slipped her hand into Tom's and he drew her against his side. They examined the shattered table and Dudie shivered. She looked round and found him staring up at the gallery, frowning.

'What is the matter?'

He shook his head and for a moment continued to search the shadows above them. 'I'm not sure,' he said at last, dragging his eyes back to her. 'I could have sworn that I saw someone up there looking down at us.' He laughed. 'It's surprising what fancies you can dream up if suggestion is planted in the mind first.'

His voice was light but she could see that he was still not convinced that there were only shadows up in the gallery.

'Shall we go up there and see?' she said, matching her tone to his. 'Nat, we're taking a look at the chambers,' she called. 'Come up with us. We haven't looked round the upper floors before.'

Nat appeared in the open doorway with a large ledger in his hands. 'I will in a minute,' he said. 'Just having a dikker through these books. Very interesten'. . . . Have you seen them, bor?'

Tom shook his head and started up the stairs with Dudie. 'There's so much to examine, I'd have liked very much to stay a while longer and go over everything thoroughly.'

The upper floor consisted of five chambers and a linen

room. From the servants' quarters a spiral staircase descended into the kitchen regions and rose upwards into the attics. The main staircase curved gracefully down from the picture gallery, which was splendidly illuminated by one huge oriel window. The rooms held their own fascination, for each was very different and clearly reflected its last occupant.

At the head of the stairs, double doors opened into the main bedchamber. This was a large and airy room, despite the closed shutters and crimson brocade curtains drawn across them. The room was tidy; obviously it had not been in use when the catastrophe happened. There was a magnificently carved four-poster bed, dominating the room like a scarlet catafalque, its rich draperies long since faded, choked with dust and cobwebs. The coverlet had been stitched in an intricate and beautiful design of trailing roses. The room was empty of atmosphere, the imprint of its occupants long gone.

They tried the door of the next room and were shocked by the contrast they found. No colour here. Nothing. Bars at the windows. No curtains to keep out the cold. No carpet on the scarred plank floor, a single iron framed bed the only item in the room. It was very cold and a smell of mould and decay pervaded the air. There were deep gouges and slash marks down the inside of the door, as though some desperate animal had been caged there. They turned away quickly, glad to close the door behind them.

'I didn't much like it in there,' Dudie said. 'Maybe it was where they kept poor crazy Amy.'

Tom made no comment but knew that he would not go in there again. He had the distinct feeling that something had hovered over him in that place, had crooned to him and stroked his head. The sounds had been within himself, he knew, but the feeling sent prickles down his spine.

'Look, look at the pictures.' Dudie started forward, pulling him after her. 'How easy it is to tell who they are. . . . Just see how beautiful the rawni in that one is. She must be Lavinia Freeland, beside Jess here.'

They strained upward, the better to pick out every detail of the four portraits in their ornate gilded frames.

'How strongly Charles resembles his father.'

Tom looked at her quickly, catching the sadness in her voice, but there was no regret reflected in her face, only spellbound absorption. He clenched his teeth hard against the rage which gripped him again. Why did even the thought of Charles Bayless have such an affect on him in this place? He stared down at Dudie, watching the rapt attention in her face.

He stood back and examined his mother's portrait. There was another one of her at Midhurst, quite similar to the face which stared down serenely at him now. This one, though, was younger and there was a tension, a watchfulness, in her perfect features which was not present in the Midhurst picture. He stroked the canvas, feeling the brush strokes that had created the curve of his mother's cheek. What a beautiful girl she had been.

Something cool touched the back of his upraised hand, holding it against the picture for a moment, and was gone. He lowered his hand and looked at it.

'Mama was lovely, wasn't she — and she's still beautiful,' he heard his voice say fiercely, and yet knew that it was not he who had uttered the words.

Dudie was still staring up at the picture of Lawrence Bayless. She smiled round at him. 'That is because you love her. Age doesn't exist where there is love.'

He shook his head in confusion. 'Dudie . . . '. How do you protest that you have not said something which both of you have just heard you say? he wondered.

The picture of Violet Bayless stared down at him with just a trace of amusement in the lovely eyes.

'Mama is old now and not ashamed of it,' he said, more to the portrait than to Dudie. 'Her beauty is in her character rather than her face these days . . . and yet, looking at this picture, everything that was in her features in youth is still there — or was when last I saw it.'

Something rushed between them and they started apart.

'What was that?' Dudie recoiled and Tom pulled her arm through his and held it tightly.

'There *are* things here, I can feel them.' He spoke slowly as though searching for the right words. 'And yet they do not frighten me as I would have expected. I have the strangest feeling of being at home. That's why I stayed last night, though I only closed my eyes to have a nap and then suddenly it was daylight.'

The remembrance brought back the subject of Moses. 'My God, I must get a message to Moses. He'll be imagining that all the ghosts have gathered to banish me to the fires of Hell by now.'

They heard Nat stamping up the stairs behind them, his heavy footfall echoing round the hall and gallery. He appeared in a cloud of dust, disapproval written all over his face.

'You'll go and get Moses later this morning, won't you, pral?' Dudie said. 'Though I shall be very surprised if that great black dinlo will find the courage to cross the threshold of this place.'

They left Nat staring up at the pictures and Tom said, drawing Dudie into the chamber where he had slept, 'What do you make of this room, then? I slept in that very comfortable chair next to the mantel and would give much to take it back to Midhurst with me.'

She wandered round, stroking the walnut bedposts as she passed. The single pane of clean glass cast a square of moving rainbow lights on to the floor, picking out the glimmer of pattern on the faded carpet in its prismatic colours.

She went over to a table containing a handsome gilt-framed mirror with an ornate girandole beside it. The surface was littered with the paraphernalia of a woman's toiletry. He had not noticed it before and was touched by the sudden feeling of closeness it gave him to that long-gone girl. It was a curiously private clutter of female accoutrement. A silver and tortoiseshell set of brush, comb, hand mirror and powder case had been pushed to one side as though the woman had risen from the dressing stool hurriedly. A silver pot had fallen, spilling its contents of long and short hairpins across the table. There was a soft blue silk reticule containing a fine lace handkerchief, a tiny hussif in an embroidered case. A spyglass enframed in fine chased silver had initials on the back . . . V. B. He picked up the comb and examined it. Entwined in its teeth was one long black hair. There were bottles which had once held colognes and fragrant lotions. The contents had evaporated long since but each bottle still held a faint suggestion of their scents.

They found another chamber, which they decided was a guest room, for there was nothing there that suggested habitation. There was only one room left to see after that. It was opposite the finely carved panels of Violet's chamber door.

'Have you noticed that these doors are all different?' Dudie said as she lifted the latch and peered into the room.

The shutters were open and daylight streamed in, giving every piece of furniture a sharp clarity. This place was smaller than the others and its window, the bay filled with a well-upholstered windowseat, looked out over the east side of the house to the paddock and Salterns woods and, just visible, the roof of a house beyond the drive and entrance gates. The single bed had a plain green coverlet. One small rug, a corner eaten away, was all the floor-covering there was. On the dressing chest stood a fine model of a brigantine, its sails stowed neatly and the name in faded gilt just discernible: *Grace*.

They stood inside the doorway, both overcome by a puzzling sense of being unwelcome.

'How odd,' Tom said, almost to himself. 'I'm getting the strangest feeling that we shouldn't be in this room. Not the way we felt in the empty room, but as though I am intruding upon some special privacy. I don't have that feeling anywhere else in the house.'

'I feel it too.' Dudie took a step forward and recoiled, falling against Tom, as though she had been hit.

367

'What in heaven's name's the matter?' Tom held her tightly against him.

'I don't know.' Her voice was muffled against his shirt. He felt the warmth of her breath against his shirt and resisted holding her closer. She drew away from him, looking confused — and turned back into the room.

'Something dealt me a blow across my head, I swear it . . . and I thought I saw a face, I think. I'm not sure at all, though.' She made as though to walk across the room towards the green damask-covered bed — and then thought better of it. 'I think something does not want us in here,' she said turning back towards Tom.

He stared at her. 'My God, what is wrong with your face?'

She put a hand up to her cheek, feeling a burning on her skin. Her fingers found long weals from eye to chin.

They backed out of the room and slammed the door behind them. He took her into Violet's chamber, where Nat was staring out of the window through the single clean pane.

Dudie went across to the table mirror and stared at her reflection in astonishment. A white-faced stranger gazed back, one side of her face scored with great swollen weals, as though some large angry creature had drawn its talons down her cheek.

Moses sat at the kitchen table. A neat row of butchery knives lay in front of him, and he spat on the whetstone in his hand and began sharpening the first knife with neat short strokes. The whole of his body trembled a long way down inside as he listened to the old man. Whatever reason might say to him, however logically it argued, the trembling continued.

He was frightened right through to the very marrow of his bones.

'C'mon now. You'n Tom 'ave ben together for a long time,' Ben Chase pleaded, elbows spread across the table from him. He was leaning forward on his arms, in his own anxiety recognizing the depth of the primaeval fear in Moses. 'Dudie an' Nat've gone over so ye won't be alone, but if they can't get Tom away then ye 'ave a much better chance than most others of taken' him. Yer nothen' to do with that family — an' yer a fairish bit stronger than most. If need be, ye can pick the bugger up and carry 'im away from there like a sack of potatoes.'

'I'm not settin' foot in that place,' Moses countered, teeth chattering in his head. They both knew that he would give in eventually, from his deep feeling for Tom. 'Dudie 'n' Nat are sure to bring him over shortly. Now that they're there, I cain't see what's botherin' you so.'

'Unless 'e 'urt 'is knee again, like ye thought last night — an' then they'll have to come all the way round in their waggon. That's near on five mile through the lanes. Take even more time.'

Someone hammered on the front door and the two men froze, eyes locked. In one movement Moses was up and across the kitchen like liquid lightening. He slipped into the cold room and closed the door without a sound. Ben pulled himself up and went round the table to the chair that Moses had just vacated. He sat down as he heard Fran creaking down the stairs to open the door.

'Oh, good day to ye, sir.' He heard the surprise in her voice. It was just a little louder than usual, the bright welcome a little too sharp. She was warning them of someone.

'Good morrow, Mrs Chase. Is your husband at home? I'd be glad of a few words with you both?'

Charles Bayless. He picked up the whetstone and began sharpening the knife with slow, practised strokes.

'Come ye into the parlour, sir, please. Ben be in the kitchen, I think — if'n 'e's not in the barn.'

'Do not trouble yourself, thank you, Mrs Chase.' Charles's voice was smooth as silk. 'I'll go to the kitchen, if I may, as I'm short of time — and come with me, if you will, for what I have to ask concerns you both.'

The door opened and he stood on the threshold,

immaculate in blue velveteen jacket and a clean froth of white ruffled shirt. In the first instant his glance slid past Ben without a word and he held the door back against the wall, looking about him with his pale snake's eyes flicking from corner to corner.

Ben stood up, wheezing his welcome and looking as pleasantly surprised as possible. 'This be a pleasure, sir,' he said, moving slowly round the table. 'Won't ye come to the parlour? 'Tis more comfortable in there.'

Charles smiled at him grimly and shook his head. 'I have no time for more than a few words with you. Pray, let us sit right here.'

Ben pulled the harvest bench forward from the wall and ushered Charles into the chair he had just left. Frances busied herself at the range, where a pot of barley broth was always brewing.

'What can we do for ye, then, sir?'

'You can tell me where the two escaped prisoners are.'

Ben stared at Charles blankly. A frown creased his weathered forehead. He scratched the thin hair on the top of his mottled head with fingernails worn short and thick.

'Sorry, Mr Bayless, but I'm not understanden' ye. Which prisoners would ye be meanen'?'

Charles put both his hands on the table in front of him, sweeping away the neat row of knives. The skin on the backs of his hands was white and slightly freckled, the fingers long and sensitive. His well-manicured nails had seen little manual labour.

'Now, let us not play games.' The lightness of his tone did nothing to hide the hardness behind the words. 'It is common knowledge that two prisoners of war escaped from one of the Langstone hulks some weeks back. It has just come to my ears that they found sanctuary here. Plenty of folks are not slow to add up the sum of recent changes around here. Item one. This place has not been so well fenced in years as it is now — done during the past few weeks, am I right? Item two. You have been very busy in your west barn, for it has a fine new floor laid in bricks

370

with a design that I have not seen in these parts. How did you learn that?'

Ben flushed and swore to himself. 'That be the way my son Georgio showed me, sir, when 'e come a visiten' from New England afore the troubles.'

'But Mr Chase.' Charles's voice was very soft, almost tender. 'Your son George was only a lad when he went over to New England, and he hardly had the chance to visit before the rebels declared war on this country. We both know that he has not been here since.'

Ben opened his mouth to protest but closed it as Charles waved aside his words.

'Item three. It has been noted that Mrs Chase does a great deal more shopping in Bosham and the Chichester markets than would seem necessary for the needs of two elderly people. I think that, because of your loyalty to that American son of yours, you have been, and possibly still are, harbouring those two men. With your permission, I shall examine the rooms upstairs. Please to accompany me, Mrs Chase.' And before either could protest their innocence further, he was up on his feet and through the kitchen door with the speed of light.

Ben remained seated at the kitchen table. He picked up the whetstone and a knife and spat on the stone before running the blade across its length. He heard Charles Bayless's firm footfalls going from chamber to chamber, with Mrs Chase following, her voice querulous at the affront. Doors opened and closed, voices became muffled. There was silence for a short time and then he heard them returning, clattering down the oak staircase.

Charles came back into the kitchen and his face was set, the pale eyes slitted. If he was disappointed he showed no sign, but returned immediately to the attack. Without a word, he strode across the kitchen and opened the cold-room door. He stood for a second, eyeing the long slab of well-burdened slate shelf and the half-carcase of lamb hanging from one of the beam hooks. Then he closed the door with a small click that sounded more like a pistol shot

371

to the two old people.

'The fact that the rooms are empty means little, sir,' Charles said to Ben coldly. 'Pray answer me another conundrum, if you will. Dudie Smith has been coming over here to tend a sick person. This is known amongst your neighbours and she has told me so herself. You and Mrs Chase look very fit to me. Tell me, pray, who your ailing visitor was — and where Dudie is now.'

Ben had had enough. He lumbered to his feet, feeling the ache of age in his hips and went across and put his arm around Fran.

'Mr Bayless, I baint a discourteous man, but ye 'ave greatly offended my wife, as ye can see, and ye 'ave violated the privacy of my 'ome by comen' 'ere, full of accusations that I be in no mind to answer. We 'ave no visitors. Some weeks back my own sister came to stay and 'ad a bad fall, from which she is now recovered and 'as returned to her home in London. That be all I can tell ye. We have no prisoners 'ere, Mr Bayless. No prisoners, nor any other mysteries . . . and now I will have no more questions from 'e unless you be accompanied by the proper authorities. Be good enough to leave my house, sir. I bid ye good day.'

They stood close together as Charles wavered. Then he left them, banging the front door after him. A piece of plaster fell from the wall and rattled on to the kitchen flags.

Ben gave Fran a squeeze. 'It's all right, my duck,' he said. 'Ye did very well indeed. I'm proud of you. Georgie would be proud of ye too.'

That name brought the smile back to her worried face. 'I nearly died when he went upstairs,' she said, clenching and unclenching her fists. 'I hardly dared to open the spare room door for fear of some clothing bein' left out or the bed rumpled from Moses lyen' on it. It was all right, though. Yer idea of always tidying up when they leave the chamber was a good one. Except that it was warmer than our room, it looked unoccupied.'

372

They remembered Moses then, still curled up behind the vegetable sacks in the cold room. He was fast asleep, doubled up in a surprisingly small ball behind piled sacks of potatoes and flour in the little nest they had made for just such an occasion.

'Ye can wager yer life on 'et,' Ben Chase said later to Moses, 'that Mr Bayless will be comen' back — and bringing the law with 'im. I think the time has come for ye to join Dudie and Nat — even if ye won't set foot in the house.'

Moses put his hand over both Fran's. 'Mistress, you have both bin the best friends a free man ever had,' he said, and the rough tenderness in his voice brought easy tears to her eyes. 'I'll take myself off after dark this evenin', if Master Tom will row me across to Hempsteddle. I'll hide in the woods till then, in case he comes back right away. Oh, that Tom, mistress. You wait till I see him — I'll paddle his head till he don' know the time of day. . . . '

9

Moses raised his hand in farewell to Ben, who was already
sculling out into the darkening river, oars dipping into
silver flurries. He watched until the old man in his tiny
bobbing shell was well out into midstream before turning
towards the woods, which stood behind him against the
opalescent dusk sky like bunched spectators before a fight,
silent, speculative — forbidding. He moved along the edge
of the field, crouching against the hazel bushes growing
thickly above the water. When he reached the bottom
hedge, which marked the boundary with Lavenham's
overgrown north paddock, he pushed himself into the
thicket and squatted down to think how best to deal with
what was before him.

The evening was warm, the air filled with the bland
scent of ripening grain. Black-winged rooks wheeled overhead and then swooped away towards their nests in the
distant trees. A bee, late wanderer after sunset, droned
lazily past his nose and settled on a leaf nearby. The field,
pale golden with tall hempen grasses in the dying light,
breathed gently, washed this way and that by the lightest
of evening breezes.

How small these English fields are, he thought, to
deflect his fear at the approach of darkness, forcing
himself to remember the long patchwork of husbanded
land that had been home since his grandfather was
brought from Africa. Two generations of bonded life. It
was their good fortune that they had been part of the
Heritage estate during much of that time, for those whites
were good Christian people and made sure that their
overseer was a man of conscience also. The young Moses

374

Abelson had known little of the cruelty and torment of the African people in bondage to the white man. He spent his childhood hunting the Mighty Hoodah through the woods and haybarns in company with Caleb and Tom Heritage, and when he was of an age to earn his keep, naturally took his place in the Heritages' grain warehouse on Boston's East Quay. He did well there, for he had shared some of Tom's schooling and quickly learned both reading and writing. Within two years he was directly under the foreman, picking up a good knowledge of ledger work whenever the chance arose.

When Tom went to sea, it was not long before Moses joined him, even though there would be no chance of advancement for him in the clipper service. Although he enjoyed learning and had no difficulty with it, personal ambition was not one of Moses' attributes. He wished to learn, for he was naturally curious about so much of what he saw around him, but there was no zealous fire burning in his belly as there was with many of the partially educated black folks. At Tom's side, he would be in the best possible company — and where better to learn the ways of the world?

Moses, proud of his freedom amongst the weight of slavery in the American colonies doggedly followed Tom into war when the Revolutionary Council declared the birth of the Federation and severed their allegiance to the English Crown.

By the time the *Free States* was captured and its crew imprisoned, Moses had found a wife, made her a home at Midhurst and given her two babies. She worked in the main house as maid to the ageing Mistress Violet, assisting Joelly Parsons, who had cared for her mistress since she had come to Boston as Desmond Heritage's new bride. Luella was young and easily given to tears as well as to laughter, but she was a fine strong girl with skin as richly shining and unblemished as a ripe plum. Mistress Violet always said it did her heart good to listen to Luella's chatter till she was scolded out of the room by Joelly. It did Moses' heart good just to think of her at all.

He sat in the thicket and drove his mind away from his lingering hunger for Louella to examine the most important issue of the moment: to get Tom out of that bad place steeped in the sins of his ancestors and on to the barque bound for Normandy in just three days' time. Then it would be only weeks before they were back in the heart of their flesh-and-blood families — and Moses could make more babies with Luella, the way it should be.

Dusk deepened, etching the horizon of distant trees and Rymans tower in an irridescent moment of purple brilliance before the last of the dying day was drawn into night shadow. The first star in that opalescent sky was joined by another and then another. Squatting in the spiky thicket, he watched the changing canopy of the sky and felt the sheer glory of his freedom, caught by the momentary perfection of it.

Even as he watched, all light melded into dusk and Moses crawled out of the hedge and made his way on hands and knees along the ditch towards the river bank and a strip of muddy sand that stretched for twenty or so yards along the Lavenham shore.

Behind him, unseen, a horseman rode down the cart-track to Newbarn, the cluster of its farm buildings little more than a wash of darkness beyond the sighing hemp.

It was too early for the moon and there was still just enough light for the keen eye, for the sky was a great roof of bright new darkness, like strong sunshine seen through the thickness of a deep blue curtain. Moses moved slowly, eyes swivelling from left to right as he went, as though to gather up every smallest movement amongst the nocturnal creatures who were only now beginning to emerge.

Charles rode his horse fast down the wide track to Newbarn. He forbore to raise his eyes for he had no wish to rest them upon the one broken Lavenham chimneypot which could be seen from this part of the lane.

He had been kept overlong in the Dell Quay office this

evening and now was late, both for the visit to Will Slaughter at Newbarn Cottage and for his meeting with Doctor Priestley at Leonie's bedside. The cough had finally become stronger than his wife's will to remain at his side, and she was rasping and bubbling feebly in her bed, all strength spent and her will to live gone. The boys hovered anxiously all day in the corridor near her chamber door, and the whole household was creeping about as though she had already given up the struggle. Exasperated with convention, longing for Dudie, he wished that she had.

A lone star shone in the deepening cobalt dusk over his head. He saw only the ruts in the track, made by the passage of the hemp waggons. Nothing penetrated the intensity of his thoughts but arrangements for the plan he was about to bring into action. He saw nothing of the distant, crouching figure that scuttled from shadow to shadow as he thundered by and melted into the thicket on the other side of the field.

The cottage, dwarfed by the high barn at its back, came into view.

'Good evening to you, Mrs Slaughter,' he said most charmingly to the stout girl who opened the door to his knock. He took off his hat the better to be recognized, and she bobbed quickly, mumbling a greeting in pleasure and embarrassment as she pushed the greasy hair back from her face.

'Is Will home yet?'

'Yas, sor . . . 'e's but newly back, just moments ago.' She suddenly realized that he was standing expectantly on the doorstep and stood aside for him to pass her.

'Go right into the kitchen, if you will, sor . . . and please excuse the state we'm in. 'Es thatchen' out the back, see.'

Will Slaughter rose from his seat by the open hearth as Charles entered the dark cave of the little kitchen, head bent for the ceiling was low.

Years of cooking had yellowed and then blackened the

lime-washed walls so that they were now of a uniform dinginess, the colour of dung. A film of grease seemed to cover everything. An odour of stale beer, burnt pig fat and body gases made him long to reach for his kerchief and hold it to his nose.

He went forward resolutely. 'Evening, Will. May we spend a few moments discussing our proposed main here?'

The man's heavily stolid face lit up. 'Oh yes, yer honour. I was awonderen' why you was visiten'. The fight between my French Spangle and Tosser Jelliff's Shropshire Red's ben agreed. I've bin down to the mill and seen 'em and 'e says 'e's right willen' . . . real keen be the look of 'un. Drummed up five other pair too, sor. 'Ave you any others in mind? We'll need a few more ter make a good gatheren' on et.'

Charles's pale eyes burned. 'Good, good.' He seated himself gingerly on a stool. 'I've been promised challengers from Sir Edwin Griffiths and Master Tertius Page. I shall be entering a couple of birds. I've just acquired a very fine Pile. Beautiful bird. Light feathers and a heel action that'll rip the throat out of anything. Just coming up to two years old now and ready for training. The other's a bit of an unknown quantity. He's a Dun — a Foulsham Downrump. I've not handled one of them before, nor even seen them in action but Lord Lennox made me a present of it.' He grinned across at Will Slaughter, seeing the man's attention, knowing that in his coop at the back of the cottage there were five Duns.

'Let us get down to the details, then, for I can promise you a good crowd of spectators and men with money in their pockets at that.'

The man's deep set eyes gleamed, a "cocker" to his last drop of blood, and he rubbed his hands together. ''Twill take mor'n a week to train 'em up, sor. Ten days, more like, so would ye be thinken' of maken' the date around Tuesday week?' Ten days. A whole life time might have passed by before Tuesday week, Charles thought.

'I'm afraid that won't be possible,' he said. 'I've to be in

London then and, in fact, am summonsed to Lord Devonshire's banquet nine days from today.' He appeared to think for a moment. 'Eight days' time, Will. It'll have to be then, as I shall be committed too fully later — and I know that Sir Edwin is to be in Paris before the end of the month.' He rose to leave and Will stood respectfully, only the gleam in his pale eyes betraying his pleasure at the coming contest.

Charles turned and appeared to hesitate, remembering something. 'That gypsy — Nat Smith,' he said slowly. 'He's always at local mains. I've seen him at most of the ones I've attended in the last four or five seasons.'

Will scratched his head. 'The one camped out on the common, would that be, sor?'

Charles nodded. 'I noted with some interest that he has one particular bird that has won at two mains that I have attended. He has moved from the common and is now camped in the north paddock at Lavenham, so I believe. Maybe you would like to let him know the date of this main, for I'd be interested in contesting that fowl of his with my Pile.'

It was quite dark by the time he left Newbarn Cottage. Not a light glimmered anywhere. Even the Dell Quay warehouse was closed. From a long way away the discordant sounds of singing filtered across the fields from the little Dell Quay tavern. He looked about him approvingly. Newbarn was secluded and remote from passers-by and would be ideal for the cock fight. Ideal also to draw Nat Smith and Dudie out into the open. Nat's fascination for cocking had been the main subject of conversation between them when he had been a welcome guest at the Smiths' fireside. It was quite possible to argue for hours on end about the pros and cons of this bird or that. Nat had a coop under his waggon and the birds he raised so lovingly were beginning to earn him a few purses.

Bait the trap and then wait and see how many mice came sniffing at the cheese, Charles thought. It was quite possible that if Tom Heritage was still in the area he might

379

also be persuaded to show himself, but it was primarily Dudie who had to be brought out. It was most unlikely that she would appear at the main, for women were rarely in attendance. But if Nat was camping at Lavenham, Dudie would be there too.

The thought of her set his pulses racing. He turned his face towards Chichester, and so absorbed was he in making his plans that it was not until he was riding past the Donnington turning that he remembered Leonie's condition.

'Tomorrow I shall leave here, I promise.'

Tom lay back comfortably in a padded chair in the withdrawing room, his feet propped up on a square footstool. Dudie had lit the many-branched candelabra which stood on an oval table close to the west window. She had closed the shutters and drawn the curtains, stirring up a great cloud of dust that had set them coughing. Now the room looked almost cosy, the warmth of the evening accentuating the slight mustiness in the air.

'Nat will be back soon,' she said, leaning over to hand him a wedge of bread upon which she had just spread a thick layer of pickled cauliflower and peach. 'If we are in luck, he will have Moses with him and then we can plan the best way to get you both aboard the ship for France. Maybe we could borrow one of the bum-boats from the quay . . . Master Chase's little cotty won't be no good for it'd have to be abandoned an' 'twould implicate him if we was discovered.'

He didn't want to think of anything as final as their departure. There were too many imponderables tied up in it. He was filled with a delicious lassitude, comfortable in this place — drawing a bitter-sweet pleasure from the sheer independence of this small and mightily determined girl who was prepared to risk her own safety for his. For the moment he was supremely happy right where he was.

'Why should we not stay here at Lavenham — the four of us?' He watched her lazily, uttering the words simply to light the explosive animation in her mobile, candlelit face.

'Oh, Tom.' The exasperation in her voice hid her own thoughts well, but he still felt them instinctively, as she must see things in men's hands. 'You don't seem to see what a dangerous position you are in. If they catch you, you'll not only be sent back to the hulks but they might even string you up for your trouble.'

She stopped, seeing the sleepy grin on his face. 'Oh, mercy, bor. Will you stop bein' a tease for just a moment?'

'Assuredly, ma'am. Would you think I was teasing if I told you that I don't want to leave here unless I can take you with me?'

She considered. 'Yes, I would think you were teasen', and cruelly too. You forget the child I am carryen'. You forget that kenners are not good places for me and I shall not live in one — ever. You are just playen' romantic dreams because you are bored with skulking in an empty house.'

'But I'm not, you see, Dudie.' He had not moved. His body was relaxed and his face almost drowsy. He might have been talking in his sleep. 'I'm not bored with all this inactivity, far from it. This place is a fascinating treasure house from Mama's past and, but for the one room upstairs, I feel most welcome in it. It would be all too easy to dwell right here quietly until peace returns to our two countries, and then open the place up properly and see whether I could not begin trading between Boston and Chichester.'

His half-closed eyes swivelled round to her. 'And I am not forgetting your situation either, Dudie. . . . What better place could you have for the birth of your child than here? Some Baylesses have been born here before, and no doubt they will be in the future. Would you not consider giving your child a proper foundation for its future? With me?'

The Watcher was suddenly angry.
What was the ridiculous fellow thinking of? Had he

taken no notice of the warnings of three generations of tragedy in this Godless place? Was it possible that he did not realize what happened to children born under this roof?

He pressed forward, forcing . . . forcing . . . battering his warning into the minds of the two figures. In the flickering candlelight, Dudie looked up at him calmly. There was no comprehension in her eyes, but for a moment he was not at all sure that he was not vaguely visible to her.

'No child of mine will ever be born within these walls, bor.' Her voice was soft and a slight huskiness made him look at her more closely.

'The house is more mokada for birth than for anything else. Your own mother was born out of it, remember. She was born in the vardo, as all Romanies should be. My child will be born in ours — and I shall not need to be subservient to any man for the sake of it.'

They watched each other covertly, he seeing the longing that was in her to go to him, she grieving at the lightness of his mood. There was no kneeling on one knee here as Charles had done, to plead for her affection. Not that that was what she wanted — let the gorgios cavort with their studied poses. The empty courtesies of court manners were not for Romany people. How good it would have been, all the same, had he uttered his proposal from the heart, rather than this casual suggestion from a feeling of pity, of responsibility for her.

He smiled at her, quite unoffended by the sharpness of her rebuff, assumed a clown's face of tragic regret and heaved himself up in his chair with a sigh.

'Before we continue this conversation, I must ask you to excuse me, Miss Smith,' he said with heavy formality. 'Nature is suddenly even more pressing than courtship. Don't move, for there are many things that must be said, and I feel that this is as right a moment as we will find. I shall not be long.'

He looked back at her as he left the room. Huge shadows cast by the candles loomed over her small figure, doing a slow weaving dance as the disturbed air of his passing set them wavering.

He stepped out of the front door on to the terrace and stood for a moment, arrested by the tranquillity. The night was brilliant, the quarter-moon attended by a million blazing pinpoints. The air was fragrant with the scent of roses, of honeysuckle mixed with the sea. The wind must be coming off the land, he thought, for within its heavy sweetness was a faint odour of stable. Tom went slowly down the weed-choked terrace steps and wandered through the archway into the stableyard, where Dudie's waggon stood, hidden by the four-square barns from prying eyes. It took a few minutes to become accustomed to the darkness in the buildings' shadow.

He relieved himself against the barn wall and was buttoning up his breeches when a movement on the far side of the yard caught his eye.

Something substantial had moved between a broken water butt and the corner of the building. He stood still, flattening himself against the barn wall, eyes straining into the black infinity of the yard.

Another small sound: a furtive swish of movement through the wild growth of weeds choking the cobbles. A pebble clattered against another. The lurcher growled from under the waggon, a long deep sound in the back of her throat. Tom held his breath, for it seemed to sound like a giant bellows in the quiet night.

He could just see the outline of the waggon. 'Nat . . . is that you?' Tom's voice grated in the heavy silence. The dog growled again and the sudden rattle of its chain echoed hollowly round the invisible walls. He stood motionless, probing the night beyond the waggon. Whatever lurked there waited also, blended with the night.

'Tom . . . are you all right?' Dudie's voice cut through the infinite moment, the anxiety in it making him turn his head.

'Tom . . . ?' She was coming to look for him. He moved stealthily along the wall with his arms outspread, working his silent way back towards the arch.

'Where are you, Tom . . . ?' She came through the archway and jumped as he put out a hand and gripped her arm.

'Shhh,' he said, with his mouth against her ear. 'I saw something over by the other gateway. I thought it was Nat but nothing happened when I called out.'

They stood close together, listening to the threatening rumbles from the dog. She growled again, dragging at her chain and making frantic outward dashes from under the waggon. Something reared up from a clump of bushes only a few yards from where they stood.

'Reckon yor li'l old ears must be full of cobwebs,' a voice said. A set of teeth flashed whitely in the dimness and Moses stepped forward and gave Tom a soft cuff with a huge balled fist. 'I'm mighty glad it was you, master.' He was breathing fast, as though he had been running. 'I spent the last two hours creeping along the banks of that murky old river on ma belly, getting myself covered in mud and bird shit and waking up all the moorhens and things that nest in them reeds. When I seed the roof of this barn yard against the stars, I reckoned I'm almost there. Then I heared a creepin' and a crawlin' like there was some mighty slithery serpent on the loose – an' then that hound of yours starts agrowlin' and carrying on. Next thing, I heared someone call out and after that Miss Dudie, ma'am. Reckon your sweet tones done save me wetten' ma breeches like I was a pickininni – specially when I hears someone waterin' the wall there.'

They grasped the big man's arms in their relief, still shaken by the tension of that creeping, unknown moment.

'Come into the house and let me try and clean you up a bit,' Dudie said, for even in the darkness the moon showed the mud glistening over most of Moses' shirt front and knee breeches.

He let her pull him through the arch, but rolled his eyes fearfully at the dark mass of the silent house towering over them. 'I'm not goin' in there. Not in the middle o' the night with all them ghoulies and ghosties hangin' about waitin' to send me to the pit.'

'Come on, old friend,' Tom laughed behind him. 'I slept here last night and had the best sleep since I was rocked in my mother's womb. It's as safe as can be and there's nothing to be afraid of.' He pushed the unwilling Moses before him as he spoke.

'Huh, you sure must've slept like a babe,' the big man grumbled, allowing himself to be hauled up the terrace steps and in through the wide door. The air was heavy in the spacious place, charged with the faint fragrance of dried leaves and old wood. He looked about him briefly and then turned back to Tom.

'The rest of yor buddies 've been worried stupid about you. That's the only reason I'm here, I tell you.'

He stopped so suddenly that Tom cannoned into him from behind.

'Oh lawdie, lawdie. . . . It's the truth then.'

In the soft shaft of candlelight streaming through the open parlour door, the jagged teeth of the shattered dining table suddenly seemed alien, shocking.

'Don't worry about it. We just haven't had time to tidy it all up yet,' Tom said. 'That happened a very long time ago and whatever was responsible for doing it is not here any longer. Come on in and see for yourself.' He went past Moses into the parlour and began dragging a chair across into the pool of light.

Moses stood and sniffed the air of the hall. 'He says there baint nothing here but I says there is,' he whispered to Dudie.

She squeezed his hand tightly. 'There may be, bor,' she said, matching his low voice. 'But now that you are here, I think we can look after him between us, don't you?'

He shivered. 'I'd go into the jaws of Hell for him if I have to,' he said grimly. 'An' I reckon that's just where we are right now.'

The Watcher turned away and closed his eyes.

They were gathering, slowly drawn together by the cloying tendrils of the Place. Lawrence's son was out there too — not daring to do battle with the forces within these walls, but drawn all the same by its magnetism, reflected so strongly through the girl. He wept then. It was the first time that tears had seemed at all possible, for although they were but an empty expression of his frustration, they were at least a human reaction.

He felt her hand on his shoulder and turned over in the bed and lay on his back, looking up at her.

'I'm losing it,' he said. 'I seem to be sliding further and further backwards and becoming less and less able to control things. How much longer will this nightmare go on, Frances, for God's sake?'

The look she gave him was filled with compassion. 'Until you have resolved what it is that you are seeking,' she said gently.

Nat was asleep in the waggon when Dudie went across at first light to fetch bread and meat. He looked hot and dishevelled and started up with an oath as Dudie patted his shoulder.

'Why'd you not come into the kenner with the rest of us?' she asked. 'Moses found his way here after Charles Bayless started threatenen' the Chases. He's turned real sour now, that sap.'

She put her hand lightly on her stomach where the child stirred with a faint flutter.

Nat grunted. 'You jus' don't know what you've got yourself tied up in with these folks.' He turned his face to the wall and closed his eyes against the sharp daylight. 'We'd best be gone from 'ere and let them fend fer themselves, the lot of 'em. Trouble, that's what they are . . . trouble fer me, pen — and worse trouble fer you.'

He had not been pleased to discover from the Chases that Moses had already left for Lavenham, even though his reasons for doing so were to protect the old couple. It was not to Nat's advantage to be scouring the countryside in search of a man he had never met, only to discover that he need not have exerted himself after all. He had never involved himself with gorgios before, except to earn a living from them when needs must. He turned over in his bunk and watched Dudie gathering the cooking utensils and food into her apron. She looked very small. Her face was serious but there was a serenity about it that was new to her. She was such a headstrong, wayward creature at times, he thought with exasperated affection. But she was still the strongest of them all, despite her slight frame. He knew that he would kill Charles Bayless before letting a hair on her head be hurt.

He appeared later in the morning and sat, munching at the bread that remained uneaten from breakfast, unwilling to join the others as they wandered over the house and trailed through the rooms as they discovered one treasure after another.

There was something about the place that had not been there before. It was as though it was slowly coming alive after a long, long sleep.

Moses sensed the change also and was afraid. He sat outside in the sunshine and prayed for their deliverance and averted his eyes from the shining faces of Tom and Dudie, busy and happy as they made a rough inventory of the house's contents. There was no attempt at intimacy between them, he saw, but there was a softness to Tom's voice, an intensity in his glance which betrayed him at every turn. And Dudie hovered close to him, the imperviousness wiped from her regard, her perfect oval face with its faint cleft in the chin alight with shining concentration. They seemed to move on another plane, quite alone with each other. The house enfolded them, inserting itself invisibly between them and their companions.

Looking up at the dusty casements, behind the wilderness of creeper, Moses had the strongest conviction that Tom and Dudie were somehow being drawn away from him and Nat — the self-appointed guardians of these two loved people — like figures seen at the end of a dark tunnel, floating away . . . diminishing before his eyes.

He rose and went down to the bank of the channel and stood with his back to the house, staring out resolutely across the water to Old Park Woods.

He was filled with terror of the night that must follow this day. He gripped the little bone cross that he wore suspended from a leather thong round his neck. He had made it from a piece of sheep's knuckle and was quietly proud of the fine quality of the carving, the little fronds of vine leaves and fruit that he had taken laborious weeks to fashion with his knife.

'Save us all,' he prayed, gripping the cross, which was warm from his body. 'Save us all and bring us back to sanity — away from this Godless place.'

The house glimmered at him, reflected in the bright water at his feet. By some odd quirk of the light it seemed suddenly to be all afire, huge shafts of white hot flame licking upwards from every window.

He spun round in fright — and found it reposing peacefully beside the oakwood, gently washed in the warm golden reflection of the setting sun.

10

Will Slaughter eventually found Nat sitting on the top step of his waggon in the centre of the overgrown stable yard and probing his back teeth with a twig.

The gypsy stared at him stonily without moving as he appeared through the archway and came across the yard, the little brindle and white terrior inches from his heels.

'Hey, good day to ye, Nat Smith. Ben looken' for you over all these blamed acres fer the past couple of hours.'

Will Slaughter was hot and he stopped at the bottom of the waggon steps to mop his damp face and neck with his shirt end. The two dogs bristled threateningly at each other but the terrier stayed close to Will's leg.

Nat took the twig out of his mouth and ejected a large gobbet of spittle. It fell with a neat *ptt* close to the little terrier's front paw. From below the waggon the lurcher growled quietly in the back of her throat, her bright eyes watching the stranger's gaitered legs intently. One word from Nat and her teeth would be sunk firmly into the back of the man's inside thigh.

'What chew want with me?' Nat demanded.

Will eyed the birdcages hanging from the waggon's tailboard. He jerked his head at them.

'Seen you at the main by Kingsmeet tavern t'other Friday. Thought you'd want to come over ter Newbarn main Thursday next week, see'en' as it's sorta close ter here. Mr Bayless, 'e said as you was campen' at Lavenham. 'E aims ter put up two good cocks. One of 'em, the Dun, 'ud give that Smokey of yours a good run, I reckon.'

Nat put the twig back in his mouth and dug at a wisdom tooth, wincing. 'I'll think on et, bor.' He watched Will's eyes flicking round the crumbling buildings in uneasy hesitation.

'Big place, ent et?' Will peered back through the archway. 'A fine house, though, one time — ye can see that. I allus wondered what twas like en 'ere, but tales was too fearsome when I was a lad. Ghosties — an' other things, so they say. . . . '

His voice trailed away as Nat still said nothing but just sat looking at him, chewing on his twig.

Will whistled to his dog and found it already pressing itself against his foot. It whined up at him, showing the whites of its eyes and shivering, one paw raised. It didn't like the place any more than other folks, Will thought, turning away.

When Will had gone, Nat left his perch and took the Smokey Dun from its cage.

'Scourings for you next feed, my kushti bor,' he said softly to the bird, stroking the proud head below the hard red stub where the comb had been severed. Only part of his attention was with the bird under his hands. The rest of him was turning over the information that Will Slaughter had brought him.

Mr Charles Bayless was interested in pitting his bird against Nat Smith's fowl. How very unlikely it was that a gentleman of his standing would go to the length of sending a messenger such as Will, chasing all over Apuldram to look for just one gypsy with a good bird. There were other contestants who could give him as good a run for his money. No, what was much more likely, seeing that it was Charles, was that the contest was bait — not for him but to draw Dudie out of hiding. It had been him, after all, as Will admitted, who had made the first suggestion that Newbarn would make a good place for a fight.

'Mr Bayless wants ter see you in action, does he? He wants too much, that gorgio. Too much. First Dudie an' now you. Well, we'll give 'im a little surprise, won't we, chiriklo? A Duckwing agin ye, eh?' He grunted with dry amusement, holding the bird up so that they stared into each other's eyes. 'A grey man's Grey Dun. Small game again a devil's bird, eh, bor?'

The Smokey cocked its head to one side, its glassy red-rimmed eyes regarding him with a rare intelligence. 'Devil's birds' lived up to their reputations with extraordinary regularity, for they were game cocks that had been placed in and hatched from a magpie's nest and were regarded by many as unconquerable. So far, the Smokey was fulfilling this expectation.

He laid the bird on the ground and, half a mind on the removal of Dudie from Lavenham, watched it peck fastidiously among the weed-choked cobbles.

Half an hour later Moses came through the archway and his eyes lit up at the sight of the beautiful creature.

'My aunt Susie's headpiece,' he said, whistling through his teeth as Nat lifted the bird up and let it spread its clipped bronze and black wings and beat the air between them with powerful strokes. 'Now, that is some gamecock. What you doin' with him? Goin' to fight him, maybe?'

Nat told him about the main.

Moses looked disappointed. 'I'd've liked to see that, but we should be over the Channel by that time, God willin'.'

'Man, I had a fine bird one time, long ago. Twas a scarlet Polecat and the only cock I ever reared on my own. Went down to a bandy-legged Bantam with one eye. Never did find another I cared for so well . . . 'cept, maybe a big ol' black rat I trained fer fightin' aboard the *Fortunée*.'

It was common knowledge that the prisoners, with little to occupy them from dawn to dusk, raced anything that moved to indulge the Rafalés' passion for gambling. Rat-racing was a regular occupation and those rats' trainers as dedicated as any.

He cocked his head at Moses. 'They still maken' their lists?'

Moses grunted. 'Reckon that's what they say they're doin'. Maybe they even believe it themselves, but ma good friend, what those two is doin' is fallin' in love — and in that tainted place that's no good for sweet wholesome feelin's as natural as theirs.'

Nat thumped a clenched fist against the side of the waggon. The Smokey, aroused from a pleasant reverie under his master's arm, squawked in protest and lashed out with his vicious beak.

Nat put the bird down at his feet. 'She's walken' into trouble, the dinelo mort.' He scowled. 'She shouldn't truck with gorgios. We're travellen' folks, see. Different from gorgios — an' always will be. Dallyen' with 'em only brings grief, bor — and I ent taken' more of it from anyone, be 'e yer pral or not. Let 'im keep 'is distance from 'er, you tell 'im that, bor, see? Or he'll have me ter reckon with. 'What's keepen' you here? Why aren't ye on yer way not to Harris's wharf? Ye could hide up a couple of days aboard ship before she sails. Why let 'im stay on here?'

'Because I caint seem to get him to hear me, that's why.' Sudden despair sharpened Moses' face. 'He is happy in the strangest way, man. Kind of dreamin', even as he speaks with you. I say somethin' to him and he is miles away and seems not to hear. And Mistress Dudie, she seems to be part of it too.'

'I reckon that house has somethin' to do with it.'

Dudie's voice interrupted their thoughts. 'Come and eat, Nat . . . Moses. I've made a good harvest mess on the hob. Quick, now, afore it spoils.'

'When are we goin' from here?'

'Well,' Tom began, but Moses cut through the slow ease of his voice, suddenly angry at Tom's almost sleepy lack of interest.

'Put it this way, Master Tom. I am leaving here tomorrow with you. I am going to Emsworth, to Harris's Wharf and I shall hide myself aboard the vessel that is takin' us to France and await ma fate in a place that at least is one step closer to ma freedom and home. All this I shall do, young master, in company with you — even if I have to break both your legs and carry you there myself. . . . This hanging about is a danger, not only to ourselves but to

Miss Dudie and to Nat, who stand to fall foul of the authorities jes' for bein' in our company. Now that your Master Bayless knows where we are, there aint no chance of us stayin' here in any safety, do you understand that?'

Tom looked at him in surprise. 'I expect he might think that we are here but he doesn't know for sure, does he?'

'Yes, sir, he does.' Moses' voice began to rumble ominously. Anger was rare with him, but the house raised a strange violence in his heart.

Tom stared at him blankly for a moment and then his eyes slewed round to Dudie. Without a word he left the table. Something took him and led him from them, guided him up the stairs and into the main bedchamber. There he stood by the window, looking down into the garden, seeing smooth lawns and orderly flowerbeds and a young woman swinging across the terrace with a basket of roses on her arm. A fine black stallion grazed close to the wall amongst the unshorn grasses. It lifted its head to watch her as she passed. The stables would be filled with horses of the Lavenham stud, for he could hear the sharp squeal and whinny of a mare in season. The odour of the stables was suddenly strong, so that it was all about him, rank, sour. . . .

He turned away from the window. It was only the house, offering him another of the little memory pictures with which it had been teasing him since his arrival.

'I have to leave,' he said to the room. 'I have another home and greater responsibilities than I owe to Lavenham.'

There was a stirring all about him, as though a mischievous breeze was tugging at his hair, his clothing.

Dudie . . . the thought of her suddenly smote him, churning the tenderness in him into sharply violent desire.

Dudie . . . he groaned, hugging himself, feeling himself invaded by a lust so alien that in its midst he was sickened to the core. He felt the hot bile rise in his throat even as the blood roared and thundered through his body. Something screamed its pleasure as the furious pulse beat in him with vast drum strokes, turning his legs to water, pouring from him in a fount of uncontrolled heat.

Dark clouds rolled away from his eyes and he was in the presence of the Fount of all Life, sliding backwards, back. . . .

They finished their stew and still Tom had not returned.

'Shall I go and look for him, do you think?' Dudie asked anxiously. 'He's had long enough to think about things, hasn't he?'

'You stay right where you are,' Nat said grimly, rising from the bench. 'I'll find him. He can't just walk away from a discussion like that. He's to leave with Moses, just like he says, see? An' you an' I'll be on our way directly. We've done it yer way up to this moment, pen, but Moses an' me — we've had enough.'

He looked into every room on the ground floor but there was no sign of Tom, nor could he see him outside on the terrace. He went up the stairs two at a time. Damned fool, he thought, hiding was not going to work. They'd find him, wherever he hid himself.

But Tom was not hiding. He was stretched out on the floor of the main bedchamber as though a great fist had felled him. His face was the colour of putty.

'Hey, bor,' Nat said, squatting down beside him and shaking his shoulder. 'What's up with 'e? Wake up. . . . '

He was breathing. His lungs pumped air slowly through his mouth in a slight snore. His eyes were closed. There was no trace of blue about his mouth. He made no response to Nat's urgings. Nor did he respond by even a flicker to Dudie's urgent pleas. He appeared to have sunk into a deep coma.

Nat and Moses glowered at each other over Tom's body as they lifted him up on to the bed. They realized he could not be taken anywhere in this condition. It was as though the house was determined to keep him from leaving, for he had been in excellent health minutes before.

Tom stirred. His eyes flew open and a thin, terrible

scream, like the squeal of a terrified animal, was forced through his clenched teeth.

Dudie pushed between the two men and leant over him to put a hand on his forehead.

'Tom, wake up . . . wake up. It's only a dream you're haven'. Fight it, bor. It'll take your sanity if'n you don' fight et. . . . '

She looked over the top of Nat's head at something beyond the bed curtains. She glowered, her face suddenly not at all the small, sweet face of Dudie Smith but that of a woman ferociously protective.

Moses, staring at her with sudden fear, saw the face of a stranger and crossed himself. 'What you lookin' at like that, Miss Dudie?' he whispered. 'There ain't a body in this chamber but us. You lookin' in the corners that way gives me the goose pimples like the Devil himself is out there grinnin' at us.'

She rose up from her crouched position beside the bed and stood very straight, her eyes still fixed at a point behind Nat.

'Not the Devil. Not that,' she said slowly. Her voice was sharp, as though she spoke to someone else. 'I see him, though. Yes — I see ye, whoever ye are. Be gone from us. We 'ave done no wrong 'ere.'

Nat and Moses looked about them furtively. There was nothing to be seen. Was the house going to claim her sanity also?

Then she blinked and bit her lip, and the colour flooded through her cheeks as she bent down to Tom once more.

'Sorry,' she muttered to them. 'I swear I saw a figure over by the door. He was quite clear for just a moment. Dressed in strange clothing, too. But he had Tom's features, I swear it. . . . '

She put her head against Tom's chest and began to weep softly.

The Watcher was deeply shaken. He held out his hand to the girl and pleaded his innocence, raked by the anguish in her face. She had seen him — she had actually seen him just then.

In the year 1802, he had been seen positively by a young human being in full possession of her senses. He withdrew when it became clear that the sight of him had gone and that no amount of protestations of his innocence would reach her. He walked on the terrace, deaf to the soft drone of bees about their business, blind to the mellow light as the sharp colours melded in a gauze of warm sweetness and the earth drowsed.

She had actually seen him.

The implications of visual contact between the years 1802 and 1953 took some time to sink in. When they did, he ceased pacing and sat on the shallow terrace steps with his back against the balustrade.

Charles trained his birds himself. He had done this since gamefowl mains had begun to appeal to him some ten years before. At first he had been content to buy birds and let Will Slaughter train them, but then the fascination of the sport had brought forth the fiercely competitive spirit of the cock-fighting Romany — a Bayless inheritance. He had one of the stables cleared and lime-washed and began to breed and train his own birds. Visiting the roost became a daily pilgrimage of expiation when the stresses of the day were put aside and he could lose himself in the fascination of fowl training and then watch his handiwork flourish at main after main.

Now he had the new Duckwing, as well as half a dozen hand-reared cocks to put through their paces. It was the Foulsham Duckwing, though, that would tempt Nat Smith, and with him Dudie, out of hiding. He took the bird from its cage, hands gentling the alarm out of the creature, his mind on the coming contest, seven days from now.

Upstairs in the house, Leonie was slowly fading away, dying without complaint or fuss, attended by her sons and servants. He felt nothing but impatience for the thing to be over. He ignored the unspoken disapproval of the household, the sadness in his wife's dull eyes.

Word had reached him that morning of an Emsworth frigate bound for Portugal which was to take on two passengers not registered on the ship's manifest. Portugal might well be the final destination, but a French port was likely to be their first anchorage.

He had the strongest possible conviction that the two strangers were Tom Heritage and the big Negro Moses Abelson. If they were, they would not get far, for he had sent a note to the captain of militia at Emsworth, suggesting investigation. Without Tom to nurse and fuss over, and when Leonie had gone, he hoped he would be able to tempt Dudie back to his side. Faint though he knew the hope was, it still gave him a feeling of lightheaded purpose.

He stroked his birds gleaming feathers and put them back, one by one, into their cloth covered pens. Then he went into the house to sit silently at his wife's bedside.

The fever which had consumed Tom so suddenly lasted for four days.

Dudie, distraught at the thought of the ship sailing without them, could do little but sit at his side, watching the strange expression flitting across his dreaming face, every instinct in her body aware of the subtly changing atmosphere all around them.

The whole place seemed different now. She felt stealth about her, as though something crept invisibly in her shadow, watching . . . growing in purpose. It gave her a deep feeling of unease, of looking constantly over the shoulder — of almost, but not quite, catching sight of the thing that stalked her.

Tom tossed on the great four-poster in the chamber, fluctuating between spasms of violent restlessness, the animal growl in his throat sometimes rising to a tortured bellow — and lying like a discarded doll, exhausted by some inner conflict which was gradually sapping the last shred of energy in him.

There were times when he knew her. Then she was aware of a terrible urgency in him, though the words that came from his mouth were unintelligible. For the most part, he was lost in some other place deep down in his mind; a place which terrified as well as gripped him.

Feeling time slipping by and the chance of their freedom diminishing with every hour, she tended him doggedly, almost resenting the occasional appearance of Moses and Nat. And the two men, having almost come to blows in the frustration of their situation, finally agreed that they could not move Tom until he recovered from his unexpected seizure. They swallowed their impatience to be gone and busied themselves with breaking up the rotting stalls in the barn for firewood.

Tom floated in a world of fleeting faces and sudden invasions of his body which scoured every nerve and sent him screaming soundlessly back into black shadows. There were times when he was aware of Dudie sitting beside him, her little pointed face anxious. He tried to tell her to go. Deivos had invaded his very soul, and his furious resistance was slowly being squeezed out of him. If he once gave in he knew that he would return to consciousness and sanity — but Deivos would be there in him, resting and waiting. Rage at the intrusion fed his weakening resistance, but even the rage was not of the same substance as it had been at first. He knew that when he came back into himself, he would not be the same again.

The Power was in him.

Halfway through the fifth day, Tom opened his eyes, focused and reached out to take Dudie's hand. She was, as usual, sitting beside his bed, drowsily listening to the light, even sound of his breathing. She started back in alarm as the hand took hers firmly and squeezed it.

'Hello,' he said.

His fever was gone, his face had losts its grey pallor and he seemed little the worse for his experience — apart from an understandable weakness. She quickly brought him broth and bread, which he ate ravenously, and he was soon out of bed, testing his legs.

'I don't know what happened to me,' he said, as she gathered up his empty dishes. The hateful faces and fears of his delirium were already receding into the back of his mind, a bad dream best forgotten.

She smiled at him, and there was an expression in her eyes that turned his heart.

'The house took you, bor,' she said. 'There have been stirrings all around your bed as though the room was filled with people, pressing against each other to get a look at you. You spoke in a strange tongue and even looked like another man at times.'

She gave him a sad little lop-sided smile. 'Your fever robbed you and Moses of your place on the ship.'

'Why should that be?' he asked, puzzled. 'I have surely not been laid low for more than a few hours?'

'Days, Tom . . . days and nights, five of them in all. Days and nights doing battle with something here in this house, and it will be the death of you if you do not come away from it.' She said no more then, for something closed behind his eyes although his head nodded in agreement with her.

Shaken by the time lapse, he dressed slowly and followed Dudie downstairs to question her further. There was a strange feeling in the middle of his chest, as though, at the smallest suggestion, his mood would flare up into white-hot rage. He clenched his teeth, holding it in. Ill temper had never been part of his nature — but then, it was the other one in him now.

Soft summer rain had scoured the pathway between the back door and the stable yard. He found Moses and Nat in an area cleared of weeds, in the act of setting two fighting cocks at each other. The calm scene and the men's intense concentration made him pause and lean against the barn wall to watch.

The birds, held astride, were set together beak to beak, then released. Moses and Nat hovered attentively as the adversaries lunged at each other, wings scything, talons and beaks darting with deadly aim.

'Watch that left spur,' Nat said to Moses. 'The muff's drag en' on 'is left there. . . . '

Something began to unfurl in Tom. Watching the birds feint and parry, the lust for blood in their beady red eyes, he felt it opening in him like a great scarlet flower.

He turned away and ran from the yard, clutching at his throat as the thing began to boil upwards from his chest. Panting, he doubled up, leaning against the wall and vomited into the long grass.

'What yo' doin' down here, master? You should be in your bed.' Hands gripped him gently by the shoulders and took his weight. For a moment, Tom could say nothing. The flower sank back, furling its fury. When he could trust himself he lifted his head.

'It's all right, Moses — I'm much better, really. It was just a momentary weakness.'

'Well, sir, it's mighty good to see you on your feet again. Thought we was going to be in this benighted place for the rest of our natural lives, I surely did. The brig left three days ago, you know.'

Tom straightened up. The shivering was almost gone now. 'Can't think what hit me. I was coming to tell you that you are all quite right and we shall be leaving this place as soon as we can arrange another berth across to France.'

The big man grinned broadly, relief making him stand taller, sharper.

'What say we go this very minute? Before you get another good reason for stayin'? Man, I jus' hate every minute of this place. Cain't help it. It's bad and I'm unclean just breathin' its air. So are you. What say we go now?'

Nat appeared beside them, looking thoughtful. He had caged the two cocks and put away the fine leather muffs with which he had protected their spurs.

'You'm lost one chance — so why not wait for a better

one? While half the countryside is busy at the main over there at New Barn tomorrow, twill be a good moment for you to slip through without be'en' noticed, see'en' as how there'll be plenty of strangers millen' about.'

They sat round the long refectory table in the great kitchen, where staff and yardsmen had sat gossiping over their dinners down the years before them. Tom said little, but Moses and Nat, wanting only to be gone, seemed not to notice.

Nat seemed happier now, suddenly more animated than Tom had ever seen him, and he realized with regret that since his escape from the hulk he had put all three of these people under enormous strain.

'We'll have to dress Moses up so that his skin is not noticed,' Tom said. 'Even at night those rolling eyes of his'd raise a battalion.'

'I could drape him in some curtains,' Dudie offered. 'There are plenty of them in the linen room, even if they'll fall to shreds before he's had them round him for long.'

'What happens when we've cleared the area?'

Three faces looked at Tom blankly. Then Nat said, 'We'll meet up with you both at, say, Ashling, north of Chidham — and make for Stansted Forest, where some of the clan are camped this month. We'll have no trouble coveren' you there, while I ask around in Emsworth an' Havant for a couple of discreet berths across the Channel. They're to be had, as the last ones were — as long as your money is good, bor. . . . '

It was — for Nat had sold to Mr Griffin of New Fishbourne a fine set of table cutlery from the Lavenham silver chest and no questions asked. No doubt Mr Griffin thought them stolen, for he was at pains to have his crest engraved on the handles. Tom patted the leather pouch at his belt and grinned at them. His mother would think it well worth the price of their freedom.

The Watcher saw them withdraw and was relieved.

He had stood close to them as they made their arrange-

401

*ments and they had not been aware of him, not even the
girl. There was some strength left, after all, in his Power
. . . but who was to say whether there would be enough for
him to get to the centre of it all?*

*He stood in the open kitchen doorway watching the four
figures moving away from the house through the archway
and into the stable yard. All round him the house was
gathering itself, manipulating unsuspecting emotions for
the horribly physical pleasure of feeding off the tragic
results.*

*'Don't come in here again,' he soundlessly begged their
retreating backs.*

Everyone was astir well ahead of dawn.

'How long do English mains run for?' Tom asked Nat,
striving to clear his mind.

The gypsy shrugged his bony shoulders, chewing the
inside of his cheek. 'Depends, bor. Sometimes 'tis all over
by dusk — ef'n the birds ent top-quality fighters. A brace
of good birds'll keep it goen' till the small hours, unless
there be time limit to et. This 'un could be like that.'

Tom nodded, satisfied. 'Could Dudie and I take the
waggon with Moses in the back and meet up with you in
the morning? You could take the boat over to Ben Chase
and borrow a mount from him and join us later in that
forest you and Dudie spoke of. Then Moses and I will be
within striking distance of one of the ports and will try and
get berths on the first vessel willing to carry us across the
Channel.'

He felt Dudie's eyes on him and turned his head from
her. He would be certain death for her if he stayed. Nat
and the Bayless clan would take care of her. Maybe one
day he could send for her.

'Don't see why not.' Nat fell silent after that, lost in his
own thoughts, and Moses, for once silent, the laughter
absent from his face, sat hunched between them in the
wavering light of the one fat lump.

Dudie perched on the edge of her bunk in the waggon

doorway. She listened to Tom's voice as he did his best to revive Moses' good humour. There was something about him that was not right at all. Something discordant that came neither from his manner, his voice nor even from what he had to say. Something else about him, some new aura that repelled and yet fascinated her.

She shivered and drew back from the candle glow. The child fluttered lightly within and she stroked it gently with the tips of her fingers.

'I will take them past New Barn around moon-up,' she said to Nat. 'By that time, the drink will have been flowen' all day an' folks will be less interested in what's passen' by.'

Tom stood up, stretched and jumped down from the waggon to relieve himself. He went across the yard to the barn wall and leant one hand against it as he unbuttoned his breeches. From inside the barn a horse suddenly neighed close to him and he started. The sound had been so unexpected and so loud that he spun round and saw the others staring across the lamplit yard with still, shocked faces.

Before he had time to open his mouth it came again: the shrill squeal of aroused stallion, and now they could hear the thump and crash of flying hooves against the barn walls.

'You've no other horse in there, have you?' he called across the yard.

Nat came over to him, his face gaunt in the dim light. 'There was nothen' in there afor nightfall save our piles of firewood, bor.' His eyes darted round the yard, searching for explanation.

It came again, and with it the all too familiar odour that had driven them from the house. The quiet night was suddenly ablaze with red light — and then, unbelievably, a gout of fire shot upward in a shower of golden sparks as the roof exploded into flame.

Tom backed away from the wall, his need forgotten. Even as he reached the waggon, old Pally, smelling the pungence of burning wood, whickered anxiously from the

403

paddock. There seemed to be more than one shrieking horse in the barn, for the sound of rage and fear gradually grew until it drowned the crackle of flames and the crash of collapsing roof timbers.

'Nat, come with me,' he shouted. 'Someone must have put a horse there. There may be a chance of getting it out.'

He ran across to the gaping glow of the open barn doors. Nat stayed where he was, rooted to the spot. There was something about the frenzy in that terrible shrilling which brought the hairs up on the back of his neck.

'There ent no 'orse in there, leastwise no liven' horse,' he said. He felt Dudie press close to him and put his arm round her shoulders.

Moses pushed past him and followed Tom towards the shimmering barn door. 'Hail Mary, Holy Mary . . . Hail Mary, Holy Mary. . . . ' He muttered the comforting formula under his breath, watching the black silhouette of Tom against the furnace of flames. It seemed to weave and fracture in the increasing heat.

Tom came to a standstill, warding off the singeing heat with a raised arm. 'It's no good,' he shouted as Moses joined him. 'Nothing could live in that inferno. It's all rotten wood in there.'

'Then why is that horse still screamin'?' Moses had to bellow into his ear against the roar of the flames and the continuing crash and screams of the burning creature.

Tom took a step forward uncertainly and then cowered back. Out of the white-hot curtain of heat a horse appeared.

It stood in the centre of the collapsing entrance, magnified in the billowing heat into huge proportions. It seemed to tower above them, jet black and enraged, its glistening body magnificent, terrible. It stared at them, lapped in flame; the pure malevolence in its rolling eyes made Moses grip Tom hard by the wrist. In the same instant the creature reared up on its haunches, the silver hooves thrusting menacingly at them.

'Run. . . . Run. . . . It'll trample us down.' Tom

jerked out of Moses' grip and turned towards the creature. The forehooves swerved towards Moses and he cried out, covering his head with an arm and sinking to his knees.

Too late to run. Tom felt the heat of the animal scorching his cheeks and scooped up the unfurling flower inside his chest. He stood against Moses' crouching shoulders and felt the sweet sensuality of the Power build up and then burst from him.

There was an explosion as though the whole of a powder arsenal had blown up before them. The great black stallion was enveloped in blue searing light. Tom closed his eyes against it and scooped Moses up, half dragging him across the yard and past the waggon.

'Run,' he shouted at the others crouching against the waggon's offside. Moses found his feet and stumbled away into the darkness ahead of Tom. Nat and Dudie panted close beside him.

They ran out of the yard and into the paddock, where Pally snorted and shambled up and down the hedge in alarm, shaking her old head from side to side. They ran the length of the north paddock, unable to find a way into Hempsteddle beyond, and finally flung themselves down, huddled together against the dense thorn hedge, Shocked and speechless, they waited for the sound of drumming hooves and that terrible squealing rage.

Silence.

Tom lifted his head and turned to where Moses was pressed into the hedge, praying under his breath. Nat and Dudie crouched against him, covering their faces.

'I can't hear anything.' He found he was whispering.

Dudie's hand crept into his and he squeezed it tightly.

'I can see no glow from the barn, either,' he said. 'Look — no light at all, no sound . . . but there must be. The barn was about to collapse a moment ago, and the roar of the flames was deafening.'

They stared blindly into total darkness. Not a sound penetrated the velvet night. No orange glare blazed beyond the paddock wall. The odour was gone and nothing stirred any of their senses other than the peace of total darkness in a grassy paddock in the middle of a summer night. A long way away Saint Mary's clock struck a single chime. The sound brought them back to reality.

'That wasn't real, was it?' Dudie's voice was low and clear in the silence.

Moses said nothing. He was still busily calling upon the clemency of the Almighty.

Nat gripped her shoulder. ''Twas nothen' from this world, I swear . . . that place be full of mullos. I'm not goen' back.'

Tom found that his breath was returning to normal. In the suddenness of shock and fear the alien thing in him had found pleasure. Now he gritted his teeth together, burying it deep inside as far down as he could.

'It seems to have gone, whatever it was,' he said.

'It must've been there,' Moses said in the darkness. 'I've burned my hand real bad.'

They stayed huddled together in the hedge for a long time, drowsing and waking fearfully, but the night remained quiet and nothing disturbed them. Before dawn, they crept back towards the yard, half expecting the terrible creature to be there still, waiting to trample them with its vicious silver hooves.

The yard was dark but for the faint glimmer of the dying lantern on the waggon, which stood as they had left it. There was no sign of fire, no sharp scent of burning wood in the air. The whole place seemed as peaceful and undisturbed as the first time they saw it.

The only sign that something had actually happened was the state of Moses' right hand and wrist. In the wavery lamp-light it looked as though the flesh had actually boiled before it burst. Dudie drew in her breath sharply at the blackened and glistening claw he held out to her. She hunted amongst her salves and liniments for something to reduce the pain, and found that her own hands were shaking so badly that she was scarcely able to take the tops off some of the jars.

They brought Pally in from the paddock, backed her into her traces between the waggon shafts and moved the waggon out of the yard and into the drive.

Dudie rekindled the lamp and handed round a flask of geneva. Moses was, by this time, in such pain that he was scarcely able to sit still. She made him drink a double tot of the fiery liquor mixed with a sleeping draught. They all drank, feeling the sharp strength of the liquor bring strength back to their tired bodies.

Nat brought the Smokey's cage up from its hook beneath the waggon. The bird seemed untroubled and blinked hopefully at him, looking for grain.

'I've to cut 'im out afore we move,' he said to Tom.

'Well, there's no point in changing our arrangements for today unless we are disturbed further. You go off with your bird and we'll follow after dark. If this place erupts again, we'll have to go before, but it would be too much of a risk for us to move along that lane against the tide of incoming cockers unless we are forced to.'

Nat shrugged and began sharpening his knife to prepare the bird for the pit. He settled down with the Smokey and gave his full attention to cutting the bird out.

Contestants were shown in the pit soon after sun-up as there were many preliminaries to be gone through before the mains and byes actually commenced.

He put the bird carefully into its cloth bag, drew the leather thong tight and stood up.

'I'm off then,' he said quietly. 'Dawn's breaken'.'

To the east, night had at last been stormed by a new day and pale streaks were just beginning to split open the black abyss.

'Nat.'

He turned, hesitating, impatient to be gone.

Tom limped across and held out his hand. 'Thank you for your help in all this. It is much appreciated, you know. Even though you'd rather we'd never been born.' Nat flashed him a look that was half amused, half irritated. 'You're all right, you an' Moses. Another time I'd have ben

407

glad to know ye, bor — but we'll not sleep sound, Dudie an' I, till you're gone.'

He turned away, the stark cut of his bony face set hard, and strode up the drive, the bundled Smokey held tenderly under one arm.

'Kushti bok, pral,' Dudie called after him. 'But leave a little luck here for us too,' she added under her breath.

A bee wandered lazily past her nose, in the direction of the orchard. It was going to be a hot day once the sun was risen.

'Jesus and all the angels,' Moses hissed behind them. He was sitting holding his injured hand by the wrist. His teeth had begun to chatter in his head like castanets.

The hand was unblemished, the skin firm and whole.

Dudie took it in hers and turned it over and Moses screamed.

'The pain is still there. . . . It feels as though the fire is still eating it away.'

Tears of pure agony spilled down his cheeks and she put her arm round his shoulder and cradled his head until he had mastered himself.

'The nerves are still shocked,' she said to him. 'It happened, whatever your hand looks like now. The barn is whole too. I shall treat the hand as though it be burned, bor, and the healen' qualities of the herbal juices will soothe those shattered nerves.'

The house seemed to shimmer lazily among the green upsurge of its overgrown gardens. The untouched roof of the great barn was just visible behind the distant outline of the stone archway.

Tom leaned against the back of the waggon. Nat was gone. Now there only remained Moses, nursing his hand. Already he seemed more comfortable, content to drowse in the waggon.

The urge to touch her was overpowering. So was the other sensation which now accompanied all his thoughts of Dudie Smith. He glowered at the distant house with its graceful archway, the brickwork already soft with rosy beauty from the first rays of the early sun.

'Midhurst,' he said quietly, and it was as though the name of that distant home could cleanse all the decay which surrounded them at Lavenham. 'O God, deliver us safely back to Midhurst.'

There was already quite a crowd of cockers and trainers assembling in the yard at New Barn by the time Nat strode past the gate, through the clutter of traps and horses and men sitting in the grass, waiting for the first contest to begin.

He nodded as someone hailed him through the throng but pushed on towards the weighing table, where he could see the weigher and his brass scales already busy at one end of the open-sided barn. Will Slaughter's leather tricorn moved a good head above his companions, turning this way and that as he watched the weighing-in and argued the betting odds with his customers. He raised his head and saw Nat. A curious expression flicked across his broad face and was quickly replaced by a nod of greeting. Nat frowned, seeing the man's eyes slide over the heads of the crowd to the other end of the barn. There were too many folk milling about for him to see who it was that Will had marked so swiftly.

He stood in line, waiting for the weigh-in with the bagged Smokey in the crook of his arm, warding off elbows and pushing bodies around him. He grunted at the greetings of his companions, in no mood for pleasantries at this stage. First he'd get the weigh-in over and then think about wetting his gullet before settling down to the serious business of matching pairs. Smokey rustled patiently in his bag, sensing the air of expectation and the presence of his adversaries all around him.

Then they were beside the weighing table and the fine set of highly polished brass scales.

The clerk looked up at him, quill poised above his registration sheet.

'Nat Smith . . . single Dorset Smokey,' Nat said, opening the bag and scooping the bird out. He placed Smokey into the scale dish, where the beautiful bird stood swaying, blinking the red rims of its sharp round eyes, disorientated by the sudden light.

'Dorset Smokey . . . Birchen Pile, yellow-breasted, clear cut with high comb, orange legs and twos in head. Grey centre nails, one eye grey walled . . . weight three pounds, nine ounces. Owner Nat Smith.'

There was a moment when the bird stood with spine fully stretched, balancing in its golden dish with consummate majesty, hooked beak raised, the long snowy neck twisted towards Nat, the black feathers on breast and clipped tail glowing with a bright emerald sheen. There was a murmur of approval about the weighing table. Then Nat scooped his bird up and made way for the man behind him. He returned Smokey to his bag and made for the back of the Slaughters' cottage, where three barrels were already being spiked by those with the first thirst of the day.

'Ah, Smith . . . we've been wondering whether you would grace the gathering. Word had it that you had already left the district.'

Nat turned slowly and touched his forehead with a grim forefinger. 'No sir, not me. Dudie, she took to the road yesterday, off to the family over New Forest way. I'll follow after Smokey 'n me've wiped the pit clean here.'

Charles Bayless smiled charmingly. There was no sign of the animosity which had coloured their last meeting.

'I've heard of the fine bird you have been rearing. A Magpie hatch too, they say,' he said lightly, eyeing the sack under Nat's arm with interest. 'I trust that my own Duckwing and Spangles will be spared to give him a fair contest.'

Nat stared after the tall, retreating figure, resplendent in grey doeskin jacket and the new stovepipe trousers.

There had been something about the look on his face that reminded him of a large grey cat making ready to pounce on its prey.

Something had been building up in Tom since before the sun reached its zenith. His head ached and the very sound of Dudie's and Moses' voices chatting as they prepared the waggon for its journey grated like sand on a raw nerve. He felt utterly listless, unable even to offer Dudie and Moses his help in battening down everything in the waggon so that they might travel with all speed.

He had the most compulsive urge to return to the house. Once there, he would never leave it again. He knew that with a cold certainty.

The Power was restless, strong in its new-found resting place within him. It drowsed, pulsing gently, only to be roused by the slightest surge of interest that he might register in anything.

He curled up and pretended to sleep.

The cowslip tea was still making Moses drowsy and he grunted, already halfway to another doze. Dudie let him sleep. There was nothing for them to do all through this day except to conserve their energies for the wild dash they must make as soon as the dusk was deep enough. Nothing but to keep their distance from the house. She climbed into the waggon and paused for a moment beside Tom. In the light of day he looked ill; the strain showed in the heavy purple smudges under his closed eyes.

Even as she stood looking down at him he stirred and turned on his back. His eyes opened. They looked at each other and she turned away, feeling the blood suffusing her cheeks.

There had been something there in his face which was quite terrifying, like looking at her own reflection in a mirror and seeing the evil face of a stranger.

The first main was started an hour after Nat's Smokey had been matched. The battle was brief as one of the cocks would not set to. After that, each contest went smoothly enough and Nat was called before the sun had climbed to the midday peak. He knew his opponent, Renard Fulke, his birds having been matched against him the previous year. On that occasion Fulke had been on a fine winning streak with a pair of silver black-breasted fowl, but one had been maimed at the end of the season and the other had lost an eye and was now a breeder only. The young Black-Red which stood against Smokey was a good-looking bird and not lacking in fighting spirit — but it was no match for the Magpie-hatched Smokey. Within ten minutes that vicious, lightning beak had ripped the jugular vein open. The Black-Red bled to death before they had removed him from the pit.

Smokey had been in the pit twice more before the sun began its downward slide towards the trees. The barrels of ale were replaced again and again, and men began to sweat and sing and mop their scarlet faces. The atmosphere, coloured by the heights of financial gains and losses on every side, pulsed with the beginnings of ale-flavoured excitement. A couple of boys started a fight out in the paddock, encouraged lustily by their companions. The crush round the pit increased.

'Mr Bayless's Grey Spangle versus Patrick Duffy's Hoxton Dun. . . . ' The Dun attacked with a vertical display of spurs and the Spangle retreated, unbalanced in the first lunge. It picked up within moments and turned in towards its opponent's right eye. They sparred and gouged at each other for twenty-eight minutes before the Dun refused on a count of forty.

Charles leaned on the pit rail and watched his feeder gather up the victorious but still furious bird. He had not been so fortunate with his Spangle which had had a leg all but severed in the previous battle.

He strolled across to his feeder.

'Good fight that, I thought, eh Walsh?' he said laying a hand lightly on the fowl's back. The man grinned at him as the head came round and the murderous beak slashed out, all recognition submerged in the great red urge to kill.

'Plenty of spirit still pumpen' through 'im, sor. Enough for another half-dozen contests. The Blackie's had enough fer today. He's young an' still needs ter feel the mat a bit more afore we set 'im at me Lord Derby's Cockalorum. Eff it pleases you, sor, would ye take a count of his contestants? I think there's two of 'em already cut out. . . . '

Charles returned to his home for luncheon. He had been invited to picnic with the Lennox party, but Leonie's condition made it necessary for him to display some show of concern. He was disappointed that young John, instead of accompanying him to the main as he usually did, preferred this day to stay at home, close to his mother's side. It was very much to be hoped that he was not, after all, going to favour his elder brother's behaviour and hang about her bedside weeping and snivelling like a limp maiden.

He looked into the sickroom and bent over the bed in the dim light of almost closed curtains. His wife lay dozing, the contours of her face sunk back against the bones of her skull. But for the flutter of breath from her half-open mouth, she might have already been dead.

He turned away, fighting repugnance at the sight of her. She had once had such liveliness, such droll sophistication. By the look of her even in the shadowed half-light, she should have been coffined a month before.

He looked into the office on East Street, agreed the sale of a parcel of land over towards Charlton, signed a sheaf of documents that awaited his attention and interviewed a prospective bailiff. By the time he returned to the New Barn main the light was going and the sound of its progress could be heard all the way from the Wittering high road.

Six birds were emerging as fit contenders for the Goodwood Gamebird Trophy, a fine silver urn which the Earl of March graciously presented to the winner of Chichester's three best-attended mains each season. It looked very much as if New Barn, though early in the fighting year, would be among the finalists.

One of Charles's cocks had been badly torn by Walter Chinneok's fowl. Two had had enough and been withdrawn. The Duck-wing had won four contests without

413

injury. He looked fresh and aggressive and was matched with a Shropshire Furnace from the Goodwood coop.

'Reckon as the Furnace, Nat Smith's Smokey an' Chinneok's Lavant Mealy be the only cocks 'ere now can measure up to 'em, sor,' the feeder said. His eyes were bright and he sweated heartily. Charles watched him closely. No feeder worth his salt touched more than a couple of tankards while his birds were in contest. The infinite care of his charges was the price of his job.

The same rule did not apply to the owners. Charles sent the man across to the ale booth with his tankard and meanwhile slipped a silver-stoppered flask from his pocket and drank from it thoughtfully. He had been drinking a mixture of ales, wines and spirits since sun-up and was floating pleasantly in a state of gentle intoxication. It was a pleasant state in which to be, he thought; if only he could remain at the same level. The other reasons for being present at the main slid through his mind, quickening his pulse, bringing a sudden dampness to his waxen forehead, and he bent quickly over the yellow silk bag in which his Duckwing, still triumphant, crouched, awaiting the next engagement. He laid a hand lightly but firmly along the bird's back and the creature, recognizing its master's touch, forbore to aim a vicious stab of its beak.

A cheer went up from the pit and general movement in the direction of the ale booth meant that another battle was over.

Charles's feeder pushed through the steam of sweating men.

'That's another down,' he wheezed with satisfaction. 'Chinneok's Mealy just refused after almost trouncen' the Furnace. Can't understand it. 'E was the better mover for near on twenty minutes, parryen' mighty canny, sor. Even drew blood close to t'other's crop an' caught em a nasty gash in the shoulder. Then suddenly 'e 'ad enough. Backed off an' just defended up close to the pit edge till pit master set the Count on en. . . . ' He saw Charles's eyes wander across the busy yard to where a small group clustered round a rangy figure.

'Nat Smith's Smokey be next in, matched to the Good-wood Furnace. That'll mean one'll rid us of the other an' then we'll take the winner.'

The human tide turned again and swept across the yard toward the pit.

Charles watched Nat, his bagged cock in the crook of his arm, approach the match master and judges. He gave his tankard to one of his young cockers and motioned him to get it filled up, then moved away from the jostling crowd into the shadow of the cottage garden.

Charles blinked his eyes to clear the slight bleariness from them. He must desist from any more liquor until after his Duckwing's battle with Smith's Smokey.

He strolled through the garden and leaned against the waist-high wall which bordered the lane. Further along the track, just beyond his vision in the deepening dusk, the outline of a waggon blocked the way, its driver arguing with a youth who had, until a few minutes before, been fast asleep in his cart pulled into the hedgerow. The waggon was large and covered.

He was about to move closer when the pit roar erupted into applause and there was a sudden outward rush for the ale booth, the hedge, and the settlement of heavily laid bets.

It was over.

The suspicious waggon suddenly forgotten, Charles pushed through the sea of overheated, odorous bodies towards his cockers. The question in the pale raised eyebrows was answered in two directions at once and his pulse began to hammer with a new excitement.

Across the pit, seen now through the thinning crowd, Nat Smith stared over the bobbing heads at him, a thin, hard smile on his lips which had little warmth in it. Whatever bile was in his soul, he had still taken the bait and Dudie would not be far behind.

'The Smokey 'ad en.' His trainer's voice was hoarse from shouting at his side. 'That Magpie Cuckoo of a

415

Smokey, 'E's blessed of a charmed life, sor. Thought the Furnace had is eye out one time, for I swear 'e took a slash right through the pupil — but there 'e is still . . . hardly spent, by the looks of 'em. We'll be lucky if'n our fowl comes out clean. We've speed on our side, I'd say, sor. Speed and 'e's a fresher bird, two of our contests be'en' byes, like.'

Charles hardly heard the man's excited stream. The waggon out in the lane was very similar to the Smiths'. Nat had said that Dudie left Apuldram the previous day, bound for the Hampshire Forests. All the same, that waggon had familiar contours.

He put a hand on the man's shoulder. 'Hold a moment, Cutts . . . I've to see someone urgently. I'll be back before long.'

'But we're third in line now, sor.' The man's voice floated back to him anxiously.

'I'll be back long before that.'

'Well, sor,' a voice said beside him. 'Your bird ready for Smokey, is he?'

There was no light, no laughter in Nat Smith's face, in spite of the casual banter of his words. The granite face, with its high cheek-bones and oily black hair dragged back behind the ears, was highlighted by the poled lantern in his hand. It gave him a look of menace that drove a knife into the pit of Charles's stomach.

He smiled coldly into the man's face. 'He's been waiting overlong, Smith,' he said lightly. 'Still, for the pleasure of such a conquest, he would have been happy to wait even longer.'

His eyes slid round Nat's head. 'Is Dudie with you this evening?' He spoke without emphasis, making conversation.

Nat shook his head. 'She don't come to cockfights. Not got the stomach fer it, like most women. She's off ter our sister's up in the Forest, where I'll be goen' after this.'

Charles shrugged and turned away with a faint inclination of the head. 'Give her my compliments, if you please,'

416

he said over his shoulder. 'If my bird wins, maybe she would accept it as a token of my respect?'

11

Tom sat on the single front step, watching the changes of light over the overgrown garden. He had allowed himself to be drawn back by the sheer beauty of the place at this time of day, just to say goodbye.

The sun set into the oaks across the river. It cast a soft pink light, hazy as the skin on a peach, through the fretwork of branches, gilding everything it touched in delicate richness. The scene from the terrace, caught in that special silence between late day and early dusk, was the essence of peace.

Man had been coming and going through this place, he thought, treading the soil since creation — worshipping here as he was doing now, bowing before the Greater Elements, the Old Ones. . . .

By the time the moon rose, he too — with Dudie and Moses and Nat — would have come and then gone, their lives altered irrevocably by the hidden violence trapped within the old house. And Lavenham? It would simply retreat once more behind its creepers and cobwebs, to decay quietly, waiting with infinite patience for the next intruder to disturb its slumber.

Regret flowed over him, an odd grief which was deeper than anything he had yet experienced. To leave Lavenham now, when he was on the brink of newness with the Killing Power as his banner . . . to leave this ancient place of homage when he could be its defender, the source of its growth and strength . . . how could he contemplate such a move? How could he permit others to make such a decision for him? The folded flower stirred within his veins and he felt the charged blood pumping languidly through his body.

The Watcher stood close to the young man, taking in the hunched shoulders, the mop of unruly hair — and felt the house pressing in on the poor wretch's resistance. He must be removed, he thought in anguish. He was prime material for disaster in which the Place would revel as it drew its strength. He dug his nails into his balled fists, trying — through the very agony from his blistered palms — to reach out to the man. Tears of frustration blurred his eyes — frustration and the sheer agony he was inflicting on the suppurating burns with his finger nails.

'Hear me, Tom Heritage . . . go now . . . go. . . . '

The sun slid away in a momentary flash of yellow and green as the shining rim glowed and was extinguished. Daylight went in the same instant, as though someone had snuffed out a vast candalabrum. The evening greyed over, lustreless and humid — a rumble of thunder, far below the horizon, growled in its sleep.

Tom looked over his shoulder, feeling the eyes that were on him. He saw the figure, and the shock was muted for it seemed that he had seen it before — many times. He studied the face, shifting round in the doorway to do so. It was male, the features familiar because they were Bayless features. The regal high-bridged nose, the finely cut bone structure, the cleft in the strong chin. Grey eyes — filled, he saw, with terrible pain. The mouth moved, the lips formed words, but there was no sound. His arm came up then, waving Tom away with agonized contortions.

'I know,' Tom said to the Being, 'I should not have come here at all and now I should not have returned, even for a moment — '

He stood up, and then noticed the open palm of the man's raised hand. It glistened whitely, raw, like un-cooked meat, and in places the fine carpal bones showed through. He shuddered, tearing his eyes away as he heard Dudie call in the distance.

'Tom?' She sounded anxious. 'Are you there? Where have you got to?'

The house seemed to hold its breath, to draw him inwards, to suck out of him the love he felt at the sound of that tender voice. It was suddenly imperative that no one should go inside its gaping door.

'It's all right. I'm on the terrace,' he shouted. 'I'm just seeing that everything is secure.'

The figure had disappeared.

Tom stood in the open doorway, feeling the danger, smelling the sharp odour of stable which filled the air with sudden menace − and he recognized it now. It was that same throat-catching stench which had accompanied the appearance of the stallion in the barn. It was as though the Place, having failed to eliminate the strangers, had decided to discard its gentle mood at last and reveal the canker at its roots.

He took the key from the inside of the door, grasped the iron handle and, holding it with both hands, pulled it sharply towards him. It gave grudgingly, the rusting hinges groaned and the great oak door closed with a hollow slam which reverberated through the building. He limped away, down the terrace steps, and went through the tall grasses that choked the carriage sweep, towards the archway. It came to him as he passed under the crumbling stone canopy that, but for the appearance of that likeness of himself, he might not have found it possible to tear himself away from the bittersweet, yearning need to remain.

'Thank you,' he said silently to the figure who was no longer there. Maybe, after all, it had simply been his own conscience, he thought.

Lightning played behind the hazy horizon. Thunder muttered a long way off. The air was so heavy, so filled with rank odours that the sweat streamed from him.

The abiding Power was a leaden lump in his chest. He breathed deeply to control it; in through his nose and out very slowly through his mouth as he hurried along the drive towards the welcome sight of the waggon.

Moses was still drowsy from his medicine and nursed his hand, casting occasional glances back down the drive.

'I feel a mighty bad feelin' about that place,' he said. 'We ain't finished with it yet, I swear,'

'It's because we are goen',' Dudie said. 'Tom is comen' with us — the house is losing its friend.'

Tom said nothing — she understood it all so well.

The stench curled over them, ever stronger as the day wore on.

'Let's be gone from here, for God's sake,' Moses pleaded for the umpteenth time. His black face had a grey tinge to it which made an old man of him suddenly.

They moved off, as agreed, once darkness had fallen. Moses stayed in the waggon, draped from head to foot in a length of ancient floral curtain, still in too much pain to make fun of his appearance. Dudie perched herself beside Tom on the top step, a brightly patterned shawl about her shoulders. Tom took the reins and gave the old horse a quick flick of the leathers on her haunches. As she went forward, casting from side to side, he caught the frightened roll of her eyes. She too wished only to be gone from this place. Crouching beside Dudie, he urged Pally up the weed-choked drive, leaning out into the bobbing lantern light to check that the wheels did not founder in some unseen pitfall. Behind them was utter silence. The moon had not yet risen but the young night was opalescent with purple afterlight, and even as they rounded the curve that would hide the house from them, it emerged — a yellow lozenge, sliding out from behind the unseen mass of Salterns Woods.

'Yellow moon, grauni moon. Count your money, riches soon,' Dudie murmured almost to herself. It seemed important to talk then, to ease the unspoken fear from between them. 'Rich man's moon, that low yellow one. The way we see it, Nat'll be having a good main over there.'

Tom grunted, turning his head from side to side as he scoured the darkness with his stranger's eyes.

'So'll all the other punters then, for they're seeing the same moon, aren't they?'

'There has to be faith, bor. There is no meanen' if there

ent faith first.'

He looked round at her then. Her voice had been light enough but the warning in her words was clear, all the same. He had been off-hand with her since his illness, speaking only when it was necessary, keeping the terrible heat in his eyes turned away from her so that she should not see what dwelt behind them. Now he looked at her directly – and let her see it there in the depths of his eyes, lit silver by the moon's soft radiance: the unfurling flower of Jess Bayless's Killing Glance. It glowed in the dim blur of his face, so close to her own that she felt the caress of his breath, at once compelling, magnetic. He turned away directly, as though he was frightened of his own potential – peering out between the horse's ears as the Lavenham gates brought them to a halt.

Dudie slipped down to wrestle them open. They were rusted, choked with great ropes of climbing brambles and Moses, hitching his curtain over his shoulder, joined her. The air was rank with the midden stench. He grasped one of the wrought-iron gates with his good hand and, giving it a mighty wrench, spat disgustedly into the grass.

'Smells like somethin' died here too. Gets right in the back of ma throat, 'nough to give a man the vomits.'

The gate moved and he swung on it with another great heave. 'Say, how did Nat move this danged thing to get the waggon in?'

Dudie stood back, panting. 'I swear it was no trouble. I opened it myself, not Nat. I pushed it and it swung back as easily as anythen'.'

The stench increased, its thick odour of rotting ordure making them gag.

'Get back in the waggon, quick,' Tom ordered them suddenly.

There was a harsh urgency in his voice that made Dudie obey him at once. Moses hesitated, peering anxiously past the waggon in the direction of the invisible house. 'Ah'll give it another heave,' he said, turning back to the gates.

They were glowing. He stared at the massive wrought-ironwork. Moments ago they had been dirty rusted things, inanimate metal which flaked under his grip. Now, suddenly, they were alive with orange heat, the beauty of their intricate design lit from within.

'Get up on the tailboard — do as I say, damn you.' Tom's voice cut through his shock and he backed away towards the now lunging Pally, crossing himself and searching with trembling fingers for his little scrimshaw cross. He was on the running board in one leap and inside the waggon a second later, holding on for dear life as Tom struggled to control the terrified swerving of the flame-dazzled horse.

'Look away. Don't watch me, for your own sake . . . look away!' His voice cut through the roar of the furnace-hot gates and they suddenly exploded. The waggon was in the middle of heat, sparks . . . a tumult of rippling shock-waves, and Tom was flaying the hindquarters of the old mare with all his strength. They rumbled, jerking and swaying into the furnace, through it, beyond it. The impetus of the terrified horse's headlong flight took them bowling up the cart track, bouncing drunkenly over ruts and boulders.

The night became still behind them, the blinding ache in their eyes all that remained of that nightmare moment.

'Oh Lawdy Lord,' Moses breathed at last,' we was surely in the presence of ol' Lucifer himself back there. . . . '

Tom said nothing but grimly flicked Pally's rump with his whip. She plunged on down the path, needing little encouragement. Rounding a slight bend, Tom hauled in the rains with an angry mutter. Newbarn lay before them, lit by a host of lanterns, both inside the cottage and out in the yard and lane. Carts, ponies and carriages lined both sides of the track so that there was little room for the waggon to squeeze by. Judging by the roar that went up from a host of throats, they had arrived just as a great victory was being witnessed. Moses withdrew hastily into the back of the waggon and pulled the folds of his curtain about his head and face.

'Give me the reins,' Dudie said quietly. Tom shifted in his seat, handed them over without another word and jumped down to lead the old mare through the mass of carts, jutting shafts and prostrate punters. A few feet past the cottage gate a cart protruded, its tailboard and rear wheels thrust into the hedge at such a sharp angle that the shaft and left front wheel completely blocked the lane. Lying comfortably under the duckboards was a sleeping youth.

Tom leant into the waggon and shook the boy. 'Come on, lad. Wake yourself and shift this cart of yours. You're blocking the lane for the rest of us.'

A sudden hush had fallen. Another main was about to begin. The boy slept on, the ale fumes in his head wrapping him in a deep, dreamless peace. Tom picked up a staff that lay close to the youth and brought it down sharply about his legs.

'Jump to it, you scurvy lout . . . get out of there and move this damned cart of yours or you'll feel the weight of this stick about your head.'

The boy stirred, groaning. He opened a bleary eye and did his best to focus. Something smote him hard in the ribs, drivin the breath out of him and he sat up and folded over with a gasp. Tom stood over him, seething with impatience. Control . . . control, ordered half of his brain as the evil flower unfurled, Don't hurt him − don't hurt the innocent.

'Do hurry, Tom. You never know who might recognize the waggon.' Behind him Dudie's voice was tight with anxiety. He began to lift one of the shafts of the obstructing waggon as the boy staggered to his feet and came forward to help. Then Moses was with them, his curtain tucked tightly over his shoulders. He held his injured hand against his chest and grasped one of the cart's shafts with the other and they began to ease the cart further into the hedge. Something blocked it and they discovered a boulder, larger than a squatting man, embedded in the bank.

Unless they moved at least another five vehicles, there was no way of squeezing through the gap. Tom, frustrated beyond words now, began to wonder whether this was not still the Lavenham influence doing its utmost to hold on to him. He could feel nothing from the place now, those whiplash inner scourgings had dropped away in the instant that they passed through the gates.

They set to once more, doggedly pushing one waggon into another, shifting a cart, backing a drowsing horse against the cottage hedge. The air was suddenly in tumult as a great roar went up from the crowd in the yard.

'What would I not give to take a look at that l'il ole main in there,' Moses mourned, gasping over a light cart as he manhandled it into the verge.

Dudie took Pally's bridle and drew her a few more feet along the lane.

'I think you'll be able to scrape past this in a moment,' Tom gasped, feeling the wheel hubs of their waggon score a deep furrow along the side of a well-polished pony trap that was roped through both wheels round the bole of a tree.

By the time Nat Smith's Smokey and the Duckwing faced each other across the mat, the crowd had thinned and then swelled again, filling up with the patronage of three nearby taverns. A few of the spectators, needing to stretch their legs and their pockets, had wandered off from Newbarn during the day, fetching up at the nearest pot-house, where they could relate in splendid detail the progress of events.

Nat's Smokey had already put a lot of money into local pockets. News that he was contesting such respected cockers as the Earl of March and Mr Charles Bayless brought in a fresh wave of spectators as night fell. By the time the two birds came together, the main had been going for nearly twelve hours.

The noise of the crowd sank to a murmur as the referee held up his hand.

'Contest between Mr Charles Bayless' Birchen Duck-wing, won seven rounds, lost one — and Nat Smith's Shropshire Smokey, unbeaten in six contests this day. Place yer bets, gents . . . if you please. Present yer birds, pitters.'

Charles's man stepped into the pit and placed the Duckwing in the centre of the mat, where the bird strutted before the crowd, rising to beat the air with its fine-clipped wings, majestic, aware of his impact. The small club head, comb raised, topped long white periwig neck-feathers gilded with a delicate emerald sheen. The bright yellow legs were encased in chased silver spurs. He turned his head arrogantly from side to side. After a minute, the trainer scooped him up and hooded him. Nat swung over the pit wall and placed Smokey on the mat in his turn.

The bird stood rock-still, staring ahead of him, and then began searching the pit with eager jerks of his long neck. He, too, sported long white neck-feathers, but his were tipped with black and glossed down over soft grey breast and wing-feathers. The clipped tail-plume would have shown a cascade of grey and marbled red feathers had they not been sheered as close as possible to the cuticle so that they stood up like a striped black and grey brush. His spurs were not of silver but of finely traced steel, so highly polished that they shone nearly as brightly as his elegant opponent's. His beady eyes missed nothing. Yellow lids framed the glassy-red glare as he raised his beak, getting wind of his adversary. The rumble of the crowd died away, for it seemed then that he would crow — and face disqualification — but he simply extended his supple neck, turning this way and that, pointing, searching.

Nat pursed his lips. He knew his bird. Smokey always took note of the air vacated by his adversary. He seemed, by this method, to be able to get the gist of him.

'Close all betten', if you please, sirs,' roared the referee over the crowd. 'No more bets now. Cockers and pitters on to the mat. Let's get on with it, gents. We ent got all night. . . . '

The two pitters placed their birds on the mat, beaks inches apart — and whipped off their hoods. The creatures immediately struck out at each other, the first feints more of a threat than any real wish to make contact at this point. Still held by their trainers, they worked themselves into a screeching rage until the Duckwing suddenly made a direct lunge and scored the side of the Smokey's head, close to one baleful red-rimmed eye. The pitters released their birds and fell back against the side of the pit, eyes glued to their protégés.

Nat heard nothing of the yells of encouragement all round him. He knew that the pit was jammed with spectators, but Smokey and the Duckwing were all that existed for him now. It was not for the money, this particular main, although he had staked ten guineas on his bird — which was near twelve months' wages — and a win would see Dudie and himself through many a lean winter. It was not even the bitter longing to take Charles Bayless off his lofty pedestal. It was simply that Smokey really was an exceptional fowl and deserved to win any prize that came his way. He crouched low, eyes glued to the thrusting birds.

With lightning suddenness they rose up, necks entwined like angry lovers, beating the air with ferocious wings — the strange, primaeval screech of their rage cutting through the encouraging yells of the spectators.

'Cut 'im out, Bayless. Go fer 'is eye then. . . . '

The Duckwing was suddenly astride the Smokey's back, gripping with iron talons, the wicked spurs slicing across the bird's right wing. Feathers filled the ring, soft white underdown, a few marbled primaries. Smokey twisted as Nat held his breath. He paused, as though to give the Duckwing a feeling of premature triumph then, snakelike, he flicked round, unseating his preening opponent. Before the startled Duckwing had time to re-establish his hold, the Smokey's vicious beak had ripped into the soft underside of its neck. They backed off and began to circle, taking little stiff-necked runs at each other, reserving their strength for the right moment. They ignored the crowd, which was getting excited. Smokey began to slow down in his movements, visibly tiring at last. He let the Duckwing bowl him over in the next feint, and for a moment the beautiful black-breasted creature stood over him for the second time, neck arched to strike. A smear of blood marred the sleek white throat-feathers. Smokey lay panting under his claw, the once shining back feathers ruffled by the vicious talons.

The air became hushed as the crowd held their breaths. The Duckwing stretched itself, ready to deliver the death blow. Charles and Nat both leaned forward imperceptibly.

There was a sudden knifelike flurry of movement in the pit. As the Duckwing struck downward with beak and spur, Smokey suddenly came to life and with a smooth movement which was almost too swift to have seen, he rolled out from under the rigid talons and was up and round, delivering a series of sledge-hammer slashes to the other's neck and breast.

There was pandemonium as the two birds, locked together in a flailing ball, jerked round the pit into the air, round again — and then the Duckwing was down. It lay on its side, one wing splayed out beneath it, an eye socket a mass of blood and torn tissue. Smokey fluttered, screeching and stabbing over the fallen bird, then shook himself vigorously to rearrange his feathers and went in for the kill.

As the roar of victory resounded round the pit, Charles pushed through the crowd and strode out of the yard towards the road. Just beyond the gate the waggon was still there — and manhandling a cart out of his way was Tom Heritage.

'Well . . . well,' he said thickly, seeing the vast shape of Moses Abelson sliding, too late, out of sight round the side of the waggon, 'good evening, cousin.'

Tom straightened and turned towards him. There was something the matter with Tom's face and Charles recoiled, as though hit.

Tom's eyes were glowing a deep arterial red. His mouth quirked into a smile. Charles, suddenly mortally afraid, raised his arm, aimed the silver knob of his walking cane at Tom's uncovered head and brought it down with all his strength, going for the temple. Too late, he saw the thing in Tom's eyes flower and explode.

Tom watched the arm rise, the utter fury and frustration in Charles's drunken face — and let the flower unfurl in him, let it well up through his body until he tingled in every extremity and felt it burst from him.

Charles collapsed slowly without making a sound, folding like a puppet at the waist and knees, sliding on to the dew-wet grass.

'Oh, dear God and all his angels,' Moses breathed behind Tom, 'Ma hand . . . the pain has completely gone. . . .'

They lost no time in rolling Charles into the verge and moving on along the lane with controlled urgency. There was no point in drawing attention to themselves by putting Pally into a canter, especially as the main seemed to have ended and the crowds would, any minute, be streaming away from the yard and following them down the lane. It took them five minutes to reach the toll road and half an hour until they were on the Portsmouth highway. Then they went fast, changing their plans as Pally widened the distance between them and Newbarn.

Dudie finally agreed to drop the two men on the outskirts of Emsworth and continue on, through the forest paths, to join her Wickham cousins and await Nat's arrival. Tom and Moses would, under cover of darkness, make for Skillet's yard. For enough gold, Hugh Skillet would do anything — even provide passage in the Channel coaler for two unmanifested passengers.

There was hardly a farewell between them, for the Tom sitting between Moses and Dudie was not the Tom she had loved. This was a harsh facsimile of that strong, gentle soul — this man seemed to smoulder. She put her arms

429

round Moses' waist and hugged him — and picked up Pally's reins as the two men climbed down on to the road.

'Good luck,' she said to Tom, who had said nothing to her, averting his eyes in the way he had done for days now. It still hurt her, and she flicked Pally's rump with the rein end and moved off before he could answer. She had an impression of his face turning at last to her as the waggon bowled away along the empty road.

Tom and Moses, still wearing his curtain, set off towards the dark mass of the harbour village. The place was wrapped in sleep. Not even a dog marked their passing. They found their way down to the coaling jetty through the criss-cross of lanes and alleyways and curled up in the lee of a warehouse to await the first pre-dawn stirrings of activity among the fishing vessels.

'Is your leg playin' up again?' Moses asked, seeing Tom rubbing it gingerly.

'Just a little. That's the longest time I've been on it since we left the *Fortunée*.'

Moses hissed. 'Oh Lord — she cain't be more'n a couple of miles away from here, either. Gives me a nasty feeling between the shoulder blades — as though that little runt, Furze, was waitin' for us jus' the other side of this wall. . . . ' He closed his eyes and his lips moved soundlessly.

'Say one for me,' Tom whispered. 'The company I've been keeping lately hasn't been too savoury, apart from you and Dudie, has it?'

Moses' great hand clamped down on his shoulder like a vice. 'That's the first crack of humour you've shown in days, man . . . feels like weeks. Oh my word, I'm so doggone glad to be away from that place of yours.'

'So am I, Moss,' Tom said quietly — and knew that he meant it with all his being. 'By the love of my family, so am I.'

They drowsed, waking as the overnight fishermen returned with their catch and the jetty slowly came to life. Tom went in search of Hugh Skillett and found him sleepily lighting lamps in his warehouse office, a huge shambling wreck of a man, so emaciated and evil-smelling that it was hard not to recoil from his greeting. At the sight of Tom's purse, heavy with the money that Nat had acquired through the sale of the Lavenham silver, he became alert and competitive. It took half an hour to persuade him to find a berth for the two of them — and then, for the sum of fifty sovereigns, he said they could join the coaling crew of his barge, which was due out on the noon tide.

It was agreed, especially as Moses' face would not be as distinctive once they were covered in coal dust. They parted with the money and went aboard to join the other stokers. By sun-up they were indistinguishable from the others and sweating freely over their shovels. Resting at the end of his shift, Tom leaned against the bulkhead in the dust-choked hold. Moses paused beside him with a huge spadeful of bright fuel.

'My word, man. You sure do make a pretty nigger. Cain't think why the Almighty made such a fool mistake as to paint you white in the first place.'

'Mr Moses!' a voice called from the open hold above them and they looked up guiltily. Who knew their names?

A head silhouetted against the morning sky. A small head, the hair whipped by a fresh breeze. The face peered down at them demurely. 'Do ye think yer brother would mind if I came down there and joined ye? Mr Skillett says I may. There's a snooper from the customs house walken' this way and I'd rather not catch his eye.'

Dudie!

Moses bounded up the ladder in four great strides and lifted her with joyous tenderness — then, mindful of her words, he carried her down into the hold under the curious eyes of the other three stokers, made a little nest of sacks for her to sit on and began to shovel coal furiously, his great body masking her from above. Tom went over and took both her hands in his, squatting at her feet.

She was able to look into his eyes now, for there was

431

nothing in them but the blaze of happiness her appearance had given him. 'I know how it was,' he said to her, 'but it's gone from me now. There was something in me while I was at Lavenham, Dudie. Something that would have hurt you — so I had to fight it, I had to seem to be rejecting you. But it really has gone now, can't you see?'

She nodded. Her eyes filled with tears but she was suddenly utterly happy. 'I know. It wasn't until after I were nearly at Wickham that I realized that there was nothing in your face when we parted at Emsworth, except sadness. I left a message for Nat with the cousins and came right back here as fast as I could because I know that it will be all right for us now, after all.'

They sailed on the noon tide, the old barque rolling even in the calm waters of the harbour. It was good to have decking beneath the feet once more, to balance the body on the soles of the feet and feel the toes doing their job of steadying the weight, Tom thought. He stood against the deck rail, holding Dudie close against him. All three of them watched the hazy green shore slide into the gathering sea mist. When it was quite gone he turned away and tucked his hand into the crook of her arm.

'When all this is behind us,' he said to her and to Moses, 'I shall finish the diaries I tried to keep while we were prisoners. No one will believe what we have gone through, but at least it will all be there as a warning for later generations.'

She nodded, and there was nothing further to add. France was in front of them — and the unknown colony beyond. She smiled at the quiet happiness mirrored in both their faces.

Part Four

1952

BAYLESS HERITAGE

1

The squadron was in sight of The Channel, with Le Havre under their left wing tips, when *Vera* took a flak burst somewhere beside Bay's head. He felt the P.47 buck and then tilt, slicing downwards in a slow curve towards the creamy ribbon of Normandy shore which merged into the grey patchwork of a choppy sea.

'Shit,' he said aloud, and slammed down on the controls with all his strength.

He had been miles away, flying with only one half of his concentration, the rest of him sitting on Granpappy's porch steps, throwing pine cones for the dogs and watching an early fall begin to paint swathes of russet throught the soft New England woods. It was almost possible to smell the first of the bonfires beyond the line of beeches that were Granpappy's pride and joy. But then the sweet, resinous scent of pine needles and windfall fruits and dried leaves had no rank bitterness like the odour which caught suddenly at his throat, jerking him back into the cockpit of his Thunderbolt. A wisp of black smoke trailed through the cockpit, before his face. He realized that the rudder bar was jammed and he had no directional control at all.

Suddenly the flak was heavy. Two more thumps jolted him against the harness, telling their own tale.

'Hey, Bay . . . you OK? Over.' Midge McCasky's voice crackled in his headphones.

'Affirmative,' Bay said, and discovered that his jaw was locked down against clenched teeth and it was quite difficult to speak. He juggled with ailerons and elevators, finding that he had some control of manoeuvre there. He broke the spin, rounded *Vera* out in a wide, shallow sweep across the rim of coastline and managed to get her pointing in the general direction of the slate grey cloud base hiding the distant English shore.

'You've taken a hit in the fuselage by the tail . . . and another up by your dome. You sure you can get back to base?'

There was a dreamy singing in his ears which made it difficult to hear his wing leader's voice. Something tickled his cheek and he flicked it away. He looked down at his hand and there was blood on it. Bright new blood. All over the inside of his fingers. He stared at his hand and then felt the side of his head. There was a jagged cut and something sharp embedded in the bone above his left ear. He looked at his hand with a certain detachment. It was now a red, wet glove where his fingers had explored the hard lips of the gash. He felt no pain at all.

'I think I took a lump of shrapnel in the head,' he said carefully to Midge. 'It's only superficial. More blood than anything. If I can keep it from running inside my goggles I'll be fine. No rudder control for the old jug, though. I'm having to use my flaps. Don't think I'll make it all the way back to Beaulieu, Midge. Any suggestions? Over.'

Another voice was in his cans now — metallic, impersonal.

'Red Fox Sierra Tango, your nearest ALG is bearing 220, ETA ten minutes. What is your IAS?'

He opened his mouth to say that he could not really see his instruments at that moment. A red miasma had settled over his goggles and he tried to rub the blood away with the sleeve of his flying jacket. It wouldn't clear. It was inside the goggles, inside the eyelids. Inside his head.

He could hear Midge's voice and another answering calmly, as though he was telling him the time of day instead of struggling to keep the very life pulsing in him. The gash in his head began to ache. He must be hallucinating, for he distinctly felt strong hands covering his, guiding the movement of the stick, nursing the jerky efforts of the stricken *Vera*, humming quietly under a ragged breath that could surely not be his own.

'Here we go . . . put your head back against the rest and brace yourself.'

A sharp odour of burning rubber filled his lungs. It was so strong — so disgustingly horrible that the sudden lurch and rumble beneath him came as a violent shock.

'This is it. She's breaking up . . . burning. Can't move out of here . . . foot caught fast.' The crescendo of sound exploded in his head and he rolled away from it, into shock waves of movement and sound. Just before he lost consciousness he had a momentary but very clear image of a woman running towards him with arms outstretched.

Her hair was on fire.

' . . . TERRA COMITIS ROGERII . . . In Cicestre Ciuitate.T.R.E.erant . . . '
The traveller mouthed the words on the brass plate slowly, taking his time over the archaic Latin text before turning to his guidebook for an explanation. 'In the City of Chichester before 1066 there were 100 sites less 2½ and 3 crofts. . . . ' How pleasing that sounded, for it projected an image of small neat homesteads with snug thatched roofs, of squires and vassals and freemen. He squinted up at the plate set into the cathedral wall. 'Modo est ipsa ciuitas in manu comitis Rogerii. . . . This City is now in Earl Roger's hands. . . . ' An extract from the Domesday Book. How strange and humbling to be reading the words written by monks from another time so remote that even the Latin of that day was already obsolete.

He turned away from the brightly polished plaque and, lifting his rucksack on to tired shoulders, left the hushed precinct of the cathedral by a side door. Mellow grey walls loomed over him in the sunshine. A milk cart passed slowly along the cobbled street, the clatter of its wheels and the horse's hooves cutting rudely through the afternoon drowsiness.

The Dolphin and Anchor Hotel suddenly looked enticing on the opposite pavement. His head had begun to throb and, recognizing the signs, he crossed the road and passed through the entrance doors. He peered through the spacious public rooms, checking for the cocktail lounge, and then sauntered across to the enquiry desk.

'Have you a room for a few days?' he asked the receptionist.

She had been trying with little success to do *The Times* crossword puzzle below the lip of the desk. She looked up at the sound of the American voice and frowned at the traveller for interrupting her train of thought. He stared back at her, hope raising his eyebrows into thick black bridges.

She saw a tall but dishevelled hiker, spiky dark hair worn longer than was approved by current fashion. No luggage except for a bulging blue rucksack strapped to his back. Obviously not suitable for a first-class hotel. She shook her head, ignoring the appeal in his angular face.

'I'm sorry, sir, but we are full for the rest of this week.' She weakened as he wilted and a look of intense weariness replaced the hope. 'Maybe the Lavant Grove could accommodate you.'

He straightened then but hovered for a moment longer beside the desk. She flushed, seeing in his grey eyes a frank understanding of her assessment of him: scruffy foot traveller with no change of clothing to present a respectable appearance in the dining room at mealtimes.

'Is it licensed?'

'Yes, of course, sir. It's a very well thought of place,' she said primly. 'Only a few minutes' walk from the Cross. You go down South Street and it is the first hotel you come to on the right.'

He turned away, leaving her with the uneasy feeling that he had eavesdropped on every thought that had passed through her mind.

It was dusk before he was settled, having walked in a circle right round the inner city, judging by the tiredness in his legs. These Limeys were not exactly putting out the welcome mat for their returning son. His head ached along the line of the old scar. He could feel the tension of the lesions all the way down the back of his neck. He flung his knapsack on to a broad overstuffed armchair and lay down on the bed. His stomach rumbled. To hell with that. He'd give his right arm for a good stiff bourbon on the rocks.

'You always gotta be a gofer, sonny.' Granpappy's creaky old voice rumbled across his tiredness. 'You want somethin' bad enough — you gofer it. Chances are that's how you'll get it too. Won't get nothin' otherwise in this life.'

True enough, Granpappy, he thought. You have to be a 'gofer', for all of this to be happening to you. You lie your way into the Air Force, bulldoze your luck through flying school, force a helluva lot of Jerries in and out of your gunsights — and all for what? All for the sake of getting your good New England feet planted on Old English soil. And what happens? You get shot out of the battle on the greatest day of the war, just as you're about to cut yourself a nice big slice of glory. He rolled over on his side and cupped the throbbing ache of his head in his hand.

The folks back home had been happy enough since his return with a Distinguished Flying Cross, won on D Day above the Normandy beaches. The fact that he had three shell splinters in his head and arm at the time raised him to hero status. From that moment on, everyone had forgiven him for every mistake that he had chosen to make in his life. All the bruised relationships, all those raging drunken scenes — all were forgiven and put down to the bad war that poor Bay had suffered.

If only they knew.

He slept and, waking, found that it was night and that someone had been in and drawn the curtains, shutting out the summer sounds of the sleepy market town. He sat up and fumbled for the bedside light. Ten after eleven. Too late to go look for a snort now. He found the bathroom, froze at the clatter of ancient plumbing when he pulled the chain, and washed the stiffness from his body. Well, what the hell — he wasn't hungry anyway, so food could wait until morning. What a blessed release it was to be able to make that observation without being coaxed and worried into eating food that tasted of cottonwool and sawdust. It was no fault of his that his sense of taste had gone in the crash so that he ate simply in order to keep life in his body.

'You're so thin, Bay,' they had wailed . . . Momma, the girls, most often of all Coral. Oh, Coral — how could he have been so weak? he wondered. To marry simply for peace's sake with no love to give her, not even a pretence of desire. Just to get Momma and the Swinburnes off his back. If she had been even a little more intelligent, the way he had treated her might have left a permanent mark, stupid little cow. As it was, the three-year travesty of a marriage was long over now, thank God. She was already Mrs Mark Brewster, and good luck to her. He drew in a deep breath and settled back into bed.

'Mrs Jenner . . . you at home?'

She had been far away, staring out of the living room window, over the trees towards the water. Once upon a time there had been a clear view of the ruined house on Copperas Point, but the oakwoods had seeded through years of neglect and gradually spread right across what had been the Salterns Lane. Now, even the old grass runway at the south end of Apuldram was throwing up young saplings to block the view from her windows. She turned away from the green curtain.

'Is that you, Mr Farndell? I'm just coming.'

He was standing beside the open back door in his normal fashion, heavy wicker baker's basket held in the crook of an arm and supported against his knee. A mouthwatering aroma of warm bread filled the small kitchen. She sniffed it appreciatively and smiled at his rosy face.

'What a lovely smell that is,' she said, reaching for her order book and flicking through the pages. 'You must be one of the most welcome of visitors to all your customers, bringing the bread even in the nastiest weather, all warm and freshly baked. I'll have a long soda and one brown cottage, please.'

She took the two loaves, pressing them against her face for a moment to inhale the warm bland smell of their baking before putting them away.

Birdsong enticed her out into the garden and she sauntered among her flowerbeds, picking off a dead head here and there, absentmindedly crumbling dried flower petals between her fingers.

'Never permit a patient's problems to intrude upon your private life.' Professor Handley had repeated that one piece of advice to his students with monotonous regularity. He was absolutely right, of course. The patients in her care had problems which were set upon destroying their mental balance, and although many of them were cases resulting from the pressures of war, there were others . . . like old Mrs Carey, whose symptoms seemed beyond help, let alone explanation. She had seen the old lady only twice but was struck by her bewilderment, for she appeared to be well adjusted in the rest of her thought assembly.

'I'm seventy-two, nurse,' she had said in despair to Frances. 'I've led a plain life with no nonsense. It's not been an easy one. Widowed in the First World War — and me with two young boys to bring up and not a jot of help from 'is family. But we managed, and I were happy enough. Never felt that things were getten' me down or anythen' like that . . . so why is this happenen' now, all of a sudden? Am I mad, do ye think? I don't feel senile or anythen' like that. Is my brain goen', nurse?'

How did you make the right noises to this kind of patient? She was a good steady woman, quite intelligent, hardy and practical. The stuff that the best English stock sprang from, as her two sons showed. Then why should such a sensible woman suddenly begin to have hallucinations? Why was it that Lavenham had this effect upon some people? The old house was little more than an empty shell these days, but once it had been an elegant mansion,

441

built with love and pride. Lavenham's roots had been filled with romance from the first moment — so why had that good and wholesome love between a gypsy and a lovely young woman from a well-to-do local family sown the seeds for death and destruction?

She had been to Lavenham many times in her life. It was, after all, the closest building to her own home, and when she was a child she had roamed the overgrown gardens and even pottered about inside the house itself. Single children, so Professor Handley had said, often create imaginary families of brothers and sisters to compensate for their own solitary situation. She must have done this without realizing her need for friendship, for she had often played at mothers and fathers in the old house. It had been an endless fount of discovery, casting round among the debris which had once been furniture.

Of course, this war had left its imprint upon the timeless silence of the crumbling house. Shortly before the Normandy landings, the fields of Apuldram had been requisitioned by the Air Ministry. They had cleared some of the scrubland south of the Dell Quay road, where three large fields made it possible for them to lay out rolls of metal landing strip. For a few excitingly noisy weeks a Czech squadron, attached to the Royal Air Force, had been based there under canvas. They were there and gone before the summer was over, simply using the temporary field as a base for the invasion of France. For the short time they were there they had used the ground floor of Lavenham as their ops room and officers' mess. All the treasures of her childhood had been cleared out and the rooms scrubbed clean. Blackout curtains replaced the splendidly musty brocade hangings which had crumbled so tantalizingly at a touch. The rest of the household furnishings, mouldering and decayed beyond use, were thrown out into the farmyard and burned.

She had only been back there once since, and the sight of empty rooms, stripped of their mystery, had disappointed and depressed her. She had never returned to explore the rooms again after that. Now — a full eight years later — she was faced with Mrs Carey and her solidly convincing description of a Lavenham that Frances could just recognize from those well-remembered furnishings — but which had not been in existence for two centuries.

The woman had appeared in the Psychiatric Department of St Richard's Hospital with a letter from Dr Morrison of Apuldram. Her notes said that she had suddenly begun to suffer from delusions after falling in the orchard of the old ruined house on Copperas Point, where she had gone gleaning for fruit. She had not seemed in the least delusive and John Painter, the resident psychiatrist, after getting negative results to most of his tests, had sent her away with a few conciliatory words of reassurance — and had quietly asked Frances, in her capacity of district nurse with special training in mental health, to visit her from time to time and watch her behaviour.

There was no getting away from the fact that Mrs Carey was a perfectly healthy and unimaginative countrywoman who, when pressed, would express the firm conviction that she had seen a vision of Lavenham in the full spate of its former glory. She had described without hesitation, its stable yard filled with beautiful gold and cream horses and the house peopled with a handsome couple, their two children and another woman, a weird, limping creature who ran from the orchard in a rolling, drunken fashion.

She was describing the first Baylesses, of course, although there was no question that she had ever been inside Salterns Cottage, where their portraits still hung.

It was not generally known that all but the daughter, Violet, had died violently. But Mrs Carey knew.

She had recounted her vision to Mr Painter in great detail. Later on, he gave Frances his notes on the subject for her to peruse. It was tiresome that even on her day off, when the garden and the summer sun should be holding her attention, her eyes strayed towards the unseen presence of that mournful house, there was nothing else that could flood through her mind with such overpowering persistence.

Not even the memories of wartime tragedies. Mother's death coming within five days of news of Father being killed in North Africa. Closing the cottage and going to live with the Ayles cousins in Oxfordshire. Meeting David Jenner and falling in love in the middle of her nursing training at the Radcliffe Infirmary in Oxford. The marriage which ended within three months, when David was torpedoed and killed at sea in 1944. She was just eighteen when overnight she became a member of a growing phalanx of mourning women.

It had seemed as though she would never unfreeze after that but she did, of course. She finished her training and returned to the cottage at Apuldram and picked up the pieces.

The day was her own; no one to call on, no callers expected.

'Here, Sandy!' She called the fox-terrier and watched him race round the side of the house and across the lawn towards her, his ears pricked eagerly. She fondled his head.

'All right, old fellow, we'll go and take a look. Come on.'

It was just an old ruined house, struggling to survive against the encroaching wave of undergrowth which spread out from Salterns Wood. The paddock which had been cleared at the end of the runway was a tangle of nettle and oak saplings. The stout pink brick and grey stone walls of the buildings rose out of chaos, grimly resisting the merciless encroachment of woodland. Most of the barn roofs had fallen in where the house joined the stable blocks in an archway. The house seemed sound, its roof and walls unchanged, though it would not be possible to venture inside without a sickle to clear a way through the shoulder-high brambles. They had not been disturbed by a soul, either human or otherwise, for a very long time. Most especially, they could not have parted to assist the passage of someone as large and squat as Mrs Carey.

But she still knew all about it. She still saw it filled with

444

sunshine and flowers and smoothly tended lawns and bees droning round the skeps in the orchard.

Frances stood looking up at the blind windows criss-crossed protectively by thick thorny rose creepers. Sandy began to bark furiously from the sprawling stableyard, and she turned towards the sound, suddenly fearful that he had become caught in the loose rubble.

In the middle of the yard, a man sat on a boulder and held his hand out to the terrier. There was an opened hip flask in his other hand. He stood up with a casual uncoiling of limbs and allowed Sandy to sniff at him suspiciously, brown eyes swinging from stranger to his mistress and back to the stranger. The man fondled the dog's curly crown gently and watched uncertainty battle with surprise as Frances took her time deciding whether or not to speak to him or to pass on by, with a nod of the head, leaving him to his own devices. He deftly flicked down the silver cap of his flask deftly and slid it into his jacket pocket with a conjurer's smoothness. Now you see it — now you don't. Something told her that his was a life filled with such deliberately provocative gestures.

He was quite tall, she saw, as he stood up. Sitting, his legs had been bent like a grasshopper's on either side of his face. A thin face, pale and aged as only the young can be when stress and pain have been too much to bear. His eyes were hidden from her behind sunglasses, but they seemed to study her with a marked intensity. He had thick eyebrows and dark untidy hair, grown longer over the collar of his jacket than by most Englishmen. There was an ugly scar on his forehead which ran up from his right eyebrow into his hair.

Sandy had completed his investigation. Finding nothing very sinister in the stranger, he withdrew. The man leant against the broken side of the mounting block. He surveyed Frances — and the lines seemed to deepen round his mouth.

She decided that she would, after all, engage him in conversation.

445

2

Planning the next move, Bay toyed with the idea of buying a bicycle to carry him to and from Apuldram. It was not more than two miles to the south of Chichester and the roads were flat, even if the tarmac was pretty badly holed and patched. All the same, that first walk out to Apuldram had proved too much for him. Lying in a scalding hot bath and luxuriating in the sensation of slowly relaxing muscles, a better idea presented itself. Why not camp at Lavenham itself? He bought camping utensils, a sleeping bag, a light canvas camp bed, folding chair, collapsible table, gas lamp and gas cooker. How many years — how many generations — since a Bayless had lived at Lavenham? he wondered. Well, the blood was there beating strongly enough in his veins, even if Bayless was only his Christian name. It was enough, though, that he was a direct descendant of Violet Bayless, who had married Desmond Heritage and founded the great family which flourished so strongly today through the eastern states of America. The romance and sheer adventure of living in those days must have fired Granpappy for decades, since it had been the old man and his stories that gripped his imagination and stayed with him like a strong, unwavering flame when the rest of his life seemed to be falling to pieces. Over the years, since Granpappy had first introduced them to his younger grandson, his ancestors had coloured his life until they become more real to him than his own parents, more flesh and blood than the weakly, pretty and empty-headed Coral.

'Settle down and let her take care of you,' they had urged. 'You'll soon forget your war. You'll feel better in your own home with your children round you and a sweet, lovely girl like Coral to give you something to work for.'

The brain damage caused by that shard of German shell made him do things that he regretted immediately, say things that should have been left unsaid, flashed images through his aching head which had no place there and filled him with anger . . . and a terrible rising fear for his own sanity. But he was always forgiven and excused because he was 'a hero', and it became a terrible, fascinating game to try and break down that fount of good will. He had done it eventually, of course, but there had been a monumental fight before Boston and the Heritages had turned their backs on him. It took eight years of drinking, whoring, stealing, fighting — even embezzling money from his own brother.

Prison had forced him to think about his situation. He had been to one doctor after another — surgeons, brain specialists, psychiatrists, psychologists. They had all been full of suggestions and theories, of course; patients expected some kind of return for their money, after all. There was no doubt that the shrapnel in his skull had left lesions in his brain which probably caused the headaches — but what about his behaviour? He was a man driven by something. Granpappy shrugged and called him a self-interested young hound who needed to grow up. He understood, which was just as well, for Bay wanted no understanding from the others.

When he was released from prison there was only one place he wanted to go: to Midhurst and the old man. The rest of the family breathed a sigh of relief, for there had been much speculation concerning his future. Granpappy was old and tired, a blind eccentric but still sharp enough to handle Bay. There was a long period of peace after that. Bay did his best to be good company, reading aloud in the evenings after the day nurse had gone home — and often trying to explain the terrors of the fantasies which haunted his sleep and sometimes his waking hours as well. The old man might be blind but there was nothing the matter with

447

his hearing. He knew the presence of despair when he heard it.

'Wasting time here, boy,' he said eventually. 'You went off to war to look at the old country an' never got to the place, apart from crashing your plane into it — that's at the root of it all, whatever you think you did. Get on over there again. I'll fund you. All these fancies of yours, they stem from what's in your blood, I reckon. That's how I see it, since it's all there in mine as well.'

The old man's face was lined in deep folds of sallow skin and mottled with age. The washed-out eyes seemed to drive their sightless perception right down into Bay's soul, to know the confusion of self-hatred which dwelt there.

'You're a bit of a throwback, I'd say, young Bayless. Always were, right from a pup, long before that crack on your head. That's just stirred it all up so that you cain't sort out what's real and what's not, not yet. You take yourself over to England for a few weeks. Go see that old homestead, find a few Baylesses to spin a yarn or two with. That'll clear the air for you, I'll wager. You're never going to find yourself here, not after the pain you've given to so many folks.'

'I'll think about it, Gramps,' he said, suddenly daunted by the possibility of a return to that dreamland. 'I'll think about it, I promise.'

Granpappy grunted and jerked impatiently at the rug across his knees. 'No, you won't, you darned little tyke. It's there in your voice. Cain't be bothered, can you? Or maybe you're just being as cussed as usual.' He had been unaccountably put out.

'Why did you never go over there yourself?' Bay said. 'You've always been more taken by those old stories than any of us, after all. Why didn't you go and see for yourself instead of filling us all up with tales of weird stones and curses and then pushing others to go see.'

The old man had stared through him, his sightless eyes boring into Bay's head like blazing grey spotlights. 'Time was, I tried,' he said eventually. 'Just plain scared of what might be there for me, I guess.'

He had died during the winter, before Bay could bring himself to make a decision. Granpappy had the last word, all the same, for he left a special codicil in his will. A comfortable sum was to be provided from the estate for Bayless Heritage to return to his roots and re-discover himself at leisure. If he did not follow the requirements of the legacy to the letter, the money would go into the main trust fund. He also left Bay the five precious volumes of the Heritage Diaries, which had been prized by every member of the family since Tom Heritage had written them.

Looking at the open disapproval in the faces of his family, Bay felt the vestiges of his affection for them drain away with the last spark of hope. There was nothing here for him. There could not be less over there in England. He bowed his head and did as Callum Heritage had wished, bleakly aware even then, that he would never have made the decision of his own free will. Granpappy had known that, too.

He bought a single ticket and flew to London without any clear plan in mind, except that he would go to Chichester and make what he could of Lavenham, if he could persuade whoever lived there now to let him browse. And he would not be returning. It seemed fitting to have chosen Lavenham, that house so hungry for souls, in which to perform his own final act.

The following morning, weary from lack of sleep, he politely refused a greasy English breakfast. He accepted tea in large quantities and asked for a cold meal to be boxed for him so that he could spend the day wandering round Apuldram. He wasted no time in finding an off-licence and filling a hip-flask with bourbon whisky. It had not taken him long to walk out of the city, for a small lane ran south to the village from the end of West Street, where it joined the Portsmouth road.

He was confused by Apuldram, for it was not the picturesque little English hamlet he had imagined. There was no village to speak of. The lane cut across barren common land and skirted the boundary wall of an extraordinary-looking house with a tower and long medieval windows. He stood at the entrance to its short drive, checking it against his map and hoping that it might even be Lavenham, because it was built like no other house he had ever seen. It was a small disappointment to discover from his map that it was called Rymans, for behind it he could just make out the stubby little wooden bell-tower of the tiny parish church. He followed the wall and found another house, set back from its gateway. This was a working farm and busy, too. He looked round as a man on a tractor swung past him through the gate. The man stared at him with stony indifference. No welcome for a stranger. Typical bloody arrogant Limey!

Outside Rymans' stone gateway the lane divided, continuing south on the one hand and curling round to the right towards the farm and the church on the other. There seemed nothing else in that direction and the Ordnance Survey map only indicated a couple of ruined cottages. There were several houses further along the lane, so he made for the next crossroads and, keeping to the survey map's directions, turned right. The fields lay flat and featureless on either side of the road. A rough cart track cut through them from north to south, leading from the distant farm buildings that he had first inspected, across the old toll road to Dell Quay, then wound away to his left, just as the woman had described. He leant on the warm wood of the farm gate and gazed out over the well-husbanded fields from where those Czech Spitfires had taken off for sortie after sortie, just as he and the squadron had done from Beaulieu.

Nothing seemed familiar. Not one tree, nor clump of summer-clad thicket sprang up from the clouded grey of memory. There was so little that he had been able to recall at all, apart from the house.

The red mist came down across his sight then. He had not had it for several weeks and the suddenness shook him.

The trees and gentle sea of corn, the sky with its soaring songbirds, the very hands gripping the top of the gate became suffused in red as though the sun had suddenly set in blood, tainting everything its light reflected. He could hear the crackle of flames, smell the acrid stench of burning metal, paint, glue. Hands covered his hands. He didn't see them but they were there. The backs of his hands felt their pressure as they guided the joy-stick this way and that, holding it firmly, strongly, against the bucking lunge of the wounded Thunderbolt.

He forced his head upwards. 'Not now. Don't start now. . . .'

It faded before the thrust of his will, leaving him drenched in perspiration. A light breeze ruffled his hair, sending a chill down the damp patch on his back, making him shiver. Keep moving, damn it, or you'll never find the darned place, he told himself.

He climbed over the gate, feeling the lethargy of long inactivity in his leg muscles. The cart track was rutted and dusty and he trudged along the softer carpet of the grass verge, eyes swinging from side to side as the contours of the land began to reflect the shape of his survey map.

New Barn Cottage was a small cluster of buildings in the middle of the wind-ruffled sea of corn. He hesitated before the little whitewashed cottage, which was dwarfed by the sprawl of untidy outbuildings at its rear. The temptation to ask about Lavenham was strong but the place seemed deserted. Maybe they were all in the fields at this time of year. He turned away from the cottage door and continued on along the track, which was curving gradually towards the thick wall of trees ahead. The track divided without warning and he took the right path, seeing disuse there, with brambles and hazel growing tall on either side. So thick was the undergrowth suddenly that he almost missed the broken gate pillars. The Lavenham entrance was too choked with brambles for easy access, so he broke a flail of hazel and used it to lay about him and carve his own passage along what had once been the carriage drive.

The day was warm, the spread of fields disturbed only by the screech of the gulls overhead, but now they seemed to wheel away, seeking their prey further off towards the water. The air was heavy and he realized that there was suddenly total silence all round him, except for the zing of blood in his own head. He moved forward cautiously — and was unreasonably shaken by the first sight of buildings ahead, pink brick merging with the soft green foliage of the trees.

He had no clear memory of when Granpappy had begun to tell him about Lavenham. Granpappy's own great-grandmother, Violet Heritage, had come from there, and the strangely ominous stories that accompanied her had touched her son, Tom, also. He had kept a diary describing the whole period of his imprisonment in Langstone during the War of Independence and for some years after. The volumes were Granpappy's most valued possession, and willing them all to his youngest grandson was a signal honour which was not approved by the rest of the family. Granpappy always said that Lavenham had left its mark on his grandfather, no doubt of that, but he had escaped to France and then back to Massachusetts, taking with him another of the Bayless clan. Boudicca Smith and Tom Heritage had wed and produced Granpappy's father, Nat, amongst other sons and daughters.

Bay's own siblings had not lost a moment's sleep over Granpappy's lurid tales of hellfire and death by a look and mad horses which vanished into thin air. The stories had always impressed Bay, though — impressed and frightened him, creating a deep fascination like walking along the top of a high wall and willing oneself not to fall. All through childhood. All through the growing-up years. All through a world war which he had joined for the express purpose of going to England to see that darned old house for himself. Well, more than that, for himself and for Granpappy, too. And he had got there, maybe drawn inwards by the influence of the house. Not as he would have wished, with time to explore and cast out the devils of a thousand story-tellers. No, he had almost literally fallen into it, crashing his Thunderbolt into the Chichester Channel as he tried to land on the little grass airfield.

They told him again and again that he had not once regained consciousness until three days after he had been taken to hospital to have the shrapnel removed from his brain. They told him that he had been so deeply concussed, so nearly mortally wounded, that he had been completely comatose. How was it then, he had asked himself ever since, how was it that he recalled, absolutely clearly, being taken from the Thunderbolt's crumpled wreckage and carried across a field to the house, which they were using as an officers' mess. He had waited for the ambulance to take him away, and known where he was. He had watched the house parade its inhabitants before him, dressing itself in the elegance it once possessed: beautiful furniture, fine pictures on the walls, a magnificent refectory table, polished like glass. He recognized the young woman with the dark hair, for there was a portrait of her at Midhurst, over Granpappy's hearth. Violet Bayless. She had stood for a moment beside him as he lay on the floor of the hall with a blanket over him. Behind her he had seen the indistinct figure of a tall, hawkish man, and at some other time had felt fear at the sight of an old woman, bent and lame, hiding her face from him.

But they said that he had not seen anyone except in his own imagination.

He had, in desperation, drawn a map of the layout of the house so that he should never forget.

Granpappy was mighty interested in that. 'Danged if I've cared much about losing my sight as a rule,' he said, 'but here's one thing I'd have loved to do, boy — check your map with the one my own grandaddy made of Lavenham. D'you really want to risk yours being wrong? Or will you go to the small drawer in the desk over there and get me the leather case you find at the back?'

Bay gripped the old man's dry hands and smiled down into the blind face. 'What I see, I shall tell you, and then we'll get Peaches in here to confirm they are the same. OK?'

He had not been at all surprised to discover that they were. Nor, when old Peaches, who had cooked for the family for over forty years, wheezily agreed that the two plans were of the same place, was Granpappy.

'It's that old thing about the eyes, you see,' he said. 'I had 'em. My daddy had 'em. Violet Bayless and her daddy had 'em. And so, I remember, do you, Bay. The grey eyes that mean something special in the Bayless family. . . . '

Well, something special had certainly happened to him in the short time that he had lain under the roof of Lavenham on that June day of 1944. Now, eight and three-quarter years later, he was back on his own terms with nothing left to lose but the one thing which he would offer in any case — and now there would be all the time in the world to investigate the house and its reputation and try to rationalize whatever he found there — if indeed there was anything, after all, to query in this twentieth century.

He pressed forward, moving towards the vague outline of the building through the trees, brushed aside a long tress of barbed bramble from his hair and found himself standing before an arch.

The main house was to his left, and what looked like farm buildings in a sad state of dilapidation sprawled outward from the arch to his right. It seemed sound enough, but he moved forward with his eyes firmly fixed on the curved bricks above his head. Then he was through and underfoot were cobbles. He went forward eagerly now, for ahead were tall grasses through which gleamed the silver-paper ribbon of the Chichester Channel.

The house seemed in remarkably good order. Where he had expected broken windows and tileless roofs he found every pane still whole and few signs of wear along the L-shaped roof. The main entrance was bounded by a terrace whose balustrade had long ago crumbled under the weight of encroaching bramble and wild rose. There was a light fragrance in the air and he sniffed with pleasure, taking in the warm afternoon with its faint aroma of flowers and sweet grasses mixed with the salts of the sea.

He pushed through spiky undergrowth and climbed broken steps on to the terrace, moved by the beauty of the view. The water curved round stunted oaks on the opposite bank and spread outward into the distance as it met the open harbour. He gazed up at the house, knowing how things were within, content to delay the confirmation of the images in his memory. Untidy rose creepers were interwoven in a glorious canopy of pink and gold over many of the windows on both floors, thrusting inch-thick arms of thorny bronze-leafed fronds across the almost camouflaged front door. He tackled them carefully with his camping knife, pruning the branches with a slanting cut and piling the sweet-scented rosewood into a bier on the open terrace.

The front door was made of oak, studded with diamond-headed iron nails, its iron ring handle quite resistant to his attempts to move it. The door was not locked, for it was jammed about an inch from its lintel. He put a shoulder to it and heaved with all his strength, but it remained firmly closed against him.

All the ground-floor windows were barred by the relentless creeper and he was not able to see into the hall or the large living room. He went round the house, cutting here, stamping grass underfoot there, but there was nothing of the inside to be seen anywhere. Nature had completely embalmed the building, preserving its privacy for the final decay. The only possible entry seemed to be by a side door which he had passed inside the archway. He returned to it and found his way barred here also, for it seemed to be locked from the inside. He pushed through the long grass towards the barns and discovered a weed-choked yard with buildings on three sides. Here, neglectful time had taken a heavy toll; the barns were roofless except for one whose enormous double doors lay open on rusted hinges. He stood inside, staring up at the sky through the gaping holes in its clay tiles. It had been a very fine building once upon a time and even now one could see, from the chaos of broken stalls, what a well-designed and functional place it must have been in its day. There were three small rooms at one end of the barn which seemed to reflect occupation in the not-too-distant past. The yard also was less choked with undergrowth than might have been expected.

He sat down on the remains of a mounting block in the middle of the yard and took the hip-flask from his pocket. He took a long gulp of neat bourbon and relaxed comfortably to let the liquor braise his throat and lungs. The late afternoon sun streamed over him. His head had stopped aching, the blood had ceased pumping deafeningly in his ears. He resisted the feeling that Lavenham was quietly inspecting this unexpected son.

Something suddenly burst from the archway and tore through the grassy yard towards him, barking furiously. His heart dived into his ribs at the sudden harsh sound, but the little terrier seemed friendly enough, quite as startled at finding a stranger there as Bay was at the unexpected disturbance.

'Come on now, Buster,' he said, holding out his hand to be inspected. 'Is this your yard? Come and check me out, that's right. See, I smell good, don't I?'

A girl appeared. At the sight of him she stood quite still. There was no fear in her, just a tense watchfulness.

'He's not aggressive,' she said shyly. 'Not normally, anyway. I think he might have a go if he thought you were dangerous.'

They smiled at each other across the yard and, feeling the faint pull of each other, were drawn closer.

She looked fragile — dark-haired and slightly built. Her surprise at seeing him there was overlaid by a show of good English manners.

'I've come over from the States to see Lavenham for myself,' he said. 'I have to lay a ghost or so, ma'am. Maybe to give it a new one, too. Does it belong to you now?'

He seemed to present no threat, for Sandy had abandoned them and was already off across the yard in search of things that scuttled. She shook her head. 'Actually, it belongs to the Church. I think the Ecclesiastical Commissioners bought up most of the Apuldram lands nearly a century ago.'

There was not a breath of air in the yard. Her hair was a mass of dark curls, blown into disarray by some other breeze.

He frowned. 'Did the Church Commissioners buy it from the Baylesses, then?'

She looked startled. Two pink smudges appeared in either cheek. 'I'm afraid I don't know,' she said. Her eyes were very intent now. 'Lavenham was certainly built by the Baylesses, but they haven't lived here for a very long time. Why? Do you know the story of this place?'

'Well, ma'am,' he said slowly, savouring her obvious curiosity, 'I do have strong ties, but the immediate one was crash-landing my aircraft here at the end of the war, when there was a grass airstrip here. I was looking for somewhere to land in a hurry and this was the first bit of England I saw — so I dropped into it, literally. They brought me out of the wreckage and into the house, and then I was taken away to hospital, but I've always remembered that house very clearly. I had to come back to put a few things straight in this confused brain of mine.'

She smiled then, and the sternness he had marked gave way to an unexpected beauty.

'I see,' she said. 'I'm sorry for having disturbed you then. It must be quite a shock to see it in such disorder. Have you been over the house?'

'No chance. All the doors and windows are either unreachable through that mad rose creeper, or else they are all locked up. I tried, but everything is firmly bolted.'

'But it's not. Or it wasn't the last time I was here.' She turned and he followed her out of the yard towards the door under the arch. 'I used to play here often when I was a child,' she said over her shoulder. 'It was wonderful being the mistress of the house amongst the old furniture

457

and crumbly curtains — but the RAF cleared it all away when they laid out the airstrip and used the ground floor as their officers' mess.' As she spoke she took the handle of the back door and turned it. The door opened with a harsh creak, which echoed away from them into the innermost recesses of the House.

'There you are. You probably missed this door. Come on in and have a browse.'

Sandy scuttled past them and into the dark passage ahead. The sound of his progress preceded them. Bay took a deep breath and followed the girl down a broad stone-flagged passage. It was dry and quite cold inside. There was a faint smell of mustiness.

He had an extraordinary feeling of *déjà vu*.

The house was little more than an empty shell. The ground floor rooms were large, with ceilings once encrusted with fine mouldings — but now what remained of the plaster cornices hung perilously over their heads, like washing on a line abandoned long ago. Dim light filtered into the long hall from a vast window which rose up the stairwell to the gallery above through a thick curtain of creeper. Wind-eddies from under the front door had swirled a flotsam of leaves from countless autumns into little heaps and wavering streamers across the stone flags.

They stood in the centre of the room, looking upwards at the still beautiful line of an unexpectedly ornate oak staircase. Bay removed his sunglasses and put them into his shirt pocket.

'There were pictures on the walls and a long dining table,' he said. His voice sounded flat, almost muffled as though he was reciting an old knowledge, repeated many times.

She looked at him, startled. 'But you said that you only came here that one time. They had taken all the old stuff out by then.'

He was miles away. There was an odd searching look in his eyes, as though he was seeing with difficulty. He appeared not to have heard her.

'In here is the big drawing room, with Jess's study beyond,' he said, making for the open door at the far end of the hall. 'There was a huge desk and shelves with ledgers and books. The curtains were very heavy yellow damask and there was a seascape in a gilt frame over the mantel. John Freeland gave that to him . . . gave it to Jess when he married Lavinia.'

She stayed where she was in the hall, her hands and feet suddenly feeling very cold.

'Who are you?' she said. 'How do you know those names? How do you know what was here before they cleared it out?'

But he heard nothing she said. With a profound shock he found himself looking at two people, a man and a young woman, and he knew with absolute certainty that they must be made to go from Lavenham with all speed. Something was growing inside the man. It was a canker as old and rotten as death itself. He recognized it with deep dread.

The young people stood in the parlour window bay, close together, the girl leaning slightly against the man's body. There was a mistiness between him and the two figures. A vast terror washed through him. 'Get out of here! Run for your lives,' he shouted at them. The words meant nothing to him, for it was as though he had been forced by some reflex in his subconscious to speak them. He was aware only of urgency. 'Hear me, damn you. Get out of this place.'

They ignored him, aware only of each other.

The great unfurling evil was here in this very room with them. His sudden recognition of it was catastrophic. It was the same unbelievable horror that had engulfed him as he and his Thunderbolt crashed into the marshy reeds which bordered the grass landing strip. That was not, as he had always thought, the terror of a close shave with death. It was the impact of his union with that absolute Power which he could now feel coursing through his veins in a burning rush.

Frances repeated the question and then noticed that the stranger was standing with an unnatural rigidity in the middle of the empty drawing room, his grey eyes bulging, unfocused — glass eyes, like those of a fish on a slab or of a carving, not a flesh-and-blood man. His arms hung limply at his sides. His face was ashen, but for the scarlet lividity of the angry wound.

My God, he's having some kind of fit, she thought, and went to him, putting her arm round him in case he should fall. He was tense, his face moist — with an almost greenish tinge round the nostrils. To her alarm, he appeared to have stopped breathing — but still he stood rooted to the spot. She felt for his wrist pulse and could find none.

Her training overrode the alarm that shot through her. 'Come on, now,' she said with a professional asperity that she didn't feel. 'Snap out of it. Come and sit down on the stairs for a moment. You'll soon feel better.'

He moved then. He gave a deep sigh and his eyes slewed round towards the sound of her voice. He looked confused, as though he had no idea who she was. She took his hand and led him out of the room and across the hall. They sat on the bottom step of the staircase and he put his head in his hands and groaned softly to himself.

'Do you suffer from epilepsy?' she asked eventually.

He jerked his head up then, as though he had forgotten that she was there.

'Sorry,' he muttered. There was a fine film of perspiration on his upper lip. 'What? No, nothing like that. Well, something like it, in a way, but the doctors say that it isn't epilepsy as they know it. Some sort of occasional electrical disturbance of the brain brought on by the head wound. Sorry . . . it doesn't often happen.'

After a little while, when his breathing had returned to normal, she stood up and held out her hand. 'You seem a bit better,' she said. 'Let's get out into the sunshine. It's rather cold in here.'

He rose obediently and allowed her to guide him out of

the hall and down the stone passage towards the bright patch of light which was the open doorway. Outside he leaned against the wall and made himself breathe deeply as he had been trained to do. The girl called to her dog.

'Come on,' she said to Bay. 'I can't leave you here like this and I have to get home. I'll drive you back to wherever you live.'

Her words had an instant effect upon him. He jerked his hand out of hers and stood still under the arch.

'I'm not going anywhere yet. I haven't finished here. I'm better now. Just leave me to sort myself out.'

He was staring at her wildly now, and the near panic in his eyes spread to her. She stepped back from him instinctively.

'All right, stay if you wish,' she said hurriedly. 'I was only trying to help.'

'That's all everyone tries to do. I'm perfectly capable of looking after myself. Just leave me alone and do your Lady Bountiful act somewhere else. I'm sick to death of patronizing women.'

She shrugged and turned away so that he would not see her hurt.

He stood and watched her picking her way through the undergrowth down the invisible drive, the little terrier leaping through the tall grasses at her heels.

For some reason he was shaking from head to foot, and the rage stayed in him. He turned away and went in search of Tom Bayless Heritage's diaries. There was something in them which very much reminded him of the two young people he had just seen.

3

At first, Bay considered camping out in the barn, but then, taking a closer look at the house, he realized that the kitchen quarters, complete with ancient cooking range and capacious wooden dresser, were quite sound and dry — and a small room leading off the kitchen itself would make an adequate sleeping place. There had been no further disturbances. It was as though the house, having warned him of its complexity, waited to discover his next move.

It was disappointing to discover that the stairs were dangerous, the wood quite rotten in several places. Some-one had already gone through, judging by a couple of gaping holes and, after gingerly testing his weight and hearing the dry crack of rotten wood underfoot, he decided to be content with the ground floor. He made himself a table of sorts from an old door supported on bricks, and was comfortable enough in the folding chair he had discovered in Pines' Ironmongery in Chichester. A camp bed, a cooking primus and two paraffin lamps was all that he needed for comfort. The stout kitchen dresser was ideal for his stock of liquor.

Rummaging through his clothing, his fingers sought and found the two packages he had tucked away at the bottom of the haversack. He picked one up and hefted it gently from one hand to the other. It was wrapped in green oilcloth and tied round securely. For a moment he weighed it in the palm of his hand, testing the solidness of it, and then returned it to the haversack. Now was not the right time to consider it, not yet. It made him think of the woman, though — think of her with regret, for she was fine-looking by any standards and had been unexpectedly understanding about his 'turn' and, instead of thanking her, he had been his usual surly self, which she had not deserved. She had asked nothing of him, had done her best to help him, recognizing right away that he had a problem. How could he explain to her what was going on in his head? She would only think he was insane. Maybe she would come back again, walking her dog. If she did, he would apologize.

He drew out the other package with reverence. It too was wrapped in oilcloth. It was a little larger than the other, lighter too. He undid the wrapping and looked at the two small books with something akin to love.

The war diary of his great-great-grandfather, Thomas Bayless Heritage, was clearly intended to be his guide in this bizarre voyage of discovery. He had read it through many times already. Meanwhile he must set down on paper his own observations of the house and the strangeness of those hallucinations which had beset him. Afterwards, when he was no longer there to feel the family's ridicule, the two documents, placed side by side, might make interesting reading for some of them.

On the makeshift table he placed a parcel of exercise books and pens, and then put the little leather-bound diaries beside them. Now was as good a time as any to begin comparing notes. He settled into the camp chair comfortably and leaned his elbows on the table.

Facts concerning his own immediate situation first, he decided, then the rest would be easier for him to set down. He would make a direct comparison with the diary all the way through.

Fact 1 His brain had been damaged – or possibly a part of its function just changed by the shrapnel wounds and the fragment still lodging there. Before the crash he had been a normal person with no extra senses, apart from the unusual colour of his eyes. There was very little concerning the colour of eyes in Tom Heritage's commentary. The first mention of them was when, as a prisoner of war on the detention hulk *Fortunée*, he had first met his

English cousin, Charles Bayless. Bay turned over the pages and paused by the entry for March 1802. . . .

> . . . The new contractor came aboard this day. It gave me great hope to recognize in him my own flesh and blood. His name is Bayless and I cannot feel anything but certainty of our kinship because of his eyes. They are of the same grey hue as my own who bears my mother's likeness. I have never seen the like in any other creature. I feel that he, too, has recognized me as his kin for there was a moment as he regarded me, when he seemed stunned. . . .

That was all. There was nothing then to indicate that the grey eyes had any deeper significance. They were simply a means of identification. As in his own case, Tom had been a straightforward and uncomplicated person until he had permitted the influence of Lavenham to draw him in under its roof. It was after that first visit that it had all begun to happen.

Fact 2 Bay's fascination with Lavenham had always been there but not as an all-consuming passion until after his crash. Before that, he had simply been fired with a child's attraction to the excitement of Granpappy's weird and chilling tales of the place. The present situation seemed to have been triggered off by that brief time when, unconscious, he had been brought to the house.

He frowned, biting the end of his pen as a thought occurred to him. No, the first time that something seemed to have reached out to him was immediately *after* he had been hit — and that was *before* his crash-landing at Apuldram. Those hands which had guided him, the overpowering presence of someone gentling the old jug in to land while he wrestled with that terrible sensation of drowning in blood inside his head. . . . That seemed to indicate that the house did possess powers of attraction outside its immediate vicinity.

Question 1 If his headwound was causing him to become a receiver of electrical impulses from Lavenham, who or what was causing him to receive those particular impulses?

'Well, I *am* surprised,' a voice said close by. 'I didn't think you really meant it when you said you were coming here to stay.'

He looked up, startled. The girl was standing in the kitchen doorway, wearing a cotton dress the colour of new young leaves. It emphasized the sleek blackness of her hair.

He covered the open pages of the diary with one hand. 'I didn't hear you come in.' Somehow it sounded like an accusation. 'I mean, you're very welcome, ma'am. You startled me, though.'

She stayed by the door. She was not afraid of him, he saw. She was just being careful. He liked that.

'It's as dark as the grave in here. How can you see to read or write? I saw the door was open and came to see if we had forgotten to close it on Tuesday. Are you really going to camp out here? I think you're very brave. You must know all the stories about it since you know so much else.'

She smiled at him then, offering forgiveness for his rudeness — and seeking it for her intrusion. He never had been able to dance to a woman's tune though, and he stood up with the barest show of courtesy.

'I know a bit, ma'am. I'll be staying to learn some more, I guess.' His eyes smiled at her, preoccupied and already straying back to the little diary.

She took the hint. 'Well then, good luck to you. I can see you're busy so I won't stay. Sorry I disturbed you. Got to be on duty in an hour anyway. I'm glad to see that you are quite recovered from your little turn. Bye for now.' She turned away, already part of the shadows.

'Thanks for helping out the other day.' He sent the words after her as though they were a parting shot rather than the show of gratitude that he intended.

She paused beyond the kitchen door. 'It was natural for me,' she said simply. 'I'm a trained nurse, you see. Goodbye. . . . '

He heard her calling the terrier out in the long grass and

465

went to the back door. She was just disappearing from view, but something made her turn and she waved, seeing him standing under the arch. He stepped back into shadow and let the house draw him inside. The sight of her had been odd. She had seemed to wobble and lift off the ground, as though he was looking at her through a heat haze. What, after all, was real? he thought. Maybe she, too, was part of the past and he was hallucinating her, together with the other shadows.

He felt a subtle change in the atmosphere the moment he closed the back door behind him. The air was cold and charged with a current which filled him with a heart-lurching apprehension. He walked very slowly along the passage, feeling the whole of his body shaking as though he had the ague.

He was aware of hypnotic singing in his ears again. The hall was ablaze with light, the whole place sparklingly clean despite the presence of that great shattered refectory table lying fragmented in the middle of the room. The table had not been destroyed before, but now it lay like a memorial to some intense upheaval.

The shadow girl was there. He could see her, and the whole room, through a floating miasma of fine mist as though this, like the other visions, was only a mirage. She was cleaning the hall with a ferocious energy as though time and the Devil himself were at her heels. There was a dreaming look on her face, a soft and contented upturning of her features as she worked.

'Who are you?' He stood close to her, but she showed no sign of awareness. Gingerly he tried to touch her but there was, as he had guessed, no substance to her. Yet there was about her a vague familiarity as though he had created her a long time before and forgotten her until now. He walked round her as she moved about, the better to examine her.

She was very small, dark-haired and foreign-looking. A little of the Mexican Indian there maybe, for her skin, though clear and smooth, had that olivine strength of texture common to those who lived out in all elements of heat and wind.

Then she was gone. It was as though a motion picture show had suddenly been switched off, and he was left standing in the empty hall on the edge of a long shaft of yellow sunlight with the echo of high-pitched singing somewhere inside his head. At the moment that she and the furniture vanished, the young man he had seen her with before appeared through the door of the main sitting room. There was a look on his face which made Bay's heart jump. Maybe he too could feel the slow pulse-beat in his head and in the very air about him.

Stifled by the brooding atmosphere, he went out into the sunshine and stood gulping in the clean salty air on the terrace, then headed for the oakwoods. The house seemed charged with sudden urgency and he had the strange feeling that it wanted him to stay within its walls all the time, that the danger he sensed would only come to him from outside.

The afternoon was peaceful, with only the faintest of sighs in the branches above his head to show that there was a good breeze out in the harbour. He strode deliberately away from the house through the high grass and soon found himself on the river bank with water lapping four feet below. Out across the water a bright red flag flapped from a buoy which lazily pirouetted on its anchor chain. Three small sailing boats were beating up towards it from the open harbour. He could just see the orange dots of their jacketed crews. But for that brief meeting with the girl and her dog he had not spoken to anyone, seen anyone for that matter, in twenty-four hours. What a blessed relief.

She had said that she lived at the end of the Lavenham drive, where it met the main road. He skirted the edge of the long straggle of woodland, following the trees where they fringed the edge of a noxious-smelling marsh. Here and there he could see signs that there had once been some sort of industry in the reed-choked basin, for there was a collapsed sea wall of sorts which protected it from most of the tide flow, and some cobbled areas remained, as though there had once been a jetty or inner stone wall. An old barn stood blind-eyed against the trees, its roof covered with rusty corrugated iron. He paused to look inside a paneless window. Long slabs of rough-hewn granite stretched away from him into the dark recesses of the place. They had been chiselled out into shallow troughs on either side of an open drain. It was difficult to see what they had once been used for. Some kind of cottage industry, long abandoned.

He made for the gate he could see at the far end of the marsh. A lane wound away from it, with a wild fringe of untended trees and shrubbery on one side and a small pasture on the other. There were birds here, he saw. Gulls swooped overhead and thrush and finch were busy in the foliage. He stood and watched them, feeling the black pit in him lift a little at sight of their elegant dance. He found it extraordinary that there seemed to be no birds of any kind close to the house.

A track cut sharply off the lane to his left. He stood in the middle of the grassy path and considered. He could just see the roofs of Lavenham from this point, and also the barns hiding the cottage at New Barn. He went on and the lane, curving slightly, thrust another building at him so unexpectedly that he stopped in his tracks. It was quite a small cottage, charming and well tended, with unusual leaded windows shaped like church arches. The walls, veiled in purple-flowering clematis, were of flint and pebble with red brick insertions — as he had seen in other buildings in the area. The front garden was a mass of colour and he dawdled beside the low stone wall, hoping that someone within would see him and come out. There was something feminine about its neatness and it was certainly close to Lavenham. He followed the wall, and the lane emerged on to a wide tarmac road. As he stood looking about him a car flashed past, raising a cloud of dust. He watched it disappear from sight round a distant bend. Somehow the twentieth century had become a blur and the sight of a motor vehicle was a dash of cold water. He put his hand on the latch of the cottage gate and pushed it open.

Inside the house a dog set up a furious barrage. That was definitely Sandy. Feeling more confident, Bay walked along the gravelled path between clumps of lavender and sweet-smelling herbs. There was a heavy Montana creeper growing round the white front door. He bent his head and pressed the doorbell, hearing it ring a long way away in the heart of the house. Sandy became frenzied.

No one came to the door and he remembered her last words: 'Got to be on duty in an hour anyway. . . . ' She was a nurse of some kind. He remembered that too, now. Funny that he knew the name of her dog but not hers. He tore a sheet of paper from his notebook and scribbled on it.

So this is where you live. Sandy is guarding you well. I came to be sociable as I have been really very remiss in thanking you for your kindness the other day. Will you call for me when you have time to waste and the pub is open? I think I must explain one or two things to you and then you might change your present impression that Lavenham is hosting a lunatic!
                                                                Bay Heritage

Bay slipped the folded note into a corner of the letterbox, then retraced his footsteps, turning off the lane onto the smaller path with confidence, knowing that it was the way back to Lavenham.

'Will you explain a little more clearly?' Frances said. Robert Crane smiled at her, a dry amusement gleaming beneath the thick, unkempt eyebrows. She sat on the other side of his desk, poring over the book in front of her.

'There is still so much of this subject that must be taken on trust if you are going to understand any of it.' His voice had a rich, smoker's wheeze and he paused to cough lustily. Chest cleared, he wiped his face with a checked handkerchief and thrust it back into an already bulging jacket pocket.

'Take that paragraph on page 228 there, where Stanson is describing the findings of his experiments on persistent activity rhythms in inanimate objects. What I am trying to get over to you is the fact that absolutely everything on this earth is alive in its own way. Stone, metals — every single thing is created out of molecular fusion and electrical attraction and repulsion. Therefore it is, in theory, possible for those now long dead to have left an imprint of themselves in the places where they lived, and it is just feasible that a person containing the same genes, in other words related by blood, might reflect these shades and the echo of their past — like a mirror, if you like.'

He sat back in his chair, watching her face as she struggled to find anything logical in his words.

'Well, I cannot see how two such different people, from backgrounds that apparently have nothing to do with Lavenham, can just suddenly become mirrors after not having been that way before,' she said finally. 'Mrs Carey says that as far as she knows her family has never had anything to do with the place. Her people do come from this area, it's true, but they have always been Selsey folk, with some from Runcton and a few scattered round the Funtingdon area.'

She sighed and stretched her back. 'The American obviously has some connection with Lavenham, I agree, because even in the few sentences I've exchanged with him, he seems to know an awful lot about it.'

'Well, find out all you can from him,' Robert Crane said. 'If you really want to investigate phenomena of this kind with any seriousness, you must go about it properly and tabulate every smallest item of information, every least suggestion of practical evidence, just as though you were a detective hunting for clues. You put down on paper all that you can — and I'll go over it now and then and keep your assessments firmly fixed in reality.' He grinned at her across the desk. 'When you are dealing with parapsychology, there is such a thick layer of superstition and sheer foolishness to wade through that, all too often, the amateur will get bogged down between fact and fiction.'

She thought about his words as she drove home. Somewhere in Mrs Carey's family tree was a person who had been involved with Lavenham in some way. She was sure of it. The trouble was, how to find out who, at what period — and the connection. But that knowledge could convince the poor woman she was not losing her wits. The immediate thing to do, however, was to see the American. There was a great deal to find out about him too, which looked as though it might be difficult as he was such a surly fellow. There seemed to be a deep anger inside him which spilt out like an exploding volcano at times — or maybe he just had no time for women. . . .

She found his note in the letterbox and read it over several times that evening. The most illuminating detail, apart from the fact that it showed a certain charm after all, was his name: Bay Heritage. That had to be the connection. 'Heritage' had an attractive ring to it, and when old Mr Freeland had mentioned it to her parents, it had stuck in her memory. That was when he had given them the three paintings which even now graced the cottage staircase wall.

'Violet Bayless married a man called Heritage,' he had said, telling them the history of each of the subjects in the oval portraits. Desmond Heritage had come over to England and fallen in love with the formidable Miss Bayless — and had borne her off to Boston before Lavenham, which had been her home through childhood, could damage her as it was apparently destroying those all around her. How astonishing it would be if this abrasive and unfriendly man camping in the old house was actually a Bayless descendant.

There was only one way to find out — but another twenty-four hours elapsed before she was able to return to Lavenham. When she did, it was to find the mercurial American in a very strange frame of mind.

The August weather had been building up all week towards thunder, filling the air with a feeling of foreboding, still and heavy with the dusty smell of harvesting. It was weather for headaches, for irrational shows of ill temper, for hot sleepless nights.

All the cottage windows were open to catch the slightest breeze and draw it through the stifling rooms. Frances sat out in the garden in the shade of an evergreen oak, sipping orange juice laced with a generous shot of gin. The long glass clinked with ice, cold enough to pearl its sides with moisture.

She had arrived home, perspiring in the hot confines of her small Fiat and cleaned the hectic day away in a long, cool bath. Now it was time to rest and unwind — and wish that Robert Crane was in the area. He never failed to cheer her up, without ever appearing to try, and she was well aware that his interest in her, fuelled by occasional nights spent together at the cottage, was deepening — which did not actually displease her. The thought reminded her of another invitation. Maybe Mr Heritage would like to mix beer and atmosphere at the tiny Black Horse Inn a few hundred yards further along the main road from the cottage.

Sandy sat close to her deckchair, panting in the shade of a tree. His long pink tongue lolled from his mouth as he watched her every movement. Now and then a drop of spittle rolled down to the tip and was gulped back into his throat.

'All right, old fellow, we'll go for your walk. Lavenham will certainly be cooler than the cottage at this time of day.' He was on his feet and waiting beside her before she made the first move, flanks heaving like bellows.

The narrow lane was like a furnace, the long grass tunnel on either side of the path burnt a sparse yellow through lack of rain. Everything crackled underfoot. It would not take much, she thought, passing through the fallen gates, to have this whole place blazing. A slither of glass reflecting the glaring sun, a cigarette stub tossed away by one of the reapers.

Sandy, imagining something darting through the undergrowth, shot off in pursuit.

The back door of the house was open again, and so, she discovered moments later, was the front door. It was propped against the wall with a piece of broken stone baluster, and the air in the hall smelt the fresher for it. The American was lying on the terrace with his head on his mattress-roll, staring out at the sparkling water. A bottle of whisky, more than half-empty, lay against his hip. He turned his head as she appeared through the doorway. For an instant his eyes were wary, as though he was not sure of what he saw. Then he recognized her and sat up.

'Hello,' he said. 'Thought you were a ghost for a moment.' He stood up with stiff-jointed clumsiness like an old man. There was an odd light in his eyes, as though he was suffering from a fever.

'I came to see whether you would like to try the local beer,' she said. 'You did suggest it in your note. I've had such a hot and sticky day, it seemed to be just the answer. It'll get you out of here for a bit, too. Have you been sitting here ever since yesterday?'

He put a hand through his hair and gently massaged the side of his head as though it hurt him. She saw that the livid scar went deep into his hair. He noticed her attention and grinned at her.

'Days like this make the old scar throb like an Indian drum sometimes. I didn't realize that this island of yours could be so hot. I swear it was always wet and misty when I was over here before. I should have waited till fall, I guess. D'you see I got the old door to open after all? Took me most of this morning. It's surely made of the hardest wood I ever saw. Sends a nice breeze through the rooms, though. It was smelling like a sewer at one time last night. As though something had died here . . . terrible. I looked everywhere, even managed to creep up those rickety stairs to the floor above, but there's nothing there.'

'Probably a bird caught in a chimney or something.' Frances repeated her invitation hopefully and he nodded.

'I'd like that. I have to fill up my water cans, in any case. Do you think I might ask you for water in the mornings, ma'am? Your cottage is so close and the folks at Newbarn might not be as friendly.'

She laughed. 'Oh, I think you'll find that they are. Come on. I'm dying of thirst — and of course I don't mind filling your water cans. If you bring them along now, we'll leave them at the cottage gate and pick them up on the way back.'

He followed her down the terrace steps obediently. He was probably not quite sober, for there had not been much left in the bottle of whisky on the terrace, but he showed no sign of drink apart from a slight unease.

'I guess they won't mind doing without me for a short while,' he said, glancing back at the house as they went through the archway.

4

They sat on the wooden seat outside the little tavern, sipping their drinks and watching the evening commuter traffic to Selsey and Itchenor building up from Chichester.

Bay seemed content to sit without talking at first. Frances watched his face out of the corner of her eye. He was dishevelled and had a pallor that suggested long ill-health. In spite of the roughness of his accommodation, he was clean and had obviously shaved that morning. The hand tightly gripping the pewter tankard had a slight shake but his fingernails were cared for and his shirt appeared to have been freshly washed. Whatever his situation at Lavenham, she guessed that he would always attend to his person. He drank his first beer like a man parched, with a grimace at its lack of refrigeration — and then quickly refilled it before she had done more than sip at hers.

'You are not at all curious about the rest of our village, or the absence of it, are you?' she said when he finally stopped fidgeting and seemed to settle. 'Wouldn't you like me to tell you all about Apuldram being wiped out by the plague?'

He shook his head. 'Seen enough plague in various forms. I came over here looking for a plague much closer to home.'

Good, she thought. Speaking in riddles could be the start of shared confidences. 'You said that you had come to trace your family connections. May I ask who they were?'

He was doing his best, she saw, to be all attention on this occasion and she flushed under the appraisal of the strange grey eyes.

He answered her question with one of his own. 'What is your name?' he asked.

'Frances Jenner.'

'Frances Jenner — nursing sister, nice cottage, dog called Sandy.' He reached across and touched the wedding ring.

She looked away from the raised eyebrows. 'No, not any more. Lost at sea.'

He nodded and passed on. Expressions of regret were neither necessary nor welcomed.

'So I learn quite a lot about you from just a few little crumbs. How long have you lived at the cottage?' He was collecting facts and storing them away as though he were not remotely interested in Frances Jenner but in the place she fitted into in his mind.

'Oh, ages . . . my parents bought it from the Church Commissioners after the First World War and I was born there.'

'Was Lavenham empty then?'

She laughed. 'Oh dear, we never stray far from Lavenham, do we? Not even when we are out of sight of it. Has it attached some sort of umbilical cord to you already, even in the short time you have been there?' She was teasing him until she saw the look on his face.

'Look, ma'am . . . Frances. I've just *got* to glean everything I can about that place from everyone around here. I can't explain why now — but I must know all there is to know. My forebears built the damned house.'

She stared. 'Your note did say your name is Heritage — and I certainly wondered whether you were a connection of the Baylesses. What a coincidence.'

'No, it's not a coincidence,' he snapped. 'I came here to clear up all the ridiculous stories that our family half believe about this place. If I have any future at all — and that's in doubt — I don't want another young Heritage being scared clean out of his wits as I was in my childhood. This Lavenham place, thousands of miles away across a vast ocean, actually coloured and disturbed that childhood of mine in a way which has affected me ever since.' He gave a humourless little grunt. 'It's a sort of obsession, I suppose. I have to try and rid myself of it, and that's why I came over here. Now I'm here I can appreciate that there really is something mighty odd about that old house — and I'm not leaving until I've found out what.'

His mercurial mood had changed again as he spoke. The fleeting gentleness was wiped out and his voice shook with hatred. She drew away from him. Robert Crane's theory of genetic memory suddenly moved a step closer to reality.

'Look, Bay — I hope I may call you that? Because I have known Lavenham all my life, I'm sure that I can help you with whatever you are trying to do. That is, if you will accept my help. After all, the people in these parts know a great deal about its history and, together with the facts that you may have, we should be able to sort it all out eventually. But please get one thing quite clear. I am not going to offer you my time and interest and receive in return the sharp edge of your tongue whenever you feel like it. I don't have to put up with that sort of thing, so here's the proviso. Either you make some sort of effort to be pleasant company — or I shall forget the whole thing, see?'

She was not angry with him. In fact, he was relieved to see that there was a suggestion of laughter in her eyes despite the stern jut of her jaw.

'I'm really sorry,' he said after a pause. He was stuck for words to explain the depression which had been his companion for the last eight years.

He emptied his tankard and stood up. 'Ma'am, can we walk? I find it very hard to sit still for long and it's a lot easier to talk with you if we are walking.'

They walked. She guided them up the road in the direction of Chichester and then they turned into a side road close to a square Georgian house set in a shambles of run-down farm buildings. 'That is where old Mary Free-land lived,' she said as they passed the overgrown drive

477

entrance.

'Are all your old houses in such a bad state? That one doesn't look much better than Lavenham — and who was old Mary Freeland?'

'I thought you might have known, as you seem to know all about the others. The Freelands were the family that the gypsy Jess Bayless married into, and it was Lavinia Freeland for whom Lavenham was built — and named.'

He had the name now. There was so much to cram into his sometimes confused mind. 'Lavinia Freeland must have been my — '

'No, she was no relation to you. Think about it. You are descended from Violet Bayless.'

'And Violet Bayless was the daughter of Amy.' He smiled grimly at her. 'Yes, I know about that incestuous bit. Granpappy told me that too, although I don't think the rest of the family is aware of it — or if they are, they prefer to ignore such shameful skeletons in their closet. It's certainly not something to shout about where I come from.'

'I don't think that it would worry anyone here.' She returned his smile. 'After all, it was a very long time ago and it is recognized that there was a great deal of incest everywhere in bygone days.'

'I expect you are wondering just why I have such a fixation about that damned house,' he said at last.

'Not really.' She spoke carefully, for the wrong answer might discourage him. 'You are the first member of that family that I have ever met, apart from some gypsy Baylesses who still camp there sometimes. There's a branch of the family living over in Petersfield, and there are others in London — rather a smart set, but they have nothing to do with Lavenham any more because the land was only leased to the family in the first place and it has been Church property for as long as I remember. I don't think that they will touch it, though. There is a lurid folk tale of some clerics meeting a sticky end there in the seventeen hundreds.'

'Well, it's quite true, as far as I know. Those three clergymen did die there — in 1754. Violet Bayless tried to have the place exorcized, and they were struck down. It was the night she ran away from Lavenham, and Desmond Heritage took her back to Boston as his bride after that.'

She laughed. 'My goodness, you Americans are such fanatics about your family details. You must have it all embroidered on your heart. Dates and everything.' Then, seeing no answering smile, she added, 'It's very interesting, though. I didn't know it was as real as that. It must have been the time that half the village reported seeing Lavenham burning, and yet in the morning there it was, large as life and no one but the dead inside.' She shivered in spite of the evening heat. A long way away, far out to sea, a mutter of thunder seemed to answer her.

They turned into the cart track leading south through the newly shorn fields to Lavenham. They could see a combine harvester at the far end of Hempsteddle, working steadily to have all the corn cut by nightfall, before the threatened storm broke. A rabbit scuttled across the path ahead of them and disappeared into the hedge, pursued by the little terrier.

'What I can't quite see is what you are going to do at Lavenham. Will you have another try at exorcizing the building?'

If only you knew, he thought. If only you realized just how deeply I need to be finished with it all — right there in that murderous house, after making sure that it will not threaten any more Baylesses or Heritages again — *ever*.

'I'm not too sure myself yet,' he said aloud. 'But I want to see what kind of threat it offers. If there is nothing left of it, that's good, but I think that something is very much still there. I have had some pretty weird flashes of some sort of throwback memory which has not happened to me anywhere else. Oh yes' — seeing the question in her eyes — 'I've had this bash on the head and I've sure been acting out of character ever since, so they say — but this is different, really odd. You'll probably have some pat explanation for it — like I'm schizo — but I seem to be able to see the folks who were here a long time back. I mean, even before this century.'

'Is that what was happening to you the first day I saw you?'

He nodded. 'That sure did put the wind up me, I can tell you. One moment I was talking to you and the next, there were these two people — and I had the strongest possible impression that the house was menacing them in some way. My God, that sounds fanciful — but I swear to you that I'm not imagining it.'

'I don't think you are, either.'

He stood still then and gaped at her. She was small in the way that that other girl had been small, strong in the delicate way that a dancer is strong.

'Don't look so startled,' she laughed. 'I'm not a believer in ghouls and ghosts and things, but it just so happens that I am a trained psychiatric nurse and one of the mysteries I'm trying to help unravel at the moment touches Lavenham and the effect that it has had on one of my patients.'

They walked on slowly as she told him a little of Mrs Carey's convictions. They passed Newbarn Cottage with heads close together, fascinated with the similarity of the two experiences.

'It's going to rain like mad in a little while,' Frances said, sniffing the sulphurous air and looking up at the yellowing heart of the leaden evening sky. 'Would you like to come back to the cottage and have a bath and some cooked food?'

Darkness would come in an hour, bringing only the great roll of towering cumulus clouds which presently reared up blackly over the horizon. Now and then a faint pink flash from within gave warning of their slow approach. The air smelt of it, dry and faintly acrid.

Frances' hair stood out from her head, charged, frizzy. He put out his hand and stroked it and felt the faint zing of electrical charge in his palm.

'Not yet. It's good of you, but I'm sure that this particular atmosphere, when the air is all charged up, is when things happen at Lavenham. I can feel it from here, right now as I'm talking to you. I can feel the pull of it, just like a magnet. I *want* to go back there, too. It's actually in my head.'

He held out his hand and she took it. For just a moment the cold grey eyes looked at her with unexpected gentleness. You cannot help me, they said, but thank you. . . .

She drew her hand away. 'Bye then. It's been nice talking to you. I'll look in during the morning and bring you some fresh bread, if you like. The baker comes about nine.'

She walked away, clicking her fingers at the bouncing terrier, and he watched as the deepening dusk slowly erased her slight figure. He let the house draw him back into its heart then, but went indoors at his own pace, resisting the urge to hasten back to the living room, where the pulse was, where the Power flowed into him with terrifying satisfaction. He was obeying its requirements, but it was going to be done by his own rules and in his own time.

This time he felt more at ease with them when they appeared again — although the sudden materializing of figures which had no place in the empty house was startling at first — for a thought had just occurred to him. Frances said that no one had lived at Lavenham since Violet Bayless left, the night that the three clerics died there. But she was wrong. Leafing through the close written scrawl of the diaries he had come to it:

. . . We explored every room, every inch of the building and found so much excellence. Dudie knew it all for it is not new to her but, seeing my pleasure, said that we should make an inventory to take back to Mama, and this we did. It took us several days. I used Mama's old chamber for sleeping and Dudie and Nat had the vardo in the stable yard.

481

That was Tom Heritage, and he had stayed here, wandering through the rooms in much the same way as the two young people were doing now. Bay suddenly felt very sure that these two people *were* Tom Heritage and Dudie Smith. They seemed to be in a kind of trance, a state which he knew, for he had succumbed to it when the house made its presence felt.

He heard the thunder gathering outside the walls, a distant disturbance of heavenly furniture. Now and then the windows were etched with stark white light. There was no darkness in the house, for his eyes could see shadowy tables and chairs, even the dreadful butchery of that refectory table in the hall. He moved with the two figures from room to room, searching their features and finding the evidence he needed.

They vanished as suddenly and silently as they had appeared, taking with them the anxiety, the certainty of disaster, which had filled him. He was left on his own with the house and that now familiar, insistent singing in his ears.

Something drew his attention to a particular spot at the far end of the long room. The whole of the ground floor was stone paved. He found himself bending down to feel the slabs with suddenly sensitive fingers. There was, he discovered, one place where two of the stones appeared quite warm against the flat of his hands. He searched the house for a suitable tool, and when dawn came, he was still hunting. He went out into the grounds, casting about him for anything strong enough not to snap under the resistance of the heavy stone slabs. He was on his hands and knees, panting over a rusty wedge of iron railing, when Frances arrived with his water canisters and a fresh loaf of bread.

His pale face was flushed, the grey eyes flinty. 'Have you something like a mallet at home?' he asked by way of greeting.

She laughed outright, ignoring his abstraction, and two dimples appeared unexpectedly in either cheek. 'You've got a very short memory, haven't you?' she said, ignoring his question. 'You are meant to say "Good morning" or "How nice to see you" at least before making demands, remember?'

He might not have heard her and she saw with alarm that he looked feverish. His movements were jerky, uncoordinated.

'Look, before I do anything, let me get you something to eat and drink. Please . . . just to indulge me. Then I'll give you all the help you want.'

She made for the kitchen without waiting for him to follow. She pumped up Bay's primus stove and poured water into a billy can. Soon the fragrance of coffee floated enticingly through the barren rooms.

'Hey, come on,' she called. 'It's ready.'

He came eventually. They sat on the broken balustrade of the terrace watching the air dance with early morning heat. When he started to talk it was, after a few hesitant sentences, as though an ulcer had burst in him and the poison poured out.

'I think that I am becoming insane.' The breath hissed through his teeth as he laughed at the words, but there was no humour, only a deep pain in him. 'Oh, I realize now that I've grown up with my foolish old granpappy's creepy stories about this house, but he told those stories as though he had been here and experienced the killing of those priests himself, as though he actually knew the feeling that Lavenham lays upon me, a sort of sucking-out of one's will to resist, a wearing-down of the spirit. One moment I see wonderful things all about me, the house at its best, the place full of happiness, and at other times it threatens and menaces in turn until I'm so confused, I just don't know where I am. Granpappy kind of told me about that, but he never came here.' He drank from the half-pint blue enamel mug in his hand. The aroma of the coffee was titillating even if he could not appreciate the flavour.

Frances said nothing. She studied him attentively and waited. A bee droned past her head and she watched it

483

settle into a cluster of pink and yellow honeysuckle on the house wall.

'I'm trying to hang on to the last shreds of good sense, Frances, and so it seems to me that because Granpappy described these sensations so vividly, these are what I am experiencing. I'm an ordinary sensible fellow by nature, and the way I figure it out is, he must have planted all of this in my subconscious. If he hadn't told me his string of stories with such zest, maybe I would be feeling pretty different about this old ruin now. Instead of which, here I am seeing things and people who are quite real to me, if not to anyone else.' He rubbed a hand across his eyes. 'My God, I'm tired now. I don't know what is driving me on in this way.' He picked up the bottle beside him and took a swig from it. 'I didn't just come here to take a look at the place. I came here to kill myself, you know.'

She nodded. 'I wondered whether something of that sort was in your mind,' she said. 'You gave the impression of someone who no longer cares about anything. That's why I came back. I thought you might be in need of company, even though you think that there is nothing much left for you.'

'But there *is* something left for me . . . now.' He sounded excited all at once. 'Ma'am, I can't explain properly. I haven't the right words but, although this place has been the death of all sorts of people in the past, all I can tell you is that the fascination I have for it is a lifesaver to me. I have to get to the bottom of it. I *have* to. It is not just my own curiosity. The house seems to want it done. Now how can that be? It has only been destructive in the past. It has been empty of living folk for a very long time, and now it wants to tell me something — I think.'

He closed his eyes against the sun. 'Look, I have to go back inside,' he muttered, rising. 'I get such appalling headaches and the sun doesn't help. Come on in. We can sit in the kitchen.'

'When did you last get some sleep?' she asked gently, seeing the lines of weariness on his face. 'Were you up with your shades all night?'

He nodded. 'I think so — can't really recall. I'll take a nap shortly. I just want to talk this out for a little longer. You don't mind, do you?'

She shook her head. The dark wiry hair stood out in frizzy curls framing her face, giving it the anxious look of a scenting deer. 'Talk all you wish. You may think you are saying things which have no sense but I am beginning to see a pattern there which, from the medical point of view, is most interesting. Once I have put it together in my own mind and maybe had a chat with my department head at St Richard's Hospital, I'll tell you more of what I think. I'll tell you something now, though. I certainly don't think that you are going insane. You have a strong streak of good old-fashioned common sense which is far tougher than you realize. The hallucinations you are having may be in your mind or they may be something quite real, but it is you and you alone who are finding reasons for not putting an end to yourself.'

She looked so earnest, trying so hard to tell him that she understood when there was no possibility that she did, he thought. She was just a nice, kindly girl putting her arms round another soul who was hurt.

'You're just great,' he said. 'My luck must have changed, because you seem to be part of the package and that's a real bonus. Just go on kicking me when I deserve it.'

He was so weary that he could scarcely keep his eyes open. She left him, knowing that he would sleep. 'I'll bring a mallet and my tyre-lever from the car when I come back,' she promised.

The morning was still heavy with storm clouds burgeoning across the horizon like vast ships' sails. It simply must break today, she thought. The tension in the air was almost unbearable.

5

The fields were all shorn now of their golden harvest and the corn stood stooked in stubble from the top of the shallow bank at the water's edge all the way across to the Witterings High Road. On the southern boundary of the little prairie a dark line of Lavenham trees bunched close and thick round the house, as though to ward off the dogged progress of that great red harvester.

There was little traffic along the Chichester channel. Bay sat in the wedge of garden beside the Crown and Anchor at Dell Quay and watched the contents of a coal lighter being transferred to three great horse-drawn waggons. Petrol rationing, even eight years after the end of the war, meant that many delivery tradesmen had reverted to their old dray horses. The wagons were high-sided, the horses those huge-shouldered creatures bred in the Middle Ages by the Suffolk, Derby and Clydesdale shires to carry armoured horsemen in times of war.

Bay surveyed the scene with idle interest. He had never seen English shire horses before and sat sipping his warm beer, marvelling at the sheer size and strength of the team of four to each waggon. The carts were thickly encrusted with coal dust, their drivers black from cap to boots but for the white flash of their teeth and the roll of reddened eyeballs. The great horses were obviously well cared for, as their coats gleamed and their fetlock feathers, freshly combed like fluffy bedroom slippers, resisted much of the mud and highway dust through which they must pass. They stood drowsily in the hot sun, blowing quietly to each other through soft pink nostrils. The clink of their studded harness brasses disturbed the early evening peace as a great head was shaken to shift attentive horse flies. Now and then a huge iron-clad hoof smote the hard-packed earth with a dull thud and a vast weight was shifted, leathers creaking, in the traces.

Frances was late.

She had looked in on her way to work that morning, all crisp and businesslike in her dark blue uniform and white collar, little blue cap stuck hastily on to the back of her head.

'Meet me for a drink at the pub in Dell Quay this evening, around six. I want to introduce you to someone. Can't stop. Sorry. I'm late as it is . . . see you later.'

He rose and took his tankard to the public bar. It was a small room, dominated by a large empty fireplace, blackened by generations of smouldering oak logs. The whole place had that special odour of stale beer, tobacco and woodsmoke which he was beginning to find most pleasant. While he waited for Fred Goodinge to fill his pewter tankard from the barrel, he leaned against the bar. There were a couple of tables and benches, but this was a place clearly intended for drink to be taken standing.

His eye was caught by a strange decoration on the wall between the fireplace and the one small window. It was a painting of a bull's head, once lavishly executed with a bold use of colour but now blackened by tobacco and fire smoke. Protruding from the end of its painted nose was a large hook. He went over to look at this oddity more closely.

Fred Goodinge put the foaming tankard on the bar top. 'D'you play ringen' the bull over in America?'

Bay shook his head. 'I'm sure we don't. How does it go?'

'See that ring on the end of the string, over your head?'

Bay looked up. A thin cord was looped over a nail. At its end was a brass ring.

'Well, you take it and swing it and see how often you can get the ring on to the hook in twenty-one throws. It's one of England's oldest games, they say. Not as easy as it looks, either. Man came in here one day from the newspaper. Says there ent more'n half a dozen bulls left in England now.'

Bay unhooked the ring and began to play idly. The ring swung outwards in a wide arc and stroked the bull's glaring eye. It was certainly harder than it looked. He was still swinging without success as the door opened and Frances looked in. He ringed the bull.

'Well done,' she applauded. 'How many tries did that take?'

'Too many to count.'

She was pink-cheeked, the dark curls abob all over her head. She looked very young and eager.

'Hello,' he said softly to her.

She took both his hands and reached up to peck his cheek. Her eyes sparkled. 'Hello yourself.' She turned her head and he saw behind her a large square man with a thick thatch of crinkly brown hair on his head and an even thicker growth of beard, which grew unchecked in reddish splendour down the front of his gingham shirt. A pair of very bright blue eyes surveyed him mildly.

'Robert, this is Bay Heritage,' she said, as he squeezed into the small space beside her. Half a dozen customers came in behind them, pressing past with a nod at Frances. They filled the room.

'Bay, I said that I wanted you to meet someone. Well, this is Professor Robert Crane. He is head of the biology department at St Richard's.'

Bay had the distinct feeling that he was a specimen under a microscope, to be inspected by two interested medics. He had been through all that so often before that he reacted automatically. He turned away from the stranger and glowered at Frances.

'What gave you the idea that I'd want to meet him? I'm not in need of any more medical attention than I've had already.' He ignored the professor, who went across to the bar and ordered drinks for himself and Frances. She shook her head at Bay and put a hand on his arm, seeing his edginess.

'He's a friend,' she said quietly. 'He's my friend and might well become yours if you make a little effort.'

Her eyes, a few inches from his own in the crowd beside the bar, hid no secret plot to involve him in anything and he held in the bitter words which hovered on the edge of his tongue. Instead, he shrugged and turned back to the bull. He ringed it twice more before joining the other two, who had gone out to the waterside garden.

The coal waggons were gone now and the empty lighter lay abandoned with its barge in the mud at the bottom of the jetty steps. The evening was fresher than it had been in the past few days. A light breeze took a curl of Frances' hair and danced it across her forehead. They sat slumped in their iron frame seats, watching the arrival of more customers.

'This place is quite popular on summer evenings,' Robert Crane said. 'It's just the right walking distance from the city for getting up an interesting thirst.' He noticed Bay's empty tankard and leaned across. 'Hurry up, young Frances. Can't have you falling behind. What's it to be? Same as before?' he said to Bay and, taking the nod to be all the reply he could expect, he went off cheerfully, the three tankards in one large fist.

Bay stared downriver to where the distant roofs of Itchenor were hazy grey smudges in the evening light.

'Bay, why are you cross at meeting Rob?'

He compressed his lips and stared away from her along the winking river.

'If you don't want to meet people, you only have to say. I shall quite understand, you know.' Her voice was low. There was no patronage in it. He said nothing but his eyes slewed round and regarded her. There was a curious lack of expression in their grey smokiness. She was sitting quite close to him, her elbows resting on the uneven red paint of the tin table between them. The corners of her mouth turned up even as he looked at her and a single dimple deepened in her right cheek. Come on, smile, she seemed to say.

'Robert has been very good to me in the past. I went through quite a difficult time when I first came to St Richard's because I had been studying psychiatric medicine at the Radcliffe in Oxford, where I did my nursing training. Then the head of the biology department retired and Rob, just out of the Army, was chosen to fill the vacancy.'

There was such a ring of gratitude in her voice that he thought, Ah, she's interested in him. This is her way of telling me to keep my hands to myself. No problem there. He had nothing of himself to offer any woman now. There was only the house to unravel — and then he'd get out of all their lives.

'So why trot him out here? You surely don't need me as an audience to your romancing.'

He had hurt her, he saw. As soon as the words were out of his mouth he could hear the bald rudeness in his tone and was instantly sorry.

She sat back in her chair, putting distance between them, two scarlet patches flaring like poppies in her cheeks. 'There is no romance. Really, you are so churlish at times. I asked you to come and join us because I thought you and he might get on well together.'

He laughed at that, a hard little bark of bitterness. Crane was coming across the grass towards them, his huge hands filled with dripping tankards. Bay leaned across the table and said quietly, 'Just let me say this. I know what you are up to and thanks, but I don't need help from him. I'm quite comfortable at Lavenham and I shall stay there for as long as it takes — and then you will not be troubled further. Just make sure he keeps off the subject of Lavenham and my phobias, will you? I don't need any more prodding and prying from quacks and oddball psychologists who seem to be more unbalanced than many of their patients.'

'Ha, are you talking about my esteemed profession?' Robert put the tankards down on the table and dug about in the pocket of his cotton bush jacket. He brought out

490

three packets of potato crips and settled down on the bench beside Frances. She picked up one of the packets and tore at the paper, feeling for the little blue twist of salt amongst the curly crisps. Bay hunched his shoulders and returned to a close perusal of the waterway.

'Psychiatry and psychology are still rather poor relations in the eyes of some of the medical fraternity in this country,' Robert said comfortably, ignoring the closed faces of the other two. 'We are on the threshold of great things over here, but at the same time we have to run a much harder gauntlet of the sceptics than most of our brethren in other branches of medical research.' He took a long draught of beer and sat back in his chair, a wisp of froth clinging to the hair on his upper lip.

'The war has presented us with more patients suffering from neuroses of various kinds than most of the other war-wounded put together. Speaking of which, Frances tells me that you are Apuldram's only plane-crash victim.'

'Yes,' Bay said eventually. 'I did drop in here around D-Day. Didn't stay for long though.'

Robert was feeling in his pockets again and this time produced a battered pipe and a dilapidated oilskin pouch. He began to pull out strands of tobacco, packing it carefully into the bowl of the pipe with loving attention. 'Got a bit mauled though, she says.'

'You could say that.'

Frances toyed with her tankard. It was irritating to find just how annoyed she was with Bay. She had hoped that this meeting might bring him out of himself but he was so dreadfully surly most of the time that a normal conversation seemed almost impossible. It was probably a mistake to have asked him to join them. The evening would have been very pleasant indeed with just Robert's company. Let the two of them do the talking then, if there was to be any at all. She was quite content to sit back and listen to Rob's skilful soothing. If anyone could make Bay behave rationally, it would be him. He was already easing things, she could see.

'D-Day. Seems another lifetime away now.' Robert tilted his chair back and swung thoughtfully to and fro, drawing at his pipe ponderously. Blue smoke signals rose and drifted away between them. 'My regiment was in Italy then. What a mess that place was left in. When did you come over to Europe? Did you see anything of the Mediterranean?'

There was, after all, no talk of health, of doctors — of Lavenham. Bay realized that he was being soothed but it was done so skilfully that very gradually he found himself responding to the gentle exchange. It sounded as though this bulldog of a Scotsman had gone through a long, nerve-racking war in North Africa and then Italy. He had not been wounded but casually let drop the fact that his wife and daughter had been killed by a flying bomb. Frances was a war widow, too. Maybe that was what they were trying to get over to him — that they had both survived their own traumas and felt competent to help him through his. He felt oddly touched. This was a whole new experience to be supported by people who seemed to care rather than be suffered by admirers who didn't.

Another round of drinks came and went and the evening deepened until the first stars appeared out of a bright deep blue evening twilight and the garden lights were switched on. It was time to go.

'Bay, will you come back with us and have some supper?'

To Frances' surprise he agreed. Robert looked delighted, which she was sure he was not. They walked back to the cottage, cutting across the fields, passing the Lavenham entrance without comment, and Bay, looking back at it over his shoulder, set his will against the urge to return there. He could feel its need of him, the siren song of something so tangible with longing for him that a lump rose in his throat. They needed him, those shadow ancestors. What might they not do without his surveillance, without that delicate balance of influence which he was just beginning to experience over their wills? No, it

492

was only the house making him think this way. They had got on with their lives before he had appeared — yes, and look what they had brought him to. . . . He hunched his shoulders and walked fast ahead of his hosts.

There was a moment just before the two figures came into view, when he suddenly realized that his will was no longer stronger than the house. If he gave in at this point, it would manipulate him utterly. He stood still on the pebbled cottage path and fastened his whole attention on the small black silhouette of a swooping bat wheeling above him, determined to remain the master of himself. For a second he was conscious of the lightning build-up of that will. Then an excitement flooded through him, welling outwards from his chest, down into his genitals, upwards into his head. Something happened behind his eyes, something hot and lethal leapt from him like the flash of a knifeblade.

The tiny bat plummeted into the grass. Bay stood rooted to the spot on the path, consumed with a terrible fear, and then went across the little stretch of front garden to where the creature had fallen. It lay with its tiny wings fully opened as though it was still in flight. He moved it gently with his foot and then turned away. He was trying to work out what had passed through him when Frances and Robert arrived.

'I'm flattered that you are so keen to get to your supper but I wonder if you'll be as eager after you've tasted it,' Frances said blithely, opening the front door and releasing the small tornado about their ankles.

Bay sat hunched in shadow. She went ahead into the sitting room and turned on a table lamp and the room unfolded into a cave of soft yellow light, agleam with well-polished woods and silver. She opened french windows on to a terrace and the dim suggestion of wide lawn, and stood smiling at them both, suddenly a small queen in her own well-loved kingdom. She looked beautiful, vulnerable, happy to be back here. Happy to have their company.

493

'Rob, will you fix us all a drink while I do a few things in the kitchen? Bay, I think it'll take me about twenty minutes or so to dish up. Would you like to take a bath?'

He did his best to shake off the sheer fright which still trembled in his chest and grinned at her, doing his best now to return her warmth.

'Am I getting a bit ripe, ma'am? I thought I'd kept the odours at bay fairly well considering the difficulties — but yes, if you don't mind, I'd really appreciate a sluice-down.'

She took him upstairs, turning lights on as she went, found a large fluffy towel for him and opened the bathroom door.

'Soap there, my father's old razor, brush and strop in the medicine cabinet, the geyser turns on here by the door . . . watch out for sudden bursts of scalding water as it's got a personality all its own and enjoys teasing strangers.'

She left him, closing the door behind her.

He ran a bath and lay in the hot water, but every muscle in his body still seemed set rigid with the shock of what had happened in the cottage garden. The soap smelled of spring flowers, a little exotic after the abrasive cleanliness of the carbolic he had brought to Lavenham with him. He washed his hair and scrubbed himself and slowly the tension eased. He had done the very thing that Tom Heritage had done — and related with horror and disbelief in his diary. He had Flamed something.

He, Bay Heritage, who had never hurt an animal in his life, had struck down a small innocent thing, just as he might have shot out of the sky anything which had been in his gun sights a few years back. But with what? It was not possible to *look* something dead; and yet that was what he had done. The bat was completely lifeless, lying out there on the damp grass, plucked out of the night sky in a motiveless execution, with a weapon of which he had no knowledge, no understanding.

Granpappy had not had it, but then none of the Family had been inflicted with it until they had been touched by

Lavenham. Great-great-grandad Tom Heritage, Violet Bayless, Jess Bayless . . . and before?

Clean, shaved, hair water-slicked into shining smoothness, he turned out the bathroom light and started down the stairs. He stopped to look at the three old pictures. Peering up at an elaborate oval frame, he stared, shocked, right into more of those cold grey eyes. It was almost as though they had been waiting for him here, away from Lavenham but not beyond the reach of its power.

His head ached suddenly, shafts of swingeing pain cutting across his skull. He should have guessed that Frances was connected in some way with the whole business. It was part of the pattern that every event was somehow linked, every person strung to the next by a common denominator.

Violet Bayless stared calmly down at him, the suggestion of humour in her impassive gaze all the more tantalizing as it echoed the look he often surprised in Frances' own.

The other two faces were strangers to him. One, very worn and discoloured, was of a foreign-looking man in plain hunting garb, one hand across his chest, gripping a furled document. The other, in a matching frame, was in better condition. The subject was young and delicate-looking, with lines already under her gentle eyes. She had beautiful hair the colour of ripe corn combed into long curls on either side of her heart-shaped face and secured with diamond clasps. Her regard was serene and blue; her hands folded, the long, artistic fingers entwined about a small posy of cornflowers in her lap.

'Do you like them?'

He started. He had been quite absorbed in his inspection. Frances stood at the bottom of the stairs looking up from the little hall, a flowered apron round her waist. There was a smudge of flour on her left cheek.

'You are part of it, after all, aren't you?'

She frowned at the rough accusation in his voice. 'What do you mean? You must be surprised to see Violet Bayless there, I know, and I didn't tell you that I had her portrait before because I wanted it to be something nice to show you when the time was right.'

'Why have you got this picture? Are you a Bayless? I thought there was something familiar about you. I just didn't realize that we were actual relations. . . . '

She laughed then. 'Now, don't go getting the wrong end of the stick. I'm not a Bayless, although one of them did marry into the Ayles family. That was my name before I married David. Jess Bayless's brother Manfri, who was his horse master, married Polly Ayles. Old Mr Freeland gave those pictures to my parents a long time ago because he was giving up his home and going to live closer to his daughter in London. He told them that this cottage had been built by Jess Bayless — he's the one on the right — especially for Violet and her mother, Amy. They had been living at Lavenham with Jess and Lavinia — she's the lovely fair one — and obviously Amy did not get on with her brother's wife and apparently the fur used to fly. They never did move in here, though, because poor Lavinia died in childbirth, but Mr Freeland thought that it was more appropriate for the three pictures to return here. It's a nice little story, you see — but there's nothing sinister about it, is there? Come on down and sample that drink that Rob poured for you.'

He followed her into the sitting room and allowed himself to be settled across a small table from Robert, who regarded them sleepily from the depths of an enormous armchair. Bay picked up his glass and found that his hand was trembling violently. Some of the golden liquid splashed across the padded arm of the easy chair. He drank the rest in one gulp.

'Sorry,' he said to Frances. 'I'm not too good with shocks, and two in one evening's all I can take.'

'Don't worry. Just try to unwind a little while I go and burn up your food. I'm sorry if the pictures upset you.' She put her hand on his shoulder and gave it a little squeeze. Then she was gone, and Robert was reaching across, refilling Bay's glass and passing over the ice bucket.

He mumbled his thanks. 'It wasn't really the pictures. It was killing that poor bloody bat,' he said suddenly. His head thumped like the inside of a kettle drum and he pressed both hands against his temples and groaned. 'God, these headaches are killers.'

'Sometimes tension, old boy. Sometimes pressure from lesions after a head wound like the hefty one you've got there. Anything painful in the head is a hellish cross to bear.'

Robert's voice seemed far away but there was something in it which made his own words easier to say. 'I killed a bat out there in the garden just before you and Frances caught me up. I don't know how I did it, but it must have been by just looking at it and exerting my will. Oh God . . . I wasn't even trying to hurt the wretched thing, just trying to focus on something so that I could resist the urge to get back to the house. One moment it was flying about over the cottage — and the next thing I knew, something seemed to burst inside my head and it dropped like a stone. My God, it was like that with those others up there on the stairs too. They had the Killing Glance. Now it's got me doing the same thing.' He pressed his fingers into his eye sockets, feeling the instant flare of pain.

'D'you want me to go and take a look at it?' Robert was sitting forward now, the sleepiness gone from his broad face. The mild eyes were attentive. There was no ridicule in them.

'I'll come with you.'

They switched the porch light on and saw a little black body right away. Robert picked it up and turned it over carefully. There was no sign of damage. He grunted and put it in the hedge.

'Dead enough, you're quite right. D'you want to talk about it?'

But the will to unburden himself had faded. Bay shook his head. 'What's the use? Something's happening to me, and by coming to Lavenham, I am entirely responsible for whatever it is. Maybe you should see the old diary I have and then you might understand what is going on. I just can't explain it now. Sorry . . . I don't feel so well.'

Frances was bending over him, front teeth biting her lower lip. Her black lashes were so long that they almost touched the smooth cream of her cheek-bone. She smiled at him and sat back on her heels. 'Good . . . that's a lot better. Thought we'd have to get you into St Richard's if you were out for much longer. How do you feel?'

He pushed himself up. He was lying on the sofa, shoes off, tie loosened. There was a steaming cup of something beside him. Across a low coffee table Robert sat back in his chair and smiled at him. He suddenly felt a rush of gratitude.

'Yes, sure . . . a lot better. What happened just then?'

'You keeled over, that's all. You've been out for nearly ten minutes. When did you last eat? Drinking on an empty stomach can play havoc, you know. Maybe we should do justice to Frances' lemon chicken — d'you feel able to chance a bite?'

Robert was obviously hungry and Bay nodded, although food was the last thing he wanted at that moment. There was scanty conversation, while Robert breezed his way appreciatively through two heaped plates of the first course and followed it up with three apples and a thick wedge of cheese. Bay ate what he could and did his best to be civil, but all the time the house called.

'It's no good,' he said when Frances had cleared away the clutter of the meal. 'I thank you both most kindly for your patience and company but I've got to get back now.' He stood up.

'Why?' enquired Robert. He leaned forward comfortably with his elbows on the table.

'I don't know . . . I just have to get back. I can't explain. I just feel real uncomfortable being away from there for long. I suppose you'd say that I've become obsessional about the damned place.'

Robert shook his head slowly and felt in his pocket for the inevitable pipe. 'No, it doesn't look that way to me. If you were genuinely obsessed with the place you wouldn't leave it at all. Nor would you speak about it in the way you do. You don't even really like it, do you?'

That made Bay pause as he moved towards the door. 'I don't know. There are times when I find myself hating it, for it is squeezing the shadow-people I see around me there, playing with them in an obscene way — like a cat with a mouse. It doesn't seem to matter what I think of it personally as long as I am there to be played with like the others.'

It was almost a relief when Robert stood up, stretching, and said with sudden firmness, taking the option away from him, 'Now, come along, old man. You've had quite a turn this evening. We'll see you back.'

He let them take him back to Lavenham. The night sky was heavy with stars. It seemed to press downwards, spilling its sheer weight of brilliant pinpoints into the black outline of the trees. Far away on the distant highway, a speeding car changed gear and, over-revving furiously, screamed away into oblivion. The silence became absolute.

There was little conversation. Robert and Bay walked together and Frances, with Sandy weaving from one side of the path to the other, trailed behind in the wake of their torches. Distant voices were raised in song from the Black Horse Inn. Light glimmered through the trees from Newbarn and a dog howled forlornly.

There was scarcely need of torches, for the moon was brilliant overhead. Everything was magnified, stark hazel rods in the hedges, gnarled silhouettes of ranging oaks — even the broken pillars at the drive entrance loomed upwards like decapitated sentries, the moulding on their crumbled plinths edged with luminous light.

'Hey, there's no need to run,' Robert complained as Bay's stride lengthened. The pools of torchlight danced before their feet. The house, invisible, watched their approach.

He was coming . . . bringing the woman with him. The other was not welcome. He would have to be made to free himself of that one.

The aged atmosphere preened itself and hid the odour within, making the empty rooms ready to receive . . .

They came through the archway and into the house through the unlocked kitchen door, harsh torchlight slashing the blackness, clothing the emptiness with infinite possibility. Robert, following Bay into the kitchen, sniffed the air. 'Hmm . . . something die in here recently?' Frances could smell it, too. An old decay, the mould of ages — and something more.

Bay placed his torch on the dresser and set about lighting his two paraffin lamps, which soon brought a more comfortable glow to the room. The presence of Bay's few personal belongings somehow underlined its stark-ness.

'Come through to the main rooms,' he said presently. 'There is more of a feeling of contact there if you're after psychic phenomena.' He went ahead of them with an anxious scurrying gait, like a dog with a strong scent, and they followed close together, watching the sudden menace of his shadow looming up the walls over their heads.

'Keep an eye on him,' Frances muttered. 'He's got the same abstracted look in his eye as he had just before he went into that trance.'

Bay hurried through the hall and made for the double doors at the far end. They were folded back against the wall as though to welcome all who wished to search the cavernous emptiness of the room beyond. Bay stood in the middle of the dusty floor, holding his lamp aloft so that every corner of the room was revealed. 'Here is the vortex,' he said, turning slowly round. 'This is where it all emanates from. I can feel it now, can't you?' His face had a

500

frowning vacancy as though he was seeing slightly out of focus.

'You all right?' Robert said sharply. Bay stood quite still, as though he were listening. The paraffin lamp swung at the end of his rigid arm. It moved on its own, for not a muscle in his body showed the slightest sign of life. Seeing the white intensity of his face, Frances shivered. He seemed suddenly to have left them, just as he had on that first day. 'He's gone into trauma again, hasn't he?'

Robert brought his torch upward, shining its full white glare into Bay's stark face. 'My God, look at his eyes.' The great irises were open in a wide, unfocused glare. They were a pure cold grey which seemed almost to glow in white intensity from within.

There was no sign of pupils.

They felt his pulse and found none. He appeared to have stopped breathing. His skin was cold and dry, as though he had been refrigerated from within. He was in a complete catatonic state, standing erect in the centre of the room with the lamp held high. The odour of decay seemed to strengthen about them. It caught at the back of the throat, gaseous as a blocked drain.

He was back in the little room beside the kitchen that had become his sleeping quarters. It was furnished now; there was a bed and a cupboard and even a chest of drawers. He did not recognize the two entwined figures in the bed, but later, when the man rolled away, he knew that it was Lawrence Bayless — for he saw the cold blue light about him and recognized that he had the Power. A moment later he sensed the new life in the girl who snuggled into the crook of the boy's arm. She smiled up at him with such touching adoration — and deep down within her the extra life pulsed strongly, something black and frightening in it.

He reached out to touch the girl; there was something about that blackness which he found at once repellent and familiar, and there beneath his fingertips, beneath the flesh of her that he could not feel, was the inheritance of something so old already that he shrank away from it in revulsion. She must not have that child. . . . There had to be some way of stopping such an unholy birth. She was so very young. There would be plenty of time for her to have others, later — but not that one.

He watched the figures stroking each other like a pair of young cats and concentrated his whole self upon the golden head of the youth, feeling the excitement build up in his body as it had between the lovers only moments before. There was no sound but he could see that the boy was angry now, and the girl cowered from him in the tumbled bedcovers, brown eyes furtive as a rabbit's. Bay watched the acceleration of the boy's Power, a mirror to the burgeoning of his own. He felt it burst from him and through the boy into the new life growing in the girl, cauterizing the putrid spark. Terminating what had scarcely begun.

There was an instant of wild, greedy ecstasy, an outflowing of sheer puissance, when everything was shafted in pulsing orange lights, licking through him, sending every nerve end screaming, blocking the two figures on the bed in a rolling miasma.

Then it passed from him. The girl lay among the sheets like a small doll flung aside by a petulant child. Her eyes, wide as saucers, stared straight up at him — and in them was an expression of sheer terror.

The youth stood up. His face too was open, unguarded. The pleasure in his grey eyes was underlined with contempt. There was a light fleck of spittle at one corner of his mouth. He looked down at the girl's body with complete satisfaction.

'You Flamed the girl,' Bay shouted at him. 'You flamed that poor skinny little kid, you bastard!'

The youth walked through him and left the room.

'It was only necessary to get rid of the child,' Bay bawled after the departed figure. 'It was the child who was bad, damn you. The child — not the girl.' He was alone in the cold room, standing beside the crumpled bed and the wraithlike figure of the girl. He had not meant that to happen. It could not have been his doing. It must have been that bastard, Lawrence Bayless. It came to him that Lawrence had been killing things throughout his entire life and would continue to remove anything that got in his way until the Power left him. He stared down into the child-woman's face and wept at the horror he saw in the dead eyes.

'He was like this before,' Frances said, trying to massage Bay's heart through his shirt and ignore an increasing feeling of nausea in the pit of her stomach. The smell of decay in the room was overpowering. 'He seemed to die right in front of my eyes, and then a few moments later he came to — and started talking quite incoherently about seeing all sorts of strange things and people.' Even as she spoke, Bay's rigid facial muscles began to slide, his arm came down hard so that Robert had to swoop to take the lamp from him, and in an instant he seemed to wilt. His shoulders bowed and he slumped to the floor and put his head in his hands. Great heaving sobs tore at his lungs.

They squatted down beside him and Robert took his wrist again. The pulse was there in full strength now, racing as though he had been running hard. The skin, which a moment before had been as cold as marble, was clammy. Bay sat and shivered violently, struggling to control the sobbing breaths.

'Watch out for sudden change,' Robert said to Frances, who had put her arm round Bay's shoulders, holding him tightly against her. 'He looks as though he could be going into spasm.'

But the shaking passed. Frances wiped his glistening face with a corner of her dress and held on to him tightly. The terrible stench had gone.

'Did you see them? Did you see what I did?' Bay said finally. His voice was thick, as though he were drunk and the words difficult to find. His teeth began to chatter.

'No, we saw nothing,' Frances said soothingly. 'Only

you — and you seem to have had some kind of turn like you had the other day. Just stay quite still for a little and let it pass.'

But he could not. He twisted round against her, staring desperately into her face. His eyes were frantic, his hands clawed at her. 'I made him kill her . . . I tried just to Flame the unborn child, but he went further and killed her, too. I hadn't meant that to happen. She was so young — too young to bear a child in any case, but it was evil and I had to get rid of it. Get rid of the bad issue and then it can't spread. You do see that, don't you?'

His voice shook and he wept again, burying his face in her shoulder. Frances looked up at Rob and felt the tears prick at the back of her own eyes. 'It's all right,' she said softly putting both arms round him and hugging him to her. 'What you did was right. It was the right thing to do. I'm sure of it because you are a good man, Bay.'

'A murderer. A bloody murderer of defenceless girls and unborn children.' He seemed quite distraught until suddenly he jerked away from them, rolled over on to his hands and knees and started to cast about on the stone pavings.

'There you are — feel it for yourselves. It's hot, you see? Here — and here it's bloody burning hot.' He grasped Robert's wrist and thrust his hand, palm down, on to the stone.

Robert frowned, feeling the heat in the ground. He was right. It was certainly warm — and in one place in particular it was very hot indeed. He pulled his hand away.

Bay turned on him in triumph. 'I told you. I told you so, didn't I? I'm not entirely off my rocker.' He was quite beside himself now and began to tear at the flags with frantic fingers.

'He can't be left like this,' Robert said to Frances over the top of his head. 'We'll have to get him back to the cottage and give him something to knock him out. Then I'll take him into Casualty in the morning before he does himself an injury. Come on, old man. I think you've had enough for tonight. You're coming back with us.'

Bay ignored him and dug and gouged with his fingers, trying to ease the stone upwards, but it had lain snugly between its neighbours for more than two centuries and was not moving now. Nails tore. Blood smeared the pale stone.

Robert stood up then, hooked Bay under the armpits and levered him on to his feet without further argument.

'Leave me, damn you. Leave me alone!' Bay rounded on him and struck out. Robert moved his head and twisted away. The blow went wide. 'For pity's sake, don't make me hurt you,' Bay gasped. He put his hands up to his face and dug the bleeding fingers into his eyes. 'I can't help it. Go quickly — Frances, take him away from me! It'll make me Flame him, I can feel it beginning. . . . '

Robert hit him once. He folded quietly and slid backwards and they caught him between them. Without a word they scooped up their torches and dragged him out of the empty room, down the passage and away from the building into the heavy heat of night. Behind them the paraffin lamp glowed from the parlour floor in a pool of soft yellow light, the blood from Bay's fingers thick black smears on the burning stones. The heat slowly drained away.

There had been no pleasure for the Place this time after all, no sucking-up of the sweet lustings from love, from death, from the acts of that gift of Power. But it would happen in time. It would happen — and when it did the pleasure, as always, would be total.

There was no fight left in him. He felt that life itself had been sucked from him by a great, all-powerful leech. He suffered himself to be put to bed, given medicine and left to sleep.

Robert and Frances made the kind of love that comes from long acquaintance, a tender coupling which lacked nothing in its intensity but was over without preamble, for their minds were already upon other matters.

505

'I cannot get his face out of my mind,' Frances said. 'He seems so utterly alone with his nightmares.' Her head was on Robert's chest and she had been listening to the deep even breathing which meant that he was thinking too. 'There is every evidence of phobia in his speech and yet he seems completely rational in every other way.'

'Did you notice how cold the air became during the time he was out?'

She twisted round and stared at him. His thoughts were away on a completely different plane from hers. 'Yes, now you mention it. That ghastly smell seemed especially strong then as well, but it had quite gone by the time we brought Bay out. I felt an odd singing in my ears at one point, too. Was that just me, or did you feel it?'

'Mmm . . . I felt it, too. Temperature change, odour, atmospheric sound waves . . . I begin to think that there is very little the matter with your patient but a hell of a lot the matter with that old house.'

'If that could be proved,' Frances murmured into her pillow, 'it would take a great weight off Mrs Carey's mind.'

'We'll bring her over there and see what happens.'

Content with this excellent idea, they slid into sleep.

Bay had gone by the time they surfaced. Frances put her head round the door of the spare bedroom and found the bed empty, the sheets flung back. It was early, for Robert had to be at the hospital by eight o'clock. They breakfasted out in the garden, listening to the special clarity of morning birdsong in the balmy air.

'I'll go over as soon as I've tidied up here,' she said. Robert studied her under the pretext of drinking his coffee. She really did look very lovely in the soft morning light. Her skin was clear and radiant in spite of the traumatic events of the previous night, and the white silk wrapover housecoat she was wearing accentuated every line of her body. He leaned across the table and kissed her, twining their fingers together across the cloth.

'We'll have Mrs Carey over to Lavenham at a time when I can be there, too, and can you see that Bay is feeling stable enough to remain at Lavenham, or we'll have to get him out of there for good. I think that would be a pity, you know. There's something there which is extremely interesting, and I'd very much like to be around to see whether he can do what he wants without exploding his mind in the process. He thinks that he is sliding down through time towards whatever it is that exists at Lavenham. I know it may sound incredible, but his brain may actually be experiencing that. Talk to him, Frances. Talk to him as though this is what we understand him to be doing — and see what he comes out with. Then try and remember enough of the conversation to relate it back to me. I'm working late this evening but if you don't mind, I'll be over at Lavenham around eight o'clock. If you can get Mrs Carey to agree, I'll pick her up on the way.'

She telephoned Mrs Carey, knowing that her mornings were spent cleaning the vicar's little house. She was not surprised at the caution in the woman's voice when she made her request.

'Well, if you really think I should, mam, I'll be free any time after seven o'clock then. Will that be all right?'

Frances smiled delightedly to herself. Oh yes, seven o'clock that evening would certainly be all right.

6

Bay was sound asleep on his truckle bed when she found him. In the dim light which filtered into the little room from the kitchen window his exhausted face seemed to have accumulated new age-lines overnight. For the first time she noticed a greying at his temples. Asleep, all the tension was ironed out of him and he looked what he was, a man in poor health who had battled with undue pressure for a long time and was now beginning to suffer for it.

She tiptoed out of the room and stood in the kitchen, leaning against the makeshift table, considering what best to do rather than disturb him. Her eye fell on the diary which he seemed to rely on for comfort. He had shown her a passage from it where Tom Heritage described his arrival with some of his crew, aboard the Langstone prison ship which was to be his home until his escape. She had been moved by the unemotional writing, the bare statement of conditions aboard the infested old hulk. Now she picked up one of the scuffed leather books and leafed through page after page of the spidery, tightly compressed writing.

It was too difficult a task, for the writing of that period was more flowing and many of the letters too alike to decipher. She flicked through the pages and eventually closed the book.

Bay slept on. She went through into the hall and stood in the living room beside the paraffin lamp still sitting in the middle of the floor, a mute reminder of the frenziedly scratching man tearing at that one paving stone till his fingers bled.

She bent down and pressed her hand flat against the

stone as she had seen Rob do the night before. Without doubt it was slightly less cold than the others. She sat down beside the stone, trying to analyse the possibilities.

The blood sang in her head. Funny, that, she thought. She had been aware of singing in the ears in this room the day before.

'Are you any closer to explaining the mystery of that warm stone than the rest of us, Madam Sherlock?'

She turned and saw him leaning against the door lintel, watching her.

'My goodness, you gave me a start!' She jumped up, slapping the dust from her skirt. 'I saw that you were fast asleep so I didn't disturb you. How do you feel? You left the cottage awfully early. You missed a very good breakfast.'

How could he answer that question in a way she would understand? For he had been away again — so far that nothing was recognizable — and who was Epona? How did he know of her when their voices were denied him?

He shrugged and smiled at her with sad eyes. 'Guess I feel like always. How would you feel with a constant pain in the head, no taste buds when you eat and a growing conviction that you're nine parts round the bend?'

'You know you're not round the bend or anywhere near it,' she said. 'Come back to the cottage with me. This place is no good for you, is it?'

He looked at her with gentleness in a kind of joyless appeal for warmth. She took both his hands and pressed them together between hers, willing him to take heed of her words. 'Please, Bay. We're meeting Robert and Mrs Carey here later this evening, but you don't have to lurk around here till then, do you? Come to the cottage and ask me whatever you want about Apuldram or Lavenham or, well, the world at large, if you wish. You aren't nine parts round the bend, just a little over-involved with this place and you really do need to get away from it now and then. Please come back with me.'

He put his arm round her and drew her against his

chest. It was a curiously impersonal gesture, as though he sought the comfort of another human being irrespective of sex. She felt the pulse-beat of his heart against her ear. They stood close, absorbing something vital from each other.

She slipped away from him and began to move towards the distant rectangle of sunlight from the open kitchen door. 'I've got a chisel at home, and somewhere in the toolshed there's a good big mallet. Just the thing for getting those paving stones up. Come and help me look for them?'

He capitulated.

They returned to Lavenham in the early evening. By that time, Bay had bathed and Frances had rinsed out a shirt for him and fed him — protesting — a dish of rabbit and mushroom pie with fresh vegetables from the garden. Lavenham had not once been allowed to creep into the conversation and both felt that a hurdle had been successfully crossed.

They bypassed the living room, although they had brought the chisel and mallet with them. It was understood by an unspoken agreement, that Bay would attack the paving stones on his own. They sat out on the terrace with one of Bay's bottles of Scotch, watching the evening sky deepen into a livid raspberry red through which the evening star suddenly shone. There was between them a soothing state of understanding, as though they had known each other a very long time.

'That portrait you have on the stairs, the one of Jess Bayless,' Bay said at last, breaking the truce. 'Do you know when that was painted?'

She shook her head. 'Well, Jess died in 1752, so it must have been painted quite a long time before that. Why?'

'I saw him, you see . . . here, of course, and in that dream state. It was horrible. A crazy old dame came into the big bedroom upstairs and attacked him with a candlestick. He was old, sitting in a chair, all wrapped up, and one side of his face looked a bit lop-sided as though he had

had a stroke. Then in she came, with her clothes hanging from her and her hair all thin and wispy and matted and that awful wild look!' Bay shuddered. 'I wondered whether there was any evidence like a death certificate as to how he died.'

She looked doubtful. 'I suppose you could write to the General Registry Office in London and see if they could trace a death certificate but it did happen two hundred years ago, you know.' He sighed. 'Yes, I know that. I suppose I'm trying to justify these wretched visions and make them more factual than they are.'

They heard Robert tooting his car horn up on the main road. Frances raised her glass to Bay. 'Here they come. Good luck.' She didn't quite know why she had said that, but he seemed to understand. His eyes smiled at her, thanking her. He took a deep gulp and emptied his glass.

'Anyone at home?' Robert's voice cut across the evening quiet. A pair of heron rose in alarm from the marshy bank and swooped away up-river in the direction of their eyrie, elegant creatures in flight, necks outstretched, the spread and strength of their wings like a Chinese brush painting in the gathering dusk.

'We're out on the terrace,' Frances called back. She jumped up and whisked the bottle out of Bay's grasp as he reached to fill his glass. 'Leave some for them,' she said. 'We're already several tots ahead.'

They came round the side of the house, pushing through the yellowing grasses. They looked strangely alike, Frances thought. They were the same height and build, the same colouring. They were calm, sensible people, Rob and Mrs Carey, and yet here they were, gathering to try an experiment which calm, sensible people would dismiss as foolish nonsense.

'Good evening, Mrs Carey,' she said. 'Come and meet our friend, Bayless Heritage.'

Joan Carey was over seventy now, a mother of sons and grandmother of grandsons. She had been Joanie Heberden of Cakeham, where the family had served many masters in

511

the manor for generations. She was respectful without obsequiousness, speaking when spoken to and then giving her answer some thought before parting with it. She looked about her suspiciously, then straightened her shoulders and turned back to them.

'Pleased to meet you, I'm sure, sir,' she said, taking Bay's outstretched hand and pumping it hard enough to make him wince. She looked at him steadily for a second or so longer than might have been necessary but then said nothing further. Robert, watching her face intently, saw a dull flush redden her neck and then her full cheeks.

'Shall we sit out here for a bit and talk,' he suggested briskly. 'Or would you prefer us to go into the house and have our chat there?'

Mrs Carey hesitated. The flush had now reached the pepper and salt hair on her forehead. She looked flustered without any intention of giving in to such weakness. 'Anywhere you say, sir,' she answered eventually. 'I can't stay long. Got me grandson's sandwiches to set up for the mornen'.'

'Then maybe we'd better leave the social part to another day and go inside right away.' Robert took her arm and ushered her in through the front door.

'Not worried about anything, are you?' he asked her in a low voice.

She shook her head. 'Nothen' I can't cope with.' She pursed her lips and walked beside him into the empty sitting room without looking to left or right.

'What was the matter when I introduced you to Mr Heritage? You looked very uncomfortable, I thought.'

'Just my imagination again, I dare say, sir. I seen 'im before, you see. I swear I seen 'im among those folks walken' about the lawns that time. 'E weren't dark then, though. I seem to think 'e wore some kind of little curly wig, if you get my meanen'. It were 'im though, I swear it.'

The other two joined them. The room was filled with the last of the evening sun, for Bay had opened the shutters and folded them back into their recesses in the

512

panelled walls. They stood awkwardly in the centre of the room, avoiding the hacked-out paving at their feet. Mrs Carey seemed suddenly to see it.

'What's that for, my goodness?' Her fingers fidgeted nervously at the little cameo brooch at her neck.

Bay answered quickly before the other had time to speak. 'I'm trying to get a few of the pavings up to check what's underneath, that's all.'

'Don't do it, sir. Leave well alone. There'm too much in this place needs leaven' alone.'

'There you are, Mrs Carey,' Frances said to her. 'There is so much that you know about Lavenham and yet you say that you've only been here that one time. How do you know that Mr Heritage should not disturb those pavings?'

The old woman took a deep breath and her voice shook a little. It was clear that she was extremely frightened. 'I don't know. Truly, I don't, Mrs Jenner, mam. All I know is that I saw those people like I'm see'en' you all now and this gentleman was with 'em. That's the same face, I know because 'e 'ad this kind of light all round 'im, just like this gentleman, only 'is light, it's sort of yellow. I know you think I'm mad, but that's all I can tell you. As fer the stones, it's not what you see but what you feel, if you get my meanen'. An' I just feel that those stones need to stay right where they are or it will be the worse for all of us.'

She was shivering now. Frances put her arm round the woman's shoulders comfortingly. 'It's all right, you know. You certainly aren't going mad. Mr Heritage has seen those same people and has described them in much the same way as you did.'

The old woman looked gratefully at Frances, comforted by the soothing words.

'Mrs Carey,' Robert said quietly. 'It's amazing that you think you recognized this gentleman. He is a direct descendant of the Baylesses who used to live here, and so it is not unlikely that an ancestor of his with a similar look about his features left some kind of imprint in the atmosphere of this place. I was very keen for you to come here this evening and am more than grateful that you've spared us the time, because I want to try a very quick little experiment. Would you be good enough to place your hands palm down on Mr Heritage's hands and keep them joined tightly together until I tell you to stop.'

She pressed her lips together in a thin line of disapproval, as though she had been asked to do something intimate with a stranger. Bay held out his hands without a word and after a moment she placed her own over them.

There was a moment of complete silence. Outside, the sun died into the trees and a warm evening hush enveloped the land.

'I know 'im. I thought I did. Now I do for sure. Lawrence. Oh, the fine young master. . . . Yes, I know ye, Master Lawrence Bayless.'

Bay snatched his hands away and backed up to the open window. The half-light slanted across his face, giving it a harsh intensity. Mrs Carey peered about her in a dazed fashion.

'Sorry, mam. I felt a little queer for a moment,' she said uncertainly to Frances. 'Like in a sort of dream. Now, what did you want me to do?'

She seemed quite unaware of what she had said a moment before. Robert and Frances looked at each other and then across at Bay, who was pressed against the casement window and still glowering at the woman like a stag at bay.

Robert sighed, shaking his head. 'We should not continue now, my dear, after all. Mr Heritage seems disturbed by our little experiment and I think that one morning might be a better time for all this. What do you think?'

Behind them, Bay slid down to the floor with a soft thump.

'Oh my, the poor gentleman's sick.' Mrs Carey went to him, with Frances and Robert on her heels. He was propped against the wall, eyes closed.

'Well, thank God he isn't in trauma, at any rate,'

Frances muttered, feeling his pulse and finding it beating fast but strongly. 'He is quite ill,' she said to the other woman. 'The war and this house have just about destroyed his health, one way and another. And I think you said something just now which gave him a great shock.'

The plump face had lost its earlier flush but she still looked worried. 'I'm sure I don't know what this is all about. It's quite beyond me — but I'd be willen' to swear that I seen this gentleman before — only then 'e was a bit different. 'E seems a nice good man here — but 'e wasn't that first time, oh no. 'E had somethen' real bad about 'im. Frightened the breath out of me, 'e did.'

'I think I'll take you back home now, Mrs Carey,' Robert said, putting his hand on her arm and turning her away from Bay. 'Mrs Jenner will look after Mr Heritage. It's not as serious as it looks. He had these turns. I'm very grateful to you for coming. You've been a great help.'

'Well I can't think how.' She sounded relieved and allowed herself to be guided towards the door. 'I'll not be sorry to go, though. There's such a bad odour about these rooms, ent there?'

'Oh, God. Did I do it again?' Then Bay remembered and his eyes darted round the empty room. 'Where are they? Wasn't your friend Robert here with that woman?'

'Yes, of course they were. You had one of your turns, that's all and did a real Victorian swoon.' She cuddled him against her, seeing the fear in him.

'Heberden,' he whispered. 'Lettie Heberden. That's who I saw.'

'Well, I've never heard that name before, but we'll ask Mrs Carey whether it means anything at all to her. She swears that she saw you too, as another chap, complete with periwig and aura. What a couple you are. She swears that you are Lawrence Bayless.'

The house settled.

It was coming to pass, just as it had been intended.

There was plenty of time. The greatest flowering of all was still a long way ahead. Now was the waiting time.

'Why are we in such a hurry?' Bay asked petulantly as they walked back up the lane in the early dusk. 'I wanted to see if I could get closer to it all, back there where the stone floor gets hot. Before you brought that woman in. . . . '

Frances tucked her arm into his, gave it an extra squeeze as he tried to draw away from her — and kept him walking.

'There was something far too immediate and too strong about your reaction to Mrs Carey,' she said, trying not to hurry but feeling the transmission of Lavenham's pull in every fibre of him. 'And about hers to you as well, but she can cope better because she is in much better health than you are. Rob has some fascinating theories about people who "see" things, as you and Mrs Carey have done. He has years of experiments to make yet, of course, but he is working on a thesis which he will put up to the Royal Medical Association, in about twelve months' time probably. I can't tell you about it as well as he can, but briefly, what it amounts to is the possibility of a certain part of the brain being capable of receiving images of the past which make the person's consciousness, though not the body, actually span time.'

He was still shivering even though the evening was warm. 'I don't understand.'

She laughed. 'No, I don't suppose you do. I'm none too clear about it myself, but Rob will explain it all when you are up to listening to such things. Meanwhile, will you stay at the cottage again? You are most welcome to stay as long as you wish.'

Her profile was close to beautiful in the soft dusk, the gentle face filled with the same dark glow, the same symmetry that mocked him from Violet Bayless's portrait. And yet they were not remotely alike, for this girl had red-gold lights in her dark hair and her eyes were the warm brown of roasting chestnuts, a little soulful at the moment as she tried to hide her determination to save him from himself.

516

'Dear, lovely Frances, how can I explain it to you? I belong to that old house back there. I feel that it contains my whole identity, that it is a blueprint of everything that went into the making of me. I know, I just know so strongly that I *must* immerse myself in Lavenham. It's part of the pattern of things — and it's what I came over here to do.'

Exasperated now, she said, 'That is simply because you know for a fact that your ancestors were there. It is not representative of you — Bay Heritage, American citizen. If you're searching for identity, I'd say that my cottage has far more identity for you if you *are* tied up with Lawrence Bayless, as Mrs Carey seems to think. The cottage was the home of his son, Charles Bayless, for many years, after all.'

'Well, there can be only the thinnest blood connection there, because I come from Violet Bayless and she was only a half-sister to Lawrence. The Boston Baylesses had all the Romany blood, didn't they? Jess's and Amy's blood in Violet. Dudie Smith's Bayless blood added a generation later. There's nothing of Lawrence in me, apart from Jess Bayless.'

They turned into the cottage entrance. As Frances opened the door into the hall the last of the sunset was filtering through the fruit trees at the end of the garden, washing everything in a faint coral light.

Robert returned, having taken Mrs Carey back to her home.

Bay got up and went out into the hall. They heard the ting of the phone receiver being lifted and then the quiet murmur of his voice. In a few moments he was back.

'Sorry,' he said to Frances. 'I've booked a call to my father. They say that there's a delay of four hours, but that's all to the good since he won't be so mad at being woken at six in the morning as he would have been in the middle of the night. I'll get them to tell me the cost afterwards and repay you, of course.'

They could get no sense out of him as to the sudden reason for the call. 'Wait and see,' was all he would say.

517

It was time for the news. While Frances and Robert sat and listened to the wireless, Bay wandered out into the garden to pace the length of the lawn as far as its well-tended herbaceous border at the far end. He knew that diary of Tom's almost by heart now. It was not necessary for him to go to it.

Dudie Smith had been carrying Charles Bayless's child when they sailed for Boston and her condition was mentioned several times in the diary.

What had happened to that child? Did she lose it, or was it the first of her five children to bear the name of Heritage? Even more important right now was the question of whether the child had survived and grown to adulthood, married . . . had its own issue.

If that child was Charles Bayless's, then Grandpappy Callum Heritage was really a Freeland Bayless with no Heritage blood in him at all — and so would he be, for the blood running in their veins was Charles's — and Charles was the son of Lawrence Bayless where the Bad Power came from.

Bay groaned and averted his eyes from the first of the bats swooping again over his head. Lavenham had marked him as surely as it had marked the others.

He returned to the living room and found Frances wheeling in a trolley on which she had put cold meats, pickles and fresh bread and butter.

'Supper time,' she said, 'Rationing makes catering quite hard sometimes but we've had long enough to think up fresh ways round the shortages and it's a challenge when you enjoy cooking, especially here in the country.' She gave Bay the full benefit of her warmest regard and wheeled the trolley in front of him. 'I know you can't taste it, but come and give your body a chance of building itself up and you'll just have to imagine how delicious this ham is that Mrs Carey has cured for us.'

'How about telling me more of this great breakthrough you are working on,' Bay said to Robert. He allowed Frances to give him a plate of lean pink ham and pickled cauliflower with a thick wedge of the excellent crusty bread.

Robert grinned at him over his own, well-loaded plate. 'So madam has been talking, has she?' he said, crinkling his eyes at Frances. 'I am working on the area of the brain that carries the sensory nerves which reflect and interpret what the eye sees and how the interpretation of that message is assessed. Look around you for a moment. See that mirror, this wall, the window over there? One reflects, one does not and one is completely transparent, agreed? It is the same with the molecular life going on around us. Some images are reflected by them, and some are not while others are seen right through something which appears to be finite — but in my opinion is not. I think that little area in your brain, containing certain molecular similarities to something over there at Lavenham, is acting as a reflector like that mirror over Frances' fireplace. In other words, the things which you are seeing are actual reflections of what has gone before. It is the same with Mrs Carey. I don't know how or why, but she must have a genetic connection with something in that place, too. We'll find that one out in good time, I expect.'

'But what about the Killing Glance? How is it possible for a human being to kill another by just looking at him?'

Robert sighed and shrugged. 'I wish I could tell you, Bay. I really do. You must have heard of such things in places like Haiti and Africa, and in China and India.'

'Yeah, I suppose it's the same thing that one hears about now and then amongst the old medicine men in our Indian tribes. I suppose you could say that the stopping of the heart by suggestion denotes a total control of the fundamental particles of life, the ability to break the electrical or cosmic current of another individual's life field. I'm afraid that's the best answer I can give on a subject which none of us knows enough about — yet.'

Frances returned with the coffee. 'It's one thing to discuss all this with Bay but how can it help him? That's surely what we are trying to do now, isn't it? I mean, look

519

at him, Rob. He's obviously low in health physically and the mental disorder was simply not there before he was shot in the head. Has his head wound upset that little area you were telling us about? I mean, where is it? His lesions are across the front of the cerebrum. I thought that part was tied up with touch and hearing and smell.'

'Agreed. Without examining Bay, I can't give a proper answer but the bits of metal removed from your skull were probably quite far in — am I right, Bay? It may be that an inner lesion is putting pressure on a specific area.'

'Maybe it's the fragment they had to leave in,' Bay suggested.

They stared at him.

'I had three operations, one here in England and two back home in the States. They removed everything but one tiny little piece which was lodged in a critical place, so they said. The options were fairly clear cut. Either they operated and removed it and there would be only a thirty per cent chance of my surviving the operation — or they could leave it where it was, and chance the possibility of personality change and various other unpleasant things.'

He closed his eyes and put his head back against the chair cushion. He looked so fragile and tired that one wrong word would snuff him out.

'As you see, that's exactly what did happen. I became an impossible person to live with, erratic and obsessional, and that's how I have been ever since I spent half an hour in that benighted house after my crash-landing. Was that all it took for those wandering molecules to fasten on to me? And why me, even then?'

'Because, maybe, they were molecular mirrors reflecting similar genes to your own and because you were in a low physical state. Because the damaged brain was sending frantic signals all over your body it was in a vulnerable state, open to invasion. I just don't know, old boy. It's no more than guesswork at this stage, isn't it?'

'Mrs Carey had no such brain damage, though.'

'No, you're quite right, but her extra sight is infinitely

narrower than yours. As far as I can make out, she is just seeing one particular scene, one set of people, one period of time. It's as though the genetic memory has opened up a tiny chink in her mind, offset by something we don't know about.'

'Well, why did she get that reaction to me?'

Robert smiled and looked pleased with himself. 'Ah, I wondered when we were coming to that. Getting you both to do that was purely experimental. The palms of the hands are slightly moist and are therefore a natural conductor. Her contact with you produced two instant reactions which were nearly identical and were an extraordinary kind of recognition. Do you remember? She called you Lawrence Bayless and you leapt away as though you'd been stung. Can you remember why?'

Bay nodded. 'Oh, yes, I sure can. She seemed to be speaking in the voice of Lettie Heberden. I have no idea how I know, but Lettie Heberden was the little servant girl that he killed, or maybe I killed when we went back to Lavenham last night.'

'Who do you mean by "he"?'

Bay opened his eyes wide. In the soft lamplight they glittered like pebbles washed by the sea. 'Lawrence Bayless. Who else?'

The chimes of the grandfather clock sliced through their silence with delicate crystal notes. Twelve strokes, Bay counted. Only another hour to wait. He took a long drink of coffee and pushed his cup across to Frances for more. 'According to the story handed down in the family, Lawrence and Violet both inherited Jess Bayless's Killing Glance, which seemed to die away during their twenties. Violet never used hers wrongly. Lawrence, on the other hand, seemed to have played around with his Gift from early childhood, and it produced quite a rift between him and his father. Then he is reputed to have killed Violet's first fiancé, Giles Croucher, in a fit of jealousy and, knowing that she would get her revenge, he ran away from home and became a pirate along with some old guy called

Benson. It sounds as though he continued to use his Power for gain until it faded, and then he was killed in a sea-fight, leaving a widow and small son in Portugal.'

'Ah, I know a bit about the story at this point,' Frances said. 'They came to live here, you see. The cottage was empty and when John Freeland wrote to tell Violet that Lawrence's son Charles had turned up here with his mother, she let them live in the cottage and apparently she paid for his schooling and quite a lot besides. I don't know what happened to him or to his descendants, but there are Baylesses, presumably of his line, in Petersfield and in London. They are quite apart from the gypsy Baylesses, of course.'

'Where are we, then?' Robert had been scribbling furiously on a scrap of paper. 'Let's see what I've got here. Jess Bayless at the top of the page, Violet and Lawrence come after him, yes?' The other two nodded agreement. 'Right then. Charles Bayless comes after Lawrence, and then we don't know what happens. Who comes after Violet?'

Bay patted the book on his knee, stroking the soft faded leather as though it were the back of a cat. 'She married Desmond Heritage of Boston and had several children, but Tom Heritage, who came over here as a prisoner of war, was her youngest son. It becomes kind of confused here, as both he and Charles were attached to Dudie Smith. She was a gypsy and a Bayless through her mother's line. Dudie was made pregnant by Charles, then went to America with Tom and married him.'

The telephone rang suddenly, cutting harshly across their concentration.

Frances and Robert sat quietly, letting Bay's voice filter through to them. 'Hello, that you, Father? — Yes, it's Bayless. I'm sorry for calling you at this hour but I get a bit confused with the time differences.'

His voice sank to a murmur . . . The seconds ticked by, then the phone clicked. It rang once, and he picked it up immediately. 'Yes, that's right. How much? Right, thanks.'

He came through the door and stood with his back to the empty fireplace, twisting the paper in his hands.

'Tom and Dudie Heritage had three sons and two daughters.' His voice was husky with tiredness. He opened the diary and scanned page after page until he came to one particular passage. 'Here it is. I knew I had seen it somewhere. It says ' . . . Dudie is four months gone with child now but there is little sign of her condition yet. All the same she did this day confess her state to Nat at last. . . . ' The rest doesn't matter but the date does. That was written in August 1802. That means that she would be due to give birth early in the New Year. Sometime during January 1803.'

They sat forward, waiting for him to tell them, knowing now what had been on his mind so intensely that he had had to know the details faster than the post could have brought a letter.

'Tom and Dudie's first child was Nathanial Charles Heritage, born on New Year's Day, 1803. It was a premature birth but the child lived. It looks as though your Mrs Carey was right, doesn't it?' His voice was filled with bitterness, his face the mask of an old man. 'I am descended from Lawrence and not from Violet.'

He sat down hard and his shoulders heaved. Robert gripped Frances as she moved to go to him.

'Bay, maybe that is the whole essence of this commitment of yours. It might not be a bad thing to wonder whether that poor misguided blighter might not be trying to put things right. Think about that, will you? I can't come over tomorrow but I'll see you on Sunday. Don't go sticking your neck out until then, eh? Let's see you settled for the night and then I'll be off. Work starts early tomorrow, Saturday or no Saturday.'

Bay was exhausted. The day had been a long one and the call to Midhurst with all its memories and associations caused the scar to throb across his temple like a hot knife. His father's voice had been sharp, not unfriendly but cool.

He had done as Bay had asked, however. What more could a son expect? There had been no enquiry about his return. There had been no regret that he was gone from them. There had been no real interest in Lavenham. Charles Bayless's son. Granpappy must have known that he was more Bayless than the rest of the family realized. Looking back at the old man's eccentricities, it came to Bay that the very knowledge of that kinship with Charles Bayless would explain his lifelong passion for Lavenham and his insistence on Bay's visit.

He allowed himself to be settled in the spare bedroom and even drank the chocolate drink Frances brought him. His taste-buds refused to acknowledge the flavour but the texture was smooth and rich and frothy.

He closed his eyes to examine the suggestion that Robert Crane had made. *Are you here somewhere, Lawrence, after all? Am I your instrument of atonement — or revenge?*

7

Bay sat on a pile of stones which had once been part of the sea wall protecting Birdham Marsh. He had gathered a little cairn of pebbles and was absentmindedly sending them skittering, one by one, across the surface of the water. The diary, as always, was open on his knee. He had slept dreamlessly, woken refreshed and breakfasted with Frances before returning, with little more than a mild token protest from her, to Lavenham. Apart from the debilitating weakness of mind and body which was always with him these days, he felt fitter than he had been for a long time.

The trouble was he knew so little of the performers in the play, beyond from those brief glimpses which the old house had given him and the contents of Tom Heritage's papers. Jess Bayless had made his fortune from night-running, married into the local gentry and established a good business in Chichester. Apart from that he knew nothing of the man, except that he had been possessed of the Killing Glance. Then there was Violet Bayless to be investigated further – and Lawrence in particular. The shock of discovering his descent from a man who had been cast as the villain in the family history was still in the front of his mind. And from Charles, too. Charles had been painted as being nearly as dangerous as his father – and yet, should not Tom Heritage have been the one to stand accused, for Charles had committed no crime, apart from falling in love outside his marriage. What had been given as the cause of death on Charles's death certificate, if Tom really had flamed him, as he had seen in his own visions.

And another thing – was it possible that he could in

some way control those flashbacks? He sensed all the time a kind of falling backwards, so that when he found himself in the role of unseen Watcher, he was witnessing something which happened slightly earlier than the time before. Then there was that odd name which kept floating at the back of his mind again and again.

Epona.

Every time he allowed himself to acknowledge it, he seemed to remember the moment of his plane crash and the sharply terrifying memory of that girl running towards him, arms outstretched, her hair on fire. Maybe she was Epona. No, somehow that did not seem to fit, any more than trying to put her into any of the periods he had witnessed so far.

With a sigh he stood up and left the serene waterscape. He followed an almost overgrown footpath through the wood, cutting away into the brush as he saw the outline of the house on his left. Everything was tinder-dry, crunching and crackling underfoot. He saw a movement and stood quite still and watched a snake slide through a shaft of sunlight, the glare dancing over the beautiful black markings on its beige skin.

His nerves recoiled. Snakes had been anathema to him since he was very young and found himself sharing his tree house with a large and — so he was eventually told — poisonous snake, which his father killed. The thing that was in him gave a fearful rolling lurch in the pit of his stomach and, even as he watched the graceful progress of this English native, the fear in him became charged as he took a step back from it. The great red flower blossomed in him. He tried to close his eyes but there was no response in his eye muscles. They were fixed upon that gleaming sliding body and he felt it burst from him — the terrible, thrilling ejaculation of death.

He saw the flash this time. It was as though the sun had gone behind a cloud and then burst from it for one instant before being blotted out by another — a second of intense radiating heat. The unhurried rustling in the dry grass

526

ceased. The snake, only visible by its movement, seemed to have gone but he knew it was over there on the woodland floor.

He waited for his heart to cease its pounding and picked up a long forked hazel branch. It was not necessary even to sweep away the undergrowth in his search. It lay beside the path. He prodded it lightly with his stick but it was dead. He left it where it was and returned to the house. Was there no way of controlling this curse? He had Flamed two creatures now, neither of which had done him any harm. How long would it be before he did the same to a human being? Darkness settled in him again. He was becoming an even greater menace, both to himself and everyone else, than he had been before he came to Lavenham.

The little Smith & Wesson Kit gun still nestled, wrapped in its green cloth, at the bottom of his camping bag. If this thing was going to take a hold of him so that he could not control it, he would put an end to himself.

He avoided the living room and sat quietly on the terrace with his enamel mug and a fresh bottle of Scotch.

That afternoon, he took the bicycle and rode into Chichester. Frances was working. Robert would not be around until later that evening. He opened a bank account with his money orders, so far untouched and bought himself some more Scotch. He was weary after his ride. Every muscle in his frail body seemed to ache and the red weal across his temple throbbed mercilessly.

There was something he wanted to do before the others came looking for him. He put the two new bottles of Scotch in the kitchen dresser and settled himself in a favoured corner of the terrace with a half-full bottle and his enamel mug. The sun was not yet at its zenith but beat down strongly on his head, making the air above the stone steps blurred with heat. Too hot for comfort. It was, he decided, no good just sitting and thinking. He took a long gulp at his drink and pushed himself up onto his feet, mug in hand.

The hall was cool and shadowed. Sunlight streamed in from the huge oriel window, cutting a delicate pattern of light and violet shade across the floor. He put the mug on one of the stairs and stood against the carved oak balusters, clearing his mind of the fuzziness wrought by the whisky. The reflection of the window seemed to billow on the floor. He closed his eyes. Jess Bayless . . . just consider Jess Bayless, he told himself. It made him a little dizzy concentrating so — not surprising, for he had put away over half a bottle of liquor in the last half-hour. All the same, there was an alarming feeling of falling so that he opened his eyes to steady himself.

The gentle daylight had vanished. The hall was quite dark, lit only by a tallow lamp.

His heart raced.

The great stone-faced hearth was bright with burning logs. He saw the soft gleam of flame reflected on skin, on the wave motion of back, on legs gripping lean buttocks.

Another coupling. Why must he always be the intruder upon the privacy of such moments? He felt the movement in his own loins reflecting the play before him. No, there must be no senseless Flaming this time, whatever the urges he could already feel thrusting for control in him. He dug his fingernails into the palms of his hands and forced the pain to hold the curling Power at bay.

He could not see enough of the figures to identify them but there was no gentleness in their joining, only a desperate, angry reaching out from both of them for something which he sensed was not theirs to take.

When it was done, the man relaxed within the woman's embrace and slept. He drew closer until he stood beside them, looking down at the two faces. They were very alike in many ways, dark and fine-featured, with pronounced cheek-bones and high-bridged, imperious noses. The woman had the makings of beauty in spite of eyebrows that were too pronounced, a mouth a mite too thin. Her right bare leg was stunted, the thigh muscle wasted so that there was a deep indentation all the way down to a badly

528

disfigured foot. She opened her eyes as he watched them and stared straight up at him with beautiful, black-lashed serenity.

Her eyes were cornflower blue and in their expression was total unguarded happiness. It was a look which he had never seen on anyone before and found now strangely moving. She was in the full flower of her youth and it was disturbing to see something lingeringly familiar about her face. As he glanced down at the ugly leg, which even now she was covering with her skirt, it came to him.

Amy.

But this was surely not the crazed and hideous crone that he had watched as she battered the old man again and again with a brass candlestick. How many years between those acts? Was this Jess, and their love-making the incestuous act from which Violet had sprung? The man, drowsing, turned in the girl's arms and the face in Frances' portrait was etched against the soft gleam of her bare breast. The dizziness was in him again. It was a very odd sensation, as though he were being whirled centrifugally. He knew that his eyes were open yet his sight seemed to be reflecting nothing but flashes and sliding colours.

He felt the knobbly top of the balustrade pressing in against his spine and leaned away from the staircase. The hall was empty again, cool and shadowed.

A new excitement filled him. Do it again and he would be certain. Jess . . . Jess Bayless . . . just go on thinking of Jess.

The dizziness enfolded him so that he groped behind him for support from the stair banister. His fingers closed round it, round the whirling flashes of rainbow lights.

He was standing on grass, grass which had been flattened by the passage of countless feet. All around him the earth had been dug in narrow deep trenches. Even as he looked about he could see men hard at work with spades and barrows. The woods had been cut back here so that the clearing would give a fine view of the channel when all the stumps had been hauled out of the earth and levelled off. He seemed to be in the centre of a building site.

Two men were standing close by, heads bent over a large plan which they held out between them. One of them turned to point towards a trench, and Bay drew in his breath, suddenly exultant. It was Jess Bayless, his young, hawkish handsomeness enhanced by the great grey eyes — his expression filled with a calm, almost dreaming pleasure.

The two men moved away then, towards one end of the site where the ground was uneven and pitted with embedded boulders. Bay, following behind, watched as they paused beside a moss-covered boulder of a lightish colour, which was so deeply embedded into the earth that little more than a couple of feet of it protruded from the protective soil. They appeared to be discussing it, for Jess squatted down as he spoke and gently stroked the mossy surface of the boulder. It was an odd gesture, Bay thought. It was almost as though the boulder were a loved thing. It was the kind of caress that Frances might give to Sandy as he sat at her feet. He leaned forward, and as he did so he felt himself drawing away. Then he was back in the hall, still gripping the upright pillar of the stair lintel.

Bay's heart thundered as though he had been running. He sat down on the bottom step and waited for it to ease. There was an uplifted feeling in him now, a thudding excitement as though he were on the verge of great things.

Just for once he had achieved something. He could project at will in roughly the direction he wanted. Maybe time and experience would make things more precise. As it was, he had done something which would surely excite Robert and Frances nearly as much as it had himself. Another thought struck him. He had also succeeded in keeping the Killing Glance under control. It came to him then that there had been no sign of it during that last flashback. The whole atmosphere of the building site had been one of lightness, happiness — freedom?

He returned to the terrace and sat on the broken balustrade with his glass replenished. As he poured out the tawny liquid and smelt the soothing fumes of it in the back of his nose, the thought passed through him that maybe he didn't need quite so much support from these bottles. Maybe he would have greater control over the projections if his mind was quite clear of alcohol.

He tilted the blue enamel mug and watched the golden stream spray out over the brambles below him and grinned, thinking of Frances. She had been most careful to avoid any mention of the way in which he knocked back his liquor but he had felt her anxiety. He was, after all, well experienced in sensing disapproval in those around him. A single drop hung on the lip of the upturned mug. He put it on the end of his tongue and savoured the warm burning sensation.

Clear head, Bayless, he told himself. Clear mind and no stimulants. Then we'll see.

He made for the living room, armed with a shovel and the chisel and mallet, for it had just occurred to him that what might be under the flagstones, if they hadn't removed it first, was the hefty old boulder. The sight of Jess's long, strong hand stroking the mossy contours with the tenderness of a lover had rung a warning bell somewhere inside his head. The flashbacks could certainly help him, but not Robert or Frances. What he needed most of all was good hard visible evidence for them to work from.

He squatted down beside the paving which had so far resisted his attempts to move it, forced the chisel into the crack which he had succeeded in making in the stone and began to hammer at it with all his strength.

'Yoo-hoo, anyone at home? Sorry I'm late.'

The daily comings and goings had already made quite broad tracks in the overgrown drive and now it was no problem getting to the kitchen door. It was closed, so Frances went round to see whether Bay was in his favourite position on the terrace relaxing in company with his Scotch and his thoughts.

There was no sign of him except for the empty bottle

and the inverted enamel mug beside it. She smiled at the sight of the mug. There was an air of finality about it, as if he had said 'no more now' — although that seemed most unlikely. She cocked an ear, hearing scraping sounds from inside the house, and went up the broken steps two at a time to investigate.

She found him in the living room. He was crouched in a hole in the middle of the room, and all that was visible of him was the top of his head. On the far side of the hole six stone slabs were neatly stacked against the fireplace. There was a sizable mound of dusty soil to one side, giving the room a sharply musty odour.

'So you managed to get the pavings up,' she said, squatting down on the edge of the pit. He gazed up at her vaguely, looking drawn and exhausted, and there was a blueness about his lips which worried her. He had taken off his shirt, and the thinness of his body was accentuated by the angular jutting of fleshless shoulder-bones. A graze on his cheek cast a livid slash down to the jawline, but there was in the pale grey eyes a feverish excitement which was infinitely more disturbing than his weariness.

'Look . . . I found it! I knew I would. I've just got to get it to stand upright now, that's all.'

She saw that he had been crouching over a half-buried boulder. It was large and pale in the dim shadow of the hole, emerging from the hard earth in which it was embedded like the tip of some monstrous monolith. It was caked with earth and, curious at the oddly smooth pallor of its surface, she put her hand down to touch it.

He knocked her away fiercely with his forearm. 'Don't do that! Don't touch it. Don't ever touch it. . . . '

She laughed her light little laugh, put out by the harshness in his voice and the sudden red glare in his eyes, but decided it was better not to cross him if he was in one of his moods.

'Sorry,' she said, standing up and moving back a little from the hole. 'It looks such a funny colour, like mottled marble, I just wondered how it felt. What is it?'

He didn't answer right away. He had been loosening the earth and then painstakingly scooping it up in his hands and throwing it over his shoulder on to the pavings. Beads of sweat had mixed with the dusty earth and streaked in dark lines down his temples to his neck. He scraped at the earth now, careful not to touch the stone as he brought more of it to light. He scooped up another handful and flung it upwards, away from her.

'Bay, how long have you been at this?' she asked.

He looked up then, and this time he seemed more aware of her. 'All day, I guess. What time is it now?'

'Well after six, you crazy thing. Come on, call it a day, won't you? Come and have a bath and something to eat. Then, if you feel like it, you can tell me why you look so excited.'

He rested his back against the side of the hole, his face tilted up towards the light. He looked oddly contented beneath his tiredness.

'Thanks, but I've got to get a bit deeper yet. I should be through before the light goes — as long as I don't get interrupted.'

'Oh, yes — I see. That's me again, isn't it? What a pest I am.'

He smiled at the teasing in her voice. There was the strangest sense of peace about him as though he were with someone he loved. It wasn't Frances. At any rate, she didn't think so. It seemed to be this one singular stone.

'You've never been that, ma'am. It's just that I'm convinced that what I'm unearthing here has a great deal to do with the whole Lavenham situation. I just feel it — the same way I feel that we must not touch it under any circumstances.'

He was so certain. It was a new experience, she realized, for one who had not been sure of anything for as long as it takes to destroy a man.

'All right. I understand. Well, I don't really, but I'll let you get on with things for now. But I'll be back after I've walked Sandy. I'm a nurse, Bay and it goes against the

533

grain to see someone doing such damage to themselves, do you understand that?'

'You know something?' Black brows, whitened with dry dust, lifted in the weary face. 'I reckon you're the most lovable, lovely person I've ever met in my whole life. One day I'm going to tell you that, see?' Then his head was down again and the chisel continued its careful gouging, everything else forgotten.

She left him in his hole, savouring the words which he had tossed out at her as though they had been a posy of flowers to catch and treasure. And it was all the more confusing to discover that she did treasure them.

The light was going. It was scarcely possible to see what he was doing now and he was so tired that he felt quite lightheaded. All the same, he was, at long last, getting somewhere.

In the dim light the stone seemed to glow in its own faint lucency. He paused and leant back against the earth wall of the pit. He would have to get a handbrush to the stone, to work the packed earth out of the cracks and indentations which pitted its otherwise smooth surface. Seen so close to, it was a most curious piece of stone. Here and there it gleamed milkily with an odd pinkish discoloration, rather like the strings and mottling found in some marbles. Maybe it *was* marble, he thought. The Romans brought plenty of it over with them, and there were presumably marble quarries in England also. Maybe this was part of a Roman effigy or pillar. It appeared to be of some length and there was definitely a cylindrical suggestion in its shape.

Something caught his eye and he peered closer. Packed with earth, which contrasted with the pale stone, were some letters. After working at the natural stone all day it was a shock to see that man had already been here before him. Bay scraped very gently with the blunt handle of the chisel at the dirty notching. A little crust of earth crumbled under the wooden scraper.

Underneath was a crudely cut heart carved between two

sets of initials. *W. T.* on the left side and *P. L.* on the right. Somehow they seemed horribly incongruous, rough lovers' carvings on something as sacred, as all-powerful as this ancient relic.

Epona, I serve. . . .

It drew him. He could feel the command registering in his brain, feel his arms lifting, hands open, fingers splayed. He placed them palms down against the sloping surface of the stone and froze in shock, limbs held rigid, unable to move any part of himself. The stone was red hot. It seared into his hands, up his arms, forcing the scream from lungs suddenly gaping for air. He seemed to be seeing things in slow motion, for before him the whole stone began to glow like alabaster lit from within, orange to pink to yellow to a creamy, white hot iridescence.

Someone was screaming, burning. . . . The whole place was falling about him, the light blinding now, every nerve shrilling in pure gouging agony. . . .

Hands were stroking his forehead. Cool, loving hands. Someone was trying to get a grip under his arms, to take him out of the place. The heat ebbed with the sound of a voice. He opened scorched eyelids and peered upward to where Frances was crouched on the edge of the hole as she struggled to lift him out of it.

He took his hands away from the stone and held them out to her mutely.

'It made me touch it. I had to touch it.'

Above Frances, a grey haze hid the sun. There was thunder in the air again. Maybe this time it would break and bring rain to clear the dust from the land.

She whistled to Sandy and when they reached the main road turned left towards the track leading to Lavenham. By the time she came round the side of the building once more she found that it was almost eight o'clock and the day was dying around her in a dull overcast. There would be no sunset tonight.

She had her foot on the lowest terrace step when the

scream made her freeze. It came again — a dreadful, agonizing bellow out of the open door of the house. She tore up the steps and inside the building.

'Bay, is that you? Bay!'

He was in the pit. She fell on her knees, shouting at him, but he went on screaming. He had both hands on the boulder, arms rigid as if to push it away from him.

'Bay, for God's sake, what's the matter?'

The pale blur of his face turned upwards to her. It was the face of a stranger, his agony contorting it into a lined grey gargoyle. His eyes were that horrifying pupil-less grey, the mouth drawn back in a rictus of pain. She shivered, feeling the alien violence in him. The room was cold, clammy as though an icy wind had just passed through.

'Oh my God! What have you done?' She stared in horror at his palms. There was little left of them, the raw hanging flesh mottled scarlet, white shafts of fingerbone protruding from the mess.

Somehow he had burned the tender inside flesh of his hands down to the very bone.

8

He sensed the presence of Frances and was comforted. Her face floated in and out of a kaleidoscope of confusing images and remained the only thing he recognized. It gradually became a very dear face. He absorbed every smallest detail, lingering over each one; the tiny mole under her right nostril, the way her eyes crinkled up into Chinese slits when she laughed. The suggestion of gold on the very tips of her eyelashes. The tenderness in her.

He did his best to respond and lifted his bandaged arms to hold on to her, to cling, limpet-like, a drowning man to a rock, for the other things he shared his confusion with only panicked him now. Amid the sliding images, he was unsure of what was reality and what was fantasy. There were frequent flashes now of a dark interior, a place without windows, and the dank odour of dried blood and rancid meat. There seemed to be something wrong with his legs, for when he tried to rise from where he lay, to distance himself from that anxious place, he found that his legs — his good strong baseball player's legs — were different, stunted misshapen things with a toeless deformity on one foot; and worse still, no foot at all apart from a hard knuckle on the other leg.

'Where are my feet?' he asked Frances desperately when next he found her in the mist.

The face smiled at him. There was no competent, starchy reply — she was not that sort of nurse. When she smiled she did it right from the heart.

'Right here, Bay dear. Two good feet on the ends of two good legs. Really — look.'

Seeing disbelief in his hollow eyes she turned back the

sheet on his bed and began to massage his feet. He felt her cool hands on straight legs, on two whole feet, counting every toe for him. He sighed and sank back into the dreaming state, knowing that it was all part of the nightmare and that he was truly whole. His feet were there and yet. . . .

'I think I'll phone the North Pallant surgery and ask Doctor Kennedy to come out and take another look at him,' Frances said to Robert. 'He's so weak, it's heart-breaking to watch his body striving and struggling with a mind which is sometimes here and other times there . . . wherever "there" is.'

Robert glanced at her keenly. There was a definite air of distraction about her this morning. Once again she had been up most of the night with Bay, which meant that she had had little sleep for almost a week now. Bay's injuries had been a severe shock, for it was impossible to accept that he had received such dreadful burns from a very old boulder which he had just excavated in the middle of the living room floor at Lavenham. But what other explanation was there? There had been no heat source in that pit of Bay's. He had not taken the paraffin lamp down there with him. There had been nothing in that pit apart from the boulder, a small pile of loose earth and the man himself. During his investigations at Lavenham, Robert found nothing very odd about the boulder. He climbed down into the pit, marvelling at the staying power of Bay's determination, for the stone must have been about five feet in depth and nearer six feet across. It was made of some unusual kind of pinky grey marble. The areas of its surface where the compressed earth had been removed had the smooth, polished look of extreme age, but the colour worried him for it reminded him of something he could not quite identify. He touched the stone gingerly with the tips of his finger tips. The stone was like silk under his touch. It was not hot as he had half-imagined it would be — but then it was not cold, either. He pressed his fingers

538

more firmly against the stone. Yes, he was right. It was very slightly warm, without a doubt. Almost like the feel of stone warmed by the sun — or the thigh of a body, newly dead. He shrugged that last thought away quickly. How strong was the power of suggestion. He'd be imagining that it *was* a body next. Somehow it seemed wise not to lay his hands over the stone as Bay had done, fingers spread. He stroked it very gently with the tips of his fingers, frowning at the unaccountable thrill it gave him to do so. There was nothing more to do or to see and he climbed out, dusting his trousers down, and left the ruined house.

It was not until he was on his way back to Chichester that it came to him. The stone reminded him in texture, colour and even marking of the placenta of an animal or even a huge human. The odd mottled effect of the pinky grey colour and the dark reddish threads of fossilized mineral deposits which covered parts of the surface in a fine tracery had all the resemblance of atrophied veins. Really, it was rather a hideous thing, whatever it was. More than that, he suddenly hated even the memory of it.

Bay made steady progress, although by normal standards it was painfully slow. A week after his accident his hands were beginning to improve and his waking periods of lucidity were longer. But the sliding away from reality continued and he was beginning to give Frances cause for fresh concern, for now and then he would try to talk to them in a tongue which neither she nor Robert could fathom out at all. She had handed over all her parochial duties to another of the nursing sisters and now devoted herself entirely to Bay, even abandoning her free time with Robert. He accepted the situation with apparent equanimity and contented himself with writing down in fine detail each small happening in the case of Bayless Heritage.

It was beginning to make very strange reading, he realized, but there was emerging a kind of rhythm which excited him intensely. He borrowed a desk dictaphone from the hospital and brought it out to Frances.

'Put this on the bedside table close to Bay,' he directed. 'If he starts to talk in that jumble of his, switch the thing on as quickly as you can and make sure that the microphone is turned towards him. I want to see whether he is just rambling incoherently or whether he is actually saying something in a tongue we don't recognize. Aaron Harlberg has agreed to check it for me.'

She understood at once and marvelled at his train of thought. Aaron Harlberg was an old friend of Robert's going back to university days, when Robert had been studying medicine, and Aaron anthropology. If anyone could help in that direction it was certainly Dr Aaron Harlberg.

Frances was in the kitchen, slicing runner beans from the garden and watching a phalanx of slate-grey cloud banking up on the horizon. There was something sulphurous and metallic about the harsh contours, she thought. They seemed solid and menacing, from the blue-black of their bases to the yellowish froth of their billowing heads. A storm of this magnitude would surely erupt into a good downpour, at least, when it came in from its stationary vigil out to sea. Whatever was in the offing was badly needed, and the parched and cracking earth would absorb a deluge in minutes, judging by the state of the paper-dry grass and wilting shrubberies.

The garden gate creaked and then clicked as someone had come through. She paused, paring knife halfway through a runner bean, and listened to the sound of approaching footsteps. Upstairs, Sandy, who had appointed himself Bay's personal guard dog and attendant, began to bark in shrill short bursts. She dropped the knife on to her chopping board and hastily opened the door lest Bay be disturbed.

Joan Carey stood in the porch, her weatherbeaten face startled, one dimpled hand raised into knuckles, ready to knock.

'That was quick,' she said. 'You must have been watch-en' out for me, mam.'

'Not me. I don't need to with Sandy around. He can hear a butterfly at a hundred paces. . . . Come on in, Mrs Carey. Nice of you to call.'

The old woman was deathly pale. There was no answering smile. Frances could feel her anxiety, and see it in the very way she held herself.

'I'm sorry to come 'ere like this, mam,' she said. 'When you didn't come to me on Friday I thought you must be sick or you'd have phoned me. But when you didn't call in on Monday either, I thought I'd better come round to you myself.'

'Oh my goodness, d'you know, I completely forgot! I do apologize. I've got a full-time patient at the moment right here at the cottage and I'm afraid that everything else has taken a back seat.' She pulled out a chair and fussed with embarrassment, making the woman sit and put down the handbag which she was clutching to her chest. If anything, Mrs Carey was looking even rounder than usual. There was a contained agitation about her which was out of character.

'It's so humid today, don't you agree? Do join me in a cup of tea or a cold drink, won't you?' Frances winced inwardly, hearing the coaxing tone in her voice. The woman seemed unmoved. She sat on the edge of the kitchen chair and gazed stonily at her. A grey lock of hair had escaped from the bun at the back of her head and clung damply to the side of her neck.

Oh dear, Frances thought, could this be trouble? 'I'll just pop upstairs and take a look at Mr Heritage first, while the kettle is on,' she said with as much cheer as she could muster. 'Now, I won't be a moment. Then we can settle down for a good long chat without interruption.'

She filled the kettle as she talked and put it on the hob. Behind her the woman said, 'You got the American here, then?' Her voice sounded as wooden as her expression.

'Yes. I'm afraid he had rather a nasty accident last week and burned himself very badly. He's improving now but it will be a while before he does any more excavating at

Lavenham.'

'I said for 'im to leave well alone, didn't I?' There was an odd satisfaction in her tone that made Frances turn round in surprise.

'Yes, you certainly did, Mrs Carey — and I only wish he had listened to you.'

'Get rid of 'im, mam. 'E's stirren' things up around 'ere. I can feel it, cain't you? Send 'im off afore it all starts reachen' out to us like in the old days.'

Frances patted the woman's broad shoulder comfortingly. Mrs Carey's flowered cotton dress, washed till the colours faded, was a tight fit. The corseted stomach heaved with evident emotion. 'Now, something's happened to you, hasn't it? Mr Heritage is quite all right, really. I'm sure he doesn't intend stirring anything up. Just wait and keep an eye on the kettle if you will, and I'll be down directly.'

She hurried away from the woman's fixed stare and went up to Bay's bedroom. He was sleeping quietly in the airless room, covered by a single sheet. Sandy sat up from the end of the bed as she appeared in the doorway. He wagged his small stump of a tail and grinned at her as though to say, 'All's well. Nothing to report.' She scratched the top of his woolly crown with loving fingers. He had become a real companion to Bay during this convalescence.

''E looks like the dead. 'Appen that's on the cards for 'im, anyway.' Frances had been regarding Bay's hollowed-out sleeping face and Mrs Carey's voice behind her cut harshly across the thought that every time she examined him he looked even more fragile than before.

She turned, frowning. 'I did ask you to stay downstairs, if you don't mind, Mrs Carey. This is a private sick-room. Please go down and I'll be with you in a few minutes.'

But the woman ignored her. She stared across the room at the figure in the bed and moved slowly to the end of the brass bedstead. Her breathing was like a wheezing bellows. 'I cain't sleep nights now. 'E's there in me 'ead all the time . . . staren' at me out of those dead fish eyes, wishen' me gone like he did poor Lettie.'

The sound of their voices must have filtered through to Bay, for he turned his head away from them and opened his eyes. For an instant they were unfocused, filled with the vague seeking that Frances had come to know as the onset of his return to consciousness.

When recognition came to him, the first thing he saw was Sandy sitting motionless at the bottom of the bed against his legs. The second was Mrs Carey. He reared up in the bed, waving his bandaged hands in front of him.

'Get her out . . . get her out . . . I don't want her here.'

His voice was hoarse and the fear in it so great that Frances leapt forward, took the woman by her great shoulders and spun her round, propelling her away from the bed with a force she didn't know she possessed.

'Come on now, see what you've done, Mrs Carey! It really is too bad of you. Just go down as I have asked and I will be with you by the time the kettle's boiled.'

The woman resisted for a moment and then allowed herself to be pushed through the doorway, but twisted round before Frances could pull the door to with her foot.

'I waited for ye over to the 'ouse every day this week. I'll still be waiten' fer ye when you're on yer feet again, just you see. You ent ruinen' my life no more, ye booger. I'll see ye in Hell first. . . . '

Frances gave her a push that thrust her into the upper hallway, away from the open door. She turned to grab the handle and pull the door to. Bay was sitting up, eyes staring in a horrified red glare. As she slammed the door between them she realized that the pupils were gone again.

'I don't know what all that was about, Mrs Carey, but I won't have it happening again, d'you understand? Come on, down we go.' And she thrust the woman's great bulk downwards in front of her, and across the hall into the sudden brightness of the kitchen. 'Now, what on earth were you up to?' she demanded as soon as they were through the door.

The woman glowered and said nothing for a moment. She was panting as though she had been running and looked like an enraged bull swaying beside the kitchen table, shaking her head from side to side as she searched for words which seemed to stick on her tongue. 'What's the use,' she muttered at last. 'I don't know how to explain these things but I'll tell ye one thing. You got 'im up there, all nice an' cosy, but 'e's the Devil himself, an' that's the truth. I'm tellen' you no word of a lie. I seen 'im over there in the big 'ouse. I seen 'im doen' things, terrible things. He's a killer, Mrs Jenner. You shouldn't 'arbour no killer an' you all unprotected an' not knowen' what I know.'

What a moment, Frances thought wearily, for Mrs Carey to be reaching her own mental crisis. This was obviously what was happening to the poor woman. She must just try to get through to her calmly and make sure that she left the cottage a little more comforted than when she came.

'I know what trouble you are having,' she said gently. 'I really do understand, you know. Try and tell me why you think that Mr Heritage is a killer.'

'I 'ad a word with me old auntie after goen' over to Lavenham that evenen'. . . . . Couldn't get the name Lettie Heberden out of my mind, you see, an' it was she told me about 'er. Said that Lettie used to work over at Lavenham as kitchen maid. She died, see? She was just dead in bed one mornen' — a good strong wench too, and they couldn't find no real reason fer 'er 'eart to fail like that. Well, not until they took a proper look. Then they found she was expecten', you see. Our line of the Heberdens come down from Lettie's sister, Annie, and me old auntie Gert had it quite clear that Lettie had told Annie that she was expecten' by the young master. I saw 'im, large as life, I did — Lawrence Bayless come back to life as your Mr Heritage. . . . '

'Now you *know* that it wasn't really Mr Bayless. It may have looked like him but you are talking about something which happened and someone who existed two hundred years ago! Try to remember that, Mrs Carey. We are halfway through the twentieth century today, not the eighteenth.'

Mrs Carey shook her head. 'We're liven' in bad times, mam. Bad times is all about us, mark my words. I'm not even certain of anythen' no more — except that I see what I see — and I reckon I know what it means, too.'

She turned and waddled away with a disconsolate droop to her bulging shoulders, up the path between the fragrant lavender, a strangely lonely figure, abandoned by reason.

Funny how strong lavender always smells just before a storm, Frances thought, with half an eye on the plump figure as she slammed the white gate behind her and plodded out of sight. She closed the kitchen door and, after some hesitation, locked it. For some reason the cottage seemed to be the centre of a state of siege, all of a sudden. She hurried back up the stairs to Bay.

He was sitting with his legs over the side of the bed, shoulders bowed so that his chin rested on his chest. He was wearing the trousers from one of her father's old pairs of pyjamas. His thick dark hair was dishevelled and stood up in schoolboy tufts. His long pointed face looked drawn and ill, like an aging leprechaun's. 'Has she gone?'

'Yes. I'm so sorry she disturbed you like that.' She sat down on the side of the bed. Sandy pressed between them. 'How are you feeling?'

He had not made any attempt to move from his bed until now, apart from assisted visits to the bathroom. He stared down at the long toes on his bony feet and wiggled them thoughtfully. 'Better, I suppose. Better right now, but God only knows how long for. I know that I'm sitting here, talking to you, feeling the scabs throbbing in my palms, feeling Sandy against my leg there. At least, I think I'm certain. I am doing all that, wouldn't you say?'

A terrible uncertainty lay upon him, revealing all too clearly the depth of his private suffering. Without thinking, she put her arms round him very gently and kissed his cheek.

'Yes, you certainly are doing all those things and you are very definitely right here with me. Would you not agree that this very forward behaviour from your nurse is real, too?'

He moved his mouth against hers. His bandaged arms went round her. She smelt of fresh flowers. The skin of her face was very smooth, cool . . . soft. The corners of her mouth turned upwards all the time. There was a cleft in the centre of her chin. Magnificently desirable.

His blood was stirring. . . .

She felt the whole of him flow into the contact of their mouths and was exalted. At last he was aware. And in the convergence of two seperate beings she recognized something quite unique between them. Her love for David had been part of the exuberance of very young adulthood; her feelings for Robert — steady affectionate comfort but never this great joyous bounding of the spirit.

'No.' His voice breathed into her mouth, against her cheek, his lips sliding along the soft curve of her jaw. 'No, this is definitely not real. I never have lovely tender dreams like this. Don't wake me up, will you?'

Sandy tired of the situation. He pushed a cold nose between them and began to lick Frances' neck. Laughing, she drew back and pushed the wet nose away. 'Hey, you jealous little beast. Who asked you to join in?'

Bay grinned. She had never seen delight on that pallid canvas before — only suffering. It created an entirely new person, someone she knew that she wanted above everything.

'My God,' he said with something like awe in his voice. 'What happened just then? I just can't seem to get my old ticker back down into my chest. I think it wants to leap out and give itself to you, ma'am. Will you accept it? It's all I have at the moment.'

He could not take her hands in his but put them wrapped in their neat bandages on either side of her face. 'Frances, I don't know how this is all going to end. I'm not sure of anything at all — except for one thing. You. You

546

are my enduring flame in all this. I've never met your kind of woman before. You've done nothing but give, in one way or another, since the first day we met. I've given you nothing but trouble in return and I can't see the future at all. Only the past. It's so unnatural.'

She leaned against him, willing him to feel the life surging strongly through her body, willing it to flow from her into him.

'You have given something to me, Bay.' It surprised her to realize the truth of it as she spoke. 'You gave me your trust right from the beginning — even if you didn't recognize it then. We have begun to build something good between us out of that, haven't we?'

'Is that what it is? Trust? From where I'm sitting, it feels like the worst fit of schoolboy passion a grown man ever had. If this is just plain old trust, I'd just hate to fall in love with you, ma'am.'

Down in the hall the telephone bell rang. 'Let it ring.' His arms tightened round her and his mouth was back, exploring the corners of hers. They ignored it for a few moments but the insistent ringing cut through their concentration.

She pulled away and stood up. 'I'd better see who it is,' she said. He watched her leave the room, an eager Sandy at her heels, listened to her footsteps hurrying down the stairs, to the distant sound of her voice. For once, every particle of himself was focused in complete gladness, upon the moment of her return. It was an extraordinary sensation.

He felt exhilarated, cleansed of all those other dark shiftings of his damaged mind. He lay back against his pillows and waited for her to return, at peace with himself and revelling in the sensation.

'That was Jenny Tregust, about one of my patients. It looks as though I'll have to nip over to Donnington for half an hour and see him. The poor old man is dying and has been asking for me for hours. I've looked after him for years now, and he used to be the gardener here. I'd want to feel that he is at peace at the end.'

She put her hands on either side of his face and kissed him very gently, a light lingering joining which still took the breath from them both again.

'I won't be long, I promise. Take great care of yourself for me. . . . '

The cottage became an empty cavern of waiting. Well, for God's sake, what did he imagine would happen when she returned, he asked himself savagely. The big seduction scene? Try getting things into perspective. She's determined that you are going to get well, even if it means giving whole chunks of herself to you as the main medicine. That is what is happening. Nothing more. She's a nurse, isn't she? She is no starry-eyed schoolgirl, dripping with love and pity for the wounded hero. That's real good — hero indeed! A man with so little hold on himself or his bodily functions that he can neither control his anger nor his desires. And that was all that this swooping sensation in his chest was — lust. Good old-fashioned male desire. He wanted that damned lovely girl with every fibre in his body. And how close the feeling was, this liquid longing, to that other feeling of pure sensual explosion which came over him when the Power burst out of him. That was all it was — bodily lust. But. . . .

He flung back the covers as anger flowed into his heightened state. God, he couldn't even have a normal male reaction to a female without that other thing homing in. He sat on the edge of the bed fighting the liquid excitement in his stomach.

There was a sound on the staircase. A board creaked.

'That you, Frances?' he called.

Silence. The Power crouched in his veins, spreading along his arms and up into his shoulders and neck. The sound came again. This time it was on the upstairs landing.

That woman. She must have come back after seeing Frances leave the cottage. She could see the Power in him, and recognized it for what it was. She must have come back as she had said she would, and both of them knew what her intention would be.

He let the great flower build up unchecked in his chest, in his head, and at the first sign of movement at the door he let it burst from him with all the nerve-screaming release of an unchecked Flaming. It exploded between them and the body fell.

There was no point in staying after that. He stepped over it with the red haze still in his eyes and the blood thundering in his ears, cushioning him against every sensation but his dream.

There was only that one reality, after all — Lavenham.

The sun had buried itself in towering stormclouds. The air quivered with heat. He made his way slowly down the stairs for there was a lightness in his movements which made each step a precarious balancing act. The eyes in the three portraits watched him go.

Mrs Carey walked slowly along the cart track across the Dell Quay road and down between Hempsteddle and its two neighbouring fields, Little Thirty and Lost Labour.

Far away below the horizon a faint mutter of thunder heralded the first weakening in the mighty cloud muster. The air was charged with dust and smelt of the bland aftermath of the thresher. On all sides the soil was shorn of its crops and lay, a golden crewcut, waiting for the plough in autumn. Crouched in the hedge as she passed, a fox stared out across the pale stubble, its amber eyes intent upon the bobbing passage of a family of rabbits along the river bank. Electricity in the air fluffed his coat out, giving him a portly, well-groomed look. He waited until the woman had passed him by and then began to creep along the hedge, crouching, intent on his prey.

I'll not see him, she was repeating to herself, I'll not go near him in Mrs Jenner's house but I'll smash his idol instead. That'll bring him out in all his true colours!

In her handbag was the bottle of Blessed Water from the convent. There had been no trouble in getting it, once she had explained that she needed it to ask for blessing on a godless house. His big chisel and mallet were still at the bottom of the hole in the living room, lying where they had been flung when he was digging. She would throw the Holy Water on to that graven thing in the pit and then set to with all her strength to smash it into a hundred pieces. That would show him. . . .

She passed through the entrance between the broken gateposts as the first drop of rain fell with a fat plop against her cheek.

The welcome was there for him, as it always was when he returned to Lavenham, even after a short walk. The heavy air was fragrant with the scent of roses and dried grass. Gulls screeched and swooped over the glassy waters of the Chichester Channel. His empty bottle of Scotch still lay on its side amongst the brambles at the edge of the terrace. His downturned blue enamel mug reminded him that he had not had a single strong drink for more than a week. Thank you for that too, my Frances, he thought.

Someone had closed the front door. He pushed it open with his shoulder and crossed the hall into the living room, leaving the oak door flung wide, for the place was musty and there was a suggestion of broken drains. He sniffed, wrinkling his nose as a strong gust of the rank odour swept across the room.

The hole seemed larger than when he had last seen it. True, he had been in no condition to assess its dimensions accurately, but he could have sworn that he had lifted three pavings one way and four the other. He stood on the edge of the hole and counted. It was still three by four and yet the circumference of the pit seemed to yawn hugely at him. In the centre, the boulder crouched like the half-bent finger of some fossilized giant. He stared at it, his skin suddenly creeping, for it seemed to him that the strangely mottled surface gleamed pinkly up at him from the shadowy floor of the hole. He looked at the thick, light wrappings on his hands and the new encrustations of scabbing seemed to contract, pulling at his raw fingers so that he cried out.

He squatted down on the rim of the hole with his throbbing hands hanging loosely on his knees.

Everything emanated from that boulder. In those lingering dreams where he was a stranger in an unknown place the stone had been there, always out of sight but somewhere near at hand, its presence acknowledged by some homing thing within himself. All the time he struggled with those images of himself dragging crippled legs over rocky ground, heard the jeers of creatures who fled from him in loathing, watched the girl who somehow belonged to him, yet was not his woman, go about her duties in the outer temple; during the passage of such dreams as those, he was aware all the time of that stone.

There was only one way to shake himself free of all this. If the stone really was the centre of his mania, he would have to destroy it.

A small sharp sound caught his attention and he lifted his head. Outside, the sky was the colour of mud. Great fat raindrops had begun to fall, slapping against the casements like a long salvo of small-arms fire. He realized that the distant discord of a storm at sea was at last turning in towards the land. That would drive out these digusting odours which hung about the place like the stink of a charnelhouse.

He sensed, rather than saw, movement behind him. Twisting as he squatted, he saw the woman as she gathered herself, arms thrust out to sweep him over the side of the pit, begin her swishing rush towards him. Her faded eyes glared, the nostrils of her bulbous nose were flared like a horse when steadying itself before leaping over a high fence. Her mouth was open, the lips drawn back in hatred.

The Power within unfurled like a striking snake before he had time to think, to try and control it. It exploded from him with all the bittersweet sensuality of its essence and she received the full force of it in her face.

He felt himself projected forwards by her weight, the monstrous breasts stifling his breath. He knew he was falling, that she was a dead weight on top of him. He thought he heard the first crash of thunder but it was probably the burning wall of the temple toppling down behind him as he swung inside, shouting for Arwyan to come to him . . .

The old man had been touchingly glad to see Frances. She sat by his bed and talked quietly to him, and watched his face slowly relax. He had been the gardener at Salterns Cottage for most of his life, certainly for all of hers, and had only retired when Parkinson's disease made working impossible. So she brought the flow of her daily life to him and, through it, he lived close to the garden and close to her. He had fallen asleep, deeply and very peacefully and, had it not been for Bay, she would have remained at his bedside until he slipped away. She permitted herself a moist-eyed remembrance of him as she drove back from Donnington. He had always been a secret ally for a lonely child. Such a dear old man.

A few large raindrops began to mix with the dust on the windscreen as she turned off the Manhood Road into the cottage drive. The sky was darkening by the minute . . . she ran for the front door and slammed it behind her as the first gust of wind hit the garden.

All the windows and doors had to be secured against what promised to be a deluge. Already the noise was deafening, the windows shivering from the onslaught of hail against the panes. Pink sheet-lightning suddenly split the overcast sky and she jumped, taken unawares by the blinding light.

'You all right up there, Bay?' she called on her way through to the kitchen. 'I'll be right up. Just battening down the hatches before we get swept away.'

A great roll of thunder exploded overhead, making conversation impossible. The whole cottage shook. If the truth were known, she didn't like thunder storms any more than Sandy did, but he would certainly be upstairs, cuddled as close to Bay for comfort as he could get. It was nice to feel the presence of Bay in the house so that both dog and mistress could go and curl up close to him until it passed.

She could see his curtains, sucked outward into the rain, slapping wetly from side to side. Oh Lord, it was coming in all over the carpet.

He was not in his bed.

She slammed the leaded window casements shut and locked them securely.

'Bay,' she called across to the bathroom. 'Are you all right in there?'

He was not in the bathroom, nor in the lavatory next door to it. She closed every window in each of the four bedrooms, while her mind raced through the possibilities. But really there was only one. He had gone back to Lavenham.

She returned to his room and was about to sit on the bed when she saw Sandy. He was lying on the floor between the bed and the wall. She might have thought that he was asleep but for the way his tongue hung from his open mouth in a rictus of snarling terror. She crouched down beside him, feeling for a heartbeat, anything at all that would contradict the evidence of her own eyes. But he was dead. His body was nearly cold.

Frances lifted him up and tried to cuddle him, but his limbs were stiffened and it was as though he wanted nothing more of her.

'Oh Sandy, Sandy.' She wept into his curly coat and knew that no vet would find anything other than heart failure in what was left of him. She carried him down the stairs and sat with him in her lap. Bay had Flamed him. It didn't matter whether he was responsible for those reflexes of his or not. He had Flamed Sandy. Sandy was dead. When there were no more tears to be shed, she rose and took the little body into the kitchen, wrapped it in a tablecloth and carried it out to the garden shed. The rain drenched them both so that her dress clung to her and the dark frizz of her hair was slicked against her scalp. She felt nothing, neither the chill of the rain nor fear of the lightning that lit her way.

She returned to the cottage then and picked up the telephone, hearing the warning in her father's long gone voice: 'Never use the phone during a thunderstorm. You might get a shock from it.'

She dialled the hospital number. 'Professor Crane, please. . . . He's gone over to Graylingwell? Oh thanks.'

She dialled the number. Her hand was shaking slightly and she steadied herself grimly. 'Unit four, please. . . . Yes, I'll hold.'

What *could* have been in Bay's mind? She was certain that he would never have knowingly hurt a hair on Sandy's head. It had upset him badly enough when he thought he had Flamed that little bat, after all. And now he had gone off into the storm. He had seemed so normal when she left him. There had even been a few moments when he showed her a Bayless Heritage that she wanted more of, much more.

' . . . Robert? Oh, thank God! I'm sorry to get you out like this but something terrible seems to have happened here while I was at Donnington. Sandy is dead, Rob, and Bay has disappeared. I think he must have Flamed my poor Sandy because there's not a mark on him.' The tears came as she spoke and left her gulping like a child into the receiver.

Robert's voice was sharp in her ear. 'Now, come on, lass, pull yourself together.'

She told him, 'I'll have to go and see whether he's at Lavenham, won't I? There's the most awful thunderstorm going on and I'm not sure what to do if I find him.'

'Look.' Robert's voice was barely audible through a series of heavy static crackles which made her glance fearfully at the instrument. 'Please don't leave the cottage. He's probably perfectly all right at Lavenham for a short while, whatever his state might be by now. I'm certain he would not have done anything to Sandy unless something made him feel threatened. I can't leave here for another half-hour, but I'll come straight out and we'll go and look for him together. And I'll dispatch Sandy for you tomorrow. All right?'

'All right.' She hung up.

But she took down the yellow wet-weather clothing of her sailing days and pulled it on, stuck her feet into woollen socks and then wellington boots, jammed a sou'wester down over her head and hunted in the telephone drawer for her weatherproof flashlight. She let herself out of the kitchen door into the deluge and dashed up the path and on to the mud-filled lane.

The wind whipped the rain into her face, blinding her. She struggled forward, seeing little but the deluge. Her progress was drenchingly slow. It took ten minutes to reach the entrance to Lavenham and another five to force her way through the battened-down undergrowth grown slimy under the unrelenting torrent.

A vivid blue flash halted her in her tracks, leaving an impression of violet purple and pink forked lightning on blinded eyeballs. In the second of its passing it had picked out the black mass of the house directly in front of her. She began to shiver violently and pressed forward towards the archway. It was impossible to see more than a foot or two ahead and she leant grimly against the driven rain, saturated to the skin now, in spite of her clothing. The pale beam of her flashlight found the edge of the left arch and suddenly the rain was a fraction less vicious. She groped for the back door handle.

The sudden quiet inside the building sent the blood pumping in her ears. Then her pulse settled and she stood in the dark passage with a widening pool of water spreading over the stone floor round her feet. She felt completely exhausted, as though she had been shaken in a drum till every muscle in her body rebelled.

'Bay,' she called out, needing to hear him in the sudden charged stillness around her. Outside the thick walls, wind devils tore at the oakwoods, lashing the dehydrated foliage, uprooting young saplings.

'Bay, are you there?' Her voice echoed back to her along the cold passage. She found she was shivering so violently that she could hear her own teeth chattering.

She went along the passage and into the black vacuum of the hall. There was an appalling stench. The storm must have stirred up all kinds of rubbish, for the smell of decay billowed round her, catching at the back of her throat so that she retched and covered her nose and mouth with her upturned collar.

'Bay . . . are you there, Bay?'

She was not quite so sure of herself now. The place felt utterly abandoned. It seemed almost to tremble with each fresh onslaught as crash after crash rattled the windows and shook the whole building. She moved forward into the living room. Another lightning flash momentarily showed her the hole in the floor. It was like a gaping pit filled with black nothing. She had the oddest feeling that if she fell into it she would go on falling forever.

She stood near the edge and aimed the flashlight beam into it. There was a body there. A great, spreadeagled body, covered in a pattern of garish flowers, flung now across the old boulder that Bay had been excavating. She gasped and crouched down so that she could see better.

The yellow beam of the torch picked out a pale thick-stockinged leg with a sensible lace-up shoe on the foot. A flowered blur of dress thrown to one side revealed a long expanse of peach celanese knicker, elasticated just above the knee. 'Mrs Carey. . . . '

Her head was twisted to one side, the hair flung across her face. Beneath her shoulder one white bandaged hand protruded. 'Oh, God help me!'

She climbed down into the pit without thinking then, digging her booted feet into the packed earth sides, hands scratching, searching for a firm grip on the stones round the lip. Somehow Mrs Carey's body seemed to fill every corner and her sliding feet met flesh wherever they tried to find a hold. She had to kick a leg out of the way, finding Bay's shoulder beneath that and digging desperately round it, before setting her weight down on the floor of the hole. She twisted her body round, dragging the weight of the woman's torso off him. He was curled up in the space beneath her body, where it straddled the boulder like a great starfish.

No movement in her. No pulse. There was on her bloated face a look of such frozen venom that Frances shuddered. The eyes were open, the mouth snarling, the teeth clenched. She averted her eyes, unable to look at such hatred in the moment of death.

She had to stand on Mrs Carey to reach the side of Bay's neck. There was a faint flutter beneath her fingertips and she dropped her head against his hair and wept in relief and the fullness of her fear.

9

He lay curled up with his eyes closed. His head ached so
badly that there was no point in opening them. He ached
all over. The throbbing in the left side of his head was like
a repeated hammer blow, relentlessly battering his temple.

It was some time before it slowly dawned on him that he
was not lying on sheets. His fingers opened and explored
– and found straw. His fingers . . . his hands were not
bandaged nor filled with the nerve-end torture of the past
week.

Shock made him open his eyes,

Darkness; but not total darkness, for light filtered
through an aperture some distance from where he was
lying.

'Good.' The voice was close to him. His eyes were
already accustoming themselves to the gloom of this place,
for he had been here before – in flashes, no more.

Someone crouched close to his feet. 'Take some food
now.'

It was a woman speaking and yet the voice had a
baritone timbre. Her bushy hair shone with fat. The faint
light from the entrance reflected the domed silhouette of
her head. He opened his mouth to refuse, but something
else came from him which meant nothing at first, then, on
reflection, he knew that it was an affirmative. His eyes
were weak and he closed them again, blotting out this new
visitation. Nothing was familiar as it had been in all those
other flashbacks. Then, he had always recognized something in his surroundings – the house, the land, even
some of the people, but here. . . . This time he must have
gone too far from his related presence.

'Here. Eat or you will be sick again.'

And now, for the first time, he could actually hear what they were saying. The shock made him open his eyes and sit up. She was beside him, an earthenware pot in her hands, holding it out to him. He did as she asked, marvelling in the wholeness of his hands. The concoction was hot, its fragrance herby and strong. He put it to his lips, tasted it and found it surprisingly pleasant, a kind of mint mixed with a thickener into a gruel. He drank it, savouring the bouquet before realizing that he had actually tasted a flavour. Texture had been his only criterion of food for so long that a return of taste was almost as great a shock as the unexpectedness of his whereabouts.

The woman watched him, squatting against a pile of hay. The gloom was easier to see through now and he returned her stare over the top of the beaker. She had flat Eskimo features but for a pronounced nose and she was wearing a short cloth tunic, caught round her waist with a leather thong. She was quite young, her breasts beneath the tunic still high and firm. There had been no child suckling yet. She had no sores about her face, her teeth seemed good and the strong smell of her was curiously enticing.

He finished the gruel and she took the pot from him. 'Where am I?' He whispered the question for it might be that he should not have asked it.

'With me,' she said. 'They came hunting you, for Ickka says it was you who desecrated Arwyan and now all the Wikken are after your blood. If the Council votes against you, it is the end. They will kill you.'

He smiled grimly. Nothing changed, even if you hid in another time, it seemed. What did the mystics call it? Karma . . . Fate?

'Why am I with you, then?'

She stroked his leg where the flesh knobbled away into a footless stump. 'You need me. You know we are both cast out, Finn, but I am not in fear of you. And I am woman. You need me.'

Frances, he thought, where are you? Don't talk of need when she is the one, not this ugly caricature of a woman, reeking of rancid head fat.

He closed his eyes again, willing himself back — away from this malodorous place. For a moment he thought that he had succeeded, for his head spun into catherine wheels of coloured sparks and a sudden pain in his temple shot across the inside of his skull — but she was still there, squatting beside him when he opened his eyes again. There was patience in her flat features. Patience edged with protectiveness.

'Listen,' he said, scowling up at her. 'I can manage on my own. I've lasted this long without a woman fawning round me. I can look after myself.'

He heaved himself out of the straw, intent now on getting away from this lair of hers before she made any stronger demands on him. The circular room had a narrow passage entrance no more than two feet wide. He had to hunch his shoulders to get through. At the entrance he glanced back at the woman. She still squatted beside the pile of straw, staring after him.

'Thanks,' he said, and swung his body out of the place on hands and forearms. God, what a way to move. But it seemed that he had always propelled himself thus for his arms and shoulders were massive and the swing of his torso from the waist effortless. He leaned against the outside of the little shelter, out of sight of the woman, and looked more closely at himself.

Both his legs were deformed, one with a great knob instead of a foot and the other with even less, for the lower leg was withered beneath the knee. What a digusting sight. He stared down at his hands, relieved that they at any rate were whole and strong. Burned hands were not part of this conception.

It must have been very early in a summer day for the sun was just beginning its climb up into a cloudless delphinium sky. A vast silence pressed about him, as though the whole world was somewhere else, broken now and then by distant birdsong. There was no sign of sea, no brine in the air. A pair of black and white oyster-catchers rose up screeching further along the small hilly ridge behind him. The woman's hut was cleverly concealed, he had to admit. It was built into the earth so that little more than its entrance was visible, the rest embedded into the bouldered side of rising ground. From outside there was little to see apart from the narrow entrance, itself camouflaged effectively behind a stand of bushes, their shiny dark green leaves a natural screen through which the light streamed downwards into the single circular room within.

She had said that she was cast out and that he was too. What did that imply? Oh, what in heaven's name had thrust him this far away from Lavenham so that he was forced to endure it for even a short time! Before, there had been brief images of this place only; he remembered them now as a distant recollection of childhood slides in the front of the mind. With this sudden thought came an awareness of violence and an ignorant fear far beyond anything that had happened to him within the walls of the old house.

Bay rubbed his eyes with his hands and, remembering the agony so recently endured, turned up his palms and examined the flat, strong, unblemished skin with the cushions hardened into thick callouses. No burns on these rough hands. No pain. No head pain, either. Inconceivable relief. He put his fingers up to his head and felt for the long scar. There was nothing but the growth of unaccustomed beard, unkempt and wiry along the jaw, and longer, finer hair from his head. He must look like the wild man of Borneo!

The thought made him smile. Would you regard me with your special blend of tenderness if you could see me like this, my Frances? Then another thought made him laugh outright, the sound winging away into the air and echoing back from the rocks. If I'm a caveman, by jiminy, what caveman ever had the kind of thoughts I'm able to indulge myself in? Maybe they haven't invented the wheel yet and I can get in there and do a good service for the whole of mankind!

'Be still.' The woman was beside him, fear stamped all over her face. She took him by the shoulders and twisted him round, thrusting him in front of her back into the shelter, down the slope of the passage. Without his legs he was vulnerable, he quickly discovered. He realized that where as he had thought her unusually tall, it was only because of his own foreshortened height. She was no taller than he but immensely strong. Her fingers dug hard into his shoulder-blades. Fear emanated from her.

He allowed her to push him ahead of her and then to shake off her grip when there was room to do so, She anticipated him this time and put a hand across his mouth, eyes flashing. A faint hissing sound came from her like a whispered growl. Her head moved and he realized that she was listening, and then he heard it, too. There was movement somewhere out there beyond the trees. They held their breaths and marked the approach of something which slid on padded feet down the slope above them and slightly to the right. She moved then, and he saw that in her hand she held a knife. She crouched close to him against the wall. He knew that he must not move, that he must keep his breathing shallow so that the air was not disturbed. The rattle of stones beneath careless feet stopped.

'Gonad . . . Gonad, come. It is only me. . . . '

The woman gave a great sigh then and the tension left her. She returned the knife to her belt, put her hand lightly over Bay's for a moment in warning and then darted up the passage to the entrance.

Bay moved quietly across the cavern, feeling his way back to the straw palliasse. There was no fire here, and yet she had brought him a hot drink and there was heat in the foul atmosphere of the place. It would be a relief to have a light, to be able to see. Something began to worry him for, sitting here in the heavy darkness, things began crowding into his mind. The girl in the temple . . . was she the

Arwyan that this one had spoken of?

His mind was filled with her then, memories flooding into his head like the turning pages of an old photo album. Dark hair, long to the waist, clear olive skin and such fine beauty in those innocent blind eyes. Long arms and hands that were not like this woman's Amazon hands but fine things grown for plucking at the music strings of her little lyre, the lyre he had made for her when they were still subject to Faed, their mother, and the tribe.

Their mother . . . she was his sister then, the girl called Arwyan. And why were they not with the tribe any more, for it seemed that the Wikken had done an awful lot of casting out.

He wondered whether this woman was his sister, also. She did not feel it. There had been something about the way she touched his leg. . . . He froze. She was returning, and as she entered the cavern light was released. He saw the fire then, on the far side. It was tamped well down with slabs of soil or peat, just a thin wisp of smoke rising from it.

'It was Kkye,' she told him. 'The women do not think that you desecrated Arwyan. Now they are thinking that she was taken by one of the Obbitii out of revenge for Ickka's victory over them last Luparia. They have gone to tell the Council what they think, for if it is so, then Arwyan must know this. But she tells only the tale of the visitation of the gods.'

For the first time he heard emotion in her voice. Relief for him was there in her eyes too, tempered with a softness he found uncomfortable. She was coarse of feature, hard-handed, and the fat which she must have combed constantly into her hair to produce such oily streaks was sharply repellent. All the same, the body of this other person which he was inhabiting regarded her with a certain different approval.

What a pair they were! He — crippled and ugly. She — just ugly, or was there something else about her that was not known? He grunted. 'It is only their word against

563

Arwyan's. It should have been clear to them in the first place that I would not rut with my own flesh.' Something occurred to him. 'Why are you cast out by the tribes?'

She straightened her back slowly. The low space made it impossible for her to stand up straight and her head, drooping, brushed the roof of the cavern. She looked away from him and fingered the knife in her belt. 'Why do you hurt me? Am I not caring for you? Have I not offered you a place by my hearth?'

There was anger in her, he saw, and the hurt was as though he had struck her. 'Look, I have no wish to give you pain,' he said carefully, trying to pick the right words. 'Why should I? You have given me sanctuary and I am well pleased. I have this thing in my head, though. Sometimes I remember and sometimes it is all wiped away and everything is strange to me. Just now, I am confused. You have told me that they cast me out because they think I desecrated Arwyan. Why did they cast you out? I want to know.'

She looked straight at him then. She lifted her head and there was about her a dignity which he found even sadder than her pain. 'You were cast out after failing your adult ordination because of your legs. You are crippled and therefore not a man . . . and I am barren — and therefore not a woman.'

He should have guessed. She was a mature young female and had no child or man. There were too many females in the clan now and the men could not find food for them all in the winter months. They had weeded out the weak and the unproductive. 'How long are you going to live out here on your own?' he asked. 'How long will they be angry with me before they decide I'm not guilty and let me go back to Arwyan?'

She shrugged. 'Does it matter? This is where I shall be always. It was my father's hut and his father's. I fought Ganna for this place and won it with honour. So why go back there to the temple? That little hole you made for yourself is too cramped for someone of your breadth. You need the space of this dwelling. Arwyan will drop her child soon. Then the Council will decide whether to let them live or to sacrifice them. What do you imagine you could possibly do for her?'

'Just be there. She is alone now that her women are gone. I have taken care of her ever since she was born. Why should I not go on caring for her now?'

She looked at him as though he had taken leave of his senses. 'Because she was chosen and took her vow to remain a stranger to man's needs — and now that vow is broken and she carries the sin inside her. It may be that it was done against her will as she says, but it may also have been done from her lust. Only the Council can decide. There is nothing that you can do any more. She is in no danger from man, for no one will approach her now. Not unless Epona directs it. The life cycle has to take its course. You know that. When Ickka and the Council see what Arwyan brings forth, then they will decide — if the women don't get to her first. Stay here, where you are safe. You are strong in all things apart from your legs. The Council may think what they will of you, but you have shown *me* how well you can hunt. You have no need of any of them.'

He was suddenly tired, weary with the things he knew and the things he did not know. It was impossible existing inside half a memory. 'Let me rest,' he said. 'I have things to think about. There is still a sickness in my head.'

She withdrew to the other end of the cavern without another word. He lay down on the pile of straw and closed his eyes.

I've got to get back, he thought, got to reach out to it . . . throw myself. . . . The dizziness crowded in, cutting across his concentration. He went down to the abyss, throwing himself forward into it.

Frances, Frances. . . .

Frances sat on the edge of the bed and put one of Bay's bound hands on her lap and slowly began to unwind the bandage. The burnt flesh was healing. The discharge was less and there were good clear patches of tender new tissue now which were beginning to scab. She took her time dressing the burns. She was rebinding the second hand when he began to tremble. At first she felt the lightest tremor in his wrist but then it spread until the bed shook with it. She gathered him close to her and held him against her chest.

'Don't go now, dearest Bay. . . . Fight it, for me as much as for you . . . Fight it.'

His eyes opened, grey sightless pools searching, searching. They stared, unfocussed, over her shoulder, and then he sighed deeply and seemed to settle into a light sleep. She held on to him, brushing his temple with her lips, feeling the light caress of his breath in her hair.

'Frances . . . '

It was so soft a whisper that she would not have heard it had he not been gathered up in her arms. She laid him back against his pillows and stroked the hair out of his eyes. They were focused now and she smiled at him. 'Welcome back.'

He crinkled his eyes at her.

He was so weak that this seemed to be the sum total of conversation just then. She remained where she was with her arm round his shoulders, his head half on the pillow, half-cradled against her arm.

Later he seemed to find more energy. 'I didn't think I would be able to get back that time. So tired . . . Where's Rob?'

That surprised her. 'He'll be here some time this evening after a lecture he's giving at Arundel. Do you feel like taking some food? You've been out for the count for over twenty-four hours, you know.'

He grunted. 'Every time I open my eyes, there's some damnfool woman trying to spoonfeed me. Can't seem to hide from the mother instinct any place.'

She let it go, for at least this showed a spark of the old crotchety Bay, which was encouraging. She simply held on to him and willed her own health and strength into his frail body. He drowsed and her position became cramped, but then he woke again and this time seemed brighter, so that she was able to move. She stood up, stretching her cramped limbs.

'How long have you been cuddling me like that?' The grey eyes watched her drowsily.

'I wasn't cuddling you, just wishing some energy into you.'

'You were cuddling me. I feel good and cuddled, so you must have been. Come back and do it some more. It's real good medicine.'

'You just lie there and get your strength back,' she said, mock-sternly. 'Then you can think about cuddling later on, when you're better able to respond to it.'

He closed his eyes and the suggestion of a smile turned the corners of his mouth up. He seemed to be at peace. 'When is Robert coming?' he said again in a little while.

'In about two hours.' She had managed to get him to drink hot sweet tea and had given him an injection. He was relaxed and sleepy but fully aware of his surroundings. 'Why all this need for Rob, all of a sudden?'

'I have to tell him where I've been. It was so strange. I went way over the horizon. . . . Never thought I'd be able to get back. Frances, how do I stay here? That other place is awful.' There was fear suddenly in his voice and he held up his bandaged hand to her. She had been tidying his bed and sat on the side, drawing him close again. He had become so thin. She was able to get her arm right round him.

'Would you like to tell me, in case you are asleep when he comes?' They regarded each other, knowing what she meant. He might have slipped away again by the time Robert came.

'I should tell him in my own way.' He was distracted now and she remembered the tape recorder. One tape had already gone to Aaron Harlberg to be analysed but there were several spare tapes with the machine. She took it out of the bedside table drawer, slipped a new spool into place, threaded the tape through the recording gate on to the second spool and stood it where he could see it.

'There we are. This tape recorder will be just the answer. Robert left it so that I could record the things you were saying while you were in coma. You seem to have discovered a new language and Rob felt that it might even be identified by a friend of his. Would you like to tell me what you have for him; you can repeat it when he comes but it'll still be there just in case.'

Bay closed his eyes. 'I love you, Frances. Did you know that? I really love you.'

She smiled down at the dreaming face. 'I think I was beginning to get the message yesterday.'

As she said it, she regretted the slip, for slowly awareness washed through him and his eyes flew open again, this time filled with sudden tragic memory. 'Oh God . . . did I dream that? What happened to Mrs Carey? Have you seen her, Frances?'

In his agitation he pushed himself up in the bed, prodding at her with his bandaged hands. She flicked the 'on' switch of the tape recorder.

'It's all right, don't get het up about it. I don't know what you remember, but Mrs Carey had an accident. Get yourself feeling better and then we'll go over it — but not now, please.'

But he was remembering even as she tried to defuse his agitation. 'For God's sake, don't treat me like a child. I had forgotten all about her — but she was there, in the house. I went back to Lavenham when you left me. I was lonesome, I reckon, wanted the company — I don't recall why I went. I remember sitting on the edge of the pit and thinking that the stone seemed to be cleaner than it had been before. It was the most beautiful mottled coral colour, like a slab of marble but of a shade I've never seen anywhere. I found I could see markings on the underside where I had last been removing earth. I was just thinking that as soon as my hands were better, I'd clear those markings, then something made me turn . . . and there was that crazy woman rushing through the door with her hands out in front of her. I Flamed her, Frances. I didn't mean to. It just happened as a sort of self-defence, I suppose. She must have hit me as I did it, for we both went over the side together. I don't remember anything after that until I came round in the hut.'

This was better, she thought. Get him on to the subject of his dream. Keep him away from Mrs Carey. He obviously had no memory at all of Flaming Sandy.

'What happened in the hut, Bay?'

He screwed up his face, trying to get the picture right. 'I was lying on straw. The woman, Gonad, came and gave me some gruel stuff. I was in some kind of cave. She was a pretty basic kinda female, not like you . . . hair glued down with fat that smelled like a hooker's armpit, a flat, crude face, square body. Strong as a bullock. I'd been ostracized by the tribe or something because I had crippled legs and feet and they thought I'd had my wicked way with their temple priestess. I know I was hereabouts, don't know why — but I was. The priestess is a strong feature. . . . I haven't seen her but she is strong in my mind.'

'Did you see the stone?' Her voice seemed to arrest his thoughts for he looked up at her, searching his mind, puzzled.

'The stone? No, nothing like it. Maybe it's with the tribe. I haven't seen them either, or Arwyan for that matter. I seem to have been Arwyan's personal guard. She's my sister, I think . . . yes, we are from the same mother. But God knows how all this fits in, Frances — or what the hell I'm doing there. Maybe this is just the rambling of a loony who's destined to watch over the sins of his ancestors for the rest of his life — and you're a wonderful girl going along with my delusions because you're the kindest, most patient woman who's ever happened to me.'

'Go on.'

But his eyes were wandering about the room again, back to their restless searching . . . unfocused. There was a long silence. He seemed to sleep. The light breeze which had followed the storm, flapped and fidgeted with the flowered curtains.

By the time Robert arrived, bursting with his news from Aaron, he had sunk back into his state of suspension. Robert examined him, shaking his head at the faint, erratic heartbeat and Bay's yellowing colour.

'He'll have to be admitted,' he said to Frances. 'He's beginning to look pretty dodgy, don't you agree?'

She nodded, biting her lip. She was nearly as washed out as Bay and he put an arm round her gently. 'You've done so much beyond the call of duty, Fran,' he said, knowing that she felt she had failed in some way, that if she had not gone off to see the old man at Donnington, Sandy and Mrs Carey might well have been alive.

'It was hardly duty.' She extricated herself gently from the arm. 'He's become quite special, I suppose. We don't really know the man at all, do we — and yet he and I seemed to be fighting his battle side by side. I suppose it makes me feel that I'm necessary to him at the moment. A nice feeling. I haven't been so necessary to anyone for a long time.'

Robert shook his head at her. Now was not the time to tell her just how necessary she was to him, too, for she didn't even see him. Her whole being was concentrated on Bay Heritage, with a woman's absolute determination to drag him back from whatever fate he had fashioned for himself. Poor bugger — but what a fascinating and unique subject he was for research.

'Just you keep him on ice until I get down to Chichester,' Aaron had said over the telephone that morning. 'I find it unbelievable that this fellow didn't know what he was saying and that the tape you sent me is not some sort of hoax on his part. You tell me he can hardly get his own language together, let alone play tricks with dead languages. Well, I'm sorry, old friend, but it's really a bit of a tall order to swallow. I'll just have to see this man for myself. From what I have been able to extract from the tape, it looks very much as though your patient is astonishingly fluent in a tongue which must have been spoken around the period that Slavo-Baltic tribes swept into southern Britain, before the waters of the North Sea and the Atlantic Ocean came together and cut Britain off from the rest of the European Continent. That language later became known as Celtic; but his version sounds a great deal earlier than that and contains a word here and there suggestive of the Aunjetitz culture. . . . '

'You just keep this fellow alive long enough for us to help him out of this state he's in, my dear,' Rob said now to Frances. 'That should show you how necessary you are to at least two of us.' He told her then how vital Bay had become to his studies and how much the tape had excited Aaron.

The ambulance from St Richard's came for Bay later in the afternoon.

10

Bay crawled out of the dwelling with greater speed than he had thought possible. Gonad was nowhere to be seen and this was as good a time as any to make himself scarce. He certainly didn't want to find himself committed to her in a moment of weakness. He reckoned she might well be stronger than he was in a fight, especially when she was wearing that openly lustful look that he'd veered away from recently. He hitched his soft leather tunic out of the way of his knees and swung off into the trees with the rolling gait of hands and body which was becoming familiar to him. He discovered a well-defined track which led right through the woods, skirting Ickka's dwelling and the long Council chamber and coming out on the far side of the temple beside the bank of a shallow stream. In a slight dip, where hazel and hornbeam entwined their branches overhead and the floor of the wood was lined with rich spongy moss, he rested, aware of a gradual withdrawal from that other time.

He sat on the ground, back against a tree, legs splayed out in front of him. They were still a shock to see — withered and misshapen below the knee, although the thigh muscles were well-developed and the rest of him was far stronger and more sinuous than he had been as Bay Heritage. He stretched out his arms and surveyed the tendons and biceps which rippled impressively as he moved. His chest and shoulders were broader too. Pity one couldn't do a swap and take the top half of Finn and the lower half of Bay and put them together.

Frances and Lavenham were becoming unreal. That was the greatest worry of all now. He reached for them wildly, drawing them out of a memory which was trying to erase them.

'Hey,' he said aloud, cuffing the side of his head. 'Don't you go getting any ideas about keeping me in this place, even with the body of Superman.' But even as he spoke it came to him that soon he would simply not have the strength to project himself back. It was not that he lacked physical power now. He knew, as Gonad obviously did, that apart from his withered legs he was as strong and as single-minded as any of the hunters in the tribe. With normal legs and feet he would have been strong enough to have challenged and ousted Ickka, to have taken his place as Headman, and none would have dared raise their spear to him. But now it seemed that he was losing the enormous inner power which was necessary to project.

Frances. He repeated the name over and over again, for it belonged so far away, and with the utterance came the image of her, the tall modish figure, clad in the simple cotton shift she seemed to wear all the time, small-breasted, small-hipped. With it came the imprint of her face with its puckish grin and the sensual cleft in the chin — and the look of melting tenderness which had lately been in her eyes when he dared to look. Lingering over the imprint of her, he stroked the supple leather of his tunic. It must be goatskin, beaten with a rounded stone for a long time after tanning, for it had the softness of quality, similar to the leathers worn by the headmen and the merchants from the blue lands across the water.

Cursing, he beat the ground with a balled fist, for there it was, happening again. This wild half-animal dream was insinuating itself across the whole of his mind, flooding him with memory pictures far sharper than the soft images of Lavenham, of Frances — even of Boston and the gentle, cunning, monkey face of Granpappy. . . .

Arwyan had made the tunic for him. She had made other things, too. In his hut was the shift of bleached linen that she had woven for him to wear on sacred days. He hated that little hovel, for it represented all that had become wretched in his existence since the men cast him out when he came to manhood.

In the year that his seedsack dropped he attended the Ceremony of Manhood up in the great hill temple of Trundl. In spite of Ickka's scepticism, he passed the first initiation ahead of all the other youths from the area, as Faed had promised Ickka he would — but then the Priest had drawn him out from the group and made him do things at which he failed. He could not run with a bolas, nor any hand weapon. He could not hunt the boar in the manner of the tribes. He was foremost in ejaculation when they tested him and proved his ability to mate, but that also was taken against him — for with such a tool and with such ability, would he not make imperfect children on all the women he covered?

Sentence was passed and his father sent him out into the forests, away from the Wikken, the people with whom he had so far shared his life. And there was no pity, for suddenly they all despised him and the girls were thrashed if they so much as looked at him. He dug out a shelter in the shadow of the temple and lived as close to Arwyan as he was permitted. She would never regard him with contempt for she could not see him. There was a closeness between them, the unity of a pain shared. She too had been singled out for segregation, although in her case the reasons were different and, as priestess of Epona's temple, she had always, since childhood, been deeply revered.

There had, of course, been times when she needed his protection, for although the temple was sacred, its outer chamber was a sanctuary for worshippers and travellers and it was not customary for callers to be turned away.

There was the time a stranger came to worship from further along the coast. This was Epona's only temple in the south. There was the large temple at Weoger, but that was many day's travel beyond the downland hills. The man came to pray for the gift of a strong horse to take him north to the land of the Coedl. He prayed for three days and took much refreshment from Arwyan and the two old women who served her. He did not see Finn in all that time, but followed Arwyan with his eyes in the way that Finn knew was bad.

He finally gathered his cloak and staff about him as though to take his leave, bowing low to her with his forehead against the ground, and then he rose and took her by the wrist and she, who had no sight, was frightened by the strange hand on her. Finn was there, watching unseen from the shadows.

The man, slathering now, unhooked his tunic and Finn saw that he was swollen. He took hold of her robe and jerked it aside, pushing her down to the ground. Finn rested his withered stumps against the base of one of the three pillars of the temple and threw his knife for, even in touching Arwyan's wrist, the man was committing the sin of desecration. The knife was slimmer than the usual knives men carried in their belts. He had given a merchant from the blue lands the hides of seven hogs for it and prized it above all other possessions. The knife flew from his hand, sent with that particular flick of the wrist that had become his personal style. The blade, honed to an infinite sharpness, caught the man in the neck, a little higher than Finn had aimed but still slicing in across the throat, severing the main neck muscles and artery.

The man fell away from Arwyan before he had even forced himself into her and Finn swung across from his pillar, emitting the little whistling call between his teeth that showed her he was with her. He patted her arm, seeing the terror on her innocent face. She had not uttered a sound throughout the ordeal. She sat up, her whole body shivering under Finn's soothing hand.

'It is safe,' he said. 'Go quickly and offer up to Epona and tell her that the danger is past — and get the women to cleanse the floor of the creature's body spill. I will do the rest.' He dragged the man out of the temple and into the grass. The traveller did not die for a long time but bled into the ground, and when there was no more blood to come from him and he grew stiff, Finn took the body from

Epona's sanctuary and dismembered it. The pieces were bones now, picked clean by the great birds of the upper air.

Ickka was pleased with him that day. Their priestess had been defended before Epona. Finn would therefore be permitted to remain in the vicinity of the temple without hindrance.

One of the old women attendants died soon after that. Her time had come, for she was older than Ickka, but the people watched in concern because there must not be three deaths at the temple in any one season. One more death would mean that Epona was angry and desired new faces in her sanctuary. Finn hung about the outer temple, anxious for Arwyan, seeing the wary faces of the tribe as they came to offer to Epona, averting their eyes from him when he grew careless and slid into their sight.

They would not harm him within the sacred precinct, whatever they thought of his appearance. He had the feeling that they were even beginning to bear him a grudging respect, and so they might not harm him if he were to go to the village. Also, it must suit them that there was a protector for their priestess, especially as he came from the same loins as Arwyan herself.

There had been two hands of boys and girls from Faed and Loc. Three had died as infants and Finn and Arwyan had been different. The others were all whole. Better, he thought, that we had died at birth, she and I, rather than coming to the fullness of our maturity, as rich in zest for spreading our seed as any — and always to be denied natural release.

'Well, there's always that Gonad,' Bay Heritage said slyly to Finn. 'She's hot enough to keep you busy with all this seed-sowing for as long as it takes.'

Frances . . . that is where I want to plant my garden. But, after all, maybe she is only the image of an eccentric mind — even in this faraway place. Am I the first Prophet? Then where is God? He continued along the path, swinging from side to side on calloused hands. A small brown pig started up and ran into the thicket in front of him. Something slithered down a tree trunk to disappear into the leafy undergrowth. There had been a flash of brillant green, marked with black.

What was so interesting to Bay was the onward flow of his thought patterns in such a random fashion, for this was the way he would best learn the body he was inhabiting. The big question was, why was he inhabiting the particular body of Finn? Why was Bayless Heritage, born in 1922, presently exchanging the sufferings of his own period for other sufferings in a period he could not identify? Robert Crane might have guessed where he was, and probably this buddy of his would know all about the language. Right now, he decided, seeing the sparkle of water in the silver daylight beyond the trees, right now he could only pray for solitude and the chance to investigate his situation without attracting attention. The sun was high in the heavens, beating down on his head with almost tropical intensity as he left the trees. The ground stretched out before him, undulating gently like the back of a snake, the skyline broken here and there by small copses of stunted trees driven backwards in a crazy drunkenness by the strength of winter gales. In the milky distance the sea gleamed like a pale blue cloud, melding in lilac softness with a dark horizon.

The temple stood close to the banks of a small stream on a slight rise. Built of wood with a simple woven beehive roof, it seemed to rear up at him from luxuriantly green long grass. A pair of white hobbled goats grazed close to its timber walls. They raised narrow heads crowned with long curling horns as he came into view, regarding him with cold topez eyes.

He sat down in the long grass, hidden from the path, so that he could assess this strange place. It was not Bay's idea of a temple, even if it might be Finn's for, to his critical eye — which had expected an edifice fashioned on the majestic lines of Greece or Mesopotamia — the little building was a disappointment. Where he had looked for marble and soaring entrance pillars, a dome at the very least and possibly the dignity of a wide flight of steps, all that he found was a modest wooden building with block stone foundations and the oddly folksy roof which not only stole its dignity but gave it the comical appearance of a straw hat. True, the roof did soar upwards sharply so that one might pretend it resembled the helmet of an ancient warrior from the solid, tree-trunk vertical walls — and the area within would probably be suitably spacious — but from where he was sitting the windowless building looked more like a grain store than a temple. Nothing in its architecture helped him to date it — not that he knew anything of architectural history, in any case. He knew he must remember the details, whatever else slipped away, to help Robert with his research.

His head throbbed and he closed his eyes to relieve them of the stark sunlight. Interesting, he thought — his pain was along the old scarline of his head wound . . . but this head had not yet sustained such injury. It quickly passed. Just a few sharp stabs as though to remind him that he was still two people.

He opened his eyes. Coming out of the trees along the temple path were three old men. He crouched low in the tall grasses and prayed that he could not be seen.

Frances was trying to convince herself that Bay was in the best place now, where all the benefits of medical science were available to help him. Rob was there, and Aaran Harlberg had arrived that afternoon and was sitting intently by Bay's bed, his gentle, beak-nosed face frowning with concentration over every word Bay muttered. He had driven down from Cambridge that morning, armed with the tape of Bay's unconscious utterances and a heavily sceptical bias. He had been there when Bay murmured a few short words, again and again. They had meant nothing at all to the medical staff, but understanding them was enough to turn Aaran's scepticism towards belief.

'The old men,' Bay had said. 'The old men bring

judgement.'

The dialect was strange, the words Indo-European. There was absolutely no doubt that the subject was deeply unconscious, that he was aware of nothing.

Telephone calls were booked to Bay's father in Boston, to tell him of Bay's declining condition — and to discover whether he had ever studied anthropology.

Frances was finally sure — as Robert was — that Bay must be away in his brain cells somewhere experiencing the echoes of his own genes.

It might be the most exciting development in Robert's research, but to her only one thing mattered now. Whatever was happening to Bay was not intended to happen to the human brain, and such strain could surely not be endured. Somehow he must be brought back to the reality of his own time — and not permitted to slide away again. What did it really matter whether Lavenham was possessed or not? Whether there really was even any such state as 'possession'? The house had done no harm to anyone for generations. It would gradually crumble away, as all things did eventually. And what did the phenomenon of Bay's extraordinary mind-warp matter to research, really? It had occurred through a unique set of isolated coincidences which they would never be able to create artificially.

This was Bayless Heritage, a sick man, being used purely clinically by Robert and Aaron, she thought with sudden horror. He was not a laboratory rat. He was a man.

She picked up his hand and kissed each knuckle of his fingers, watching his face for some sign that he was aware of her. He seemed to resist her hold on his hand for a moment, and then the corners of his mouth turned up in a dreaming smile. He did feel her, did need her. Her throat tightened on tears that must not be shed. Rob was a dear man but a boffin up to his eyebrows. She needed a partner who would be her complement. Someone to enjoy things with, to share things with . . . to love.

She settled down in the chair beside Bay's bed and

began to talk to him quietly about the cottage and the garden and Sandy. He was somewhere near to the surface, she was sure, and there might be a chink through which her voice pictures could slide, jolting him back to her.

He lay flat on his stomach in the long grass, waiting for the old men to go. The fact that they were there and well past their fruitfulness meant that word was being sent from Ickka. The women must be a danger then, for it would have been natural for the senior women to have borne such messages to Arwyan. She must be in danger from the women. He listened for sounds of approach, his ear pressed hard against the dry earth. No one came and eventually the messengers departed, shuffling slowly out of sight along the wood-paved approachway. He waited, senses honed for the sounds of their passage to fade, and then eased himself through the underbrush to the temple steps. He hopped upwards with ease. He had taken those three steep steps countless times. He swung into the outer courtyard of the temple and sat down with his back against one of the three timber pillars which supported the roof.

'Arwyan.'

The place seemed to be deserted and one part of himself looked round with interest while the other simply sat, waiting for her to show herself and whistling that special call to her through the broken edge of his centre teeth.

The beautiful carved tree pillars rose upwards round him like a vertical racecourse of flowing silver horses. He had thought the building would be dark within because of its lack of wall apertures but now he saw that the tree trunks which formed the stout outer walls were not butted together but had been placed at a slight angle so that daylight shone through narrow-angled spaces between them. The outer chamber was light and there was a cool current of air flowing through. It brought with it a strange odour which made his heart thump suddenly against his ribs. It was the same smell of horse which had constantly bothered him at Lavenham while he was digging in the living room.

He sniffed the warm air. The odd thing was that although he recognized it, what had seemed a most unpleasant odour at Lavenham was no longer so displeasing. In fact, it was as though he had lived with such a scent for a long time and that he found it, if not pleasant, at least comfortingly familiar.

Then he saw her, and the unexpectedness of her drove the breath from him. In the same instant, he realized Arwyan was the source of this strong equine body odour. It was the primary reason that she had been selected for the temple at such an early age. None of the others had her kind of body scent. She smelt of that rare and precious creature that they worshipped through Epona Horse.

She was fine-featured while all about her were broad and flat-faced. Her skin was milky and unblemished, making a mockery of Gonad and the others. The rest of the tribe, or the few of them he had so far seen, were leathery and slow, hard-beaten by the elements. But Arwyan — Arwyan had the grace of a ballet dancer and the innocence of a child. There were just two things that stopped her short of perfection as he saw it — the extraordinary body odour which emanated from her so strongly and the fact that the lovely hazel eyes were blind.

He knew this instantly, even as he rose up on to his stumps. She walked through the arras towards him with perfect ease and confidence, her head tilted back, testing the air for the telltale scents of strangers, and her eyes were great unfocused orbs set deep within long black lashes. She was heavily with child.

'Finn, they have voted you clear of the sin. Did you hear them?' He took her hand so that they had contact with each other and she sat down in the forecourt with him. 'I was outside,' he said. 'I did not trust their visit. They will never convict me of sins I have not committed — nor you.'

The great sad eyes filled with tears, which spilled down her cheeks. 'Why will they not believe me? How can I prove my truth?' She placed a hand on the great bulge beneath her breasts. For a moment it curled into a hard fist and she raised it as though to strike at herself. He took

581

her hand and gently unwound the fisted fingers.

'You know,' he said, and she nodded.

'Nothing must be different. The laws of the temple were laid down by Epona before life began. Man begets man. Creature begets creature. There must be continuity but not integration. It is not permitted. Sin will be struck down. Epona is to be obeyed in all things.' Her sing-song voice recited the litany of their belief and he joined her quietly, taking the lead as her words faltered. 'The servants of Epona are as the servants of Deivos. They shall remain unknown to man, save only through intercession.'

'Every time I say this prayer I live my pain again.' She put her head down and wept quietly.

He patted her gently, suddenly foolish and inadequate in the presence of female tears, just as he had always been with his sisters' tantrums at Midhurst. The cloth of her robe was fine muslin, and through it he felt the lumpiness of scars under his hands. He pushed her hair to one side and hissed at the sight of the great red weals across the back of her neck and down her arms. Someone had beaten her unmercifully with what must have been a sharp-edged instrument. The scars were almost healed, but some of them must still be tender for they were an ugly dark red and there was still moisture about one arm scar.

An attack like that had surely all but killed her. He searched for words which would not give her pain, which would not show her his complete ignorance. 'Tell me what happened again. My head is dizzy and the pictures go from it.'

She straightened her back with a sigh and smiled at the sound of his voice. 'Poor Finn, you have enough of a burden without me making things worse. Are you sure you remember nothing? You said the same thing to me just two moons past. I repeated the same words then that I told you after it happened to me. Is it all wiped away?'

Frances, where are you? he thought. Why do I have such feeling for this lovely girl who is my sister? Has she been caught at Lavenham all through the centuries with

582

nothing to show for her existence but the throat-catching stench of her?

'Tell me,' he said. There is nothing in my head but strange fancies.'

'Then you are lucky. I pray to Epona every day and night to take away from me the memory of that day but it is here still, and now the result of it is the final shame.'

But as she told him he remembered and in remembering was revolted. ' . . . and I had no knowledge that I was being watched. I always know, Finn. I always sense when there is a presence, but this was different. I was putting fresh grass on my pallet, right there inside my bedchamber, beyond the offertory where no person apart from the priestess or her attendants ever come. I think I was bending to sniff at the fresh scent of the grass, it is so good, the first growing after winter — and then a snarling grunt came just behind me.'

She stopped as the words were uttered. He watched her wipe her hands on the sides of her robe as though to cleanse herself of the memory. She licked her lips and when she spoke again her voice wavered. 'The next thing I knew, I was being flung forwards by a great weight and something in a horse pelt was over me and biting into my neck and then I felt the hot thrusting of it and the agony — and then it was all agony. . . .'

Arwyan listened to the sounds of his horrified retching. 'You did that last time also,' she said when he had finished. There was uncertainty in her voice. 'Am I truly so disgusting now? Am I disfigured?'

She put her small hands up to her face and pressed her fingers into the soft flesh of her cheeks. 'It was not man. I would have known. It was Epona.'

It was what she had said from the very beginning, and yet Epona was equine and creature cannot make life with human. Can it?

He put an arm round her and stroked her hair. It was oiled as Gonad's was, but Arwyan had crushed wild lavender into her oil before combing it through her hair.

The fragrance was strong and clean, almost strong enough to cover her own scent.

'I have tried to tell you the whole truth as it happened — even though I try every moment to forget it. Do you understand how it is with me now? The women are gone so I must get water myself, I must gather in the temple offerings myself, I must find wood from the pile in winter when you are not there. I know my way about from every stone and hole in the ground, so that does not worry me, but I cannot see who may be lurking behind the wood store, at the spring, in the outer courtyard. There is a fresh terror beyond every step I take. I tremble to move — and the child is starting to drop. When I bring it out, will that be the moment which decrees the death of both of us? For I shall not know what comes from me. I am so frightened.'

He held her close to him. Poor kid. He had thought his own nightmare situation the worst that man could experience and yet here was the most innocent of girls, desecrated beyond belief and living in a far more horrifying darkness than his own would ever be. 'You are not alone,' was all that he could say to give her comfort. 'I'm here now, and even if they convict me after all, I shan't go away from you again while there is life in me. I promise on the hand of all the gods.'

As he said it, it came to him that this might mean that he could become trapped in this very moment and that he would then have to remain with her, both as Finn and as Bay, until her child was born and their future decided by Ickka. Panic gripped him. He just had to get back to Robert and Frances for it was now imperative to try to explain his involvement with these archaic people who had been responsible for all that went after, and most of all for the stone. It might be that if he was not able to reach the stone from this end, they might be able to get rid of the thing from theirs. But if he could not get back to tell them, how would they ever know?

The stone. He had actually forgotten all about it in the

last hours. There was no sign of it in the forecourt, only the three timber piers made from the whole trunks of sweet-scented conifers which supported the roof.

Arwyan sighed beside him. 'I must give the midday libation,' she said. There were dark lines beneath the beautiful sightless eyes. He studied them as he steadied her on to her feet. In some lights they were the colour of the forest in sunlight but now in the shadowy forecourt they were flecked with shades of the purple hills. They reminded him of the portraits of Violet Bayless, the same long dark lashes, the same wide, open gaze.

There was a spreading wet patch where Arwyan had been sitting. At the moment that he saw the puddle she groped through her gown. 'The waters are breaking,' she said. 'It is the time.'

During the afternoon Bay was given an exhaustive series of X-rays and finally an electrocardiogram. When he was wheeled back into his room, he showed signs of a return to consciousness. Frances had cut short her visiting list and returned to the hospital and Bay's little side ward.

'He's making a splendid effort to come out of it,' the nurse told her. 'He seems to be floating just beneath the surface, as though he will wake at any moment.'

They stood on either side of the bed, watching the muscular changes in his face, the occasional fibrillation of eyelids, the whispered mutterings. The tape recorder hissed quietly beside the bed. 'I forgot to change the reel this morning and Professor Crane was very cross about it.'

The nurse was elderly, trained before the war which had brought technology to her door. She disapproved of these gimmicks in medicine. Lives had been cared for and saved for generations before all the razzamatazz of the new machinery. She could not see that listening to a sick man's ramblings was going to benefit him in any way. But Professor Crane and Professor Harlberg had some bee in their bonnet about the poor fellow, so she tried to follow their technical instructions as well as she was able.

Though Arwyan's labour was in its earliest phase she was clearly suffering a growing discomfort already. She had wanted to go out into the open air and bring forth her child in the long grass but Finn had forbidden it and led her through the arras which separated the outer chamber from the sacred quarters and she, mindful only of what was happening within herself had taken no heed of the fact that Finn was still with her — in the presence of the Ultimate Sanctity.

The inner chamber was partitioned into three sections which between them protected a fourth. As in the outer forecourt, where the worshippers gathered to offer to Epona, there were three more ornately carved timber pillars supporting the beehive roof, but the sections were divided only by fine bleached cloth, embroidered with a design of trees and corn — and beautiful bounding horses. He was astounded at the work of these curtains for the detail, the soft colours, all suggested an unexpectedly fine quality of artistry and colour dyeing, not to mention a lifetime of devoted labour. Arwyan went through the curtains on the left of the inner sanctum into her sleeping quarters. There was a raised stone form in one corner, a cooking fire and a strange contraption which Bay recognized as a weaving loom.

'Did you make those curtains?' he asked in astonishment. She was sitting on the edge of her sleeping form, head bent. Her hair had escaped from the red plaited cord with which she had looped it away from her face and hung about her shoulders like a heavy black mantle.

'The sanctuary hangings? Yes, I made them.'

'But how was that possible? You have never seen grasses, never seen corn, nor even a horse.'

Her head came up then. The discomfort had eased. 'The women tacked the shapes and I followed with my thread.' She seemed to realize then that they were within the sanctuary confines. 'You should not be here!' she said sharply. There was fear in her voice. The odour of horse was overpowering in this inner place, lit only by fat lamps.

He felt great unease and shifted from hand to hand. 'I must stay with you,' he said simply. 'You have no women now to attend you, only me.'

'I don't need anyone. I must do this thing by myself. It is usual. Please leave me. Stay in the outer chamber if you must but keep away from the sanctuary if you value your life. Epona's wrath is without limit if she is disobeyed. Stay out, please. It is the best way you can help me.'

'I promise I will go, but let me make provision for returning without being seen. Please?'

Pain turned her features into the rictus of an animal. He swung across to the wall and began to move round the building, examining the great tree trunks which made it so secure. It was interesting to see that several kinds of timber had been used in an almost haphazard fashion, as though the builders of the temple had to be content with whatever was at hand. He counted oak and beech and even pine. . . .

Pine. Soft wood. He returned to two pine trunks and finally selected the larger of the two in a kind of storeroom where hay and food and sanctuary oil was kept. He drove his knife into the wood and then eased it out. No — that would take too long. He searched the untidy clutter of discarded gifts and empty pots in the store and discovered flint tools and a kind of hammer.

It took him a long time to cut a square wedge out of the pine trunk just large enough to squeeze through. He put the wood back into the aperture he had made then, just like a cork into a bottle and tapped it firm, praying that it would not be readily noticed from outside. Arwyan heard the sounds of his industry but kept her distance. She completed her temple duties listlessly and ignored him. He left her when the work was done, torn between doubts and certainties. He would only be in the way now, in this most sacred of all female rituals — but she should not be having pain yet. That thought nagged at him.

He went through the curtains and lingered in the offertory for it too, was lit by fat-lamps and their wavering

587

glow gave the place a certain mystery. Bay looked round with interest at the carved wooden horses in every stage of movement which decorated the walls — but from Finn came a terrible leaping fear in this inner sanctum and a straining to obey Arwyan's orders and leave it to its secrets.

Light streamed through the cloth curtains from the temple entrance and a wayward breeze stirred the flaming sentinels in their bowls of liquid fat. He paused, hefting his weight on to one broad hand, and reached out with the other to draw the curtain open a few inches. There was only one lamp in the inner chamber and he moved forward just enough to feel the curtain drape itself across his shoulders. The chamber was small and circular, about ten feet across. It was bare of anything but the lamp bowl which had been placed on the floor at the foot of a central stone pillar.

The floor in the inner chamber was not tamped-down, brick-hard earth as the rest of the temple was. This room had been paved with pale stone which gleamed in the soft yellow light of the lamp. He raised his eyes slowly. It was only then that he noticed how the light reflected the markings on the pillar. In the same instant he saw that it was not, after all, a support pillar, as the other six were. It rose upwards for twelve feet or so, its top almost lost in the unlit gloom of the domed roof.

It was not made of granite but of a curiously beautiful mottled pink and grey stone. As Bay's mind registered his recognition of the stone and stretched out his hand to stroke it, Finn gasped at the horror of his own actions and raised his eyes in supplication, to beg for mercy at his own iniquity. The cold carved horse face looming above him seemed to swoop downwards and he pushed himself backwards, out of the sanctuary, across the offertory and the forecourt and on to the steps of the temple. The crash which accompanied his flight had not, after all, been the monstrous toppling of that affronted Presence. A huge black cloud had built up in the western sky and now leaned heavily over the land. The gods of the air were angry with him. They would hunt him down with their silver spears, wherever he went. What had possessed him to trespass into the sacred place when he knew full well that he would pay for it with his life?

He swung down the steps and moved fast along the log road, away from the temple, away from Arwyan. At least her life and the life she was bringing forth need not suffer for his folly. He must go to Ickka and tell him of Arwyan's hour before the gods meted out his punishment.

Bay freewheeled and let Finn propel him forward. His mind was on something quite different. He had seen the stone.

And he had seen what was on the other side of it, now. The face of Epona, part human, part equine, with terrible flaring nostrils and gaping mouth, teeth bared.

But it was more than that, for it had been sculpted by the hand of a vicious master and the very mottling on the marble surface had been used to terrifying effect.

The recollection of that one brief upward glance was etched into his memory. Shuddering, he saw it still. The eyes in that monstrous head, bulging beneath a deep brow, were carved in every detail through a vein of palest grey. There were no pupils, just great glowing orbs in the pinkish stone.

Grey eyes of that peculiar pallor by which the Baylesses identified each other.

Eyes like a graven image of his own.

11

Bay moved as fast as his stumps allowed him. Finn was obviously used to this pace, for his breathing was not laboured although he was pushing himself to the limits of movement. The track was obviously well used, the earth flattened by the passage of countless feet. A sound to his left stopped him in his tracks but it was only a pair of young deer who, hearing his approach, veered away from the path. He took the weight off his stumps and listened to the sound of their crashing retreat. Pity he didn't have his spear, he thought. One of them had a fine pelt. Rested, he swung on along the track until it curled away to the right and here he left it, cutting into thick undergrowth.

It was cool in the woods. Above the trees, slate-coloured clouds reared upwards, gathering themselves for the downpour he could already smell in the air, a damp acidity like mouldering moss.

He must warn Iccka of the coming of Epona's choice, for it was now quite clear in his mind that she had indeed communicated her wishes to him there in the temple. How else would he have had the courage to draw back the curtain of her sanctum and behold her image so coolly? It must have been she who filled him with strange visions and with the troublesome sensation of duality, she who used him now as her messenger, knowing that her people would destroy him if he failed to get to Ickka as she wished.

He pushed through the brambles and on to the secret paths of the little forest pigs and so to the rear of Ickka's hut, knowing the men were away hunting and the women occupied with tanning and baking and weaving for the great feast after the next full moon. He would wait for Ickka and confront him alone.

He smelt the camp before he heard it and heard the women before he saw it. He stopped and squatted low in the thicket, knowing that the camp of the Wikken was only a spear-throw away, visible through the undergrowth. He settled back on his rump, content to wait until Ickka and the men returned.

There were several small huts and a communal fireplace in the open ground, round which they were now grouped, and a long barn where they met to discuss problems, mete out justice to those who warranted it, feast in winter and rut with the young women when the barren land began to bud once more.

The Headman's hut was closest to the barn. Like the others, it was little more than a hole in the ground with a woven canopy over the top, but it had the distinction of the Headman's tree beside its doorway, a young beech which had been planted as a sapling and draped with the beads and little pieces of woven cloth representing a supplication for favour. Ickka had been Headman for a long time now and the tree was the height of three men. When he had first taken Faed she had been very young and filled with strange talents. She had carved designs on the bark of the living tree, telling the story of the greatness of Ickka, his superiority in the hunting field, the hardness of his command of the tribe, the kindness of his heart when life was taken from them, the fertile richness of his loins, which had made many children on three women. All his accomplishments were carved into the bark of the sacred tree.

Finn sat and waited for the man who had banished him, the man who was his father. It would have been good to have been Ickka's son had his legs been whole, for he was stronger than his brothers, broader of chest and far more clever in the hunting field. But then they would never agree with his hunting methods. He worked to a plan, as they often did not. They stalked their prey without

591

thought for wind or noise, and when they lost it were disappointed and often turned on each other. Finn had learned as a young boy that time was the best ally and patience the next best. He had never gone after game and returned empty-handed. But who knew that, apart from Arwyan and Gonad and himself?

Bay, tasting the sadness in Finn, was chastened by the absolute acceptance in his soul. His own situation was not unlike Finn's for Bay had also been rejected by his family — but it had been entirely his own fault and still his bitterness was so strong that death seemed the only escape. Finn, knowing his own strength and patience, was content to abide by the Headman's dictate — and wait until a moment of weakness came to the tribe.

He wasn't such a dumb cripple after all, Bay thought.

The back of Ickka's hut blocked his view of the communal ground in front of the huts, where the women worked with the children at their sides. From where he crouched, he could hear their shrill cackles of laughter and a quick burst of crying as a child was chastised for some small misdeed.

There would be plenty of young females around that fire. The part of him that was Finn dwelt upon the desirability of half a dozen females all grouped together, waiting for the mating time like ripe fruit on a tree awaiting the picker.

A piercing trill came from far off and a woman suddenly appeared between the huts. She stood still, her body tense as she listened, sniffing the air. A baby in the crook of her arm sucked sleepily at her breast. The trill came again. Iccka was coming in.

Finn moved then. He scuttled forward and pressed himself against the side of the Headman's hut. He put his ear to the thatch and listened. No one inside. With consummate care he began to separate the woven hazel twigs which, packed with mud and moss, kept much of the rain out when the heavens washed the forest. It took some time to make a gap sufficiently large for him to wriggle through. The hut was dark inside and it took more precious moments for his eyes to accustom themselves to the gloom. It was stiflingly hot, for someone had forgotten to throw back the hide which covered the entrance. In summer the fires were kept alight outside if the weather was dry. He curled himself up in a tight crouch beside the raised sleeping place and waited. A long way away, summer lightning danced against the grey sky and thunder muttered in the distance.

Arwyan, Bay thought. What was happening with her now? He had been gone from the temple for several hours. Maybe he should have made Gonad go to her, after all. She was, of course, quite as likely to kill Arwyan as any of the other women — but if he were to agree to stay with her later, maybe she would help him to protect Arwyan until the child came forth and they could be judged. Too late now. In any case, Ickka must be told, must be there to make his judgement. If the child brought forth was of the god, they would know. If it was made by man it would die — and so would Arwyan.

His head throbbed suddenly. Red flashes brought his hands up to his eyes. The double images were in his mind again. He heard Faed's voice close by and Ickka's deep rumble answering her. They were approaching the hut.

There were six of them grouped round the bed now. Robert and Aaron, Dr Peter Redway from Pharmaceuticals and John Fellows, the ward physician. Beside them, waiting for instructions, were Sister Wall and Frances.

'Well, I think we're all agreed then.' Robert's eyes flicked round each face, over the rims of his half-lens spectacles. 'We'll give the Genera D4 a try and keep a full observation of the patient's reaction. If he shows any sign of degeneration, ten milligrammes of Matrizone to be injected into the upper arm as soon as his blood pressure starts to fall.'

Redway nodded and passed over his pad for signature. Dr Fellows stood against the side of the bed, Bay's charts in his hand. 'What are you going to do with him ultimately?' he asked, as Robert scribbled. 'Surely he should be in Graylingwell, rather than here.' His tone implied that he was one of those who did not agree with experimentation on fringe subjects.

'I think not,' Aaron said crisply. 'Professor Crane is based in this hospital, the new equipment is here — and we are not dealing with a defective mentality but a quite extraordinary possibility which we will endeavour to observe under the very best conditions.'

John Fellows said nothing. As far as he was concerned this American had flipped his lid, as the Yanks would have called it — and all this new interest in genetic brain regression was just another of the countless oddball ideas that these 'New Wave' boffins were coming up with these days. Not far from the bin themselves, some of them, though he had to admit that Robert Crane had always seemed a most balanced chap.

'Sister, when Dr Redway sends these drugs up to you, both Professor Harlberg and I wish to be here to observe Mr Heritage's reaction, so would you ring my office immediately? I shall be in the lab until three-thirty and then I'll be working in the office.'

Robert had had a hard battle getting either Redway or Fellows to agree to try the Genera D4 on Bay. It had not been passed for general use in hospitals and permission had had to be sought from the Heritage family — which had wasted another vital twenty-four hours. Now the family were waiting for another call from Robert.

Frances had shaken her head in disbelief when she heard that they were thinking of flying over to England. Bay would not, she was sure, want his mother and father to come now.

'He has been a very sick person for so long now.' Charles Heritage's voice had sounded metallic over the transatlantic telephone, the words all jangled together with atmospheric crackle. 'We decided to go along with his plan to fly over to England because he was in such a nervous condition that to disagree only disturbed him to violence.'

'Ah.' Robert picked up the word quickly. 'Are you saying that he has shown signs of this violence before, Mr Heritage?'

The ether thinned and he could hear the voice on the other end fading and flowing in waves. ' . . . not actually hurt anyone except for that one attack on his wife.'

'Can you tell me about that?'

'We-ell . . . it wasn't really an attack exactly because he did say that it had only been his intention to put her over his knee and give her a good spanking, but it seems she struggled and must have punched his temple where the scar is because he went berserk and gave her two black eyes, a broken rib and a lot of nasty bruising.'

It sounded to Robert as though Bay had had more provocation than was being admitted. 'I see. And that's all?'

The crackling line intimated that yes, that was all.

Poor devil, Rob thought, when the crackling finally cut them off altogether. Bay had said nothing at all about his past except a few little comments now and then to Frances. He had always been loyalty itself concerning Coral, his ex-wife, but one couldn't help getting the impression of a petulant child who had probably richly deserved the spanking he had tried to give her.

Frances had been sitting beside Bay for some time. She viewed the coming experiment with mixed feelings, for the Genera D4 was a brand new drug, discovered by the Nevern Institute of Cambridge, and had successfully brought animals in deep coma back to normal consciousness. It had not, however, been tried upon a living human brain.

'Bay, darling, they think they've found something to help you at last.' She settled down to chat to him, when the others had gone, as though he were on the other end of a telephone. She held his bandaged hand in hers, lightly polishing the tips of his uncovered fingernails with the flat of her thumb, and willed his eyes to open.

Ickka entered the hut, stooping as he flung the hide cover aside. As he did so he became aware that he was not alone. His hand went to his belt dagger and he backed against the wall, eyes raking the shadows as they became used to the dark.

'Ickka, it is Finn. May I speak with you? It is Arwyan's time.'

Ickka's taut shoulders relaxed. The anger left his eyes and he returned the dagger to its sheath, keeping his fingers round the bone hilt.

'Leave me,' he rasped through the doorway to Faed. 'I am with Finn. When Gered comes, bring him here, and Innes and Opha also. Keep the women clear.'

She crouched in the open doorway for a moment, baring her teeth at the shadowy Finn. He was not her son any more, had not been her son since the day he was cast out. There was no feeling for him now, only for the protection of the women from him.

'Don't waste time growling at Finn,' Ickka roared, aiming a fist at her face. 'Go!'

She retreated, rubbing the cheek where his knuckle had grazed her and hissing her disapproval.

Finn was still squatting against the wall at the far end of the hut. He had not moved a muscle.

'What do you want?' Here it is, Finn thought. Speak with your mind, not with your heart.

Nasty-looking character, Ickka, Bay observed, longing to escape from this cramped and stinking pigsty. He already looked too old for the job, although, judging from the hair on his genitals, he couldn't have been much older than Bay himself. That meant Finn was probably not more than nineteen or twenty.

'It is Arwyan's time, Ickka. She has no attendant at the temple except when I am there, and now she will bring out the child and you must come and make judgement.' He hesitated as Ickka said nothing but stared through the gloom with baleful red eyes. There was a droop to his shoulders. Ickka was, Bay realized, thoroughly frightened by the whole business of Arwyan and her issue, for he must make a correct judgement or else the Wikken would take sides and fight — and he would be slaughtered.

Finn pressed his plea home. 'I believe that Epona has put the child into her. I think she has been telling the truth, for there is no point in lying to me, is there? Ickka, please give her protection from the women until you have seen what she brings forth. If it is a child sacred to Epona, Arwyan must suckle it and care for it until it is old enough to take her place — '

'I know all that better than you, Broken Dog,' Ickka growled. 'You disobeyed my command in coming here. Why did you not get that empty bladder who fawns round you to bring the news?' 'There was no time. Arwyan's waters broke and she was in pain at once. Her burden is too large for her and she needs help so I had to come.'

Ickka moved across the hut to stand over Finn, keeping his eyes averted from the withered stumps of his son's legs. 'You have fool's courage,' he rumbled. 'For you know that I will punish you. This place is forbidden you under any circumstances. Gonad should have come. There can be no help for Arwyan, for none of the women has Epona's blessing, now that the old ones are gone. I shall cut the cord of Arwyan's cub myself if it is a sacred child, but if it is not, Epona will mete out the punishment and the women will choose a new priestess.'

He poked a finger into the hard muscle of Finn's arm. 'Half a man,' he said, and kicked out at the shorter stump of Finn's leg. His foot, calloused and hard as stone, caught a tender nerve above the thick heelskin of the stump and Finn jerked back, hissing with the sudden pain. His hands shot upwards round Ickka's neck and in a moment the two of them were rolling on the earth floor, kicking, gouging, fangs bared and lunging for muscle flesh. Something hit Finn on the back of his head and he went down in a dead weight across Ickka's body.

'Just as well Faed told me to see you as soon as I came back,' the young man said to Ickka as the Headman, chest

597

heaving, struggled out from under the cripple's great body.

They dragged the unconscious Finn out of the hut, into the evening light. Distant thunder rolled closer and all eyes were raised. High above them fork lightning stabbed the burgeoning belly of menacing night cloud. It gave the felling of this stunted giant new meaning, for the gods were gathering to see him justly punished. They fell to their knees and pressed their foreheads into the musty ground.

'It is an omen,' Faed said, as they waited for the terrible voice of the skies. When it came the ground shook and the air was filled with the smell of hot metal and the sounds of the people's fear.

'You saw the colour,' Ickka said to his people. 'It means that we are to see some terrible portent. Finn came here bearing news that Arwyan is bringing out her child. He disobeyed me, for I forbade him to come within half a league of this place and for that — and the attack he has just made upon me — he will be punished by Deivos himself.'

'But Deivos is here now with us,' Faed said to him above the keening wail of women. 'We cannot go forth when Deivos marches the heavens in anger.'

'Do as I say, woman,' Ickka snarled at her. 'Deivos will have this creature here on which to vent his anger. It is necessary that Arwyan is seen to bring out her child. Finn says that she has had pain from the breaking of waters. That can only mean that Epona will punish her with a bad birth. She may take her life. She may take the life of the seed. We must be certain that all is done correctly or she may well take more lives still.'

The woman bowed her head.

'Take him,' Ickka said to the returned hunters. 'Tether him out there on the hill so that Deivos can see him clearly and vent his rage upon him alone. Then we will go to the temple.'

It took four of them to lift Finn's body. They dragged

him out of the camp and up on to the open ground behind the village. They bound his wrists with leather thongs and drove wooden pegs into the ground, binding the thongs to the pegs. They bound the thongs loosely round his neck and pegged them also into the ground on either side of his throat. They bound his withered stumps and spread them as they had his arms and pegged them also into the ground.

As they left him, another shaft of lightning forked down into the trees and an answering explosion in the heavens came soon after. A fat raindrop hit the side of Finn's face but the blow to his head had been a hard one and both he and Bay were still far away.

The four small bottles were delivered from the hospital pharmacy during that quiet period in the early afternoon when patients are resting and doctors and staff are lunching in shifts.

Frances rang the call bell. She had not gone down to the canteen to eat because Bay seemed restless and there was always the hope that he might open his eyes and recognize her at any moment. She continued a desultory stream of chat to him, repeating the same things over and over again until Aaron suggested that her voice be taped, so that there was some respite for her. Now she sat, listening to her own voice urging him to put out a hand, take hers and grip it and know that she was right beside him. She was far beyond the refuge of tears. Looking at his wasted face and hollowed cheeks, reason told her baldly that if he could not be resuscitated he would slowly die. Maybe that was already happening.

'Bay is living another existence somewhere else, which is using up all the energy in his system,' Robert had told her.

'If he were to die in that other life, Rob — what would happen to him here?'

He had stared down at Bay, frowning. 'I don't know. I have reasoned my way in and out of half a dozen theories already on that one and I still have no idea. It could be that

599

he'd be released and would return to consciousness here. That's the answer which seems most logical to me — but then this life force of ours is not always as logical as we would wish and it could well be that his life would be extinguished at all levels.' He smiled at Frances and leaned across the bed and brushed her temple with his lips quickly, lightly. 'With luck and a few other factors, we won't know the answer to that one because we shall get him back and fight like navvies to keep him here this time, see?'

She glanced across at the charts which told their own story. Bay's heart was slowly failing, blood pressure dropping — hope for him diminishing.

Sister Wall poked her head round the door. 'Getting tired?' Her smile was bright, professional and in a hurry. 'Do you want a break? I'll get Nurse Hammond in when she's finished the baths.'

Frances shook her head and tapped the white parcel. 'No, I'm quite all right. I just wanted to let you know that the drugs for Bay have arrived. They'll be the Genera D4 and Matrizone for his injections this afternoon. I signed for them as the messenger couldn't see you in your office.'

'No, I'm a bit pushed with a patient down the other end right now. I'll be back in time for Professor Crane though.' She was gone again with a crisp rustle of skirts and the soft plodding footfall of speed without haste so characteristic in busy hospitals.

Frances took one of Bay's hands and turned it over to peer under the light dressing which still protected the burns. They were improving slowly, but how much faster would they be healing if the rest of him could only fight back? She put her cheek to the flesh of his lower arm and then laid it back beside his thigh. 'Not long now, My darling . . . '

His eyelids flickered and he blew his cheeks out as though he was running. At their side the soft whir of the tape recorder purred on relentlessly. The microphone attached to the metal back rest of the bed picked up a word that she did not hear.

'Frances . . .'

She brushed the limp black hair off his forehead and turned to adjust the sound of her voice on the little portable recorder. He puffed again and for a second his eyes opened, showing only the bloodshot whites. She was slightly turned away and saw nothing.

'Frances. . . .'

The cruel flail of the rain brought him back to consciousness. It fell on his upturned face with relentless persistence, drowning his eyes, battering his body, cooling the thunderous ache on the left side of his head. It smote him like a swarm of furious wasps. He thought he must be drowning and lashed out wildly with his arms. It was then that he discovered that they had tied him down. He was blinded by the water and even shaking his head from one side to the other was not enough to clear his vision. Something reverberated in the distance. It was followed by a flash that seared right through his closed eyelids, filling his head with a weird blue afterlight, and was followed with earth-shaking immediacy by a cracking explosion directly overhead.

Finn shook against his ropes with terror. Thunder, Bay thought. One heck of a storm and the bastards have pegged me out in it. He kept his eyes closed and gave his attention to the rest of himself. He was tied down by his wrists and thighs and neck, pinned against a hard slope, which was at least one advantage in the torrential rain. His hair was in his eyes, slicked down across one side of his face. He tried to shake it away but the thing across his throat prevented movement. Another violent flash was followed by a double thunderclap, one rolling into the path of the other. A smell of cordite and mould permeated the liquid air. He breathed through clenched teeth, blowing the water out of his mouth and then quickly drawing in a breath before it filled again.

Finn cringed within. The gods were speaking, and

never had he heard such anger in the heavens. He seemed to shrivel, to freeze all thought, all feeling, consenting to his punishment with quaking acceptance.

The aggression, the anger, was all Bay's. He struggled against leather thongs which only tightened more in the rain. He twisted his wrists inside their sling grip, back and forth . . . back and forth. It occurred to him that if he could continue to do that for some time, he might just be able to ease his hands out — providing the downpour continued, for it was actually giving him lubrication to ease them through the thongs.

'The gypsies are back in Salterns Wood. I saw the smoke from their fire this morning. They're late this year, for some reason.'

Frances' voice. It couldn't be so because she was not in this time.

'Doctor Redway says that the dressing on your left hand can be reduced tomorrow. . . . '

He lay still, straining for the sounds which had intruded across his concentration. Impossible as it was, her voice seemed to have broken through to him here. He blew upwards with all his might and tried to open an eye into the driving rain. Through wavering water he could just make out the line of trees and the huts of the Wikken below. It couldn't have been Frances.

He lay and searched his mind all the same, reaching out desperately. Frances, bring me back, he willed. I must come back. . . . There was a moment when he began to feel that singular spiralling dizziness which accompanied the switch in time — but then it went and there was nothing more, and yet he had the curious feeling that something had become thinner between his presence and his future. There was a membrane dividing something which seemed to be changing its density.

'Bring me back, oh God, get me out of this.'

Finn cowered against the streaming ground, feeling the little rivers of water channelling down between his shoulder-blades and thighs. What would they be doing at the temple? The futility of it all engulfed Bay. Wherever he was, in whatever life, in whoever's body, it seemed that he was only there to face despair. There had been no hope for him as Bay Heritage and now there seemed even less as crippled Finn. For pity's sake get on with it and put an end to me, one way or the other, he thought.

As another violent flash cut through his eyelids, he shivered against the streaming ground and roared his own frustration and terror right back at the tumultuous heavens.

The room was full of people.

'Just move your chair a little, if you will, Fran,' Robert said, and she stood up and moved back as he asked, clenching her teeth on the resentment flashing through her at the sudden intrusion of strangers around Bay. She became cut off from him as the white-coated figures moved in round the bed and the business of trying to resuscitate the patient was set in motion. There was so little to see from where she stood beside the window, apart from a bank of white backs . . . the murmur of Robert's deep voice and Dr Fellows' answering monotone. Then the white wall parted and Robert was beckoning to her.

'Come and stay close to him, Frances. He has always responded to you best and your face should be the first thing he sees when he opens his eyes.' He smiled at her.

She stood against the neat white bed, close to Bay's head.

'I have just given him a single shot of this new stuff, which is not only a stimulant to the heart but also gingers up the old brain.' Robert sounded so casual, he might have been talking about a miracle cosmetic she thought. They had turned off her recorded voice. There were now two microphones strapped to the bedhead.

Without warning, Bay's body began to jerk.

'He's going into spasm. Give me the relaxant, nurse, quickly please.' Robert seemed so cool. She glanced sideways at him and was surprised to see bright beads of perspiration pearling his forehead.

The spasm passed. The rasping breath and the soft whirr of the recorder were the only sounds in the room. The breathing became ragged, as though Bay was running, and Frances looked anxiously across at Robert, who shook his head reassuringly at her. 'He's all right,' he said softly, fingers on Bay's pulse. 'He's responding now. Do your talking thing and we'll see whether he is close enough to take it in.'

She knelt down then, pushing away from her the others who crowded round the bed. She put her head close to Bay and laid her hand on his upper arm and began to talk to him, and then there were no others in the room, only Bay and Frances — and this time he was going to hear her.

'Bay, the gypsies are back in Salterns Woods. I saw the smoke from their fire this morning. They're late this year, for some reason. I wonder why that should be because they usually appear in time to help bring in the harvest. . . . '

His chest began to heave in deep rhythmic breaths like massive bellows. She watched its movement as she talked, and stroked his forehead. It was damp under her hand, damp and hot and the breaths became a groan. He moved his body as though struggling against some terrible weight.

He seemed to be so close now to them. 'Bay, open your eyes. You're back, really you are. Just open your eyes and see for yourself.'

Behind her, Robert said to the nurse, 'The minute he regains consciousness, give him the next injection. The very moment he opens his eyes, d'you understand?'

Bay's head was moving from side to side as though to escape the attentions of something on his face. Frances felt behind her for the wet flannel with which to mop his face.

'Keep talking, for God's sake!' Robert's voice snapped across the bed at her. 'Never mind about the bloody cloth. Just keep talking.'

'Open your eyes, Bay . . . we're all here. You're absolutely fine now, back with us again, and we won't let you go. Just try and open your eyes.'

'I can't . . . they're full of water.'

The sound of his voice, cracked and hoarse, was such a shock that her heart flew up into her throat. 'Rob, he said something!' She had never really thought that he would come back. He was so frail, his colour so bad. She leant forward and kissed the side of his face and gently swabbed both eye sockets with the cool flannel. 'There you are then, I've wiped it away. Now try. . . .'

He opened his eyes and closed them again.

'Injection nurse, quickly now!'

Frances took no notice of the excitement, the swift movements of the medical staff all round her. She was aware only that he had answered her, that he was close to her again. A great fount of relief flooded across the quiet sea that had been the beginnings of grief and she pressed her body hard against the hospital mattress, feeling the metal frame against her ribs. He opened his eyes again and stared at the ceiling. Slowly the vague grey pupils focused and he turned his head and looked at her. He gave a sigh of complete exhaustion. The traveller had come a very long way.

'Ma'am, I'm sure glad to see you. Can you get these things off my wrists?'

The tears were back then, pricking their way past the dam of her determination, to course down her face and on to his wrapped hand. 'It's only your burn dressings,' she said, clearing the huskiness from her voice. 'Just rest, Bay. You've had such a long journey.'

He grinned at her then, his face like a ravaged elf's. 'Kept hearing your voice . . . in the middle of all the other things. I'm sure glad I didn't dream it after all.' He seemed to notice the tears then and raised his fist and brushed her wet cheek with his bandages. 'Have you been raining on me for long? Back there I was in the middle of a thunderstorm and just about drowned in the deluge. Didn't realize it was the tears of a good woman.' He closed his eyes then and turned his head away.

'Give him another ten milligrammes, nurse,' Robert's voice rasped across the silent room. 'Don't let him slide back now, for God's sake.'

The lank head shook from side to side on the pillow. 'I'm right here, old buddy. Just sorting my wits out. I've got to try and tell you something.'

Bay looked at his hands and all the time it was coming back to him, flowing through his head like a tidal race. Now the two levels of memory fused together and smote him, invading every last space in his brain so that he groaned at the pain of it. 'My head. God, it's killing me.'

Something pricked his arm and he smelt the clean odour of surgical spirit, and soon after that the pain eased and his breathing became less laboured. 'I've got to draw you a building,' he said. 'I don't know enough about history or pre-history to be able to tell you where I've been, but while I can remember, I've got to draw it. It's real weird, I promise.'

Robert nodded then and turned his head as a dark man with a neat goatee beard leaned over his shoulder and murmured in his ear.

'It's all so clear, you see,' Bay told Frances, his head pillowed against the inside of her shoulder. She nodded, trying to keep the anxiety out of her eyes and failing dismally. It was difficult, Bay found, to focus on Robert in the blurry sea of all those other faces so he fastened his whole attention on Frances' pale little heart-shaped face and found it the best medicine, anyway. 'I've see the stone, Frances. I've actually seen it and it's in this temple place, a wooden temple. Can you imagine that? I always thought temples were made like the Greek ones, and here's this place a bit like a bee-hive with a woven roof and in the middle, in a sort of inner sanctum, there's this kind of totem. And Frances, they worship the horse there. They worship Epona, Goddess of the Horse.'

He didn't hear the sharp exclamation from Aaron, didn't hear the soft nasal voice asking the nurse to check that the recorder had plenty of tape still to run. All he wanted to do now was to talk — to share that other place with Frances and Robert Crane so that they could one day make something of it, so that they might, with their strong unbiased minds, come up with the answer to Lavenham for him.

'You know, it's funny, but that old house seems hardly important any more.' He was surprised to find this so. 'Just the other day it was the most important thing in my life, the only thing, I guess, but now . . . there's another life being led somewhere inside me. Raw and dirty and full of lice — am I covered in them now, Frances? — and as basic as it's possible to be, and yet I'm kinda getting used to it.'

He closed his eyes again then, to think about what he had just said — because it was true and it had not occurred to him until that moment. When he had found himself in Finn, all he had wanted to do was to get back to Frances, to warm himself in the love he could feel growing in her. Now, suddenly, lying in the clinical cleanliness of his little side ward, surrounded by doctors and nurses, all devoting themselves in their different ways to bringing him back to health in Chichester, England, he experienced a small keen pang for that knife-edge on which Finn lived.

Comparing Finn's life with this sterile twentieth century complaisance, there was much to be said for the simplicity of the Wikken's beliefs, the total faith they invested in their peers and each other. When one measured the constant dangers and terrors of their everyday lives against the absolute security of his own, he was moved by the dismal unimportance of the very things which had caused him to destroy his marriage, his relationships with others, his very need to exist. He should not, he thought wearily, even be here. What was happening to Arwyan? She needed him more than any of the people in this clean white place needed him, even more than Frances did. Arwyan had no guardian except for that crippled brother — and Gonad, barren or not, was still a woman with plenty of fire

607

in her. And then there was Ickka, aging early, as they all aged. Who would follow him as Headman? No one had Finn's power or even realized that he was capable of leading the Wikken, but he knew that he was — and so did Bay.

'Bay, tell us about the stone.' Robert's voice cut through his drowsing thoughts and he opened his eyes. Frances held a beaker of tea to his lips and he drank and was glad of the hot, sweet fragrance. His stomach rumbled, complaining.

'I'm kinda hungry,' he said in surprise. 'Is it time to eat soon?' They all laughed round the bed, easing their own tension, and the sound of it brought out another picture from his mind, of sitting on the bottom step of Granpappy's graceful staircase with his brother and sisters, listening to the tall tales of the old man's youth, wonderfully exaggerated, embroidered into the epic adventures of heroes.

A tray of soup and buttered toast appeared from somewhere and he let Frances feed him, watching her face as she lifted the spoon to his mouth, catching her eye and holding her glance with his until a warm flush stole through her cheeks.

He asked to be propped up on more pillows and they lifted him. What a poor, weak specimen the twentieth-century Bay was. He raised his arms and inspected them with wry amusement. 'You know, I'm a real cute guy back there in the olden days,' he said with a grin. 'Mind you, I can't get about except by swinging along on my hands and kind of paddling with my knee stumps because I'm crippled, but from the knees up. . . . '

He tried to flex his muscles at Frances and failed. 'Well, I may not amount to much right here, judging by the way this miserable body's losing its looks — but over there I make Johnny Weissmuller look like Stan Laurel.'

The man with the little goatee beard came forward with paper and coloured crayons. The room emptied as the crowd filtered away once the miracle had happened, leaving only Robert, Frances and this man who was unknown to him. Bay relaxed against his pillows, fighting a weariness which was slowly washing through his whole body. Tell them everything he could first, he decided, sleep after.

'Mr Heritage, my name is Aaron Harlberg. I'm a friend of Robert's and he asked me to come and help to identify the period of your dreams.'

Bay opened one eye and viewed the stranger bleakly. 'They aren't dreams, you know. They are as real as this moment. If the others are dreams, then so is this.'

Aaron nodded. 'I know. Your brain appears to be undergoing a quite extraordinary duality, Mr Heritage, and I am privileged to be a witness. It is projecting its own genetic memory, we think. What we both would like to do, quite apart from bringing you back to full and permanent health, is to correlate every scrap of this experience that we can gather from you and try to back it with evidence, write a paper on the subject for later publication. It's going to be a bit difficult finding hard evidence — but your mention of that stone could be a very great help. The stone at Lavenham has lain there for a very long time and has still not been raised, so no one — including yourself — can have any idea of its history. However, you say that you have seen the stone in that other time? Could you describe it to me? Size, colour, any identifying marks? Its function and age?'

Bay nodded. 'It's there, sure enough. That sort of mottled pinkish grey marble seaming is fairly distinctive and, although I only had a quick glimpse before the other me shot away from it like a rabbit with buckshot up its tail, I saw that it was a double-headed sculpture. One side was a female face, high bridge to the nose, wide nostrils, thick-lipped mouth. Not much to look at as far as women go. The other face was terrible. It was a kind of human horse face with the most horrible expression I ever saw. I'm not surprised poor old Finn did a bunk. It was a real vicious piece of sculpture, that one. I couldn't say whether it had been there a long time or whether it was new, but something I do know — I wouldn't want to get into the bad books of that totem. Come to think of it, the life those folk lead is a pretty vicious struggle all the time. Can you imagine a blind girl as lovely and fragile as Arwyan being attacked today by a horse and actually sexually assaulted by it? I mean, is that possible?'

Aaron shrugged. 'One would think not, but there is no doubt that there is a certain breed of donkey which is used — or was in the bad old days — for exhibition purposes with young women in North Africa and the Middle East. It is not beyond the realms of possibility, I suppose, for some stray stallion — they were all as small as our moorland ponies you know, at one time — to have come upon her. That would imply, of course, that her scent is the sexual one which mares exude when they are in season.' He grimaced and Frances shuddered at the nightmare thought of that bestial attack on a blind girl. 'Don't talk about it any more,' she begged. 'It isn't your problem now, is it?'

Bay shrugged. It was understandable for someone like Frances to be shocked at such a horrendous act. But it had happened and Arwyan had survived it. Her shoulders and neck still bore the terrible scars of that coupling. The question crossed his mind whether Frances would have coped as well as gentle Arwyan had.

He drew the temple for them by holding the soft crayon between both wrapped fists. The picture he produced was wobbly and out of perspective, but every detail that he could remember was there, added painstakingly in answer to Aaron's quiet probing.

'I have to ask you something,' Bay said, when it appeared that he had exhausted his supply of information. Aaron was staring at the little pile of drawings on his lap. Bay tucked his throbbing hand into Frances' and looked from her to Robert. 'I have had no sign at all of the Killing Glance in that other place,' he said. 'I know that I am infected with it, just as Tom Heritage and the Baylesses were. What do you think caused such an affliction? Why should we suffer such a curse, those of us with the grey eyes?'

Even as he said the words something occurred to him. 'I did see one thing on that damned totem. The eyes on the side which represented the human head were carved through a grey seam in the marble. But surely that would not have any relevance?'

'I don't think that you should take this Killing Glance too seriously, Mr Heritage,' Aaron said. 'I'm afraid that my view is that you have been led to believe in it by the accounts in your forebear's diaries. They believed in all sorts of things in the olden days which we see in a different light today, you know.'

Frances felt Bay stiffen. Oh why had he said that? she thought. Why had he not couched his disbelief in more gentle phrases . . . ? 'Aaron hasn't seen it happen, so of course he is a sceptic,' she said quickly.

'Well, my dear, have you?'

She shook her head, and her mind was filled with the memory of Sandy's stiff little body . . . and Mrs Carey's dreadful, hate-filled face, caught in the very moment of her own intent to kill. 'No, but I have seen the results.'

She could feel every muscle in Bay becoming rigid. 'Maybe I should try and show you!'

Aaron smiled at Bay with great kindness. 'I think you should not waste your energy trying to prove something to me which is really unimportant, Mr Heritage,' he said gently. 'This power to inflict harm on others has been talked about amongst witch doctors and sorcerers since time began. I am very much more interested in the other things you are being good enough to show me.'

Bay stared at him and drew all his strength up into his head, felt the stirring of that latent red flower deep down in the very depths of his being. He willed it upwards into his head — but the strength was not in him any more. It flickered and sank out of mind. Tiredness dragged at his eyelids like lead weights, overcoming his concentration.

'Haven't the muscle any more, I guess. Just feel so tired I could sleep for a month.'

Robert finally brought the interview to an end. 'Time you had a wash and then a good rest,' he said, seeing the fresh lines of exhaustion in Bay's face.

'What if I slide away again while I'm asleep?' Bay asked. 'There's so much I've got to go back for, to try and help that poor kid, Arwyan, and to get rid of the stone, I guess — but after that, after I've got rid of that darned totem, which I'm sure is at the base of the whole business, I want to be here. There's too much unfinished business to see to in Bay's life too, I reckon.'

Robert looked at them both, Bay lying close to Frances and her hand tucked into the crook of his arm. He nodded shortly. 'The drug we used to help you back here is very much at the experimental stage and we are not at all sure, either about the side-effects or how much we can pump into the human system before it reverses itself but, judging by the success of the two injections we gave you today, we should be able to give you one more course of two or three shots in twenty-four hours' time without putting you at risk.'

He gave Bay a gentle pat on the shoulder. 'See you tomorrow, old man. It's good to have you back.'

When Robert and Aaron had gone, Bay said to Frances, 'There was one very good reason why I had to get back, you know.'

She was looking so young, sitting beside him brimming with relief. There was a glow about her face which seemed to light up her eyes, her skin, even to highlight the red and gold shine in her glossy dark hair.

'I had to tell you again that I really do love you more than I can say. I finally realized that during the transition. I think that this transition thing I go through must be the greatest danger period for me. I feel as though I'm dying, and I have to haul myself away from giving in to it somehow. So, in order to get here to tell you that a caveman from way back wants you more than life itself, I had to put that life at risk to reach you. But it's true, Fran.'

They stayed very close, talking softly, heads almost touching. Then his weariness reached out and Frances saw that he was almost asleep.

'I'll go now,' she whispered. 'I'll come back this evening for a short time, but then I'll try and spend most of tomorrow with you.'

He opened his eyes sleepily. 'And the day after — and the day after that.'

'We'll see.' She tiptoed towards the door.

'Listen, there's one thing that could wreck everything, the way I see it,' he said, and she turned. 'If I get rid of that old totem it will mean that the future will change — because it will not be lying about waiting to catch folks down the centuries any more, will it? Suppose it changes us too? I wouldn't want to feel that you and I never met after all, not when I've spent my whole miserable life so far messing it up because I hadn't met you.'

'Darling Bay.' She came back into the room and planted a kiss on his upturned mouth. 'You just said that to bring me back then, didn't you?'

She tasted of summer fruit. 'No, I didn't but it was worth it all the same. I meant it, though. If you see Rob again before you come in this evening, will you ask him to think about it and come and talk if he has time. I don't want to change history — only to remove a destructive element. And Fran — talk to him about the Killing Glance too, yes? I know his friend thinks it's all a big ego-trip of mine, but it isn't, is it? I really did those awful things, didn't I? I really Flamed those creatures and Mrs Carey.'

'Who knows,' she said quickly, seeing his fresh agitation. 'If it isn't with you in that other time, then I expect we'll be able to sort it out here too. Just rest on that. I'll talk to Robert about it all, I promise.'

He let out a deep sigh and relaxed against his pillows. A nurse came in with a bowl of water and a towel.

'I'll be back this evening,' Frances said to the staff nurse on duty. 'He must be monitored all the time still, so could you be sure and see that someone is in there with him?'

She climbed into the little Fiat and swung out of the hospital gateway, feeling good for the first time in what seemed like years.

Bay closed his eyes and slept.

About an hour later he was aware of the whirling churning chasm once more. 'No!' he shouted at it. 'I'm not ready. Stay back.'

But it rolled towards him, as inevitable as a tidal wave, and he was swept into the dropping whirlpool of lights and nausea and there was nothing he could do then to resist it.

12

The call came through from the hospital as she stood towelling herself after her bath.

The whole of her body had felt tense with emotion long held in check, and as she lay in the cool fragrant water, soaping herself and smoothing the creamy lather over her skin, she wallowed in the most profound relief at Bay's return. True, he was still very dangerously ill and there was his growing urgency to relate every small detail of his experience. It was as though he needed to prove himself beyond even his own doubts. Well, he had certainly impressed Robert and Aaron. They were, at that moment, over at the old house, trying to move the stone and take a look at the markings Bay had begun to excavate on its underside. They would look in at the cottage on their way back to Chichester.

She lifted her sponge up and slowly squeezed the water from it, watching the froth splash down onto the shining skin of her stomach. Once he was well, she would marry Bayless Heritage — if he asked her. She was very sure now that he would.

She sat up, tugged at the bath plug and jumped out. As she dried, humming to herself, the telephone began to ring downstairs.

He was cold. His whole body shook with dank chill. His teeth chattered in his head. He couldn't move. The rain had stopped and the air, though still and humid, was at least quiet now. The thunder, still muttering a long way off, had moved on along the coast to vent itself upon other settlements.

A hand gripped his wrist and he jerked away from it, turning his head from the expected blow.

'Be still. I am trying to free you.'

He opened his eyes then. It was quite dark. There were no stars in the black vault of the sky, no moon to thin the void into shadows. He lay and concentrated on the hands which tugged at his wrist thongs, the deep ragged breathing close to his head.

'They are swollen with the rain. I'll have to cut them. Lie still or I might cut you too.'

'Gonad?' he croaked, feeling the wisp of her breath across his forehead, recognizing the body scent of her.

'Be still, I said. Do you want us both dead?'

He felt the blade of her knife slip between his wrist and the agonizing pressure of the thongs and begin to saw back and forth into the cuts already biting his flesh. He gritted his teeth and waited, and then his left hand was free and she moved across to the other side of him and began to feel down his arm to the second peg and thong. He realized he must have been here for hours, judging by the pain in his shoulder when he lowered the free arm from its outstretched position. He lay quietly flexing his fingers and arm muscles while Gonad sawed through the other thong. The blade nicked him, all unseen, and he growled at her. She felt round the curve of his shoulders and began cutting his neck thong. It took a long time to release him and then he found he could not support himself at first. His eyes, accustomed to the flat black night now, saw the silhouette of trees against the unlit sky, and the faint outline of Gonad as she half dragged him across the slope below the hillcrest and down into the hazel brush.

'Come, we must leave here. Dawn is not far away and they have been all night at the temple. Arwyan was still inside when I came away to find you, so she had not brought forth her child yet. I heard Ruwen calling for the Goddess. She was inviting the women, challenging Arwyan to reveal her child, urging Ickka to go inside and bring her out. I think they will stir themselves up until he

616

is forced to appeal to Epona herself.'

The circulation returned to his arms, bringing sharp pain with it — but pain was a welcome spur, making him move faster with Gonad at his side.

They pressed through the trees, pausing now and then to sniff the air, to listen to the earth for sounds of movement in their vicinity. It began to rain again. The soft patter of raindrops on the foliage above became a steady hiss. Thunder still threatened below the horizon. 'The wind has changed,' Gonad said beside him. 'The gods will follow us now.' There was fear in her voice where before there had been none.

Finn gripped her shoulder. 'Go back to your hut,' he said. 'You'll be safe there. I must do what I can for Arwyan. It would be better for us all if you were not to be seen. If I come out of this with my life, I shall offer it to you, for you have earned your claim to it.'

She rubbed herself against his arm and then loped onward. 'I shall stay,' she said shortly as he caught up with her. 'If the gods take you in punishment, they will take me too, for there would be nothing left for me if you were not here.'

The night was hot, the wood airless. Even the rain, falling steadily, did nothing to cool it. They were both panting as they pushed through the undergrowth, the sodden leaves slapping against their faces. They heard the sound at the same time and froze, crouching low into the bushes.

From a distance came voices, not the singing that usually accompanied the entire tribe's presence at the temple, nor the haunting keening of the women when they went to offer after the death of one of their people. Finn, straining to listen through the rattle of the rain, felt the hair rise on his arms, across his chest. The screams of the women, the baying of the men must mean that Arwyan had brought forth issue and that it was unacceptable to Ickka. He burst away from Gonad and flung himself forward towards the sounds of animal hatred.

Frances was back in the airless little side ward, crouching beside the bed. It was as though she had never left it, as though this day's short-lived triumph had simply been part of her imagination.

She rested her cheek against Bay's arm. It was hot and dry and there was little flesh on it. His breathing was shallow, the colour of his skin like old parchment.

After the call from the hospital she had flung on bra and pants, a cotton shift and sandals and run all the way from the cottage to Lavenham.

She had found the two men sitting on the edge of the pit, Aaron hunched over his notepad sketching with the small precise strokes of his pedantic nature, Robert puffing away at his pipe and watching him. They both looked hot and streaked with dusty perspiration.

'We managed to turn the thing,' Robert said as she came through the door toward them. 'Come and look.' But she cut through his words.

'No time to talk about that now. Bay's gone back into coma. The hospital just rang. I'm going in now. Are you coming?'

They hurried back to the cottage and Robert's car. Lavenham, Frances thought, as she followed in the Fiat, had seemed like a neglected elderly relative as they left — dank, unbeautiful and crumbly. If the house had been human, she decided, it would have looked like an ancient and wrinkled crone — all strength spent.

They made haste through the hospital corridors, up in the lift and found Sister and two nurses with Bay. 'Dr Fellows has just left to make his report.' she said waving away the nurse who was sitting beside the bed with a stethoscope round her neck.

Robert examined Bay carefully — pulse, heart, eyes — and then scanned the charts and drugs sheet. He caught Frances' eye and shook his head. Bay was now in deep coma, maybe the deepest yet. It was going to be touch and go trying to bring him back now. He drove one fist into the palm of his hand then, frustration getting the better of him for the first time. 'God, I'm sorry, Frances old dear.' He patted her shoulder awkwardly as Aaron bent over Bay's face, his ear close to the half-parted lips. The change between Robert and Frances had not been discussed but both were acutely aware of it now. 'We'll keep him under intensive surveillance and, although we can't risk another injection of the D4 for twelve hours at least, there are other stimulants we can try. But we can do little more than try to keep him stable until then.'

'He's not stable now, though, is he?' she said without looking at him. 'His pulse was a hundred ten minutes ago and that's a little higher than it was at the previous count. I expect it's still rising. He feels much too hot and his breathing is so shallow.'

He said gently, 'Do you want to stay here tonight? I'll square it with Sister if you'd like to.'

She nodded gratefully. 'You never know . . . he might surface enough for me to talk him back. It helped before. He said it did. He said he could hear me for ages before he came to.' Tears pricked her eyes. They slid together down her cheeks, met on her chin and fell unheeded onto the green bedcover.

'Just see that you get some kind of rest, there's a good girl.' Rob cleared his throat of its constriction. Poor lass, he thought. Widowed when she was little more than a green girl and now facing the possibility again. He had not needed her to spell it out to him that Bay was the one she had chosen. It was far deeper than simply the response of a woman to the needs of a sick man. They both, it seemed, had a special need of each other. He left them. He needed her also but now was not the time to bring that up.

Aaron, looking from one to the other, fingered the notebook sticking out of his pocket and followed him.

Finn pressed himself against the hard wood trunking of the temple wall. The front entrance and forecourt were thick with men and women grouped close together, their torches sputtering and hissing smokily in the fine rain, borne aloft over heads thrown back in collective anger. They must have been joined by some of the hill tribes, Finn thought, for there were only four hands of adults to the Wikken and out there in the tamped-down open space in front of the little temple there must have been twice that number at least.

Gonad had not obeyed him. She had not returned to her dwelling but had followed him doggedly, several paces beyond the wrath of his slinging arm, hissing her defiance when he snarled at her over his shoulder. Now she skulked on her stomach beneath a holly bush, watching the shadow that was Finn insinuate itself like a snake along the foundation of the back wall. In the reflections from the torches on the other side of the temple he seemed to be giving very special attention to one part of the wall. The rain was slight now, little more than a fine mist. She blinked a drop of water out of her eyes. When she looked again he was gone.

Finn found the trap by running his fingers up and down the bark of each great tree trunk. The glow of the torches was quite ineffectual so close in to the wall and he had to guess at the place, for it was too dark to take a count of the trunks. The one he had cut from inside the store was two hands away from the corner from the left and five hands from the right. It had taken him hours of quiet whittling with his knife and the flint cutting edge of his hand spear to fashion the little hidden aperture. Bay had been in charge of that operation, Finn thought grimly, Bay with his keen eye for precision had hammered away with his flint, getting a chiselled angle square cut into the softer pine trunk of just one tree panel. He looked about him, listening to the undulating baying of the people at the temple entrance. There was no sound from within. He put his shoulder to the loosened wood and flung himself against it with the whole of his weight. It gave, throwing him forward. As he began to push his torso through the aperture the scent of Arwyan's body came strongly to him.

He landed in a shower of dried grasses, grazing his jaw

on the sharp edge of the timber. Before there was time to fight his way through the sea of straw he heard the weak sounds of Arwyan's expellation. He hefted the wooden wedge out of his way and swung across the storeroom, thrusting from him anything that stood in his path. The fat-lamps had gone out in the offertory, but there was still a glow from the inner sanctum where the great stone stood. Its soft luminosity filtered dimly through the dividing drapes into Arwyan's sleeping chamber.

She was on the floor, lying on her side, knees drawn up tightly under her chin. She had removed her tunic and lay naked, curled round the bloated sphere of her stomach like nymph round a huge overripe plum.

'Arwyan, I'm back,' he said crouching beside her, taking the discarded robe and wiping the damp hair from her face. She went into spasm as he spoke and the terrible pushing, bursting sounds came from her again.

'It will not come,' she hissed between breaths. 'It will not come. . . .'

He heaved himself across to the empty lamp bowl. Beside it the oil ewer was half full and he emptied it into the bowl and cast round for a fresh wick. No wicks. Behind him Arwyan let out a long grinding moan and he swung back to her. From her buttocks something protruded. The contractions seemed to have stopped. He wiped her face again and she stirred, moving her head feebly. 'I cannot bring it out,' she whispered. 'I have no more strength left.'

'Yes, you can,' he said fiercely. 'You're doing much better than you think. It seems to be coming by the feet, that's all. If I can get light, I will help to pull it from you. Where are the wicks?'

'The store. . . . ' Her whisper was so faint that he scarcely caught the words before another contraction drove the breath from her. He swung away through the curtain, unmindful that he tore a section as he went. He found a reed basket filled with the little plaited wicks and dragged the whole thing back with him. Flame next. The

621

sounds of her travail were agonizing. Cursing his legs, cursing the situation, cursing everything, he hopped, bowl in one hand, into the inner sanctum and took light from its single flame.

'Bloody thing,' Bay said to the foot of the marble column in passing. 'Bloody superstitious evil thing.'

He brought the light back to Arwyan and set about helping her. With the next contraction the baby began to appear and a tiny foot projected from her. With infinite care he hooked his fingers into her and felt the other twisted up inside. His mouth was dry. Perspiration streamed from him, for what he was trying to do might be wrong. He was ignorant in such matters, but instinct simply said to pull. The next contraction jerked her knees upward and he thrust fingers and thumbs into her and tugged.

The second foot and both legs appeared. For a moment he was too occupied with checking his sister's half-hidden face to look closely at them. Then his eyes were drawn to the tiny protruding legs and he froze.

They were covered in dark hair. The feet were perfect in every way except that they were not human feet. They were pale hoofs encased in a fine bluish membrane.

Behind him a voice grated, 'So you *are* part of this evil, then, for we left you lying out on the hillside and yet you are here with her. This *is* your guilt. You are proof of it.'

Ickka.

Finn jerked round, still in shock at the monstrous thing that was trying to free itself from Arwyan's fragile body. The Headman stood at the open curtain, deep fear making his face the mask of a gargoyle.

'You're a fool,' Bay snapped at him. 'Rant and rave all you want but let me get this thing out of Arwyan first. And stay where you are,' he added, as Ickka took a step forward. Something in the pent-up rage in the cripple's voice stayed the Headman. He was in terror, entering this most sacred of places where he knew that no man must come. He muttered his pleas for forgiveness to Epona under his breath and, hearing the thin wail of weary agony from Arwyan and seeing the swift movements of her crouching brother, took a step nearer.

Finn rounded on him, snarling. 'Keep your distance or I'll cut you. . . . '

Ickka stood rooted, his eyes bulging at the shining thing that Finn was withdrawing from the girl. It came in a rush and with it a gout of bright blood. It slid from her across Finn's calloused stumps and he was crouching in blood and mucus and staring down in shaking revulsion at the thing in the shining membrane.

The head was human. It was pink and neat, the little shell ears flat against its perfect baby skull. It was pressed against the limp animal legs, the whole little body folded over inside its envelope.

Ickka gasped. He pushed Finn aside and gaped down at the little creature. 'Epona has given us her child! She is the Sacred One and has created herself out of the womb of her unworthy servant. . . . ' He kicked out at Finn with his foot. 'You — look to the woman, for she must suckle this precious child of Epona. I shall tell the people and then I shall come and take the child to show to them.' He went then, his face filled with ecstasy.

The thing moved on Finn's legs, a tiny hoof kicked and an edge of the membrane tore. At the same time the afterbirth came away, and with its expulsion Arwyan gave a deep sigh and seemed to settle into the straw. Finn backed away from the creature and went to Arwyan, shaking her by the shoulder.

'Are you all right? It is over.' She seemed to have fallen into a deep sleep for she did not move and he bent and looked more closely at her. The strain had gone from her face and she looked serene and lovely, lying on her side and the damp hair framing her face with dark tendrils. The length of the eyelashes was such that they touched the soft white skin of her cheek-bones. She was not breathing. He pressed his hand against her chest and heard no heartbeat. He bent and put his ear to her mouth and felt only the faintest flutter of breath.

Outside, a great roar went up from the people, and he turned as Ickka strode back into the chamber, the triumph of this glorious miracle shining in his face.

'She is weak from her labour. It was too big for her. Look, she is ill,' Finn said. 'This terrible thing shows the truth of her words, but it is an abomination, Ickka. The Wikken must not venerate such a creature. Look at the evil in it. It has poisoned the respect of her people for the time of its growing, it has lived off her body, sucking it dry and now it will take the last thing she has to offer it — her life. Is there anything more you can do to what is left of her?'

The contempt in his voice, the sheer bitterness and disrespect towards Epona's offering to the people, made Ickka gape. He stood beside Arwyan's curled-up body, over which Finn had flung her robe, and just for a moment there was a deep uncertainty in him. Then he bent down and scooped up the little creature, peeling the silken membrane from it as he did so.

'Don't touch it like that,' Bay screamed, as full understanding suddenly burst through into the mind that was Finn. But it was too late.

Ickka stripped off his own soft leather waist-cloth and wrapped it round the little body. He held it in the crook of his arm and bore it away from Finn as proudly as a man carrying Epona herself. Finn stared after him, seeing the little hoofs kick out under Ickka's hand.

He swung after the stocky figure. 'Don't look at it. Don't look into its eyes. . . . ' But even as he shouted the words, even as he thrust his way through the hangings in the wake of the triumphant Ickka, even as he bellowed the warning, he knew that it was too late. The ecstatic Ickka was bent only upon bringing the new Epona to her people.

From the sulphurous night one brilliant blue flash scythed downward, burning his eyeballs. Something black slammed between him and the figure of Ickka standing on the temple steps, holding aloft the tiny half-human foal. Sound exploded all round him and he found himself flattened against the earth floor. There were screams from outside, the screams of frightened gulls rising in flight from a predator. There was a red light in the upper air, the acrid smell of burning.

But he had seen in that one second the glare in the perfect little face of the tiny mutant, seen the power burst from it straight into Ickka's transported face, seen the shadow of the great marble monolith scything downwards upon them.

The centre of evil was not the lightning-struck stone. It had been created out of beautiful marble, the gift of some wealthy merchant from over the blue water, and erected in all humility for a deity lovingly worshipped. No, the beautiful coral stone was not the evil but only the executioner. The power, the vortex of all hatred, was in the little creature crushed with Ickka as lightning struck, in the moment of the stone's fall.

He crawled away from the fallen totem, back into the inner sanctum, searching through the smoke for Arwyan. The whole building was burning. It would be a suitable pyre for Ickka. It would burn that terrible little body and ensure that its soul did not enter the earth and lie there, waiting for the moment to emerge.

The acrid smoke billowed before a gout of flame. Through it a figure staggered, arms outstretched, mouth open in a terrible soundless scream. Her hair was alight, and even as he saw her, she was gone as her face was lapped in a tongue of orange fire.

He had seen her fleeing through the swirling smoke like that once before. She had come running towards him in the moment after his plane crashed and he was lying, stunned, across the remains of the port wing. Even as he held out his arms to her she fell and the stench and heat drove him back, eyes streaming, past the blackened bodies — down the steps.

He crawled away, skin blistered, blinded by pain and his own tears, and made for the blessed coolness of the stream.

It was when that sudden shaft of terrifying blue light from the Gods of Night struck down at the temple that Gonad finally understood Finn's real mission. The truth of it was almost more blinding than the monstrous spear which came out of the darkness with no more warning than the patter of gentle rain upon them all — and a single, deafening crack which pressed stone weights against eyeballs and eardrums.

When Finn had left her and disappeared into the temple, she remained for a while hidden in the thicket. She sat and thought about the completeness of his disappearance, for it was as though he had simply melted into the night without a flicker of movement. But then the Wikken raised their voices again and she could hear them urging Ickka to enter the sanctuary.

'Bring out the woman . . . bring out her child, Ickka. Show us Epona's chosen one or the fruit of her guilt.'

She slid out of her refuge then and stole through the trees round to the front of the temple and joined the crowd as they pressed about Ickka. She knew that he would be against entering the sacred offertory, where only those in trouble went to plead for Epona's help, for he was a man who had deep convictions and knew right from wrong with great clarity. That wisdom of his was, after all, why he was still Headman, for he was ageing now and one would come soon to challenge his leadership. There were several men who might lead by bravery but none who could match skill in the hunting field with Ickka's tough and fair-minded counsel. She stood tight-lipped as those around her shouted.

'Why do you not urge Iccka also?'

She shook her head at the bent old man at her elbow, whose creaking voice broke each time he joined it with the others. 'Ickka is a good and wise man,' she said shortly. 'If he is unwilling to enter the sacred place then he has good reason and is right not to do so.'

The old man frowned over this and then nodded his head. 'It is so. He is too good a leader for us to throw so willingly upon Epona's wrath, as she has always been a hard mistress.' He leaned heavily on his stick and stood back from a sudden surge forward by the crowd.

Ickka was going up the steps, the men and women at his heels. He turned on the top step and held up his hands, and the voice of the crowd wavered and died about him. When there was silence he spoke to them in a voice which carried right across the open ground to be deflected back by the trees. The rain, so fine that it was little more than mist, whispered across the clearing, making the torches hiss and gutter.

'I shall go and ask Epona for her counsel.' His voice trembled with the depth of his fear. His face was gaunt in the flickering torchlight, the hair thin and sparse where once it had been a shining mane of golden curls. His beard was red, streaked with grey on either side of his mouth.

'I shall go alone. No one is to follow, for if I have made a sinful intrusion, it is I who must suffer, not you. I shall find the woman. With Epona's blessing I shall bring you an answer.' He bowed his head and turned and was swallowed up by the darkness of the temple. The crowd drew back, waiting. The anger was gone now and uncertainty replaced it. They fidgeted in the warm night and became restless. Pink flashes in the sky far away beyond the sentinel downland hills still charged the air, filling them all with a nervous need for action. Gonad trembled, for now was the moment when two great spirits would engage. Ickka and Finn.

It was fitting that this should happen in the sight of Epona, for she would make the final choice.

'Why are you here?' Kkye said beside her, and she jumped, for her thoughts were shot with fear just then.

'I heard the people's voice,' she said to the girl who was her sister and who now was to wed Ickka's brother. 'I came to see the justice. I do not think that Ickka should have entered the temple, for what will happen if Epona takes him?'

Kkye, her torch smoking between them, grinned at her

627

and a slither of saliva trickled down the side of her mouth to her chin. 'The men will compete for the leadership.' There was swift pleasure in her voice, for to see men fighting was pure carnal excitement to the women and put them into a frenzy which only cooled in rut.

Gonad turned away and Kkye took a fresh brand from under her cloak and put flame to it from the other.

Finn never hesitated to enter the temple, Gonad thought. He had gone to support Arwyan with all the conviction of a man guided by divine blessing and now it was all suddenly quite clear to her. Finn, cast out and imperfect, Finn rejected as she and Arwyan had been, Finn the withered one with all his strength, with all his strange visions . . . Finn had been chosen by Deivos to replace Ickka and to lead the Wikken. The thought filled her with excitement and she began to push towards the front of the crowd.

She had gone no more than three paces when Finn's voice came from inside the darkened sanctuary and she stopped in her tracks, the blood pulsing in her head.

'Don't touch it like that. . . . ' The hoarse terror in Finn's voice boomed out hollowly from the unseen sanctum and the people, shocked by the desperate tone, sheered away from the steps like a flock of frightened birds, fearful now of Epona's wrath.

It was then that it happened.

Ickka's tall figure burst from the darkness into the guttering torchlight, his face transfigured with excitement. In his arms he held a small bundle, which he held aloft.

'Here is your priestess!' he screamed, his whole body trembling as he raised up the thing he carried, so that it hung between his hands, blocking his face from their sight. They saw the little creature cradled between his hands, the baby head hanging back, the little hindquarters covered in damp hair, kicking weakly. They fell to the ground and covered their heads, but before the first knee had touched damp earth the heavens opened and the temple seemed to disintegrate before their eyes.

Something red burst from the little body to explode in Ickka's entranced face, and in the same instant a great forked tongue of blue flame cracked out of the void above their heads, the blast flinging men, women and children across the clearing in a terrible crashing, singeing tumult of sound. Gonad felt as though a mighty hand had thrust her down against the ground. When she lifted her eyes, the blood singing in her ears, the imprint of that violent blue fork was still branded upon her vision.

Where, moments before, the clearing had been filled with excited men and women, now there were only the scattered bodies of the stricken. Ickka lay face down where he had stood at the top of the temple steps, across his body the monstrous pink shape of a single shining stone pillar. There was no sign of the newborn child.

Gonad shivered against the earth, for she had seen it etched in red light like a bursting poppy in that instant before Deivos spoke. The head and shoulders were human but the feet were tiny hoofs and the legs had the fetlocks and pasterns of a foal.

Epona had shown the people that Arwyan was innocent and then recalled her miracle.

The whole temple building was on fire, great greedy tongues of white-hot flame roaring upwards into the night, impervious to the rain. There had been no thunder following the single bolt of lightning. It was as though it had never been, but for the roaring inferno silhouetted against the night.

The man and women of the Wikken moaned among the trees, for there had never been a catastrophe of such magnitude within living memory. Ickka had been right to think that Epona would punish him for his trespass. Now she was punishing the whole tribe with the destruction of its Headman and its temple. She would not have a presence amongst them hereafter — and they were denied their leader.

Gonad knelt on the ground, arms wrapped round her

body and rocked herself as she gave vent to a new grief. Finn . . . had he also been taken as part of the great punishment?

'Are you as foolish as all the others, after all?' Bay said gruffly beside her. 'I did think that you would have more faith in me.'

She raised her head and squinted through the eye-smarting smoke at him. He was almost black as a forest boar but his teeth gleamed like cowrie shells.

'Come on,' he urged. 'Let's get away from here. There's nothing more to be done till morning. I've got some things to tell you and it's not going to be easy. It might have been Finn who went in there, Gonad — but this is Bay who has come out of it. D'you understand? I am to be called Bay now.'

'My dear old friend, please try and understand,' Aaron said to Robert, his tiredness showing itself in his exasperation. 'I can only submit such a theory against hard evidence, and in this case you must admit that we have precious little.'

'But we do have some,' Robert insisted. 'Look — the little we do have is quite remarkable. We have the drawings, the tapes and the corroboration of at least half a dozen people — and Bay Heritage is still alive and may come up with more.' He thumped the arm of his chair as Aaron shook his head. 'Well, dammit, you Armenian pessimist, take a look at what we've got for yourself.'

'I have.' Aaron was quite unperturbed by Robert's wrath. He had known him for a long time. Robert had always been the one who ferreted out the angles, but it was Aaron who invariably kept him in a state of perspective. 'I've been weighing the pros and cons ever since I heard the first tape, or I wouldn't be here now. I'll tell you exactly what we have. Nothing. We have a language being spoken which would suggest the kind of speech one might expect from the old Indo-European tongue but I can only speak hypothetically. Next we have a man coming out of a deep coma and describing with commendable detail the kind of scene which, again hypothetically, we would associate with the Bronze Age cultures of, say, the Aunjetitz or Lausitz people. Your Mr Heritage was extremely accurate in describing the drinking vessels and lamps as he saw them, and there is certainly a close similarity to the kind of artefacts we are excavating on the sites of the Beaker Folk. Then there's the temple which he was at such pains to draw for you. That also seems to reflect the little which is known of the architecture of that same late Bronze Age, as do the weapons and clothing he has described to us.

'So far so good — except for two things, Robert, old friend, which I'm very much afraid will make the writing of a paper on this man's situation very nearly impossible. The first is that we only have his tape describing the monolith in the temple, and his discovery of the dual carving of the head as he describes it. There is not any indisputable proof that his forebears did not put that thing there under the floor and pass down details of it by word of mouth from one generation to the next, is there? It was probably not done that way — but it could have been. Yes?'

Robert nodded, frowning deeply.

'Right. Then there is the other matter. Frances tells us that Bay, wherever he is at the moment, is going to do his best to get rid of that stone. If he succeeds, there will then be no evidence of any kind to support your theory. I'll go even further. If he gets rid of the stone or whatever it is that has been poisoning that one place and one genetic strain, then the subject in its entirety will have ceased to exist.'

Robert sighed and screwed up his face, hating to agree with the obvious. There was so much here. Aaron would never believe in Bay's use of the Killing Glance theory although he did admit that certain cultures used it even in the twentieth century. He was as impressed as any of them by Bay's language and by his pictures, but he was quite right to apply sceptic argument to everything.

It still quickened his pulse, all the same, whenever he thought of what they were witnessing. Genetic brain warp — the continuing signals of something which had emitted tremendous power a very long time ago and which was still spanning man's non-spatial continuum which he calls time, repeating itself in the descendants of those initially involved. A kind of genetic echo, allied to physical similarities among related humans.

Now there were a few precious shreds of evidence. The question was, how might those shreds hold up under the examination of a sceptical world?

'Let's do our best to get the poor bugger back to the land of the living at this end and try some electrolysis to erase the whole thing from that overworked mind of his. Then he might even respond naturally under hypnosis.'

'It's what Fellows has been recommending all the way through the case, you know.'

'Come and get some fresh air,' Robert said to Frances.

She had been sitting huddled up beside Bay's bed for most of the day and looked close to exhaustion. She hesitated and he said quickly, 'Look, old dear, if you go on in this way, you won't be much good to Bay when he wakes up and really needs you. He's miles away at the moment, so let him be while you recharge your own batteries. What you should have is a good long sleep, some nutritious food inside you and a blow of fresh air. How about letting me take you back to the cottage, where you can have a nice relaxing bath, and then we'll go for a quiet stroll and stop off at the pub for a bite?'

She found she was too tired to explain that she wasn't hungry, she couldn't sleep and she didn't think that her legs would carry her ten yards. Bay was in a deeply comatose state. He had been that way for fifteen hours now. They were going to try one more set of injections of the Genera D4 later in the evening. It was probably a sensible idea of Robert's to take a break first. She rose from her chair beside Bay's bed, trailed her fingers along his arm and then followed Robert out of the room.

The cottage was filled with the scent of roses. There was one particularly fragrant climber on the west side of the house which her mother had planted a long time ago. It produced, in great abundance, perfectly shaped deep pink roses with a white centre to each petal. The scent was strongest in this grey humid weather, she found. It was so rich and heady that she felt purified. She stood at the open french window, drinking in deep breaths of it.

'Robert, I know you'll think I'm still dwelling on Bay, but would you mind if we went to Dell Quay over the fields?'

'You mean, would I mind if we went to Lavenham.' He crinkled his eyes at her. She was as tense as an overstrung violin. He resisted the urge to gather her up and run from Apuldrum as fast as he could carry her. 'Well, why not? It might be just as well to batten down the place and bolt those doors in any case. That stone of Bay's is probably going to be a pretty valuable item for the local archaeologists once this is all resolved, so we'd better try and keep it safe from prying eyes.'

'Or until Bay wipes it out.'

He nodded. 'That, too. Come on, old thing.'

They walked slowly and there was little conversation between them. The old house lay dejectedly beneath the low grey canopy of muggy afternoon sky, exuding an air of crumbling desolation which she was sure she had never felt before. Strange how one's mood alters everything, she thought. Lavenham had always been a place of tempting mystery and beauty until this moment. Now, suddenly, with the memory of two grotesque bodies in the yawning pit, flung across that horrible stone, she could only think of it with loathing.

They pushed open the door under the arch and went through to the kitchen.

'Don't you think we ought to gather up all Bay's things and take them back to the cottage?' she said despondently, seeing the dresser littered with the casual clutter of his occupation.

They packed everything into his haversack, which they found hanging up behind the door in the dark little bedroom. It also contained Tom Heritage's diaries and the Smith & Wesson revolver. Robert hefted the little handgun from one palm to another for a moment and then put it back. The precious diaries were wrapped in oilcoth.

'I'll take care of these for the time being, if you don't mind,' he said. 'There's a lot of material in them that I'd be interested to read at leisure, as I imagine they'll be very valuable as a reference source, judging by the year they were written.'

'I suppose it's all right.' She sounded doubtful. 'If anything happens to Bay, though, I think they should be sent back to the family. They are Heritage property, after all.'

She wandered away then, forcing herself to go across the hall and into the long drawing room. What a dreadful scar the excavation made in the room, she thought. It had seemed so perfect when she was a child, for then the furniture was still in place and somehow it had not mattered that it was all decaying gently around her. That had been part of the magic, after all. What would Jess Bayless have thought if he could have seen his house now, so pitifully abandoned and gradually falling down?

She stood on the edge of the pit and looked down at the stone. It was not as large as she had thought at first for, half-buried, it appeared to have greater length. It was about four feet long and maybe two feet in circumference. Another piece of the stone lay under it. Aaron and Robert had managed to turn it slightly so that part of the underside was visible. The carved section that they had all been so excited about was very worn but, squatting down, she could make out the curl of an upper lip and the full lobe of a human ear. What had Bay said? A double-headed sculpture? That meant that the other face was on the underside. She examined the thick lip, wondering whether she was looking at the female face or the half-equine one.

Judging by his comments, she hoped that it was the female.

The pit was in deep shadow, for little light seemed to filter in through the dirty casements. Something caught her eye and she leaned closer, the better to see it, but then her eyes seemed to mist over and for an instant she could have sworn that something moved down there. She sat back on her heels and put her hands up to her eyes.

'What's up?' Robert said from the doorway.

She found she was shaking. Her mouth was so dry that she had to lick her lips before she could answer.

'I don't know. Nothing, really. I could have sworn I saw something under the stone then . . . like a small animal. The leg of a little creature or something. I could have sworn it moved, too.' She laughed shakily. 'I'll be seeing Bay's horse goddess next. I must be more tired than I thought.'

Robert leaned over her shoulder. 'Can't see much down there. Must have been the light. Come on now, old thing. You've had your sniff around the house. Let's buck up our stumps and get to the pub before it fills up.'

She averted her eyes from the stone as she stood up. It was a relief to be taken in hand and told what to do. The last weeks had been quite a strain.

They locked the front door from the inside and slammed the back door as they went out. Frances could hear the hollow echo of the crash resounding through the house behind her as they left.

Robert tucked her hand into the crook of his arm and walked her briskly down the drive. It had given him a considerable shock to see that something actually was protruding from under the fallen pillar. It was not the fetlock Frances had seen, but at first glance it certainly did look remarkably like a leg-bone of some kind.

13

The people had fled, taking those who had been struck down with them. The clearing was empty but for the blazing building, and even that was beginning to die in great gouts of smoke under the gentle persistence of misty rain.

They crouched in the little shelter that had housed Finn for the years since Ickka had cast him from the Wikken. Gonad squatted beside the opening, hunched in watchfulness like a cat, feeling the tension, waiting for movement. She understood nothing except that out there across the clearing the temple smouldered, incinerating three bodies — and one of them was Ickka.

'What will happen to the Wikken?' she ventured. Finn was in an odd mood, crouching at the back of the hut, communing with his thoughts. He had changed in the last days, gaining stature, so that it was almost as if he was preparing himself for something. He had said that he was no longer Finn and she believed this because of the change in him. He had said that he was someone else called Bay. Was Bay the one sent by Deivos to lead the tribe away from the dangers of their existence?

Finn had been huddled against the further wall ever since they ran in, away from the stampeding terror of the others. She tried again. 'Why are you Bay when before you were Finn?'

He looked up then and grinned at her. This new mood seemed very odd for he had never so much as given her the slightest grimace of friendship before. She resisted the urge to stretch out and stroke him.

'Poor Gonad. How am I going to explain all this to you?

I don't suppose I shall ever get you to understand what's going on — and why should you?' He shifted his weight from one haunch to the other and settled lower on to the ground. 'Now listen, and try to make something of what I am saying, for this is very important. Out there in the temple is Arwyan. She died when she brought forth that creature. Later on I shall mourn, but now there is no time because Finn is in terror inside me and I — who am Bay — can only influence Finn's mind when it is in this frozen state. Finn will soon shake himself out of his fright and then Bay will have no further use here. I belong elsewhere, you see. I have a life I nearly threw away and a woman who needs me, so I have to get back — and I must try and use Finn's physical strength, his good healthy body power, to do that.'

She stared blankly at him, eyes uncomprehending. It didn't matter. There was a kind of peace between them. He went on, 'I thought, when I saw the creature Flame Ickka and the totem crash down on them both, that that was the answer — that the stone was broken and its power would be broken, too. That it was the end. The flames would be their burial mound and nothing would be left to carry on down the years. But I was wrong. I've had time to think and now I see that this is exactly what happened before. The remains of that filthy little creature must have decayed and inhabited the earth of that spot, beneath the stone. . . . Maybe it didn't even decay but lay there waiting in a sort of hibernation. Whatever happened last time must be changed, you see. I must remove that creature to another place so that it cannot possibly infiltrate this soil.'

She tried hard to understand his words but it was just not possible to envisage one body inhabited by two men — Finn and this new commanding Bay. She raised her eyes to him and let him see the trust there. Comprehension was not necessary, only faith.

He moved then, burrowing beneath the pile of skins which was his bed and bringing out a tangle of hempen rope. He tugged at it and then stowed it in his belt. There was a mightiness about his movements which made her bow her head before him. She felt his hand on her hair.

'Come with me,' the flowing voice commanded. She did as he said, drawn by the sound of it and followed him out of the hut.

The first streaks of day were just splitting the night sky in shards of pearly light. They showed the dim shape of smouldering timber which had once been the pride of the Wikken. Gonad hung back then, feeling the spirits and their desolation, but Bay swung ahead of her.

'Hurry,' he called over his shoulder. 'There isn't much time and I need your arms and legs.' He was irritated by her fear of him. 'Come on, you stupid woman. Stop cringing and crawling like some beaten cur and do as you're told.'

She had no knowledge of his words then, for strange things were coming from his mouth, but there was no need for words when the sound of his impatience was so clear in his voice. She loped forward and trotted beside him over the uneven ground and along the planked footpath. He paused in the act of hefting his body up the steps. Heat still radiated from the blackened mess. The great pillar, which had been hewn and polished from that beautiful foreign stone, had broken into several pieces as it toppled over. The lightning must have struck the totem, rather than the roof, for the whole thing had been split from the fall and the heat. A large piece of the totem had struck Ickka across the back, felling him in its downward passage. The underside of his body had been partially protected from the fire by the angle of the stone, but most of his back, head, arms and legs were burnt to the bone. Even as Bay took in the dreadful red glistening of intestines beneath the broken cage of charred ribs, the first of the blowflies homed in and settled on the mess.

A blackness flowed over him. He was looking upwards from his hospital bed at the face of the young nurse bending over him. Nice heart-shaped face, with a small full mouth pursed in concentration.

Then he was back, crouched over Ickka's body, and the momentary flash was gone. It came to him then that Bay was dying back there in that hospital bed and Finn was gaining in strength and conviction.

Frances . . . I need you. Don't let me go.

But how could she help? How could anyone help him?

Bay's blood pressure began to rise soon after midday. By 1.15 the nurse who was sitting with him rang for the ward sister, and Dr Fellows was sent for. He examined Bay thoroughly.

'I'm afraid he's approaching some kind of crisis,' he said to the sister. 'Try and find Professor Crane, will you?'

She was ready for that. 'I have the number of the pub he is lunching at,' she said. 'I'll see whether he is still there.'

Robert was on the point of deciding whether to follow an excellent jugged hare with cheese and coffee, or another of Gales Best, when he was called to the telephone.

'Your patient is in trouble,' Fellows said to him and reeled off the list of temperature, pulse and blood-pressure readings.

'Oh damn, damn,' Robert cursed under his breath. Why did these things have to happen when one was miles from anywhere. They didn't even have the car and would have to go back to the cottage for it.

'Look,' he said, making decisions in a rush. 'We'll be at least half an hour getting back. Give him a full-strength shot of the Genera D4 and monitor every breath he draws. I'll be with you as fast as I can.'

'Come on,' he said to Frances, waving her away from the dining table and ignoring the alarm in her white face. 'Can you run all the way back to the car? Bay's having a relapse.'

I've got to get hold of what remains of that thing, Bay said to himself, gritting his teeth and steeling himself to ignore the stench of burnt flesh which pervaded the whole temple site. I must take it away from the temple, scatter its ashes far and wide so that nothing could ever again grow its evil culture anywhere.

The charred pillars which had held aloft the roof-tree stood out of the black slime of ash mixed with the night's rain like lonely sentinels guarding an empty treasure. It was still too hot underfoot for him to search for Arwyan.

'Here,' he said to Gonad, who has been hovering at the bottom of the steps, head bowed against the sights she dared not see. 'Come up and help me to get the stone off Ickka.' But she shook her head.

'I dare not,' she whispered. 'That is Epona's stone and she has punished Ickka. I dare not touch it and undo what the gods have done.'

'You'll bloody well do as I tell you!' Bay roared. 'Get on up these steps and take the other end of this thing. It's only a blasted bit of marble, you stupid cow.'

His voice echoed round the clearing. A piece of charred wood fell with a crash behind him, and Gonad scuttled up the steps and grabbed the hot stone with shaking, sliding hands. Somehow even the wrath of Deivos and Epona was better than the wrath of this unpredictable flesh-and-blood deity.

Between them they began to push, thrusting against the boulder with all their strength.

They ran. Robert took Frances' hand and together they panted down the tarmac road, turning right on to the cart track leading south between Hempsteddle and Big and Little Thirty fields. Their breathing became ragged and Frances gasped, 'I can't keep this up. You go ahead and I'll follow in the car.'

He grunted and pounded on, gripping her hand all the tighter, dragging her with him. Their feet smote the uneven path like pistons.

'It's you he'll want to see if we bring him out of it, even for a short while. And it's you who'll have the best chance of saving the poor fellow now, not me or anything that we can pump into him.'

Her lungs burned her. There was a pain in her side which was growing. Nearly at Newbarn — soon be in sight of Lavenham, she thought. Wait for us, Bay. Wait for me. . . .

They could not shift the stone at first but then Bay said. 'Rock it, Gonad, like this. Push — relax. Push — relax. That's right, harder now, harder. . . .'

They rocked the coral pillar and at last felt movement beneath their hands. Gonad stared down at the beautiful rich marbling. She had never seen such smooth perfection, never even imagined such colour, like the rosy radiance which filled the skies sometimes as the sun set. I am touching Epona, she said to herself. I shall never be the same. This is sinful and I shall be struck down. But the thought no longer held fear for her. She was doing the bidding of Finn, who called himself Bay, and this Bay was stronger than anyone in all the land. If he said that it would be all right for her to handle Epona's image, then it would be so. She slipped in the ashy mud and the stone rolled away from what remained of Ickka. They crouched on either side of it, panting, eyes sliding away from the mess of his fleshless back.

'Here.' Bay held out the tangle of rope to her. 'Take up two of the pathway planks. Cut them to the length of your arm and rope them together. How far are we from the sea?'

She looked confused. 'Sea? What is sea?'

'The big water, then. Whatever you like to call it. How far are we from it?'

'At the pace of you it is about the time it will take for the sun to climb from that treetop to the branch of the old oak, no more.'

'Half an hour.' he estimated. 'Why is the sea so far away? Never mind. I must get the horse thing's ashes first. Stand well out of the way.'

'Gonad,' he called as she went to do his bidding. She looked round at him. Her face was blank, with a kind of dreaming trance in her eyes. 'Get me a large urn from my hut first. The one I keep the oil in.'

She went, and he watched the swift loping run she used, her body bent forward, hands trailing. Let's get this done. he thought, then Gonad can have Finn back and do her damnedest with him.

Frances. . . . His head was suddenly whirling and he felt himself falling. Not now, for Pete's sake, he begged, Oh God, don't let it happen now — Not until I've finished. Keep a grip on this reality, he told himself. Only this one. There is no Frances, no Lavenham, no twentieth century. Shout obscenities. Kick someone . . . keep the action going *here*.

He kept his eyes open, made himself move, beat himself across the chest and roared the first thing that came into his head across the dripping shell of the temple.

'Pardon me, boy . . . is this the Chattanooga Choo-Choo . . . ?'

The place echoed hollowly with the sound and Gonad sprang from the little hut and came tearing towards him, the wide-mouthed urn clutched in both arms. 'What is the matter? Why are you crying in that way?'

'ABCDEFGH — I've got a girl in Kalamazooooo. . . . ' Keep the sound coming, he thought. Doesn't matter what you sing . . . just keep going.

The feeling passed. The rainbow lights cleared, leaving in their wake an upward surge of confidence, as if a great weight had been lifted from him. He could see what was to be done clearly now. There were really no great hazards ahead, for he was definitely Bay, with Bay's intellect and Bay's powers of perception, which were infinitely greater than any of these simple creatures'. He squared his shoulders, gave Gonad a dazzling smile of enormous sweetness and breathed a sigh of relief. 'Give the urn to me and get on with roping that timber together.'

She did as she was told. He began to move the glutinous mass of charred bone and slimy entrails which had once been the Headman and now covered the tiny body of the human foal.

It was there. He could see the hairy gleam of a haunch, the pink dimpled curve of a baby elbow. He managed to shovel away the congealing raw flesh which had been Ickka's shoulder. The neck had parted company with the head and Bay's stomach rose at sight of the half-face, its features burned beyond recognition.

Beneath the shoulder-bone, the baby lay unscathed. As he pulled the heavy mass away and thrust it to one side he saw the tiny body, smeared with Ickka's blood, nestling beneath his protective shield. It was a perfect baby. The flesh was firm and round, the little face reflecting some of the beauty of its mother, the mouth a tiny rosebud, the little fingers curled into fists. The smooth pink stomach was where it changed, soft human skin merging into the fine silky hair of newborn foal as it became miniature haunches.

He reared backwards with a dry hiss which made Gonad, sawing away at the grey seasoned path planks, look up sharply. 'Are you burnt?'

He shook his head, eyes glued to the tiny body. Not only was it unscathed but it was breathing.

He pushed himself away from it very slowly, his mind racing. Stone . . . Ickka – and beneath Ickka, this abomination, generated by a chance mating between creature and human.

The last piece of the jigsaw fell into place and he saw the whole thing then. No, it was not the stone which was possessed of that one concentrated drop of absolute evil. It had never been the stone. The stone had simply been the inanimate protector of . . . whatever remained of this thing, conceived in the union of total carnality and innocence, and denied life at the moment of birth. There was a terrible logic in assuming that the one gene which made this creature utterly impossible would also strive through timeless aeons to regenerate itself again, however long it took. And it had, gradually evolving itself as a concentrated influence – and Bayless Heritage, with the metal in his brain and his personal despair, all his anger and growing hatred of himself as well as his fellow man, was the carrier of the seed.

Cause and effect were face to face.

The rage stirred behind his eyes then. This was the thing that had destroyed lives like a disease down the centuries, snuffed out the beautiful like of Arwyan, having used her innocent body in which to grow.

Well, you disgusting deformity, he thought, this is where you change course. This is curtains, once and for all. He grasped the creature by its neck, sickened by the parody of its tiny helplessness. The pouting baby mouth drew back from teeth like pointed pearls, the eyelids flew open, and from the horror of huge grey Bayless eyes the Power unfurled in a violent scarlet flame. Something rushed out of him, holding the great undulating tongue as it reached for him, weaving — seeking. His own Power was there. It had not left him. It poured from him, holding it . . . was stronger, for it had grown in its maturity with each carrier. His head pounded, the blood thundered through the screaming vessels of his brain. Then it wavered and in an instant his strength burst through the shield.

The two pairs of grey eyes scoured each other for a fleeting, terrifying instant of combat before the hideous compulsion died in the huge pupils and blood spurted into the sockets, drowning the great irises as it welled up and spilled out down the baby cheeks.

Bay grasped the little body by its slender foal's legs and swung it round his head and brought it down again and again against the stone, seeing nothing of the scarlet pulp of its head and chest, knowing only that this thing must be destroyed utterly.

When the rage cooled in him he flung what was left of the body across the stone and hunted feverishly through the smoking timber for wood still smouldering. The rain had almost quenched the blaze but there were still plenty of glowing splinters of well-seasoned oak. He built a cairn of half-burnt wood round the shattered, exploded body and put a light to it.

Dr Fellows held the little phial up to the light and pierced the soft seal with his hypodermic needle. He drew pale golden liquid very slowly out of the bottle and then flicked the hypodermic with a practised fingernail.

The nurse beside him took Bay's arm and wiped the skin with a spirit soaked pad of cottonwool. She still had her stethoscope round her neck. There was no exchange of words. He found an artery and pierced the skin of Bay's forearm with all the skill of an experienced dart player. He depressed the plunger slowly, leaning over Bay as he did so.

Their faces were only inches apart when the American's sunken eyes opened. It gave the young nurse quite a turn, for Mr Heritage had large eyes of a rather odd colour, a pale grey which reminded her of a fish on a market slab. It obviously gave Dr Fellows a start too, for he straightened his back with an exclamation.

'I've done it!' the man on the bed gasped. His voice was quite strong. He seemed to speak normally. 'I've done it. I've done it. . . . '

It all happened so quickly then that she could not grasp what she was seeing. The patient's face seemed suddenly to suffuse. The lips drew back into an animal snarl and a terrible redness came from the eyes, flooding straight across the doctor's unguarded face. Even as she saw his body pitch forward in terrible slow motion, something more dreadful was happening to Bay Heritage's face, for it darkened and reddened and blood began to spurt from his eyes, from his nose — to well up out of his mouth. Even as she registered this, his head split open like an overripe tomato flung against a wall and exploded across the pillow.

She blinked in sheer disbelief.

'Nurse Allen, are you day-dreaming or something? We've three admissions this morning. Please hurry up and see that this side ward is ready for Mr Terry.'

The young nurse nodded. 'Sorry, Sister. I could have sworn I saw something just then . . . but I can't remember what it was now.'

Sister Wall smiled. Nurse Allen was a good girl and would make an excellent SRN one day. She was not usually given to day-dreams. 'Too much burning the candle at both ends, I dare say. Is this ward ready?'

The girl looked round her. 'Yes, I've checked everything.' She followed Sister out of the door, smoothing the pristine pillows and spotless undersheet on the bed in passing. 'Funny though. I could have sworn. . . .'

The stench of crackling flesh was rank in the still morning air. The burning of the creature was now a ritual. Bay squatted close to the pyre, never taking his eyes from it, ready to Flame it again at the slightest suggestion of returning life. There was none.

Gonad, her little raft ready for Bay's inspection, dared not speak to him. He was dispatching the creature which Epona had sent and then taken back — and this was right and proper, for Arwyan had been his flesh and blood and Epona had left him unscathed when all else in her temple had been eliminated.

She watched him through the curtain of her hair. He looked like the avenging Deivos himself, the depth of his anger engraved in grim lines upon a strong young face grown suddenly old. The very strength and pride of him seemed to have increased tenfold, exciting the blood in her veins.

'Bring me the urn,' he said at last, when the sun had crept up the sky and the flies were swarming like black dust over Ickka's remains. She did as he commanded and he took a piece of bark and began to scoop the little pile of body-ash off the top of the stone, where he had incinerated it. He tipped all the ash into the oily urn, brushing up every last particle until the stone was clean but for the scorch-marks upon its polished surface.

He carried the urn down the steps, balancing it on one shoulder and descending with that curiously graceful swinging movement of his body. 'Lift it for me now.'

She did so, and found it easy enough to carry. He made a loop of the remaining rope and slung the little raft she had made on to his back.

'Take me to the nearest blue water,' he said then. 'I shall send this out to sea with a flame in it, when the tide is going out, and we will watch until we can no longer see its light. Then we will go from this place and claim the Wikken, and see what they think of a Headman with withered legs.'

He put his hand on her breast as she lifted the urn on to her shoulder. There was still a glimmer of the red rage in his eyes but she knew then that he wanted her to stay.

Frances flung herself down in the dry grass and lay flat on her back, eyes closed, panting as she waited for her lungs to slow their painful heaving. There was no sun, for low grey clouds hung like overloaded sacks above the trees. The scent of brine and freshly cut corn filled her nostrils.

'I thought you said you were fit!' Robert complained beside her. She rolled over and snuggled her head into his lap. Sandy watched them for a moment and then wandered off into the long grass in search of a good scent.

'I was before I married you.' She grinned up at him with unladylike pleasure. 'Give me a bit longer than these few days and I shall have got into step with the requirements of a husband — including being chased all the way from Dell Quay for the benefit of health and beauty.'

He pinched her nose and bent over to kiss the pinkness he had made of it. 'You're quite healthy and beautiful enough without having to chase me all round Apuldram, Mrs Crane. You can have me anywhere you like without half-killing yourself for it. How about here?'

But she sat up primly and dusted the grass-seeds from her cotton dress. 'No, not here. This is a funny place. It has a feeling about it that's sort of old and wise. I'd not make love here, even with you. When I was growing up I used to come here when I needed to think.'

'Come on.' Robert stood up and took her hands and pulled her against him. Apuldram was a delightful little place but there were no strings here to tug at him as they did Frances. He put his arm right round her, whistled for the little terrier and they walked slowly across the shorn field away from the Chichester Channel and back towards the bridle path, Sandy coursing busily between the verges behind them.

'I hope this hasn't been all a sentimental journey for me and just plain boring for you,' Frances said.

He sniffed the air appreciatively and shook his head. 'Not on your life, darling. You've a large family, and spending one's honeymoon exploring some of its old stamping grounds without the intrusion of relations is a pretty painless way of learning the wife's family secrets.'

A thin wisp of smoke rose through the stunted oaks on their right. 'Looks as though the gypsies are back,' Frances said, pointing.

They walked slowly, arms entwined, and passed the little encampment, set just short of the trees between the path and the saltpans. There were three waggons. The ponies had been tethered some distance from the camp, where the grass was more lush and there was shade. Sandy had learned a long time ago that it was wise to avoid them and did so now.

'Good afternoon,' Frances called as they passed them by.

There were several tousle-haired children romping in hay that the harvester had left. They had made round nests with high walls, much as she remembered doing in childhood, and peered shyly at her from within. Two youngish women with kerchiefs round their thick black hair crouched beside a sullen fire, and an old man was hard at work making a basket beside a pile of dried reeds. A very old woman was sitting in the doorway of one of the waggons, propped up by pillows and wrapped round with shawls and a dirty army blanket. Heads turned and watched them until the thicket hid them.

'Friends of yours?' Robert asked, teasing.

'No, not really. They always camp there at this time of the year, and as I haven't been here for a long time, it was nice to see that they haven't let a world war change their habits.' She frowned then. 'Funny thing, though. Did you notice the old woman?'

'Smelt her. I don't know about much else. Why?'

His wife wrinkled her nose. 'I'm not really sure, but did you notice her eyes? Her face was as wrinkled as an unironed vest but her eyes — they were very large and the most odd shade of grey. And Rob, I swear they had no pupils! It gave me quite a turn. And I had the strangest feeling that I've seen her somewhere before.'

A Selection of Arrow Bestsellers

☐ The Lilac Bus	Maeve Binchy	£2.50
☐ 500 Mile Walkies	Mark Wallington	£2.50
☐ Staying Off the Beaten Track	Elizabeth Gundrey	£5.95
☐ A Better World Than This	Marie Joseph	£2.95
☐ No Enemy But Time	Evelyn Anthony	£2.95
☐ Rates of Exchange	Malcolm Bradbury	£3.50
☐ Colours Aloft	Alexander Kent	£2.95
☐ Speaker for the Dead	Orson Scott Card	£2.95
☐ Eon	Greg Bear	£4.95
☐ Talking to Strange Men	Ruth Rendell	£5.95
☐ Heartstones	Ruth Rendell	£2.50
☐ Rosemary Conley's Hip and Thigh Diet	Rosemary Conley	£2.50
☐ Communion	Whitley Strieber	£3.50
☐ The Ladies of Missalonghi	Colleen McCullough	£2.50
☐ Erin's Child	Sheelagh Kelly	£3.99
☐ Sarum	Edward Rutherfurd	£4.50

Prices and other details are liable to change

ARROW BOOKS, BOOKSERVICE BY POST, PO BOX 29, DOUGLAS, ISLE OF MAN, BRITISH ISLES

NAME..

ADDRESS..

....

....

Please enclose a cheque or postal order made out to Arrow Books Ltd. for the amount due and allow the following for postage and packing.

U.K. CUSTOMERS: Please allow 22p per book to a maximum of £3.00.

B.F.P.O. & EIRE: Please allow 22p per book to a maximum of £3.00

OVERSEAS CUSTOMERS: Please allow 22p per book.

Whilst every effort is made to keep prices low it is sometimes necessary to increase cover prices at short notice. Arrow Books reserve the right to show new retail prices on covers which may differ from those previously advertised in the text or elsewhere.

Bestselling SF/Horror

☐ The Labyrinth	Robert Faulcon	£2.50
☐ Night Train	Thomas F. Monteleone	£2.50
☐ Malleus Maleficarum	Montague Summers	£4.50
☐ The Devil Rides Out	Dennis Wheatley	£2.50
☐ The Shadow of the Torturer	Gene Wolfe	£2.95
☐ Contact	Carl Sagan	£3.50
☐ Cobra Strike (Venture SF 17)	Timothy Zahn	£2.95
☐ Night Visions	Campbell, Barker, Tuttle	£2.95
☐ Bones of the Moon	Jonathan Carroll	£2.50
☐ The Island	Guy N. Smith	£2.50
☐ The Hungry Moon	Ramsey Campbell	£2.95
☐ Pin	Andrew Neiderman	£1.50

Prices and other details are liable to change

ARROW BOOKS, BOOKSERVICE BY POST, PO BOX 29, DOUGLAS, ISLE OF MAN, BRITISH ISLES

NAME...

ADDRESS...

....

....

Please enclose a cheque or postal order made out to Arrow Books Ltd. for the amount due and allow the following for postage and packing.

U.K. CUSTOMERS: Please allow 22p per book to a maximum of £3.00.

B.F.P.O. & EIRE: Please allow 22p per book to a maximum of £3.00

OVERSEAS CUSTOMERS: Please allow 22p per book.

Whilst every effort is made to keep prices low it is sometimes necessary to increase cover prices at short notice. Arrow Books reserve the right to show new retail prices on covers which may differ from those previously advertised in the text or elsewhere.

Bestselling Fiction

☐ Hiroshmia Joe	Martin Booth	£2.95
☐ The Pianoplayers	Anthony Burgess	£2.50
☐ Queen's Play	Dorothy Dunnett	£3.95
☐ Colours Aloft	Alexander Kent	£2.95
☐ Contact	Carl Sagan	£3.50
☐ Talking to Strange Men	Ruth Rendell	£5.95
☐ Heartstones	Ruth Rendell	£2.50
☐ The Ladies of Missalonghi	Colleen McCullough	£2.50
☐ No Enemy But Time	Evelyn Anthony	£2.95
☐ The Heart of the Country	Fay Weldon	£2.50
☐ The Stationmaster's Daughter	Pamela Oldfield	£2.95
☐ Erin's Child	Sheelagh Kelly	£3.99
☐ The Lilac Bus	Maeve Binchy	£2.50

Prices and other details are liable to change

ARROW BOOKS, BOOKSERVICE BY POST, PO BOX 29, DOUGLAS, ISLE OF MAN, BRITISH ISLES

NAME. . . . .

ADDRESS. . . . .

. . . .

. . . .

Please enclose a cheque or postal order made out to Arrow Books Ltd. for the amount due and allow the following for postage and packing.

U.K. CUSTOMERS: Please allow 22p per book to a maximum of £3.00.

B.F.P.O. & EIRE: Please allow 22p per book to a maximum of £3.00.

OVERSEAS CUSTOMERS: Please allow 22p per book.

Whilst every effort is made to keep prices low it is sometimes necessary to increase cover prices at short notice. Arrow Books reserve the right to show new retail prices on covers which may differ from those previously advertised in the text or elsewhere.

Bestselling Thriller/Suspense

☐ Hell is Always Today	Jack Higgins	£2.50
☐ Brought in Dead	Harry Patterson	£1.99
☐ Russian Spring	Dennis Jones	£2.50
☐ Fletch	Gregory Mcdonald	£1.95
☐ Black Ice	Colin Dunne	£2.50
☐ Blind Run	Brian Freemantle	£2.50
☐ The Proteus Operation	James P. Hogan	£3.50
☐ Miami One Way	Mike Winters	£2.50
☐ Skydancer	Geoffrey Archer	£2.50
☐ Hour of the Lily	John Kruse	£3.50
☐ The Tunnel	Stanley Johnson	£2.50
☐ The Albatross Run	Douglas Scott	£2.50
☐ Dragonfire	Andrew Kaplan	£2.99

Prices and other details are liable to change

ARROW BOOKS, BOOKSERVICE BY POST, PO BOX 29, DOUGLAS, ISLE OF MAN, BRITISH ISLES

NAME...

ADDRESS..

....

....

Please enclose a cheque or postal order made out to Arrow Books Ltd. for the amount due and allow the following for postage and packing.

U.K. CUSTOMERS: Please allow 22p per book to a maximum of £3.00.

B.F.P.O. & EIRE: Please allow 22p per book to a maximum of £3.00

OVERSEAS CUSTOMERS: Please allow 22p per book.

Whilst every effort is made to keep prices low it is sometimes necessary to increase cover prices at short notice. Arrow Books reserve the right to show new retail prices on covers which may differ from those previously advertised in the text or elsewhere.

Bestselling Fiction

☐ Saudi	Laurie Devine	£2.95
☐ Lisa Logan	Marie Joseph	£2.50
☐ The Stationmaster's Daughter	Pamela Oldfield	£2.95
☐ Duncton Wood	William Horwood	£3.50
☐ Aztec	Gary Jennings	£3.95
☐ The Pride	Judith Saxton	£2.99
☐ Fire in Heaven	Malcolm Bosse	£3.50
☐ Communion	Whitley Strieber	£3.50
☐ The Ladies of Missalonghi	Colleen McCullough	£2.50
☐ Skydancer	Geoffrey Archer	£2.50
☐ The Sisters	Pat Booth	£3.50
☐ No Enemy But Time	Evelyn Anthony	£2.95

Prices and other details are liable to change

ARROW BOOKS, BOOKSERVICE BY POST, PO BOX 29, DOUGLAS, ISLE OF MAN, BRITISH ISLES

NAME...

ADDRESS...

....

....

Please enclose a cheque or postal order made out to Arrow Books Ltd. for the amount due and allow the following for postage and packing.

U.K. CUSTOMERS: Please allow 22p per book to a maximum of £3.00.

B.F.P.O. & EIRE: Please allow 22p per book to a maximum of £3.00

OVERSEAS CUSTOMERS: Please allow 22p per book.

Whilst every effort is made to keep prices low it is sometimes necessary to increase cover prices at short notice. Arrow Books reserve the right to show new retail prices on covers which may differ from those previously advertised in the text or elsewhere.